Pitcher

a novel by

Michael E. Cook

TELEMACHUS PRESS

PITCHER

Cover Designed by Telemachus Press, LLC

Cover Art:
Copyright © iStockPhoto/485509621/IPGGutenbergUKLtd
Copyright © Kevin M. Mccarthy/dreamstime/53165030

Published by Telemachus Press, LLC
http://www.telemachuspress.com

Contact the author at: cookorourkeseries@gmail.com

ISBN: 978-1-945330-48-3 (eBook)
ISBN: 978-1-945330-49-0 (Paperback)

Library of Congress Control Number: 2017932621

Fiction / General

Version: 2017.02.18

Table of Contents

Pitcher

Chapter One

Robert W. Parker was born in the spring of 1950 in a suburb of Columbus Ohio. He was the only son of Robert G. and Mary Louise Parker. The W in Robert's middle name did not stand for anything just as the G in his father's middle name did not stand for anything. Robert G's father's name was Robert T and the T stood for nothing so Robert G continued the tradition. Robert G. Parker was a veteran of the war in the Pacific and a decorated Marine. He had joined the Corps in 1942 immediately after high school graduation. He saw action on Tarawa, and several islands that were taken in the island hopping campaign. His last action was on Iwo Jima. He was only seventeen when he joined.

His parents knew that he would join as soon as he turned eighteen, so they signed for him to join. He and Mary were high school sweethearts. They were married when Robert came home from the war. He took a job working a swing shift at a factory, and Mary was a housewife. They tried to have children right away but were not successful. Finally, Robert W. arrived. The Parkers considered themselves to be Catholics but the only time they went to church was when someone died or someone got married. Robert W. was baptized as an infant.

Young Robert grew up in a good neighborhood. They lived within a few blocks of a city park and not far from the local school. At an early age, young Robert, now called Robbie, took an interest in baseball. This was good because his father also liked baseball. At the age of five, his father bought him his first glove and they started playing catch together. Columbus had a minor league team called the "Jets" and he and his father went to a game every once in a while. His father was also a fan of the Cincinnati Reds and at least four times a year, he went to Crosley Field. When Robbie was six, his father started taking him to the games.

His father had a good friend from the Corps who was a farmer now and lived just south of Columbus. The farmer had another friend who was also a veteran and the two of them were Reds fans too. They took turns driving when they went. Some of the times, there were double headers. They made these trips to Cincinnati until 1963. That year, his father's friend died from lung cancer and the other man was killed in a car crash. After that, the Reds games were watched on TV. There was one thing that Robbie would never forget. The year that the Reds went to the World Series and played the Yankees, his father somehow managed to get some tickets for a game. The Reds lost the Series, but it was still a great thrill for Robbie.

There were plenty of boys in the neighborhood and Robbie was always able to round up enough boys for a game. A few years later, some of the local businesses got together and started a Little League. It was for boys aged 10–12. When Robbie turned 10, he tried out for a team and made it. He was worried that since he was only 10, he would be setting the bench a lot. When the coach saw what he could do on the field and in the batter's box, he made him a starter. He played 2nd base and was the lead- off hitter. Robbie did very well and at the end of the season, his batting average was .350 and he had committed only two errors. His father and mother attended every game that they could. Whenever his father couldn't attend because of work, his mother attended alone.

After baseball season ended that year, Robbie's dad decided it was time for him to learn how to shoot. "A man needs to know how to shoot," his dad always said. "You just never know what might happen in this world." They would go to his dad's friend's place and shoot on his farm. The weapon they used was a bolt action .22 rifle with open sights. His dad always started out with a safety lesson. Then he showed him how to line up the sights. "You squeeze the trigger," he would say. "You don't pull it. Once you get your sights lined up on the target, your concentration should be on tip of the front sight blade."

When Robbie was ready to start shooting, he was in what is called the off-hand position. "Dad, I can't hold the rifle still," Robbie said.

"That's to be expected," his dad said. "No one can hold a rifle perfectly still. What you must learn to do is time your squeeze. Watch the movement of the muzzle of the rifle. Say for example your movement is kind of like a figure eight. Try to time the squeeze for when you get back to where the center of the eight is. Do you understand what I'm saying?"

"I think so Dad," answered Robbie. The target was a juice can about fifty yards away. Robbie took his time and then fired. The can was hit dead center.

"That's good son. Now do it again only a little faster," said his dad. Robbie worked the bolt and chambered another round and fired. The can was hit again. "Excellent Son," said his dad. "Now you don't need to worry about this right now, but that can is not shooting back at you. Now go ahead and crank off some more shots." Robbie did very well his first time out. On the way back home his dad told him how good of a shot he was. "We'll come out every once in a while and take some target practice," he said. "When you get a little older, I'll let you shoot my M1." Robbie was excited about this. He knew that the M1 was the standard rifle of the military during WWII and Korea and had a shell that was huge compared to a little .22.

~~~~

When Robbie was 11, his baseball coach moved him to shortstop and to number three in the batting order. He had another good year batting .375 and only one error. He also had hit ten home runs.

Robbie had a good growth spurt when he turned 12. The coach decided he would give Robbie a chance at pitching. His father showed him how to throw a curve ball and he mastered it very well. He threw it from what his father called the three quarters position and sidearm. He also learned a pitch that he called a drop ball. He threw it from straight overhand. It would come in like a straight pitch and at the last minute, it would drop down without curving. In the big leagues, they called it a sinker. The first game of the season, Robbie struck out twelve and gave up only one hit. He also was batting cleanup now and hit two home runs that day. When he wasn't pitching, he played third base. At the end of the season, his batting average was over .400 and he had not lost a game when he pitched. He had hit fifteen home runs. His team won the league and came in second in an invitational tournament.

~~~~

The VFW sponsored what was called "Teener" baseball for boys aged 13 – 15. This was a big jump for the thirteen-year-olds. The pitching rubber was now 60 ft. 6in. from the plate and the bases were 90 ft. apart. In little league, the pitching rubber was 45 ft. from the plate and the bases were 60 ft. apart. Robbie convinced himself that he would not try out as a pitcher, but would go for second base. One of the teams picked him and he spent his first season as a second baseman. His

batting average was not what he wanted it to be. Most of the pitchers were 15 year
olds and could throw a lot harder than he had expected plus they had a higher
variety of pitches. His batting average was pretty low until toward the end of the
season when he brought it up to .280. He had been batting seventh in the lineup
at the beginning of the season, but toward the end, he was moved up to lead-off.

~~~~

Something happened when he was in the eighth grade that he wasn't too sure
about how he should react. He was in a seventh period study hall when the assistant principal came into the room and told them that the President had just been
shot. Some of the students openly cried and some even screamed and yelled
"why? why?" Robbie was not sure what he should do or think. Why would anyone shoot the President? When Oswald was caught, his father said, "That son of a
bitch was in the Corps too." Robbie had never heard his dad cuss before. When
Jack Ruby shot Oswald, his dad said, "I just bet this is some kind of conspiracy."
Johnson was sworn in as President and the world went on. Robbie never paid any
attention to politics or the news, but when he saw Johnson giving a speech on
TV, he always thought his speeches were boring.

~~~~

At 14, Robbie's coach moved him to shortstop and he was still the lead-off hitter.
Toward the end of the season, the coach started using him as a relief pitcher at
times. He did well and saved every game he relieved. His batting average was over
.400 again for the year and he had hit five home runs. His coach informed him
that he would be pitching the next season.

　　Robbie had a good growth spurt. When the season started, he was 5 ft. 10 in.
and weighed 160 lbs. He had an excellent year as a pitcher and played third base
when he wasn't pitching. His team won the league that year and he was selected
for the all-star team. The all-star team won the state wide tournament that year.
Toward the end of the season, Robbie was pitching an exhibition game against a
team who considered themselves to be semi-pro. They were men who had played
high school and American Legion ball and were hoping to move up to a minor
league team. The home plate umpire was the coach of the local American Legion
team. He liked what he saw in Robbie and asked him if he would play for him the
next season. "You've got a great curve ball son," he said. "I like the way you work

it around. Next season we'll make you even better." Robbie shook the man's hand and told him he'd see him next season.

When Robbie was a sophomore, he decided not to play baseball for his high school. His dad wanted to know why. "Dad, the other boys tell me that the coach is a total jerk," Robbie began. "He does not and will not let the sophomores play. His pitchers always bat last and he never even lets them have batting practice. I will not be a bench sitter. I'll do my playing for the Legion."

"If that's what you want son," his dad said. "It's your decision." That year the high school team had a dismal record. Many of the juniors on the team said that they wouldn't be playing the next year. This coach was a bum.

Robbie's first year in Legion baseball was a great learning experience. He soon discovered that he couldn't just blow his pitches past the hitters. There were a lot of good hitters in this league and some good pitchers too. Slowly he learned the weaknesses of the hitters. With his coach's help, he learned how to pitch each batter. He found out that he couldn't be a strike- out pitcher so he learned to keep the ball low and rely on his infield. He won a lot of games that season and never struck out more than five batters in a game. He played shortstop and third base when he wasn't pitching and batted third in the line up. His team didn't win the league, but they came in second.

~~~~

That fall, Robbie's dad took him out to shoot the M1. They went to the same farm where his friend had lived. The man's wife was still there and she didn't mind if they took some target practice. Robbie's dad started out with a safety lesson first. This rifle was totally different and Robert made sure Robbie knew everything about this rifle before it was time to shoot. "What kind of sights are these dad?" asked Robbie. "How do you line them up?"

"This is what you call a peep type sight," Robert began. "You center the front sight blade in the rear peep sight. Now sling the rifle and we'll go set up a target at around two hundred yards."

"Two hundred yards, that's a good ways off dad," said Robbie.

"When you join the Corps, and I figure you will, you'll find out that two hundred yards is not far at all," said Robert. They set up the target. Robert drew about a ten inch circle in the center for a bull's eye. Then they paced off two hundred yards. "We'll start off in the off hand. Now make sure the safety is on and load this clip like I showed you. The sights are set for me right now, but that doesn't mean they're set for you. Not everyone sights in exactly the same. Now practice sighting in before you shoot." Robbie sighted in a few times and said he was ready. "Now listen to what I tell you," said Robert. "This will make you a very good marksman. Breathe. Relax. Aim. Slack. Stop. Squeeze. Do you understand?"

"I think so Dad," answered Robbie. "I'll take a deep breath and hold it for a while and then let it out. Then I'll relax and aim. Then I'll take the slack out of the trigger and stop. Then I'll squeeze."

"All right Son, fire when you're ready," said Robert. Robert had a pair of good binoculars and was ready. Robbie took his time and fired. "Nine o'clock in the bull about two inches in," said Robert. "Take two more shots and we'll see what kind of group you have." Robbie took his time and cranked off two more shots. "Both in the bull about two inches from the first shot," said Robert. "One's about an inch higher than the first and the other's about an inch lower. That's very good shooting for the first time out. Move the rear sight two clicks to the right and finish off the clip." Robbie put the safety on and adjusted the sight. When he was ready, he began firing again. Every shot hit the bull. It was about a three inch group and closer to the center of the bull's eye. "That's very good son," said Robert. "Let's move that sight one more click to the right and then you can try some rapid fire. You load up that clip again and I'll go put up a fresh bull for you." Robert had Robbie get down in the prone position and showed him how to use the sling to help steady the rifle. When he was ready, Robert explained what he wanted. "Now I want you to fire these eight rounds fast, but I want them accurate," he said. "For now, accuracy is more important than speed. Now fire when you're ready." Robbie took some deep breaths and then started firing. Robert wanted him to fire fast, but he did not expect Robbie to fire as fast as he did. Eight rounds were fired in less than fifteen seconds. "Let's walk down to the target," said Robert. "I can't quite make out what you did." Robbie put the safety on, slinged the rifle and they went to the target. "Not bad at all," said Robert as they got closer. "Looks like all eight are in the bull. Not bad at all." On the way back home Robbie told his dad that the M1 didn't kick as much as he thought it would. "That's because it's gas operated," said Robert. "The gas makes the bolt work and that action lessens the recoil. The old '03's kicked like a mule. I fired them before I fired the M1."

At least twice a year after this, they went out to fire the M1. They shot at 200, 300, and 500 yards. Robert was sure that when Robbie joined the Corps, he would qualify as an expert rifleman.

~~~~

In his junior year, Robbie gave in and decided to play high school baseball. After the very first practice, he wished that he had not decided to play. Practice was an unorganized mess. Where was the coach? The second practice, Robbie finally saw the coach. "You pitchers go run some laps now," he said. "You infielders take a little infield practice then we'll do a little hitting." Robbie watched the so-called infield practice as he was running his laps. There wasn't one boy who could catch a ground ball. Batting practice was pathetic too. Someone was lobbing in pitches that a six year old could hit. The pitchers never touched a bat. It was like this until the first game. Then it got worse. Robbie was third in the pitching rotation and sitting on the bench about did him in. When it finally came time for him to pitch, it was an away game. He had always heard about home town umpires but never believed it until now. No matter what he threw, he couldn't throw a strike. Several times he split the middle of the plate with a belt high fastball and if the batter didn't swing, it was a ball. He kept waiting for the coach to go argue with the umpire, but it didn't happen. He decided if he was going to get anyone out, he would have to give each hitter a perfect pitch to hit and hope the infield or outfield would do something. He was wrong. The final score was 12 – 0. When they got back to their school, Robbie went straight to the coach with his uniform in his hands. "I cannot and will not play for you," said Robbie. "I might just go to the school board and see if they'll fire you. You must just be here because they couldn't get anyone else. Well having no one would be better that having you. I'm not supposed to cuss so I'll leave now."

"Get your ass outta my office," said the coach. "We don't need a wise ass like you anyway."

Robbie went home and told his dad what had happened. "I can go to the school board and complain if you want," said his dad. "If you really want me to, I think we should get with some of the other players parents and see what they say."

"I guess not," said Robbie. "Most people don't want to rock the boat. Sooner or later, they'll get rid of him. Besides, I'll still be playing Legion ball this summer."

"All right son, we'll let it go for now," said Robert. "Do you think you'll have any new pitches this coming season?"

"I think I'll try a knuckleball," said Robbie. "I can throw one now, but I never know where it's going. I might try it sometime when there's no one on base and we're way ahead."

"That's sound wisdom," replied Robert.

~~~~

Legion ball was good that summer. Robbie's team did well and Robbie's pitching got even better. He was still not a strike- out pitcher, but he got the job done. During the season, he had several innings where he only threw three pitches. That's a pitcher's dream. His team won the league that year and did well in the tournament. When the last game of the season was over, Robbie had a talk with his coach. "Coach, I won't be back next year," Robbie said. "I'll be joining the Marines after graduation."

"Is this something you just decided?" asked the coach.

"No, I have always thought that I wanted to be a Marine," said Robbie. "My dad was a Marine. I think his dad was a Marine."

"Well the best of luck to you," said the coach. "You know about that thing that's going on over there in that place called Vietnam. You might just end up there."

"I know coach," said Robbie. "If I do, I'll do my duty. You've been a good coach. Best I ever had. I hope you do well next season."

"You take care of yourself now," said the coach as he extended his hand to Robbie. Robbie shook his hand and then left for home.

School would start shortly and Robbie decided he should get himself some new clothes. He had noticed that his clothes had seemed a little tighter and his pants a little shorter but he just figured that they had shrunk from being washed a lot. He hadn't weighed himself all summer or measured himself either so he decided he would do it before he went clothes shopping. When he got on the scales he was very surprised. "One hundred and seventy five pounds," he said to himself. "How could that be? I'm not fat. How did I gain fifteen pounds?" Then he measured himself. "Six foot," he muttered. "How could I get taller and not notice it? I wonder what my waist is?" Robbie pulled out a tape measure. "Thirty-two inches," he said to himself. "Not bad at all. Hey Mom, did you notice that I got two inches taller and gained fifteen pounds this last year?"

"I knew you grew some but I never mentioned it," she answered. "I figured you kept track of that."

"Well I reckon I will from now on," said Robbie. "My shoes been feeling a little tight too. I suppose I'll move up to a size twelve."

"Well you know what they say about the size of a man's hands or the size of his shoe don't you?" asked Mary.

"Yes I do Mom but I never expected to hear it from you," replied Robbie.

"Mom's are people too Son," Mary said.

Chapter Two

It was 1967 and Vietnam was in the news on a regular basis. Several boys from the area had been killed. Robbie started watching the evening news whenever he could so he could learn whatever he could about Vietnam. One evening he and his dad were watching the news and there were a few scenes of some Marines in the field. "What's this thing in Vietnam all about?" Robbie asked his dad. "They never really say on the news."

"I'm not sure myself," said Robert. "There's this fella in North Vietnam, Ho Chi Minh, and he's a communist. He wants the south to be communist too. I guess the south doesn't want to be communist and we're over there helping them out. People over here are scared to death of communism. There's something called the "Domino Theory." They think if one country falls to communism, more will follow."

"So what's so bad about communism?" asked Robbie.

"Don't they teach you anything in school these days?" said Robert. "In communism, there are no free elections. There is no religion. You go along with the government or they send you off to a salt mine or shoot you. That man Stalin had thousands of people killed when he was in power."

"So how could a man like that stay in power?" asked Robbie.

"He killed everyone who opposed him or who he thought would oppose him," answered Robert. "If a country's got no free elections, you can't vote someone out."

"So what was Korea all about?" asked Robbie.

"Well after WWII, Korea became a divided country," answered Robert. "The north became communist and the south didn't. The north invaded the south and the U.N. sent troops to stop them. Then later on, Red China got involved. It's still a mess over there. They signed some truce, but the war is not officially over. If you want to know more about Vietnam, you best go to a library and look it up. I do know that Vietnam used to be a French colony before WWII. The Japanese came in and ran out the French. After the war, the French went back in and tried to establish their authority again. The Viet Minh went to war with the French and finally got them kicked out. I believe the Viet Minh were communist. When the war finally ended, the country was divided. The north became communist and the south stayed free. A few years later, a group called the Viet Cong was trying to take control of the south. They were definitely communist. We sent our advisors over there to help the south. Things got bigger and bigger. The north started sending troops down to help the Viet Cong. The first of the Marines landed at Da Nang in 1965. It has just grown and grown. Seems like it may never end. Well anyway, I'm not positive on some of this stuff. You should look it up. One thing I do know for sure. If you do end up in Vietnam, you remember that it's their country. They know their way around and you don't. Just cause the people over there are a lot smaller than us, don't mean they can't fight. I knew a lot of fools that used to think that about Japs. Most of them are dead."

"Thanks dad, I'll look up some stuff tomorrow at the school library," said Robbie. The next day at school, Robbie spent a whole study hall period in the library. Most of what his dad had said was true. He convinced himself even more that he should go help those people who didn't want to be communist.

~~~~

Robbie had been driving since he was sixteen, but he never drove much. He was close to the school and the ball park so he walked most of the time. When school began, he decided it was time to get a part time job. His dad had showed him how to tune up their car and change the oil. He also learned how to work on the brakes and wheel bearings. He landed a job at a gas station. He worked two evenings a week and on the weekends. He mostly pumped gas and changed oil, but he also did brake jobs and tune ups when it was needed. He saved every penny he made. The gas station was only eight blocks from home so he walked some of the time. When the weather was bad, his dad or mother took him to work. The family only had one car, and Robbie was hoping to buy his own car before too long.

Robbie never dated but he was always interested in girls. He always talked to the girls at school and he knew that some of them liked him but he didn't want to ask them out when he had no car. He made up his mind that he would have his own car by spring and would go to the Prom. He told his parents his plan. "Well that's a good plan son," said his dad. "I have something else for you to put into your planning."

"What's that Dad?" asked Robbie.

"As far as I know, you don't know how to dance," said Robert. "You need to learn how to dance. The women love a good dancer."

"That's true," added his mother. "Your father is an exceptional dancer. We'll teach you."

"No one dances like you did back when you were young," said Robbie. "If I do that, the kids will think I'm crazy."

"No they won't," said his mother. "If you learn to jitterbug well, you can do anything on the dance floor. You'll see. I'm telling you. The girls will love you."

"All right you two," said Robbie. "We can start tomorrow. I got some homework tonight."

The very next night after dinner, the dance lessons started. All the furniture was moved out of the way in the living room and the carpet was rolled up and moved. The hardwood floor was exposed. Robert went over to the record player and pulled out his and Mary's favorite old song. It was "In the Mood." He started it and he and Mary went to dancing. Robbie was downright amazed. His dad was smooth on the dance floor. He and his mother just moved perfectly together. When the song ended, Robbie gave them a standing ovation. "I think you're right you two," said Robbie. "If I can learn to do that, the girls will love me. Do it again, then I'll give it a try." Robert started the song again and this time he threw in a few more moves. He was good. "I don't know if they'll appreciate those moves at the Prom," said Robbie. "They'll think all the boys will be trying to look up my girls dress."

"Don't worry about that," said Robert. "If you do it right, she'll be moving so fast that nobody'll see anything."

~~~~

The record was started again and Robbie took the floor with his mother. He was very awkward at first. "Feel the music," his mother said. "Let it move you. Clear your mind and feel the beat. It will move you." Now watch your dad and me one more time. Watch how fluid his movements are. Watch how he leads me." Robbie stepped back and watched his parents one more time.

"I can do this," Robbie said. "I can do this. When I pitch it's a good fluid movement. If I can pitch I can do this." The record was started again and Robbie took the floor. His mother could tell that he was gaining more confidence with each move. After about a half hour, Robbie was very confident and wanted to try some of the moves where his dad flipped his mother over his shoulder and around his waist.

"I believe I've had enough this evening," said his mother. "We'll try those things next session. You're working tomorrow so we'll cut us a rug the next evening."

"I suppose cut a rug means dance, right?" asked Robbie.

"Yes it does Son," said his dad. "Now if you don't mind, I'm gonna have a slow dance with this good looking woman here."

"Go ahead you two," said Robbie. "I'll get cleaned up and head to bed. I'll dream about dancing tonight."

The next dancing session went very well. Robbie's confidence grew some more. He wasn't as good at moving his mother around as his father was, but he knew he would improve. They even played some different songs this time. Robbie found out that you could dance this way to rock and roll songs.

It didn't take Robbie very long to save up enough money to buy a car. There was a woman a few houses from them whose husband had died and she was selling everything and moving out of state to be nearer to her children. They had two cars. She drove a 1966 Chevy Impala and her husband drove a 1960 Oldsmobile. The Oldsmobile needed some work and she didn't want to invest any money in it. When Robbie found out it was for sale, he went to her and made an offer. She accepted. Robbie got such a good deal on the car that he was able to pay for his insurance too.

The car needed a tune up, brakes, and a muffler. Robbie had it ready for the road in no time. This car was a dream to drive. Robbie loved the fluid speedometer. This car was slow out of the hole but on the top end it would fly. He and his dad took it out in the country one day to see what it would do. They got it to 115mph. "Now don't ever do that again," said his dad. "Don't ever tell your mother we did this either." They were about an hour away from home. Robbie took this time to have a personal talk with his dad.

"Dad, you know that I haven't dated before," started Robbie. "I have never kissed a girl before. I want to make sure I do things right."

"If I was you, I'd tell the first girl I wanted to kiss that I wasn't very experienced and I wouldn't mind some direction and help from her," said his dad. "Let her teach you. Have her tell you what she wants. Follow her lead. When you do make moves, be gentle and smooth. See how she responds to your moves. You'll be able to tell if she likes them or not."

"What if she laughs at me?" asked Robbie.

"I doubt that'd happen," said Robert. "Even young girls get tired of boys going after them like they're sacking a quarterback. I think she'll like your honesty."

"I'll give that a try," said Robbie. "Now I got something else to ask you."

"O.k., ask away," said Robert.

"I know about sex and how to do it, but how will I know if she's ready for it?" asked Robbie. "I wouldn't want to do it with someone who didn't want to do it with me."

"She'll let you know," said Robert. "Girls want to have sex too. It's not just a guy thing."

"So how often do you and Mom have sex?" asked Robbie.

"Gee, I never expected you to ask me that. Most kids don't want to think about their parents having sex. Well you asked me so I'd say probably five to six times a week," answered Robert. "If it weren't for trick work, it would be more. When we first got married, that's all we did. I mean three, four or five times every day. We did that till you came along."

"So you must have been some kind of machine?" said Robbie.

"No not really," said Robert. "You're mother was and is a good motivator. Now let's get to something very important. Sex is good but you don't want to end up being a father yet. If you get to where you think it might happen, make sure you have some protection. I have also heard that someone is working on or has developed a birth control pill. I don't know much about that. I do know that rubbers work. You don't want to be a daddy and you don't want to get the clap or something worse."

"We have rubbers at the gas station," said Robbie. "I'll get some and keep them in the car so they'll be there if I need them."

"Well I'd start asking some girls out if I was you," said Robert. "It's a long way to the Prom. When you go to the Prom, you want it to be special. You want to make sure you take the right girl."

"I'll get started on that next week," said Robbie. "The drive-in's still open. I'll see if I can get a date."

They didn't talk again until they had gotten home and were having the evening meal. "What did you two talk about today?" asked Mary.

"Sex," answered Robbie very quickly. "Dad was very informative."

"I'm sure he was," said Mary. "So if you're going to go out and try out what you've learned, please be careful."

"I will mom. I will," said Robbie.

That night, Robbie thought and thought about who he would ask out. He decided on Cindy Tyler. She was a senior too and did not have a steady boyfriend. She was very nice and attractive and was in several of his classes. They had a history class last period every day. Before the class started, he asked her if she would meet him in the student parking lot when class was over. She agreed.

As soon as class was over, Robbie went to his locker and got what books he needed and went to the parking lot. Cindy was there in a few minutes. "What is it Robbie?" asked Cindy. "Are you going to ask me out?"

"Well since you brought it up, yes I am," said Robbie. "I got my car now and I was wondering if you'd take in a movie at the drive in this Friday with me."

"I can't Robbie," said Cindy. She could see that he was starting to look unhappy about this. "It's not that I don't want to. My parents are going someplace and I have to babysit. I can go Saturday if you want."

"That would be o.k.," said Robbie. "I have to work at the station till 6 PM. That should give me time to get the gas and oil smell off of me. So I'll pick you up at 7:30."

"That will be fine," said Cindy. "Now when you pick me up, you have to meet my parents. My dad's a little grouchy at times but he's all right. Well I'll see you at school again tomorrow." They said their goodbyes and headed home.

Robbie gave his parents the news at dinner. "I got me a date for Saturday night," he said. "It's Cindy Tyler. She's a senior too and is in some of my classes."

"I know who that girl is," said Mary. "She's an attractive girl. I hope you two have a good time."

"Thanks mom," said Robbie. "I think we will. We know each other pretty well already. She'll be easy to talk to."

"Be a gentleman son," said his dad. "Women appreciate a gentleman."

"I will Dad, I will," said Robbie.

When school started the next day, Robbie discovered that almost everyone knew that he and Cindy were going out. It kind of aggravated him at first, but when he saw Cindy for the first time that day and she smiled at him, he got over it. The week flew by quickly and it was Saturday now. He got home as quickly as he could and cleaned himself as best he could. At the dinner table he kept asking his mom if he smelled like oil and gas. "You smell just fine," she said. Robbie wolfed down his dinner and went to his room and made sure his clothes looked all right.

Cindy only lived ten blocks away. Robbie didn't want to get there too early and appear eager. He timed it so it was exactly 7:30 when he knocked on the door. Cindy's father answered the door. "Who are you and what do you want?" he asked.

"I am Robbie Parker sir and I'm here to take Cindy to a movie," said Robbie. Robbie extended his hand to Cindy's father. He looked reluctant at first, but he shook Robbie's hand.

"My name's Bill," he said. "Come in young man. She'll be down in a minute." Cindy's mother came into the room now. Robbie introduced himself to her too.

Cindy's father was looking Robbie over and sizing him up. "What are you gonna do with yourself when you get out of school young fella?" he asked Robbie.

"I'll be joining the Marines right after graduation," said Robbie.

"You know you'll be going to that Vietnam place," said Bill. "Been several boys killed over there this year."

"I know that sir," replied Robbie.

"Well just why would you want to go over there?" asked Bill.

"Someone's got to help those people," answered Robbie. Cindy came downstairs.

"You're not talking politics, are you Daddy?" asked Cindy.

"No not really," answered Bob. "Just sizing up this young man here."

"Well does he meet your approval?" asked Cindy.

"He'll do," answered Bill. "Now you two go on now. We expect you home at midnight."

"I'll be home by then daddy," said Cindy. "Goodbye mom. Let's go Robbie." When they got to the car, Robbie opened the door for Cindy. She was impressed. When he got in, she slid over right next to him and gave him a hug. Things were starting out well. "What's playing tonight?" she asked.

"I have no idea," answered Robbie.

"Well, it doesn't matter," she said. "We probably won't see it anyway." Robbie wasn't quite sure what to think now. It seemed that Cindy might not be the sweet innocent girl he thought she was. It wasn't crowded at all at the drive-in, but Cindy insisted that they park in the back row. It wasn't quite dark yet. Robbie asked her if she wanted some popcorn or something. "Sure, get us some popcorn and a soda," she said. Robbie went to the concession stand and returned with the popcorn and sodas. It was dark now and the previews of coming attractions were playing. As he headed to the car, he couldn't see Cindy. When he got closer he could see that she was in the back seat. He climbed into the back seat too.

"I thought we'd be more comfortable," she said. "There's more room back here. This is one big back seat." Cindy slid over close to him and grabbed some popcorn. They both ate the popcorn and actually watched the movie for a while. When the popcorn was gone, Cindy took the empty container and the soda cups and set them on the floor. Then she looked at Robbie and smiled. Then she unbuttoned her blouse and put her arms around his neck. Robbie remembered what his dad had told him.

"I'm not very experienced at this," said Robbie. "I'm willing to learn."

"You just lay back and enjoy the ride," said Cindy. "I'll take care of you." Robbie reached into a pocket and pulled out some rubbers. "You won't need those," said Cindy. "I'm on the pill."

"Then we'll be twice as safe," said Robbie as he unwrapped one of them.

"Suit yourself, I know I don't have the clap," said Cindy. A good while and three rubbers later, they were getting dressed. "You can take us for a burger and then take me home," said Cindy.

Robbie took her to a diner and they had a burger and some fries. Neither one of them said much. As Robbie stopped the car in front of her house, Cindy put her arms around his neck and ran her tongue down his throat. "Walk me to the door now," she said.

Robbie opened his car door and came around and opened her door and walked her to the front door. "I had a nice time," he said. "I'll see you at school on Monday." Then he gave her a short kiss and backed away before she could run her tongue down his throat again. She told him goodbye and went inside.

~~~~

The next Monday day at school, it seemed like everyone knew about his date with Cindy. Several of his friends told him that they were going to start calling him Woody. "Why Woody?" he asked.

"Cause of that wood you used last night," his friend Brad said. "Besides, your middle initial is W isn't it." Robbie just shook his head and walked away. Before he had gotten to his first class of the day, three girls had asked him out. He finally had a chance to talk with Cindy during lunch break.

"It sounds to me like you told the whole world about our date Saturday night," said Robbie.

"I did not," said Cindy. "I told Betty and she promised to keep it secret."

"Well it's sure no secret now," said Robbie.

"Well look at it this way," said Cindy. "You're going to be the most popular guy in school now. Just enjoy it while you can. When can we go out again?"

"I'm kind of ticked at you right now," said Robbie. "I think I'll check out some of these other girls."

"Screw you Robbie Parker," Cindy said.

"Maybe after these other girls have had their chance," said Robbie as he chuckled and walked away from her.

For the next few weeks, Robbie was living in a young man's fantasy world. He had at least two dates each week. He didn't have to spend much money because all the girls wanted to do was go somewhere and park. Sometimes they went to someone's house if they knew the parents were not home. Robbie's dad was right. Girls like sex too.

~~~~

It was early winter now and the dating slowed down some. Robbie paid more attention to the news when he could. More boys were getting killed in Vietnam. The Marines were doing some heavy fighting on some hills that were near a combat base called Khe Sanh. The army had their hands full along the Cambodian border. With Christmas getting nearer, Robbie felt a little empty. He had been with all of these girls, but there was not one that he felt any attachment to. He decided that it was for the best. He would be leaving for the Marines right after graduation anyway.

A lot of things happened in early 1968, The combat base at Khe Sanh came under siege by thousands of NVA, and the Viet Cong and NVA had launched the Tet Offensive. Almost every Provincial Capital and big city in the country had been attacked. The NVA had taken the city of Hue and the Marines were trying to take it back. The American Embassy in Saigon was overrun by some Viet Cong. Somewhere during all this, Walter Cronkite came on the news and said the war was a stalemate. Robbie didn't understand this. How could it be a stalemate? Sure a lot of Americans were killed, but thousands of VC and NVA were killed. On Mar. 31, LBJ came on the news and said he would not seek, nor would he accept, the nomination for President.

On April 4, 1968, Martin Luther King was killed. There were riots all over the country, even in Cincinnati. Robbie didn't understand this either. There were very few black kids who attended his school. They all seemed nice to him. What was all this hate about? Robbie asked his dad about the riots. "What's this all about?" he asked his dad.

"Inequality I guess Son," said Robert. "Things have been a lot different down south than they are up here. We been integrated for years. The schools in the South were segregated. Blacks were supposed to go to the back of the bus or give up their seat for a white person. There were separate rest rooms and drinking fountains. You name it, they kept it separate."

"How could someone be like that?" asked Robbie.

"They were raised that way," said Robert. "They had to learn it. There's a lot of folks around here who don't care for people of color. You just don't hear about it much because there's a lot fewer black people around here. Haven't you ever wondered why certain people live in certain sections of the city?"

"I guess I never thought about it much till now," said Robbie.

"Well when you get in the Corps, you'll be around more boys from every-where," said Robert. "You'll probably have some blacks, some Chicanos, and some American Indians. Maybe even some Japanese or other Orientals. Anyway, always remember this. You'll all be Marines and when the shit hits the fan, you'll need each other."

Robbie turned eighteen on April 10. As soon as he could, he went to see the Marine Recruiter. He signed up for two years and asked if he could leave for Boot Camp one week after graduation. The Sergeant at the office told him that would be fine. All he had to do before then was to go to Fort Hayes and take his entrance examination and physical. That evening, his dad took him to the American Legion post for a couple of beers. His dad had been a member of the Legion for a long time but he did not go there on a regular basis. Sometimes when they had a dance on a Saturday night, he and Mary would go and dance some. Maybe once a month, his dad would go have a beer with the boys, but his dad wasn't much of a drinker. He didn't smoke either. Robbie had asked him years ago why he didn't smoke. "I smoked a little when I first joined the Corps," his dad answered. "When I got into combat, a lot of the fighting was at night. I decided I didn't need to take any chances smoking and give my position away so I quit."

At the Legion, some of Robert's friends were there. They joined them and Robbie was introduced to all of them. "I hear you're gonna be a jarhead," one of them said.

"I never heard Marines called that before," said Robbie. "But if that's what they call them, then I guess I'll be one."

In Ohio the drinking age was 18 for 3.2% beer. You had to be 21 to drink anything else. Robbie had never drank before. Some of his friends went to a few parties and had gotten drunk and such, but Robbie never did. His dad ordered him a Pabst Blue Ribbon. Robbie decided he liked it. After the first beer, Robert's friends had to leave. Robbie and his dad had the whole place to themselves except the bartender. "Dad, if I ask you something, will you answer it?" asked Robbie.

"Depends on what it is," answered Robert.

"Well, I'd like to know how you got your Bronze Star during the war," said Robbie.

"That's easy son," said Robert. "I got it by not getting killed."

"C'mon dad, you can do better than that," said Robert.

"Well not getting killed was a good part of it," said Robert. "All the men in my squad got killed or wounded that night. My squad was assigned to hold this spot on our line. About 2 AM, I heard the thumps from mortar rounds being dropped into their tubes. We knew we were going to get some incoming and then the Japs would be coming in right after that. We thought we had a little time after the barrage stopped to get ready for them, but we were wrong. They had already slipped within fifteen yards of us. It was so dark, we had no idea they were there. As soon as the incoming stopped, they were on us. I opened up with the .30 cal. We killed them as fast as we could but they kept coming. It was hand to hand most of the time. When the CO found out that our position was in trouble, he sent a couple of fire teams to help out. When it was finally over, me and one other man were the only ones left from my squad who could even stand. Both of us were wounded. There were thirty dead Japs all around our position. Like I said, I got it by not getting killed."

"So were you a machine gunner dad?" asked Robbie.

"No, I was just a rifleman, but the .30 cal. was at my position that night," answered Robert. "Our machine gunner had been killed the day before. So now that you're officially entering the Corps, you better start getting yourself into better shape. I know you're in pretty good shape now, but you don't get up at zero dark thirty and run three miles before breakfast. You can't do push ups all day long. You'll be surprised at what they'll make you do. The stronger you are, the easier it'll be and it will not be easy."

"I'll do my best," said Robbie.

"You'll do your best and then some," said Robert. "They'll get it out of you."

Robbie started training the very next morning. He got up an hour earlier and ran two miles. Then he cranked out all the push ups he could do and then all of the pull ups he could muster. He intended to increase this a little each day and add a few more exercises. He even called the Marine Recruiter and asked him what exercises the Marines did for their Physical Fitness Test. On the evenings he wasn't working, he did his routine then too. By the second week, he was running three miles in eighteen minutes. He passed his entrance examination and his physical the second week also.

One Friday evening as he was finishing up his run and almost home, a very rough sounding car went down the road past him. Right in front of his house, the car backfired and came to a halt. An attractive young dark haired girl was behind the wheel screaming some strange words and beating on the steering wheel. Robbie went over to see if he could be of help. "Excuse me Miss, may I give you a hand." said Robbie.

"Only if you are a mechanic and don't cost much," said the girl.

"Well I am a mechanic and I work cheap," said Robbie. "Now you put the car in neutral and I'll get you off the street. Turn left into that first driveway." She did as instructed and Robbie shoved the car into his driveway. "My name is Robbie Parker and this is my house," said Robbie. "And may I have your name?"

"Yes you may," she answered. "My name is Maria Rios."

"Well Maria, I'll pop the hood on this thing and see if we can get you running," said Robbie. Just as Robbie popped the hood, his dad came outside.

"Who's your new friend and what's the problem son?" said Robert.

"Dad, this is Maria Rios and her car broke down in front of our house," said Robbie. "By the way it was sounding, I'm pretty sure I know what the trouble is." As Robbie put his head under the hood, his mother came out carrying several glasses of iced tea.

"I brought tea for everyone," said Mary. "Would you like some young lady?"

"Thank you very much," said Maria. "I'd like a glass of tea."

"Mom, this is Maria Rios and her car broke down in front of our house," said Robbie.

"Well Maria, you picked a good place to break down," said Maria. "Both of my men know their way around a car. I'll get us some lawn chairs and we can sit and watch the men work." Mary got two folding lawn chairs from the garage and she and Maria sat down and watched the men work. She and Maria had some small talk while the men worked.

As soon as Robbie put his head under the hood, he spotted the problem, or problems. The spark plug wires were hooked up in the wrong order and the distributor cap was cracked. He put the wires in their proper places and started the car. It started right off but was still very rough. "We need to get you a distributor cap," Robbie said to Maria. "The car will run some, but there's no guarantee it would get you home. Once we get you a new cap, the carburetor needs some adjustment. I can get a cap down at the station where I work but they're closed now. I can have you up and running by 10 o'clock in the morning."

"I can't just leave this car here," said Maria. "I couldn't intrude on you. I'll make a call and get some help and get it towed."

"Nonsense," said Mary, "that car's not hurting anything there and Robbie can give you a ride home. Can't you Robbie?"

"Yes mom, I can take Maria home if she doesn't mind," replied Robbie. "You wouldn't mind, would you Maria?"

"No I wouldn't mind but my grandparents might," said Maria.

"And why is that?" asked Robert.

"It is because I am Puerto Rican and you are white," answered Maria. "I live with my grandparents and they are very traditional. They don't think that anyone should be with someone who is not the same race."

"Well you and are I not getting married right this minute," said Robbie. "Let me take you home. If I would do anything out of line, you wouldn't have to worry about your grandparents. My parents would kill me." Robbie went inside and washed his hands and came back outside. He got his car out of the garage. "Your chariot awaits," he said as he opened the door for her. Maria was speechless but she got into the car. Robbie closed the door. "Be back as soon as I get her home," said Robbie as he was leaving the driveway. "Which way?" asked Robbie.

"I live on the south side," said Maria. "The easiest way is to get to High Street and go south. "I'll tell you where to turn."

They didn't talk much. When they got to Maria's house, Robbie got out and opened her door. "I'll need your phone number so I can call you when your car is ready or I can just pick you up in the morning and take you to my house," said Robbie.

"What will this cost me?" asked Maria. "I cannot pay much."

"The distributor cap won't cost much at all," said Robbie. "I will get it for a discount where I work. It won't be more than three dollars."

"Here is my phone number," said Maria. She had gotten into her purse and found some paper and a pencil and had written down her number. "I thank you for your kindness. I must go in now. This is not always a good neighborhood."

"You should hear from me by ten," said Robbie. "Goodnight to you."

As soon as Maria went into the house, her grandparents gave her the third degree on the white boy and the car. She convinced them that the white boy was just some nice boy giving her a helping hand. She informed them that his parents were very nice too.

When Robbie got back home, his parents asked him if he got her home all right. He informed them that she was delivered without incident. "That young lady is very beautiful," said Robert. "You need to ask her out."

"Your father is right," said Mary. "She is one very beautiful girl. You would be a fool not to ask her out."

"So it doesn't bother you that she is Puerto Rican?" said Robbie.

"Why would that bother us?" asked Robert. "My folks were English and your momma's folks didn't mind."

"Mom's folks were English too," said Mary.

"That's true but at times they probably thought I was the devil himself for wanting their baby girl," said Robert.

"I will most likely ask her out tomorrow after I get her car done," said Robbie. "And yes, I can see that she is one good looking girl. She's got to be the best looking girl I've ever seen."

The next morning Robbie was at the station at eight o'clock when they opened and got the distributor cap. By nine o'clock, the car was running like it was brand new. Robbie cleaned himself up and called Maria. Maria's grandmother answered the phone. "Hello, this is Robbie Parker," Robbie said. "I have Maria's car ready. May I please speak to her?" She never said a work to Robbie, but he could hear her yelling something in Spanish. Maria picked up the phone.

"This is Maria. Is that you Robbie?" Maria said.

"Yes it's me," he said. "Your car is good to go. I can pick you up in a half hour."

"That will be fine," Maria said. "I'll be waiting out front."

"O.k., see you shortly," said Robbie. Then Robbie yelled out to his parents that he was leaving to get Maria and left.

When he got there, Maria was sitting on the front porch. She headed to the car as soon as he stopped. Robbie got out and opened the door for her. As she got in and sat down, she reached into a pocket and pulled out three dollars. "Here's the money I owe you," she said. Robbie looked into her eyes, but didn't say anything. After they had gone a few blocks and were at a stoplight, Robbie looked into her eyes again.

"Keep your money," said Robbie. "It was a privilege to do it."

"No, I must pay you for your work," said Maria. "I cannot be indebted to you." The light changed and Robbie took off.

"Well how about this," Robbie began. "I'll take your three dollars if you go out with me."

"I can't go out with you," replied Maria. "I don't know you."

"What do you mean you don't know me," said Robbie. "I'm Robbie Parker. I fixed your car. You've met my parents and you know where I live. I have been a perfect gentleman."

"That's not what I meant," said Maria. "People need to know each other more before they do things together."

"Well around here people get to know each other better by going out and doing things together," said Robbie. "Tell me what you want me to do so I can take you out and I'll do it."

"You must meet my whole family and they must approve of you," said Maria. "That would be my grandparents, my brothers, and my sisters."

"Sounds all right, when can I meet them?" asked Robbie.

"I will talk to my grandparents when I get back home and if they agree, you will be invited to Sunday dinner tomorrow," said Maria.

"I will look forward to it," said Robbie. Not much more was said the rest of the way to Robbie's house. When Robbie pulled into the driveway, his mom and dad were sitting on the front porch reading a newspaper. Robbie opened Maria's car door for her.

As she was walking to her car, Robbie's dad spoke. "Has that son of mine asked you out yet?" he said.

Maria was embarrassed for a second then she spoke. "Yes he has Mr. Parker, but he must meet my family first," Maria answered.

"As it should be," said Robert. Mary sat there and smiled.

Robbie opened Maria's car door for her. "I'll call you this afternoon after you've had a chance to talk with your family," said Robbie as she got into her car. "Or I can give you my number and you can call me."

"You can call me," said Maria. "I will expect your call around four o'clock."

"O.k. Four o'clock it is," said Robbie. "Be careful driving back home." Maria smiled at him and left.

"I wish I would have paid better attention in Spanish class," said Robbie to his parents after Maria had gone. "It could come in handy if I get invited to dinner."

"You'll be invited," said Mary. "That girl likes you already. I can tell. Her folks will too."

"That's right son," said Robert. "Anybody can see that girl already likes you. Don't worry about the Spanish. I would say that everyone in that family probably knows English and they will speak it around you so they can make sure you understand what they mean and say. Besides, I don't think anyone ever learned to speak any foreign language the way they teach it in the schools. All they wanna do is conjugate verbs all the time."

"So when you get invited to dinner, will you be able to get off work?" asked Mary.

"Sure, I'll trade times or days with one of the boys," said Robbie. "They won't mind."

Chapter Three

R obbie called Maria at exactly four o'clock. Maria answered the phone. "Hello, this is Maria. Is that you Robbie?" she said.

"Yes, it's me," answered Robbie.

"Dinner is at one o'clock," said Maria. "I will see you then."

"One o'clock it is," said Robbie. "Goodbye Maria."

"Goodbye Robbie," Maria said.

"Well, I'll be going to dinner," Robbie said to his parents. "Should I take a gift or something for the family?"

"I think you should take some flowers for Maria and her grandmother," said Mary. "Flowers are always good when you're not sure about a gift. You should dress nice and be on your best behavior. In other words, just be yourself."

"Yes Son, just be yourself," added Robert. "You'll be fine."

"I'll have to get the flowers today," said Robbie. "The flower shops will be closed tomorrow."

Robbie went to the flower shop and got a half dozen yellow roses for Maria's grandmother and a half dozen red roses for Maria. Mary assured him that they would be all right the next day. When he went to work that evening, the first thing he did was get someone to trade times with him. Of course everyone was curious about why he needed to trade. Robbie just told them it was a personal matter and he would not explain further.

Robbie wore his nicest clothes for his dinner date. He thought about wearing his suit but that would be a little overboard. He even shaved. He normally only shaved about once a week when his dad would say something about getting some milk and letting the cat lick it off. Robbie was a little nervous when he left the house but as he got closer to Maria's house, he got his confidence back. When he pulled up to the curb, he could see that several people were peering out the front window. He got his composure and went to the front door. Before he could knock, the door opened and Maria stood there. "Hello Maria, it's good to see you again," said Robbie. "I brought you these red roses. I hope you like them."

"It's good to see you again too and I do like the roses," said Maria. "Please come in and meet my family." Robbie came in to find everyone there in the living room. Maria introduced her grandmother first.

"Mrs. Rios, I brought you these yellow roses," said Robbie. "I hope you are not allergic or anything."

"No young man, I am not allergic," she said. "I will take these and Maria's roses and put them in some water, and thank you."

Maria introduced her grandfather next. "Grandfather, this is Robbie Parker," she said. Robbie extended his hand and they shook.

"You have a nice firm handshake Robbie," said grandfather. "A good handshake tells a lot about a man."

Next Maria introduced her two sisters, Elena and Rita. They looked to be about fifteen and sixteen. Robbie was amazed. Maria's sisters were very beautiful too. Next came the two brothers, Roberto and Migel. They were both in their early twenties. Robbie shook hands with both of them but he could tell that they would be hard to like. Grandmother announced that it was time to eat. Maria showed Robbie where sit. They had a long rectangular table. The grandparents sat at each end. Robbie was in the middle on one side with Maria to his left and Elena on his right. Roberto, Migel, and Rita sat across from them. "Do you say grace at your house?" grandfather asked Robbie.

"Not as often as we should," answered Robbie.

"Are you Catholic?" grandfather asked.

"Yes I am," answered Robbie. "But I must tell you that my family does not go to Mass regularly. I was baptized when I was small."

"It is good that you were baptized," said grandfather. "Now I will say grace and we will eat."

As soon as he was done with the prayer, the food started getting passed. Robbie had no idea what anything was but when he began eating, he knew it was very good and had to say something. "Mrs. Rios, I have never eaten anything like this before but I must tell you that it is so very good," exclaimed Robbie. "Maybe my mother could have your recipes."

"She can get them from Maria," said grandmother. "She did most of the cooking for this meal. I just helped."

"Well maybe I can have Maria give them to my mother if we are allowed to get to know each other better," said Robbie. Robbie looked over at Maria and she smiled at him.

Roberto joined in on the conversation now. "So Robbie Parker, what are you going to do with yourself when you get out of school?" he asked.

"I have joined the Marine Corps and I will be leaving for Boot Camp one week after graduation," answered Robbie.

"Just why would anyone join the Marine Corps?" asked Migel. "We've had some friends killed in Vietnam already. There's a lot of protesting going on all over the country."

"I know about the protesting and such but someone's got to go help those people over there," said Robbie. "The Soviets and the Chinese are supplying arms to the North so the whole country can become communist, so we are helping the South."

"It's true that the Soviets and Chinese are arming the North but they haven't sent in ground troops," said Roberto. "Why should the United States?"

"When I get into the Marines, it will be my duty to do what I am told," said Robbie. "The military doesn't make foreign policy. So Roberto and Migel, do you know that you have a good chance of getting drafted?"

"All right, all right, that's enough about that," said Grandmother. "Let's have some decent conversation and enjoy our food. So Robbie, what have you done with your life so far?"

"I started playing baseball when I was small," started Robbie. "I love baseball. I played little league, teener ball, and American Legion ball. My father taught me about cars and I work at a filling station part time."

"We are happy that you were able to fix Maria's car," added Grandfather. "Maybe you can show her brothers how to properly tune up a car." Robbie knew then that it was one of her brothers who had wired the car improperly and hadn't noticed that the distributor cap was cracked.

"So what position did you play?" asked Migel.

"I mostly pitched and when I wasn't pitching I played the infield," said Robbie.

"What kind of pitches do you have?" asked Migel.

"I have a fastball, a sinker and I threw my curve three different ways," said Robbie. "I also had a knuckleball but I hardly ever threw it because I never knew where it would go."

"How fast was your fastball?" asked Roberto.

"I have never been clocked, but it wasn't that fast," answered Robbie. "I'd say maybe 85 to 87. I wasn't a strike out pitcher. I tried to work the hitters by keeping the ball low and working their weak spots. I had a good infield behind me."

"You know some of the best players in the world are from Cuba," said grandfather.

"I know they are," said Robbie. "Maybe some day they will play here in the Majors." Maria hadn't said one word during the meal, but when it was over, she finally spoke.

"So my family, does Robbie meet with your approval?" asked Maria.

"You have my blessing to see this young man," announced her grandparents. Elena and Rita nodded their heads yes but Migel and Roberto didn't speak or respond. After a few minutes of silence, Migel spoke.

"If my baby sister wishes to see this young man, I will approve," said Migel. "But he must know that if he mistreats or hurts her in any way, he will pay."

"That goes for me too," added Roberto.

"So why don't you two take a ride and go to the park or something?" said Grandmother. "The girls and I will clean up. Now you two run along. Remember Maria, you still have to go to work later."

Maria thanked everyone and she and Robbie took off in his car. "So what do you do for work?" asked Robbie.

"I am a shift supervisor at a McDonald's," answered Maria.

"I bet that's a tough job," said Robbie. "I bet it's hard to keep good help."

"Yes it is," said Maria. "We use a lot of young people and it's hard to get them to work at times. We're always short help. Someone's always calling in or not showing up. I'm hoping that one day I will have my own restaurant."

"That would be great," said Robbie. "I already know that you are a great cook. What was it that we ate anyway?"

"It was just jerked chicken with a few other things," said Maria. "I'm glad you liked it."

"It was really good," said Robbie. "So are you still in school?"

"No, I graduated last year," answered Maria. "I thought about college but I could never afford it. Besides, I want to cook. They don't teach that at most colleges."

"I hear they have culinary schools and such but I have no idea where they are or anything," said Robbie. "You could probably teach them a thing or two."

They arrived at the park and Robbie parked the car and got out and opened Maria's door. "Let's just walk around for a while," said Robbie. "We can walk around the lake and watch the swans and the ducks." It was a nice warm, sunny April day and there were several people in the park. People were walking their dogs and children were playing on the merry-go-rounds and swings. There were some young couples laying on blankets and making out. A few elderly couples were sitting on benches and watching the swans. They had gone about halfway around the lake and not said a word, and then Robbie noticed something. They were holding hands. Maria must have realized this at the same time. They stopped walking and looked at each other. Not a word was spoken. Robbie put his arms around her and pulled her to him. She responded and put her arms around his neck. They pulled themselves together and kissed very passionately. "Oh my, I'll feel that kiss for a long time," said Robbie. Maria smiled and they kissed again. Maria gently pulled away from him.

"There is something I must tell Robbie," said Maria. "You must know this before our relationship goes any farther."

"What is it Maria?" asked Robbie.

"You may not want to be with me any more after I tell you," said Maria.

"You're not a mass murderer are you?" asked Robbie.

"Be serious Robbie," said Maria. "This is very important for you to know."

"O.k., I'll be as serious as I can be," said Robbie. "Now please tell me what it is that I must know."

"I got into trouble when I was fifteen," Maria began. "I got pregnant and had a baby. The baby was stillborn. I was young and foolish. The doctor told me I could not have any more children."

"I'm sorry you lost your baby," said Robbie. "Did the father of your child give you any help or anything?"

"No, he just wanted in my pants and as soon as he got what he wanted, he moved on," said Maria. "As I said, I was young and foolish. I thought I was in love. So do you find me repulsive now?"

"Why would I find you repulsive?" said Robbie. "No one's perfect. I'm no angel myself. I have been with a lot of the girls in my senior class. So do you find me repulsive now?"

"No I do not," answered Maria. "But I want to know how you have been able to be with so many girls."

"Well I just started dating last fall," Robbie began. "On my first date I went out with this girl who I thought was nice. We went to the drive-in. I started suspecting that she wasn't sweet and innocent when I got back from the concession stand and she was already in the back seat. I told her that I wasn't experienced and was willing to learn. Well she was all over me. We had sex three times that night. She bragged about it to her friends and after that they all wanted me too. This is a true story."

"I hope you used some protection," said Maria.

"I did," said Robbie. "I think I'm done with those girls now. I haven't been on a date for a good while. Speaking of dates, I would be honored if you would go to the Prom with me."

"I have never been to a Prom," said Maria. "Are they fun? Do I need a formal dress?"

"Well I've never been to a Prom either," said Robbie. "As far as I know, the girls wear formal dresses and the guys wear tuxes. They usually have a band and everybody dances, or a few dance and several people watch. Do you dance?"

"Yes, I love to dance," said Maria. "I have been dancing for a long time."

"Then we should have a great time at the Prom," said Robbie. "Will we be going?"

"Yes we will," answered Maria. "I will need some help finding a dress and I'll want to get my hair done."

"Well you and your hair are beautiful just the way they are," said Robbie. "I can take you to some stores and see about dresses. If money is a problem, I can help out."

"I have money," said Maria. "I'm not sure about what style of dress to buy."

"From the pictures I've seen from last year's Prom, all the girls wore long dresses," said Robbie. "Some were low cut and some were not. I think you should wear low cut and short."

"Robbie, I don't want to look like a tramp," said Maria.

"I assure you," said Robbie. "You will not look like a tramp. You will look absolutely gorgeous."

"It's nice that you think that," said Maria. "Now kiss me one more time and then take me back home. I have to go to work." Robbie didn't need any more coaxing. He pulled her to him and kissed her again.

When they stopped in front of Maria's house, he thought about kissing her again, but didn't. He got out and opened Maria's door for her. "The Prom is in two weeks," said Robbie. "How about we go out again next Friday or Saturday."

"Call me on Wednesday," said Maria. "I will know what my work schedule is by then. Good bye Robbie Parker. I'll be thinking of you."

"Good bye Maria Rios," said Robbie. "I'll be thinking of you too."

When Robbie got home his mother was sitting on the couch watching television. "So how did it go?" asked Mary. "Did they approve of you?"

"Yes they did," answered Robbie. "Maria and I are going to the Prom. Where's Dad?"

"He's over at the Legion Post," said Mary. "He wanted you to join him if you didn't get back too late."

"I'll go there right now," said Robbie. When Robbie got to the Legion, Robert was sitting with several of his friends. Every one of them was drinking Pabst Blue Ribbon. "Hey Charlie, bring my son a Pabst," Robert yelled to the bartender. "Pull up a chair Son and tell us how it went today."

"It went good today dad," started Robbie. "Her grandparents approve of me and we'll be going to the Prom. We'll have a date next weekend too."

"That's good son," said Robert. "I knew that girl liked you. She sure is a looker. Reminds me of your mother when we were young."

There were four other men sitting at the table and all of them were veterans. Two of them were with the army in WWII and the other two were in the Corps and served in Korea. They all knew Robbie was joining the Corps so they all had to give him advice on just about everything. Robbie drank three beers while he was listening to them. He was about to get another one when the bartender announced that it was closing time. They always closed early on Sunday unless there was a big event or something. All of them left and as Robbie was about to get into his car, his dad asked him. "Are you o.k. to drive?"

"I'm good dad," Robbie answered. "Have you got any beer at home? Maybe we can have another one when we get home. Maybe Mom can join us."

"I got a six pack at home," Robert answered. "That sounds good."

When they walked in the door at home, Mary took one look at them. "Looks like you two could use another beer," she said. "Have a seat and I'll get us one. Why don't we sit out back. It's a nice day." Mary got the beers and Robert rounded up some lawn chairs. "So how was the Legion today men of mine," asked Mary.

"It was interesting," answered Robbie. "I got all kinds of advice from dad's friends. I should be able to skip right over Boot Camp and go kill Commies. No seriously Mom, Dad's got some good friends."

"Veterans stick together Son," said Robert. "Always remember that."

After Robbie finished his next beer, he knew he had a little buzz going. He could tell that his dad did too. Everything seemed funny now. Every time one of them said something, they all laughed. Robbie started thinking about Maria again. "I want to have some more dance sessions before the Prom," said Robbie. "I want to make sure I still have my moves. Maria loves to dance too."

"We'll have some sessions this week and next if you want," said Mary. "I bet Maria can show you a few moves too."

"Speaking of moves, why don't you and me go try some out right now?" Robert said to Mary.

"All right by me," said Mary. "Robbie, you can have another beer if you want. Your dad and I will be busy for a while. I'll fix us something to eat later."

"Go on you two. I'll sit here and think about Maria," said Robbie. He sat there for a good while thinking of Maria the whole time. He wasn't sure if he should have another beer or not, but he got one anyway. It went down easy. His thoughts of Maria got better and better. He decided it was time to go take a leak. He felt a little woozy when he got up. He stood there for a minute and then headed to the bathroom. He made it there o.k. Then he went back outside and sat down. Maria was back on his mind. The next thing he knew, his mother was tapping him on the shoulder.

"Come on Robbie. I made us something to eat," she said. "You nodded off for a while. Are you all right?"

Robbie yawned a little and stretched his arms. "I'm o.k. Mom," said Robbie. "I just been sitting here dreaming about Maria. Had me a good dream too."

"Well dream your way to the dinner table," said Mary. "Don't want it getting cold."

Robbie ate his food without saying a word and then excused himself. "Mom, Dad, I had a good day today. Thank you," he said. Then he went to his room. It was only around eight o'clock, but Robbie decided to take a shower and go to bed early.

The next morning when he got up, he felt great. He went out and did his running and exercises and then showered and ate breakfast. "Are you feeling all right this morning?" Mary asked him. "You've never drank that much before. You didn't get sick or anything did you?"

"No Mom, I'm o.k.," answered Robbie. "I got a little woozy after that last beer, but that was it. I feel really good today."

"That's good," said Mary. "Have a good day at school today. We can dance some this evening if you want."

"Sounds good Mom," said Robbie. "See you this afternoon."

The school day started out good, but as the day wore on, Robbie knew he didn't want to be there. That afternoon when Cindy Tyler cornered him, he knew for sure that he didn't want to be there. "What is it Cindy?" Robbie asked her. "Just what is it you want from me?"

"Why haven't you asked me to the Prom Robbie Parker?" Cindy asked.

"Because I don't want to take you to the Prom," answered Robbie.

"But I'm the first girl you ever screwed," said Cindy. "You should ask me since I was your first."

"Yeh, but I wasn't your first Cindy Tyler," said Robbie. "I think you were screwing me more than I was screwing you. You shouldn't have any trouble finding someone to take you to the Prom. Everyone knows that you put out. Now look, I'm glad that I lost my virginity with you, but that's as far as we go. Now please excuse me. I don't want to be late for class."

"You're an ungrateful bastard," said Cindy.

"I might be considered ungrateful by some people but I am no bastard and don't ever call me that again," proclaimed Robbie. "Now please excuse me." Robbie left and went into his classroom. Cindy just stood there a little dumb-founded. Robbie's friend Brad walked by and saw Cindy with the strange look on her face.

"What's up Cindy?" Brad asked. "You looked like you just saw a ghost."

"That Robbie Parker pissed me off," said Cindy. "He doesn't want to take me to the Prom."

"Well I'll take you to the Prom," said Brad. "That is if you'll go with me."

"I guess I will," said Cindy. "Nobody else has asked me. I can't figure out why."

"Well don't worry about that anymore," said Brad. "We'll have a great time. I'll get with you later and we'll get everything set up. Gotta get to class now."

Wednesday rolled around and Robbie gave Maria a call. Maria was free Saturday afternoon and evening. "Why don't I pick you up at one o'clock and we can go to the park again," said Robbie.

"That would be fine," said Maria. "I liked it at the park with you. I'll see you Saturday." Robbie was scheduled to work Saturday evening so he got someone to trade with him again.

"She must be something," said the boy he traded with. "I don't mind working anyway. My girl and I just broke up. This'll gimme a few more bucks for the next girl I take out."

"Well I appreciate it," said Robbie. "You might get more time anyway after I leave for the Marines."

"Yep, I probably will till they get someone else hired," the boy said. "Who knows, maybe I'll join the Army or the Navy. I can't afford college. I suspect that if I don't do something, I'll get drafted sooner or later. Don't wanna be in no Marine Corps though. I hear them guys are crazy."

"Well thanks for trading with me," said Robbie. "I guess I'll find out if Marines are crazy or not before too long."

Robbie had a couple more dance sessions before Saturday. He felt very confident. Mary could see that he was confident. Robert wasn't there because he was working 2nd shift. "That Maria is going to fall in love with you son," said Mary. "You are one smooth fella on the dance floor."

"Thanks mom. You and dad are some great teachers," said Robbie. "Did you get along with your parents as well as we get along?"

"No I didn't Robbie," Mary began. "My father was a hard man to like. I mean we loved him but he was just so hard to like. He was always negative about everything. I never ever saw him show my mother any type of affection. He acted like she was his servant and she waited on him hand and foot all the time. He never hit her that I know of but there were times when I thought he might. I would have hit him with a ball bat if he did. He never talked to me about anything other than to tell me to do something. He really never did like your father. I don't know why. Your dad was always a perfect gentleman."

"Maybe that's why," said Robbie. "Maybe he thought Dad was just putting on a show to impress him and he was really one wild kid when he was out of sight."

"Well I do know that my mother loved him," said Mary. "It about did her in when he died. It's probably a good thing that she died not long after him. I think she was having a breakdown. So back to you and Maria. Try to remember in the heat of passion that you will be leaving a week after graduation. If you think you are in love for the first time, it will hurt when you leave her. It will be a hurt like no other. I'm sorry Robbie. I was remembering what it was like for your father and me. He was gone for a long, long time."

"Don't worry mom," said Robbie. "I do know that I have some strong feelings for Maria and I know she likes me. I'll be able to handle whatever happens."

~~~~

Saturday came and it was a beautiful day. There wasn't a cloud in the sky and it was almost eighty degrees. Robbie wore some blue jeans, a T shirt and some sneakers. When he got to Maria's house and was making his way to the door, Maria came out before he got there. Robbie was shocked. Maria was even more beautiful than he had remembered. She had on a very well fitting T shirt and sneakers. She also wore a pair of well fitting shorts. They weren't what they called short shorts, but they weren't much longer than that. Robbie kind of stood there for a minute staring at her. "What is it Robbie?" said Maria. "Is something wrong?"

"No, nothing is wrong at all," said Robbie. "You are just so beautiful. I mean it. You are gorgeous."

"So you like the way I look," said Maria.

"I'm not dead," said Robbie. "Of course I like the way you look."

"Well we better get going before my grandfather comes out here to see what's goin on," said Maria. They made their way to Robbie's car. Robbie opened the door for her. As soon as he got in, Maria slipped over right next to him. Robbie looked over at her and smiled. Then he started the olds and they headed to the park. They didn't speak much till they got to the park.

"I brought a blanket today in case we wanted to lay in the shade for a while," said Robbie.

"Let's walk a bit first," said Maria. "I like walking with you." They took off walking around the lake. "I found myself a prom dress," said Maria. "I found it at the first store I went to."

"Are you going to tell me about it or will it be a surprise?" asked Robbie.

"We'll let it be a surprise," answered Maria. "I know you'll like it. It will go with any color tux you wear. I will tell you this though. If you buy me a corsage, it will have to be a wrist corsage."

"That's a good thing to know," said Robbie. "So did your grandmother approve of your dress?"

"Yes she did," said Maria. "My sister's think it's beautiful too. My grandfather said that we had to get some pictures taken at the house before we leave that day."

"I figure my parents will want pictures taken too," said Robbie. "So here's what we'll do that evening. I'll be at your house at six o'clock and they can take some pictures. Then we'll go to my house for pictures. Then we'll have dinner at a nice restaurant. I'll have reservations made. Then we'll go to the Prom and dance ourselves silly."

"What will we do after that?" asked Maria.

"I'm not sure yet," said Robbie. "Several of the kids are having after Prom parties. When the time comes, we'll see what we want to do. Make sure your parents know that you will not get home till way late."

"They already know that," said Maria. "Now are you renting a tux or do you have one?"

"My dad has one," said Robbie. "It's older but it still looks good. We are about the same size so if it fits, I'll wear it. If not, I'll get one rented."

"So you are a dancer," said Maria. "You're not one of those boys who stands around and watches others dance."

"I'm a dancer," said Robbie. "You'll see."

"So who taught you how to dance?" asked Maria.

"My parents," said Robbie. "My dad is one smooth fella on the dance floor. I would have never believed my parents could dance like that. They are very good."

"Well I intend to make you an even better dancer than you are now," said Maria.

"I can't wait," said Robbie. He pulled her to him and kissed her. By her response, Robbie could tell that she wanted some more. He obliged her. He pulled away from her and looked into her eyes. "Let's finish walking around the lake and then lay on the blanket for a while," said Robbie. "Then maybe later we can get something to eat. Is there anything you would like to eat?"

"How about we get a pizza," said Maria. "You like pizza don't you?"

"I love pizza," said Robbie. "There's a new place not far from here. We'll give it a try."

They spent a lot of the afternoon making out, but Robbie did find out a lot about Puerto Rico. He also found out that Maria's parents had died and that was why they lived with the grandparents. Grandfather and Grandmother keep hoping that the brothers will get married and move out one day. About five thirty, they both decided they were a little hungry so they went to the pizza place. They took a table in one of the corners. Robbie pulled out a chair for Maria. She was impressed. A young waitress brought them some menus and asked if they'd like something to drink while they read the menu. "They have beer here if you want one," Maria said to Robbie. "It won't bother me if you have a beer."

"I'll just have a coke," said Robbie. "If you'd like a beer I'll get one for you."

"I'll just have a coke too," said Maria. "I drank a little at one time but anymore the only time I drink is if we have some wine with dinner at home."

"So how old are you Maria?" asked Robbie.

"I'm nineteen," she answered. "I just turned nineteen in February. My birthday is on Valentine's Day."

"That'll make it easy to remember," said Robbie.

"So you think you'll be wanting to remember my birthdays," said Maria. "I'm glad. I hope we can have many birthdays together."

"I hope so too," added Robbie. "Now do your parents know that you aren't supposed to drink wine in this state till you're twenty one?"

"They know. They think Ohio has some silly laws," said Maria. "They think as long as you act responsible, age doesn't matter. Besides, I only get a glass or two of wine when we have it anyway. So I like my pizza with everything but anchovies."

"That's the way I like it too," said Robbie. The waitress came back with their drinks and took their order. They talked about anything and everything the whole time at the pizza parlor. When they were finished and about ready to leave, Maria started asking Robbie questions about his future.

"Have you thought about what you might want to do after you get out of the Marines?" Maria asked.

"No, not really," answered Robbie. "I signed up for two years because that was the shortest time allowed. That way if I don't like it, I figure two years isn't all that long. Then if I did decide I like it in the Marines, I could stay in and make it a career."

"You have a lot of confidence in yourself Robbie Parker," said Maria. "I know that whatever you do you will be good at it. Now I think you should take me home now."

"It's early yet," said Robbie. "We can take in a movie or something."

"I know but if I am with you much more today I will want to sleep with you," said Maria. "I don't think that we should do that yet. Now please take me home. I have had a wonderful day."

"O.k., I'll take you home," said Robbie. "I have also had a wonderful day. The prom is a week away. May I see you sometime before them."

"I am off work on Wednesday," said Maria. "You can come over that evening and we can get some ice cream or something."

"Sounds good," said Robbie. They went to the car and of course Robbie opened her door. When he got in she slid over close to him. Robbie sat there for a minute and did not start the car. They turned and faced each other. Robbie pulled her closer to him and began kissing her passionately. She did not object. "I wanted to do that now and not be tempted to do it in front of your house," said Robbie.

"I appreciate that Robbie," Maria said. "Although I think you and I both will be tempted when we get there." Robbie started the car now. When they got to Maria's house, Robbie parked the car at the curb and went around and opened Maria's door. He walked her to the door and then gave her a quick kiss on the lips. Maria pulled him to her and whispered in his ear.

"I will have a hard time sleeping tonight," she said. Then she backed away and smiled at him and went inside.

Robbie went back to his car and just sat there for a minute. "I'll have a hard time sleeping too," he said to himself. Then he started the car and headed home. His parents were on the couch watching TV when he got home.

"How was your day?" Mary asked him when he came inside.

"I can't imagine how anything could be better," said Robbie. "Maria is one nice girl."

"So have you got everything set up for the Prom?" asked Robert.

"Yes we do Dad," answered Robbie. "I gotta make sure your tux will fit me and that's about it. I'll be going to her house around six so her people can take some pictures. Then we'll come back here so you can take pictures. Then she and I will go out to a nice restaurant and then go to the Prom."

"Have you picked out a restaurant yet?" asked Mary.

"Yes, I'll make a reservation at Engine House No. 5," said Robbie. "I hear that's a nice place."

"It is," said Robert. "Your mother and I have been there a couple of times. Do you need any money or anything?"

"No, I'm good dad," answered Robbie

"Do you have any plans for after the Prom?" asked Mary.

"There will be several after Prom parties," said Robbie. "We're just going to see how things go and decide later."

"Well if you would go to a party and have a little too much to drink, don't hesitate to call us," said Robert. "We know you got a good head on your shoulders but sometimes good heads get careless too."

"I won't be getting drunk," said Robbie. "I want to have all my wits about me when I'm with Maria."

"That's a good thing," said Robert. "Tell me, do any of them kids in your school smoke that pot stuff?"

"I don't really know Dad," answered Robbie. "I haven't been around anyone who was smoking it but that doesn't mean no one is."

"They say on the news sometimes that some of our boys in Vietnam are smoking that stuff," said Robert. "I don't know. I think if we'd have had that stuff in the Pacific, I'd been too scared to try it. If I was gonna get shot at or blown up, I'd want to know what was going on around me."

"I'll be smart dad. Don't worry," said Robbie. "It's early yet. Think I'll change my clothes and do some running and stuff." Robbie got his clothes changed and then went outside and started running. After three miles he felt really good so he ran three more. Then he did his push ups, pull ups, and bends and thrusts. He still felt good after all this so he took off and ran another mile. It was almost dark when he got home. He let his parents know he was back home and then took a long shower and then went to bed. Thoughts of Maria kept him awake for a while, but it wasn't long till he was asleep. He woke up around six thirty. He put on some fresh running clothes and took off. This time he ran about eight miles. He did his exercises and then went back home. His parents were sitting at the kitchen table having some coffee.

"Can I make you some breakfast?" asked Mary.

"I'll just get some cereal," said Robbie.

"Nonsense, if you're going out and doing all that running and such, you need a good breakfast," said Mary. "Now sit down and have some coffee while I make some bacon, eggs, and potatoes."

"You know I don't drink much coffee," said Robbie.

"You will," said Robert. "You'll need it. That's one thing I always liked about a field mess hall. Them boys knew how to make good coffee. The stuff we had at camp was terrible, but whenever we had a field mess set up, we had good coffee. Your mother makes good coffee."

"My mother taught me," said Mary. There won't ever be any of that instant stuff in our house."

"So what are going to do today son?" asked Robert.

"I don't really have any plans," answered Robbie. "Maria's working today and I have all my school work done. Maybe we can watch a ball game."

"How about we go out and do some shooting?" asked Robert. "It's sunny today and it's not supposed to get real warm. It'll be a good day for shooting. It could be the last time you shoot before you go to Boot Camp. I figure after the Prom you'll be spending every spare minute you have with Maria."

"You're probably right dad," said Robbie. "We can go right after breakfast if you want."

Robbie did very well at two and three hundred yards, but when they got to five hundred yards, he had a few out of the bull. "You can't be thinking of Maria when you're shooting son," said Robert. "You need your concentration on that front sight blade, not Maria's figure."

"It's hard dad," said Robbie. "It's hard."

"I know son," said Robert. "I always had a hard time shooting cause I was always thinking of your mother. I told myself that the better I shot, the quicker I could get home to her." Robbie loaded up another clip and took aim. All eight went in the bull at about a five inch group."

"That's good shooting son," said Robert. "Now let's pick up our brass and such and get back home. Your mother and me have a date this afternoon."

"So are you going somewhere?" asked Robbie.

"Yes we're going somewhere but we're not leaving the house," said Robert.

"I understand," said Robbie. "Maybe I'll go the park and catch a little league game or something after I clean the rifle."

Mary had dinner waiting on them when they got home. Robbie ate his meal and then cleaned the M-1 and gave it a good oiling. Then he walked to the park. There was a little league game being played. It was only the second inning so Robbie took a seat in the small bleachers and watched. "Man, those boys look small," he said to himself. "Was I that small when I played little league? I reckon I was." Robbie's coach from his Legion team was the home plate umpire. He saw Robbie watching the game and went over and talked with him between innings.

"So you'll be leaving home real soon won't you?" he said.

"I'll be leaving for Boot Camp one week after graduation," said Robbie. "How's your team going to be this year?"

"I think we'll do well," said the coach. "I got a left hander who can throw ninety. He's a little wild sometimes but he'll come around."

"Ninety, that's pretty fast," said Robbie. "I wonder if I could hit a ninety miles per hour fastball on the inside corner just under the letters."

"I think you could," said the coach. "Once you got used to that speed, you'd do well. Well better get back. If I don't see you again, keep your head down and don't be no hero."

Robbie watched three more innings and then left. The people in the crowd didn't act the same way they did when he played little league. They were screaming and yelling at the kids and the coaches and umpires. Robbie decided he better leave before he got into it with some kids parents. As he was walking home, his friend Brad came driving by. "Need a lift?" he said to Robbie as he stopped his car by the curb.

"No, I'm good," said Robbie. "You know I only live a few blocks from here."

"That's true," said Brad. "So have you got a date for the Prom?"

"Yes I do," answered Robbie.

"Well who is it?" asked Brad. "It's not someone from our school is it?"

"No, she's not from our school," answered Robbie.

"Well what's her name. Maybe I know her," said Brad.

"You'll meet her at the Prom," said Robbie. "So who are you taking?"

"I thought the whole world knew," said Brad. "I'm taking Cindy Tyler."

"Well I didn't know," said Robbie. "I hope you have a good time."

"Is that all you have to say about Cindy?" asked Brad. "I figured you'd have to say something about her screwing the hell out of you on your first date."

"I don't have to say anything about Cindy," said Robbie. "She's the one who told the whole world about our date. What you two do is your own business. So you want to come over to the house for a beer. We might have some in the frig. You are eighteen aren't you?"

"Yes I am and a beer sounds good." said Brad.

When they got to Robbie's house, Robbie had Brad go around the house to the back. "You go on and have a seat out back," said Robbie. "I'll go in and get us a beer if there's any." When Robbie went into the house, he could hear his parents having their date. "I hope I like being with whatever woman I end up with as much my as my dad likes being with my mom," Robbie thought to himself. There were four beers in the refrigerator. Robbie took two of them and went out back. "This is Blue Ribbon," said Robbie. "That's what we drink at my house."

"Thanks," said Brad. "My old man always drinks Strohs. He lets me have one every once in a while. So you'll be in the Marines shortly. Are you getting nervous or anything yet?"

"No, not yet," said Robbie. "I imagine I will the day before I leave and on the way down there to Parris Island. I've heard all kinds of horror stories about Boot Camp. I reckon I'll find out for myself. So what are you gonna do after graduation?"

"My folks tell me I'm going to Ohio University in Athens but I haven't even applied yet," said Brad. "I have no idea what I would want to be or anything. I think college would be a waste of time unless a person knew what they wanted to do. I have heard that OU is a big party school. That might be fun. If I go, I reckon I'll find out."

"I've heard that about OU too," said Robbie. "College is an expensive place to go if all you want to do is party."

"Well my parents say they'll pay for it," said Brad.

Robbie's dad came out the back door with a beer in his hand. "Are we going to need more beer?" asked Robert. "It's Sunday. Can't buy beer on Sunday around here."

"No, I won't need any more. How bout you Brad?" asked Robbie.

"Well I could always use another beer," said Brad. "I could go to my house and get some of my dad's Strohs. He'd probably let me have some if I told him I was drinking with Robbie's dad."

"Remember we have school tomorrow," said Robbie.

"My dad wouldn't let me have enough beer for us to get plastered," said Brad. "You two sit tight. I'll be back shortly." Brad finished the beer he was drinking and took off.

"What's Brad doing after graduation?" asked Robert.

"He doesn't know for sure," answered Robbie. "His folks want him to go to Ohio University and they say they'll pay for it, but Brad thinks he shouldn't go to college unless he knows what he wants to do."

"Well that makes sense," said Robert. "College costs a lot. A person should have an idea what they want before they spend that much money."

"So how was your date dad?" asked Robbie.

"I'll tell you one thing Robbie boy," said Robert. "If you get a woman that's as good as your mother, you'll be one lucky man. So it apparently doesn't bother you to ask your parents about their sex life. That's good. Maybe more parents should talk to their kids about sex. Maybe some people would get along better. There's a lot of couples who lose interest after kids come. That's wrong."

"So dad, have you ever thought about being with another woman?" asked Robbie.

"Take a good look at your mother," said Robert. "Just why would I want anyone else with her around. Now I look at other women and such, but I have never even had one thought about being with someone other than your mother." Mary came out the door now and had a beer in her hand.

"So what are my men talking about now?" asked Mary. She went over and sat on Robert's lap.

"We were talking about sex darlin'," said Robert.

"So do we need to go back inside," asked Mary.

"Maybe later," said Robert. "I think we already had a good date today. We were also talking about college. Brad doesn't know what he wants to do with himself after school."

"Well he'll get it figured out," said Mary. "That is if Uncle Sam doesn't help him make up his mind." Brad pulled into the driveway and came around back carrying a six pack.

"Dad said I could have this," said Brad. "He wants you, Mr. Parker, to make sure I don't drink it all myself."

"Well we wouldn't want you to get into trouble so we'll all help you," said Robert. "I haven't had a Strohs since forever. Might be nice for a change."

"You all go ahead and take one," said Mary. "I'll put the rest in the frig." Mary put the beers in the refrigerator and put the empties in the trash.

Robbie took a sip of the Strohs. He paused a minute and then took another sip. "I think I like this stuff better than the ribbon," said Robbie. "There's not much difference, but I think it's better."

"It's not bad beer," said Robert. "Better remember what good beer tastes like cause you might not get any good beer some places. I don't know how the military handles drinking ages. Used to be they would let you drink at the enlisted club even if you weren't the legal age for that state. Don't know what they do now. Should be that if a man is old enough to serve, he should be able to get a drink if he wants one." Mary came back outside and went back to sitting on Robert's lap. Brad seemed kind of surprised by this but he never said a word.

The boys got to talking about baseball and the Cincinnati Reds. They all decided that Pete Rose would set a record some day, but the Reds would need to make some changes if they wanted to be a sound team. When the beer was gone, Brad excused himself and went home. Robert promised him that he would repay his father for the beer. Mary went inside to get dinner started. Robert and Robbie stayed outside for a while.

"So the Prom's getting closer," said Robert. "You got everything all set?"

"Yes dad, we're all set," said Robbie. "I'll see Maria on Wednesday and if anything needs taken care of, we'll get it done."

"Maria seems like a real nice girl," said Robert. "You two will have a great time. If she's a really good dancer and you learn some new moves, you can show your mother and me. Let's go in now and see if the Red's game is on. We can watch while your mother finishes dinner."

The Red's game wasn't on but there was a Yankee's game on. They watched it anyway. "I don't like the Yankees," said Robert. "Never did. My dad never liked the Yankees either. I never did like the American League either. Maybe if Cleveland had a good team more often I would watch them some."

About an hour after dinner, Robbie decided he would go out and run and do his exercises. He had drunk three beers but wasn't worried that it would affect his performance. It didn't. He ran five miles and felt like he hadn't even broken a sweat. He did his exercises and then showered and went to bed early. He got up early and did his running and exercises. Monday and Tuesday seemed to drag on and on. Finally it was Wednesday. At 6:30 PM, Maria and Robbie were sitting in the parking lot of a Dairy Queen drinking a milkshake.

"I have missed you Robbie," said Maria. "I can't wait to dance with you. I feel like a little kid who just can't wait for Christmas."

"I feel that way too," said Robbie. "I hope the next two days don't seem as slow. I have to work Thursday and Friday so that should keep my mind occupied some. So how have things been at your house? Is everyone there o.k.?"

"Everyone is o.k.," started Maria. "My brother Migel got himself engaged but they haven't set a date yet. Rita and Elena both will be attending a Prom. Rita's is this weekend and Elena's is next weekend. My grandparents are kind of worried about them. It's kind of nice that they are. That way they won't worry about me. Do you think your parents worry about you?"

"I'm sure they worry about me but they trust me," said Robbie. "They know I won't do anything too stupid. Robbie looked into Maria's eyes. She was already close to him. He began kissing her again and again. The kisses seemed to last forever. After a good while they were startled by a car horn. Robbie finally realized that he had bumped the horn while they were making out. Then he looked at his watch. They had been making out for well over an hour. "I think I better get you home," said Robbie. "If we stay here and keep this up, someone might call the law on us."

"If we got arrested, do you think they could put us in the same cell?" said Maria.

"I doubt it," said Robbie. "But if they did, maybe we could ask for some curtains too."

Maria looked into his eyes and smiled. "Well give me another good kiss and then take me home," said Maria. Robbie obliged her. When they got to Maria's house, he opened her door and walked her to the door. The he pulled her to him and kissed her. It wasn't a long kiss but it wasn't a short kiss either. Then he pulled back a little. "I'll be here at 6 PM Saturday," said Robbie. "I'll be thinking of nothing but you till then." Maria gave him a kiss on the cheek.

"I'll be missing you Robbie," she said as she went inside.

Chapter Four

Saturday finally arrived. Robbie got up and did his running and exercises. He showered and then had a big breakfast. He had a lot of school work to do so he got right on it. That took up the rest of the morning . He spent a couple of hours cleaning his car. Then he went to the flower shop and picked up the corsage he had ordered. He spent some time making sure his dancing shoes were perfectly shined. Robert had showed him how to do a spit shine. He looked over and over at the tux to make sure it was perfect. He shaved and showered around five o'clock and then got dressed. Once he was dressed he had his mother check him out to make sure everything was perfect. "I've got me some good looking men," Mary said as she was checking him out. "Maria is one lucky girl." Robbie didn't say a word as he smiled at her. "Now have your dad give you the once over and then go get your girl," said Mary.

Robert took one look at Robbie. "All of the girls, not just Maria will love you," said Robert. "You got some good genes. Now go get your girl." Robbie thanked them, got the corsage and then left.

When he arrived at Maria's house and started to the door, he could see that several people were peering out the window. Maria's grandfather answered the door when Robbie knocked. "Come in young man," he said. "Maria will be down in a minute. You look nice. Maria will be pleased." Robbie looked up as Maria was coming down the stairs. He was speechless. He finally spoke. "Oh my, you are so beautiful," he said. "Oh my." Maria's dress was strapless and was around four inches or so above her knees. Robbie didn't know what type of material it was but it fit her like a glove. It showed all of her curves perfectly. It was royal blue in color and had some designs on it in the right places. She smiled at him as she came down the stairs.

"I take it you like the way I look," said Maria as she approached Robbie and kissed him on the cheek. "Do you like what I had done to my hair?" Robbie was so taken by the dress that he hadn't noticed her hair. He gave it a look.

"It's really nice," said Robbie. "It goes very well with your dress and it enhances your beautiful face. I like it. I brought you this corsage. Let's put it on you and get those pictures taken. Robbie helped her put the corsage on her arm and Maria put a yellow rose in his lapel.

"You are very handsome tonight Robbie," said Maria. "I'll probably have to fight off the other girls." Robbie smiled at her and gave her a kiss on the cheek. Then the whole rest of the family stood around while Grandfather was taking pictures. Rita was wearing her formal dress but her date was not there yet. She was beautiful too. When they were finished, all of them told Maria and Robbie to have a fun evening and enjoy themselves. Not one word was said about getting home at any certain time.

When they were out the front door, Robbie gave Maria his arm and escorted her to the car. He opened and closed the door for her. When he was in the car, Maria slid over next to him and put her arms around his neck and kissed him. Then she smiled at him and then kissed him again. "We better be going now," said Robbie. "We'll have plenty of time for this later." He smiled at her and then started the car.

When they arrived at Robbie's house, his parents were all ready with the camera. "You two have got to be the best looking couple I've ever seen," said Mary. "Everybody at that Prom will envy you two."

"Yep, they both got good genes," said Robert.

The pictures got taken and Maria and Robbie left for their dinner reservation. When they arrived at the restaurant, all eyes in the place were on the two of them. There were also other couples there who were going to Proms. The hostess showed them to their table and a waiter came and took their drink order.

"I don't know what to eat Robbie," said Maria. "I've never been to a nice restaurant like this before."

"This is a first for me too," said Robbie. "I think we should try something that we've never had before. Let's not get a steak. We can get that at home any time. Why don't we start off with a shrimp cocktail. I hear these places sometimes have specials too that aren't on the menu."

"Shrimp cocktail sounds good," said Maria. "We'll see what the specials are." The waiter came back with their drinks which were iced tea and then told them what the specials were. One was some type of steak that they had never heard of and there were two fish specials. One was halibut and the other was mahi. "Why don't one of us get the halibut and the other get the mahi," Maria said. "Then we can kind of share."

"That sounds good," said Robbie. He told the waiter the order and the waiter thanked him and said he'd be back shortly with some bread. Robbie couldn't take his eyes off Maria. "I always knew that you were beautiful," he said. "But I just can't help myself. A guy would have to be dead for ten years to not know how beautiful you are."

"I'm glad you think so," said Maria. "You are one good looking man yourself." They leaned across the table and kissed. Robbie looked around the dining room. All eyes were still on them.

"We must be popular tonight," said Robbie. "Everybody is still watching us."

"You just wait till we get on the dance floor," said Maria. "They'll really get an eye full."

They both agreed that their meals were probably some of the best they had ever had. Robbie left a good tip for the waiter and they left for the school. When they arrived at the school, they could hear that the band had already started playing. Robbie escorted her inside. Once again, all eyes were on them. The first couple they met when they went inside was Brad and Cindy. Brad took one look at Maria and his tongue about hit the floor. "Just where did you find this goddess?" asked Brad.

Brad and Cindy, this is Maria Rios," said Robbie. "Maria, this is Brad and Cindy."

"I'm very pleased to meet you," said Maria. "You both look nice."

Robbie could tell that Cindy was a little upset because Brad couldn't take his eyes off of Maria. "Let's go mingle some Brad," said Cindy. "Please excuse us." They left but Brad kept looking back at Maria. "Do you think he's screwed her yet?" said Cindy to Brad.

"Now how would I know that?" asked Brad. "But who wouldn't want to. She's fabulous looking."

"Well how do I look to you?" asked Cindy.

"You look good," said Brad.

"Nice of you to finally notice," said Cindy.

Robbie took Maria around and introduced her to some more of his friends. There were a few couples on the dance floor trying to dance but the band wasn't playing anything that was good dance music. They were playing a lot of what everyone was calling acid rock. Robbie knew the boys in the band so he decided he would talk with them and see if they would play more songs that were good dance songs. When they finished the song they were playing, Robbie went up and had some words with the lead singer. "You guys can play this new stuff really well," said Robbie. "You sound just like Jimi Hendrix and I would have sworn that was Eric Clapton a while back. My friend, your music is good, but it's not dance music. We came here to dance. Would you play some rock and roll that we can dance to?"

"We surely can," said the lead singer. "We've been playing this new stuff because we thought everyone would want to hear it. We know a bunch of older rock and roll stuff that's great to dance to. Now as soon as you tell me who this hot girl is, we'll start playing."

"Maria, the lead singer here is John Townsend," said Robbie. "John, this is Maria."

"I'm definitely pleased to make your acquaintance lovely lady," said John. "Now show me what you can do on the dance floor." The band broke into "Run Around Sue."

Robbie and Maria grabbed each other and had at it. The whole floor cleared and everyone was watching them. Most of the kids looked like they had never seen jitterbugging before. Robbie spun Maria around his waist a couple of times and flipped her over his shoulders and then pulled her underneath him between his legs. Everyone was clapping along and cheering. When the song ended, everyone gathered around them begging to learn how to dance like that. That is, everyone but Cindy Tyler. She stayed back and kept Brad from the crowd. "What's your problem?" asked Brad. "Them two can dance. We should learn how to do that. Even if you're ticked at Robbie, don't mean you can't learn to dance like that."

"I already know how to dance," said Cindy. "I'll show you when they play another good song."

The next song they played was "Brown Eyed Girl." Robbie and Maria had at it again. The others watched for a while and then decided to give it a try. Brad was surprised. Cindy did know how to jitterbug some. He tried to follow her as best he could. Some of the couples picked it up pretty quick. Others didn't but didn't give up. The next song was a slow one, "Walk Away Rene." Every couple in the place danced to it.

"You are a very good dancer Robbie Parker," said Maria as they were dancing. "When they play some fast songs again, we'll throw in some tango and some rumba. I'm sure you'll pick it up very quickly."

"I believe I could do anything when I'm with you," said Robbie. He bent down and kissed her. Their lips stayed together for the rest of the song. When the fast songs started again, Maria showed Robbie some tango and rumba moves. He picked them up easily. They danced every song. After about two hours, the band took a break.

"I need to go to the ladies room," said Maria. "Would you show me where it is?"

"Come on, I'll show you," said Robbie. "The men's is just down the hall. I'll go too." When Robbie went into the men's room, Brad was in there.

"Where did you find that girl?" asked Brad. "She is gorgeous. She's a Spic isn't she?" Brad could tell by the look on Robbie's face that he had said something wrong.

"Brad, we've been friends for many years," started Robbie. "Maria is Puerto Rican. She is not a Spic. Do not use that word around me. If you do, I will hurt you."

"Gee, I'm sorry Robbie. I didn't mean anything by it," said Brad. I guess I wasn't thinking."

"No, I don't guess you were," said Robbie.

"Say, did Maria go to the restroom too?" asked Brad. "Cindy's in there. She's jealous of your girl. She might say something nasty to her."

"Maria's a big girl and can take care of herself," said Robbie. "If Cindy says the wrong thing to Maria, she might just punch her out."

"That would be something, wouldn't it?" said Brad.

"Yes it would," said Robbie. "Let's hope it doesn't happen."

In the ladies restroom, Cindy and Maria were both at the mirrors touching up their makeup. Cindy kept looking over at Maria. "If you've got something to say to just say it," said Maria.

"I was just curious," started Cindy. "Has Robbie screwed you yet? You know he's screwed a lot of the girls who are here now."

"Our sex life is nobody's business but ours," said Maria. "If you want the whole world to know about yours, which I hear that you do, that's up to you. I will tell you this though, when Robbie and I make love, I get off three times before he gets off once. Now please excuse me. If I hear that you've said something bad about myself or Robbie, I will hit you so hard that you won't wake up till next Tuesday." Maria left the restroom. Robbie was outside waiting for her.

"So was Cindy in there too?" asked Robbie.

"Yes she was," answered Maria. "We had some words. I'll tell you about them later. Right now let's get back on the dance floor." The band had just started up again and the dance floor was filling up. They danced the whole time till the band took another break. During the break, they got invited to several after Prom parties. The first song they played after the break was a slow dance. They held each other tightly.

"So what would you like to do after this?" Robbie asked Maria. "Some of the parties might be fun."

"I would rather spend my time with you alone," said Maria. "I would like to spend the whole night with you." Robbie had been wanting to sleep with Maria after the first day that he met her, but she surprised him when she said this.

"Are you sure that is what you want?" Robbie asked her. "I have wanted you. We need to be sure."

"I am sure," answered Maria. "I know we have not known each other for long, but I know my feelings and I think you feel the same."

"I do feel the same," said Robbie. "When we leave here, we'll go get us a motel room. I'll make love to you all night long. When morning comes, we'll start over again."

"Let's go now," said Maria. "We've danced enough." Robbie took her arm and escorted her out to the car. Other couples looked at them as if they knew what they were going to do.

They found a small motel on the west side of town and got checked in with no problems. Once inside the door, they were all over each other. Clothes went flying all over. "I've got some rubbers," said Robbie.

"You won't need them," said Maria. "I was told by that doctor that I couldn't have any more children."

"Well let's use them anyway just in case he might have made a mistake," said Robbie.

"All right," said Maria. "I'll help you put one on."

They made love for hours. Just when one of them was about to nod off, they would get going again. They must have fallen asleep somewhere around 5 AM. The motel was not far from the road and when the morning work traffic started, they woke up. They picked up right where they left off. Check out time was eleven o'clock so around ten, they decided to take a shower and then get dressed. The shower lasted almost an hour. Neither of them had a change of clothes so they put their Prom clothes back on. Robbie left off his jacket and tie.

"Let's go get some breakfast," said Robbie. "I'm hungry. Will that be o.k. or should you get home?"

"Let's go eat," said Maria. "My grandparents will not be worried."

There was a small diner nearby and they decided to go there. "I'll have some coffee this morning," said Robbie. "I drink coffee at home once in a while but not often. Do you drink coffee?"

"I usually have a cup or two in the mornings that I go to work. I'll have some this morning." said Maria. "When I'm not working, I sometimes drink hot tea. So what are you having for breakfast?"

"I think I'll have some pancakes, sausage, and eggs," said Robbie. "I hope they have good pancakes. How about you?"

"I believe I'll have a cheese omelet and some hash browns," said Maria.

They sat there sipping their coffee and just looking into each other's eyes and smiling. They ate their food without saying a word. They sipped some more coffee after their food was gone. When they decided that they had enough coffee, Robbie took Maria home. When he stopped in front of her house, Maria put her arms around his neck and looked into his eyes. " I love you Robbie Parker," said Maria.

"I love you too," said Robbie. "When can I see you again?"

"Call me tomorrow evening," said Maria. "I'll know my work schedule by then." Robbie escorted her to her front door. He pulled her to him and kissed her passionately.

"I'll be missing you Maria," said Robbie. "I'll call tomorrow around six."

"I'll be missing you too," said Maria as she went inside. Maria's grandparents were sitting on the couch in the living room as she came inside.

"We'll assume that you had a very good time," grandmother said.

"Yes I did," said Maria. "Robbie is a wonderful dancer and a perfect gentleman. Now please excuse me. I need to take a nap. We were up all night."

When Robbie got home, his mother was home but Robert was working first trick. "You had a good time didn't you?" asked Mary.

"Yes I did," answered Robbie. "I'm in love too. It sure feels good."

"Maria must be in love too," said Mary.

"She is," said Robbie. "She surely is."

"Well did you learn any new dance steps last night?" asked Mary.

"I sure did," answered Robbie. "Maria showed me some rumba and tango moves. I'll show you and dad soon. Now if you don't mind, I need to sleep a little. We were up all night."

"That'll be fine. Just leave the tux on the clothes hamper and I'll get it to the cleaners," said Mary. "I'll wake you later for dinner if you're still asleep."

Robbie woke up around three thirty when his dad got home from work. He put on some clothes and went to the living room. He saw his parents in the kitchen necking. He went to the couch and turned on the television. They didn't have cable. With their antenna, they could get three channels. There was an old western movie on one channel. The Cubs were playing the Dodgers on another channel, and "Gone With the Wind" was on the other channel. Robbie had seen "Gone With the Wind" a bunch of times but he decided to watch it for a while. Scarlet O'Hara had just found out that Ashley Wilkes was going to marry Melanie. "I can never understand this," Robbie said to himself. "Ashley is such a wimp. I don't get it. He can go to war and kill people but he can't handle Scarlett. And just why would Rhett Butler love Scarlett? She's a bitch." Robbie was still mumbling to himself when Robert came into the living room.

"So your mother tells me you had a great time and you're in love," said Robert.

"Yes I did and I am," said Robbie.

"That's good," said Robert. "You'll be leaving in less than a month. You should spend as much time with her as you can. Maybe you should give notice on your job."

"I was thinking about that," said Robbie. "I figure I'll tell them tomorrow that I'll work two more weeks. Maria finds out her work schedule tomorrow for the week too. I'm sure we'll do what we need to do so we can be together. So what's for dinner Mom? I think I could eat a horse today."

"I was thinking I'd make some spaghetti," said Mary. "Both of you men seem to like my spaghetti."

"You make the best sauce I ever had," said Robbie.

"Same for me," said Robert. "I should have been Italian. I do love spaghetti."

The two men watched the movie while Mary made the spaghetti. She made a big batch because the men sounded like they would eat a bunch. They did. After dinner, Robbie decided that he wouldn't do his running and exercises. He would just do some walking. He told his parents what he was doing and took off. He came back about dark, took a shower and went to sleep.

The next morning he got up early and did his routine again. He was very popular at school. Everybody kept telling him what a great time they had at the Prom and how good looking Maria was and what great dancers the two of them were. Even the girls were giving compliments. After school he went to work and the first thing he did was talk to his boss about his quitting notice. His boss told him that if he wanted work only one more week instead of two it wouldn't be a problem. Robbie told him that he would go ahead and work the two weeks because Maria didn't always know her work schedule. Just because he would be off, wouldn't mean that she would be off too. At 6 PM he called Maria from the pay phone at work. Maria answered the phone.

"Hello, is this Robbie?" she began.

"Yes it's me," answered Robbie. "I have missed you. Do you know your work schedule?"

"Yes, I'll be off Thursday and all day Sunday," said Robbie.

"That'll be great," said Robbie. "I'm off work Thursday and we're closed on Sunday. I'll pick you up at five and we can get something to eat. Will that be o.k.?"

"That will be fine," said Maria. "I love you Robbie. I will see you Thursday."

"I love you too Maria," said Robbie. "See you Thursday."

Tuesday and Wednesday seemed to drag on forever. Finally it was Thursday. Robbie picked Maria up at 5 PM. As soon as they were in the car, they were all over each other. After about fifteen minutes they decided it would be a good idea to not do this in front of Maria's house. "So where would you like to eat this evening?" asked Robbie.

"Why don't we walk in the park some and then go back to that pizza parlor," said Maria. "I liked it there."

"Good idea," said Robbie. "That was some good pizza we had."

"How was school this week?" asked Maria. "I would bet that you were Mr. Popular on Monday."

"I was," said Robbie. "I got compliments all day long on how good looking you are and what good dancers we are."

"Dancing is not the only thing we're good at," said Maria. "I'd like to do that again soon." Robbie looked at her and smiled. As soon as they were out of the car at the park, Maria pulled him behind the biggest tree she could find and was all over him. He did not object. Out of the corner of his eye, Robbie saw a police car going through the parking lot very slowly. He pulled away from Maria, took her hand, and they started walking. The police car went back out to the street and left.

"Do you supposed he was watching us?" asked Maria.

"Maybe, I don't know," said Robbie. "A lot of kids come to the park and smoke pot sometimes. At least I've heard that. Maybe he was hoping to make a bust."

"Well let's walk some and then go eat," said Maria. "So what did your parents say when you got home Sunday morning."

"Actually they just asked me if I had a good time," Robbie began. "I told them I had a great time and that I was in love."

"What did they say about that?" asked Maria.

"My dad thought I should give my notice at work so I could spend as much with you as possible since I will be leaving shortly," said Robbie.

"Your dad seems like a good man," said Maria.

"He is," said Robbie. "He and my mother were high school sweethearts when he joined the Marines in WWII. They got married as soon as he got back. So tell me about that conversation you had with Cindy Tyler."

"Well Cindy asked me if you had screwed me yet," started Maria. "She said that you had screwed a lot of the girls who were there that night."

"So what did you say to her?" asked Robbie.

"I told her that our sex life was none of her business," said Maria. "I then told her that if she wanted to broadcast her sex life to the world that was her business. Then I told her that when we did have sex, I got off three times before you got off once."

"That was a nice touch," said Robbie. "Anything else?"

"I then told her that if she said anything bad about you or me, I would hit her so hard that she wouldn't wake up till Tuesday."

"Another nice touch," said Robbie. "Now about this getting off, how was it for you when we made love?"

"Robbie, I got off so many times that night I didn't count," said Maria. "You are a great lover."

"I had a great lover to work with," said Robbie. They stopped walking and kissed. They walked around the lake and then went to the pizza parlor. They ate and spent another two hours there sipping cokes and talking. About dark Robbie decided he had better take Maria home. He also had a paper to write for school tomorrow. When they got to Maria's house they made out a little.

"How about we make a day of it Sunday," said Robbie. "I can pick you up at ten and we can go to a State Park and spend the day."

"I've never been to one," said Maria. "Where's a good one?"

"I was thinking we could go to Hocking Hills," said Robbie. "Old Man's Cave is down there. There's several parks in Hocking Hills. There's gobs of hiking trails. We could do some hiking and maybe spend some time in the woods. There's a restaurant at the lodge too."

"Sounds like we could have a really good time," said Maria. "Pick me up at ten. Now walk me to the door. Robbie walked her to the door. Once there he pulled her to him and kissed her.

"I love you Maria. I will see you Sunday," said Robbie.

"I love you too Robbie. I'll be missing you till Sunday," said Maria.

When Robbie got home he went straight to his room and wrote his paper for school. He didn't care if it was good or not. His grades were high enough that there was nothing he could do that would keep him from graduating. The rest of the week flew by quickly. When Sunday morning came, Robbie's mother was surprised that Robbie didn't get up and do his exercise routine. "So why aren't you doing your routine this morning?" asked Mary.

"I'm picking up Maria at ten and we're going to spend the day at Hocking Hills," said Robbie. "We'll be doing a lot of hiking."

"That's a nice place," said Mary. "I haven't been there in years. There are some ledges at Old Man's Cave that some kids have fallen off. Be careful."

"Don't worry Mom," said Robbie. "You didn't raise no fool."

"No I didn't," said Mary. "You should take some water and a blanket with you."

"I got everything covered Mom," said Robbie.

"Well you have fun today," said Mary. "Your dad and I might go to a movie this evening so if we're not here when you get home, that's where we are."

"O.k., I'll see you later," said Robbie.

Robbie picked up Maria at ten and they were on their way. It would take a little over an hour to get to Hocking Hills. It was a pleasant drive. The only problem that Robbie had was that Maria kept sticking her tongue in his ear. He didn't mind, but it was distracting. When they got to Hocking Hills, they decided they would go to Old Man's cave first. When they got to the parking lot, the place looked deserted. There was only one other car in the whole parking lot.

"I know what I want to do," said Maria. "Grab that blanket and let's slip into the woods over by that picnic area." Robbie didn't need any coaxing. They found a good spot and put down the blanket.

"I don't get poison ivy. Do you?" Robbie asked Maria.

"No I don't," answered Maria. Then they were all over each other. An hour later they were laying there holding each other. Several more cars had pulled into the parking lot and some people with families were setting up for picnics.

"We probably shouldn't make so much noise," said Robbie. "More people are showing up."

"It's hard to be quiet when I'm with you Robbie," said Maria. She began kissing him and they were at it again. When they were finished, they decided they were hungry. They got dressed and headed to the car. Several people saw them come out of the woods.

"They're just remembering what it was like when they were young," said Robbie when he saw the people watching them. "They knew what we were doing." Maria stopped him and kissed him hard.

They drove to the lodge and had their meal and then came back to the parking lot. They found a stand that had trail maps on it and took off on one of the trails. "This is a nice place," said Maria after they had been hiking for a while. "I'm glad we came here."

"I like it too," said Robbie. "It is nice here, especially with you. He pulled her to him and kissed her. They hadn't seen another person on the trail since they first started. They looked at each other and smiled. Robbie took her by the hand and they ran into the woods about fifty yards off the trail. There was a large down log so they made use of it. When they were finished, they dressed and went back to the trail. They didn't talk much. They just looked at each other from time to time and smiled. The trail made a big loop and about a hour later, they were close to coming back where they started. There was still no one on the trail. They stopped and looked at each other. "Should we go again?" asked Robbie. Maria didn't say a word. She just smiled and grabbed his arm and led him off the trail. A good while later, they were back at the car. "I'm hungry again," said Maria. "Let's get something to eat."

"Is the lodge o.k. or would you want to find another place?" asked Robbie.

"The lodge is all right with me," answered Maria. "Do you want to do any more hiking after we eat?"

"Why don't we just find a nice spot and lay on the blanket for a while. How does that sound?" said Robbie.

"That sounds good to me," said Maria.

They had their meal and then found a nice spot not far from the lodge. They laid the blanket down and laid on their sides facing each other. Robbie pulled her to him and kissed her. "Will you write me when I'm in the Marines?" asked Robbie.

"Of course I'll write you," said Maria. "You're my man aren't you?"

"I reckon I am," said Robbie. "I know I'll be busy in Boot Camp but I'll write you every chance I get."

"How long is Boot Camp?" asked Maria.

"Boot Camp is eight weeks and then infantry training is after that," said Robbie. "I think infantry training is maybe two weeks to a month. I'm not sure. Then after the infantry training they send you to school or training for whatever your MOS is."

"What is MOS?" asked Maria.

"That stands for Military Occupational Skill," answered Robbie. "If you're just going to be in the infantry, you're done after infantry training. They'll give you orders telling you where you'll be stationed after training."

"So will you get a leave after all your training?" asked Maria.

"The recruiter told me that in the military you get thirty days leave a year," said Robbie. "I figure they'd let me have a leave after I was done with training, especially if I was going to Vietnam."

"So if you did go to Vietnam, how long would you be there?" asked Maria.

"A tour of duty is thirteen months for a Marine," answered Robbie. "Now they have some rules about getting wounded. I heard that if you get wounded too many times, your tour is over, but I don't know how many times that is. I do know that if you get severely wounded, you would probably get a Medical Discharge and maybe some kind of disability."

"You won't let anything bad happen to you, will you?" asked Maria.

"I'll do my best to keep anything bad from happening," said Robbie. "I want to come back to you in the same condition I was when I left."

"I want that too," said Maria. "I'll be missing you every minute you're gone. So when will you be leaving?"

"Graduation is the first Sunday in June," said Robbie. "That's in two weeks. I leave for Boot Camp the second Monday in June. So I have a week after graduation to do whatever I want."

"I have a few days of vacation time coming," said Maria. "Would you like it if I took a few days to be with you?"

"That would be wonderful," said Robbie. "We can spend the next two weeks figuring out what we can do."

"I saw a sign when we first got to Hocking Hills that said cabins," said Maria. "When we get ready to leave, let's drive over that way and see what they look like."

It was getting late now so Maria and Robbie headed back to the car. Then they drove over to where the cabins were. "Those cabins really look nice," said Maria. "Maybe we could stay in one of them sometime. If they have stoves and refrigerators, we could bring some food and I can cook for us."

"That would be great," said Robbie. "Let's go back over to the lodge. They should have information about the cabins." They got back to the lodge and some people there were very helpful. They found out the cabin rates and what was in them. They also found out that all the cabins were booked solid for the next two months. There were a few openings before Fall, but during Fall, they were booked solid. A lot of people go there to see the Fall foliage. "Maybe some day we'll get us a cabin," said Robbie. "It would be just you and me and the trees and no one else."

"I will look forward to that," said Maria. "Now I think we better get home. You have school tomorrow and I have work early." They didn't say much on the drive back home. They just looked at each other and smiled from time to time. When they stopped in front of Maria's house, they kissed for a good while before Robbie walked her to the door. At the door, Maria put her arms around his neck and kissed him some more. "I'm off Saturday and Sunday so I'll expect you at ten or eleven Saturday morning if that's all right," said Maria.

"I'll be here," said Robbie. He kissed her one more time. "I'll be missing you till then," said Robbie as he was leaving.

When Robbie got back home, his parents were in the living room watching television. They were on the couch and Mary was sitting on Robert's lap. "How was your day?" they both asked at the same time.

"We had a good day," answered Robbie. "How was your day? Did you go to a movie?"

"We decided to stay home and snuggle instead," answered Mary. "So is Maria taking it well that you are leaving soon?"

"I think she is," said Robbie. "If she is upset, she's not showing it yet."

"Well it'll start showing up more the closer that time gets," said Mary.

"You're probably right Mom," said Robbie. "She's going to take some vacation days the week before I leave. I'd like for us to go somewhere and be together those days."

"You're not thinking about getting married are you son?" asked Robert.

"I would never do that to Maria," said Robbie. "It wouldn't be right to get married and then leave like that. We haven't talked about it anyway. I would say that if I asked Maria she would say yes without any hesitation. I think we'll talk about it right before I leave. I think it would be best. If we're meant to be together, we can wait till I get back or till I get out of the Marines."

"It's good that you're thinking with the right head son," said Robert. "So are you all ready for your final exams and such?"

"I am," said Robbie. "I don't think I could flunk any of my classes if I tried."

"That's good," said Robert. "Well your mother and me are going to bed now. We'll see you tomorrow."

The week flew by very fast. Robbie got up early every morning and did his running and exercises. This was his last week at work too and the boss had a little going away party for him. Saturday at ten, Robbie was knocking on Maria's door. Grandfather answered the door and asked Robbie to come inside for a while. "Have a seat young man," grandfather said. "Maria will be down in a minute. So when is it you'll be leaving?"

"It'll be the second Monday in June," said Robbie. "Graduation is Sunday June 2nd and I leave Monday the 10th.

"You know Maria will be missing you while you're gone," grandfather said. "We wouldn't like it if you left and forgot about Maria."

"That would never happen Mr. Rios," said Robbie. "I haven't said this to Maria, but I'm hoping that we could get married when I get out of the Marines, or if I go to Vietnam, after I get back from there. I haven't discussed this with Maria. I was going to do it the week before I leave."

"That is honorable young man," said grandfather. "I'll tell Maria to come downstairs now. I told her to stay up there while we had our talk. Maria, you can come downstairs now. Go with your young man and have a nice day."

After they were in the car and driving away, Maria asked Robbie why her grandfather needed to talk with him. "Your grandfather is a good man," said Robbie. "He wanted to make sure that I wasn't going to be some guy who just used you and then left. I assured him that I wasn't that type of person.

"And just how did you do that?" asked Maria.

"I was hoping to discuss this with you when we're together before I leave," started Robbie. "But I can't hold it in anymore. I was hoping that we could get married after I get out of the Marines, or if I go to Vietnam, after I get back from there. I love you Maria Rios. I'd like to spend the rest of my life with you."

"I would like to spend the rest of my life with you too Robbie Parker," said Maria. "I'll wait for you no matter how long it takes."

"I don't have a ring to give you," said Robbie.

"I don't need any ring," said Maria. "I know I'll be with you. Now pull over to the curb somewhere and kiss me for a while. Robbie pulled over and they kissed for a good while. Robbie happened to look down on the sidewalk and saw the red fire hydrant.

"We've got to move before I get a ticket," said Robbie. "This is a no parking zone. There's a fire hydrant right there." Robbie pulled away from the curb. "What would you like to do today?" he asked.

"We don't need to do anything special," said Maria. "Why don't we just go to a mall and do some window shopping. We can pretend we're buying things for our first apartment or house."

"That would be nice," said Robbie. "That could give me an idea of what your tastes are like."

They spent the rest of the day looking at all kinds of furniture and house appliances. A salesman at a mattress store was sure he had a sale when they spent over an hour trying out different beds. They had dinner at a Frisch's and then Robbie took her home. At the door, she kissed him as always and then stood back and looked into his eyes. "I would like it if you went to Mass with me in the morning and then stayed for Sunday dinner," said Maria.

"I'd like that too," said Robbie. "What time is Mass? Some of the churches have it at several different times."

"We can go to 11 AM Mass," said Maria. "Then I will fix dinner when we get back."

Robbie kissed her again and then turned and left. "I'll see in the morning," said Robbie.

Robbie showed up at Maria's the next morning wearing a nice jacket and tie. Maria wore a very nice looking dress too. "Will anyone else be going to Mass with us?" asked Robbie.

"No, they already went to early Mass," said Maria. "Let's go."

Robbie could not remember the last time he went to Mass. He had almost forgotten about the Holy Water and all the kneeling and such, but he survived it. When they got back to the house, Maria had him take off his jacket and tie and have a seat in the living room while she changed her clothes and went to the kitchen to make dinner. Grandfather was in the living room watching television. "The Reds game should be on shortly," he said. "Are you a Reds fan?"

"Yes I am," answered Robbie. "My dad used to take me to Crosley Field once in a while. Do you know who's pitching today? I hope it's Jim Maloney. I like to watch him work."

"I like him too. He's fast and he's got a good sinker," said Grandfather. The game started and after three innings they were called to the dinner table. The two brothers were not present. Grace was said and food was passed. Then Robbie asked about the brothers. "They're with their women," said grandfather. "I sure hope they get married soon and move out." Grandmother let out a little giggle. There was not much talking during the meal. When it was over, Robbie and Grandfather went back to the game and Maria and Grandmother cleaned up. Maria came in and watched the game with them when the kitchen was back in order.

"So do you like baseball?" Robbie asked her.

"I do," said Maria. "Maybe you and I can play catch sometime. I can throw a curveball too."

"Well you'll have to show me sometime," said Robbie. It was getting late when the game ended so Robbie decided he should go home. They went out to the front porch for their goodbyes.

"I'll be working next weekend because I'm going to ask to be off the Friday, Saturday, and Sunday before you leave," said Maria. "I'll get a day off during the week but I won't know which one till Tuesday. Call me Tuesday around 6 PM and I'll know. We can do something then."

"I'll call you then," said Robbie. "I'll be missing you Maria."

"I'll be missing you too," said Maria.

Maria was off on Thursday. Robbie picked her up at 5 PM. They went to the park for a while and then had a meal at the pizza parlor where they had gone two times before. They sat there for a good while sipping cokes and talking. "Will you get any more days off before next weekend?" asked Robbie.

"I should get Monday or Tuesday off," said Maria. "I'll find out Saturday evening at work. I will call you from work. Now since graduation is Sunday, don't go out partying with the boys and have a hangover on Monday in case I'm off Monday. I'm sorry I can't go to your graduation."

"It's no big deal," said Robbie. "We wear those silly robes and hats, get a piece of paper, and then realize that some day we'll have to grow up."

"Well maybe the ceremony and such is silly, but getting the diploma is not," said Maria.

"I know that," said Robbie. "I know education is important. Speaking of which, I want you to teach me some Spanish. I took it last year, but all I learned was how to conjugate verbs."

"Why do you want to learn some Spanish?" asked Maria.

"I figure that there will be some Chicanos wherever I go in the Marines," said Robbie. "It would be nice if I knew a few words so if I was around some of them and they were jabbering in Spanish, I might know what they might be saying."

"So you would like to know if they're bad mouthing you or not," said Maria.

"I guess so," said Robbie. "If I go to Vietnam, I hope to learn some of that language too. That might come in handy."

"That would be wise," said Maria. "Now take me home. I have an early shift tomorrow."

They were on the front porch saying their goodbyes. "I'll call Saturday evening. When we get together again, we can talk about what we should do on those three days we're together."

Robbie kissed her again. "I'll be missing you Maria," said Robbie.

"I'll be missing you too Robbie." said Maria.

Maria was to be off on Monday. Robbie would pick her up at 10 AM and they would spend the day together. Sunday was graduation. It dragged on and on. Some guest speaker gave a long and boring speech and then the Valedictorian gave a speech that would have put a church revival to sleep. Afterwards, Robbie went over to Brad's house for a couple of beers. Some other members of the class were there too. Cindy Tyler was there. She didn't speak to Robbie at all. Robbie finished his second beer and then went home. He had another beer with his dad. They talked a good bit while they sipped their beers. "So dad, I know you went in the corps right after graduation," said Robbie. "How soon after graduation was it?"

"I was just like you," answered Robert. "I left for Boot Camp a week after graduation. I wanted some time with your mother before I left."

"Did you get a leave before you went overseas?" asked Robbie.

"No I didn't," answered Robert. "After training, I had so many days to get to California. Can't remember how many but it was only a few. I slipped home to see your mother for a day before I left."

"You probably didn't get any leave during the war did you?" asked Robbie.

"We didn't get leave but we got time at a base somewhere for a rest once in a while," answered Robert. "They don't keep men constantly on the line without a rest once in a while. But sometimes it's a long time between rests. Then when you're not on the line, you're always training or something. They won't let you get out of shape. After you've been in combat for a while, they put new men with the experienced men so they can learn. A lot of men wouldn't even talk to the new men. They didn't want to know their names or anything. I guess they thought it was easier that way if they got killed. I imagine it's still like that. I expect you'll find out."

"I expect I will," said Robbie. "Well I hope that if I get sent to Vietnam that I can get a few days leave or something before I go."

"I expect you will," said Robert. "The men down at the Legion with sons in the service say that the boys get a leave before they go overseas or after their training."

"I hope so," said Robbie. "I'll be with Maria most of the day tomorrow. We'll be figuring out what we want to do when we have those three days together."

"If you need any money for something special, I'll help you out," said Robert.

"I have enough dad. Thanks for the offer," said Robbie. "Would you mind if Maria went with us to see me off?"

"Sure, she can go with us if she wants," said Robert. "Do you know if there are any other boys going to Parris Island with you?"

"The recruiter told me there would be ten of us leaving that day for the Corps" said Robbie. "I don't know if we're all going to Parris Island or not."

"Well you're as ready as you're going to be," said Robert. "You've never flown before. I hope you don't get sick. You used to get car sick once in a while when you were little. I've never been on a jet before. Anything I was ever in had props. Sometimes it was rough. Sometimes it wasn't."

"Well I'm going to go ahead and shower and get to bed," said Robbie. "I'll be picking Maria up at ten and I won't be home till late."

"I'll be on second trick tomorrow," said Robert. "I'll see you at breakfast."

Robbie picked up Maria at ten. When they pulled away from her house, Maria was hugging Robbie tightly and kissing him all over. Robbie was almost ready to tell her to back off a little because it was interfering with his driving. After a few blocks, she slowed down some. "Let's just go to the park for a while," said Maria. "We can have some Spanish lessons."

Robbie smiled at her. "The park it is," he said. When they got to the park, there were three police cars in the parking lot. They had a car surrounded and a young long haired man was next to the car and he was handcuffed with his hands behind his back. The police were doing a search of his car. In a few minutes, one of the cops help up a clear plastic bag with some stuff in it that looked like grass clippings .

"That's pot," said Maria. "Someone was smoking some pot not long ago. I can smell it."

"So that's what that stuff smells like," said Robbie. "If that guy had that much of that stuff, he must have been trying to sell some. I supposed he'll be in jail for possession and distribution or whatever they call it."

"Well those cops won't be watching us make out," said Maria. "They'll be back at their station patting each other on the back for this big bust. Well let's get the blanket and go have some lessons."

Robbie was amazed at how well Maria was at helping him. She had a notepad and was writing phrases down for him. She also showed him how to correctly pronounce the words. She made sure he knew some good cuss words. About one o'clock they went to a Frisch's for some lunch. Afterward, they went back to the park and picked up where they left off. After a couple of more hours, Maria decided that Robbie had enough lessons for the day. They talked about anything and everything. Every once in a while, she would kiss him, but most of the time was spent talking. About six o'clock they decided they were hungry again. This time they went to the diner where they had breakfast after Prom night. They took their time with their meal. It was dark when they left the diner. Maria needed to get home. She had an early shift the next day. When they stopped in front of her house, she put her arms around his neck and smiled. "I would like for us to spend our three days in a nice downtown hotel," said Maria. "It won't cost as much as you might think. I can help pay too."

"I would like that too," said Robbie. "Money is not a problem. "I'll make us a reservation at the Hyatt Regency. We'll check in Thursday and check out Sunday. Does that sound o.k.?"

"Yes it does," said Maria. "What time do you have to be at Fort Hayes on Monday?"

"I have to be there at 6 AM," said Robbie.

"Walk me to the door now," said Maria. Robbie opened her car door and walked her to the front door. They faced each other and then kissed passionately. "I'll see you around four o'clock on Thursday," said Maria after the long kiss.

"I'll be missing you till then," said Robbie as he turned and headed back to the car.

When Robbie got back home his parents were at the kitchen table playing poker. They were using real money too. "So are you squared away on your last days here?" asked Robert.

"Yes I am," answered Robbie. "So you're playing poker. I guess I never learned to play. I suppose I should have."

"I should have taught you a long time ago," said Robert. "After you get out of training, there will always be someone wanting to gamble some. Sit down for a while and we'll teach you. I'll teach you how to play five card stud, seven card stud, and draw. Forget all them other games and don't play with people who want to have all kinds of wild cards or share the pot or anything like that."

"All right dad, let's get started," said Robbie.

The first thing Robert did was make sure the Robbie knew what hands were the highest. Then they played five card stud. Robert showed him how to bet . After several hands, Robbie had a fair idea on how to play the game. Then they played several hands of seven card stud. Robbie thought he picked up a fair knowledge of the game. Then they played draw. Robbie found out it was a lot different when you couldn't see the cards on the table. Robert taught him how to draw his cards and how to bet. He explained to him how it was not a good thing at times to try to draw to an inside straight. He tried to teach him how to bluff, but Robert explained to him that being a good bluffer could take some time. Robbie decided he could handle himself if he got into a game.

"I always used to set myself a limit," said Robert. "When I lost, say $20, I would quit. If I would win $20, I would quit. Someone will always be saying to let them have a chance to win their money back. They already had that chance. Forget them. Maybe they set you up making you think you're a winner and now they'll try to clean you out if you keep playing. It's a shame, but some boys are just not honest, especially when it comes to money. Everybody will always make about the same amount of money. Someone will always want to bum money from you. Don't be lending your hard earned money. I knew so many guys who always sent their money home and never had any on them. Then they always bummed off someone else and never paid anything back. Then when they went home, if they didn't get killed, they had a nice little pile waiting on them. Another thing, don't ever leave your locker or foot locker unlocked. I mean never. In Boot Camp if a Drill Instructor sees anything unlocked, you'll think you're already in the war. I think you know what I'm saying. People will steal. That's just the way it is."

"I got you Dad," said Robbie. "Now I'm going to clean up and get to bed. Maybe we can play some more poker before I leave. Goodnight Mom, Goodnight Dad."

"Goodnight Son," said Robert and Mary.

The next three days flew by quickly. Robbie and his parents played poker a few more times. Robbie tried bluffing a few times but he couldn't fool his dad. Robert showed him several ways how people cheat at cards. Robbie was convinced that he would do o.k. if he got into a game. Finally, Thursday arrived. Robbie picked up Maria and they went straight to the hotel. They were amazed when they got to their room. They had a king sized bed, a huge jetted tub, double sinks in the bathroom, a huge television, and a kitchenette. After they were done looking at their amenities, they were all over each other. About two hours later they were in the jetted tub. Neither one of them had ever been in one and they were really impressed. After another hour they decided they were hungry and ordered some room service. After their meal, they made love some more. They fell asleep in each other's arms. It was daylight when they woke up and they picked up right where they left off. They got some room service for breakfast and after that, they made love till early afternoon. They decided to leave their room and go downtown for some lunch. They found a nice bistro and had a nice lunch and then did some window shopping. They window shopped for a couple of hours and then went back to their room. They spent about two hours in the jetted tub before making their way to the bed. For dinner, they ordered some room service again. A few hours after dinner, they went to a downtown bar they had seen during their window shopping. The bar was having a good band that night and they intended to do some dancing. They had a wonderful time. The band played some really good songs that were good for dancing. They started dancing when the band started and they danced until the band took a break. Robbie thought that he might have to get mean with some guy who kept asking if he could dance with Maria. After the fourth time he asked, Robbie had a few words for him. "The lady here told you no four times," said Robbie. "Now please leave us alone or I will hurt you."

"Sorry man," the guy said. "She's one fine girl. Thought I'd give it a try."

"Well you tried now git," said Robbie. The guy mumbled something to himself and then went across the room somewhere. They never saw him again after that. The band played another set and they danced again until the band took another break. Then they went back to their hotel. They made love well into the night and fell asleep in each other's arms.

Saturday was pretty much a repeat of Friday. The lovemaking was intense and often. They did go to a different place for lunch. When Saturday night rolled around Robbie could tell that Maria was getting a little teary eyed. "This will be our last night together before you leave," said Maria. "After tomorrow, I won't see you for months."

"Are you coming with us to see me off?" asked Robbie.

"No, we'll have our goodbyes tomorrow," said Maria. "I don't want your parents to see me cry all over you."

"I understand," said Robbie. "Check out time is eleven o'clock tomorrow. We'll hang out together most of the day after we leave the hotel. I should spend a little time with my parents then too."

"You should," said Maria. "We can have dinner together somewhere tomorrow and then you can take me home. I will cry all over you but I know you'll come back to me. I have some pictures of myself for you. Do you have any pictures for me?"

"I have some of my senior pictures in my wallet," said Robbie. "I hope they will do."

"They will be fine plus I have our Prom pictures," said Maria. "I hope that one picture will not get you into trouble if you take it to Boot Camp with you." Robbie went through the pictures slowly. There were six of them. In four of the pictures Maria was wearing tight T-shirts and short shorts. In one she was wearing a very skimpy bikini. In the last one, she was stark naked laying across a bed in a suggestive pose.

"Oh my," said Robbie. "You are so beautiful. I better not take that picture of you naked with me to Boot Camp. I suspect they'll make us empty our pockets and show everything we're carrying when we first get there. I'm sure they'd appreciate your beauty too, but they might not appreciate me carrying that picture on me. I best leave that picture at home for a while."

They made love well into the night. The next morning they had room service for breakfast and then spent the rest of their time in the jetted tub. They were both teary eyed when they checked out. They walked downtown and had some lunch and then went to the park. They laid on a blanket and held each other for hours. Robbie was hungry now and wanted to get something to eat, but Maria was upset and nervous and said she couldn't eat. "You can take me home now," said Maria. "I need to have a good cry and I want to do it in my room at home." Robbie took her home. They hugged and kissed on her front porch for a good while until finally Maria needed to go have her cry. "Goodbye Robbie. Make sure you come back to me in the same condition you are now," said Maria. Then she kissed him one more time and went inside.

When Robbie got home, his parents had just sat down for their evening meal. "Come on and join us," said Mary. "This'll be your last home cooked meal for a good while."

"I guess it will," said Robbie as he sat down.

"So how's Maria doing?" asked Robert. "I imagine she's pretty upset."

"She is," said Robbie. "She won't be seeing me off in the morning. She didn't want to cry all over us."

"She'll be all right," said Mary. "You two love each other. You'll be coming back."

"Would you drive the Olds once in a while and make sure she stays pretty Dad?" asked Robbie.

"Course I will," answered Robert. "Your Mom and me may try out the back seat sometime."

"Whatever Dad," said Robbie. "Make sure you clean up any mess you make. I reckon I'll get to bed shortly and try to get as much sleep as I can," said Robbie. "There's no telling what may go on tomorrow."

"I don't know for sure but I'd say you'll fly to Charleston, South Carolina and then take a bus to Parris Island," said Robert. "They'll probably be a bunch of you at Charleston. It may take hours of waiting too. I would say there will be a Marine there to tell you what to do. He'll be a Corporal or Sergeant. This will be the first person that starts screaming and yelling at you. Just do what he says and when he says. You'll be all right."

Robbie finished eating, took a shower and then went to bed. He tried his best to get to sleep. Finally about 1am he fell asleep. The next thing he knew the alarm clock was ringing and it was 4:30 AM.

Chapter Five

Robbie got up and dressed, shaved, and went to the kitchen. His Mother was fixing him a nice breakfast. His Dad was sitting at the table drinking some coffee. Robbie poured himself a cup. "Do I need to take anything with me?" Robbie asked.

"No son, you don't," answered Robert. "They'll give you everything they want you to have. Just take your wallet and your driver's license if you want and some pictures of Maria." Nothing else was said as they ate breakfast.

When it was time to leave, Mary gave Robbie a big hug and a kiss and told him goodbye. "I'll stay here and have a good cry," she said. "Your dad will see you off."

When they got to Fort Hayes, Robbie knew where he was supposed to go. He gave his Dad a firm handshake and told him goodbye. "Don't take no shit off any other recruits and don't take no shit off anyone who don't outrank you," Robert said as Robbie walked away.

There were ten of them going into the Marine Corps that day. Robbie found out that he was the only one of the ten who was going to Parris Island. They took him to the airport and gave him his tickets and his instructions. He would fly from Columbus to Washington D.C., then to Atlanta, and then to Charleston, South Carolina. Robbie had never flown before and he felt a little sick during takeoff. He tried to sleep a little but the seats weren't very comfortable. He felt sick again when the plane was descending to Washington D.C. At D.C. he had to change airlines. He had a hard time finding his way, but he made the flight all right. He felt really sick when they landed in Atlanta. He had to change airlines again but this time he had two hours till his next flight. As soon as he stepped into the terminal at Charleston, he spotted a Marine Corporal. There were several other young men with him. Robbie went to him and showed him his papers. Robbie was told to sit with the other boys and keep his mouth shut. Only the Corporal didn't use polite words. After a couple of hours several more boys arrived. The Corporal took a head count and then he herded all of them onto a bus. They were not allowed to speak on the bus.

After what seemed like hours they passed the Main Gate at Parris Island. A few minutes later, the bus stopped in front of this old two story building. When the door of the bus opened, about five or six Marines wearing Drill Instructor hats ran up on the bus and started screaming and yelling at them. They got them off the bus and had them go inside and stand around some tables. It was a big room and the tables were around the outside perimeter of it leaving the middle area open. The Marines wearing the Drill Instructor hats kept screaming and yelling at them. After a few minutes, one huge Sergeant told all of them to empty all of their pockets onto the tables. Robbie did as instructed. There was a big boy right across from Robbie. When he emptied his pockets, Robbie could see a switchblade knife in front of the boy. Three of the Marines saw the switchblade too. They ran over to the boy and proceeded to beat the hell out of him. Then they dragged him away. Robbie never did see that boy again. "Just what the hell did I get myself into?" Robbie said to himself.

After the Marines inspected the recruits belongings, they were told to put their things back in their pockets. Then they herded them out and made them stand on some yellow footprints. Next came the haircuts. Robbie never had long hair. It was maybe four inches long on top and tapered some on the sides. His sideburns were short. Robbie was amazed to see what his bald head looked like. They couldn't have cut it any shorter unless they used a straight razor. His head was bleeding in a few places where the barber, if you could call him that, dug the clippers into his scalp. Then they herded them to a mess hall and got them fed. Everyone was yelling at them. Even the servers in the chow line hollered at them. Robbie never knew that he could eat a meal in three minutes or less. After the meal, they went back out and stood on some yellow footprints again. After a while they were herded into another old wooden building. This time it was their barracks. There were bunks stacked two high on both sides and it was open in the middle. There were three Marines in the barracks. They were told where to stand and then one of the Marines spoke. "I am Staff Sergeant Brown," he began. "I am your Senior Drill Instructor. I am not DI or Sarge. These other two are Sergeant's Taylor and Cummings. They are your Assistant Drill Instructors. You will do exactly as we say and when we say or we will kill you. The first word out of your mouth will be "Sir" and the last word out of your mouth will be "Sir." Do you understand?"

Everybody answered, "Sir, yes Sir."

Then the Senior Drill yelled, "I can't hear you." This yelling went back and forth for a good while. This is not exactly how the conversation went though. Every other word out of the Drill Instructor's mouth was fuck, fucking, or another obscene word. Robbie had heard cussing before but never anything like this. Then the Senior Drill Instructor proceeded to tell them how low they were. "You people are not even people," he began. "You are so low that you'll have to get promoted to become maggots. You are the scum of the earth. I will make Marines out of you or you will die trying to become Marines. Your momma is not here. Mary Jane rotten crotch is not here. I am your mother now. When I get through with you, you will have muscles in your shit."

The first couple of days were spent getting shots and all medical attention. Uniforms, all gear, and rifles were issued too. Robbie was impressed with his M-14. They started physical training right away. The very first thing they did was a three mile run. The run didn't bother Robbie but he had never run in combat boots before. He was amazed at how much out of shape a lot of the other recruits were. The Marine Corps used several different exercises to get the recruits into shape. There were push-ups, sit-ups, pull-ups, and side straddle hops which was the Marines version of jumping jacks. But there was one exercise that the Marine Corps used extensively. This exercise was called bends and thrusts. This was the Corps version of the squat thrust. A bend and thrust is like a squat thrust but when the a person goes down and kicks his legs back, the feet stay together and the back is not kept straight. The back bends allowing the belly to sag to the ground or almost to the ground. Most Marines called this exercise bends and mothers.

The Marine Corps had different words for common things and places. The recruits had to learn them quickly. The most important one is that a rifle is called a rifle or a weapon. It is not a gun. Calling a rifle a gun can have grave consequences. A hat is not a hat. It's a cover. The bathroom or restroom is a head. The floor is the deck. The ceiling is the overhead. The wall is the bulkhead. Where the recruits stayed in the barracks was the squadbay. It had two sides. The right side was called the starboard side and the left side was the port side. The recruits could not call themselves by name. They were to refer to themselves as "the private."

There was no wasted time in Boot Camp. Every day was spent learning something new. When the recruits weren't in some class or eating, they were drilling or exercising or scrubbing something. Robbie figured if they scrubbed those old wooden floors any more, there wouldn't be any more floor at all. There was a few minutes before lights out when a recruit could write letters and such.

One thing they preached constantly was that if one person screwed up, the whole platoon screwed up. The Marine Corps is a team and a team must work together. After the first week, some of the recruits who couldn't keep up or catch on were sent to what was called "Motivation Platoon." Robbie didn't know what it was, but he was sure he never wanted to go there. All the running and physical fitness didn't bother Robbie when they were just doing it. What started to bother him was when someone screwed up and they had to do a bunch more. There were eighty to ninety recruits in Robbie's platoon, but at graduation, there were only seventy of them left.

Robbie had been at Parris Island for a week now and he was still amazed at how the Drill Instructors slaughtered the English language. Just when he thought he had heard a brand new phrase loaded with cuss words, they surprised him. There were days when Robbie tried to count how many times the Drill Instructors said "fuck," but he kept losing count. Then he tried to keep track of how many times they would say "fuck" in one sentence. This became too difficult too.

Robbie had written his parents a couple of times and he wrote Maria every other day. In the middle of the second week, Robbie finally got some mail from home. His parents told him to keep up the good work and do his best. The letters from Maria had a little perfume on them so Robbie took a little guff from the Drill Instructors. At the end of the second week, the Senior Drill Instructor told them that he wanted them to give him pictures of their girlfriends. Of course the girls were all called Mary Jane rotten crotch. All of the pictures would be put up on a board for all to see. That way, they could all see what they were getting none of. They called this board the "Hog Board." Robbie gave the Senior Drill Instructor one of the pictures of Maria in the tight T-shirt and short shorts. He wasn't going to part with the one of Maria in a bathing suit. When he handed the picture to the Senior Drill Instructor, he looked at it for a few minutes. "Why would this good looking Spic bitch be with you Private Parker," he asked.

"Sir, she's Puerto Rican Sir," said Robbie.

"And I said she was a Spic bitch Private Parker," said the Senior Drill Instructor.

"Sir, she's Puerto Rican Sir," said Robbie. Robbie was getting very ticked off. He could forgive the Senior Drill Instructor using the word Spic, but he couldn't forgive the word bitch.

"What's the matter with you Parker?" asked the Senior Drill Instructor. "You want to hit me don't you."

"Sir, the Private does want to hit the Senior Drill Instructor, Sir," said Robbie.

"Go ahead Parker. Take your best shot," said the Senior Drill Instructor.

"Sir, the Private does want to hit the Senior Drill Instructor, but the Private believes that if he does, the Senior Drill Instructor and the Assistant Drill Instructors will beat the shit out of the Private," said Robbie. "Then the Drill Instructors will throw the Private in the Brig, Sir."

"Private Parker, you are now squad leader of the first squad," said the Senior Drill Instructor. "You will make sure that they don't fuck up ever again."

"Sir, yes Sir," said Robbie.

Robbie tried his best but he couldn't always keep his squad at its' best. At least they would get stronger with all the extra bends and mothers they had to do. When they had bayonet training, the recruits fought each other with pugil sticks. Pugil sticks were wooden poles about as long as a rifle with big pads on both ends. The recruits wore football helmets and crotch protection and then tried to beat the shit out of each other with the pugil sticks. Since Robbie was a squad leader, he had to fight his whole squad. He got knocked down once but he got right back up and put the other man down and kept him down.

The Marine Corps is considered an amphibious force so Marines are supposed to know how to swim. They were taught "drown proofing" which is a way to keep yourself from drowning. To qualify as a first class swimmer, they had to drown proof for an hour. To qualify as a second class swimmer, they had to swim several laps in the pool with a rifle around their neck. Robbie didn't swim much but he knew how and was comfortable in the water. He qualified as a first class swimmer. Robbie was sure some of the other recruits would drown, but at the last minute, an instructor would take a hook and pull them out of the water.

Robbie actually liked the obstacle courses and he really liked this thing called the "slide for life." The recruits climbed up on this platform that was maybe thirty to forty feet high. There were ropes from the platform to the ground maybe two or three hundred feet away. The ropes were over some water. The recruits had to slide down the ropes and not fall in the water. They were to start down the rope in one position. Then go a certain distance and change to another position. After some more distance, they would change to another position. A lot of recruits got wet on the "slide for life."

Time went by and Robbie kept thinking it would get easier but it was the opposite. The more they got done, the more they did. They got sort of a break when they got mess duty. Robbie didn't know it, but all recruits pull a week of mess duty. All those people in the mess hall who were always yelling at them were just recruits too. Robbie ended up working in the pot shack. Mess duty went from zero dark thirty till zero late thirty. During the week of mess duty, one of recruits in Robbie's platoon slashed his wrists with a razor blade. He had gone into the head and done it and then went up to the Senior Drill Instructor and just held out his bloody arms. A lot of choice cuss words were spoken by the Drill Instructors. The recruit was hauled off somewhere. They never saw him again. The day after the incident, the platoon had a class on the proper way to slash your wrists.

The Marine Corps is very big on close order drill. The Drill Instructors in the Marine Corps can call some very interesting cadence. By week five, when Robbie's platoon marched, only one heel hitting the pavement could be heard when they marched. The platoon was getting good.

When they got to the rifle range, the Senior Drill Instructor told them that the highest shooter would make Private First Class at graduation. Robbie knew it would be him. After all the classes and snapping in, they started live firing. They would have four days of firing and the fifth day would be "qualification day." They started with the 200 yards slow fire which was the off-hand position. Then came the 200 yard rapid fire which was the sitting position. Then they moved back to 300 yards. There was slow fire in the sitting and the kneeling position and then came rapid fire in the prone position. The 500 yard slow fire was last. It was in the prone position. The recruits were given starting dope (windage and eleva-tion) for their weapons. There were shooting instructors for each recruit and after several rounds, the instructor would give the recruits dope corrections. Robbie was in the black right off with a tight group but he was at three o'clock just in the bull. The instructor gave him some changes and he was dead center. Robbie's Senior Drill Instructor had noticed that Robbie was in the black and came over to watch him. After the last shot of slow fire, the Senior Drill Instructor spoke. "Private Parker, who taught you how to shoot?" he asked Robbie.

"Sir, my father taught me. He was a Marine Sir," answered Robbie.

"What weapon did he use?" asked the Senior Drill Instructor.

"Sir, it was an M-1 Sir," said Robbie.

"Well Private Parker, I can see that you will qualify with no problems," said the Drill Instructor. "You will make sure that your squad qualifies too."

"Sir, my squad will qualify Sir," said Robbie.

Robbie shot a qualifying score the first day of live firing. In the Marine Corps you are either unqualified, a Marksman, a Sharpshooter, or an Expert. On Monday Robbie was a Marksman. On Tuesday, he was a Sharpshooter. On

Wednesday, he was an expert. On Thursday his score increased and on qualification day it was even higher. Robbie ended up having the highest score in the Battalion. He would be a PFC at graduation. His whole squad qualified too.

The recruits had been getting their hair cut every week. During the seventh week, they got their hair cut, but his time only the sides got skinned. It was this way on the eighth and last week. Graduation finally came. The Drill Instructors talked to them now like they were real people. They were now Marines. They sat around that day and the Senior Drill Instructor called everyone's name and told them what their MOS (Military Occupational Skill) was going to be. "PFC Parker, 0300 infantry," he said to Robbie. Robbie's bunk mate was told he would be a 2500. "You're gonna carry radios on your back," said the Drill Instructor. "Your life expectancy in a fire fight is about fifteen seconds."

The next day, they were loaded up and taken to Camp Lejeune for ITR (Infantry Training Regiment). The very first thing they did was send them to Camp Stone Bay for a week of mess duty. Robbie was in the pot shack again. After that week, they went to Camp Geiger. There they began their infantry training. They were issued M-16's now. They learned infantry tactics and learned all of the infantry weapons currently used. When they were issued the M-16, the first thing an instructor told them was that this rifle was not made by Matte Mattel. Robbie wasn't sure he would like the M-16, but it was sure lighter than an M-14 and a man could carry a whole lot more ammo with this thing. He had heard stories about the M-16 jamming a lot. The instructors told them that those problems had been corrected. All they had to do was keep it clean and it would work.

Infantry training wasn't bad for Robbie. They did a lot of forced marches. Every where they went, they force marched. One day they had to crawl under barbed wire while machine guns fired over their heads. There were also explosive charges in pits not far from where they were crawling. Robbie thought someone might panic and try to stand and run, but no one did. When they went to the gas chamber, Robbie discovered that snot could hang from his nose clear to the ground. Robbie was told his MOS was 0311. That's an infantry rifleman. Some of the other men became machine gunners and mortar men. When ITR was over, they got their orders. Robbie was going to Staging Battalion at Camp Pendleton. Then he would be sent to WESTPAC, which was Western Pacific. This always meant that they would be sent to Vietnam. At Staging Battalion, they would find out if they would be in the 1st Division or the 3rd. Robbie asked for permission to speak to the Company Commander so he could find out about leave and such. Robbie asked for ten days leave and received it. He also had a few days travel time to get to Camp Pendleton. Robbie got himself to the nearest airport and got himself headed home. At the airport, he called home and told his parents when his flight was expected in Columbus. He tried to call Maria several times, but the line was busy.

It took a while, but Robbie finally got to Columbus. Mary and Robert were waiting at the gate. Mary ran to him and hugged and kissed him. Robert stood back and when she was done he hugged Robbie and gave him a firm handshake. "Welcome home Marine," Robert said. Robbie had on his uniform. His dad eyeballed the Expert Rifleman badge. "I knew you would shoot expert," he said.

As they went through the terminal, Robbie noticed that he was getting a lot of stares. Robert noticed that Robbie had noticed and told him not to worry about it. "There's a lot of anti war sentiment around," Robert said.

"I'm not worried about it," said Robbie. "I just want to get home now. It's been a little while. I've missed you guys."

It was late when they got home. Robbie and his dad sat down and had a beer while his mom made something for them to eat. "You didn't lose any weight did you?" asked Robert.

"I think I actually gained some," said Robbie. "But I haven't been on a scale for a good while. I'll weigh myself in the morning."

After the meal, Robbie told them all about Boot Camp and ITR. "I just never dreamed that anyone could cuss like that," said Robbie. "I hope it didn't rub off on me too much."

"You won't offend us if a few words slip out once in a while," said Robert. "When you're in Vietnam, I'm sure you'll hear plenty of cussing. Probably do a lot yourself."

"I think I'll have another beer and then take a shower and get to bed," said Robbie. "I'll be seeing Maria as soon as I can tomorrow."

"She'll be glad to see you," said Mary. "I called her a few times to see how she was doing. She sure missed you."

Robbie drank his beer and they talked some more about Boot Camp. Robbie told them about the guy who slashed his wrists and how they were given a class on how to properly slash your wrists. When the beer was gone, Robbie excused himself, showered, and went to bed. He slept like a baby.

He woke up before daylight the next morning. After he relieved himself and before he dressed, he got on the scales. "Damn, I gained ten pounds," he said to himself. "How in the hell could I gain weight after all that?" He got dressed in civilian clothes and went to the kitchen. Robert and Mary were at the kitchen table drinking coffee. Mary got Robbie a cup.

"How did you sleep, son of mine?" asked Mary.

"Like I haven't slept for a long time," said Robbie. "It was good. I didn't dream about Drill Instructors at all."

"I bet you dreamed about Maria," said Robert.

"I surely did," said Robbie. "I hope she's not working today. After I eat something, I'm heading to her house. Please don't be offended if you don't see me for a while if Maria and I hook up."

"We won't be," said Mary. "We were young once too."

Robbie finished his breakfast, brushed his teeth and left for Maria's house. It was not quite daylight when he got there. Maria's car was parked in front of the house. There were no lights on in the house yet. Robbie waited fifteen minutes and then went to the door. He gently knocked on the door and waited. A few minutes went by and no one came to the door. He knocked again. After a few more minutes, Maria's grandfather came to the door. He opened the door, took a look at Robbie and smiled. Then he yelled out. "Maria, get up. Your young man has come home," he yelled. The he shook Robbie's hand and invited him inside. Robbie could hear Maria running around in her room. She came charging down the stairs wearing a robe. She ran to Robbie and jumped up on him and wrapped herself around him and began kissing him. No words were spoken. They kissed until they were out of breath. "Go get yourself dressed," said Grandfather. "Robbie and I will have some coffee while you are getting dressed." Maria gave him another kiss and went upstairs. Grandfather and Robbie went to the kitchen. Grandfather poured Robbie a cup of coffee. "How was Boot Camp?" he asked Robbie.

"Eight weeks of pure hell," answered Robbie. "Infantry training was tough but not as bad."

"Are you going to Vietnam?" asked Grandfather.

"Yes I am," answered Robbie.

"When will you be leaving?" Grandfather asked.

"I have ten days leave and four days travel time to get to Camp Pendleton for Staging Battalion," answered Robbie. "I think Staging is two weeks or something like that and then I go."

"What is Staging Battalion?" asked Grandfather. "Haven't you just finished training?"

"Yes I have finished my training," said Robbie. "Staging Battalion is where they refamiliarize everyone with weapons and tactics. They also run you through some Vietnam like places. I guess so maybe you'll have an idea about booby traps and such. I think we'll get a bunch of shots too."

"Now how long is that you'll be gone?" asked Grandfather.

"A tour of duty for a Marine is 13 months," answered Robbie. Just then Maria came downstairs. Robbie stared at her for a while. "You are just so beautiful," said Robbie.

"You two don't have a whole lot of time before Robbie leaves," said Grandfather. "Go on now and enjoy each other." They told Grandfather good bye and then went to the car.

When they were both in the car, they were all over each other. After a good while they stopped and just looked at each other. "I know what we should do while you're home," said Maria. "I'd like to see if we could get a cabin at Hocking Hills."

"That's a great idea," said Robbie. "I still have some literature in the car. We'll call and see if they have one available." They went back into Maria's house and called. There was a cabin available. Maria went to her room and got some clothes packed. She told her grandparents she would be gone for a week or so and not to worry. Then they left for Robbie's house.

Robbie's parents were still at the kitchen table when they arrived. They invited Maria to have some coffee with them while Robbie packed some clothes. Robbie was ready to go in just a few minutes. "We'll be at a cabin in Hocking Hills," said Robbie. "We'll be back in a week or so." They told his parents good-bye and then left.

On the drive down, Maria couldn't keep her hands off Robbie. As soon as they got into their cabin, the clothes went flying. After what seemed like hours, they lay next to each other almost completely exhausted. They stared at each other without speaking. Maria spoke first. "You look good with your hair that short," said Maria. "You have a nice shaped head. If you would ever go bald you would still be a fine looking man."

"Thank you," said Robbie. "I doubt if I would ever go bald. No men on either side of the family were bald. You would be beautiful with short hair too but I do love your long dark hair. I love the way it hangs over your breasts when you're on me. I love it when it blows in the wind. What I love the most is that it's your hair and I love everything about you." It wasn't long and they were at it again. They fell asleep in each other's arms. When they woke up a few hours later, they decided to go get something to eat. They went to the lodge. After they ate their meal they decided to go to a small town they had gone through on the way there. There was a small store there and Maria decided that she wanted to cook a little while they were at the cabin. They bought coffee and enough stuff for breakfast for their stay. They also bought some lunch items and some food for two dinners. They would eat at the lodge the rest of the time. When they got back to the cabin, Robbie asked Maria if she had asked to be off work or if she just took off with him.

"When you were having coffee with Grandfather, I called work and told them that my man was back home and that I would need to be off for a week," said Maria. "I had some time coming because I have been working extra hours since you've been gone. They didn't mind me being off."

The days at the cabin seemed to fly by. When it came time to check out, they both were a little teary eyed. Maria pouted almost all the way back home. As they were standing on her front porch saying their goodbyes, Maria told Robbie to call her tomorrow evening and she would know her work schedule. They kissed again and Maria went inside.

It was around lunch time when Robbie got home. His mother made him some lunch and ate with him. "Your father gets off at 3," said Mary. "He'll want you to go down to the Legion for a beer when he gets home."

"That sounds good," said Robbie. "So how was it around here without me in the house for three months or so?"

"When you father was at work, the house seemed very empty," said Mary. "It wasn't the same as when you were at school and your father was at work. It seemed a lot different."

"Probably because you knew I wouldn't be home any time soon," said Robbie. "You know that a tour of duty in Vietnam is 13 months don't you?"

"Yes I do," answered Mary. "I'm not worried about that. I have faith that nothing bad will happen to you. I also know that you are a grown man and after your military service, you will be leaving home. That's as it should be."

"So did you and dad do any dancing while I was gone?" asked Robbie.

"We went dancing on July 4th," answered Mary. "They had a band over at the Legion. They weren't bad. We had a good time. There was a lot of other women there who wanted to dance with your father."

"I bet there was some other men who wanted to dance with you too," said Robbie. "You're a good looking woman Mom and you can sure dance."

"Both of us did dance with some other people," said Mary. "Some of them were a little too drunk so we didn't dance very long. Oh, I can't remember if I told you before but your friend Brad joined the Army. He left home about a month or so ago."

"I guess I never wrote him when I was gone," said Robbie. "There wasn't a whole lot of time for writing so the time I had was for Maria and you and dad."

They sat at the table and talked and talked. They were still talking when Robert got home. "So can I take my son out for a beer?" said Robert.

"You surely can," said Mary as she went to him and then kissed him. "Don't be too late. I'll be making a nice dinner tonight."

"We have our orders son," said Robert. "Let's go."

There were several of Robert's friends at the Legion. They all sat together and told stories about some of their old war buddies. The more beer they drank, the more stories they told. When it was time to leave, all of the men wished Robbie well and told him keep his head down. When they got home Mary told them that by the time they drank another beer, dinner would be ready. They did as instructed and had another beer. Robbie didn't know what his mother had fixed but it sure looked good. He took a bite. "Damn Mom," he said. "This is fucking good." Then Robbie realized what he had said.

His Dad let out a laugh. "Yep, this stuff is fucking good. What is it?" Robert said.

Mary let out a laugh too. "It is fucking good isn't it," she said. "It's shrimp alfredo. I've never made it before. Glad it turned out."

"Well we are too," said Robert. "Robbie, you'll have to come home more often if we can get food like this every time you come home."

"I made a cheesecake for dessert too," said Mary.

"That sound great Mom," said Robbie. "You know, while I was gone, I never even thought about the food being good or bad. I just ate it. I can't remember any of the food I ate except breakfast. I know I ate a lot of taters and SOS and eggs and ham."

"You were hungry son," said Robert. "You would have probably eaten whatever they had no matter what it looked like."

After dinner and dessert, they all sat at the table and had coffee. They talked well into the night. Finally, Robbie told them good night and cleaned up and went to bed. Robbie slept well again and didn't wake till eight o'clock. After breakfast, he decided the first thing he had to do was get his flight to California scheduled. He had six days total left, but it might take two of those days to get to Camp Pendleton. He had to report on a Monday. He scheduled a flight for Saturday.

That would give him an extra day if there was some kind of trouble or anything. That left him with four days counting today.

The four days flew by. Robbie and Maria spent all the time together that they possibly could. Maria went with Robbie to see him off this time. Maria and Mary put out a lot of tears as Robbie boarded the plane.

Chapter Six

When Robbie got off the plane in California, he spotted several other Marines. He went to them and asked if they were headed to Camp Pendleton. They were. One of the Marines was a Sergeant. He had been there before and he knew the best and cheapest way to get there. All of them were going to Staging Battalion. They all were wearing their uniforms and they could see that the Marine who knew the best way to Pendleton had already served in Vietnam. He wore all of his ribbons which included his Vietnam ribbons, a combat action ribbon, a purple heart, national defense, and some other ones that Robbie didn't recognize. While they were waiting on a bus, all of the other Marines were questioning the veteran. "I was over there in 65 – 66," the Sergeant said. "I was a machine gunner. I was with the very first Marines that landed at Da Nang. I guess things have really heated up since then. Any a you boys grunts?"

"I am," answered Robbie. One of the other guys said he was a radio operator and the other two said they were artillery.

"I'm Bob Harper," said the Sergeant. He extended his had to Robbie.

"I'm Robbie Parker," said Robbie as he shook hands with Bob.

`"Well Robbie Parker, when you get out to the bush, you listen to the guys who have been there," said Bob. "Listen and learn from them and maybe, just maybe, you'll live through it. Now you over there that said you was a radio operator. I bet they told you in training that the life expectancy of a radio operator wasn't very long. Well they weren't kiddin'. When you get hit, one of the first things they try to do is knock out communications. After that, they try for automatic weapons."

The bus finally came and they all boarded. The ride to Pendleton took a while. Once there, the Sergeant knew exactly where to go. They got checked in all right. There were a few other Marines there. They all went around and introduced themselves to each other. Then they found the mess hall and had a meal. Robbie sat next to the Sergeant. Robbie wanted to ask all the questions he could think of about Vietnam. After a few of them, the Sergeant had enough. "Look, I'd say it's different now than it was in 65 and 66," he said. "As I said before. When you get to the bush, learn from the men who are there."

"So if you were there in 65 – 66 and It's 68 now, you must have re-enlisted didn't you?" asked Robbie.

"I lost my head back in 67 and re-enlisted," he said. "I guess if I don't get myself shot to hell, I'll make a career of it."

"Did you volunteer to go back or did you get orders?" asked Robbie.

"I volunteered," said the Sergeant. "They was using me as an instructor for infantry training out here. They must have thought I was important or they probably would have sent me back a long time ago. Anyway, I got tired of not doing my fair share and here I am. You know how to play Back Alley?"

"What's Back Alley?" asked Robbie.

"It's only the best card game a Marine can play when he's not playing poker," said the Sergeant. "When we get back to the barracks, I'll show you. Maybe some a them other boys'll know how to play. Back Alley is kinda like Spades only a lot better." They got back to the barracks and the Sergeant got out a deck of cards. There was another Marine who knew how to play. Between the two of them, they showed the boys how to play. "Now when you get to where you know what you're doing, you get some money involved," said the Sergeant. "We won't worry about that yet."

The barracks filled up the next day and on Monday, they got started. Robbie had just finished his Infantry Training so he had no problems with anything, but a lot of the personnel were not grunts and needed the training. Robbie wasn't impressed with the trails that had the booby traps and such. He asked Sergeant Harper about booby traps. "Well I'll tell you the truth Parker," said the Sergeant. "I never saw a booby trap when I was over there. Someone else had always tripped them before I came close. They were there, but I never saw them. Never saw them sticks. These were all mines. Blew the hell out of us."

Time went by quickly. One of the last things they did was get a bunch of shots. They left California on a commercial airline, Braniff Airlines. They were crammed in it like sardines. The plane stopped in Honolulu for a while and then went to Manila for a stop. Then they went to Okinawa.

In Okinawa they got all of their paperwork straightened out. Some men wanted to write wills and name their beneficiaries. Robbie found out that he was considered a sole surviving son and he didn't have to go if he didn't want. He signed some form that said he would go. They hung around Okinawa for a day or two. There was no liberty but some of the men knew how to sneak out. Robbie stayed on base.

Most of their gear was stored on Okinawa. Robbie had orders for the 1st Marine Division. They flew to Da Nang on Braniff Airlines. When they got close, the land that Robbie could see was covered with bomb craters. Strange looking mountains seemed to spring up out of nowhere. They were met when they de-planed. Robbie found out that he would be with the 5th Marines at some place called An Hoa. They got their money converted and then they took them to some hootches and told them a chopper would take them to An Hoa in the morning. They showed them where a mess hall was so they could get a meal. The mon-soons were starting but it hadn't rained a lot just yet. Robbie didn't sleep much that night. Several times they went to bunkers when some rockets slammed into the area. Small arms fire could be heard all night. Some of it was close and some of it wasn't. It rained hard the next morning and the chopper didn't come. Finally later in the day, it let up some and the CH-46 came. As they flew to An Hoa, Robbie was amazed. The number of bomb craters was staggering. There were rice paddies and water buffalo everywhere. Little villages showed up every so often. The mountains and hills were covered with thick jungle. "How am I gonna hump around in that shit?" Robbie thought to himself.

The chopper landed and they were met and told where to go. The new men were still in their stateside uniforms and they all felt out of place. It wasn't long and Robbie finally got to his unit. A tough looking 1st Sergeant talked to them for a bit. "Do what you're told. Learn from the men who've been here and you might just live through this," he said. Then the new men were assigned to their platoons. Robbie's Platoon Sergeant was a very big black man. He was on his second tour and was a squad leader when the Marines retook Hue. Robbie never found out until later that Staff Sergeant Benjamin was from Cincinnati. He had been a foot-ball star in high school and turned down a scholarship at the University of Cincinnati to join the Corps. He was intending to become a Drill Instructor after this tour of duty. As a Platoon Sergeant, he did not fraternize with the men much. That made it a lot easier when certain orders had to be given. S/Sgt. Benjamin took Robbie to his tent and introduced him to his squad leader. "Parker, this is Lance Corporal Sims. He's your squad leader," the S/Sgt. said. "Sims, show him around and get him all his equipment." The S/Sgt. then left.

"Hey Parker, where you from in the world?" asked Sims.

"I'm from Columbus, Ohio," answered Robbie.

"Not another fuckin' buckeye," said Sims. "Seems we got more buckeyes than anything around here."

"Well I may be from Ohio but I'm not an Ohio State fan," said Robbie. "I follow baseball, not football. I'm a Reds fan."

"Good man," said Sims. "I'm a Reds fan too. I'm from Kentucky, just outside a Covington. Ever play any ball?"

"Hell yeah," said Robbie. "I played from little league up to Legion ball."

"What were you? You look like a third baseman ta me," said Sims.

"I pitched mostly," said Robbie. "When I wasn't pitching I played third and short."

"That's great," said Sims. "I was a catcher. Maybe we can see if we can get us some balls and gloves. I'll see what you got. You're lucky you got me for a squad leader. A lot a these guys won't hardly talk to new guy. I don't understand that. Everybody in this outfit gets hit sooner or later. That's just the way it is. You'll get hit too. The trick is to not get hit too bad. Three hearts and you can go home. I only got one. That's enough." Sims pulled up his right pant leg and showed Robbie the scars from the shrapnel wounds. "Well let's go get you some gear," said Sims. "We'll get you some jungles first. Then we'll get your web gear. After that we'll get you a rifle and ammo."

As soon as Robbie got his jungle utilities and boots they went back to the tent so he could get out of his statesides. Then they got his web gear. "Those damn packs they give us are from WWII," said Sims. "We'll steal you a rucksack from the Army or you can get a pack from some NVA you kill sometime. Both a them are better'n what we get." They went to the armory to get Robbie a rifle. The rifle that was handed to Robbie looked like it had seen a lot of use. There was absolutely no bluing left on it. The front sight was bent almost flat and the rear sight was loose.

"I'm not taking this piece of shit," said Robbie. "I may be new here, but I'm not taking this thing."

"And just what's wrong with that rifle?" asked the armorer.

"The front sight is bent all to hell and the rear sight is loose," said Robbie. The armorer grabbed the rifle from Robbie. He reached into a tool box and grabbed some needle nose pliers. He used them and straightened up the front sight some. Then he took another tool and tightened up the rear sight. Then he handed it back to Robbie. Robbie took one look at the front sight and handed it back to the armor.

"I'm not taking that rifle," said Robbie. "That front sight is still bent some. You got a lot of rifles in there. Just give me another one."

"You fuckin' grunts," said the armorer. "Just who in the fuckin' hell do you think you are?" Sims stepped in now.

"Look asshole, just cause you're short don't mean you can act this way," said Sims. "Now you get my man a decent weapon or me and my squad might just pay you a visit real soon."

"You mother fuckers," said the armorer as he handed Robbie a different rifle. Robbie inspected the rifle and accepted it. Nothing else was said as they left.

"Why was that guy such a shithead?" asked Robbie.

"You'll find out that a lot of these rear pogues don't like us grunts," said Sims. "They think that we think we're better'n them. I don't like some a the pogues cause they don't get stuck with all the shit that we do. Whenever we're back here and not in the bush, we work our asses off. We're always filling sandbags and rebuilding bunkers and such. We burn shitters. We have perimeter guard at night. We run patrols out of here too. The pogues don't do any a that shit. Now let's get you some magazines and ammo." Robbie got twenty one magazines and four bandoliers of ammo. "Soon as we get back, you go ahead and load up them magazines," said Sims. "Never know when you'll need'em around here." They went back to the tent and Robbie started loading up his magazines. "Only put eighteen rounds in each magazine," said Sims. "Fillin'em clear up can cause jams. Before you load a magazine in your rifle, smack it against your helmet or something if you have time. That'll make sure the rounds are seated good. Now after you get'em loaded, put the magazines in the empty bandoliers." Robbie finished loading up.

"So what's next?" asked Robbie.

"Well they should be takin' all the new guys out for some indoctrination," said Sims. "They'll put you behind somethin' and fire some rounds over your head. They'll probably fire an M-16, an M-14, maybe an M-1 carbine, and an AK-47. You'll find out that an AK makes a very distinct sound." Sims was right. It wasn't long and they rounded up the new guys in the platoon and had the indoctrination. As soon as the AK was fired, Robbie knew what it was. He had heard that same sound in Da Nang.

When Robbie got back to the tent, there were several other men there. Sims spoke. "Guys, this new guy is Robbie Parker," said Sims. "Don't fuck with'm. He's a Reds fan too." Robbie went to each man and shook their hands. They gave their names but Robbie knew he wouldn't remember them right away.

"What have you boys been doing today?" asked Robbie.

"We been burnin' shitters," two of them answered. "You'll be doin' your share soon."

"We lucked out boys. None of us got perimeter tonight, " said Sims. "But we're goin' on patrol tomorrow."

"Tell me about this patrol if you would," said Robbie.

"Well there's patrols run out of here every day," started Sims. "It's usually a platoon. We go out to wherever they want us to go. We go out one day and come back in the next. Sometimes we set up ambushes. Sometimes we don't."

"So where's the NVA or VC or whoever we're looking for?" asked Robbie.

"Them mother fuckers are everywhere," said one of the other men. "You can kill a bunch of 'em in one place and go back the next and more of 'em'll be there. They wanna kill us bad."

"Don't be scarin' the new man," said Sims. "He'll find out soon enough." Just as he finished talking, they could hear a plane coming. "We'll be going to a bunker shortly," said Sims. "Whenever one a them C-130's comes in, we get some incoming." As soon as the plane touched down the incoming started. Some rockets came in first and then some mortar rounds. "Them are 82's," said Sims as he lit a smoke in the bunker as the mortar rounds hit by the runway. The plane unloaded quickly and got away without being hit. The incoming stopped as soon as the plane lifted off. "We'll get some more a that tonight," said Sims. Men from the other squads in the platoon started showing up now. Some of them introduced themselves to Robbie.

It was getting late so all of them went to the mess hall. Afterwards, some of them went back to the tent. Robbie didn't know where the other ones went. He was sure he smelled some pot on the way back. After he got back to the tent, he decided he would write a letter to Maria and one to his parents to let them know he was there and all right. Sims came over to him. "Go ahead and get them canteens filled tonight," said Sims. "Be one less thing to do in the mornin'. Make sure you take your malaria pill ever day. Some guys say they don't take'em cause they give'em the shits. Don't listen to that. Take your pills. You'll have the shits most a the time you're here anyway. If you get water out in the bush from a stream or whatever, use your halazone pills. We'll get some grenades and C-Rats in the mornin'. Now one more thing and I'll shut up. When we get incoming tonight, and we will get it, take your rifle and ammo to the bunker with you. Never know when them little fuckers'r comin' through the wire. Now get as much sleep as you can. Them artillery batteries here'll be shootin' tonight. It won't be long and you'll be able to sleep through the outgoin' and wake up for the incomin'." Robbie was looking at Sims with kind of a blank stare. "What is it man?" said Sims. "You got a question?"

"I was just wondering," said Robbie. "I know I smelled some pot on the way back from the mess hall. Do many of the guys smoke that stuff?"

"Nobody in the squad does now that I know of," said Sims. "We had a few that smoked some when we got back from the bush, but they're gone now. Some are dead and some rotated. I never did that stuff. I know some guys that take that Obesitol stuff. It's supposed to be like speed. Never tried it either. I like my beer and a little whiskey now and again. I got relatives that make moonshine. Just for personal consumption mind you. Are you a drinker?"

"I have some beer once in a while," said Robbie. "Not regularly though. Never been drunk before."

"Well we'll fix that one a these days," said Sims. "We got us a club here. It's not much, but they got beer."

Robbie tried to sleep but there was just too much on his mind. When he finally dozed off, the artillery batteries cut loose. They fired for a good while. When they finally stopped, small arms fire could be heard. Some was close and some wasn't. He got up once and looked out towards the perimeter. There were green and red tracers everywhere. He laid back down. He didn't know if he was asleep or not when the incoming started but he grabbed his rifle and ammo and followed the others to the bunkers. Sometime before daylight, Sims gave him a nudge and told him to get up. They would be leaving shortly. Robbie got up and got ready. He put his poncho and poncho liner and a pair of socks in his pack. He put on his flak jacket and helmet and his bandoliers of magazines and ammo. He carried his pack outside. Sims got him some C-rats and three hand grenades. He put the C-rats in his pack and put it on. He put the grenades in his flak jacket pockets. "Keep your interval when we get movin'," said Sims. "If you see somethin' that looks out of place or not right, let someone know. Don't pick up nothin' that looks like it could be a souvenir unless it's off a gook you killed. Could be booby trapped." Robbie nodded his head yes. "That fella up there with the Platoon Sergeant is our Platoon Commander, 1st Lt. Conrad," said Sims. "He's been with us for a while. He's all right. Now I haven't said nothin'

about any fire teams. There's only eight of us in the squad so we got two teams.
You're with me."

There were four squads in the platoon, but none of the squads were up to
strength. Besides the eight of them in Sims squad, one squad had nine and another one had eight also. The other squad only had seven men. A machine gunner
and his a-gunner went with them. One of the men in Sims squad carried a grenade
launcher and wore a .45. A captain came out for a few minutes and had some
words with the Lt., and then they were ready to move out. No one said "lock and
load" but Robbie heard rounds being chambered so he loaded up. They moved
out in a staggered column. Sim's squad was the third one back. Sims was in the
middle of his squad. The machine gunner was right in the middle of the column
and Robbie was right behind him. The a-gunner was to the gunner's right.

The area they were in was kind of open and brushy. There were some small
tree lines. Every time they got near a tree line, the men seemed extra cautious. It
rained hard for a while but had slacked off some. After a couple of hours, they set
up a perimeter and ate some C-rats. After a half hour or so, they were moving
again. They had been moving for another hour when the point man thought he
saw something. It was checked out and nothing was found so the column moved
out again. It wasn't five minutes when they started receiving heavy fire from the
right and front. Before Robbie could hit the deck, something struck his rifle and
almost ripped it out of his hands. While he was going down, his rifle took another
hit. The fire was very intense and if anyone was giving any kind of orders, Robbie
couldn't hear them. Robbie got his wits back and looked at his rifle. It had been
hit in the forearm and the gas tube was ripped up. The spring in the stock was
hanging out. He had no weapon to fire. He looked to his front at the machine
gunner. He wasn't moving. Robbie crawled up to him. He had been shot through
the head. The a-gunner had been hit in the chest and wasn't moving. The Marines
were returning fire now.

Robbie crawled over to the a-gunner. He was dead too. Robbie looked at
Sims and could see his lips moving but couldn't make out what he was saying.
Robbie crawled back over to the machine gunner. Robbie was getting some belts
of ammo off of the gunner when the Platoon Sergeant came by. He was working
his way down the line telling the men where to direct their fire. He was on his
knees crawling and right next to Robbie when he was hit. The bullet hit him in his
left thigh. He screamed in pain. As the Platoon Sergeant was looking at his wound
to see how bad it was, another bullet tore through his right arm. Robbie crawled
to him. He was bleeding terribly from his leg. The bullet had gone through and

had shattered the bone. Robbie pulled the S/Sgt.'s belt off of him and made a tourniquet. Then he grabbed a battle dressing out of the Sergeant's pack and wrapped it around his leg. Robbie could see pieces of bone sticking out of the holes as he wrapped the dressing around the leg. He grabbed a dressing out of his pack and put it on the other side of the leg. He crawled back over to the gunner and got a dressing from his pack and crawled back to the S/Sgt. and wrapped it around his arm. Bone was sticking out of the wound. Robbie then crawled back over to the dead gunner and was getting the machine gun when he saw three enemy soldiers working their way toward them on the left side. One of them was carrying an RPG. No one else had seen them and they were getting close.

Robbie reached into his flak jacket and pulled out a grenade. He pulled the pin and threw it as hard as he could toward the soldier with the RPG. The enemy soldier must have seen the grenade coming and he hit the deck. The grenade exploded and right after it did, there was a secondary explosion. Robbie thought he saw a head flying through the air. Then Robbie threw another grenade. More enemy soldiers were moving toward them on the left now. Robbie threw his last grenade. Sims had heard the explosions and turned to look at what was happening. He now saw the enemy soldiers. Fire was still very intense from the right and the front. Sims crawled to two of his men and had them cover the left side. One of them had been hit in the leg but he wasn't bleeding badly and could still do his job. They threw grenades and laid down a good base of fire. Several enemy soldiers were killed or wounded but they kept coming. Robbie picked up the machine gun and crawled as far forward toward the enemy soldiers as he could. When he cut loose with the M-60, the enemy soldiers started to pull back. Robbie emptied the belt of ammo that was in the gun and loaded another one. The enemy soldiers were still pulling back. Robbie stood up and charged them firing the machine gun. "Get the fuck down Parker," Sims began yelling. "Get the fuck down." Robbie had fired the belt of ammo and was loading another one when something struck his left shoulder and knocked him back a little. He straightened back up and loaded his last belt of ammo. He fired a few bursts and then got down. The fire from the right and front was still coming but was not as intense. Robbie felt something or someone touching him. He looked to his left. Sims had crawled up to him and had brought two more belts of ammo for the M-60.

"Let's try to move to our left now and see if we can get some more a them gooners," Sims yelled. "They're startin' to pull back. Maybe we can get some." As they got closer to where some of the enemy soldiers had been, they both saw an arm come up from behind some brush. There was a grenade coming toward them. Sims and Robbie hugged the ground as best they could. The grenade landed about twenty feet from them but didn't go off. Robbie and Sims held their breath.

"Gimme one a your grenades," Robbie said to Sims. "I'll get that fucker." Sims gave Robbie a grenade. Robbie pulled the pin and got to his knees and threw it. When he got to his knees, the enemy soldier fired at him several times but missed. Robbie could see the enemy soldier clearly now. The grenade was about to hit him when it exploded. The enemy soldier was torn to bits. When the grenade went off, two other enemy soldiers got up and were running away. Robbie cut loose with the M-60. They both went down. Robbie and Sims worked their way to the column's right hoping to see some more enemy soldiers. As they moved, they finally noticed that it was quiet. The enemy had fled. They sat down for a minute. Robbie took a drink from a canteen and offered one to Sims. Sims looked at him hard. As Sims was taking a drink, they heard a thump as something hit the ground near them. They both spotted the grenade at the same time and hugged the earth. When it went off, the force of the blast rolled Robbie over onto his back. Robbie checked himself but he wasn't hit. He looked over at Sims and could see blood on his rear end. Before Robbie could examine the wound, some shots were fired at them. Dirt was being thrown on them as the rounds missed. Robbie figured out where the shots had come from and cut loose with the 60. A lone enemy soldier got up and started running away. He darted from tree to tree before Robbie finally cut him down. Then it was totally quiet.

"Just what in the fuck did you think you were doin' standin' up like that with that much fire goin' on," Sims yelled at him. "Are you fuckin' nuts?" Robbie never said a word. "You know you saved our asses today," said Sims. "Them fuckers woulda cut us ta pieces." Robbie still didn't speak. "You got blood all over your face and there's some on your left shoulder," said Sims. "Take off that flak jacket and I'll have a look."

"I'm all right," Robbie yelled back at him. "You been hit in the ass. Shut up and lay there while I take a look." Robbie took a knife and cut Sims pants open so he could see the wound. There was a big rip on his left cheek and a few small holes that probably had shrapnel in them. His right cheek wasn't touched. Robbie grabbed a dressing from Sim's pack and covered the wounds as best he could.

"Now take off that flak jacket and let me have a look at you," said Sims.

A bullet had caught the top of Robbie's left shoulder. It had ripped his flak jacket and just grazed his shoulder. Sims looked at Robbie's face. There was a piece of black plastic stuck just below the cheek bone on the right side of his face. "I'll get the Corpsman to look at you when he gets done with the others," said

Sims. "You know them gooks you killed were probably new guys. They was bad shots and a NVA soldier who's been in the shit for a while won't get up and run like them boys did. I was here three months before I seen a live one. Yeh we got shot at a lot and we killed a lot of 'em but I never seen'em till they were dead. Anyway, I never seen anybody throw a grenade like you. How that hell could you throw it that far and accurate. I'm gonna start callin' you "Pitcher." I'll tell everyone to call you that before that medivac bird gets here."

A perimeter was formed and a medivac was called. The platoon had three killed and eight wounded. Three of those were quite severe. There were twenty dead enemy soldiers that they could find. As the men were searching for enemy casualties, single shots could be heard every so often.

The medivac bird came. It was a Ch-46. There was a Corpsman on the bird to take care of the wounded on their way to the Evac Hospital. There was no firing as they loaded the wounded and when the bird lifted off. The Corpsman took a look at Robbie now. "That's a piece of your rifle in your face there," he said as he pulled it out. "You'll need some stitches. I'll do that when we get back in. You just got grazed on your shoulder." He took something and cleaned the wounds as best he could. "You'll be fine," he said.

The Lt. was on the radio and was trying to get them to send a chopper out to get the platoon back to An Hoa. Robbie heard him yelling to someone on the radio. "I've lost eleven men today," he yelled. "If we get hit again, we'll get wiped out." Just then it started raining again. The platoon got back into a staggered column and headed back to An Hoa. Robbie broke down his shot up rifle and tied it to his pack. He carried the 60 and two belts of ammo on the march back. They went back a different way than the way they had come. They made it back without incident. It had rained the whole time. Robbie stashed the 60 and his gear in his tent and went to get his face stitched up. It took eight stitches. As the Corpsman was stitching him up he spoke.

"You're that Parker fella aren't you?" he said. "You saved the Platoon Sergeant's life when you put that belt on his leg. That bullet nipped his femoral artery. He told me and the Lt. what you did out there with that 60. He said you saved our asses. Thank you."

"You're welcome," said Robbie. "I was just trying to stay alive."

"Well I'm glad you were there," said the Corpsman. "Now you try and keep your shoulder and face clean. Even the smallest little scratch can get infected over here. Now I hope I never have to work on you again."

"I hope that too," said Robbie as he was leaving. When he got back to the tent, the other men in the squad were figuring out who would be the next squad leader. A guy named Bill Towers figured that he had been there the longest. He was a L/Cpl. "If it's all right with the rest of you, we'll just figure I'm it till someone says otherwise," said Bill. "Parker, Sims said we was to call you "Pitcher" on account a the way you can throw a grenade. He said you saved our asses today. We thank you. Now I'm gonna go see the Lt. and make sure we don't have perimeter tonight."

Robbie sat down on his cot and was about to start a letter home when Towers came back. "We don't have perimeter tonight," he said. "We'll be fillin' sandbags all day tomorrow if it don't rain. We'll be goin' out on an operation day after tomorrow. We'll be out there for more than a month. Pitcher, the Lt. wants to see you right now." Robbie never said a word and reported to his Platoon Commander.

When he reported to the Lt., the Lt. told him to follow him and they were going to see the Company Commander. There was no formal saluting or attention standing when they reported to the Captain. "Captain, this is PFC Parker," said the Lt. "He's the man I told you about."

"Parker, S/Sgt. Benjamin told some story to the Lt. here about some crazy wild man who patched him up and then picked up a 60 and stood up and charged the enemy," started the Captain. "He said he saw you personally kill five of them for sure and maybe even more. He said you needed your ass kicked for standing up like that when the fire was so intense but what you did saved the platoon. He said you should be decorated. I agree. The Lt. here will write everything up and you will make sure it's accurate. We'll be putting you in for a Bronze Star. How does that sound?"

"I don't know sir," said Robbie. "I'm sure other men deserve a decoration more than I do. I was just trying to stay alive."

"That's what we do over here," said the Captain. "We all just try to stay alive. You went a little above and beyond. Now we know that you can handle that 60. Would you like to be a gunner?"

"No sir, I wouldn't," said Robbie. "I can handle it but if there would be a jam or something, I might not be good enough to fix it. I know we're going on an operation day after tomorrow. I'll take the 60 till you get a replacement if that's all right with you."

"That'll be all right," said the Captain. "I can't blame you for not wanting to carry that thing. It's a might heavier than a 16. I hear your rifle got shot up too.

Get to the armory and get yourself a .45. We'll get you another 16 when we get some more replacements. Now you and the Lt. go work on your citation. Dismissed."

They went to the Lt.'s tent and began. "Now don't get all worked up by all this fancy writing," said the Lt. "They always use lines like, "with complete disregard for his own personal safety" and such. Now tell me everything that happened and in the order it happened. Then I'll get it written up and have a clerk type it up." Robbie did his best to tell everything to the Lt.

"I still don't feel right about this," said Robbie. "I only been in country a few days."

"Would you feel better about it if you had been here twelve months and were getting short?" asked the Lt. "I bet not. You'd have kicked your own ass for doing something like that after you realized that you might have gotten killed. You're a good man Parker. Don't think too much about all this. Now go get yourself that .45."

Robbie left the Lt. and went back to his tent and got his shot up rifle. "What's up?" Towers asked him. "What'd the Lt. want?"

"I gotta get me a .45," said Robbie. "I'll be humpin' the 60 till a replacement comes. They're puttin' me in for a medal too."

"No shit," said Towers. "How bout that boys. Pitcher here is a hero."

"Knock it off will you?" said Robbie. "I don't feel right about it."

"Well I seen some a what you done Parker," said Towers. "You're a crazy fucker standin' up like that. But it did save our asses. Besides, something like that might look good on a resume some day. What medal is it?"

"Bronze Star," said Robbie.

"Far out," one of the other men said. "Far out." Robbie left for the armory.

The fella that had given Robbie the shit about the rifle was there. "So what the fuck do you want now?" he asked Robbie. Robbie handed him the shot up rifle.

"Gimme a .45," said Robbie. "I'll be humpin' a 60 till a replacement comes."

"So you're that guy," said the armorer. "Words been goin' round bout you. They say you saved that platoon's ass. You may not like me but I respect you whether you think I do or not. I'll get you the best damn .45 I got. When you need a 16 again, I'll get you the best one I got if I'm still here. I only got a month to go." Robbie extended his hand to the armorer and they shook.

"I'm Robbie Parker," said Robbie.

"Steve Nelson," said the armorer. They gave each other a nod and Robbie went back to his tent. All of the men then went to the mess hall.

That evening, Robbie wrote letters to Maria and his parents. He told them he was going on an operation soon and he would do his best to write. He told them that the monsoons had started and it would be hard to keep paper dry. He fell asleep easily that night but it wasn't long and the incoming started. They got some three different times that night. First time it was rockets. The second and third times were 82 mortars. The artillery fire from the base woke him up too, but he managed to get back to sleep quickly.

It wasn't raining the next morning so the men went to their assigned area and filled sandbags and rebuilt some bunkers. They worked some in the afternoon, but it started raining again so they lucked out.

Chapter Seven

The operation they were going on was a big one. Several battalions were involved. They were going out into some place they called the "Arizona." Robbie had his pack as full as he could get it. It was full of C-rats and some extra socks. He had some soap, tooth paste and tooth brush, flashlight, paper and pen wrapped in some plastic, and a few other things. His poncho and liner was tied to his pack. He also had an e-tool fastened to the pack. He had three canteens and a first aid pack. He carried one belt of ammo in the 60 and two strapped across him. He had four hand grenades in his flak jacket pockets. Another man carried two cans of ammo for the 60 besides his own weapon and ammo. Other men had extra belts strapped across them.

They were at the pad at daylight expecting to load shortly. It was raining, but the rain got harder and harder. The choppers were delayed. Finally after three hours or so, the rain slacked up and the birds came. Everyone loaded up and the birds took off. Robbie knew that his platoon was short on men but he figured all the platoons were in the same boat. They had a new Platoon Sgt. He came from another company. He was supposed to be good man and was on his second tour. His name was S/Sgt. Rojas.

They were told to expect a hot LZ when they landed but it was not. They formed up and moved out. It wasn't long before they made contact. Robbie's whole company was pinned down and had taken several casualties. Whenever they tried to make a flanking move, heavy fire stopped them. A forward observer with the company called in a fire mission and began walking the rounds closer and closer to their position. Robbie thought he was doing a good job. After what seemed like a hundred rounds were fired, the mission stopped. The Marines waited a while. A squad was told to make a flanking move. As soon as they moved, over half of them were cut down. The firing started again all over. Artillery was called in again. This time the FO walked the rounds to within a hundred and fifty yards of their position. A battery of six 105's was doing the firing. On their second adjustment, there were several secondary explosions. The FO told them to fire for effect. There was one more secondary. The FO kept the battery firing. As soon as the barrage stopped, the Marines moved. They took some fire but nothing like they had taken before. They assaulted the enemy position and took it. It wasn't easy. The NVA were in a series of bunkers. Whenever one bunker was taken, another one opened up on them. When it was over, the company had taken five killed and twenty wounded, some seriously. Two of the KIA happened after the firefight had ceased. A booby trapped mortar round was responsible. There were thirty dead NVA that they could find and there were several blood trails. Medivacs were called. The choppers came and left without taking fire.

The company moved the rest of the day without any contact. They dug in as best they could in the mud and set up for the night. Some ambushes were set up. About 2 AM, one of the ambushes opened up on a squad of NVA killing three of them. Another one was wounded and in the morning, they took him back to the company. They didn't have anyone with them who could speak Vietnamese, so they patched the NVA up as best they could and kept him tied up. When they resupplied, they would send the POW back on one of the choppers. Some of the other companies had Kit Carson Scouts with them but Robbie's company didn't. He had heard that they had one a while back but he had been killed. Kit Carson Scouts were enemy soldiers that had come over to the other side through the "Chieu Hoi" program. They were either VC or NVA. Robbie did know that some of the men weren't quite sure they could trust a Kit Carson Scout. Robbie figured he'd find out for himself.

They moved out the next morning. After about an hour there was an explosion at the front of the company. The point man had tripped a booby trap. He was dead and the next man was seriously wounded. A perimeter was formed and a medivac was called. As the chopper was landing, it started taking fire. It was from some sort of heavy machine gun and was over five hundred yards away. Robbie could tell where the fire was coming from so he opened up with the 60. He fired two belts of ammo at the position. The firing slowed but didn't stop. The CO had gotten a hold of a gunship and it was on the way. When the chopper got there, he cut loose with mini-guns and then a 40mm cannon. No more fire came from that position. They put the POW on the medivac bird. They put something over his head and tied his hands and feet and then tied him to something in the chopper so he couldn't get loose. After the chopper left, they moved out again.

They moved in the direction the heavy machine gun fire had come from. When they got to where the fire had come from, they found two dead NVA and a 12.7mm machine gun that had been completely ruined. The NVA weren't really recognizable. The mini-guns had completely shredded them to pieces. One of the Marines discovered that what was left of the machine gun had been booby trapped so they blew it in place.

There was no contact for the rest of the day. They set up a perimeter and dug in for the night. About midnight, they started taking some 61mm mortar fire. Someone thought they saw the flash from the tube. They returned fire with their own 60mm mortar. After several rounds, the incoming stopped. That night one of their own ambushes was ambushed. One man was killed and two were wounded, but not seriously enough to be medivaced. The Corpsman stitched them up. They would be getting resupplied tomorrow and the chopper was told there would be a permanent routine medivac.

The resupply bird came and all the supplies were distributed. The chopper came and went without taking any fire. The CO had spent a lot of time on the radio talking to other units. A large force of NVA had been spotted and all of the units would try to force them to a position where the Marines could annihilate them.

The NVA weren't going to be forced anywhere. This was their territory. They had bunkers, holes, and tunnels all over the place. They were always well camouflaged and hard to spot. They knew every crack and crevice and hill and stream and could usually slip away. There were several small actions, but not the big fight the Marines wanted. Several NVA were killed, but the Marines took casualties too. The rest of the operation was like this. Some unit was always in contact somewhere. Some of the fire fights were fierce but the enemy almost always slipped away after inflicting casualties. The operation went on. After a month and a half, Robbie's company was choppered back to An Hoa. They had taken more casualties than some of the other companies. In Robbie's squad, Towers had been killed and three others had been wounded. Robbie's old squad wasn't much more than a fire team now.

When Robbie got back to their tent, he got a good surprise. Sims was there. Robbie looked at him and smiled. "How in the hell are you?" said Robbie as he went over and shook Sim's hand.

"I'm good," said Sims. "I got some light duty for a while but I'll be back out there in no time. So how was it out there?"

"You been out there," said Robbie. "I reckon it was just like it always is."

"How bout let's go get us a beer," said Sims. "I'll buy."

"Sounds good," said Robbie. "Let's go."

They had a few beers at the club. Someone had an eight track tape player and was playing some Motown music. "I wish I was dancing with Maria right now," said Robbie as he nursed his beer.

"If I was with my girl right now I'd skip over the dancin'," said Sims. "You got a picture of your girl?"

"Sure do," said Robbie as he pulled out a picture of Maria and handed it to Sims.

"Jesus Christ," said Sims. "Just how the hell did you get a woman that looks like that. That woman is drop fuckin' dead gorgeous."

"Yes she is and she is my woman," said Robbie. "We're gonna get married when I get out of the Corps."

"You shouldn't have shown me that picture," said Sims. "I'll be havin' evil thoughts for a long time."

"You got a girl don't you?" asked Robbie.

"Course I do and she's not bad lookin', but she don't compare to that woman a yours," said Sims.

They had just started another beer when the Platoon Sergeant, S/Sgt. Rojas came into the club looking for Robbie. "Parker, the Platoon Commander wants to see you right now," he said.

"I had me a few beers," said Robbie. "He won't care if I been drinking, will he?"

"I doubt it," said Rojas. I think he's had a little himself."

Robbie made his way to the Platoon Commander and reported. "Don't worry about formalities," said Lt. Conrad. "Stand at ease. Your Bronze Star has been approved. Congratulations Parker. You're a good man. You are also now a L/Cpl."

"Thank you Sir," said Robbie as the Lt. reached over and shook his hand. "Will there be anything else?"

"We will be getting several replacements tomorrow," said the Lt. "You won't have to lug around that 60 anymore, although you are very good with it. Now go on and have a few more beers and enjoy yourself. We'll be out on patrol day after tomorrow."

"Thank you again Sir," said Robbie. Then Robbie left and did as the Lt. instructed. He went back to the club to have a few more beers. Sims was still there and was getting a little drunk.

"So what's up?" asked Sims. "You in trouble or somethin'?"

"No, no trouble," answered Robbie. "They approved that Bronze Star and I'm also a L/Cpl. now. And we got replacements due in tomorrow and I can give up that 60."

"Well Pitcher, you're a bona fide real fuckin' hero now," said Sims. "I think we'll get us a good drunk on to celebrate."

"Well I don't know about the celebrating, but I think we'll get drunk anyway," said Robbie.

The boys did get drunk and had bad hangovers for most of the next day while they were burning shitters. There was no drinking later that day. The platoon would be on patrol the next day. Sims wouldn't be going because of his light duty, but he would be ready for the next operation.

The platoon did not have any firefights on the patrol but one man was killed and two were wounded from a booby trap. One of the wounded men was Lt. Conrad. He had shrapnel wounds in both legs.

When the next operation started, there were a lot of new faces in the platoon. One of them was their new Platoon Commander, Lt. Byers. The Platoon Sergeant, S/Sgt. Rojas, stuck to him like glue and made sure he didn't do anything foolish or make any foolish decisions. This operation wasn't much different than the last one. There were a lot of fierce fire fights and several men were killed or wounded. There were also some casualties from booby traps and snipers. Several NVA or VC were killed or captured too. Robbie had walked point several times and was getting better at spotting booby traps or things that didn't look quite right. It seemed like this operation would never end.

On Thanksgiving Day, hot chow was sent out to them. They had turkey and dressing and some of the trimmings. The men really enjoyed it. Robbie was used to C-rats, but this stuff hit the spot.

The operation finally ended in mid December. The monsoon rains were starting to slow some. There was to be a USO show sometime when they were out of the bush. Everyone was excited when the show came. It was a Philippino band and they had a couple of good looking girls that danced with them. They didn't speak very good English and couldn't pronounce a lot of the words to the songs they played, but they could play their instruments well. The girls wore mini- skirts and bathing suit tops. Of course the men loved it. Robbie was up front. These girls reminded him of Maria. As the band played, one of the girls kept motioning for Robbie to come up and dance with her. Robbie obliged her and got up on the stage and danced with her. She was amazed at how good a dancer Robbie was. The crowd cheered them on. When the song was over, the girl pulled Robbie to her and whispered into his ear. "You can fuck me for $5.00," she whispered. Robbie smiled at her and pulled her to him and whispered into her ear.

"You can pay me when we're done," said Robbie. The girl let out a little laugh and gave Robbie a kiss on the cheek. Robbie then got off the stage. After the show was over, Robbie heard that the girls had made a good bit of money before they left. Robbie hoped that none of the men got the clap.

It was a good thing that the monsoon rains were slowing because on the next operation, one of the men in Robbie's platoon had gotten a copy of the December '68 Playboy. Cynthia Myers was the Playmate and the whole Company was in love. Every time the magazine was passed from man to man, there was a standing order. There were to be no pages that were stuck together.

Bob Hope would be having his show soon and certain men would be allowed to go. The men who had been there the longest were the ones allowed to go. Robbie had only been in country for almost four months but with all the new faces he was one of the ones who could go. He decided not to go. Sims went and thought Robbie was crazy for not going. "I hear Ann Margaret's gonna be there," said Sims. "Are you fuckin' nuts? It's Ann Margaret. Besides, it'll get you outta this shit for a little while."

"It'll just make me home sick," said Robbie. "You go on now. Don't forget to come back."

The New Year came and the 5th Marines were spending a lot of time in the "Arizona." Everyone was getting concerned that the VC and NVA were planning for another big TET Offensive. Patrols were always out looking for the enemy and trying to find supply stashes. There were a lot of fire fights and a lot of men were killed or wounded from booby traps. Robbie's platoon was on patrol near the end of January when they were ambushed. The enemy hit them hard from three sides and then vanished. Three men were killed and six were wounded. Robbie was one of the wounded. He had been shot in both legs. A blast from an AK-47 on full automatic caught him as he was crawling over to help another wounded man.

At the Evac Hospital they told him he was very lucky because the bullets had not struck bone. He would be healed up in no time. He was in the hospital when the TET Offensive began. It wasn't near what the "68 TET was but the VC and NVA still attacked a lot of key installations and cities. They were beaten back but there were a lot of casualties.

Robbie was all set to go back to his unit when he got some infection in his legs. It took three weeks or so for them to say he was well enough to go back. While he was fighting his infection, the ammo dump at An Hoa got blown up by enemy sappers. The base was also under siege for almost two weeks. Robbie wanted to be there helping his friends.

A few days before Robbie was scheduled to go back to his unit, his mail caught up with him. It had taken a good while to catch up because of the offensive. He received several letters from Maria and his parents. He read Maria's letters first and he read them in the order that they were postmarked. Then he read his parent's letters in the same order. There were six letters. The first two were typical letters. They wanted to make sure he was all right and everyone back home was fine. The third letter told him that his friend Brad had been killed around some place called Pleiku. The fourth letter was a typical letter. In the fifth letter they told him that they had been notified that he had been wounded but not seriously and he would be healed in no time. Then came the sixth letter. It was from his mother. It went as follows.

My Dearest Son,

There is no good way to tell you this so I will do the best I can. Maria is dead. She was at a Convenience store one evening and there was an armed robbery. The robber had gotten the money from the register and was leaving when he noticed Maria's purse. He demanded that she give it to him and she refused. She actually hit the robber upside the head with it. He shot her three times in the chest and then shot another person in the store. The police arrived very quickly and there was a shootout. The robber was killed. I am so deeply sorry. I told Maria's grandparents that I would tell you. I know this will be hard for you to take but I know you are a strong young man and you will be all right over time. Your father and I both loved Maria too. I am sorry that I do not have the words that need to be said to comfort you because I know that whatever is said will not be enough.

We love and miss you,

Mom and Dad

Robbie was in total shock. He checked the date on the last letter from Maria and compared it to his parent's last letter. The letter from his parents was dated two days after Maria's last letter. He started crying. He cried so loud that a nurse came over to check on him. "What's wrong Marine?" she asked. "Is there anything I can do?" Robbie couldn't talk. He took the letter from his mother and handed it to the nurse. Robbie was now crying uncontrollably. The nurse read the letter and she began crying too. Both of them cried for a good while. Another nurse came over to check on them. "We'll be all right shortly," said the first nurse. "We're having a good cry. We'll be all right." The other nurse left. After about fifteen minutes, Robbie finally quit crying. "You must have loved Maria very much," said the nurse.

Robbie struggled to get out his words. "We were going to get married after I got out of the Corps," said Robbie.

"I know how you feel," said the nurse. "I lost my husband at Dak To in '67. I cried for weeks. When I read your letter, I was crying for my husband again. I will always miss him just as you will always miss Maria." Robbie sat up in his bed and hugged the nurse and cried a little more on her shoulder. He pulled away after a few minutes. The nurse smiled at him. "My name is Helen Carter," she said. "I've got my rounds to make but if you need someone to talk to or need anything, I'll be there for you."

"I'm Robbie Parker and I thank you for being here," said Robbie. "I'm going to try to sleep now if I can. Thanks again." Helen gave Robbie a smile and then left for her rounds. Robbie cried a little more but finally got to sleep.

When he woke up several hours later, Helen was standing next to his bed and checking his legs to make sure the infection wasn't returning. "Good morning Robbie Parker," she said. "How are you feeling now?"

"I'm not sure what I feel right now," said Robbie. "I want to cry some more but I know it won't help anything."

"Well I'll be back in a while and we'll have time to talk if you'd like," said Helen.

"That would be nice," said Robbie. "We'll talk then."

Helen was back in a couple of hours. Robbie was allowed to walk some so they went to a room that looked like it was some sort of conference room. They went in and sat down. "This is just a room where we bring wounded men who are having problems," said Helen. "I don't just mean from their wounds. There's a lot of men who just don't want to go back to their units. They're tired of death and killing. They just want to go home."

"I can understand that," said Robbie. "It's not very pretty out there."

"Well tell me all about yourself," said Helen. "Tell me everything from when you were small and up to now." Robbie began telling his whole life story to Helen. The more he talked the better he felt. When he thought he had told her everything, he asked her to tell him about herself.

Helen was born in Hawaii. Her mother was Hawaiian and her father was white and a doctor. Helen had always wanted to be a nurse. She was in nursing school when she met her husband to be. His name was Paul. He was an officer stationed at Schofield Barracks. They had a whirlwind romance and were married. It was good for a while but he finally got orders for Vietnam. He had been there for five months when he was killed on hill 875 in Nov. 67. Helen spent some time grieving but she finished her schooling and then decided to join the Navy. Her tour in Vietnam was almost over. She would be stationed at the Naval Hospital at Pearl Harbor when she rotated.

"That'll be great for you at Pearl Harbor," said Robbie. "You'll be home."

"Yes, it'll be nice," said Helen. "I know I'll be missing my husband more when I go home. We had a house that my father had given us. It will bring back memories again." Then Helen changed the subject. "You'll be going back to your unit in three more days," she said. "Will you be all right out there?"

"I'm sure I will," said Robbie. "I know I'll have Maria constantly on my mind, but when I'm out in the thick of things, I'll have my head on straight."

"That's good to hear," said Helen. "Now let's get you back. The doctor will be wanting to look at you shortly." The three days went by quickly. He and Helen talked a little every day. Robbie got extremely embarrassed one of those days. Helen was a very attractive woman. Her skin tone, hair color, and body features, all reminded Robbie of Maria. One day when they were talking and Robbie was laying in bed, he looked down and noticed that he had a huge hard on. He turned over onto his belly as quickly as he could. Helen let out a little giggle. "That happens here more than you might think," said Helen. "Most of these men haven't been near any women for months." Robbie laughed too.

On the day that Robbie left the hospital, Helen handed him a slip of paper. "This is my address in Hawaii," she said. "I want you to write me and let me know how you are." Robbie thanked her and was on his way.

Chapter Eight

When Robbie got back to An Hoa the place looked like it had been rebuilt some. Some of the bunkers looked almost new as they had newer looking sandbags on them. On his way over to report in, he saw Sims and some other men. They were burning shitters. Sims saw him and went to talk with him. "Just where in the hell you been Pitcher?" said Sims. "You missed all the fun around here. We coulda used you."

"I would have been back sooner but I got some infection," said Robbie. "I'll go report in and I'll be over to help you boys." When Robbie went to report in, Lt. Byers was in a meeting with all the officers. S/Sgt. Rojas was the only one there. "So you're back Parker," said Rojas. "It's a good thing. We'll be needing you. We're going back out in the "Arizona" and try to find them little fuckers. They done a number on us while you were gone. I'll tell the Lt. you're back. Your squad is burnin' shitters. Go help them."

"All right Sarge," said Robbie. "I seen them on the way here." Robbie went back to where the squad was burning shitters and pitched in. Some of the men he had never seen but they all had stories to tell him about what had happened in his absence. They all went to the club that evening but they didn't get drunk. Robbie saw a small book over on another table and went to see what it was. It was a Vietnamese phrase book. It had common words and phrases in it and explained how to pronounce the words. Robbie asked around to see if it belonged to any-one. No one claimed it so Robbie put it in his pocket. Robbie spent some of his spare time looking at the book and trying to remember some of the words and phrases.

In a few days they were on another operation. This time they had a Kit Carson Scout with them and an interpreter. Whenever he could, Robbie tried to pick up words that the Kit Carson Scout had said and then he would see if he could find them in the book. Most of the time he had no luck but other times he did. One day they captured a VC and Robbie wasn't far away when the Scout began asking the VC some questions. Robbie could see that the VC eyes were filled with pure hatred for the Scout. He spit on the Scout once. When he did, the Scout knocked him down and began kicking him viciously. It seems that this Kit Carson Scout was from some village and was worried that the VC would kill his family. The Scout couldn't get the VC to talk. After a while, the Scout and the VC walked away somewhere. Robbie couldn't see them or where they went. After a while there was a single shot. The Scout came back but not the VC.

The next several days, the Company had a lot of contact. They were killing some VC and NVA but were taking several casualties. One day Robbie heard a chopper flying over and looked up to see a four man recon team hanging from a ladder under a CH-46. Apparently they had gotten into some shit and had to get out quick. Shit was right. The recon team had spotted a good sized force of NVA not far from where Robbie's company was. They had radioed in the position and gotten the hell out of there. The company went looking for them.

It wasn't long before they found them, or at least the NVA found the company. The company started receiving mortar fire from 82's. Several men were wounded. Then the NVA assaulted the Marines. The Marines formed a perimeter and fought hard. Their 60mm team mortar was firing as fast as they could. Some of the NVA had gotten close. Robbie could hear one of them shouting commands. He fired a full magazine from his M-16 at where he was sure the man was. He thought he heard the man gasp but it was hard to tell with all the firing that was going on. All of a sudden, five NVA soldiers charged his position. Robbie cut down two of them with his M-16 but the other three still charged. Robbie was about to change magazines when he heard a voice behind him. It was S/Sgt. Rojas. He handed Robbie a K-bar and told him to use it. Robbie tucked the knife in his belt. The three NVA must have been out of ammunition because they didn't fire another shot as they charged. Their bayonets were fixed on their AK-47's. Rojas had a .45 and he shot two of the NVA when they were about ten feet away. The one remaining came straight for Robbie. As he got closer, Robbie took his M-16 and pushed the NVA's rifle to the side. Robbie didn't have time to put a fresh magazine in his rifle. He dropped his rifle and pulled the K-bar from his belt with his right hand and stuck the blade of the K-bar deep into the NVA's gut. The NVA dropped his rifle and fell to the ground. He tried to get back up but Robbie took the K-bar and cut his throat down to the bone. As the NVA lay there dying, Robbie grabbed his M-16 and loaded a fresh magazine. A few more NVA had charged but were cut down. After some very intense fighting, the NVA withdrew. The forward observer called in artillery and they were firing on suspected routes the NVA could be taking as they withdrew.

When the fight was over, there were forty dead NVA within fifty yards of the company's position. There were blood trails everywhere. The Marines had five men killed and twenty wounded. Robbie went over to the three NVA who had charged him and checked their AK's to see if they were empty or not. All three of them had rounds in the magazines that were in their rifles and they still had more loaded magazines on them. "Why in the hell didn't they fire," Robbie said to himself. "They must have been so gung ho that they wanted to kill us with their bayonets or maybe they were just plain stupid. Well, they're dead and I'm not." After the artillery quit firing, helicopter gunships came in and raked the area with their mini-guns and rockets. Medivac birds came and took out the wounded and dead. Resupply was ordered because the company had almost exhausted all of their ammunition. Everything was needed from rifle and machine gun ammo to mortar rounds. Grenades and .45 ammo were also short. They set up a perimeter and waited for the resupply.

As they were waiting for resupply, Rojas went around checking on his men. He handed Robbie a sheath for the K-bar. "You're a squad leader now Parker," said Rojas. "I'm moving you over to second squad. Blevins got killed. Give Sims a goodbye kiss and move over to second squad." Robbie never said a word. He told Sims the news and went over to his new squad.

The supplies didn't arrive till almost dark so the company stayed put for the night. The next morning they went looking for the NVA again. They found more blood trails and several booby traps were found. No contact was made but in the afternoon they started receiving sniper fire. Two Marines were wounded and the Kit Carson Scout was killed. Some of the other units on the operation had made contact but the enemy didn't stand for a long fight. They ambushed units and faded away.

The rest of the operation did not produce the results the Marines wanted. There were several short and fierce firefights but the enemy always faded away. Several more casualties came from booby traps and sniper fire. Robbie had two men in his new squad wounded before the operation ended.

When they finally got back to An Hoa, Robbie realized something as he was walking to the platoon's tent. He had been in country long enough to take an R & R. He remembered that at one time he was hoping Maria and he could meet in Hawaii. What would he do now? Maybe he would just take one of those in country R & R's. A lot of the guys always talked about how great Bangkok was but Robbie didn't want to be with some whore. Maybe he wouldn't take an R & R. He stashed his gear and cleaned his rifle, then he and Sims and some of the others went to the club. They all sat there and never said one word while they drank their first two beers. Then Sims spoke. "So how's that good lookin' woman a yours Pitcher," said Sims. "I bet you two'r goin' to Hawaii on R & R soon."

Robbie had not told Sims or any of the men that Maria was dead. He had a hard time holding the tears back. Finally he spoke. "My Maria is dead. She was killed during a robbery at a Convenience store back home," said Robbie. "I found out when I was in the hospital."

"We are so sorry man," said Sims. "I wouldn't have said anything like that if I had known."

"It's not your fault," said Robbie. "You didn't know. It was hard to swallow."

"Well you still got your act together Pitcher," said Sims. "You done good out in the bush."

"Well I reckon I should figure out what I should do about an R &R," said Robbie. "I suppose I could do one a those in country things."

"Those girls in Bangkok'll take care of you," said Sims.

"I reckon they would but I don't want any whores just yet," said Robbie. The boys had a couple more beers and went back to their tent. Robbie decided he would write a letter home and then one to Helen Carter. His letter home told them that he was a squad leader now and not to worry about him. His letter to Helen was hard to write. He wanted to thank her for helping him and he wanted to choose the proper words. He thought and thought and then started writing. The letter went as follows.

Dear Helen,

I want to express my thanks to you for helping me at a very hard time in my life. You were so nice to me and I will never forget your kind words. I have been well and have been able to keep my mind on my work. I won't tell you about the bush but I will tell you that I am a squad leader now. I have been here long enough to go on R & R but I have no idea what I should do. I had been hoping that Maria and I could meet in Hawaii. Now I don't know what I should do. Most of the guys here have been going to Bangkok. I guess if you want to pay for a woman it's up to you, but I couldn't do that. I could just take one of those in country deals but I'd just be around a bunch of drunks. I can do that here when we're not out in the bush. Enough about me.

How is Pearl Harbor? It must be great to be back home. I know you said you would have some memories at the house but I know that over time all of those memories will be the good ones. Is the hospital a good place to work? I suppose that some of the wounded from here end up there when they are well enough to travel. Hawaii is probably a nice place for anyone to spend their recovery days. Is that beach at Waikiki as nice as I have heard? I have heard that the north shore is one of the best places in the world to surf. Not much surfing in Ohio. Well I have taken a lot of your time so I'll say good-bye now. Once again, thank you for your kind words and help. I consider you a good friend.

Many, many thanks,

Robbie

The platoon spent the next day filling sandbags and rebuilding bunkers. The next night they had perimeter guard. They burned shitters the next day. While they were burning shitters, Robbie heard someone yelling for him. It was Sims. "Hey Pitcher, they finally got us some gloves and a ball," said Sims. "After chow this evening you can show me what you got."

Throwing a baseball again really made Robbie feel good. The gloves and the ball weren't the best but they would do. It didn't take long for them to get warmed up. Sims was impressed with Robbie's curve ball and the speed on his fastball. "I bet you coulda been in the Majors," said. "You got about the best curveball I ever did see. I know I couldn't hit it. How fast you reckon that fastball is. I'm guessing close to 90."

"I don't think I can throw 90," said Sims. "I think I'll try a knuckleball. Be ready. I never know where it will go." Robbie threw a knuckleball the next pitch. Sims couldn't catch it. It went past him high. There was an outhouse not too far behind him and the door was open. The ball went in, bounced off the back wall and right into one of the holes. "Shit, let's find something to get it out with," said Robbie. "We can't afford to lose that ball."

"I'll go get a rubber glove from a Corpsman," said Sims. "He should be able to part with a glove." Sims went for a glove and Robbie opened up the back of the outhouse and slid out the shitter. Sims was back in no time with a glove and retrieved the ball. They cleaned up the ball the best they could and continued playing catch.

The next day the platoon went on patrol. Robbie's squad took the lead on the way out. There was no contact all day long and no one tripped any booby traps. They put out an ambush that night and nothing happened. They headed back a different way the next day. Robbie's squad was in the rear. They were about a click from the base when a single shot was fired. The very last man in the column was hit. The men fired up the area all around them but no more shots were fired. The Corpsman did his best but he couldn't save the man who had been hit. Some of the men made a litter out of a poncho and some bamboo and they carried the body to the base.

It wasn't long until they were back in the "Arizona." This time it seemed like there was an endless supply of mines and booby traps. Contact was made on a regular basis and a lot of VC and NVA were killed. Lt. Byers was badly wounded and S/Sgt. Rojas was in charge of the platoon. Two weeks later, Rojas was wounded. The senior squad leader was temporarily put in charge of the platoon till replacements arrived. Sims hoped that replacements would come soon . He was still only a L/Cpl. but he was next in line. Two days later, some replacements were choppered out to them. One was a new Platoon Commander for Robbie's platoon. Another one was a Sergeant and he was their new Platoon Sergeant. His name was Sgt. Coleman. He had just returned to duty. He had been shot in the arm a few weeks ago. The Platoon Commander, Lt. Green, was green. The men hoped Coleman knew his shit. There were other replacements too. They were new guys that had just arrived a few days ago. Robbie knew how they felt. Another good thing happened when the replacements arrived. The mail came with them. Later on when the mail was passed out, Robbie got a letter from Helen Carter. As soon as he got the chance, he sat down and read it. It went as follows.

Dear Robbie,

It was good to hear from you and I am so glad that you are doing well. I love it here in Hawaii. Pearl Harbor is a great place to work. We have such a good staff there. I'm o.k. at the house. The memories are good but at times it seems so empty. As far as your R & R goes, I have an idea. You can come here and stay at my house. I could use the company. I would be working at times so you would have some time to yourself. You will have your own room and I know you would love it here. I'll show you all around the island. You would not be intruding. Get your R & R scheduled and let me know when to expect you.

Your friend,

Helen

Robbie was totally surprised when he read the letter. Visiting Helen had never crossed his mind. He stood some extra hole watch that night because he couldn't sleep. As soon as he got the chance the next day, he went to the Company Commander and asked what he had to do to put in for R & R. The Captain told him that everything would be taken care of when they got back. Robbie immediately wrote a quick letter to Helen telling her he would be there and he would get her the dates as soon as he could. The letter went out on the next resupply bird.

The next two weeks seemed to drag on and on. There was some contact from time to time but nothing major. When they got back to An Hoa, Robbie went straight to HQ and made sure they knew about his R & R. Things moved fast. Robbie would be going to Hawaii in two weeks. Robbie fired off a letter to Helen and hoped she would get it in plenty of time. Robbie went back to his tent. Sims was there. "Let's play some catch," said Robbie.

"Sounds good," said Sims. "I'll go get the stuff." Sims was back shortly and they went out and started throwing. "You got a strange smile on your face Pitcher," said Sims. "What's up?"

"I'm going to Hawaii in two weeks on R & R," said Robbie. "I'll be staying at some nurse's house. I met her when I was at the Evac Hospital. She works at Pearl Harbor now. She lives there too."

"Are you in love again?" asked Sims.

"It's not like that," said Robbie. "We just became good friends. She was there when I got that letter telling me that my girl was dead. Her husband was killed around Dak To last year. We had a good cry together."

"I won't say nothin' else about it," said Sims. "You'll have a good time for sure. I'll be gettin' short when you get back. I'll only have a month left. Hell, I'm already short. Maybe I can get me some job in the rear for a while. Maybe they'll let me burn shitters the whole time till I go. That wouldn't bother me. Not too many booby traps around the shitters."

"Shut up and throw the ball," said Robbie. "You lived this long, you'll make it the rest of the way."

"Yep, I've lived and I got the Purple Hearts to prove it," said Sims. "Hope the women don't mind that big scar on my ass."

"And why would they mind," said Robbie. "It's such a nice ass."

"Shut the fuck up and show me that curve ball," said Sims. As soon as Robbie threw the curve, they heard a plane coming. They got their weapons and ammo and went to the bunkers. As soon as the plane touched down, the rockets started landing. Then came the 82's. The plane unloaded and took off without being hit. Robbie and Sims were playing catch again a few minutes later.

There was a lot of incoming that night. Everyone was expecting a sapper attack but none came. The platoon was on patrol the next day. This was the first time that anyone could remember that a patrol had gone out and come back in without any contact or taking any casualties. This was short lived. The platoon that went out the next day had two men killed and three wounded. Three VC had been killed.

Robbie was in the bush when he was choppered out for his R & R. He was a nervous wreck. He hadn't heard back from Helen. Maybe the plane will crash. Maybe this. Maybe that. "Shut up Parker," he mumbled to himself. "Everything will be all right." The flight to Honolulu seemed to last forever. Everything was all right. The plane landed and Helen was there. She gave him a hug and they went to her car. Her house was on the north side of the island. Robbie couldn't believe how beautiful everything was. Helen's house was on a small hill and there were no other houses very close to it. There was a lot of bushes that Robbie didn't recognize around it kind of like a privacy fence but they didn't block any of the views. "This place is beautiful," said Robbie. "I have never seen anything like this."

"I like it too," said Helen. "Let's go inside and I'll show you the place and your room." The inside of the house was beautiful too. There were all kinds of plants that Robbie didn't recognize. His room was very nice too. He even had his own bathroom. There was a big picture on the wall in the living room. "That was your husband and you?" Robbie asked.

"That's us," said Helen. "That was one of our wedding pictures."

"You were a beautiful bride and he was a very handsome groom," said Robbie.

"Thank you. We were a good looking couple weren't we?" said Helen.

"Yes you were," said Robbie.

"Well why don't you put away your clothes and such and then we can set out and have a beer," said Helen.

"O.K.," said Robbie. "A beer sounds good. I'll be ready in a few minutes."

In a few minutes they were setting in the back yard drinking a cold beer. They talked about anything and everything. Helen fixed them a nice dinner that evening and Robbie helped her in the kitchen. After dinner they took a walk all around the neighborhood. Robbie was amazed at how green everything was. Palm trees were everywhere. They were sitting in the yard again talking till after dark. Around ten o'clock, Helen said she had to go to bed because she had an early shift in the morning. She showed Robbie everything he needed to know and told him goodnight.

Robbie decided he would go to bed too. He went to his room and got undressed and was about to get in the shower when he noticed a bathroom scale. He hadn't weighed himself for a long time. He stepped onto the scale. "Jesus H. Christ," he yelled. Helen heard him and came running to see what was wrong. Robbie was standing there naked still on the scale.

"Sorry, I didn't mean to startle you," said Robbie. "I just found out that I've lost over twenty five pounds since I've been in country." Then he realized he was naked and grabbed a towel and covered himself. Helen let out a good laugh.

"Well if you've lost over twenty five pounds, you're still looking pretty good," said Maria. "Don't worry about it. Once you get back home the weight will come back. Now sweet dreams. See you around 3 to 3:30 tomorrow afternoon."

Robbie took a shower and went to bed. He fell right to sleep. He woke up a few hours later but went right back to sleep. Then he started dreaming. He and Maria were at a cabin in Hocking Hills. They had made love and fallen asleep in each other's arms. While he was sleeping , Robbie sensed that he was being watched. He opened his eyes and saw Maria standing next to the bed watching him. He could see her naked silhouette in the moonlight. He watched her watching him. She did not know that he was awake. He reached up and pulled her down to him. They made love till they were exhausted.

Robbie woke up around seven o'clock. He reached for Maria but she wasn't there. Then he realized that he had been dreaming. He got up and dressed. Helen had left him a note on the kitchen table telling him where everything was and told him again when she would be back. Robbie fixed himself some coffee and breakfast. He spent the day relaxing. He walked around the neighborhood some and talked to a few people. They were very nice. He made himself a sandwich for lunch and then decided he would sit down and write a letter to his parents. He told them he was in Hawaii on R & R but he said he was just staying with a friend who lived there. He actually wrote two letters. One was for his mother and the other for his dad. The one to his mother was a typical letter with no gory details about the bush. In the one to his dad, he broke down and told him a lot of the things that had happened over there. He asked his dad not to say anything to his mother. He had just finished them when Helen got home. He was sitting at the kitchen table.

"How was your day?" she asked when she came through the door. "Did you sleep o.k. last night?"

"I had a good day and I slept really well last night," answered Robbie. "I had the best dream. Maria and I - - - - ." Helen cut him off.

"Robbie, we need to talk. That was not a dream you had last night," said Helen.

"What do you mean that wasn't a dream?" asked Robbie.

"That was me watching you last night," started Helen. "When you reached for me, I went to you."

"How could that be?" asked Robbie. "How could I not know that it was you?"

"When you saw me, you wanted so much for me to be Maria that I was Maria to you," said Helen. "Before you say anything please let me talk for a while. It has been almost two years since Paul and I have been together. I have not been with another man since. I haven't dated or anything. When I saw you naked on the scales yesterday, I started thinking about Paul. I always liked to watch him weigh himself. He was always naked when he did. He wanted his weight to be accurate. He was in very good shape. Your physique and his are almost identical. I lay in bed for hours thinking about his touch. I needed him. I convinced myself that you were him. I watched you for a long time while you slept. I needed Paul. You reached for me and I went to you. I do not regret it."

"Wow, I'm not sure what to think," said Robbie.

"Don't think," said Helen. "Just make love to me."

Helen sat down on his lap and they wrapped themselves together. They made love till they were exhausted. Eventually they made their way to Helen's bedroom. They lay there holding each other. They caressed each other while they were looking into each other's eyes. Soon they were making love again. They fell asleep and didn't wake for hours. When they did wake up it was five in the morning. They picked up where they left off. An hour later, Helen was on top of

Robbie caressing his chest. "You'll be late for work if we keep this up," said Robbie.

"No I won't" said Helen. "I took a few days leave. When my tour was over, I was allowed thirty days leave. I didn't feel the need to take all of them since I live right here on Oahu. I only took twenty days. Today I asked for another week and they approved it. I want to spend my time with you. Is that all right with you?"

"Yes it is," said Robbie as he wrapped his arms around her. "I keep thinking I should feel guilty but I don't. Do you feel guilty at all?"

"I did a little last night but I don't now," said Helen. "Right now I need you and I hope you need me."

"I do need you Helen," said Robbie. "And I'm glad that you need me."

"Well let's get some coffee and have some breakfast," said Maria. "Today I'll take you to the north shore and maybe teach you how to surf."

"So you're one of them surfer girls," said Robbie.

"Yes I am," said Helen. "I'm a native born Hawaiian. Of course I can surf."

After breakfast they went to the north shore. Helen said the waves were good today. They were probably too big for a beginner but Robbie could try if he wanted. Helen had on a skimpy bikini and when she caught her first wave, Robbie had no idea how she kept from losing it. She was right. She could surf and she was good. She caught several waves and then came in for a rest. She explained to Robbie as best she could how to surf. He decided he would try it. He was out there a long time and caught several waves but he never got all the way up. He got tired and paddled in. "You did good," said Helen. "I'd say one or two more times and you'll be getting up no problem."

They had lunch at a small café and then went home. They spent the whole afternoon making love. They stopped and had some dinner in the evening and then sat out in the yard and had a mixed drink. Robbie didn't know what it was but it had pineapple in it and was good. Helen told Robbie that she wanted to have a serious talk with him.

"Robbie, we need each other right now but I want something from you," said Helen.

"What is it that you want?" asked Robbie.

"I don't want you to fall in love with me," said Helen. "It will be very hard but I don't want to fall in love with you either."

"Are you worried that I might get killed?" asked Robbie.

"That's a good part of it," said Helen. "Maybe I am feeling guilty. I'm not sure."

"I think I understand," said Robbie. "Not falling in love with you will be very hard. Whatever happens between us, I will always consider you one of my best friends."

"How old are you Robbie Parker?" asked Helen.

"What's the date?" asked Robbie. "Seems like dates run together for me anymore."

"It's April 20," answered Helen.

"Wow, my birthday was the tenth and I clear forgot it," said Robbie. "I just turned nineteen."

"You seem older than that to me," said Helen. "I know thirty year olds who aren't as mature as you. You know I'm older than you don't you?"

"I know you are and I also know that you are an Officer," said Robbie. "I always heard that enlisted men weren't supposed to fraternize with Officers."

"Is that what we've been doing? We've been fraternizing," said Helen. "I'd like some more fraternization please."

"I wouldn't want to displease a superior Officer," said Robbie.

The rest of Robbie's R & R sped by. Robbie was convinced that someday he might live in Hawaii or at least visit there regularly. At the airport when Robbie was leaving, they kissed and hugged and promised to write each other as often as they could. Robbie sat there on the flight back thinking the whole time that he was one lucky man.

Reality set back in when the chopper landed at An Hoa. There was another operation going on and Robbie would be sent out to "Arizona" on the next re-supply bird. When the bird landed, the first face he saw was Sims. His squad was to unload supplies. "Just how in the hell are you Pitcher?" said Sims. "Did you get any while you were gone?"

"Did you get any while I was gone?" asked Robbie.

"Fuck you Pitcher," said Sims. "If my balls get any bluer they'll bust." Robbie laughed and then went to the Platoon Commander to let him know he was back.

"Good to have you back Parker," said the Lt. "We need more experienced men out here. There's booby traps damn near everywhere we go. Snipers too. Your squad's over there at six o'clock. When we move out shortly, your squad's in the lead." Robbie nodded his head yes and went to his squad.

They moved out a half hour later. Robbie had Bob Sours on point. He had been in country for two months. Robbie was in the middle of his squad. After an hour, Bob motioned for them to stop and motioned for Robbie to come up. Bob was facing Robbie as he came forward and was down on one knee. Robbie was only twenty feet from Bob when the firing started. It came from the front and the left side. Sours was struck in the back and fell forward. Rounds hit all around Robbie but he wasn't hit. Robbie crawled forward to Sours. He was dead. Robbie yelled for his squad to return fire. Robbie saw some movement about fifty yards to the front and he threw a grenade at it. He saw a hat go up in the air. The firing increased all up and down the line. Two more men in Robbie's squad were wounded. They were yelling for the Corpsman but he didn't come. Robbie crawled to the closest man and put a dressing on his shoulder wound. Then he crawled to the second man and put a dressing on his side. Robbie heard a plink and his helmet was knocked off. Robbie was getting really pissed now. He put his helmet back on and started cussing as loud as he could. Probably no one could hear him because of all the firing. He reached into his flak jacket and pulled out two more grenades. He threw them as hard as he could toward the firing. Then he took the grenades from the wounded men and threw them too. "That's enough of that shit you mother fuckers," Robbie yelled over and over. Then he took his M-16 and fired magazine after magazine. When his ammunition was gone, he took the ammunition from the wounded men and fired it too. There was a thump and Robbie looked to his left and there was a grenade a few feet from him. He picked it up and threw it as hard as he could. It went about thirty feet before it exploded.

The 60mm mortar team was firing as fast as they could. The firing slowed some but didn't stop. Robbie was out of grenades and ammo and was starting to crawl down the line when he saw Coleman working his way toward him. He handed Robbie three bandoliers of ammo and six grenades. "Figured you could use this stuff," said Coleman. It was hard to talk and hear.

"Most of the firing from the front has quit or slowed," said Robbie. "I'll take my squad and see if we can get on their left. Don't let nobody shoot us." Coleman gave a nod and started crawling back. Robbie and his squad worked their way forward and then started working to the enemy's left. There was a lone NVA somewhere taking pot shots at them and he was close. Nobody could spot him. Robbie threw three grenades as far as he could toward where he thought the shooter might be. The squad waited a few minutes and then moved again. No more shots were fired at them. They had moved a few yards when an RPG was fired at the column. Robbie spotted where it had come from and started for it. He was crawling when he saw the NVA raise up to fire another RPG. Robbie took aim with his M-16 and fired. The NVA was struck in the head. Another NVA picked up the launcher and was aiming it when Robbie fired again. That NVA went down too. Robbie's squad was about a hundred yards from the enemy position. Other NVA figured that something wasn't right and began firing toward Robbie's squad. They weren't sure where they were but they were hoping to hit anyone who was out there. One NVA got careless and stuck his head up too high. Robbie cut him down. The firing in his squad's direction ceased. Robbie moved his squad forward another fifty yards. He had every man in the squad throw a grenade at the same time. When the grenades exploded, the squad moved another twenty yards and threw another grenade. The squad stayed still with their rifles ready. The firing got slower and slower and then finally ceased. Robbie had his squad stay put while he worked his way back to the column.

The Lt. had been wounded and Coleman was taking charge. "Give me three more men and I'll check out the area," said Robbie. "I got one killed and two wounded."

"Grab whoever you want and get it done," said Coleman. "Watch for traps."

Robbie grabbed three men from the platoon and went back to where his squad was. "All right, we're going through their positions," said Robbie. "Be ready for anything and watch for traps. Don't touch nothing. As they got closer, they could see that there was a series of bunkers. They couldn't be seen till they were almost right on them. Robbie hand signaled back to the column that more men should move up and help them. Another squad moved up. It took a good while but they checked out all the bunkers and destroyed them. There were RPG's and a lot of ammunition in them too.

A perimeter was set up and medivacs were called. As soon as the medivac bird touched down, they started taking mortar fire. The bird took off before any of the wounded were loaded. Robbie could hear the CO screaming on the radio. "You get the fuck back down here and get my men outta here," he kept yelling. The chopper ignored him and left. It wasn't more than fifteen minutes and a couple of gunships showed up. They were on the radio with the CO and asking where the mortar was. They made a couple of passes around the area. Some NVA must have been a new guy because he opened up with a machine gun on the gunships. The chopper pilots saw the tracers and cut loose with rockets and miniguns. The firing stopped. The medivac bird returned shortly.

Besides Robbie's squad and the Lt., three other men in the platoon were wounded. The rest of the company had three killed and six wounded. They found fifteen dead NVA and a lot of blood trails.

After resupply the next day, they moved out again. They had no contact, but they found several booby traps and a huge supply of rice. They blew the traps and destroyed the rice.

They didn't move for the next two days. Robbie couldn't remember not moving unless they were waiting for resupply or medivac. He wondered what was up. The first day they didn't move he went to Coleman and asked if he knew anything. He told Robbie that they were waiting for other units to get in position and then they would be doing a big sweep somewhere. Robbie nodded his head and started back to his squad when Coleman spoke again. "Parker, I'm gonna get with the CO and tell him you should be decorated," said Coleman. "You're a fightin' son of a bitch."

"I never did nothin'," said Robbie. "I didn't do any more than anyone else."

"I saw you. I know what you did," said Coleman. "Look at your damn helmet. All that nothin' you did killed some NVA and saved some men." Robbie just shook his head and went back to his squad. He looked at his helmet. There was a dent in the right side of it and the camouflage cover was ripped where the bullet grazed it.

Coleman went to the CO and told him all that Robbie had done and that he should get a Bronze Star for his bravery. "Parker you say," said the Captain. "He got himself a Bronze Star in his first firefight."

"He's a good man Captain. Now he'll have two Bronze Stars" said Coleman. "I never seen anybody who could throw a grenade like him."

"Well we'll get it written up when we get back in," said the Captain. "He's a L/Cpl. isn't he?"

"Yes he is Sir," said Coleman.

"Well tell him he's a Corporal now," said the Captain. "Good men should be promoted."

"I'll tell him Sir and thank you," said Coleman. Coleman went straight to Robbie and told him the news. "You're a Corporal now Parker," Coleman said.

"What's that pay?" asked Robbie.

"I forget," said Coleman. "Maybe three, four, five dollars a month more."

"Well I won't spend it all in one place," said Robbie. "Maybe with all that money I can hire me a butler to carry all my gear around for me."

"Don't be an asshole Parker," said Coleman. "You're a good Marine. I know it and you know it."

"I guess I'm just feelin' bad about losing my men," said Robbie.

"You can't take things personal," said Coleman. "Men get killed here. If it wasn't for men like you, more of them would get killed. You're the senior squad leader now. Sims is short and he's only a L/pl. If anything would happen to me, you might find yourself Platoon Sergeant till a replacement could be had. I'll do my best to keep that from happening. I told the Captain that you should get another Bronze Star."

"Coleman, I heard once that If an enlisted man got the Medal of Honor, Officers would have to salute him. Is that true?" asked Robbie.

"I heard that once too but I couldn't tell you if it's true or not," said Coleman. "Anybody that I knew that got that medal, got it posthumously."

"Well I'll do my best to make sure that I don't get it either way," said Robbie. Coleman let out a laugh and left.

Robbie left his squad and went to see Sims for a while. "You're pretty damn short," said Robbie. "They'll be sending your orders pretty soon."

"Should be any day now," said Sims. "I need to find me a hole and stay in it."

"I've known you for months and I don't know your first name," said Robbie. "Just what the hell is it?"

"It's Carl," said Sims. "Let's exchange addresses and phone numbers. We won't be that far apart. Maybe we can hook up sometime when you get back."

"Sure, we can take in a Reds game and go get drunk somewhere," said Robbie. "What are you gonna do with yourself when you get home?"

"When I get back to the world I'm gonna sleep for a full week," started Carl. "Then I'm gonna get my gal and have her screw me senseless for a month. Then I might go find a job. I got an uncle who runs a lumber yard. He said he'd give me a job when I got back. Won't pay much but I won't need much. I never have wanted a lot of things."

"Sounds good man. Hope that works out for you," said Robbie.

"I heard a hot rumor that you're a corporal now," said Carl.

"That's no rumor," said Robbie.

"How bout that medal rumor?" said Carl.

"That's no rumor either," said Robbie.

"Damn, you're gonna be just like Chesty Fuckin' Puller," said Carl. "You'll be the fuckin' Commandant before you know it."

"You gotta stay in to be Commandant," said Robbie. "I'm not gonna be a lifer. I'll do my share and get out."

"So what'r you gonna do when you get back to the world?" asked Carl.

"Right now I have no idea," said Robbie.

"You never said nothin' bout your R & R," said Carl. "How was it?"

"Pure heaven," answered Robbie. "That's all I'm saying. I better get back now." Robbie got back to his squad and made sure they had their assignments. Then he sat down and wrote Helen a letter. It would go out on the next bird.

Not a lot happened on the rest of the operation. There were a few small firefights but most of the casualties came from mines and booby traps. Before the operation was over, Robbie lost another man in his squad. Before the operation ended, Sims had gone. Robbie was out on a short patrol when Sims left on a resupply bird.

The first day back at An Hoa, the platoon got the day off. They had perimeter that night but they had the day off. Robbie hunted up someone to play catch with him. It was a guy from Detroit. He was a black man and everyone called him Bad Ass. He said he was in a gang back in Detroit. His real name was Larry Johnson. He had played Legion ball too. He was a shortstop. He and Robbie got along great. Larry had been in country six months. He had one purple heart. In fact, there was probably not one man in the platoon with two or more months in country that didn't have at least one purple heart. Larry loved his Motown music too. Robbie thought there might a few fights once in a while with some boys who liked their country music, but they always ended up laughing at each other. Robbie didn't like country music either so he ignored it as best he could.

The next day the whole platoon was burning shitters. After chow that evening, Robbie, Larry, and a few others from the platoon went to the club. They were laughing and having a few beers. Not far from them was a table with four black Marines setting at it. One of them looked over at Larry. "What you doin' settin' with them white boys Bad Ass?" he said. Robbie stood up.

"If you see a boy over here, you better come over and kick his ass," said Robbie.

"What'd you say white boy?" the black Marine said.

"You fuckin' heard me," said Robbie. "Now come over here and kick my ass."

"Whoa, whoa, whoa," said Larry. "This man is my friend and if you fuck wit him, you fuck wit me. Now git up and let's git it done, or you shut the fuck up and leave us alone."

"Calm down bro'. Calm down," the black Marine said. "We didn't mean nothin'."

"I'm not your fuckin' bro'." said Larry. "You wanna be my bro', you best act like my bro', not some jive ass ghetto nigger. Did your momma raise you to be like this? I don't fuckin' think so. Are we good now?"

"We good," said the black Marine. Nothing else was said. The four black Marines finished the beer they were drinking and left. Robbie and the boys had a couple more beers and they left.

"We'll keep an eye out for them mo'fuckers," said Larry. "They might try and jump us but I doubt it. They know me and what I'm like when I get ta fightin'." Nothing happened that evening.

Robbie's platoon went on patrol the next day. They had another new Platoon Commander. Robbie didn't worry about what his name was. He was a new guy and Coleman would take care of him. They had no contact on the way out. They set up an ambush that night and they killed one VC and wounded another one. They were halfway back when they started taking fire. It was quick and intense and then they were gone. One man was killed and two were wounded but not seriously. They found a blood trail but there were no bodies found.

The next day back at An Hoa, a bunch of replacements arrived. Robbie got three new men for his squad. They seemed so young to him. One of his men was a Chicano from Texas. He was friends with a new man who was in one of the other squads. He was a Chicano too. Robbie took all his new men and got them supplied. The squad had the day off but would be filling sandbags tomorrow. That evening after chow, Robbie and Larry went to the club for a couple of beers. When they got back to the tent, the two Chicanos and two other new guys were smoking pot in the tent. Robbie was furious. "You sons a bitches get that fuckin' shit outta here right fuckin' now," said Robbie. Nobody moved. Robbie went to the closest one who was smoking and picked him up by the front of his shirt and took him to the door of the tent and threw him out. The other three got up now and were heading out the door. The Chicano in Robbie's squad said something in Spanish to Robbie. Robbie remembered the lessons he had gotten from Maria. The Chicano had told him that his father was a pig and his mother was a whore. Robbie went to his cot and reached for something underneath. It was his K-bar. He put the knife right on the Chicano's throat. "You dirty rotten fuck," started Robbie. "You can call me whatever you want but if I ever hear you say anything bad about my mother and father, I will slit your throat from ear to ear. I'll swear that a VC come in through the wire and did it. Do you fuckin' understand me?" The new man wasn't quite sure what to say or do. He was shaking a lot. He nodded his head yes and went outside.

"Damn, you a crazy fucker," said Larry. "I'm glad you on my side."

"Nobody, and I mean nobody slanders my family," said Robbie.

"I fuckin' guess not," said Larry.

During the night, they started taking mortar fire. Robbie rounded up the new men as best he could and got them to the bunkers. Some of the new men were not in the tent. Robbie wasn't going to go look for them. When the incoming stopped he went back to the tent. He waited a good while but the new men still didn't show up. He got a flashlight and went looking for them. It wasn't long till he found them. About a hundred yards from the tent and behind another bunker, he found four bodies. It looked like a mortar round had landed right in the middle of them. Robbie figured they had been smoking pot when the first mortar round hit right in the middle of them. Three of them were dead. The fourth one was still alive but his left arm was missing just below the elbow. He should have bled to death but for some reason he hadn't. Robbie took the man's belt and made a tourniquet. The man who had slandered Robbie's family had both of his legs blown off. Sgt. Coleman saw someone moving around with a flashlight and came out to see what was up. "I bet them fools were smokin' pot when that first round hit," he said when he saw the bodies. "That's them new guys isn't it."

"Yes it is," said Robbie. "What kind of letter do you write to them boy's mommas?"

"You lie," said Coleman. "Well you go get a Corpsman and I'll get these bodies taken care of." Robbie told the wounded man to stay put. The wounded man was alert now and sat down and cried. Robbie gave him a firm look before he left for the Corpsman. "You're gonna have to live without that arm because you just had to have a joint," said Robbie. "You done that yourself. The NVA mighta supplied the round, but you sat there and let them do it. You gotta live with yourself."

Chapter Nine

Before the next operation, the company had a new Commanding Officer. His name was Capt. Dearborn. This was his second tour and Sgt. Coleman had served under him on his first tour when the Capt. was a Platoon Commander. Coleman said that the Capt. knew his shit. He was aggressive, but he wasn't stupid. He knew when to move forward and when not to. The first operation under his command went very well. They had good body counts and casualties weren't high.

The next operation started off badly. The first day out the company had been ambushed and casualties were high. Sgt. Coleman and the Platoon Commander were killed. Robbie was the senior squad leader so he was the acting Platoon Sergeant. The Company received mortar fire during the night. The forward observer called in mission after mission on suspected enemy positions but as soon as the missions stopped, the mortars started again. They were being cut to pieces. Right before daylight, the mortar fire ceased. Medivac birds came in and took out the wounded and surprisingly they didn't take fire.

For a full week after that, the company had no contact. A few booby traps were found. They were dug in for the night and had ambushes out. About two hours before daylight, a few shots could be heard. Gradually the firing increased till it was deafening. The NVA were trying to overrun them. They attacked one side of the perimeter and then another. They were trying to find a weak point. Robbie moved all along the perimeter giving his platoon encouragement and telling them to keep down and make sure of their targets. They killed a lot of them but more kept coming. "How can they do that?" Robbie asked himself. Some NVA had made it through the perimeter and were probably looking for the CP.

Robbie heard AK's cracking inside the perimeter. He told his squad leaders to stand firm and he took off looking for the NVA who had penetrated. An AK cracked and he went that direction. He had moved a few yards when he heard some of the NVA talking to each other. They were close. He laid on the ground and waited. He rolled onto his back and had his rifle ready. There wasn't much moon but as he looked toward the sky he could see shapes of men coming toward him. There were four of them. The first one almost stepped on Robbie. He never saw Robbie as he opened up and killed all four of them. Robbie moved to the CP and told the Capt. that NVA were in the perimeter. Robbie heard more AK fire inside the perimeter and went looking. This time they found him first but for some reason they missed when they fired at him. There were three of them. Robbie flipped his 16 on full auto and cut loose. He made sure they were dead and worked his way back to his platoon. The men were still holding firm, but some were wounded. Robbie swore he heard a bugle and the next thing he knew, a bunch of NVA were charging his platoon. They couldn't kill them fast enough. Some of the fighting was hand to hand. Robbie emptied a magazine but before he could load another one an NVA was almost on him. He took his rifle like a club and slammed into the NVA's head. The NVA went down but wasn't dead. Robbie grabbed the soldier's AK and smashed the stock of it into his head. More NVA came. Robbie fired the AK till it was empty and then used it as a club. The NVA started pulling back. Robbie picked up his rifle but the stock was broken. He got a rifle and some more ammo from a man who was too badly wounded to fight. Daylight was starting to break now. There was no firing anywhere on the perimeter now except in front of Robbie's platoon. Robbie got with his squad leaders. "It seems like the gooks think this is a weak spot in the line. We're gonna change their minds. When I give the word, we'll all open up on anything in front of us that could have a gook behind it," said Robbie. "Then we'll move forward in an arc firing as we go. Every man needs to keep track of the men beside him so no one gets too far ahead and accidentally gets shot. I'll be in the center. I'll send one man to the CP to tell the Capt. what we're doing. That way he can have men plug up the holes on our ends as we move. Now get back to your men and when you hear me yell, open up."

Robbie waited till the squad leaders were back to their squads and then let out a yell. They opened up all at the same time. When they did, a few NVA got up and ran. The platoon got up and moved forward in an arc firing as they went. More NVA took off running. Several of them were cut down. Robbie didn't want to over extend the platoon so he stopped after less than a hundred yards. He had everyone get down and get the best cover they could find and fire at anything that could hide the enemy. He sent a man back to tell the mortar team to start dropping rounds in front of his platoon. He also had the man find the forward observer and have him start firing up the area about two hundred yards in front of his platoon. The mortar team was firing in no time. They fired every round they had. Right after the last mortar round was fired, the arty started coming in. The FO fired up the whole area on Robbie's side of the perimeter. A few secondaries were heard. They stopped the arty after the area was worked over pretty good. There was an air strike coming now. There were two planes. They came in low from Robbie's rear. When they dropped their loads, Robbie was sure they would hit the Marines but they didn't. The napalm was a good sight for the Marines. It got real quiet after the planes made their last pass.

Robbie moved his platoon back to their original position. The Corpsman looked after the wounded and Robbie went to the CP. The CO had been wounded in the right shoulder but he was still giving the orders. "Parker, I'm not quite sure what you did over there but I think it saved a lot of Marines," said the Capt. "How come you're not a Sergeant or an Officer? You're a fightin' son of a bitch. What woulda happened if they would have hit us on the other side or another place while you were advancing over there?"

"Captain, it seemed to me that the largest concentration of NVA was in front of my platoon," answered Robbie. "I took a chance."

"Well some of my Officers want me to fire your ass up for making that move on your own," said the Capt. "I told'em they were supposed to be officers and gentleman and they should admit that you did good and maybe saved our asses. They're young yet. If they live, they'll learn. Parker, you're a Sergeant now. Keep up the good work."

"Just tryin' to stay alive Sir," said Robbie. "What are the orders now?"

"Medivacs are coming and resupply," the Capt. said. "After we get resupplied, we'll sweep the area and see what we can find." Robbie went back to the platoon to tell the men what they were going to do. When the medivac birds came, he went over to help with the wounded. He was helping load a wounded man when a single shot was heard. Robbie was knocked backwards. He looked down and blood was coming from his stomach area. He turned over and got on his knees and tried to stand. When he did, another bullet slammed into his back. Blood was coming out of his mouth now. Men on the perimeter couldn't spot the sniper but they were firing everywhere hoping they would get lucky and hit him. As Robbie was laying there, another bullet slammed into his left thigh. A

Corpsman and another man picked up Robbie and put him on the chopper. The sniper fired no more shots. The Corpsman worked on Robbie as best he could. The bullet that had struck him in the back had hit a lung and passed through. The Corpsman tried his best to plug the wounds.

When they got to the Evac Hospital, the doctors and nurses were ready for them. A doctor took one look at Robbie and said that he probably couldn't be saved. They had to work on the men they knew for sure that they could save. They left Robbie laying there on a cot. In a few minutes, a Chaplain was there. "I see by your dog tags that you are a Catholic," he said. "I am here to give you your last rights if you want."

"Padre, I'm not gonna die," said Robbie. "With all due respect, get the fuck away from me."

"As you wish my son," said the Chaplain.

Captain Dearborn was there waiting to be taken to surgery. He had heard what the doctor had said about Robbie and then the Chaplain. He started yelling at the top of his lungs. "Nurse, nurse, get me a fuckin' nurse right fuckin' now," he yelled. Finally a nurse came.

"What is it Captain?" she asked.

"You see that man over there that your fuckin' doctor said was gonna die?" asked the Capt.

"Yes I see him," said the nurse.

"Well you go tell that fuckin' doctor if that man dies without him or another doctor tryin' to save him, when I get outta here, I'm gonna rip off his fuckin' arms and beat him to death with them," said Dearborn. "Now do as I fucklin' say and I mean right fuckin' now." It wasn't a full minute and Robbie was taken to surgery.

Robbie was in surgery for a very long time. The bullet that had struck him in the back had gone through his left shoulder blade and his left lung. It passed through and tore up two ribs on the way out. Another bullet went through his stomach and out his back just missing his spine. The other bullet shattered the femur bone in his left thigh. By all rights, Robbie should have been dead. Robbie didn't regain consciousness until the next day. He opened his eyes and a nurse was looking at him. She called for the doctor. The doctor looked at Robbie's chart. "You're a very lucky Marine," said the doctor. "I guess maybe it was divine intervention. Anyway, there'll be no more combat for you. Your healing process will take a long time. Soon as you're well enough to be moved, you'll be going to a stateside hospital." The doctor gave Robbie a smile and left. Robbie went to sleep.

When he woke up the next morning, Capt. Dearborn was beside his bed. "They tell me you're gonna live Parker," he said. "I'm glad. You're one hell of a Marine. I'm putting you in for a decoration. You'll get it too or I'll be kicking someone's ass. Robbie didn't say anything. He just reached up with his right arm and shook Dearborn's hand. He tried to talk some but it hurt. Just breathing hurt. Dearborn talked a little more then went back to his bed. After a while, they gave Robbie some morphine. There were a lot of very seriously wounded men in Robbie's ward. Robbie was thankful that he had all of his body parts. As they days went on, his pain wasn't as bad. He woke up one morning a week later and Bad Ass was standing there beside his bed. Robbie looked at him and smiled. "How in the hell did you get here?" asked Robbie.

"I had me a bad toothache and they sent me here to see a dentist," said Larry. "Got it pulled out and I'll be goin' back next bird. Thought I'd stop in and see how my white boy's doin'."

"Well your white boy is getting better," said Robbie. "Soon as I get well enough to travel, they'll send me to a stateside hospital."

"Maybe they'll send you ta Pearl Harbor," said Larry. "I hear that's a nice place ta heal up."

"Yes it is and I know someone who works there," said Robbie.

"I bet that person's a nurse," said Larry.

"She surely is," said Robbie.

"Well Pitcher, I best git goin' or I'll miss my bird," said Larry. You heal up good now."

"Gimme your address and phone number," said Robbie. "Maybe we can look each other up sometime."

"Sure thing," said Larry. "I'm half way now. I'll make it the rest of the way." The men exchanged addresses and phone numbers and Larry was on his way.

~~~~

A week and a half later Robbie was at the Naval Hospital in Pearl Harbor. Helen somehow found out he was being sent there and was there to meet him. She had made sure that Robbie would be in her ward and under her care. When Robbie first saw her he wanted so much to run to her and hug and kiss her but that wasn't possible. It would still be a good while before they let him try to walk on his leg. Helen was with him every time she got the chance. Every day when her shift was over she visited with Robbie for hours before she went home.

Two weeks later Robbie was laying in his bed when three Marines in dress blues showed up. There was a full bird Colonel, a Major, and a Sergeant Major. Some Naval Officers were there too. Helen came over to see what was going on. "Gentleman, this is my patient," said Helen. "Is there something we can do for you?"

"You are Sergeant Robert Parker aren't you?" asked the Colonel.

"Yes Sir I am," answered Robbie.

"Sergeant Parker, for your bravery and leadership while in combat you have been awarded the "Silver Star," said the Colonel. "I take great pleasure in reading the citation." It was a long citation. When the Colonel was finished, Robbie looked up at him.

"Did I do all that stuff?" asked Robbie.

"Yes you did Sergeant" answered the Colonel. "Captain Dearborn was your Commanding Officer and he wrote the citation. He also said that if it wasn't approved, he would raise hell all the way to the Commandant of the Marine Corps. Congratulations Sergeant." All of the Marines and Naval Officers shook Robbie's hand and left. When they were gone, several other patients in the ward came over and shook Robbie's hand.

"How did that make you feel?" Helen asked Robbie after the other patients were done shaking his hand.

"I don't feel any different," said Robbie. "I was just trying to keep me and my men alive. I don't feel the need for medals. Seems like every time I did something, someone wanted to give me a medal."

"You mean you have other medals?" asked Helen.

"Yes, I have two bronze stars," said Robbie. "Of course I have my purple hearts, three of them, maybe more. I don't know how they figure them. I got shot three times last time. Is that three or just one big one. Don't matter. Then there's all that other stuff."

"Well we're going to have to get you stronger so you can stand up straight when you wear all of them," said Helen. Robbie let out a good laugh.

Three weeks later, they let Robbie walk a little. He used a walker. It hurt a good bit but Robbie thought it was good to move around on his own. The day after he first walked , he got a big surprise. As he was walking with Helen, he looked down a hall and his mom and dad were walking toward him. Mary let out a yell and ran to Robbie. She hugged him and kissed his cheeks and they both started crying. Even his dad started crying. No words were said right away. They all just looked at each other and smiled. After a few minutes of silence, Robbie introduced Helen. "Mom, Dad, this is Helen Carter," said Robbie. "We are very good friends."

"We are very pleased to meet you Helen," said Mary. "Looks like you've taken good care of my son." Mary gave Helen a big hug and kissed her on the cheek. Robert gave her a good hug and kissed her cheek also.

"I'll take you to a place where you can sit down and visit," said Helen. "Robbie has been on that leg long enough today and needs to get off his feet.." Helen took them outside to a nice place with soft chairs and plenty of shade. "I'll be back after a while to get Robbie," said Helen. "He has some therapy that will last an hour or so and then you can have him back." Helen then left.

"I sure didn't expect to see you two here," said Robbie. "I am so glad to see you. I think I might cry again." They all had a short cry.

"Well your mother always said she wanted to see Hawaii," said Robert. "We never wanted to be here under these conditions though. They notified us that you were sent here and here we are. So how are you doing son?"

"I'm getting better all the time," said Robbie. "Did they tell you about my wounds?"

"No they didn't. They just said you were seriously wounded," said Mary.

"Well I'll tell you," started Robbie. "One bullet went through my shoulder blade. Then it went through my lung and then two ribs. Another bullet went through my stomach and out my back. The other one shattered the bone in my thigh."

"Where did you get wounded the last time?" asked Mary.

"I got shot through both legs," said Robbie. "The bones weren't touched. I also got wounded another time that you never knew about. It wasn't much more than a scratch. I was only in country a few days and in my first firefight. My rifle got hit and a piece of the plastic forearm got stuck in my face. That's what that little scar is. That same day a bullet grazed my left shoulder."

"Well you're alive and you'll be healed before you know it," said Mary.

"I would say that as soon as I'm good enough to travel home, they'll give me a Medical Discharge," said Robbie. "I'll probably have a limp the rest of my life and I've lost some of my lung capacity."

"You know that John Wayne lost a lung to cancer and he did fine," said Robert. "If I know you, you'll get yourself strong and that limp'll be gone in no time."

They talked a while longer and then Helen came to get Robbie for therapy. "I'll bring Robbie right back here," said Helen. "Is there anything I can do for you before we go?"

"We'll just stay right here," said Mary. "I think we kind of have some jet lag."

"We'll be back in an hour or so," said Helen as they were leaving.

"So what do you think? How does our boy look?" Robert asked Mary.

"He's lost a lot of weight but I think he looks good for all that's happened to him," said Mary.

"He's got good genes," said Robert as he leaned over and kissed Mary. They sat there and talked the whole time till Robbie came back.

"How long are you two intending to stay in Hawaii?" Helen asked Mary and Robert.

"We'll only be here a couple of days," answered Mary.

"Do you have a place to stay yet?" asked Helen.

"We got a rental car at the airport and came straight here," said Mary. "We were going to get a hotel later."

"Well forget the hotel. You can stay at my house," said Helen.

"We couldn't do that," said Robert. "It wouldn't feel right."

"Nonsense," said Helen. "It's settled. After my shift is over, we'll visit with Robbie some and then you can follow me to my house. You'll like it there."

That evening, they all bid Robbie goodbye and headed to Helen's house. Robert and Mary were amazed at how beautiful everything was. When they got there, Helen gave them a tour of the house and showed them to their room. Then they all went outside for a beer.

"How did you meet Robbie?" Mary asked Helen after a short while.

"I was a nurse at the Evac Hospital when Robby was wounded last time," said Helen. "I was on duty when he got the letter about Maria. I asked him what was wrong as he was crying and he handed me the letter you had written. I read it and started crying too. You see, I was crying for my husband again. He was killed in Nov. 67 over there. We had a good cry together. We talked a lot and became good friends while he was a patient. When he left I gave him my address and told him to write me. He did. He spent his R & R with me. It was a wonderful time. I asked him not to fall in love with me and I said I didn't want to fall in love with him but that's been very hard not to do."

"Well I'm glad you found each other," said Mary.

"I'm glad too," said Helen. "Did you know that your son is a hero?"

"What do you mean?" asked Robert.

"Well the other day some Marine Officers and a Sergeant Major and some Naval Officers came to the hospital and presented Robbie the "Silver Star," said Helen. "I found out from him later that he already had two bronze stars."

"I knew he'd be a good Marine," said Robert. "What do you think of that Mary. Our boy done good."

"I knew he would," said Mary. "He's got good genes. How about we take you out to dinner tonight Helen? It would only be right since you're letting us stay here."

"We can do that," said Helen. "I'll give you a tour of the island so you can do some things on your own when you're not visiting Robbie."

"That would be wonderful," said Mary. They had a great time that evening.

Back at the hospital, Robbie started thinking hard about what he would like to do after he was discharged. He kept thinking that he should do something that everybody always needed and the demand would never stop. But what would that be? Just what would that be? That night he had several nightmares. In the dreams he was filling body bags. There seemed to be an endless supply of body bags and bodies to put in them. He dreamed these dreams until he woke up in the morning. Helen was right there when he woke up. "Good morning Marine," she said. "No more breakfast in bed for you. From now on you have to walk to your meals."

"Sounds good," said Robbie. "Let me go to the head and then I'll go eat." Robbie did his necessaries and then Helen walked with him to the mess hall. "How were my parents last night?" asked Robbie.

"You have some really good parents," said Helen. "You are a lucky person. I just love your mother. She is so nice and sweet. And I can see why she loves your father. They are good people. I know they made love last night too. I heard them."

"They're active," said Robbie.

Robbie ate his breakfast and then had some therapy. He was feeling stronger every day. He was glad he wasn't left handed. If he was, it would probably be a very long time before he could ever throw a baseball. He had a good visit with his parents that day. Their flight back was early the next morning so they said their goodbyes that evening. Robbie told them he would be home when he was discharged.

Robbie continued to heal well and a week later he graduated to a cane. He said it made him look distinguished. Almost every night he was having nightmares about the dead and filling body bags. He didn't think that the dreams upset him. After all, he had helped fill a lot of body bags. He decided he would tell Helen about the dreams and see what she said. "I'm not the person you should be talking to about this," said Helen. "If you'd like we can get you an appointment with a psychiatrist."

"You mean a shrink don't you?" asked Robbie.

"Call them whatever you want," said Helen. "I guess I call them shrinks too at times. Anyway, it wouldn't hurt anything if you talked to one. They are here to help us."

"Sure, why not? Let's get me an appointment," said Robbie. "Some people think dreams mean something. Maybe the shrink can help me figure things out."

"I'll get on it right now," said Helen. "In the meantime, you get to your therapy. I'll see you after a bit."

Robbie went to therapy and Helen went to her supervisor so arrangements could be made for Robbie to see the psychiatrist. Robbie's appointment was in three days. Every night before his appointment he had the same dreams. He felt relieved when the day of his appointment finally arrived, but he was very nervous when he first was with the doctor. Robbie walked into his office and looked around. There was no couch. "I thought I was supposed to be laying on a couch when we did this," said Robbie as he walked in.

"You've seen too much TV," said the doctor as he let out a little laugh. Then he extended his hand and he and Robbie shook. "I am Doctor Phil Dawson. I have all these degrees you see on my wall plus I have spent some time on the ground in Vietnam. Of course I wasn't out with the grunts but I have spent a lot of time in bunkers because of incoming and I have seen my share of the dead and wounded. I think you and I will understand each other. Do you feel more comfortable now?"

"I do Doc. You don't mind if I call you Doc do you?" asked Robbie.

"That's fine," said Phil. "That's a lot better than some things I have been called. Now what do you think brings you here?"

"Well I have been having these dreams where I am filling body bags," said Robbie. "There is always an endless supply of bags and bodies to put in them. I have these dreams every night."

"When did these dreams start?" asked Phil.

"Maybe two weeks ago I think," said Robbie.

"And you never had any dreams about anything like this before then?" asked Phil.

"No, not really. I had dreams about things that have happened over there but nothing like this," answered Robbie.

"So what have you been thinking about in the last few weeks here?" asked Phil

"I have been thinking about what I should do after I get discharged," said Robbie. "I figure I will be getting a Medical Discharge as soon as I'm good enough to travel."

"So what have your thoughts been about what you will do?" asked Phil.

"I have been thinking that I should do something that there will always be a demand for," said Robbie. "It's got to be something that everyone will need sooner or later. For the life of me I have no idea what that could be."

"You were thinking about your future career and then you started having these dreams about bodies and body bags," said Phil. "Think for a minute. What does everybody do sooner or later?"

"They die," answered Robbie.

"That's right," said Phil.. "Everybody dies. There are no exceptions. Then what happens?"

"Most of the time there is a funeral and they get buried," answered Robbie. "Oh shit! I couldn't do that. I couldn't be a mortician. No way!"

"You have done your share of filling body bags, right?" asked Phil.

"Yes I have," answered Robbie. "More than I want to count."

"Well maybe, just maybe you are feeling that better care should be given to the dead," said Phil. "Maybe the bodies should be treated with more respect than being thrown in a bag and left to lay until the next bird comes in and takes them somewhere else where they wait some more."

"I guess I didn't feel right just putting a friend or a fellow Marine in a bag," said Robbie. "So Doc, why did you think of morticians?"

"There are other things that people must do no matter what," said Phil. "They must eat. They must sleep. They must do their bodily functions. So if you want to feed people, do you own a grocery store? Do you raise the food? What food would you grow that everyone must have? What type of beds would you make that everyone must have? What types of toilet would be the ones everyone would need? After needing and using all these other things, they will die. As I said before, there are no exceptions."

"So Doc, are you saying that I should be a mortician?" asked Robbie.

"No Robbie, I am not saying that at all," said Phil. "All I am saying is that everyone will die sooner or later and there are no exceptions. Did you worry about dying when you were in country?"

"Maybe when I first got there," said Robbie. "But I can't remember worrying about it later. I did worry about others getting killed and I was always thinking about what I could do to prevent it."

"Well you're a leader. You take charge," said Phil. "That has been shown by your record. What did you do before you joined the Marines? Did you play sports?"

"I loved baseball," answered Robbie. "I started in Little League and played up through American Legion Ball."

"You were a pitcher weren't you?" asked Phil.

"Yes I was," answered Robbie. "But I played the infield when I wasn't pitching."

"You must have been a hitter too if you played other positions when you weren't pitching," said Phil.

"I always had a good average," said Robbie.

"Did you have a good relationship with your parents?" asked Phil

"My parents are the best," answered Robbie. "They came here and visited me not long ago. It was good to see them."

"Was your father a Marine?" asked Phil.

"Yes he was," answered Robbie. "He and my mother were high school sweethearts when he joined the Corps. They got married when he got back home."

"So did you have good relationships with women before you joined the Marines?" asked Phil.

"Are you sure you want to hear this stuff?" asked Robbie.

"Well I think I need to know as much about you as possible," said Phil. "But if you don't want to talk about your love life that's o.k."

"I don't mind," said Robbie. "I just don't want to sound like I'm bragging."

"Go ahead and brag," said Phil. "We have time."

"Well I didn't start dating until my senior year," started Robbie. "I went out with this girl that I thought was a real nice girl. She was good looking too. Anyway, I got some advice from my dad before the date. I told him that I didn't have any experience and I wasn't sure about things. He told me to explain to the girl that I hadn't been around and I would like it if she helped me out. Well that's what I did and she surely did help me out. We were at the drive in and she had her way with me three times. She told one of her friends about it and the next day at school, the whole school knew about it. Well I must have done something right because after that, the girls were all over me. I never went out with the first girl again. Later on I met Maria. Her car had broken down if front of our house and I got it running for her. We started dating and we were in love. We were going to get married when I got out of the Corps." Robbie stopped and let out a tear.

"What happened with Maria?" asked Phil.

"She was killed during an armed robbery at a convenience store," answered Robbie. "It was hard to take, but I did it. I have someone else now. We are very good friends but we haven't discussed any further plans. Hey, I forgot to tell you that my parents taught me how to dance. They said that women loved a good dancer. They were right. When Maria and I went to the Prom, all eyes were on us. Everyone wanted us to teach them how to dance like that. It'll be a while before I can dance like that again."

"I have a feeling that you'll be dancing again in no time," said Phil. "I know I will," said Robbie. "I'll get myself strong and it'll be like I never had a limp." Robbie hesitated for a moment. "Can I go now? I'd like to be by myself for a while and think."

"That's fine," said Phil. "Would you like to come back in a week or so?"

"I would," said Robbie.

"Just stop at the receptionist's desk and she will set up your appointment," said Phil. "If something would happen and you felt the need to see me sooner, I will make myself available."

"Thank you Doc," said Robbie. "I'll see you in a week." Robbie got the appointment made and went back to his ward. He had therapy in an hour. Helen was making her rounds and came over to Robbie.

"So how did it go?" she asked.

"It wasn't anything like I expected," said Robbie. "We can talk about it when your shift is over today."

That evening they went outside and talked about Robbie's visit with the psychiatrist. "So you weren't there very long Robbie," said Helen. "What did you talk about?"

"He wanted to know why I was there and I told him it because of the dreams I have been having," started Robbie. "Then he asked me when they started and I told him it was about the same time I started wondering what I should do after I get discharged. I told him I have been thinking that it should be something that people will always need and there will always be a demand for."

"So what did he say?" asked Helen.

"He asked me what everybody does sooner or later," said Robbie.

"Well that's easy," said Helen. "They die."

"That's right. Everybody dies," said Robbie. "There are no exceptions. They must eat, sleep, and have bodily functions. Then they must die."

"Did he tell you that you should be a mortician?" asked Helen.

"No he didn't," answered Robbie. "He was just telling me that people will always die and the bodies must be taken care of. That is always certain."

"So could you be a mortician?" asked Helen.

"I have no idea," answered Robbie. "I guess I did feel bad about the way we had to handle the dead bodies. The bags seemed so impersonal and disrespectful. Maybe I do want to take better care of the dead. Some young man's momma has got a right to see her son how he once was."

"Well I'm sure that whatever you do you will do it well," said Helen. "I'm going to leave now. I'll be seeing my parents this evening. I haven't told them about you yet. I think I will this evening. "I'll see you tomorrow." Helen gave Robbie a kiss and left.

That night Robbie dreamt about his first firefight and putting the tourniquet on S/Sgt. Benjamin's leg. Then he dreamt about the four new men who had been smoking pot when the mortar round landed in the middle of them. But he did not dream about bodies and body bags. In fact, he never had one dream about bodies and body bags in the days leading up to his next appointment with the psychiatrist.

On the day of his appointment he went into Phil's office and shook his hand and sat down. He had a smile on his face. "Why are you smiling Mr. Parker?" asked Phil.

"I'm not sure," answered Robbie. "I feel good right now. I haven't had one dream about bodies and body bags since our last appointment."

"So what kind of dreams have you had?" asked Phil.

"They've been about things that happened over there but there were no bodies and bags," answered Robbie.

"Will you be sad when you get your discharge?" asked Phil. "Do you think you'll feel guilty about not serving out your full time?"

"No, I don't believe so," said Robbie. "I've done my share and maybe a little more."

"I've seen your record," said Phil. "It's most impressive. How do you feel about all those decorations?"

"I don't think about them," answered Robbie. "I was just trying to stay alive and keep my men alive. That's all. I wasn't looking for any glory or fame."

"How do you think you'll feel when you go home and there are anti-war protests everywhere?" asked Phil.

"I couldn't say right now," said Robbie. "I remember getting some nasty looks when I was in uniform and got home on my leave before I went overseas. I hear it's a lot worse now."

"It is worse," said Phil. "I've heard about soldiers and Marines and Sailors getting spit on and being called baby killers and things like that. Could you handle that?"

"I've been called about every name that you could think of but I will not tolerate being spit on," said Robbie. "I would probably find myself in jail if I would get my hands on someone who spit on me."

"What if it was a woman?" asked Phil.

"I don't know," answered Robbie. "I just don't know."

"Well let's just hope that none of this happens for you," said Phil. "Will you be glad to go home?"

"I will," said Robbie. "I miss Ohio."

"Well Robbie Parker, you seem like you have your head on straight," said Phil "I think you will be fine when you go home. I don't believe we need to see each other again. And as I said before, if you need me, I'll make myself available to you." They shook hands and Robbie left.

~~~~

Three weeks later Robbie was told that he would be getting a Medical Discharge. He would have orders to California and then be discharged there. When he told Helen the news, she asked him if there was any way that they could discharge him in Hawaii. She wanted him to herself for a few days before he went home.

It took some doing but Robbie got discharged in Hawaii. Everything was done right there at Pearl Harbor. He was given all his back pay and travel pay. The only thing he didn't have was his uniforms. His stored gear had never caught up with him. It would be shipped to his home when it was located.

Robbie spent five days with Helen before he went home. Helen still had three days leave left for the year. She worked the first two days then took her three. Robbie met her parents on the second day. Robbie thought they were very nice and polite. Helen's mother was full blooded Hawaiian and she was beautiful.

They made love every time they had a chance. Helen assured Robbie that she would take it easy on him. On the third day Helen was acting like her back was hurting her. "What is it?" asked Robbie. "Did you wrench your back or something?"

"I think I did," said Helen. "Maybe I have been a little too energetic. I'll take it easy and slow from now on."

"I can handle easy and slow," said Robbie.

Helen took Robbie to the airport on the day he was to leave. They both got a little teary eyed. "You know that I love you don't you Helen?" said Robbie.

"I know that you do," said Helen. "I have tried not to love you but it's no use. I love you Robbie. "Let's be together as soon as we can." They kissed passionately and then Robbie boarded his plane.

Chapter Ten

Robbie's parents picked him up at the airport in Columbus. There were a lot of hugs and kisses and handshakes. They were surprised that Robbie was not in uniform. "My stored gear never caught up to me," said Robbie when his father asked him why he wasn't in uniform. "It'll be sent to the house when someone figures out where it is. Let's go home."

"You're moving along pretty good with that cane," said Robert. "If you want, we can get you a nice fancy one. Make you look more distinguished."

"I'm not figuring on using this cane for very long," said Robbie. "I'll work at getting myself stronger every day. I expect to be dancing like I used to in less than a year."

"That's a good attitude Son," said Robert. "I'd say you'll get it done."

"We'll be having spaghetti for dinner this evening," said Mary. "I thought it would be appropriate for your first meal back. I know how you and your father love my sauce."

"That's great Mom," said Robbie. "I don't think I've had spaghetti anywhere since I left home. I do love your sauce. I love both of you too, very much." Mary broke out in tears now. "What is it Mom?" asked Robbie. "Did I say something wrong?"

"No son, it's just that I am so glad you are alive and home and in one piece," said Mary.

"I'm glad too Mom." said Robbie as he hugged Mary again. No one spoke as they drove home. Robbie's Oldsmobile was sitting in the driveway. Robbie got out of the car and walked around his car. "She looks good dad," said Robbie. "You kept her cleaned up for me."

"The gas tank's full too," said Robert. "And I changed the oil a few days ago. You're good to go."

"I reckon I'll drive around in a day or two and see what's changed since I left," said Robbie.

"Well there sure are a lot of changes," said Robert. "There's new malls all over the place. They keep building new highways and outerbelts. I've been lost a few times myself. Why don't we have a beer while we're waiting on dinner. I've been drinking Strohs mostly ever since Brad brought over that six pack that day."

"Have you seen Brad's parents at all since he was killed?" asked Robbie.

"I ran into his mother at the grocery store a while back and tried to talk to her," said Mary. "She seemed very bitter so I left her alone."

"Maybe I'll go talk to them sometime," said Robbie. "Maybe I can ease their minds. Maybe I'll make them even more bitter. I hope I can help." They drank their beer and dinner was ready. Robbie wolfed down his spaghetti and asked for more. They all watched a little TV and then Robbie went to bed early. He slept really well his first night back home.

When he woke up the next morning, he was overcome by the smell of his mother's coffee brewing. He got himself dressed and went to the kitchen. Robert was at the kitchen table anxiously waiting for his first cup. "You got a whiff of that coffee didn't you?" said Robert.

"Yes I did," said Robbie. "It sure smelled good."

"Well it's ready now," said Mary. She filled a cup for each of them and sat down. "What would my men like for breakfast this morning?" asked Mary.

"How about some pancakes and sausage," said Robbie. "I haven't had a pancake since I can't remember when."

"That 's o.k. by me," said Robert.

"Coming right up," said Mary. Mary worked on breakfast and Robbie and his dad sipped their coffee and talked.

"What are you going to do on your first full day back?" asked Robert.

"After breakfast I thought I'd just take a nice walk around the neighborhood and maybe the park," said Robbie. "Then this afternoon I thought maybe we could go over to the Legion for a bit if you're off today dad."

"I took a few days off since my boy was coming home," said Robert. "We'll go the Legion whenever you say."

Robbie finished his breakfast, thanked his mother for the fine meal, grabbed his cane and took off on his walk. After a couple of blocks, he decided that most everything still looked the same. There were several different cars in driveways.

There were some new fences and some of the houses had changed color. Several of the people he saw knew him and waved to him as he walked by. At one house a Jack Russell Terrier came charging out at him and tried to nip him on the heels. Robbie yelled at the dog to back off but it wouldn't. The dog had ahold of his pants leg and wouldn't let go. Robbie finally took his cane and smacked the dog in the head. About the time he was smacking the dog, the owner of the dog came out the front door of her house to see what was going on. "Why did you smack my dog?" asked the older woman. The dog ran to the woman and she picked it up.

"Your dog tried to bite me ma'am," said Robbie. "I was just walking down the sidewalk and your dog came after me. I defended myself."

"Well we'll see about that," said the woman. "I'll be calling the law on you. Shame on you for hitting my little dog."

"My name is Robbie Parker," started Robbie. "I live just down the street. When you call the law I'll be glad to talk with them. You owe me a pair of pants." Robbie showed the woman where the dog had gotten ahold of his pants leg and ripped them. "These pants cost me $10," said Robbie. "And another thing, I'll be walking this way on a regular basis. Have your dog under control or I'll have the Humane Society haul it away. Now good day to you." The woman mumbled something to herself and ran into her house. Robbie continued his walk.

Robbie walked for several hours. He was getting tired and decided to head back home. When he turned the corner and got on his street, he could see a police cruiser setting in his driveway. "So that old bitch did call the law," Robbie said to himself. "Well this'll be interesting." When Robbie entered his house, he recognized the policeman right away. It was a boy he had gone to school with. His name was Jerry Tomlinson. He had been talking to Robbie parents. Robbie went to him and shook his hand. "I see you made it back," said Jerry. "It's good to see you again."

"So why are you here?" asked Robbie. "I know you didn't just come here to welcome me back home."

"A Mrs. Wilson down the street called in and claims you beat her dog," said Jerry. "Tell me what happened."

"I was taking a walk this morning," started Robbie. "When I got down to that woman's house, her dog came after me. I yelled at it to back off but it wouldn't. The dog got ahold of my pants leg and wouldn't let go. I smacked it in the head with my cane. She came out the door just as I was smacking it." Robbie showed Jerry his torn pants. "That woman owes me $10 for these pants," said Robbie.

"You were on the sidewalk, right?" asked Jerry.

"Of course I was on the sidewalk," said Robbie. "That's where you're supposed to walk."

"I'll go have a talk with her," said Jerry.

"Maybe you should talk with some of her neighbors and see if anyone else has a complaint about that dog," said Robbie.

"I was going to do that anyway," said Jerry. "I'll probably be back over here shortly."

"I'll be here," said Robbie. Jerry left and Robbie sat down on the couch.

"Looks like you had a nice morning," said Mary.

"I did except for that dog," said Robbie. "I should have broken that little shit's back. Excuse the language."

"I would probably have done that too," said Robert. "The language seems appropriate." It wasn't even a half hour and Jerry was back.

"Well I talked with several of the neighbors and it seems that none of them have anything good to say about that dog," said Jerry. "I told the woman that if her dog caused any more problems it would be put down. Oh, and here's $10."

"Thanks Jerry, I appreciate it," said Robbie.

"I'll be rolling now," said Jerry. "And Robbie, I am glad you're home. Take care now."

Robbie took his DD-214 with him when they went to the Legion post so he could go ahead and become a member. Several of Robert's friends were there and they all sat together and told a few war stories. One man would tell a story and then they would all keep saying that they were the old farts and would be dying out soon and they needed the Vietnam vets to keep things going. Then another man would tell a story and then it was back to needing the Vietnam vets. This went on for several beers. Then someone decided they should have some shots. Robbie hadn't ever had whiskey before and he was still only nineteen and not of legal age to drink it in Ohio. No one cared. They all had a few shots anyway. When it was time to leave, Mary came and picked them up. As soon as they got home, they had another beer. Mary joined them. Robbie fell asleep on the couch that night.

Robbie was sure he would have a hangover the next morning but he didn't. He just felt really worn out. After a couple of cups of coffee, he was fine. He spent the morning getting signed up for his VA health care and getting his disability pay straightened out. After lunch, he went over to talk with Brad's parents. Both of them were home. They invited Robbie inside and Brad's mother brought everyone some iced tea. Robbie was hesitant to start speaking. When he was finally ready to speak, Brad's dad spoke. "Can you tell me why my boy died?" he asked. "I mean what is this all about and why are we over there anyway?"

"I always thought it was about communist aggression," said Robbie. "I guess you could talk and talk about it forever. The protesters say this and the government says that. All I know is that all I did over there was to try and stay alive and keep my men alive. That's what we did. Try to stay alive."

"I see you got wounded," said Brad's dad. "Are you gonna need that cane the rest of your life?"

"I hope not," answered Robbie. "I hope to be dancing again before too long."

"Brad said you and that girl of yours were really good dancers," said Brad's mother. "We heard about what happened to Maria. That was a shame. Seems crime's picked up around here in the last year or so."

"I was in the hospital recovering from other wounds when I found out about Maria," said Robbie. "It about did me in."

"So you were wounded more than once?" Brad's dad asked.

"Yes I was," answered Robbie. "The first time a bullet grazed my left shoulder and a piece of plastic off my rifle got stuck in my face." Robbie showed them the scar on his face. "The next time I got shot through both legs," said Robbie. "Then the last time I got shot in the stomach, the left lung, and then my left thigh."

"It's a good thing you weren't over there any longer or they'd have run out of places to shoot you," said Brad's mother.

"So did they tell you how Brad was killed?" asked Robbie. "Or did they just say he was killed in action somewhere?"

"They said it was a booby trap," said Brad's father. "They said that a man tripped it and him and Brad and another man were killed. They said it was a 155 round. I don't know how they could tell that once it blowed up. Brad was pretty torn up. We had a closed casket."

"I'm so sorry for your loss," said Robbie. "We lost a lot of men to booby traps. Seems they were everywhere."

"Nixon says we're going to start having troop withdrawals and let the Vietnamese do their own fighting," said Brad's dad. "What do you think about that?"

"I don't really know what to think," said Robbie. "I was never really around any South Vietnamese troops so I don't know if they're any good or not. I was always hearing that they were useless. Nixon said a lot of stuff to get himself elected. I expect we'll see what happens. I suppose that if we do pull out and the South falls, we'll all wonder why the hell were we there in the first place."

"So Robbie, what will you do with yourself now that you are a civilian?" asked Brad's dad.

"I'm not quite sure," said Robbie. "There's one thing I might try but I want to make sure that it's what I want."

"I believe things will work out for you," said Brad's mother.

"Well I think I'll be going," said Robbie. "I hope I didn't upset you by coming over."

"It's probably always upsetting to talk about the death of a loved one," said Brad's mother. "But we are glad that you stopped in and we hope the best for you."

"Thank you, I miss Brad too," said Robbie. He shook Brad's father's hand and gave his mother a hug and then left.

When Robbie got back home, Mary asked him how it went with Brad's parents. "It went well I thought," said Robbie. "They wanted to know why Brad died and of course I couldn't really tell them a good answer. I think they just want to make sure that he didn't die for nothing. I did get them talking a little and I think they are more at ease when they talk about it than they might have been before. They told me how Brad was killed and that they had a closed casket. They asked me what I thought about troop withdrawals. That was about it. We wished each other well and then I left."

"It's nice that you went over and talked with them," said Mary. "I remember when your father was gone. So many families were losing sons. It seemed like it would never end. I held my breath every time I saw someone on a bicycle, a western union man, or a military car going down the street. So your father has one more day off. Why don't you two do something? Maybe the Jets are playing today."

Robbie and his dad went to a Jets game that evening. They lucked out. The season was almost over and this was one of their last home games. There was also a rumor going around that this would be their last year in Columbus. The rumor didn't specify if they were moving to another city or if they would be disbanding. Anyway, the Jets won and the men had a good time.

The next morning after breakfast, Robbie took another walk. When he got to Mrs. Wilson's house he could hear that little shit barking but he couldn't spot it. He stopped for a minute and looked. The dog was on top of something and looking out a picture window. Robbie could see that the little booger was baring his teeth at him. Mrs. Wilson apparently was in another room when the dog started barking and she went to see why he was barking. She picked up the dog and looked out the window to see Robbie standing there. Robbie waved to her. She gave him the finger and moved away from the window. "If that woman's not careful a house might fall on her," Robbie said to himself. He finished his walk and after lunch he decided he would visit a VFW Post that wasn't far away. He told his mother where he would be and left.

When he got to the VFW there were several cars in the parking lot. He found an unlocked door and went inside. He had entered the bar. A bartender was behind the bar and there were three tables with three or four men at them and there was a very old man setting over at table by himself. The bartender spoke. "What can I do for you young man?" he asked. Robbie walked over to him.

"My name is Robbie Parker. I just came in here to look around," said Robbie. "I've never been in here before." Robbie extended his hand to the bartender. They shook.

"Well I'm pleased to meet you young man. Name's Jake Canton," said Jake. "Can I get you a beer or something?"

"I'll take a strohs," said Robbie.

"Comin' right up," said Jake. "I'm not s'posed to serve anyone who's not a member, but I'd say you're a veteran. You got that cane and your hair is shorter than most young men around here."

"I am a veteran," said Robbie. "Just got my discharge."

"You look like a Marine to me," said Jake. "You can always tell a Marine when you see one."

"That's right. I was a Marine," said Robbie.

"I was a Marine too," said Jake. "Glad to know you. So how's things over there. Are our boys doing any good?

"We've been killing more of them than they have us," said Robbie.

"You said your name was Parker, didn't you?" asked Jake.

"Yes I did," said Robbie.

"I know your father if his name is Robert," said Jake.

"That's him," said Robbie. "How do you know him?"

"Your dad and me was in some of the same scrapes," said Jake. "We was in the same company for a while. I never really got to know him but I knew who he was and he knew me. I was in your dad's company when he got his Bronze Star.

After that scrape there wasn't many of us left so they put us all in other units. How is your dad? I haven't seen him since we left Iwo Jima."

"He's doing good," said Robbie. "You should come over some time and see him. I know he'd like that. We both belong to the Legion. I bet if he knew you were here he'd join here too. I know I'm going to join here. I have my DD-214 with me and if you have an application, I'll get signed right up."

"We always keep some behind the bar," said Jake. "We'll get you signed up."

Before Robbie had the application filled out, several of the men in the place were coming over to him and introducing themselves. They all wanted to buy Robbie another drink. Every one of them told Robbie that the Legion needed the Vietnam Vets because the old farts would be dying out soon. A man sitting by himself never left his chair. He sat there and started bitching about Vietnam Vets. "You Vietnam Vets don't know shit," he was saying. "All you did was go over there and smoke that dope. That's why them boys is getting killed. They're high and they don't know what's going on. You don't know a damn thing about combat."

"Who in the hell is that?" asked Robbie.

"That's ole Jessie," said Jake. "He's one of our WW1 vets. He gets a little cranky once in a while. We try to ignore him when he gets like this."

"I believe I'll have some words with ole Jessie," said Robbie. Robbie walked over to Jessie's table. He faced ole Jessie and extended his hand. "They tell me you're Jessie and you were in the Great War," said Robbie. "I'm Robbie and I was in a war that's not so great." Jessie cracked a smile and extended his hand to Robbie. They shook.

"Pull up a chair young fella," said Jessie. "Hey Jake, bring this young man another beer and I'll have another shot." Jake brought over the drinks. "So tell me young man. Was you a Marine?"

"Yes sir I was," answered Robbie. "My dad was a Marine too."

"Don't be calling me sir," said Jessie. "I used to work for a living."

"So tell me Jessie," started Robbie. "What makes you think that all the boys in Vietnam are smoking pot?"

"It's the damn news," aid Jessie. "You never hear anything good on the news. Everything is always gloom and doom. A bunch of our boys got killed here. A bunch got killed there. They don't hardly ever say one word about how many of them VC or NVA our boys killed. They even showed a bunch of soldiers smoking pot on the news."

"Well Jessie, I can assure you that nobody in my platoon was a dope head," said Jessie. "One time back at the camp we had some new guys smoking dope.

We got some incoming and three of them got killed when a mortar round landed right in the middle of them. There were four of them. The one who didn't get killed had his arm blown off. That's the extent of my knowledge of our boys smoking pot. If anything else went on I didn't know about it. Did you boys have any trouble with booze or anything during the Great War?"

"We had a lot of boys who got drunk every time they had the chance but we didn't get many chances in the trenches," said Jessie. "I don't know of anyone that got killed cause they was drunk."

"What was your rank?" asked Robbie.

"I was a Sergeant," said Jessie. "I was in the Marines for ten years before we got into the war. I loved it. I would have made it a career but I got shot in the hip at Belleau Wood. I see you got a cane. You must have been hit too."

"Jessie, I've been shot five times," said Robbie. "The first time it just grazed my shoulder. Second time was in both legs. Then it was in the stomach, left lung, and then left thigh."

"Damn boy, you been shot to hell," said Jessie. "I count that as six times."

"Well that one in both legs might have been just one bullet," said Robbie. "I didn't get a chance to ask the shooter." Jessie cracked another smile. They talked some more. After about an hour, Jessie said that he had to go.

"I best git home now," said Jessie. "The wife gets a little testy if I'm gone too long. I reckon she worries bout me."

"Well it was nice meeting you," said Robbie. "I'm sure we'll have another drink together soon." Jessie left and Robbie went back to the bar."

"Ole Jessie's taken a liking to you," said Jake. "That's amazing. He don't like very many people."

"It was my sense of humor and personal charm," said Robbie. "Ole Jessie's really a nice man. I believe I'll have one more beer and then hit the road." Jake got Robbie another beer. Robbie went to pay him.

"That's already covered," said Jake. Robbie drank his beer and then headed home. His dad was home from work and dinner was almost ready.

"I met a guy today who was in your company during the war," said Robbie.

"Who was that and where did you meet him?" asked Robert.

"His name is Jake Canton and he was tending bar at the VFW," said Robbie.

"Is that so," said Robert. "I remember him. He was in another platoon. I never knew he was from around here. I'll have to get over there sometime and see him. Not very many of us lived through all that."

"I also met a WW1 vet," said Robbie. "Everybody kind of avoids him at the VFW. They say he's grouchy and don't like too many people. Anyway, I got to talking to him. He's really a nice man. He's just upset about the stuff they always flash on the news. He was shot in the hip at Belleau Wood."

"He was a Marine then," said Robert. "The Marines killed a lot of Germans at Belleau Wood but they took a lot of casualties too."

"Dinner's ready," said Mary from the kitchen. "You men can tell war stories after dinner."

That evening Robbie decided to write a letter to Helen. It went as follows.

My Dearest Helen,

I arrived home o.k. It's great to be in Ohio again. I haven't done a whole lot since I've been here. I joined the American Legion and the VFW and met some interesting people. One of my friends from school was killed over there and I went to talk with his parents. I was hoping to make them feel better but I don't know if I did or not. I did get them talking some. They seemed very bitter about Brad's death when I first got there. They didn't understand why he died and why we are over there in the first place. I couldn't give them a good reason for anything. I told him that we were just trying to stay alive. I haven't set down and thought about what I will do with myself yet. I have plenty of time for that.

How have you been? I have missed you immensely. I know you do not have any leave time left this year so I will come over to see you after the first of the year. That's not too far off. Maybe by then my limp will be better and we can do some surfing. Or you can do some surfing and I'll watch. I loved watching you surf. You and the wave were like one. Both of you were beautiful. I can't wait to hold you close to me again.

Love and Miss you.

Robbie

Robbie got up the next morning and decided he would take a drive. Before too long he found himself on the south end of the city and not far from Maria's grandparents house. Robbie pulled up to the curb in front of the house. "Should I go see them?" Robbie asked himself. "Me visiting might just get them upset. Should I or shouldn't I?" Robbie decided to visit them. He went to the house and lightly knocked on the door. Grandfather answered the door. He smiled at Robbie and shook his hand.

"Woman, come see who's here," said Grandfather. "Grandmother came from the kitchen and started crying when she saw Robbie. She went to him and gave him a hug.

"We are going to the graveyard this morning and visiting Maria," said Grandmother. "You are welcome to go with us."

"I would like that," said Robbie. No more words were spoken until they were in Grandfather's car headed to the graveyard.

"I see you are using a cane," said Grandfather. "Were you wounded badly?"

"I was," said Robbie. "Besides the leg wound I was hit in the stomach and the left lung. I was given a Medical Discharge."

"Well you are still very young and you have plenty of time for your body to get stronger," said Grandfather. "I watched you with the cane and I would say that before too long you will not need it."

"I'm hoping that too," said Robbie.

They arrived at the graveyard and went to Maria's grave. There was a nice headstone. On it was carved her name and the dates of her life. Then it said "Sadly Missed by All." Grandmother placed some flowers on the grave and they all had a good cry. When they arrived back at the house, Robbie was invited for lunch but he told them that he needed some time by himself. Robbie gave Grandmother a hug and kiss and shook Grandfather's hand and left. He had no idea where he wanted to go. He just drove. After about a half hour he pulled over to the curb. He had never been in this part of town other than to drive through it. He grabbed his cane and got out and started walking. On both sides of the road were big, older, beautiful houses. After a couple of blocks, he saw this huge older house. It was brick with a slate roof and different colored windows. Robbie got closer to look at it. It wasn't a house at all. At least it wasn't a house right now. It was a funeral home. The sign out front was behind a huge oak tree and Robbie didn't see it till he got closer. The sign said "Fulbright's Funeral Home." Robbie stopped on the sidewalk and looked at the place. He thought it was beautiful. "This is a nice looking place," Robbie said to himself. "This is what a funeral home should look like. Some of the new ones look very impersonal. They should just put a sign out that says "you stab'em and we slab'em." Robbie noticed that there was a big Marine Corps emblem in one of the downstairs window. As Robbie was looking at the emblem, he noticed that someone inside was looking at him. A few minutes later, a middle aged man came out the front door and walked toward Robbie.

"You seem pretty interested in this building son," said the man. "Is there something I can help you with?"

"No sir," said Robbie. "I was just admiring the place. I think it's beautiful."

"Son, first off, don't call me sir. I work for a living," said the man. "And yes this place is beautiful. My grandfather built this place in 1900. My father remodeled it in 1944 and I keep it looking nice. I'm Abner Fulbright."

"I'm Robbie Parker," said Robbie as he extended his hand to Abner. They shook. "You must have been a Marine," said Robbie. "We're the only ones that I know of that say "don't call me sir, I work for a living." Plus you have that Marine Corps emblem in the window."

"Once a Marine always a Marine," said Abner. "Every man in our family was a Marine."

"Same in my family too," said Robbie. "Maybe one day when I have my own family the boys will be Marines too."

"My son was a Marine," said Abner. Abner was having a hard time holding back tears. "He was with the 5th Marines. He was killed at Hue."

"I was with the 5th Marines too," said Robbie. "I just got back home a few days ago. I got a Medical Discharge."

"So where was your father during the war?" asked Abner.

"He was at Tarawa and several other islands," said Robbie. "His last action was on Iwo Jima."

"I was at Guadalcanal, Peleliu, and Okinawa." said Abner. "There were other islands but I can't remember their names. Let's go inside to my office and have something to drink. You're not in a hurry are you?"

"No, I have no set plans for today," said Robbie. They went to Abner's office. "I have fresh coffee or I can get you a coke if you'd like."

"Coffee's fine," said Robbie. "I don't drink much soda anymore."

"I bet you like your beer," said Abner.

"I do like my beer," said Robbie. "But I don't drink on what you could call a regular basis. I used to have a few beers with my dad when I turned eighteen. He took me to his Legion Post. I joined that Post just the other day. I joined the VFW too. Everyone kept wanting to buy me drinks."

"I drink a little on a hot summer day and I'll have a nice wine with a good meal," said Abner. "I never did join the Legion or the VFW because I don't drink much."

"Even if I didn't drink I would have joined them," said Robbie. "I was a baseball player and both the Legion and the VFW sponsor teams."

"I guess I never thought about that," said Abner. "I suppose another reason for not joining is because in this business, you never know when you will be working. People don't die by a schedule. Things have to be set up. You have to meet with the family and relatives to get everything going. There's viewings and most of them are in the evenings because of how people work. Then there's the funeral. You never know what day they will be."

"Don't you have other people working for you so that you don't have to do everything yourself?" asked Robbie.

"This is a small outfit," said Abner. "I do have some other help but I don't have anyone who wants to take charge if you know what I mean. My son would have come into the business. I have a daughter and she wants no part of this business. If something ever happened to me, my wife would sell the business. So tell me young man, what are you intending to do with yourself now that you are a civilian?"

"You probably won't believe this but I have been considering becoming a mortician," answered Robbie.

"Why would you consider that?" asked Abner. "There's so many things out there a young man could do."

"When I was in the hospital recovering from wounds, I was having these dreams where I was constantly filling body bags," said Robbie. "There was an endless supply of bodies and bags. At this same time I was thinking about what I should do after the Corps. I decided it should be something that there will always be a demand for. People will always die and someone will always have to take care of the bodies. There are no exceptions."

"You're right about that," said Abner. "We all die. There are no exceptions. So how hard have you thought about this Robbie?"

"Not hard enough to make up my mind yet," answered Robbie.

"Tell you what, why don't I give you a nickel tour of this place," said Abner. "We don't have any bodies here right now so you don't have to worry about that."

"Believe me, I've seen way too many dead bodies," said Robbie. "It wouldn't bother me. If I thought it would, I wouldn't be here in the first place."

"All right, let's go," said Abner. Abner showed Robbie everything. An hour later, Robbie was shaking Abner's hand telling him goodbye. Nothing else was said as Robbie left.

That evening at dinner Robbie's folks asked him about his day. "I went to Maria's house," said Robbie. "I went with her grandparents to the graveyard. We had a good cry. Then I ended up at a funeral home."

"Why in the world were you at a funeral home?" asked Mary. "Did someone you know die recently?"

"No Mom, I was just driving when I ended up in this neighborhood and there were older beautiful houses all over," said Robbie. "This one huge house was actually a Funeral Home, Fulbright's Funeral Home."

"I know that place," said Robert. "That is an older beautiful building."

"Well Abner Fulbright is the owner," said Robbie. "He saw me out front looking at the place and came outside to see if I needed anything. He was a Marine too. His son was killed at Hue. We talked a good bit and he gave me a tour of his place."

"Did it give you the creeps?" asked Mary. "Were there any bodies there?"

"No Mom, there were no bodies and I didn't get the creeps," said Robbie. "I have actually thought about becoming a mortician. I want to do something that everyone will need sooner or later."

"Well everyone will need taken care of sooner or later," said Robert. "There are no exceptions. If a person could stomach it, it would be an honorable profession. If you did decide to do this it wouldn't bother your mother or me. You'd have to get used to hearing this though."

"What's that dad?" asked Robbie.

"How's business? Dead?" said Robert.

"Nothing wrong with a little humor," said Robbie.

The next day Robbie went back over to Fulbright's. He wanted to talk with Abner about mortician school. Abner was glad to tell Robbie what he knew. "The best place to get a degree in the state is the Cincinnati School of Mortuary Science," said Abner. "They'll teach you everything you need to know. You can get an Associate's Degree in a full year or a Bachelor's Degree in a year and a half I think. An Associate's Degree is all that's required in this state to practice. That's all I have. If I were you I'd go down there and talk with them. I have some old cards with their address and phone numbers. Take one." Robbie took a card.

"I believe I'll drive down there and talk with them," said Robbie.

"Tell you what Robbie Parker," Abner began. "You go down there and get your degree and I'll give you a job. You won't get rich here but it would give you a good start. Besides, Marines should help out their fellow Marines."

"Semper Fi," said Robbie and he shook Abner's hand. "I'll drive down there tomorrow and talk to those people. I'll see you after I get back and let you know how things went."

"I'll look forward to seeing you," said Abner. "Drive safely."

Chapter Eleven

R obbie got up early the next morning and was on his way to Cincinnati. It was a long drive but Robbie enjoyed it. He hadn't been to Cincinnati since the last time he and his dad had gone to a Reds game in 1963. He found the school easily and he went to the admissions office. They sent him to an advisor who could tell him everything he needed to know and answer any questions he might have. Then they gave Robbie a tour of the school. Robbie made up his mind that he would attend the school.

Everything was set up in semesters. The fall term had already started so Robbie would have to wait until the next semester. It would start Jan. 11. There would be 3 semesters in a calendar year and he could get his Associate's Degree by the end of the year. If he decided to get a Bachelor's it would take another semester after that. Robbie went ahead and filled out his enrollment application. They told him he would receive a formal letter informing him if he was accepted or not. They assured him he would be accepted. Robbie found a chili parlor and had some Cincinnati chili before he drove back to Columbus.

His dad was just leaving for second trick when Robbie got home. They waved to each other as Robert was pulling out of the driveway. Robbie went inside. Mary was sitting at the kitchen table looking at a recipe book. "What's up Mom?" asked Robbie. "You going to make something new?"

"I thought I'd try a new recipe," said Mary. "When you cook all the time you kind of get in a rut. Something new gets you out of it sometimes. So how was that school?"

"I went ahead and got signed up," said Robbie. "The next semester starts in January. I'll start then and I could be done by the end of the year. That'll get me an Associate's Degree. If I go another semester I can get a Bachelor's. I should get a formal letter shortly saying that I have been accepted. Once I get that letter, I'll need to get signed up for my GI Bill."

"You'll need to get an apartment down there too," said Mary. "They can be expensive depending on where you want to live."

"I know, but I don't need much," said Robbie. "A roof, a bed, a kitchen with a stove, a bathroom, and I'm set. Maybe when I start looking I could find someone who would share with me."

"Well be careful if you do that," said Mary. "Not everyone's as honest as you are."

"I know that Mom," said Robbie. "I've been around."

"So if you don't start school till January you'll have a lot of time here before you go," said Mary. "What will you do with yourself?"

"I'm thinking that I might do some volunteer work at the VA," said Robbie. "They have volunteers that do odds and ends. I can get coffee and talk to people."

"That would be very admirable of you son," said Mary. "So have you talked to Helen since you've been home?"

"I wrote her a letter the other day," said Robbie. "Of course I told her that I loved and missed her. I'll tell her all about school after I get my acceptance letter. I wish she had more leave coming this year. I'd fly over and see her again."

"I would say that leave or not you should go see her," said Mary. "Once school starts in January you'll be tied up for a while. You won't want to wait until the end of the semester or spring break or whatever they give you down there. She normally works a five day week I bet. You could go for a few days around her days off and still see plenty of her. I wouldn't wait till Thanksgiving or Christmas though because I hear that it's a very busy time flying to Hawaii then. I'd go before then if I were you."

"Sounds like you're trying to get rid of me," said Robbie.

"No son, it's just that I know what it's like to be without someone for a long time," said Mary. "I want you to be happy."

"Well you talked me into it," said Robbie. "You can figure on me being gone maybe the second week of November."

The next day Robbie went over to Fulbright's and gave him the news about the school. "You know, if you'd like to get a head start on things you could come over and help me out some," said Abner. "Of course you can't do certain things but you can watch and learn. I could even pay you a little. Would you be interested in that?"

"Yes I would," answered Robbie. "When could we start?"

"Well give me your phone number and I'll give you a call," said Abner. Robbie gave Abner his phone number and then was on his way. Robbie went straight home. He wasn't home for a half hour when Abner called. Robbie's mother had answered the phone.

"Robbie, Abner Fulbright's on the phone for you," said Mary. Robbie thanked her and took the phone.

"Yes Abner, this is Robbie," said Robbie.

"We have our next customer," said Abner. "I am meeting with the parents of the deceased on Thursday at 10 AM. I would like for you to be here if you can make it."

"I'll be there," said Robbie.

"I should tell you Robbie," started Abner. "The deceased is a soldier who was killed in Vietnam. His body is being shipped here. Wear some nice clothes if you have them."

"I'll see you Thursday," said Robbie.

"So what did Mr. Fulbright want?" asked Mary.

"Well Mom, I'm going to be helping him out some before I go to school," said Robbie. "I hope to learn some things. Thursday we're meeting with the parents of a soldier who was killed in Vietnam. I need to see if some of my good clothes fit."

"I'd say your clothes should fit," said Mary. "They might even be a little big. You haven't gained back all the weight you lost over there yet."

Robbie went through his good clothes and found what he thought would be appropriate. His suit had been covered by a plastic cover and still looked good. His mother ironed a shirt and a tie for him. Robbie shined up his good shoes.

Thursday rolled around and Robbie showed up a Fulbright's a little early. Abner was impressed that Robbie showed up in a suit. "Suit looks good on you," said Abner. "Customers appreciate it when we dress respectfully. Now what we'll be doing is listening to the people and they'll tell us what kind of service they will be having. Like will the service be held here or a church or will there even be a service at all. Sometimes they just have a graveside service. We offer suggestions. We go over casket selections. Will there be a viewing or not. After all of that and anything else that could come up, we talk about pricing and payment. Sometimes that is difficult. Sometimes it isn't."

"I'll be a good listener," said Robbie.

"Now when we get started I will introduce you and say that you are a new employee and learning the business," said Abner. "If someone would ask you a question, it's all right for you to answer if you can or if they want your opinion that's all right too." The parents of the deceased arrived and they went into Abner's office. They were the Millers and their son's name was Thomas. Abner introduced himself and Robbie to them and they all shook hands.

Things went very well. They would have a viewing and there would only be a graveside service. There would be a color guard with a twenty one gun salute. Mrs. Miller couldn't make up her mind on the casket she wanted. Mr. Miller said it was up to her. Mr. Miller noticed that Robbie was using a cane. "Why are you using a cane young fella?" asked Mr. Miller. "You're not old enough for a cane. Were you a soldier?"

"No Mr. Miller, I was a Marine," answered Robbie.

"Same difference," said Mr. Miller.

"We don't think so," said Robbie.

"So you think Marines are better than soldiers?" asked Mr. Miller.

"Of course I do," answered Robbie. "Shouldn't a man always think that his outfit is the best?"

"I guess you're right son," said Mr. Miller. "Our Tom was Airborne. He thought they were the best. So how bad did they shoot you up?"

"Bad enough that I got a Medical Discharge," answered Robbie.

"Well I hope you can get so you don't need that cane some day," said Mr. Miller. "I hope all them hurt boys get better and I hope that my boy and all them other boys don't end up dying for nothing." While Robbie and Mr. Miller were talking, Mrs. Miller finally made up her mind about a casket. Then they all went back to the office to discuss pricing. Abner gave them the prices and no one objected. They all shook hands and the Millers left.

"That was an easy one today," said Abner. "Some folks want to argue and argue about everything. I have actually told some people to take their business elsewhere. We're a small outfit. We don't do volume business. Our prices are our prices. They are what we have to charge to make a profit so we can make a living."

"I can understand how some folks would argue pricing," said Robbie. "Some people are just that way. They want everything as cheap as they can get it."

"Well you did good today," said Abner. "You didn't get into an argument with Mr. Miller about who was better. What you said was good. Miller liked it.

You'll do good in this business. Now when the body gets here, I'll call you and you can come and watch what we do to get it ready."

"Will I be needed for anything after that?" asked Robbie.

"I want you to come to the viewing," said Abner. "You can help greet people and offer sympathy. Sometimes if we have a huge crowd we need to get more chairs out. We don't ever know that till it happens. A lot of people pass through the line, look at the deceased, shake hands with the relatives, and then leave. Others stay and chat for hours."

"Well give me a call when the body arrives," said Robbie. "I'll be here."

It was lunchtime when Robbie got home. Robert was on first trick so he wasn't there. "How bout I take my best girl out to lunch?" said Robbie to his mother.

"I can't turn down an offer like that," said Mary. "Why don't you change your clothes before we go?"

"I will," said Robbie. "I'd have to send everything to the cleaners if I wore it when I ate. We're going to the Olive Garden. I'm a little sloppy when I eat Italian food. You should know that after washing my shirts when we have spaghetti."

"You and your father both," said Mary. "You can tell me all about this morning on the way to the Olive Garden." Robbie got changed and they were on their way. "So how was it this morning?" Mary asked as they were driving down the road.

"It was all right," said Robbie. "All we did today was talk about the service and the viewing and such. They picked out a casket and we discussed prices."

"Did that go well?" asked Mary.

"It did," answered Robbie. "We had no problems at all. When the body arrives, Abner will call me and I'll go over and watch what he does to prepare the body. Then I'll go to the viewing and help out." They pulled into the Olive Garden parking lot. "Let's talk about something else while we're here Mom," said Robbie.

"All right by me," said Mary. They went inside and were seated. Mary looked and looked at the menu. "I can't make up my mind," said Mary. "I don't know what a lot of this stuff is."

"We'll order you a glass of wine and that will give you some more time," said Robbie. "Then if you want, we can ask the waitress what certain things are and if she can't help we'll ask for the manager." The waitress was back in a few minutes and asked if they would have anything to drink. Mary ordered a glass of the house red wine and Robbie ordered a beer. The waitress wanted to card Robbie but when she saw his cane, she changed her mind. Robbie saw her looking at the cane. "I'm nineteen," said Robbie. "In our illustrious state I can only drink 3.2%." The waitress let out a giggle and returned shortly with the drinks.

"She's a cute girl son," said Mary. "She'll be after you."

"Yeah I know," said Robbie. "It's a curse to have such good genes and look this good."

"Don't make me laugh while I'm sipping my wine," said Mary. "I don't want to waste any."

They placed their order and had a good meal. Robbie could tell that Mary really enjoyed herself. "I'll have to tell Dad to take you out more often," said Robbie.

"I guess we could go out more often," said Mary. "I don't mind getting out of cooking once in a while." The waitress asked if they were finished. They said they were and she soon came back with the check. Underneath the check was also a slip of paper. On it was the girl's name and phone number. "I told you that girl would be after you," said Mary when they got to the car.

"And I told you I had good genes," said Robbie. They both let out a good laugh. When they got home Mary started doing some laundry and Robbie set down and wrote a letter to Carl Sims. He figured Carl would tell him he was crazy if he wanted to be a mortician but Robbie told him anyway. He told Carl that since he would be in Cincinnati that maybe they could get together down there somewhere since Carl lived around Covington. He had just finished his letter when Robert pulled into the driveway. He came into the house and went to Mary. He gave her a good kiss.

"What's for dinner tonight?" asked Robert. Mary kissed him again and then took his arm and led him to their room. "I guess we're having dessert first," said Robert.

Two days later the body of Thomas Miller arrived. Abner called Robbie and Robbie had his first lesson on body preparation. There was a huge crowd at the viewing. Several people made their rounds and left but more of them stayed. More chairs were needed. Thomas had a lot of friends who were in the military. Many of them wore their uniforms. One of them was a Marine Corporal. Robbie introduced himself. The Corporal had been with the 5th Marines but was in a different Battalion than Robbie. Both of them had spent a lot of time in "The Arizona." Several of the other young people who came were definitely anti-military. Robbie overheard several of the comments they made to the people in uniform. He thought that the men in uniform did a very good job of controlling themselves. Robbie figured that if they hadn't been at a funeral home, some people would have been punched out. After a couple of hours, the crowd started filtering out. Someone must have put out the word that Robbie had been in Vietnam. He was standing by the door telling people goodbye when some long haired young man with a scraggly beard approached him. "How many babies did you kill?" he said to Robbie. As quickly as he said those words he was gone. Robbie was taken totally by surprise by those words.

"Just who the fuck are you to be saying that to me?" said Robbie to himself. "You fucking piece of shit. You don't know a damn thing about anything." The crowd was almost gone now. Abner could tell that Robbie was ticked off about something. He went over to him and stood by him as the last of the people left. The Thomas's spent a little more time at the casket and then they left.

"You did good today Robbie," said Abner. "You will do well in this business. I can tell. I did see that you were upset about something but you didn't let it get the best of you. What was it?"

"Oh some long haired guy asked me how many babies I've killed," said Robbie. "Before I could react he was gone."

"It's most likely good that he left quickly, isn't it?" asked Abner.

"I guess so," answered Robbie. "I don't think I would have smacked him but I might have had a heated argument with him."

"Well it's good that he did leave quickly," said Abner. "This is not the place for quarrelling."

"Will I be needed for the funeral?" asked Robbie.

"No, my other help will take care of everything else," said Abner. "I will give you a call when you are needed again."

"Thanks, I'll see you then," said Robbie. Robbie went to his car and drove straight home. It was around 7:30 PM when Robbie came into the house. His parents were in the living room watching TV. Mary was sitting on Robert's lap. "That's great," Robbie thought to himself. "Them two really love each other."

"Hey Dad, how about you and me going over to the VFW now," said Robbie. "Mom can come too."

"What do you say?" Robert said to Mary. "Should we go to the VFW with our son?"

"All right by me," said Mary. "But you remember, you are still on first trick."

"I'll make sure things don't get out of hand," said Robbie. "I'll get my clothes changed and we can go." When they got to the VFW, Jake Canton was there. He wasn't tending bar but was at a table with a couple of other men. As soon as Robbie and his parents headed for a table, Jake spotted them and came over. He recognized Robert right away. Robert recognized Jake too. They gave each other a hug and a handshake and then stepped back and looked at each other.

"Just how in the hell have you been gyrene?" said Jake. "I wish I'd have known you better and that you were from around here. We're some of the ones who made it back. It's awful good to see you again."

"Likewise Jake," said Robert. "Jake this is my wife Mary. You already know Robbie." Jake took Mary's hand and kissed it.

"I'm pleased to make your acquaintance Mary," said Jake. "Robert sure got himself a beautiful woman."

"Why thank you Jake," said Mary. "Is there a Mrs. Canton?"

"Yep, she's home watching her TV shows," said Jake. "She won't come here much unless we're having a dance or something. She likes to dance. I'm not too good but I get out on the floor. How about you two. Are you dancers?"

"Yes we are," answered Mary. "Robert is Mr. Smooth on the dance floor."

"That's great," said Jake. "We'll be having a "Halloween Dance" shortly. You two should come. Are you a dancer Robbie?"

"I am," answered Robbie. "These two taught me. Probably not much good right now but I'm hoping to get rid of this cane one day soon."

"I bet you could still cut a rug some," said Jake. "We got a good band lined up. They play all kinds of stuff. They play a lot of rock and roll too."

Ole Jessie was sitting at a table by himself several tables away. Robbie excused himself and went over to his table. "Hey Jessie, Come on over and meet my parents," said Robbie. "Everybody at that table was a Marine except my mother. Come on over."

"All right young feller, I'll go," said Jessie. Jesse picked up his glass and went to Robbie's table.

"Mom, Dad, this Jessie," said Robbie. "Jessie, this is Mary and that is Robert." They all shook hands. "Jessie, what is your last name? I know your first name is not Ole and your last name is not Jessie."

"It's Horner," said Jessie. "Jessie H. Horner. The H don't stand for nothing."

"None of the men in our family have real middle names," said Robert. "We just have letters. Mine is G. Robbie's is W, and my father's was T." They had been talking and had not had anything to drink yet. Robbie went over to the bar and got everyone their drinks. He also got Jessie another shot of whiskey.

"The bartender said you drank Jack Daniels so that's what I got you Jessie," said Robbie.

"I thank you young man," said Jessie. "I figure if a man's gonna drink whiskey he should drink good stuff, not some rot gut. This'll have to be my last one though. I been here a while already. Wife'll be calling here telling them to send me home."

"She cares about you," said Robbie.

"I reckon she does," said Jessie. "This gettin' old stuff isn't much fun though, but I had me a good life. So young man, What are gonna do with yourself now that you're a civilian?"

"How bout you take a guess," said Robbie. "I bet you couldn't guess in a million years." Jessie started guessing. After a while Jake started guessing too. Then they gave up.

"Well I don't want any bad remarks or anything when I tell," said Robbie. "I want both of your words on that."

"Well we know that you're not gonna be a ballet dancer," said Jake. "Go ahead and tell us. We promise we won't say anything bad."

"All right, here goes," said Robbie. "I'm going to mortician school."

"Damn, I never expected to hear that," said Jessie. "Hell, I'll be needin' you before too long."

"I don't think I could do that," said Jake. "But it sure as hell is something that all of us will need sooner or later. Good luck with that."

"Thank you," said Robbie. "I hope I won't see you in the future as a customer."

"I hope so too," said Jake. "I hope I got a ways to go yet."

Jessie was just finishing his whiskey when the phone behind the bar rang. The bartender yelled out that it was time for Jessie to head home. Jessie said his good byes and left. They all had a couple more beers and talked for another hour and then Robert decided it was time to head home. He and Jake shook hands again and he told Jake that he would probably be at the Halloween Dance.

The next day, Robbie's acceptance letter from CCMS arrived. He located a local Veteran Representative and got signed up for his GI Bill. A letter from Helen had arrived that day too so when he answered it, he could tell her about starting school and coming over for a visit. His letter from Helen and the acceptance letter cheered him up some. He was feeling a little ticked about what the long haired guy had said to him at the funeral home. He forgot all about that when he read Helen's letter. Of course she missed him terribly and couldn't wait to be together again. She also said that things seemed to be slower at the hospital. There was still a lot of wounded coming from Vietnam but now it wasn't a steady stream. They came in spurts. He wrote his reply to Helen's letter after he got home from seeing the Veteran's Rep. It was afternoon and he decided he would take a walk. When he got to Mrs. Wilson's house he could hear her dog barking again. When he looked at the front window of the house, he could see Mrs. Wilson holding the dog and giving him the finger again. "I wonder where that bitch's husband is," Robbie said to himself. "He probably ran off or is dead. Hope she don't have any kids. If she did they probably ran off to get away from her." Robbie shrugged his shoulders and moved on. When he got home Mary informed him that he had missed a call from Abner. Robbie immediately called him back.

"We have another one," said Abner. "Can you be here tomorrow at 10 AM?"

"I'll be there," said Robbie. "Well Mom, Abner needs me tomorrow."

"I hope it's not that person who was in that bad wreck I heard about this morning," said Mary. "They showed the car on the news. It was mangled terribly."

"I guess I'll find out tomorrow," said Robbie.

Robbie was at Fulbright's at a quarter till ten. The deceased was the person who was in the bad wreck. She had lost control and ran off a highway. The car had gone down a steep hill and rolled several times before crashing into a wall of rocks. When the parents of the deceased girl arrived, Abner introduced himself and Robbie and they got started. The girl's mother could not quit crying and the father wasn't helping much. "I should go up there and beat the hell out of that son of a bitch," said the father. "I knew from the start that he was no good."

"Would you two like some time alone?" asked Robbie.

"We'll be all right," said the father. "I just gotta do some bitching right now. Do you mind listening?"

"We're here to help you," said Robbie. "If you need to vent some, go right ahead."

"Well like I said, I always knew that son of a bitch was no good," said the father. "I could tell by the way he was always looking at other women that he was no good. But my daughter loved him and wouldn't listen to us. She said she was a big girl and it was her life. Well two days before the wedding she caught him screwing her best friend and roommate. She called us and said she was coming home."

"Well there is nothing that I can say at this time that would probably be of comfort," said Robbie. "I was not acquainted with your daughter but I am sure by what you have said that she was a very special and wonderful girl. I know she will be deeply missed. I know you loved her very much."

"Thank you young man. I believe the Mrs. has calmed down some so we can probably get started," said the father.

Everything went smoothly now. It would be a closed casket so there would be no viewing. A funeral service would be held at the funeral parlor and then they would proceed to the graveyard. A medium priced casket was picked out and there were no problems with the prices. The couple thanked Abner and Robbie and were on their way. "You did good again today," said Abner. "You didn't say a lot but what you did say was good. You'll do well. Now come back tomorrow morning around nine. We'll do what we can with the body."

"I'll be here," said Robbie.

When Robbie got home Mary was sitting at the kitchen table peeling some apples. "I'm making us a pie," said Mary. "How was your morning? Was it the person from that bad wreck?"

"Yes it was," said Robbie. "The parents were pretty upset but they calmed down some."

"I guess if you're going to do that for a living you'll see a lot of upset people," said Mary.

Robbie was at Fulbright's at nine. When he saw the girl's mangled body it kind of reminded him of some of the things he had seen overseas. The funeral service was short but there was a larger than expected crowd. Robbie heard the father of the deceased girl say, "That son of a bitch better not show up here." The girl's former fiancé didn't show up and everything went smoothly. Robbie was not needed to go to the graveyard. Abner would call him again when he was needed.

Robbie went home and changed his clothes and headed to the VA Hospital. He talked to the person who was in charge of the volunteers that day. They would be glad to have him despite his irregular hours. They were especially pleased because he was also a veteran. He could start whenever he wanted. They told him he could be a gopher. He would go see patients and ask if they needed anything. If they did, he would go get it for them. Hence the name gopher, go for this, go for that. Robbie told them he would start right away so they made him a name tag so other employees and volunteers would know that he was supposed to be there. Another volunteer showed Robbie around. The volunteer let Robbie know that there was a possibility that some patients could be violent. Those individuals lived in a certain dormitory. He decided he would go there first. A nurse saw him and went with him for a while as he and the other volunteer walked around asking patients if they needed anything. Most of the patients he saw that day must have been really drugged up or something. They didn't talk or wouldn't even look at Robbie. A lot of them were older too. Robbie figured they were WW2 vets. Robbie had heard at one time that some of the patients were there because they had gotten syphilis and now had paresis. Robbie could see that some of the patients were there because they had suffered severe head wounds. Robbie went to another dormitory. The patients in there seemed pretty happy but still wouldn't talk to Robbie. Robbie spent around four hours at the dorms and then went to the office where he had started out and told them he was leaving for the day. He would come back tomorrow if he could.

At the dinner table that evening Robbie didn't talk much. "What's going on son?" asked Mary. "Did something bad happen?"

"Yeh, what's up Son?" You're awful quiet," said Robert.

"Well I went out to the VA and did some volunteer work," said Robbie.

"That's very admirable Son," said Mary. "How was it out there?"

"Well I'm going to be a gopher," started Robbie. "I just ask people if they need or want anything and go get it if I can. I went into two dorms today. The men in the first one were dad's age or maybe a little older. Some of them were just like vegetables. Couldn't get one of them to talk or look at me. In the other dorm all of them seemed real happy."

"Probably drugged up," said Robert. "I bet some of the ones that was like vegetables had syphilis. Some of them others might have had shell shock and never come out of it. Some of them probably had bad head wounds too. I knew a guy who worked over at the VA after the war. I don't know for sure what his job title was but he helped deliver meals to some of the patients. Whenever a patient was done with his meal, this guy had to make sure he got all of the silverware back. Someone didn't do their job one day and this guy got stabbed in the back with a fork. Needless to say, he didn't work there after that."

"Well I'm going back tomorrow unless Abner calls and needs me," said Robbie.

The next morning after breakfast Robbie went back out to the VA. A person who was in charge of the volunteers told him he could go anywhere. Since he had already been to two of the dorms he could go to different dorms or he could go to different waiting areas. These would be waiting rooms for examinations and such. Robbie went to the lab waiting area first. There were about twenty men waiting to get blood work done. Robbie could hear some of them bitching about having to wait in line. "Can I get something or do anything for anyone here?" Robbie said so all of them could hear.

A somewhat fat and unshaven man looked up at Robbie. "Just who in the God damned fuckin' hell are you?" he said to Robbie. "This is the waitin' line for the fuckin' lab. We can't have nothin' before blood work. Are you fuckin' stupid or what? Robbie got right in his face.

"You have no reason to talk that way to me you stupid old fart," started Robbie. "Now if you want to have a cussing contest I know I can whip your fucking ass. If you just plain want your ass whipped, I can do that too."

"I'm gonna whip your ass boy," said the man as he was starting to stand.

Robbie took the end of his cane and put it on the man's chest and shoved. "Sit the fuck back down shithead," said Robbie as he shoved the man back into his chair. The man started back up out of his chair. "Where's urgent care around here," said Robbie. "Somebody better tell them that they'll have a patient shortly and he's gonna need stitched up." Just then they called the man's number for the lab.

"You're lucky boy. I gotta go now," said the man.

"I'll be right here when you get done," said Robbie. "Ask them if they have any extra blood while you're in there cause you're gonna need it." The man shook his head and went into the lab.

"I don't like that loud mouth either," said a patient who had been sitting beside the shithead. "I see him sometimes out here when I have lab work. My name's Roscoe Samuels. What's yours?"

"I'm Robbie Parker. Pleased to meet you Roscoe," said Robbie.

"I see you got a cane," said Roscoe. "Are you one a them Vietnam Vets?"

"Yes I am," said Robbie. "Just got discharged not long ago. Thought I'd come out here and do a little volunteering."

"Well this place can use all the help they can get," said Roscoe. "Not that I'm complaining or anything. I'm glad they look after us vets. It just don't seem like they can keep help out here. Every time I come out I see a different doctor. Probably don't pay enough to keep doctors out here. Now there are some good doctors here. They retired from their other practice and come out here to work. Trouble is, they're getting old and will retire from here too."

"Well I just got signed up to come out here for my health care so I can't say anything good or bad about this place," said Robbie. The shithead was finished in the lab now and came out. He walked over to Robbie.

"I gotta be somewhere else right now or I'd stick around and kick your ass," said the shithead.

"You go on now," said Robbie. "I wouldn't want you to be late. But chew on this for a while. My Grandma's been dead for a lotta years and I doubt if you could whip her ass." Shithead shook his head and left.

"What's that guy's name?" asked Robbie.

"I like shithead," said Roscoe. "But his real name is Randy White."

"Why's he like that?" asked Robbie. "What did he do in the war?"

"I don't know why he's such an idiot," said Roscoe. "He's all wind anyway. He was an Army Supply Sergeant during the war."

"In the rear with the gear," said Robbie. "Probably tells war stories all the time. So, would anyone here like me to get them something like a magazine or anything?" Just as Robbie finished talking, the person in charge of the volunteers walked over to him.

"I'd like to see you in the office," he said. "Please come with me."

"Oh no, I'm going to the principal's office," said Robbie. The patients who were still there and waiting on lab work started laughing.

"Leave him alone," said Roscoe. "That fat fuck needed someone to straighten him out."

"Gentlemen, please excuse us," said Robbie's boss.

"Don't let him spank you," yelled Roscoe as they were leaving. "He might want you to spank him back." The other patients laughed again.

When they got to the office, the boss asked Robbie to have a seat. "I got a call that said one of my volunteers was getting into it with a patient," said the boss. "We will not tolerate anyone giving a patient a hard time. Do you understand?"

"Tell you something there Mr.," started Robbie. "I will not allow anyone to call me names and threaten me. That goes for everyone, patient or not."

"Mr. Parker, if I get any more reports about your bad behavior, your services will not be needed out here," said the boss.

"Well don't you worry yourself at all," said Robbie. "If I git into it with anyone else out here, patient or otherwise, I'll quit and save you a speech."

"I don't understand your attitude," said the boss.

"It's not an attitude. It's just the way I am," said Robbie. "I won't allow myself to be abused whether it's verbal or physical. If you don't mind if someone calls you names and threatens you that's your business. I'm not that way."

"Well try to control yourself as best you can," said the boss.

"I always do," said Robbie. "I'll be here a couple more hours and then I'm leaving. I'll be back when I can." The head of volunteers didn't say a word. He just nodded his head as Robbie left the office. Robbie went back over to the lab waiting area. Roscoe was still there waiting.

"You didn't get a paddlin' did you?" asked Roscoe.

"No, he just cracked my knuckles with a yard stick," said Robbie.

"Don't worry about that fella," said Roscoe. "He's just a volunteer too. I hear he was a clerk typist in the army. Probably don't know which end of a rifle the bullet comes out."

"Well there's gotta be people like that," said Robbie. "You know how the government is about paperwork. You gotta have paperwork. So you've been waiting a good while haven't you."

"I'm next," said Roscoe. "I didn't mind the wait. Someone put a show on for us this morning anyway. Well they just called my number. Maybe I'll see you around sometime."

"Nice meeting you Roscoe," said Robbie. "Take care of yourself."

~~~~

Three weeks went by and Robbie was fairly busy at the funeral home. The first week there had been two funerals. The second week there had been three and three again during the third week. Robbie had only been out to the VA two times during those three weeks. There had been no incidents. Robbie received a letter from Carl Sims. Carl was doing well. He got his job at his uncle's lumber yard and had married his girlfriend. He was looking forward to seeing Robbie. Robbie was a little concerned because he had not received a letter from Helen. It had been a good while since he had written her. Was something wrong.? Why hadn't she written?

Chapter Twelve

The last time Helen and Robbie had made love, she had complained of having some pain in her back. She just assumed that she had wrenched her back or injured a muscle or something. During the next few weeks the pain had gotten worse and had spread to her hips. She talked with her father and told him her symptoms. He recommended that she see a specialist. This specialist sent her to an oncologist. The news was not good. Helen had bone cancer and it was spreading fast. Any treatment they did would not save her. She would be lucky if she made it another year. The pain would become unbearable even with the strongest pain medications available.

When Helen told her father and mother the news, they sat down and had a good cry. "You need to tell your young man," said Helen's father. "He should know."

"I just can't tell him," said Helen. "He has already suffered a terrible loss. Another one could do him in."

"He still should know," said her father. "Robbie's a good man. He has a strong mind."

"Would you tell him for me Papa?" asked Helen. "I don't have the strength."

"We'll wait a few days and give you some more time to think about it," said her father.

"That will be fine," said Helen. "Maybe in a few days the shock of this will have worn off some. Thank you Papa."

A couple of days later, a big storm was expected and the waves on the north shore would be huge. Warnings would be posted letting surfers know the danger. Helen took her board and went to the north shore. There were a few surfers there but none of them went out. By late afternoon all of the other surfers had gone. Helen got on her board and paddled out to catch the waves. The next morning Helen's board was found on the beach. The surfers that had found it knew for sure that it was Helen's. Helen had been a regular here for many years and she was very well known. They also recognized her car in the parking area. Later that day her body was spotted by another surfer as it was being tossed about in the waves. A small memorial service was held two days later.

Helen's parents grieved for a few days and then decided that Robbie should know. Her father sat down and wrote Robbie the following letter.

My Dearest Robbie,

I am having a hard time getting these words out. There is no good way to say this. Our beautiful Helen is gone. We discovered that she had bone cancer. It was advancing quickly. Helen couldn't bring herself to tell you. They had told her that she might only live another year even with the best treatment available. I hate to think that my daughter took her own life but she went out surfing by herself and her body was found the next day. We had a small memorial service for her. I know there is nothing that I can say that will help your pain. I know that you two loved each other deeply. If there is anything I can do for you please let me know.

William Carter

Robbie had been at the funeral home for most of the day. When he got home his mother told him that he had received a letter. It was from Helen's father, not Helen. Robbie took the letter and went to the living room. He sat on the couch and stared at the letter wondering why the letter was from Helen's father and not Helen. After a few minutes he opened the letter. As he read, the tears began flowing. Robbie dropped the letter on the floor and curled up into a ball and cried loudly. Mary had been in the kitchen and came out to see what was happening. She saw the letter on the floor and picked it up. As she read it, she began crying too. Robert had just gotten home from work. He came into the house and heard all of the crying and rushed into the living room to see what was happening. "What is it?" Robert cried. "Why are the both of you crying?"

"Helen's dead," said Mary. "Robbie just got a letter from her father." Robert started crying too. They all cried for several minutes. Robbie finally spoke.

"Is there something wrong with me?" said Robbie. "Am I cursed? First Maria and now Helen. Why? I don't understand."

"None of us will ever understand why some people are taken from us," said Robert. "But don't ever think that you are cursed. Some day that special someone will come along and you will have a wonderful life together. I wish I was better with words."

"You're doing fine," said Mary. "All of the words in the world cannot help right now. Time is the great healer." Robbie didn't say another word. He uncurled himself and stood up and hugged his parents. He spent the rest of the day in his room. He didn't come out for dinner that evening.

The next day Robbie called Abner and told him he would not be available for a few days and explained why. Abner had no problems with this. Robbie ate a little food that day but he felt that his stomach was tied up in knots and he had no appetite. The next day he decided he would go to Cincinnati and go apartment shopping. Mary suggested that he should stop at the school and check their bulletin board. Maybe there would be someone who would be attending and they would like a roommate to help share expenses.

Robbie found the student's bulletin board and there was one person who had a two bedroom apartment and needed another person to help split costs. Their previous partner would be graduating at the end of this semester and moving out. Robbie wrote down the phone number and then went apartment shopping. There was absolutely nothing available within a five mile radius of the school. That is, there was nothing available where Robbie would be willing to live. It wasn't because of ghettos or anything. They were all nice places. It was that they were just way too expensive. Robbie found some houses where he could rent a room but he wouldn't even have his own bathroom and there were no close laundromats. Robbie spent almost the whole day in Cincinnati. It was after five o'clock now and Robbie headed for home. It took him a good while to get out of Cincinnati because of rush hour traffic. When he got back home his parents were just finishing their dinner.

"Pull up a chair son and tell us about your day," said Robert. "Have some of your mother's spaghetti. I think it's better that it usually is."

"Believe I will," said Robbie. "I kind of feel like my appetite is coming back." Mary got Robbie a plate and before he said another word it was empty. "That was good," said Robbie. "I'll have some more." Robbie filled his plate again but before he started eating again he told his parents about his day in Cincinnati. "Didn't have any luck today," said Robbie. "I took a number from a bulletin board at the school. There was someone who wants another roommate to share expenses. The person who had shared with them would be graduating and moving out. They didn't say anything about themselves but it is a two bedroom apartment. It could be a girl I guess."

"I suppose you'll find out when you call," said Mary. "It won't matter what sex that person is as long as you two can get along."

"Well I'll call that number in the morning," said Robbie. "I think I'd like a beer now. Would you two like to join me? That is if we have any."

"I've been keeping a six pack in the frig here lately," said Robert. "That way it's there if you want it. No driving involved." Mary put the dirty dishes in the sink and they all had a beer. "That Halloween Dance at the VFW is getting closer," said Robbie. "You reckon you'll feel up to going Son?"

"I'll most likely be going," said Robbie. "I want to see you two tear up the dance floor. Who knows, maybe I'll get out there a little if I can find me a partner."

"I'm sure there'll be girls there," said Mary. "They'll see you and your good looks and be all over you."

"Yes and if there's too many of them I can beat them off with my cane," said Robbie. They all laughed. Robbie finished his beer and excused himself. He took an early shower and went to bed. The next thing he knew it was morning. Robbie was surprised that he had slept that long and that well. He had his breakfast and went for a walk around the neighborhood. When he got to Mrs. Wilson's house he could hear her dog barking. He saw the dog through the window but Mrs. Wilson was not there giving him the finger. "The old bat's probably taking a dump and can't come out to see it's me," said Robbie to himself. "Oh well, even old bat's gotta go too." Robbie finished his walk and got back home as his mother was fixing some lunch. Robbie ate his lunch and then decided to make his phone call. An answering machine picked up.

"This is Brandy Wisecup," it said. "Leave your name and number and I'll call you back when I can." Robbie left his name and number and said what the call was about.

"Well did you get ahold of anyone?" asked Mary.

"I got an answering machine," said Robbie. "Some girl named Brandy Wisecup was on the machine."

"So maybe she's the one with the apartment," said Mary.

"We'll see if she calls me back," said Robbie. "I suppose I could live with a girl. She's probably nice and has a boyfriend and such. I reckon I'll find out if she calls."

It was three o'clock in the afternoon when the phone rang. Mary answered the phone and yelled for Robbie. "It's the call you're expecting," said Mary as she handed the phone to Robbie.

"This is Robbie Parker," started Robbie. "Is this Brandy?"

"Yes this is Brandy," said Brandy. "If you are serious about sharing the apartment I think we should meet. Are you available this coming Saturday?"

"Yes I am," said Robbie. "Why don't we meet at the school and we can have lunch somewhere and talk if that would be all right with you."

"That's fine with me," said Brandy. "Would 11:30 AM be good for you?"

"Yes, that's good for me," said Robbie. "I will see you then and thanks for calling."

"We'll meet right at the bulletin board," said Brandy. "Goodbye."

"I'll be going back to Cincinnati on Saturday and meeting Brandy," said Robbie. "We'll be going to lunch and discussing things."

"I hope things work out for you," said Mary. "If they don't there's still plenty of time to find a place."

Saturday came and Robbie was at the school. He had gotten there a little early and took another look at the campus. At 11:25 he was at the bulletin board. No one else was around. At exactly 11:30 a girl arrived. She was tall, five foot eight or nine, long blonde hair, and very well built. She was not beautiful but she was very good looking. She walked over to Robbie. "Robbie Parker?" she said.

"Yes, I am Robbie Parker and you are Brandy Wisecup?" said Robbie.

"I am Brandy," she said as she extended her hand to Robbie. "Well let's have our lunch and talk. Is there any place special you'd like to go?"

"No, you pick the place and I'll drive," said Robbie.

"All right, there's this little diner I like to visit once in a while," said Brandy. Brandy hadn't noticed Robbie's cane when she first saw him but she saw it as they walked to his car. She never said anything about it. When they got to Robbie's car, he opened the door for her.

"You don't need to do that," said Brandy. "I'm perfectly capable of opening my own door."

"I can see that you are but the men in my family open doors for women," said Robbie. "That's the way we were raised."

"So will we argue about who picks up the lunch tab?" asked Brandy as she got into the car.

"No we won't," said Robbie. "We aren't on a date and you're not my wife. We'll go dutch."

"Well I like your car Robbie," said Brandy. "My dad had a big Olds like this. I drove it a lot when I first started driving. Now I drive a Volkswagen bug. Gets very good mileage." They arrived at the diner and Brandy was out of the car before Robbie could get her door opened. He did open the door to the diner. They got their food ordered and Brandy started asking Robbie questions about himself.

"So you will be a student at CCMS?" asked Brandy.

"Yes I will," answered Robbie. "I'll be starting the next semester. I intend to get my Bachelor's."

"Why do you want to be a mortician?" asked Brandy. "Is it a family thing for you?"

"No, it's not a family thing," said Robbie. "I decided to do something where there would always be a demand. People will always die and the bodies will always need taken care of."

"So being around stiffs doesn't bother you?" asked Brandy.

"I've been around a lot of death," said Robbie. "It doesn't bother me."

"I bet you're a Vietnam Vet," said Brandy. "I noticed your cane but didn't want to say anything."

"Yes, I am a Vietnam Vet. I just got discharged not long ago," said Robbie. "Can we please not talk politics?"

"Well I'm against the war myself but we won't discuss it," said Brandy. "So Robbie, would you be a good renter? Will there be any financial problems? Are you neat? Will you cleanup your own dirty dishes? Do you have any bad habits that I should know about? Do you drink and do you smoke dope or drop acid?"

"There will be no financial problems," started Robbie. "I have my GI Bill and disability pay, plus I have plenty of money saved. I am currently working at a small funeral parlor in Columbus right now. I am a neat person and I clean up my own messes. I have a beer once in a while but I have never used any drugs. I don't steal and I would hurt anyone who steals from me. I won't allow anyone to slander my family. Now maybe you should tell me about yourself."

"Well I'm here to carry on the family business," started Brandy. "My family has been in the business since the 1870's. I'm from Toledo. I am a neat person outside of my room but I am a slob in my room. I cook some and I always clean up my messes. I have been known to get drunk once in a while and have smoked pot on occasion. I don't buy it. If I go somewhere and someone else has some and offers it to me, I usually have some. I won't drink a beer from the frig that I know is not mine. I have boys over from time to time but there is no one serious. How about you? Is there a girl in your life?"

"Not right at the moment," said Robbie.

"I find that hard to believe," said Brandy. "You're a nice looking fellow."

"I'll tell you this right now and we will never discuss it again," said Robbie. "My girlfriend just recently died. She had bone cancer. There was another girl before her that I was going to marry after I got out of the service but she was killed during an armed robbery at a convenience store when I was overseas."

"I am so sorry," said Brandy. "I will never ask you about anything like this again. So Robbie Parker. I bet you were a Marine. You look like a Marine to me."

"Yes I was a Marine," said Robbie.

"So what was it like over there?" asked Brandy.

"You don't really want to know," said Robbie. "We were all just a bunch of young men trying to keep ourselves and each other alive. We won't discuss this anymore either."

"So you were apparently wounded," said Brandy. "Will you always need that cane?"

"I fully intend to throw this cane away one day," said Robbie. "I used to be a really good dancer and fully expect to be cutting a rug in no time."

"What's cutting a rug?" asked Brandy. "I never heard that before."

"It's dancing," said Robbie. "I guess it is an older saying."

"So you think you're a good dancer," said Brandy. "I love to dance too. Maybe one day we can cut a rug. So let's finish eating and I'll show you the apartment." They finished their food and headed to the car. Brandy beat Robbie to the car so he couldn't open the door for her.

Robbie was impressed when they got to the apartment. It was totally furnished. Both bedrooms had a queen sized bed. There was plenty of closet space and a huge chest of drawers in both bedrooms. The living room furniture was nice and there was plenty of cookware and utensils in the kitchen. There was also a washer and dryer. At first Robbie thought that the rent was high but when Brandy told him that the water, electric, and heat was included in the price, he realized that it was a very good price. "I will stay here if you'll have me," said Robbie.

"You can start moving in a couple of days before the semester starts," said Brandy.

"Will I need to sign anything like a lease or something?" asked Robbie.

"To be all legal and such we should have you sign something," said Brandy. "But I've got a good lawyer in the family and he can take care of just about anything or anybody. I will give you a receipt every month when you pay me."

"I can pay the first month's rent now if you'd like," said Robbie.

"Just give me half now and the rest when you move in," said Brandy. Robbie paid her and she wrote him out a receipt. "Would you take me back over to my car?" asked Brandy. "I'll need it shortly."

"Let's go," said Robbie. Again Brandy beat Robbie to the car so he couldn't open her door. The apartment was only two miles from the school so they were there in no time.

"So we have each other's phone number so if anything comes up or happens we can call," said Brandy. "I hope nothing does and we'll see each other in January."

"I hope so too," said Robbie. "See you in January."

Robbie got home and gave his parents the news. That evening Robbie and his dad went to the VFW. Ole Jessie was there at a table so they sat with him. Jake was tending bar that evening. They were enjoying their drinks and talking when Randy White came in. Randy hadn't noticed Robbie. He sat at the bar. "There's that shithead," said Robbie. Robert could see that Robbie was looking at Randy.

"So you know Randy?" asked Robert.

"Yeh, I met that shithead at the VA a while back," said Robbie. "We had some words."

"That doesn't surprise me," said Robert. "I'll just about bet he called you a couple of names and was gonna kick your ass."

"Yep, that's about right," said Robbie.

"Well don't worry about him," said Robert. "He's a big blowhard. He's always saying he's gonna kick someone's ass. He used to hang out at the Legion a good bit but several of the fellas politely asked him not to come back unless he could control that loud mouth of his. I've almost punched him a few times." After a few minutes, they could hear Randy giving some lip to Jake at the bar. Randy was gonna kick Jake's ass.

"Get the fuck outta here and I mean right now," yelled Jake. "Don't ever come in here again when I'm tending bar. I won't serve you. Now git." Randy finished his drink and left without saying another word. They needed more drinks at their table so Robbie went up to the bar to get them.

"What was that all about?" Robbie asked Jake.

"That was just Randy being Randy," said Jake. "That man is just an asshole. I'm tired of it. He can go be an asshole somewhere else."

"Maybe when he was a baby his momma used to rock him to sleep using big rocks," said Robbie. Jake let out a laugh.

"Well whatever she did didn't do any good," said Jake. "Maybe he took asshole lessons somewhere. Something happened sometime to make him this way. He'll probably straighten out when he's about to die. So do you know him?"

"Yeh, I had a run in with him when I was out doing some volunteer work at the VA," said Robbie. "I found out what a sweet guy he really is."

"So what did you think of the VA?" asked Jake.

"It's too soon to tell," said Robbie. "I went out a couple of times and then we got busy at work so I haven't been back in over three weeks. I'll probably get back out there soon unless work gets busy again."

"So you're working at the funeral home huh?" said Jake. "How's things going for you so far?"

"It's been good so far," said Robbie. "The worst thing that's happened so far was when we had a service for a soldier who was killed in Vietnam. As everybody was leaving, some long haired guy asked me how many babies I've killed."

"Did you punch his lights out?" asked Jake.

"No, he was gone before I could even think about what he had just said to me," said Robbie.

"Some of the things that people been saying and doing to the Vietnam Vets is a disgrace," said Jake. "I don't understand it at all."

"I don't understand either," said Robbie. "I better get these drinks over to the table. Ole Jessie'll be dying of thirst." Robbie took the drinks over to the table.

"So Jake kicked the windbag out?" asked Robert.

"Yep, he did. He said Randy was just being Randy," said Robbie. "So Jessie, how's your wife doing?"

"She does all right," said Jessie. "Her arthritis is starting to act up more now that it's a little cooler outside. She won't take them pills they give her for the pain. She's funny about taking pills."

"So do you two have any children?" asked Robbie.

"We had a boy and a girl," said Jessie. "We lost them both during the war. Our daughter was over in England and got killed in an air raid. Our boy was killed on Guadalcanal. He was a Marine too. He knew Chesty Puller. You heard of him haven't you?"

"Sure, every Marine knows who Chesty Puller was," said Robbie. "I'm sorry for your loss. I hope I didn't stir up bad memories."

"No, I was just thinking about them two again," said Jessie. "Seems like whenever it starts getting close to Veterans Day I start thinking about them two real hard. Our girl Denise was a nurse. She went over and joined up to help out the British way before we was even in the war. Jessie Jr. joined the Corps the day after they bombed Pearl Harbor. We was proud of them two. Still are." They all had another drink and left.

Things were very busy at the funeral home and Robbie didn't get out to the VA till almost Halloween. There were no incidents at the VA. Robbie still couldn't get some of the patients in the dorms to talk with him. He saw Roscoe Samuels one day as he was waiting for an eye examination. They talked for a few minutes.

Robbie was looking forward to the Halloween Dance at the VFW. He made up his mind that he was going to get out on the floor and see what he could do without hurting himself too badly. Robbie hadn't had a haircut since he had been home. His hair was maybe four inches long on top and was getting a little scraggly around his ears. He went to the barber shop that his father and he had always used. The same barber, Ole Red, was still there. He was sitting in the barber chair reading a Playboy. He recognized Robbie right away. "I reckon if you're in here you're not gonna let your hair grow and be one of them hippie types," said Red.

"I don't think so," said Robbie. "I don't think I could stand to have my hair blowing in my face. It would get in the way when I'm kissing some girl too. Just give me a trim around the ears and leave the top alone. No white sidewalls either."

"I can do that," said Red. "So how's the world treating you since you been home?"

"All right I guess," said Robbie. "I've been working at Fulbright's. I'll be going to mortician school in January."

"How's business at Fulbright's? Dead?" said Red.

"You know Red, that the first time someone's said that to me since I've been working there," said Robbie. "I doubt it'll be the last. So does your wife know you're looking at that Playboy?"

"Hell, she buys them for me," said Red. "She figures if I look at them young girls and get all worked up, it'll help her out."

"Sounds like sound wisdom," said Robbie. "I remember when someone in my platoon got a copy of the December '68 issue with Cynthia Myers. Everyone was in love."

"I still have that issue," said Red. "That woman's got about the best set of tits I ever did see."

"Yeh, we had a standing order that when the magazine got passed around, there could be no pages stuck together," said Robbie. Red let out a good laugh.

"I guess that could be a problem," said Red. "We better talk about something else. I might have to close early and go home."

"So Red, I bet your business is way down since so many guys are letting their hair grow," said Robbie.

"It sure is," said Red. "The old timers still come in regularly, but the young boys and men either don't get their hair cut at all, or not very often. Maybe it's a phase. Things'll change in a few years. I had a nephew of mine go to that Woodstock thing back in August. That boy musta taken some a that LSD when he was there cause he's been really strange ever since then. All he wants to do now is get high. My sister can't get him to do nothing. Maybe they'll draft his ass. I'd kick his ass out if he was my kid."

"So what are your kids up to?" asked Robbie.

"Both of the girls are school teachers now," said Red. "They graduated from Ohio State last year and one of them is in Dayton and the other one is in Martin's Ferry. It hurt us bad sending both of them to college at the same time. The wife got a job and helped out. She quit her job right after they graduated. Having twins is tough but if you only want two kids to start with, you get it over quicker. How many kids you figurin' on cranking out?"

"I have never thought about that," answered Robbie. "I guess maybe as many as I can afford."

"If you wait on what you can afford you'll never have any," said Red.

"I have a lot of years to think about a family," said Robbie. "I'm still only nineteen."

"Well you're a full grown man," said Red as he was cleaning the hair from Robbie's neck and shoulders.

"What do I owe you?" asked Robbie.

"Same as it was last time you was here," answered Red. "Still $3.00."

Robbie handed him $4.00, thanked him, and left.

~~~~

When they got to the VFW for the Halloween Dance, the parking lot was packed. "Got us a good crowd," said Robert. "There should be plenty of young women here tonight. You'll have your hands full son." Robbie just smiled at his mother and they went inside. The band was set up in a corner and a large area was cleared for a dance floor. There was one empty table in the back and a lot of people still not seated so they grabbed it. Robbie went to the bar and got them all a beer. The band got tuned up and was about to start. Robert took a look at the band. "Them boys all have long hair," said Robert. "I hope they don't play a lot of that new stuff. They call it acid rock don't they?"

"Yes they do Dad, but I bet they'll play what the crowd wants," said Robbie. "You know these older Veterans won't put up with music they don't like."

"That's true," said Robert. "That band'll mix it up or they won't get asked back."

Robbie started looking around the place. He was surprised. There were a lot of good looking young girls there. He was under the impression that nowadays young people didn't want to hang out with older folks. "Don't think too much Robbie," he said to himself. "You're here and they're here so just have a good time." It got quiet. Someone went to the stage and made a few announcements on the microphone and then the band started. Robbie about fell out of his chair when they started with "Runaround Sue." "Just like the Prom," he mumbled under his breath.

Robert grabbed Mary's arm and led her to the dance floor. They were the first couple dancing. Robbie could tell that the crowd was amazed at his parents abilities. Robbie was about to get out of his chair and ask a girl to dance when a nice looking blonde tapped him on the shoulder. "Hi, I'm Tina," she said. "Let's go." Robbie was surprised. He smiled at Tina and stood. Tina saw his cane as he laid it on the table.

"I'm Robbie," said Robbie. "Don't worry about that cane. I think I can get around some without it." He took her arm and they went to the dance floor. "Can you jitterbug?" Robbie asked Tina.

"I never have," said Tina. "I'm willing to learn."

"Well hang on and follow me as best you can," said Robbie. "I won't be as smooth as that other gentleman out here but we'll do fine." There was only one verse left in the song when they started but they made the most of it. When the song ended, There were still only two couples on the dance floor.

"Let's stay out for the next song," said Tina. "You're good. I don't want you getting away just yet."

"We'll see what they play," said Robbie. Robert and Mary stayed on the floor too and waited for the next song. The band broke into "Fortunate Son." Robert and Mary looked at each other for a moment and then went back to their table. Robbie and Tina had at it. Soon there were other younger couples on the dance floor. Robbie didn't know what type of dance they were doing but they were having fun. "That's what dancing is all about," Robbie said to himself. The song ended and everyone clapped and cheered. Robbie was about to tell Tina he needed to sit for a while and rest his leg, but the band broke into a slow song. Tina gave him the right look and he stayed. She pulled herself close to him. When the song ended, Robbie took her arm to escort her to her table.

There were three other young girls at the table. Tina introduced them to Robbie. "Robbie, this is Anna, Debbie, and Sharon," said Tina. "Girls, this is Robbie."

"I'm pleased to meet all of you," said Robbie. He pulled out Tina's chair for her. "Thank you for the dances Tina. Maybe we'll dance some more this evening."

"You can't leave now Robbie," said Tina. "You need to stay here with us. We're not letting you get away."

"Well let me get my cane and I'll be right back," said Robbie. Robbie went to his parent's table. "I'll be joining those young ladies over there," said Robbie to them. "I'll probably see you back on the dance floor in a bit after I rest my leg some."

"You better make sure you give all of those girls a chance," said Mary.

"I will Mom," said Robbie as he was leaving.

When Robbie had left to get his cane, the girls were talking among themselves. "Where did you find him?" Sharon asked Tina. "That man can dance. I mean he's good."

"I bet that's not all he's good at," said Debbie. "They say that guys who can dance are real good at other things if you know what I mean."

"I know what you mean," said Tina. "You are acting like little girls. Cool your jets." Robbie was at the table now.

"What were you girls talking about while I was gone?" asked Robbie.

"We were talking about you," said Anna. "You have any friends around that look as good as you and can dance as good as you?"

"Sorry, I'm it," said Robbie. "There's nobody else like me around. Just kidding. That older couple that you saw on the dance floor were my parents. They taught me how to dance. Some of the guys I went to school with could dance well, but I haven't seen any of them since I've been home. One of them was killed over there."

"All of us girls have a relative or know someone who was over there," said Tina. "How was it over there? What did you do over there?"

"I was a Marine grunt," answered Robbie. "All we did over there was try to keep each other alive."

"What's a grunt?" asked Anna.

"That's an infantryman," answered Robbie.

"So apparently you were wounded," said Tina.

"Yes, more than once too," said Robbie. "Now let's talk about something else. What are you ladies going to do now that you're out of school? I assume you're out of school."

"We are out of high school and all of us are going to college," said Tina. "Sharon and I are at Ohio State and Anna and Debbie go to Capital University. What are you doing now that you are a civilian?"

"You girls could never guess in a million years," said Robbie. "Maybe two million."

"I give up already," said Tina. "Tell us."

"Well I'm going to be a mortician," said Robbie.

"Oh gross, I could never do that," said Debbie. "A corpse would flip me out."

"Me too," said Anna. "How could anyone do that?"

"Hey, people are always going to die and the bodies will always need care," said Robbie. "Somebody's got to do it. I can handle it."

"So do you go to a school for something like that?" asked Tina.

"Yes, I'm starting at the Cincinnati College of Mortuary Science in January," answered Robbie. "I've been working some at Fulbright's Funeral Home already."

"So you have a lot of time before you leave," said Tina. "Maybe you can take me out sometime."

"I might," said Robbie. "I'll tell you right now that I'm not interested in a full time relationship."

"Why's that?" asked Debbie. "Did some girl do you wrong?"

"No, that's not it," said Robbie. "Actually it's none of your business, but I'll tell you anyway. While I was overseas, the girl I was going to marry was killed in an armed robbery. That seems like a long time ago. Not long ago, another girl I loved died from bone cancer."

"We're sorry for your losses," said Tina. "I'm not ready for a serious relationship either. We could go out and just have a good time."

"And don't forget about us," said Debbie. "We have no intention of being serious yet either."

"We'll see," said Robbie. "Who wants to dance now?" Before the other girls could answer, Tina grabbed Robbie and took him to the dance floor. "You're not the least bit forward, are you Tina?" asked Robbie.

"Not the least bit," said Tina. "I saw you first." They danced two songs and then went back to the table.

"I'm next," said Anna. "As soon as you're rested, we're going."

"Your wish is my command," said Robbie. The band played three more songs and then Robbie and Anna went to the dance floor. The next song was a slow song. Robbie pulled Anna close. Anna was a very well built girl. Her dress was very tight and showed off her curves. She put her head against Robbie's neck. Robbie could feel himself getting aroused. Anna could feel him too.

"Is that a big stick in your pocket or are you glad I'm here?" asked Anna.

"Hey, I'm not dead," said Robbie. "Maybe we better go sit down."

"No, let's finish this song and do one more," said Anna as she kissed him on the neck. That kiss made things worse. Robbie held her even tighter. It wasn't because he wanted her, even though he did. He just didn't want the whole world to see what he had going on down below.

"It's a good thing the lights are low," said Robbie. "Everyone would know what I was thinking if they weren't."

"You know we can get out of here for a while," said Anna. "What kind of car do you have?"

"I didn't drive tonight," said Robbie. "I came with my parents."

"Well you might not be leaving with them," said Anna. "Tina drove all of us here but I'm sure she wouldn't mind taking you along."

"I'm not ready for that," said Robbie.

"It sure didn't feel like that to me," said Anna. "I never said anything about getting married. I'd just like to have some good sex with you."

"What about Tina and the others?" asked Robbie.

"I'd say that they want some sex too," said Anna.

"Well maybe another day but not tonight," said Robbie. "I'll get everyone's phone numbers before we leave tonight." The song ended and the band announced that they were taking a break. When they went back to the table, Robbie held his arms and hands in front of him and stayed close behind Anna.

"I'm next," said Debbie. "Soon as they start back up, I'm next." Robbie never said a word. He just sat there and smiled. Sharon had gone to the bar and gotten all of them another beer.

"Did I miss anything?" asked Sharon.

"Just that I'm next," said Debbie. "I guess that makes you last."

"Well, save the best for last," said Sharon.

"You know there's other guys here," said Robbie.

"Yes, but they don't move like you," said Tina.

The band was back in fifteen minutes. Debbie took Robbie's arm and led him to the dance floor. They danced two songs and then went back to the table. "I'll rest my leg for a while and then Sharon and I will have at it," said Robbie. The band was playing some country songs now. A lot of the older folks were up dancing now. After ten minutes, Robbie decided it was time to dance and he escorted Sharon to the dance floor. The next song they played was a country song and it was a slow song. Sharon pulled herself tight against him. All four of these girls were very attractive. Robbie could feel himself getting aroused again. Sharon could feel him too. She looked up at him and smiled. Robbie tried to think of something else. Who won the World Series last year? Who's the best shortstop in baseball? What's the formula for finding the area of a circle? Nothing worked. The next song was another slow song. "What's this," Robbie said to himself. "No band ever plays two slow songs in a row." Sharon was not about to let Robbie go just yet. Finally the song was over. They went back to the table. "All right ladies, I give up," said Robbie. "I'll spend the night with one of you."

"Why not two of us," asked Anna.

"I don't know about that," said Robbie. "I've never done that before."

"You'll know what to do I'm sure," said Sharon. "Now how are we going to do this?"

"One at a time or not at all," said Robbie. "Make up your mind."

"I found him first," said Tina. "He's mine."

"Well you girls can figure out the rest," said Robbie. "I'd like to go now if we could."

"Can you girls get a ride home or do you need me to take you?" asked Tina.

"You go on," said Anna. "We'll get us a ride. You have fun now." Phone numbers were exchanged.

Robbie went over to his parents and told them what was happening. "Make sure you have some protection," said Mary. "We'll see you tomorrow." Tina and Robbie left. Tina's car was a 1966 Corvair. Robbie had never been in one and was kind of amazed. Tina had an apartment on the west side of town. It took them twenty minutes to get there. As soon as they got inside the clothes went flying. When they woke up the next morning they were laying on the kitchen floor. They had not made it to the bed. Tina decided they should do something about that so they started all over again. This time they started in the bed. Around ten o'clock Tina made them some coffee and breakfast. Tina looked at Robbie and smiled. "That was nice wasn't it?" said Tina. "I think you needed that. I know I wanted it."

"Well you sure as hell got it," said Robbie. "I need to go home and get some rest. Can you take me home shortly?"

"Sure, I'll take you home," said Tina. "When do you think we can do that again?"

"I don't know," said Robbie. "I never know my work schedule. Abner Fulbright calls me when we get customers. Sometimes we're really busy and other times we aren't. I'll have to wait and see." They finished their breakfast and Tina took Robbie home.

"I'll tell the others to be ready for a great time," said Tina as she was leaving Robbie's house.

Robert and Mary were at the kitchen table having some coffee when Robbie arrived home. "How was your evening and night?" asked Robert.

"It was interesting and intense," answered Robbie.

"Which one of them did you end up with?" asked Mary.

"Tina," answered Robbie.

"Does she have a last name?" asked Mary.

"I suppose she does but I don't know what it is," answered Robbie. "She doesn't know my last name either."

"What about them other girls?" asked Robert.

"There's Debbie, Anna, and Sharon, and I don't know their last names either," answered Robbie. "Apparently they just want me for sex. This must be some of that free love I've heard about. Anyway, last night was just meaningless sex."

"I hope you used protection," said Robert. "If a girl is going to give it away that easily, she must do it regularly and have different partners."

"I always use protection Dad," said Robbie. "I'm not ready to be a father and I don't want the clap or something worse. You know, I just don't understand why them girls were after me. There were plenty of young men there."

"There were a lot of young men there, but there wasn't one of them who could move like you on the dance floor," said Mary. "They probably figured if you could move like that on the dance floor, you would be good at other things."

"Would you think that if you saw a man dancing good?" asked Robbie.

"I have your father," answered Mary. "I know he's good. So will you see the other three girls sometime?"

"I'm not sure," answered Robbie. "I'm starting to feel a little guilty now. It hasn't been long since Helen has been gone."

"Well Son, those young girls were very attractive," said Mary. "They could be hard to resist. I'm sure Helen wouldn't want you to become a priest."

"I could never be a priest," said Robbie. "I'd be breaking my vows regularly. Whose idea was it that priests or nuns couldn't have sex? That doesn't make sense at all. Aren't people supposed to be fruitful and multiply?"

"Yes they are," said Robert. "That stuff about abstinence has got to do with purity or something I think. I thinks it's silly too. Anyway, if you're going to be a lady's man, keep your wits about you. There could be jealous ex boyfriends and such out there. If you see all of them girls, then that could be multiplied."

"I'll be thinking with the right head," said Robbie.

Chapter Thirteen

Business was slow at the funeral home so Robbie was able to go out to the VA several times in early November. Some of the patients in the dorms were finally starting to talk to Robbie. One patient came up behind Robbie and grabbed him but Robbie stomped his foot and he let go. The patient went right back to his bed and laid down. A nurse had seen what had happened and didn't seem concerned. The next time Robbie saw that patient, they talked as if nothing had happened.

Veterans Day came and there was a parade in town. Robbie and his parents went to watch. There were some war protesters around but they weren't doing anything out of line. Things got busy at the funeral home the next two weeks. Robbie never made it to the VA those two weeks. At one of the viewings during those two weeks, Anna showed up. Robbie never knew her last name so he was surprised when he saw her there. He was helping greet people when Anna came in with some people who appeared to be her parents. She was wearing clothing that Robbie thought was a little inappropriate for a viewing, but Robbie thought she was looking really good. She was wearing a very tight fitting black dress. It was well above the knees and low cut. She wore a strand of pearls around her neck. When she saw Robbie, she excused herself from her parents and went over to talk with him.

"Why haven't you called me?" asked Anna. "I've been thinking about you. I bet you've been thinking about me too."

"Hey, I'm not dead," said Robbie. "I must say, that dress you're almost wearing fits very well. Don't you think it's a little much for this."

"I believe in advertising," said Anna. "If you got it, show it. I've been thinking that I might get a job at a strip club. I hear a girl can make a lot of money doing that."

"Well we can't be talking about that right now," said Robbie.

"Well I expect to get a call from you in the next day or two," said Anna. "If I don't, I'll go right to your house. I know where you live. Tina told all of us."

"You'll be hearing from me," said Robbie. "Now why are you here? Is the deceased a relative or something?"

"No, he was just a good friend of the family," said Anna. "I'm going to go pay my respects now. Don't forget to call me."

"I won't forget Anna," said Robbie. "Expect a call day after tomorrow." Anna smiled and got in the receiving line. Robbie stayed out front greeting people. Through a window he could see Anna mingling with people. He could see that most of the men had a hard time not looking at her. After about a half hour, Anna and her parents left. As they were leaving, Anna put her right hand on the left side of Robbie's face and smiled. She never said a word.

After everyone had left, Abner came over to Robbie. "Who was that captivating young girl?" asked Abner. "It looked like she knows you."

"I met her at a dance a while back," said Robbie. "Her name's Anna and I don't know her last name. The deceased was a friend of her family."

"Well you watch out for that girl," said Abner. "She looks like she could hurt you bad."

"Yes she does," said Robbie. "I reckon I'll have to find out."

"Well be careful," said Abner. "You're young. You'll be all right."

~~~~

Robbie's time with Anna was about the same as it was with Tina. The only difference was that Anna was very acrobatic. Robbie was amazed at some of the positions that Anna could get into and not hurt herself. They had some coffee and breakfast and talked a little the next morning. "So what do you think Robbie?" asked Anna. "Do you think I'd do all right as a stripper?"

"I think you could make plenty of money," said Robbie. "You have a figure that a lot of girls would die for and the way you can move is amazing. You say you like to advertise. You'll do well."

"Would you pay to see me?" asked Anna.

"I don't have to or need to," answered Robbie. "But I'm sure others would."

"I think I'd be a hooker too if I could be choosey when it came to my clients," said Anna. "I really like sex but I need good looking men."

"Well maybe one day down the road you could be a really high class call girl and have good looking rich men as your clients," said Robbie.

"That would be nice," said Anna. "If I can keep my looks, that might just happen. Speaking of happening, I think we should have at it again." Robbie never objected. An hour later, he was driving home.

~~~~

Thanksgiving came and Mary prepared a very fine meal. They had a big turkey and all the trimmings. Mary made pumpkin pie that was to die for. She made it out of real pumpkin, not canned pumpkin. They would have wonderful leftovers for several days. Cable TV had been in town for a while and Robert had gotten it installed for an early Christmas present. Robbie was never a big football fan, but with the cable, there were several games on. Robert had made sure there was plenty of beer on hand so they all enjoyed the games with a beer in their hands.

The next week Robbie decided to do some Christmas shopping. He had been to several different jewelry stores looking for something for his mother. He didn't want something really expensive. It needed to be something he thought she would really like. He was almost out the door when he almost ran into a girl who was coming in. He excused himself and started to move on and then he saw that it was Debbie. She was looking at him and hoping that he recognized her. He looked at her and smiled. "Hello Debbie, it's good to see you again," said Robbie. "How have you been?"

"I've been good Robbie," said Debbie. "I've thought about you some. I hope Tina and Anna didn't scare you off. Those two can be really aggressive at times."

"I guess you could call them aggressive," said Robbie. "So are you doing some shopping now?"

"Yes, I'm looking for something for my mother," said Debbie. "I want to get her something nice that I know she'll like. It can't be too expensive."

"That's what I'm doing too," said Robbie. "Why don't we get some lunch and do some shopping. That is if you have time."

"I have time and lunch sounds good," said Debbie. "There's a little bistro right down the street that has good food."

"Sounds good to me," said Robbie. "Let's go."

They went to the bistro and ordered their lunch. They did not speak to each other until after they had ordered their food. They both had some iced tea while they were waiting on their food. Robbie spoke first. "So Debbie, why did you ladies end up at the dance at the VFW?" asked Robbie. "I would think that girls with your looks would be at some big party somewhere."

"We have been to some really big parties the last couple of years," said Debbie. "We all decided to do something different this year. Our fathers all belong to the VFW. It was a little tame compared to what we've been doing. So are you a party animal?"

"No, not really," answered Robbie. "I guess I don't really like crowds that much but I do love to dance."

"Well you're very good at that," said Debbie. "Hey, before I forget to tell you, Anna took a job at a strip club. She works on weekends. She's been there a couple of weeks. She's made a lot of money so far. She says she really likes it. I couldn't do that. I am not an exhibitionist."

"She told me she was considering doing that and asked me if I thought she would do well," said Robbie. "I told her that she would do very well. She also said that she would like to be a hooker if she could be choosey about her clients."

"She has never said that to me, but it doesn't surprise me," said Debbie. "That girl likes her sex. She said that you were very good too. So did you have a good time with her and Tina?"

"I don't like to talk about my sexual experiences with other people," said Robbie. "Even if it was just meaningless sex, it was still personal. If they want to talk about it, that's their business. So Debbie, do you have a last name?"

"Yes I do," answered Debbie. "It's Ryan. And do you have a last name Robbie?"

"It's Parker," answered Robbie. "So Debbie Ryan, what kind of jewelry does your mother like?"

"She likes necklaces that aren't big and flashy," answered Debbie. "I bought her a necklace a few years ago that was just a gold chain with an ivory carved elephant on it. She loved it. I decided later on that I shouldn't buy anything made of ivory. I never knew about all the poaching that goes on in Africa. Anyway, my mother really liked it. She still wears it a lot. What does your mother like?"

"I think she's kind of like your mother," answered Robbie. "She doesn't like big and flashy. My parents visited me when I was in the hospital in Hawaii. I know she really liked the palm trees."

"I was in a store this morning that had just the necklace she would like," said Debbie. "It was a gold chain with a very small palm tree on it. The palm tree was gold too. We can go back to that store after our lunch if you'd like."

"That would be great," said Robbie. Their food came and they ate and had an enjoyable time. Robbie was kind of surprised. Debbie never said one word about having sex. "Would you be offended if I got the check?" asked Robbie.

"No, I will not be offended," said Debbie. "So this is kind of like a date, huh Robbie?"

"Maybe," said Robbie. "Maybe we can a real date another time."

"Maybe we can," said Debbie. "Now let's get that necklace for your mother and then I'll have time for one more store. I have a paper to write for school." Robbie paid the check and they went to the jewelry store where Debbie had seen the palm tree necklace. It was only two stores from the bistro. Robbie bought it and then they went to the other store.

The other store was about five blocks from the bistro so they just walked. They did a little window shopping and talking as they went. Debbie couldn't find anything that she thought her mother would really like. "Well I've got to get going now," said Debbie. "It was nice having lunch and shopping with you."

"Yes it was," said Robbie. "I hope you find something nice for your mother."

"I'm sure that I will," said Debbie. "Well my car is over this way. Thank you for lunch."

"You're most welcome," said Robbie. "Maybe we can go on a real date sometime."

"I'd like that," said Debbie. "Give me a call."

"I'll call you when I have an idea what my work schedule will be," said Robbie. "That should be in a day or two."

"I'll look forward to your call," said Debbie. She came close to Robbie and kissed him on the cheek. She backed away for a second and smiled. Then she turned and left. Robbie smiled at her and then walked to his car.

The next morning Abner called Robbie. They had two customers. Robbie went to the funeral home and he and Abner met with the relatives of the deceased and got everything set up. Robbie would be tied up every day this week but he would be free on the weekend. When he got home that afternoon, he went right to the phone and called Debbie. A woman answered the phone. "This is Robbie Parker," said Robbie. "Is Debbie there?"

"This is her mother," said the woman. "She's in class right now. I can have her call you or you can call back this evening. Her class is over at four but she doesn't always come straight home."

"I'll try back this evening around six," said Robbie. "And thank you Mrs. Ryan."

"You're welcome young man," said Mrs. Ryan. "I'll let her know you called as soon as she gets home. Goodbye."

Mary had heard Robbie on the phone. She looked at him and smiled after he hung up the phone. "So you're going on a date or something?" asked Mary.

"I reckon so," answered Robbie. "I ran into another one of those girls I met at the dance while I was doing some shopping. We're going out on a real date. We're not just going to hop in the sack."

"Well I hope you have a good time," said Mary. "There's a surprise for you in your room. I had a hard time dragging it in there. I think your stuff from the Marine Corps finally got here." Robbie went to his room. There were two sea bags leaning against the bed.

"Yep, that's my stuff," said Robbie. "Amazing, after all this time it finally got here."

"So will all of your decorations and citations be in there too?" asked Mary.

"They should be," answered Robbie. "I'll go through this stuff right now."

The first bag was all stateside uniforms. The second one had everything else in it. There was a pair of jungle boots and a set of camouflaged utilities and a bush hat on top. Next was two pair of stateside combat boots and a pair of dress shoes. Next came some small boxes. They contained all of his medals, citations, chevrons, rifle expert badge, and emblems. His platoon book from Boot Camp was there along with the Marine Corps Manual and his notebook from the rifle range. The rest of it was all cleaning and shaving equipment. Mary stopped by to see how he was doing.

"Is everything there?" she asked. "That looks like a lot of stuff."

"I think it is," said Robbie.

"You know we can get some frames and mount your citations on the wall if you'd like," said Mary.

"I don't think I want to do that right now," said Robbie. "I think I'll repack most of this stuff and keep out the things I might need some time."

"So did you get all of your medals and ribbons?" asked Mary. "I remember your father had a bunch of ribbons that he wore besides his Bronze Star."

"I believe they're all here," said Robbie. "Let's see. There's the Silver Star, two Bronze Stars, and three Purple Hearts. Then there's the Combat Action Ribbon, Presidential Unit Citation, Vietnam Service Medal, Vietnam Campaign Medal, Vietnamese Cross of Gallantry, Vietnamese Civil Action Ribbon, and the National Defense Service Medal. Damn, I never even heard of some of these."

"Maybe you should mount all of your ribbons like you were going to wear them on a dress uniform," said Mary. "That way if something came up and you wanted to wear your uniform for something, they would be ready."

"I could do that, but I'm not even sure what order they go in," said Robbie. "All I know is that the most important ones go first. After that I would have no idea."

"I bet that if you wanted to find out, a Marine Recruiter could help you," said Mary. "Or maybe there's another Marine Vietnam Vet over at the Legion or the VFW who would know."

"I'll see Mom," said Robbie. "I'm going to repack most of this stuff now." Mary could see that Robbie was a getting a little upset now.

"I'm sorry. I didn't mean to be a pest," said Mary. "I'll leave you alone now."

"You're not a pest Mom," said Robbie. "Sometimes I get a little upset when I think about everything that happened over there. I'll be all right shortly." Mary smiled at him and left.

Robbie put everything but his citations and medals in the sea bags and shoved them into the closet. He put the citations on the dresser and laid down on his bed. He laid there and stared at the citations. After about fifteen minutes, he got up and went over to the dresser. He picked up the one that was for his first Bronze Star and started reading. As he was reading, he started remembering what happened that day. He remembered the blood flowing from S/Sgt. Benjamin's leg as he put on the tourniquet. He also remembered the bones sticking out of Benjamin's leg wound and his arm wound. He quit reading and he swore that he could here Sims yelling at him. "Get the fuck down Parker. Get the fuck down." Then he felt himself being knocked backward a little as a bullet hit his left shoulder ripping his flak jacket and grazing his left shoulder. "What was that all about?" Robbie said to himself. "How could I feel that bullet hitting me. How could I hear Sims? He's not here. Get it together Robbie. You're home now." Robbie laid back down on his bed. He tried to think of something good. The next thing that popped into his head was when he cut the NVA soldier's throat with the K-bar that Rojas had given him. Robbie was getting pissed off now. He tried to think of other things but the war kept coming back. The next thing that popped into his head and wouldn't leave was when the mortar round had landed in the middle of the four pot smokers. Robbie couldn't get this out of his head. He kept saying what he had said to the man who had lost part of his left arm. He wasn't aware that he was speaking out loud. Mary came back to his room.

"Are you all right Robbie?" asked Mary. "I heard you talking. There's nobody else here is there?"

"Not that I know of Mom," said Robbie. "I think I was having some of them flashbacks or whatever they're called. I was talking to some boy who had part of his arm blown off. I'm sorry. Do we have any beer?"

"You father has been keeping some on hand," said Mary.

"Well how about you and me having one together?" said Robbie.

"You father should be home any minute now," said Mary. "Why don't we wait till he gets here and we can all have one together?"

"Sounds good Mom," said Robbie.

"You know Son, your father had terrible nightmares for a lot of years after he came home," said Mary. "I think he still has some every once in a while."

"He's never done anything crazy has he?" asked Robbie.

"No, he did think about seeing a shrink once, but decided against it," said Mary. "I guess he feels that he has everything under control. If you ever feel that you're being overwhelmed by things that happened over there, your father and I will be glad to talk about it with you. They have shrinks at the VA and they have support groups. Don't hesitate if you think you need help. You're a strong man Son. You will be all right." Just as she finished speaking, Robert pulled in the driveway. He came into the house and went to Mary and kissed her as he always did.

"So how's things with the two of you?" asked Robert. "I'm kind of thirsty. Why don't we all have a beer. I even picked up some more on the way home. Have you got dinner planned?"

"Nothing definite," said Mary.

"Well why don't we drink some beer and order a pizza for dinner," said Robert. "That one place has free delivery."

"I don't mind not cooking," said Mary. "Pizza sounds good. Is pizza all right with you Robbie?"

"I like pizza," said Robbie. "And I like beer too. Sounds good." Robbie got all of them a beer and they all sat down in the living room. "My stuff from the Corps finally made it here," said Robbie. "Two sea bags of it."

"Your stuff probably just sat somewhere and was forgotten for a while," said Robert. "I knew a lot of men who never did get their stuff after they had been wounded. A lot of them never cared either. They were just glad to be alive and home and nothing else mattered. We always said that if you can make it through all of this, then the rest of your life will be easy. Of course we spiced it up with some different words."

"You mean you guys cussed," said Robbie sarcastically.

"We sure did," said Robert. "Good cussing has been around for a long time. Where do you think your Drill Instructors learned to cuss? Good cussing has been passed down from generation to generation. Some people are real masters."

"You know when I was in Boot Camp I tried to count how many times the Drill Instructors would say "fuck" in a day," said Robbie. "But I couldn't keep count. Then I cut it down to how many times they would use it one sentence. Every time I thought they set a record, they would break it." Robbie and Robert started laughing. After a moment, Mary joined in the laughing. They finished a beer and then Mary ordered the pizza.

"It'll be here in a half hour," said Mary.

"That'll give us time to nurse another beer," said Robert. Robbie got them all another beer. "So how are all of those girls you met at the dance doing?" asked Robert. "Have you been out with all of them yet?"

"I've been with two of them and I think you already know that," said Robbie. "I'll be going on a real date with one of them this weekend."

"What do you mean real date?" asked Robert.

"I mean we're not just hopping into the sack," said Robbie. "We'll go to a movie and dinner or something like that."

"That one girl that was holding on to you so hard when you were dancing looked like she was a girl who could hurt you," said Robert.

"That was Anna," said Robbie. "She probably could hurt someone. Debbie, the girl I'm going out with this weekend told me that Anna got a job at a strip club and she really likes it."

"I couldn't do that," said Mary. "I don't want anyone looking at me but your father."

"Well if Anna is the one I think she is, she'll do well at a strip club," said Robert. "That girl was built. All four of those girls were built but there was something about that girl that really stood out."

"It was probably her tits dad," said Robbie. "And the fact that she probably only has a twenty two inch waist makes them look even bigger. She has a beautiful ass too."

"All right you two, it's time to talk about something else," said Mary. "You two will be wanting to go to that strip club and see that girl."

"I've already seen that girl," said Robbie. "I don't need to see her again."

"Yeh, and I've got you woman," said Robert. "Why would I need some young girl when I've got me a real woman." Mary let out a giggle and went to Robert and sat on his lap. The doorbell rang just as Mary sat on Robert's lap. Robbie went to the door. He took the pizza and paid the delivery person. He also gave him a tip.

"Let's eat in the living room and see if we can find a movie to watch," said Mary. "I'll get us some plates and napkins. One of you see if there's a movie on." Robbie turned on the TV and started going through the channels. They had a choice of two movies. One was a James Bond movie, Goldfinger. The other one was a western, "The Big Country." They decided on the western.

"I've seen this movie a few times but I really like the music to it," said Mary. "Plus Gregory Peck and Charlton Heston aren't bad to look at."

"Jean Simmons is cute too," said Robert. Robbie made sure everyone had some beer and they ate and watched the movie. The movie wasn't over at six o'clock. Robbie excused himself and went to the telephone.

Debbie answered the phone on the first ring. "Hello, this is Debbie. Is this Robbie?" she said.

"Yes, this is Robbie," Robbie said. "Are you free this Saturday evening?"

"I am," answered Debbie. "What do you have in mind?"

"I thought we might go out for a nice dinner and then maybe take in a movie," said Robbie.

"That would be nice," said Debbie. "What time can I expect you?"

"I'll pick you up at 6:30," answered Robbie. "I need your address." Debbie gave him her address and they said their goodbyes.

Everything went smooth at the funeral home that week. Robbie got up early Saturday morning and made sure his car was all cleaned up inside and out. He got out some nice clothes and made sure they didn't need ironing or anything. After lunch he took a walk around the neighborhood. Mrs. Wilson's dog was in the window barking at him again, but he didn't see Mrs. Wilson. When he got back home he watched TV until it was time to get ready for his date.

He arrived at Debbie's house at exactly 6:30 PM. When he knocked on the door, Mr. Ryan came to the door. "Hello, I'm Robbie Parker," said Robbie as he extended his hand to Mr. Ryan. "I'm here for Debbie." They shook hands. Robbie had left his cane at home.

"Come on in young man. Name's Frank." said Mr. Ryan. "Debbie will be down in a minute. Have a seat." Robbie took a seat on the sofa. "Debbie tells me that you're a Vietnam Veteran and you were wounded."

"Yes Mr. Ryan," said Robbie. "I got back not long ago. I was a Marine and I was given a Medical Discharge."

"I was on an aircraft carrier in the Pacific during the war," said Mr. Ryan. "I made it through the war without getting wounded. I was one of the lucky ones. So Debbie tells me you're going to be a mortician. That's something that there will always be a demand for."

"That's one of the reasons I decided on that," said Robbie. "People will always die. There are no exceptions." Mrs. Ryan came into the room now.

"Hello young man, I'm Debbie's mother Olivia," she said.

"Pleased to meet you Mrs. Ryan," said Robbie as he extended his hand to her. "I'm Robbie Parker." They shook hands. Debbie came downstairs now. Robbie looked at her and smiled. "Good evening Debbie," said Robbie. "You look really nice this evening."

"Why thank you Robbie," said Debbie. "Mom, Dad, we'll be leaving now. I hope I don't wake you up when I get back home."

"You two go on and have a good time," said Olivia.

"Nice meeting you both," said Robbie as they went out the door. When they got to the car, Robbie opened the door for Debbie. She was impressed. When Robbie got in she slid over next to him.

"So where are you taking me?" asked Debbie.

"Do you like Italian food?" asked Robbie.

"Yes I do," answered Debbie.

"Good, we're going to Tony's on South High St." said Robbie. "I've never been there. Have you?"

"No I haven't," said Debbie. "I see that place all the time and have never even thought about going there."

"Well let's hope they have good food," said Robbie.

They never said another word until they were seated in the restaurant. A waiter brought them some menus and some water. He asked if they wanted anything else to drink. They both ordered iced tea. "I don't know what a lot of this stuff on the menu is," said Debbie. "The only Italian food I've ever had is spaghetti or lasagna."

"I don't know a whole lot more than you do," said Robbie. "I do know that if it's alfredo something or other, it's most likely good. We can always ask the waiter. They might have some specials too." The waiter brought their iced tea and told them about the daily specials. Robbie had him explain what certain things were. Debbie ordered some shrimp Alfredo and Robbie had something with veal in it. After they ordered, they just looked at each other for a while. Debbie was the first to speak.

"So I bet you never met Tina's or Anna's parents did you?" said Debbie.

"No, no parents," said Robbie. "It's probably best that those two have their own apartments. Will you be staying with your folks until you graduate?"

"I will," answered Debbie. "As long as they don't mind me being there, I'll stay. I really couldn't afford to move out right now anyway. Tina wanted me to share with her but I decided against it. I would probably end up partying too much and neglecting my studies. How about you Robbie? Will you stay at home for a while?"

"You know, I haven't really thought hard about it yet," said Robbie. "I already have a job all lined up after I graduate. I'll probably move out as soon as I can."

"Do you have any brothers or sister?" asked Debbie. "I was an only child. I think my parents will really miss me when I do move out."

"I'm an only child too," said Robbie. "I suppose my folks will miss me when I'm out of the house for good. I'm sure they missed me when I was in the Marines. So Debbie, what's your major? What do you want to be when you grow up?"

"I'm a business major," answered Debbie. "I haven't really decided where to go with it, but with business, there's a lot of things you can do."

"I think that I'll be taking some business classes too," said Robbie. "It's part of the curriculum."

"That makes sense," said Debbie. "Maybe one day you'll be running your own place. Who knows, maybe you'll have places all over the state. Maybe you'll get so big that all you'll have to do is own everything. You'll have good people to run everything for you. You just check the books regularly and be nice to your people and customers."

"I suppose that would be nice," said Robbie. "I have learned a lot already from Abner Fulbright. You have to know how to talk to people and not everyone is the same."

"I have no doubt that you'll be very successful one day," said Debbie. "You're not just a good talker, but you're a good listener too."

"That was nice of you to say," said Robbie. The waiter brought them some bread and their salads. They didn't talk much as they ate their salads. After the waiter took away their salad plates, Debbie spoke.

"I see you didn't bring your cane this evening," said Debbie. "Will you be all right without it?"

"I believe so," said Robbie. "If my leg gets to aching too much, I'll just have to take it nice and easy."

"Would you mind if I asked you about your wound?" asked Debbie.

"I don't like to talk about it but since this is a first date I will tell you," said Robbie. "Then we won't have to talk about it ever again. Is that fair enough?"

"Yes, fair enough," said Debbie.

"I have been shot several times," started Robbie. "I was over there less than a week when I got shot the first time. A bullet just grazed my left shoulder. Five or six months later, I got shot through both legs and I was lucky. The bullet or bullets never hit bone. The last time I was shot three times. The first time it was through the stomach. I was knocked backwards when I was hit. When I turned over and was trying to get up, I was shot through the left shoulder blade. The bullet also went through my lung and tore up two rib bones. As I was laying there, another bullet hit and shattered my thigh bone."

Debbie was crying now. Robbie pulled out a handkerchief and handed it to her. "Please don't cry now," pleaded Robbie. "I'm all right now. It's over. I lived. Please don't cry." The waiter was concerned and came over to the table to see what was happening.

"Is everything all right here?" he asked. "Can I get something or do anything for you?"

Debbie finally got the tears stopped. "I'm all right," said Debbie. "There's nothing wrong here. We were just discussing some things that happened in Vietnam and I got upset. I'll be all right. Thank you for your kindness."

"My brother is over there now," said the waiter. "His tour will be up shortly. We're hoping that he makes it home o.k."

"We hope so too," said Robbie. "Thanks for your concern."

"You're welcome and your food will be out shortly," said the waiter.

"I think I'll go to the ladies room and fix my face," said Debbie. "I bet my makeup is running after that."

"It's not and you still look good," said Robbie.

"I'll go and see," said Debbie. Debbie was gone a few minutes and returned.

"See I told you," said Robbie. "You still look good."

"Thank you Robbie and I'm sorry for crying," said Debbie. "It's just that I can't even begin to imagine what it would be like over there let alone get shot."

"Well we're done with that," said Robbie. "No more depressing talk. So would you like a movie after dinner or would you rather go dancing or something?"

"Let's see if we can find a movie," said Debbie. "I have no idea what's playing. We can drive around and see and if there's anything we would want to see. If there's not, we could do something else. I already know you're a good dancer."

When their food arrived, they stared at it for a little while. "This is almost too pretty to eat," said Debbie. Then she tasted her food. "Oh my, this is good. Give me your fork and I'll give you a taste."

"That is good," said Robbie. "My mother made something like this once and it was good but not like this. Don't tell my mother what I just said." Robbie took a bite of his veal. "Oh my goodness but this is good," said Robbie. "Give me your fork and I'll get you a bite."

"That is wonderful," said Debbie. "I need to learn to make things like this. Of course if I did, I'd end up weighing 300 pounds. Darn this stuff is good."

They didn't talk much as they were eating. They were enjoying their food too much. They traded bites several times. When they were finished, the waiter took their plates and asked if they had saved room for dessert. "Why don't we get something and share it?" said Robbie.

"That sounds good," said Debbie. "I like my sweets but I don't have much room left." The waiter brought the dessert menu and they decided to get a tiramisu. They each ordered a cup of coffee. When the tiramisu was gone, they both agreed that it was excellent. Robbie paid the check and left a good tip and they were on their way.

The first movie theater that they found was playing a Lee Marvin and Clint Eastwood movie. It was "Paint Your Wagon." "I'd like to see that movie if you don't mind," said Debbie. "It's a musical. I'm guessing some guys don't like musicals."

"I don't mind," said Robbie. "I like Lee Marvin and Clint Eastwood. Did you know that Lee Marvin was Marine in WW2 and got shot in the butt when he was on Saipan?"

"I never knew that," said Debbie. "I have heard that some big stars were in the war but I never knew who. Anyway, it'll be interesting to see if Lee Marvin can sing. I figure Clint Eastwood can but I wonder about Lee Marvin."

"Well lovely lady, we'll be finding out shortly," said Robbie. Robbie parked the car and they got in line to get their tickets. "Must be a good movie," said Robbie. "There's a lot of people in line." They got seated just as the previews of coming attractions started playing.

The only time that there was no laughter in the theater was when someone was singing. People were talking and laughing as they exited the theater. "So what do you think?" asked Robbie. "Can Lee Marvin sing?"

"He was good in the movie," said Debbie. "I liked it."

"I liked it too," said Robbie. "I've only seen one other musical before. That was "South Pacific." That one red headed guy who was their partner in the tunnels was in South Pacific too. I think he played "Stewpot" in it."

"I remember him now," said Debbie. "He was the guy who sewed the things for Mitzi Gaynor."

"That was him," said Robbie. "You know that movie was about sex and racism don't you?"

"I guess so, "said Debbie. "The men weren't getting any. Mitzi fell in love with the older guy and the young Marine Lieutenant wouldn't marry Bloody Mary's daughter because she was a native girl. I guess I never thought about that before now. Well anyway, this movie was about sex. I liked it."

They got to the car and Robbie opened the door for her. When he got in, she slid over next to him. They looked at each other for a moment and then kissed. "Would you like to do anything else this evening?" asked Robbie.

"I've had a nice time," said Debbie. "You can take me home now." Robbie kissed her again and then started the car. When they got to Debbie's house, he parked the car, opened her door, and walked her to the front door.

"I've had a real nice time tonight too," said Robbie. "Would you like to do something again next weekend?"

"Yes I would," said Debbie.

"I'll give you a call when I know my work schedule," said Robbie. "if something comes up, you can always call me too." He pulled her to him and kissed her again. She wrapped her arms around him and held him tightly for a while. Then she pulled back and looked into his eyes and smiled. She gave him a short kiss and then went inside."

The next evening, Debbie got a call from Sharon. "So how was your date with our boy?" asked Sharon. "Did you get laid?"

"First off Sharon, he's not our boy," said Debbie. "Just because Tina and Anna tried to screw him to death doesn't mean he's ours."

"You didn't get laid," said Sharon. "I can tell. You think you like that guy don't you?"

"Robbie's a very nice guy," said Debbie. "We're going out again next weekend."

"Well I'll leave him alone," said Sharon. "Remember what we said when we were at the VFW. None of us were looking for a serious relationship."

"I remember," said Debbie. "Robbie said that too. Anyway, it won't be long until he'll be leaving for his school in Cincinnati. He's a nice guy and I think we like each other's company."

"Sounds like serious stuff to me," said Sharon. "I'll tell Anna and Tina he's hands off."

"You don't need to be doing that," said Debbie. "Robbie's an adult and can do what he wants."

"Well I doubt if Anna would have time for him anyway," said Sharon. "She's getting a lot, and I mean a lot of guys now that she's a stripper. She's trying to talk Tina into doing it too."

"Tina would be good at it," said Debbie. "I can just see them two on the stage at the same time. They would probably end up getting arrested."

"Well I'll leave you alone," said Sharon. "I've got work to do. This one professor I have actually wants papers on time. Who does he think his is? You take care now."

"You too. I'll talk to you later," said Debbie.

Chapter Fourteen

There was only one customer at the funeral home the next week. Robbie made it out to the VA one day to do his volunteer work. He called Debbie on Tuesday and they set up a date for Saturday. He would pick her up at 6:30 PM again. Robbie also finished up his Christmas shopping this week. He bought his mother a few things for the kitchen. He had a hard time buying gifts for his father. He ended up getting him a set of cuff links with his initials on them and an expensive wallet.

As the week wore on, he found himself getting excited about his date with Debbie. He decided that he was beginning to like her. He also thought that he didn't want to get too attached to her because he would be leaving for school in about three weeks.

Saturday came and Robbie had their date all planned. They would have dinner at another nice restaurant. Then they would go to a small neighborhood bar and have a beer. After that, they would go to a club and do some dancing. He felt good when he knocked on the door of Debbie's house. Debbie answered the door. She was not all dressed nicely like she was going on a date. She was barefoot and had on some very snug fitting jeans and a T-shirt. Robbie could see that she wasn't wearing a bra. She took his arm and led him inside. "My parents aren't home," said Debbie. "They won't be back till close to ten. Let's go to my room."

"Is this what you really want?" asked Robbie.

"Yes it is," answered Debbie. "I have thought and thought and this is what I want." She led him to her room. Once inside, she closed the door. She had him stand beside the bed as she slowly undressed him. She took her time and kissed him all over as she undressed him. Robbie was very excited now. He wanted to grab her, undress her, and take her to bed, but he controlled his urges and let her continue. Debbie gently kissed and caressed the scars from his wounds. Robbie couldn't take it anymore. He grabbed her and pulled her to him. He kissed her hard and pulled off her T-shirt. Then he began kissing her neck and breasts. He kept his mouth locked to hers as he pulled at her jeans. He bent down and pulled the jeans from her legs. He leaned around and gently kissed her bottom as he removed her panties. On his way back up to her mouth he gently kissed the inside of her thighs. He locked his mouth back to hers and picked her up and laid her on the bed. They wrapped themselves together and became one.

An hour later they were completely covered with sweat. They were wrapped together and completely exhausted. No words were spoken. They just smiled at each other and kissed from time to time. After a few minutes, Robbie could see that Debbie was about to nod off. He took his right hand and caressed the side of her face. She opened her eyes and smiled. "Let's get in the bathtub," said Debbie. "I feel like soaking in the tub with you."

"Sounds good," said Robbie. She took his hand and led him to the bathroom. Debbie's room was actually a master bedroom. She had her own bathroom. There was even a double vanity. The bathtub was the old style with the claw feet. Robbie thought it was perfect for two people. They lay there soaking but soon they were making love again. After another hour they decided to get out of the tub. Robbie enjoyed drying off Debbie. When they were dry, they went back into the bedroom. Debbie wrapped her arms around him and kissed him gently.

"Let's not go out tonight," said Debbie. "Let's just order a pizza and watch a movie on TV."

"That's fine with me if that's what you want," said Robbie.

"That's what I want," said Debbie. "I want you to myself. We better get dressed though. My parents might come home before the time they said."

"They might not take it too kindly if we were naked eating pizza and watching TV when they came in the door," said Robbie.

"They know I'm not a Nun," said Debbie. "But that would probably upset them." They got dressed and Debbie ordered the pizza. Robbie turned on the TV and went through the channels looking for a movie. They had their choice between a John Wayne movie, "The Sands of Iwo Jima," or "Miracle on 34th Street." They watched "Miracle on 34th Street." They sat close on the sofa and watched the movie. "Natalie Wood was a cute little girl wasn't she?" said Debbie.

"She was," said Robbie. "She grew into a fine looking woman too, and Maureen O'Hara is drop dead gorgeous. I always liked her. I always wondered how red her hair actually is."

"I'd say that they might color it up some for the movies and such, but I think it's really red," said Debbie. "So why don't you tell me what actresses you think are beautiful and I'll tell which actors I think are very handsome."

"You can go first," said Robbie. "I need to think a bit."

"O.k., there's Gregory Peck, James Garner, Sean Connery, Paul Newnan, Steve McQueen, Jimmy Stewart," said Debbie. "I can go on and on."

"All right, here goes. Let's see. There's Sophia Loren, Janet Leigh, Debra Paget, Doris Day, Rhonda Fleming, Barbara Eden, Kim Novak," said Robbie. "I could go on and on too."

"I noticed you didn't say Marilyn Monroe," said Debbie.

"She was a beautiful woman but I just never liked her," said Robbie. "Maybe it was all those silly roles she played. I don't know. I remember I thought she sounded really sexy when she sang happy birthday to Kennedy."

"I think a lot of people thought that too," said Debbie. "Most of them were men. I bet Jackie never liked it." Just then there was a knock at the door. Robbie answered it and it was the pizza delivery person. He paid him and tipped him and Debbie got them some drinks. They went back to watching the movie while they ate their pizza. There were a couple of slices of pizza left when Debbie's parents got back home.

"I guess you two didn't go out on the town," said Frank.

"No, we decided to stay in and watch TV," said Debbie.

"It's nice seeing you two again," said Robbie to Debbie's parents. "There 's going to be some pizza left. You both are welcome to some if you'd like. I can't eat any more."

"I'm full too," said Debbie. "You guys help yourself."

"Save it for your lunch tomorrow or something," said Olivia. "We had plenty to eat tonight. I think we'll go ahead and turn in. You two enjoy your movie. Goodnight."

"Goodnight," said Debbie. "See you in the morning."

Debbie's parents turned in and she and Robbie watched the movie. When the movie ended, Robbie figured it was time to go home. "I better go now," said Robbie. "Can we get together next weekend?"

"We can," said Debbie. "But the next week I'll be gone. We always go visit relatives out of state during Christmas week. We've been doing that for a lot of years. I actually enjoy seeing my relatives. We usually get home by the 28th."

"It's nice that you enjoy your relatives," said Robbie. "Well I'll be going. Why don't we figure on 6:30 PM Saturday again. If something comes up, I'll call you or you can call me." Robbie walked to the door. He pulled her to him and kissed her. "I'll see you Saturday," said Robbie. He kissed her again.

"I look forward to it," said Debbie. Then they kissed again and Robbie left.

~~~~

They were really busy at the funeral home the next week. They had four customers. One of the funerals was going to be on Saturday. One of Abner's regular workers had asked to be off and Abner let him go. He wasn't expecting that much business. It seemed hectic, but they got through the week all right. The funeral on Saturday was for someone who was very well known and liked. There was a huge procession. The weather cooperated and Robbie made it home by four. He had plenty of time to get ready for his date. He got himself ready early and talked with his parents while they were eating their dinner.

"So how are all of them girls doing?" asked Robert.

"Well the one working at the strip club is making plenty of money," said Robbie. "That's Anna. I haven't seen her again. I think she tried to talk Tina into working at the strip club, too. Now I'm dating Debbie. We've been on two dates so far. I haven't heard anything about Sharon."

"So do you like Debbie o.k.?" asked Mary.

"She's nice," answered Robbie. "She a lot different than Tina and Anna. We're going out this evening and then I won't see her till after Christmas. Her family always visits relatives around Christmas."

"Well you'll probably get to see her again before you leave for school," said Robert. "Maybe you'll be going to a big party somewhere for New Years."

"Will you two be doing anything for New Years?" asked Robbie.

"I got a bottle of bubbly and your mother and me are staying home," said Robert.

"That sounds nice," said Robbie. "I never knew you drank champagne."

"We don't," said Mary. "We just thought we'd try some this year. If we can't stand it, we'll open some beer."

"I've never had any but I hear it sneaks up on you," said Robbie. "Something about them bubbles I guess. Well I'm taking off now. See you two tomorrow."

"Have a nice time," said Mary.

Debbie's parents were home this time when he knocked on the door. Debbie was ready and they left after Robbie told Olivia and Frank that is was nice seeing them again.

"Is there anywhere you'd like to have dinner?" asked Robbie when they got into the car. She slid over next to him and kissed him.

"We can go back to Tony's if that's all right with you," said Debbie. "I liked it there."

"I liked it there too," said Robbie.

When they arrived at the restaurant, they were seated at the same table they had on their first date. They had the same waiter. "Welcome back," the waiter said as he poured them some water and gave them some menus. "Would you like something to drink while you're choosing your meals? I'll go over the specials when I come back with your drinks."

"I think I'll start off with a beer and then go to iced tea with the meal," said Robbie. "Would you like a beer Debbie?"

"I believe I will," said Debbie. "I'll have some iced tea with the meal too. Do you have Michelob?"

"Yes we do," answered the waiter. "And you sir?"

"I'll try a Michelob too," said Robbie.

"Very good sir," said the waiter as he was leaving."

"Is Michelob any good?" asked Robbie. "I usually drink Strohs or Pabst. Don't remember what we had overseas. I think it was Black Label or something."

"I like Michelob," said Debbie. "But I'll drink whatever is on hand." The waiter returned with the beers and took their order. Robbie took a sip.

"Not bad, I can drink it," said Robbie.

"Well I think it's supposed to be premium beer," said Debbie. "It costs a little more than the cheaper stuff. It's probably the same as Budweiser. I can't drink Budweiser. It gives me a headache."

"I've think I had some Budweiser at a club or somewhere. I remember not liking it," said Robbie.

"So Robbie, we haven't talked about last weekend," said Debbie. "What are your feelings about what we did?"

"It was wonderful," said Robbie. "We just didn't have meaningless sex. We made love to each other and it was beautiful."

"I never thought I'd hear a guy say anything like that about sex," said Debbie. "Where did you come from? How did you learn to talk like that? You're making me want you again." Robbie smiled at her and leaned across the table and kissed her. "Just where did you come from?" said Debbie when Robbie sat back down. "The woman that lands you will be one lucky lady." Robbie smiled again and took a sip of his beer. "I'm talking too much," said Debbie. "You talk for a while."

"You're doing fine," said Robbie. "I like listening to you. I think the guy that ends up with you will be one lucky guy. You're beautiful, smart, polite, interesting, sensible, and you're a great dancer. I could go on and on."

"Please do," said Debbie.

"All right, you are also a wonderful lover," said Robbie.

"That's enough now," said Debbie. "I'll be wanting to get a hotel room. We're saved. Here comes the waiter with our food."

They couldn't pronounce what they were eating but they thought it was very good. They skipped dessert and went to a small neighborhood bar for a beer. They nursed their beer for an hour or so and then went to a club. Debbie knew the band that was playing that night. They were supposed to be very good. Debbie and Robbie took a table and waited for the band to start. A very attractive waitress took their drink order. Debbie could see that the waitress was eyeballing Robbie. "I know that girl," said Debbie. "She's nice. She goes both ways."

"What do you mean both ways?" asked Robbie.

"I mean she likes men and women," said Debbie.

"Oh, I see," said Robbie. "Well if you go out and you go both ways, you have a good chance of hooking up one way or the other or both. Maybe she's checking you out."

"She knows I don't like girls," said Debbie. "I think she was with Anna one time though." The waitress brought their drinks. Robbie went ahead and paid her. He didn't want to run a tab.

The band finally started. They were very good but they didn't play very many songs that were good dancing songs. Robbie and Debbie danced every song that they thought was danceable. When they finally took a break, Debbie went to the stage and asked the lead singer if they could play some different songs. He had no intention of playing anything different. He informed her that if she didn't like his music, she could go somewhere else. Robbie was over at their table while Debbie talked with the singer. He saw Debbie give him the finger and then come back to the table. "What was that all about?" asked Robbie.

"That idiot said he would play what he wanted to play and if I didn't like it, I could go somewhere else," said Debbie. "I reminded him that he was here for us, not himself. Then I gave him the finger."

"So are we going somewhere else?" asked Robbie.

"Why don't we?" said Debbie. "I feel like dancing."

"Your chariot awaits," said Robbie.

They went to two more places. In the first place, the band was playing a lot of acid rock. At the second place, the band was mixing it up a good bit so they stayed. They found a table toward the back and took a seat. They had just sat down when they heard someone yelling Debbie's name. It was Sharon. She hurried over to their table. She had some long haired guy with her. They sat down with them just like they were invited. The long haired guy was definitely high on something. His eyes looked like a Los Angeles road map. "Hey guys, what's up?" said Sharon. "And this is, hey, what is your name?

"What?" answered the long haired guy.

"I said, what is your name?" said Sharon.

"Oh, my name, uh, let's see, oh yeah, my name, uh, it's Roger," he finally answered.

"Well Roger, do you have a last name?" asked Sharon.

"Last name, huh, oh yeah, it's Smith." answered Roger.

"Well Roger Smith, this is Debbie Ryan and Robbie Parker," said Sharon.

"Far out man," said Roger. "Far out."

"So Roger, have you been partying all day?" asked Debbie. "You look like you've been at it for a good while."

"Sure have," answered Roger. "Drank about all day yesterday. Then I started again this morning. I dropped some acid a few hours ago and I had some killer weed about an hour ago."

"How come you're still awake?" asked Debbie.

"It's cause they cut that acid with speed, man," answered Roger.

"So Roger, how long do expect to live?" asked Robbie.

"What kind of a question is that, man?" asked Roger. "I figure I'll get old someday."

"Well if you do what you're doing on a regular basis, you might not make it," said Robbie.

"Bummer man," said Roger. "This dude's bummin' me out. Let's go smoke some pot."

"You go on," said Sharon. "I'm staying here."

"I'm outta here, man," said Roger. "See you around." Roger left and mixed in with the crowd. They didn't see him the rest of the evening.

"Where'd you get that one?" Debbie asked Sharon.

"In here, just a little while ago," answered Sharon. "He's wasn't bad to look at. I'll get me another one before too long. So have you guys had sex yet?"

"What do you think Robbie?" asked Debbie. "Should we tell her?"

"Hey, I don't talk about my sexual encounters, but if you want to, it's your business," said Robbie.

"Well, Sharon, Robbie is a great lover. He's the best I ever had and probably ever will have," said Debbie.

"You're lying," said Sharon. "You guys haven't done it yet. I can tell. So can I take your man out on the dance floor?"

"Go get your own man," said Debbie. "Robbie's with me right now."

"Fine, be that way," said Sharon. "I'll go get one. I'll call you tomorrow." Sharon got up from the table and became lost in the crowd.

A waitress finally found her way to their table and took their order. As soon as their drinks arrived, they went out on the dance floor. They danced for three songs and went back to their table. They had only been sitting for two songs when the band started a slow song. Debbie took Robbie's arm and led him back to the dance floor. "We gotta dance to this song," said Debbie.

"All right by me," said Robbie. They held each other tightly as they danced. Debbie could feel that Robbie was getting excited. She looked up at him and smiled. "Hey, what can I say?" said Robbie. "You feel good and I'm not dead."

"I'd like to spend the night with you," Debbie whispered in Robbie's ear. "I'm sure Tina would let me borrow her apartment if I asked her."

"I'd rather not go there," said Robbie. "I can get us a hotel room. They don't cost that much."

"Let's go," said Debbie. They left the dance floor and went to Robbie's car. Debbie was all over him before he could even get the car started.

"Slow down," said Robbie after about five minutes of some heavy making out. "We'll have all night." They kissed one more time and Robbie started the car.

It took about fifteen minutes to get to the hotel. Once inside their room, the clothes went flying. Their room was on the end of the building and the room next to theirs was vacant. It was probably a good thing because they were very loud most of the night. They finally nodded off around 4 AM. Robbie woke up around eight. Debbie was still asleep. She was on her right side facing away from him. Robbie got on his right side and got behind her. He started kissing her ear and neck. He gently caressed her breasts. She awakened and turned to face him. They made love for an hour. Afterwards, they both got into the shower. It was a nice long shower. They didn't talk as they got dressed. They checked out of the room and went to Robbie's car. Robbie opened her door and when he got in, she slid over next to him.

"Let's get some breakfast," said Robbie. "I'm hungry. Is there anywhere special you'd like to go?"

"Any diner will do fine," said Debbie. "I need some coffee." There was a diner just a few blocks from the hotel. The parking lot seemed very full. When they went inside, all of the booths and tables were occupied. "We can sit at the counter," said Debbie. "I don't mind."

"All right by me," said Robbie. A waitress was right there so they had some coffee in no time. Debbie ordered a pecan waffle and Robbie ordered a ham and cheese omelet and some hash browns. They sat there sipping their coffee and looking into each other's eyes.

"I liked being with you all night," said Debbie. "I have been with several guys, but I have never spent a full night with a guy. Up until I met you, I have never known a man I wanted to spend the whole night with. I'm not making you uneasy, am I?"

"No Debbie, I'm not uneasy," answered Robbie. "I think we both had a very good time last night. I'm glad that you liked being with me. I feel the same about you."

"I'll miss you when you start your school," said Debbie. "When does your semester start?"

"I don't remember the exact date, but it's the first full week right after New Years," said Robbie. "I'll need to move into my apartment a couple days before classes start."

"That school will probably be a breeze for you," said Debbie. "You've probably already learned a lot from Fulbright's."

"That's true," said Robbie. "I've seen about everything there is to see and do in that line of work. I've worked with the relatives and gone over billing. I guess the only thing I haven't seen or been around is cremation. I think we have some classes on that. I'd say that before too long, there will be a lot of cremations. Well anyway, let's talk about something else. You'll be gone for Christmas and several days visiting relatives, right?"

"Yes, my family takes off the week of Christmas and visits relatives," said Debbie. "Sometimes we just all go to someone's house, and other times, all of us rent houses somewhere. This year we're all going to Florida. I have an aunt down there. She has a huge house so there's plenty of room for all of us. I have some really nice relatives."

"That sounds like a good time," said Robbie. "I don't have any close relatives that I know of. I was an only child. So were my parents. My grandparents on both sides are gone. I had plenty of friends when I was growing up. I haven't seen too many of them since I've been home. I guess a lot of them are away at college or working somewhere. One of my close friends joined the Army and was killed in Vietnam. I talked to his parents when I got home. Let's change the subject. Why don't you give me a call when you get back from your trip and we can get together. We'll have a few days before I go to school. Maybe someone will invite us to a New Year's Eve party."

"I had a terrible hangover after the one I went to last year," said Debbie. "I remember Anna having her own little orgy. The guy I was with passed out before midnight. I never went out with him again after that. It wasn't because he passed out. It was because I finally decided that he was a bum. What did you do last New Year's?"

"I was on a date with Uncle Sam," answered Robbie.

"I guess that was a different kind of party," said Debbie.

Their food arrived and the waitress refilled their coffee cups. They didn't talk as they were eating. They had one more cup of coffee after their food was gone. When their cups were empty, Debbie leaned over and kissed Robbie on the cheek. "You can take me home now," said Debbie. Robbie paid the check and they were on their way. When they got to Debbie's house, Robbie parked the car and went around and opened Debbie's door. He walked her to the door and then pulled her to him. They smiled and looked into each other's eyes. Then they kissed several times. Debbie then stepped back from Robbie and smiled. "I'll call you when I get back," said Debbie. "I'll miss you."

"I'll miss you too," said Robbie as he turned and left.

~~~~

There were two customers for the funeral home during Christmas week. Robbie had some good lessons on how some people act when there's a death of a close one during a major holiday. He also made it out to the VA one time. He tried to see as many of the patients in the dorms as he could. Robbie and his parents also went to Mass that week. Some of Robbie's old acquaintances from school were at

Mass. They had the usual conversations. How have you been? What have you been up to? Are you in college? Where are you working? They all knew that Robbie had been in the Marines and that he had been given a Medical Discharge. They were all a little shocked when Robbie told them he was going to be a mortician. Then they all said typical things like, let's stay in touch, let's get together sometime, or I'll call you. Jake Canton and his wife were invited over to the Parker's for a dinner a couple of days before Christmas. After the meal, the men stayed at the dinner table telling war stories while the women went to the living room. Robbie didn't join in on the war stories. He just listened.

Christmas day at the Parker's was just the way it had always been. They got up in morning and had some coffee. Then they opened presents. Robert and Mary slipped back to their room for an hour or so before Mary got busy making their Christmas feast. It was a good day at the Parker house.

Abner called Robbie the day after Christmas. They would have a soldier who had been killed a few days before Christmas. The parents of the soldier were very bitter and nothing that Abner or Robbie said helped. At the viewing, Robbie could tell that many of the people who attended were very anti-war. At first, the parents didn't want to have a color guard and the shots fired, but the morning of the funeral, they changed their minds. Abner had to rush to round up the color guard.

Debbie called Robbie the morning of the 29th. "Come over to the house around six," said Debbie. "My parents are going out to dinner and then taking in a movie. We'll have the house to ourselves for a few hours."

"I'll be there," said Robbie.

When Robbie knocked on the door of Debbie's house on the 29th, Debbie answered the door. She was wearing a long bathrobe. She grabbed Robbie's arm and pulled him inside. Once he was inside, she closed and locked the door. Robbie had taken his cane with him because his leg had been aching some. He laid the cane on the sofa. Debbie opened the robe and put her arms around Robbie's neck and locked her mouth on his. Robbie moved her arms so he could get the bathrobe off of her. Debbie was wearing some very sexy panties and a very fancy type of bra that Robbie had never seen before. He peeled off his jacket, picked her up, and carried her to her bed. She sat on the edge of the bed and he stood as she undressed him. He stood her up and began kissing her all over. He worked his way down and when he got to her panties, he pulled them off with his teeth. He stood back up and unfastened her bra. They wrapped themselves together and fell onto the bed. After a good while, they lay in bed looking into each other's eyes.

"I guess you missed me," said Robbie.

"I did," said Debbie. "I knew I would miss you but I didn't expect to miss you as much as I did. I know when we first met I said that I wasn't interested in a serious relationship, but it has been very hard trying not to become serious with you."

"I know what you're saying," said Robbie. "I'm having a hard time too."

"Could it be that all we have between us is sex?" asked Debbie. "I've thought about that a lot."

"It could just be the sex," said Robbie. "But I think we would still like each other without the sex. We do have some good love making though, don't we? I mean that's what I think about it. It's not just sex. We are making love to each other."

Debbie really liked what Robbie had said and she was all over him again. An hour later, they were soaking in the bathtub. They had been in the tub around fifteen minutes when someone knocked on the door. "Did you hear that?" Debbie asked Robbie. "I think someone knocked on the front door." Before Robbie could say anything, there was another knock on the door. "Who would that be?" said Debbie. "The neighbors would never knock this time of day. If they needed something, they would call on the phone." As soon as Debbie finished talking, there was another knock at the door.

"Could be somebody trying to find out if there's anyone home," said Robbie. "A lot of houses get robbed around the holidays. You stay in the bathroom and lock the door. I'll go have a look." Debbie gave Robbie a look of despair. She got out of the tub and wrapped a towel around herself. Robbie went back to her room and threw on his pants. Then he went back to the bathroom. "Now lock the door and stay inside," said Robbie. "Don't come out till I tell you." Debbie did as instructed. Robbie worked his way to the living room. The lights were on in the living room and the blinds and drapes were closed. Robbie could not see outside. He went to the sofa and got his cane. Just as he picked up his cane, he heard a sound. It was coming from the front door. Someone was trying to pick the lock. Robbie glued himself to the wall by the doorway. When the door opened, he would be behind it and couldn't be seen by the intruder. Robbie waited patiently. Finally the door opened. A medium sized man wearing dark clothes and a ski mask entered. He eased inside and looked around. When he was satisfied that no one was home, he moved away from the door. Robbie moved swiftly. He stepped from behind the door and cracked the intruder on the back of both of his knees with his cane. The intruder's legs buckled and he fell to his knees. As he was falling to his knees, he turned his head a little to see Robbie behind him. Before he could react or say anything, Robbie cracked him on the head with his cane. The intruder was knocked out and slumped to the floor. When he fell forward, his head banged into a coffee table. Robbie always wore his military web belt. He took it off and was using it to tie the intruder's hands behind him. Just as he finished tying the man, someone grabbed him from behind. This person was huge. He picked Robbie up clear off the floor. When he did, Robbie's head hit the ceiling. Robbie struggled as hard as he could. The man's grip was loosening. As Robbie was slipping down, he took the back of his head and struck backwards as hard as he could. The man let out a groan and let go of Robbie. Robbie turned to face this intruder. Blood was pouring from his nose. Robbie picked up his cane and cracked the intruder on the outside of his right knee. The intruder screamed in pain and fell to his right. As he was falling, Robbie cracked his head with his cane. He was unconscious before he hit the floor. As he was falling, his head struck an end table. After the man fell, Robbie looked around to make sure there were no more intruders. He was surprised to see Debbie standing there. "I thought I told you to stay in the bathroom," said Robbie.

"I was scared," said Debbie. "I heard all the noise and I didn't know if you had been hurt or not. I had to come and see."

"How much of this did you see?" asked Robbie.

"I came out of the bathroom just as you smacked that fella with your head," said Debbie. "I saw him drop you and then you put him down with your cane."

"Well you've seen too much," said Robbie. "Now I need some rope or something to hog tie these two with. Get me something and then we'll call the police." Debbie left the room and returned with some rope. It was clothesline rope. Robbie tied the big man first. He tied his hands behind him and then tied his feet together. Then he tied the man's feet to his hands. He left his belt on the other intruder. He tied the man's feet together and then tied his feet to his hands. Debbie called the police. Debbie and Robbie got dressed before the police arrived.

The police were there in fifteen minutes. One of the policemen who came was Jerry Tomlinson. He was the cop who had talked to Robbie about the dog incident. He recognized Robbie right away. "So what do we have here?" asked Jerry. "Looks like you've been busy." Jerry looked at Debbie. "Is this your house Miss?" asked Jerry.

"Yes, I live here with my parents," answered Debbie. "They went out this evening."

"And you were here with Robbie?" asked Jerry.

"Yes, we were in my room when someone knocked at the door," answered Debbie. "They kept knocking even though we didn't answer the door."

"Then what did you do?" asked Jerry.

"Robbie suspected that someone might just be checking to see if anyone was home so they could break in," said Debbie.

"And then what happened?" asked Jerry.

"Robbie told me to lock myself in the bathroom while he checked things out," answered Debbie. "That's what I did."

"What did you do Robbie?" asked Jerry.

"All the lights were on and the blinds and drapes were closed," answered Robbie. "I got my cane and hid so that when the door opened, I couldn't be seen. After that one by the coffee table got the locked picked, he came in and looked around. After he cleared the door, I hit the back of his knees and buckled his legs."

"Why is he unconscious?" asked Jerry.

"He must have hit his head on the coffee table," answered Robbie.

"Sure," said Jerry. "Then what happened?"

"I took off my web belt and fastened his hands behind him," started Robbie. "I was grabbed from behind by that big fella. I never knew he was there. He picked me up and I banged my head on the ceiling. I struggled and he was losing his grip. As I was sliding down, I banged his nose with the back of my head. He let go of me then. I picked up my cane and cracked the outside of his right knee. He fell."

"So why is he unconscious?" asked Jerry.

"He must have hit his head on the end table," answered Robbie.

"Yeh, of course," said Jerry. The two intruders were regaining consciousness now. Jerry bent down beside the one by the coffee table. "Got anything to say fella?" asked Jerry.

"I got plenty to say," said the intruder. "We was out for a walk when for no reason, this crazy man with the cane attacked us. He knocked us out and drug us inside and tied us up."

"That's right. That's just what happened," said the big one. "That fucker's crazy."

"Yeh, and I'm the King of Spain too," said Jerry. The intruders were cuffed and taken out to the cruisers. Jerry gave Robbie back his belt. "You two have a pleasant evening now," said Jerry as he started to his car.

"Don't you need to do fingerprints or something?" asked Debbie.

"Did you see their hands Miss?" asked Jerry. "They were wearing gloves. We did find some lock picking tools on them. They both had switchblades on them too. They're going to jail. You take care now."

When the police cruisers were out of sight, they closed the front door and sat on the sofa. "Why didn't you tell the policeman that you hit that man in the head with your cane?" asked Debbie. "Those two were knocked unconscious," answered Robbie. "I did tell him that I knocked them down with my cane. That's good enough. We don't need some sleazy lawyer saying I attacked them when it wasn't necessary."

"I guess so," said Debbie. "I hear some lawyers can twist things around pretty good." Just as Debbie finished talking, her parents got home.

Debbie's mother saw some blood on the carpet. "What happened here?" she asked. "Why is there blood on my carpet?"

"Two men broke into the house," answered Debbie. "Robbie took care of them. The police came and took them away."

"Are you all right Baby?" asked Debbie's father.

"Robbie had me lock myself in the bathroom while he took care of things," answered Debbie.

"Thank you young man," said Frank. "We're so glad you were here. Who knows what might have happened if you hadn't been here." Both of Debbie's parents took turns hugging Robbie.

"I'll call the insurance company in the morning and see what they say about the carpet," said Olivia. "Are you sure you're all right Baby?"

"I'm fine Momma," said Debbie. "You and Daddy can go on to bed if you want."

"All right," said Olivia. "We'll see you in the morning." Frank and Olivia left and went to their room.

"How often do they call you Baby?" asked Robbie.

"Only when something important happens," answered Debbie. "I thought we should get a pizza but I don't think I can eat right now. We can order one and you can eat if you're hungry."

"I'm good," said Robbie. "How bout I just go home. You look like you need to be alone with your thoughts."

"I think I do," said Debbie. They got close to each other and kissed. Robbie started out the door. "I'll probably call you tomorrow," said Debbie. "I'm expecting to get invited to a New Year's Eve party. Would you want to go if I do?"

"I would if you're going to be there," said Robbie. "Give me a call, party or not. We can still get together again before I leave for school." Robbie went to her and kissed her again. Then he left.

When Robbie got home, his parents were in the living room watching TV. "I got a call a while back," said Robert. "Someone I know has one of them police scanners or whatever it's called. They said there was a break-in at this certain address and two people were taken into custody. That address is close to where that girl Debbie lives."

"It wasn't close Dad," said Robbie. "It was her house."

"Well tell us all about it son," said Mary.

"Well Debbie and I were together when we heard someone knocking on the door," started Robbie. Debbie's folks were out for the evening. The kept knocking on the door even though no one answered. I suspected someone wanted to break in. I had Debbie lock herself in the bathroom. I got my cane and hid so when the front door opened, they couldn't see me. The lock got picked and one guy came in and looked around. When he cleared the door, I took him down with my cane. I hit the back of his knees with it. Then I cracked his head with it. I had just tied his hands behind his back when another guy came through the door and grabbed me from behind. I cracked his nose with the back of my head. He let go of me then. I took him down by hitting the side of his knee with my cane. As he was falling I cracked his head. We tied them up and called the cops."

"You've had a full evening," said Mary.

"I didn't tell the cops that I cracked their heads with my cane," said Robbie. "I said they hit their heads on some furniture, which they did."

"That was probably smart," said Robert. "You don't want some lawyer saying you hit them when it wasn't necessary."

"That's what I told Debbie when she asked me," said Robbie.

"I thought you said she was locked in the bathroom," said Robert.

"She was," said Robbie. "But she got scared after a while and came out. She saw me take out the second guy."

"Well at least she knows you're a capable guy," said Robert. "A lot of people panic and have no idea what to do. I think you did good."

Word got out about the break-in at Debbie's house and the local news reporters were after Robbie. They wanted him to be on the local TV channels and tell what happened and everything. Robbie would have no part of it. He politely told all of the reporters to please leave him alone. One particular reporter was getting very pushy. "The people have a right to hear some good news once in a while and see a real hero," he kept saying.

"Look you, why don't you just post my picture everywhere with my address so when those two get of jail, they'll know exactly who I am and where I live?" said Robbie. "Now please leave me alone."

~~~~

Debbie called Robbie. They would be going to a party on New Year's Eve. The party was starting late so Robbie wouldn't pick her up till around 10 PM. When Robbie went to pick up Debbie, her parents had to thank him all over again and tell him about what the insurance company had said. Finally they got away from the house. "Where we going?" asked Robbie.

"A friend of mine is a friend to this guy who is an Assistant Professor at Ohio State," said Debbie. "We're going to the professor's house."

"What's he a professor of?" asked Robbie.

"Philosophy," answered Debbie. "I'm pretty sure it's philosophy."

"Well give me some directions," said Robbie. "Do we need to bring anything? I can stop and pick up some beer."

"I was told that nothing was needed," said Debbie.

They arrived at the party house in about fifteen minutes. The house was a nice, big and fancy, two story house. "Philosophy must pay good," said Robbie.

"Maybe someday you'll have a nice big house like this," said Debbie. "Now let's go in." Robbie had his cane with him because his leg had been aching again.

They knocked on the door and as soon as it opened, a cloud of pot smoke came rolling toward the door. A man about 30 with long scraggly hair let them inside. He was wearing blue jeans and had on a sweatshirt with a big peace symbol on the front and back. "Come on in," he said. "I'm Jeff and this is my place."

"I'm Debbie Ryan and this is Robbie Parker," said Debbie.

"Well feel free to move around and mingle," said Jeff. "There's plenty of alcohol in the kitchen and I'm sure you can smell the pot. I think someone's got some acid if you want that too." Jeff left and went to another room. Debbie and Robbie went around and tried to mingle with the people. There was only one person there that Debbie knew. She was the person who told her about the party. Sarah was her name. She took them around and introduced them to everyone. Robbie was feeling uncomfortable. He really didn't want to be at this place since there were drugs present. He also felt out of place because he was the only guy who didn't have long hair.

"I don't like it here," said Robbie to Debbie. "I feel out of place. What if the cops come?"

"Try to relax," said Debbie. "Have a beer or two. If you still feel uneasy after that, we can leave."

Robbie got both of them a beer and then they sat down on a couch. Everyone kept trying to get them to smoke some pot. After a while, Jeff came into the room. He saw that Debbie and Robbie wouldn't smoke. He walked over to them. "What's a matter man?" said Jeff. "Isn't this weed good enough for you?"

"I don't smoke that stuff," said Robbie. "You do whatever you want."

Jeff finally noticed Robbie's cane. "You have that short hair and you're using a cane," said Jeff. "I'd say you just got back from the Southeast Asian War Games. I bet you were a Marine too."

"I was a Marine and I just got back not long ago," said Robbie. "What of it?"

"It just amazes me that they get fools like you to join up and go be cannon fodder so the big war machine can make millions and millions of dollars," said Jeff. "That's a civil war over there. We have no business being there. You know that Michelin and other tire companies are getting rich from the rubber plants over there."

"First off Jeff, this may be your house, but it doesn't give you the right to call me names," said Robbie. "And I never had the pleasure of meeting anyone from Michelin while I was over there."

"I never called you any names, man," said Jeff.

"You called me a fool and I don't appreciate it," said Robbie. "Jeff, thank you for your hospitality. We'll be leaving now."

"Calm down Robbie," said Debbie. "Jeff doesn't mean to insult you. We don't have to leave yet. Please sit back down."

"Debbie, I'm leaving now," said Robbie. "If you want to stay, you'll have to get a ride home from someone else."

"That's right man," said Jeff. "Just run off and leave your woman. She'll be fine here with us. You go ahead and leave. Just remember what I said. All those guys who got killed over there died so the war machine could stay rich."

"So you're a philosophy professor," said Robbie. "What is philosophy? Isn't that where you just sit around and bullshit? You don't know shit Jeff. You're not even in the real world. You hide yourself so you don't have to go out and get a real job. You bullshit young kids so they can learn how to bullshit. And they pay you too. Unbelievable!" Robbie could tell that he struck a nerve with Jeff. Jeff went right up to Robbie and started pointing his finger at him. He kept saying the same things over and over about the war. After a while, his finger was poking Robbie's chest. Robbie started backing up. He was in a doorway when he stopped. "Please quit poking me with your finger." asked Robbie. Jeff didn't stop. "I'll ask you again," said Robbie. "Please quit poking my chest with your finger." Jeff didn't stop. "All right, that's enough," said Robbie. Robbie reached out and grabbed Jeff's finger with his right hand. Then he bent it backwards. Jeff went down to his knees and yelled in pain.

"Let go man," said Jeff. "Let go of my fucking finger."

"Are you going to quit poking me with it?" asked Robbie.

"Yeh man, I'll quit," said Jeff. "Now let go."

"You didn't say please," said Robbie.

"All right man, please, please let go of my finger," said Jeff. Robbie let go of Jeff's finger. Jeff stood up and shook his hand around. Then he took some type of stance.

"I have a brown belt in tae kwon do," said Jeff. "I'm gonna kick your ass."

"You have a black belt in running your mouth too," said Robbie. "Well come on and kick my ass." Robbie was still standing in the doorway. Jeff threw a punch at Robbie's face with his right hand. Robbie knew the punch was coming and quickly moved his head a little. The punch missed and Jeff's fist crashed into the wood on the door frame. Robbie could tell by the sound that Jeff had broken some bones. He backed away a little and cursed Robbie.

"You son of a bitch," yelled Jeff. "You're mine now." Jeff turned sideways and attempted a sidekick at Robbie with his right leg. Robbie knew that as soon as he turned sideways, he would try the kick. When the kick came, Robbie got ahold of his right foot. Jeff danced around on one foot and didn't know what to do. He cursed Robbie again.

"That's enough," said Robbie. Robbie kept ahold of Jeff's foot with his left hand and arm. He raised up his right elbow and crashed down into the side of Jeff's knee. He let go of Jeff and he fell to the floor. "Now you son of a bitch," said Robbie. "You just showed all these nice folks why you wear those peace signs."

"I'm filing charges on you," said Jeff. "I'm calling the law right now."

"No Jeff, I think I'll be calling the law," said Robbie. "They'd have a blast here with all these illegal drugs in your house. There's probably some underage drinking too. I imagine Ohio State won't look too kindly on one of their professors being involved with drugs and alcohol. Now thanks for the pleasant evening. I hope I didn't spoil your party. Debbie, I'm leaving now. Are you coming?"

"No Robbie, I can't go with you," said Debbie. "I need some time to think about all of this."

"That's fine," said Robbie. "Don't get yourself arrested while you're here." Robbie left and Debbie sat down on a couch and wondered what had just happened.

Sarah came over to her. "That guy you were with is really intense, isn't he?" asked Sarah.

"I didn't know that," said Debbie. "He's always been kind and gentle. He did take out those two guys who broke into our house, but that was a different situation. Maybe he's really one of those violent types."

"You're losing it girl," said Sarah. "You're man didn't do anything wrong. Jeff wouldn't back off. Robbie asked him nicely two times. And then all he did was grab Jeff's finger. After he let go of Jeff's finger, Jeff cursed him and threatened him. Jeff threw the first punch and missed. Then he tried to kick Robbie. Robbie just defended himself. Where were you girl? Didn't you see any of this? Robbie's a good man and if you can't see that, you got a screw loose."

"Maybe I do," said Debbie. "Can I get a ride with you when you're ready to go."

"Sure, I'm leaving right now," said Sarah. "This party has lost its' allure."

~~~~

The days between New Year's and when Robbie had to leave for school seemed to drag. Robbie had told Abner that he wouldn't be working since he was leaving shortly. He thought about calling Debbie but decided against it. He and Robert went to the Legion and VFW one more time before Robbie left so he could tell everyone goodbye. Three days before classes were to start, Robbie called Brandy and told her when to expect him. She would meet him at the apartment and help him unload and give him his key.

Chapter Fifteen

When Robbie arrived in Cincinnati, Brandy was there as expected. She helped him unload and was surprised by the amount of stuff that Robbie had brought. There wasn't much at all.

"You're not a material person are you?" Brandy asked.

"I don't need much," said Robbie. "I'll get things down here as I need them. After I put my clothes and things away, I'll be going to a grocery store."

"I'll go with you," said Brandy. "I need a few things. Do you like chili? I don't mean Cincinnati chili."

"I like chili," said Robbie.

"Good, I made a big pot last night," said Brandy. "We'll be able eat off of it for a couple more days. That's what I like to do. I make stuff that will last a few days so I don't have to cook all the time."

"That makes sense," said Robbie. "I never really cooked much other than frying stuff. Maybe you can show me a few things."

"I will," said Brandy. "The more you learn, the less I'll have to do." Robbie started putting his clothes away.

"I have a question," said Robbie. "How do we handle the bathroom?"

"Don't worry," said Brandy. "I'm not the kind of girl who leaves her underwear all over the bathroom. You put stuff like your shaving things and toothbrush and stuff on one side of the sink and I'll put mine on the other. There's two sets of towel racks. One is yours and one is mine. There's a small closet in the bathroom too. It's got four shelves. Two are yours and two are mine. We'll take turns taking out the trash. A week for you and then a week for me."

"Sounds like you have it all figured out," said Robbie.

"I don't think we'll butt heads," said Brandy. "The TV is mine. We don't get cable, but we can get several channels with the rabbit ears. I don't watch much TV anyway."

"Neither do I," said Robbie. Robbie finished with his clothes and put his things in the bathroom. "Well, that's good for now," said Robbie. "Let's go to the grocery now." They went down to Robbie's car. Brandy made sure she got there first so Robbie couldn't open the door for her. They went to a Kroger's. Robbie bought the food he thought he would need for a week or so. He also bought toilet paper, paper towels, soap, dish detergent, and laundry soap. He already had plenty of notebook paper and pens that he had brought from home. Brandy picked up the few things that she needed. Robbie put everything in its' proper place when they got back home. They both sat on the sofa and relaxed.

"So how was your Christmas?" asked Brandy. "Were you with your family?"

"Yes I was," answered Robbie. "It was just me and the folks but we had a good time."

"My folks have a house on Kelley's Island," said Brandy. "That's in Lake Erie not far from Port Clinton if you didn't know. Well we went there for a couple of days. I didn't like it all. It was too cold up there."

"Well it's nice that they do have a house there," said Robbie. "It'd be nice to have another house where you could get away at times."

"Well I like it up there in the summer," said Brandy. "But that wind will hurt you up there in the winter time. I guess the lake can freeze over too but I've never been there when it did. I'm hungry now. Do you want to try some of my chili?"

"Sure, I'll give it a try," said Robbie. Brandy heated it up and they ate. "This is pretty good stuff," said Robbie. "Did you really make it?"

"I really did," said Brandy. "I make a great spaghetti sauce too. I won't eat that canned stuff."

"I love spaghetti," said Robbie. "What else can you make?" Before Brandy answered, the telephone rang. Brandy answered. It was her father.

"Hi Daddy," said Brandy. "Do you need something? Yes, my new roommate is moved in now. We just got back from the grocery. Yes Daddy, I love you too. Bye Daddy. My daddy said to tell you hi. This reminds me. We never talked about the telephone. We split the basic bill and we each pay for our own long distance calls."

"That's o.k. with me," said Robbie.

"Will you be giving this phone number to any girls?" asked Brandy.

"I don't know yet," answered Robbie.

"Sounds to me like you might have had a falling out with someone," said Brandy. "Tell me all about it."

"Why are you so interested in my love life?" asked Robbie.

"I guess I'm just nosey," answered Brandy. "It's the way I am. So are you going to tell me?"

"All right, I was dating this one girl," started Robbie. "We were starting to get serious even though we both said that we did want any serious relationships. We had a few dates and had a really nice time. We went to a party on New Year's Eve. It was hosted by some guy who was a philosophy professor. Anyway, he was a horses ass. He found out I was a veteran and called me a fool and said a few things I didn't like. He kept provoking me. He didn't like what I said about him and his job. He took a swing at me and missed. He thought he was a karate man. He tried to kick me. I grabbed his leg and foot and then smacked the side of his knee with my elbow. He went down. Then he said he was calling the law on me. I informed him that I would be calling the law. There were a lot of drugs there and probably some underage drinkers. I thanked him for his hospitality and left. The girl I was with was upset by all of this and wouldn't leave with me."

"So did you call the law?" asked Brandy.

"Of course not," answered Robbie. "I never heard from the girl after that either."

"What did she have to be upset about?" asked Brandy. "If what you told me is the truth, then you didn't do anything wrong."

"Well maybe she didn't think I needed to smack his knee since I already humiliated him," said Robbie. "Maybe she thinks I am prone to violence. I don't know. I may as well tell you about the two guys who broke into her house."

"Oh yes, I need to hear this," said Brandy.

"Well we were at her house. Her parents were out for the evening," started Robbie. "We heard someone knocking on the front door. No one was expected. We didn't answer. They kept knocking and knocking. I told her that it may be someone wanting to break in. They were just making sure no one was home. I had her lock herself in the bathroom. I took my cane and got beside the front door. I would be right behind the door when they came in and wouldn't be seen. They picked the lock. One of them came inside and looked around. He didn't see me. At the time, I didn't know there was two of them. I cracked the first one across the back of his knees and put him down. As he was falling, I cracked his head with my cane. His head also hit the coffee table as he fell. I was tying his hands behind his back when another guy grabbed me from behind. He was a big fella. My head actually hit the ceiling when he picked me up. I struggled and his grip loosened. I smacked his nose with the back of my head. He let go of me. I took my cane and smacked the outside of his right knee. When he fell, I smacked his head with my cane. His head hit an end table when he fell. I didn't know it, but the girl had come out of the bathroom. She saw me take out the second guy. She wondered why I smacked his head with my cane. Anyway, I hog tied them and she called the police. I told the police all that had happened. A cop asked my why they were unconscious. I told them that the first one hit his head on the coffee table as he was falling and the other hit his head on the end table as he was falling. All the cop said was "sure." It was kind of funny when those two came to. They said they were outside walking when I attacked them and drug them inside and tied them up."

"So will there be a trial for those two?" asked Brandy. "Will you have to go back and testify?"

"I have no idea," answered Robbie. "They had lock picking tools and switchblades on them. I guess if it would happen to go to trial, I'll have to go."

"Well it sounds to me like if someone broke into here, you would protect me," said Brandy.

"I reckon I would," said Robbie. "That is unless I was ticked at you or something."

"Well I'll try not to get you ticked at me," said Brandy. "Anyway, I see no reason why your girl should be upset by anything that happened. Maybe she would have felt better if them two would have tied you two up and stole everything. Maybe something worse could have happened."

"So we were talking about your cooking skills before Daddy called," said Robbie. "What else can you make?"

"First off, no one calls him Daddy but me," said Brandy. "My younger sisters call him father. His name is Wendel. His friends call him WW."

"Interesting, my middle initial is W," said Robbie. "It doesn't stand for anything though. So back to the cooking."

"All right Robbie W, I make a lot of stir fry stuff," said Brandy. "You know, oriental stuff. I do a lot of different things with chicken. My pot roast is excellent. I cook fish several different ways. There's a lot of things I can do."

"If you're as good as you say, maybe later on we can make a deal," said Robbie. "You do all of the cooking and I clean up."

"I might take you up on that," said Brandy. "I really don't mind the cooking. It's the clean up that's a pain. We'll see. So, it's Saturday night, what say we go out and see if you can really dance."

"I don't know," said Robbie. "I'm kind of tired."

"Sounds to me like you're all blow and no show," said Brandy.

"All right, but you get to drive," said Robbie.

"No problem," said Brandy. "There's this band I like and they're playing at this one club. I think you'll like them. They play a lot of songs that are good dancing songs."

"What time will we be leaving?" asked Robbie. "It's seven now. Maybe I can catch a few Z's before we go."

"We'll leave around 9:30 to 10:00," said Brandy. "You'll be able to nap for a bit. I'll go ahead and shower while you're sleeping. I'll wake you at nine if you're still asleep."

"Sounds good," said Robbie. Brandy left to clean up and Robbie stretched out on the couch. He was soon asleep. The next thing he knew, Brandy was poking him on the shoulder trying to wake him up. He finally opened his eyes. Brandy was standing beside the couch. She was wrapped in a towel that just barely covered her. Robbie looked at her and smiled. "I think you're trying to seduce me, Mrs. Robinson," said Robbie.

"What was that? What did you say?" asked Brandy.

"That was from "The Graduate," said Robbie. "You know, with Dustin Hoffman."

"Yes, I know the movie," said Brandy. "Are you saying I'm old and look like Mrs. Robinson?"

"No, I don't think you look old," said Robbie. "I'm sorry. I'm not sure why I said that. It just popped out."

"I really didn't mind," said Brandy. "I was just seeing if I could get you going. I guess I did. I'll get dressed now." Brandy walked away toward her room. Before she got to the door of her room, she started removing her towel. Robbie watched her. She seemed to be teasing Robbie. She removed the towel in such a way that Robbie was not able to see anything before she closed her door.

"That was a nice towel you almost had on," said Robbie as he got up off the couch. He heard Brandy let out a giggle. Robbie took his shower and soon they were on their way to the club.

The club was very crowded. Brandy seemed to be very well known. A lot of people, men and women, told her "hi" as they were looking for an empty table.

They found a table near the back and sat down. They had just sat down when two other girls joined them. They were friends of Brandy's. Brandy introduced them. "Tonya and Josey, this is Robbie Parker," said Brandy. "He's my new roommate." Robbie stood and shook hand with both of them.

"I'm pleased to meet any friend of Brandy's," said Robbie.

"Robbie tells me he's a good dancer," said Brandy. "I intend to find out."

"If he is, can we borrow him too?" asked Josey.

"That's up to him," said Brandy. Before Robbie could say anything, a waitress came to get their drink orders. She was a very attractive girl. She was wearing hot pants and a very snug fitting blouse. She took their order and left. The girls could see that Robbie was watching the waitress. "She's got nice legs doesn't she?" said Brandy. "Her ass is cute too."

"Hey, I'm not dead," said Robbie. "She's an attractive girl, but so are all of you."

"So you'd be staring at us if we had on hot pants and a tight blouse," said Tonya.

"I said I wasn't dead, didn't I?" said Robbie. "Now if I try hard enough, I can sit here and imagine what you all would look like if you were dressed like that. In fact, I don't have to try too hard."

"I like this guy," said Josey. "Keep him around for a while." Their drinks came and Robbie paid the waitress and tipped her.

"You didn't have to do that," said Brandy. "This was my idea."

"Well you can get the next round," said Robbie. They had taken a few sips of their beer when the band started playing a song that Brandy really liked. It was also a good dancing song. Before she said a word, Robbie had her hand and was leading her to the dance floor. Robbie decided he would make a good impression and really got down to business. Brandy was really impressed. She had never danced with anyone who could move like this. After a little while, the other dancers on the floor moved out of the way so they could watch them. Robbie had Brandy over his head, around his waist, and between his legs. Then he used some moves that Maria had taught him. The song was actually over but the band kept playing so they could watch the dancers too. The normally three and a half minute song lasted almost ten minutes. When the band finally stopped, the whole placed cheered for the couple. Robbie and Brandy stood in the middle of dance floor like a figure skating couple. Robbie took a bow and Brandy did a little curtsy. They started back to their table. Just as they got to the edge of the dance floor, the band started a slow song. Robbie smiled at Brandy and took her back to the middle of the dance floor. They held each other tightly as they danced. Brandy looked up at Robbie.

"You weren't kidding," said Brandy. "You are an exceptionally good dancer. Where the hell did you learn to dance like that?"

"My parents taught me," answered Robbie. "I also learned some moves from a girlfriend."

"Well I'm impressed," said Brandy. "I don't know if I'll share you or not."

"Well I'll have to rest my leg a bit after this," said Robbie. "It's aching some." Robbie kept hoping that the song would be over soon. He could feel himself getting excited and he knew that Brandy could too. She looked up at him again and smiled. "Hey, I told you I wasn't dead," said Robbie. Brandy just smiled and held on even tighter. Finally the song ended and they went back to their table. Tonya and Josey were just returning too. They had been on the dance floor too. The guys that had danced with them didn't stick around.

"So when do I get a chance?" asked Josey.

"He needs to rest a bit," said Brandy.

"Why? He looks healthy to me." said Josey.

"Because, my dear Josey, Robbie is a Veteran," said Brandy. "He was wounded and he needs to rest his leg."

So you were in Vietnam," said Josey. "I can't imagine what it was like for you. I'm against the war myself."

"We don't need to discuss the war this evening," said Robbie. "I'll be ready to dance again shortly."

"So you were hit in the leg?" asked Tonya.

"I'll say this one more time ladies," said Robbie. "We won't talk about the war or anything related to the war."

"Geeze, you sure are touchy," said Josey.

"Look Josey, you seem like a nice girl," said Robbie. "Please don't talk about the war or anything related to the war. Can you do that for me?"

"Yes I can, but I don't know if I will," said Josey.

"Well then I guess I can't dance with you," said Robbie.

"Well I'll go find someone else," said Josey. "Come on Tonya, let's go."

"Hey, you can go if you want," said Tonya. "I want to dance with Robbie at least one time."

"Suit yourself," said Josey. "I'll be around." Josey left and blended herself into the crowd.

"I apologize for Josey," said Tonya. "She can be hard headed at times."

"We all can," said Robbie. "My leg's rested now. We can dance now." Robbie escorted Tonya to the dance floor. Robbie didn't use all of his moves, but he used enough to make sure Tonya was impressed. When the song was over, he escorted her back to the table.

"You can have him back now," Tonya said to Brandy. "I would like to slip back and get a slow dance with him. I'll go see what Josey is up to now. See you later."

"So how was Tonya?" asked Brandy.

"She followed me fairly well," said Robbie. "She wasn't near as good as you though." They finished their beer and ordered another one. When the waitress set the beers on the table, she had some napkins that she set the beers on. Brandy paid her. When Robbie picked up his beer to take a sip, he noticed some writing on the napkin. He picked it up to see what it was.

"I bet it's her name and number and what time she gets off," said Brandy.

"Close, it doesn't have what time she gets off," said Robbie.

"How does it feel to have women chasing you?" asked Brandy.

"It's a curse," answered Robbie. "I'm just kidding. Let's dance." They went back out on the dance floor. They danced for three songs. They were about to leave the floor when the band started playing another slow song. They stayed for it. When the song ended, the band announced they were taking a break. Brandy and Robbie went back to their table.

Several people who knew Brandy stopped at their table and talked for a while. All of the girls wanted to know where Robbie learned to dance so well. Even some of the guys said they wished they could dance like that. There was one guy named Clark who came by and had apparently been a former boyfriend of Brandy's. Robbie could tell by their conversation that their relationship didn't end well. He kept calling Brandy a bitch and a spoiled brat. He was a little drunk too. Robbie was about to insist that he move on when Brandy stood up and punched him right in the nose. He went down hard. Blood poured from his nose and was all over his shirt. "You fucking bitch," he said as he was getting back up.

"I'd back off if I was you," said Robbie.

"And just who in the fuck are you?" said Clark.

"I'm the guy who's going to hurt you if you don't leave Brandy alone," said Robbie. Robbie stood up now.

"I don't need any help with this ass hole," said Brandy. "She let fly with a left hook and caught Clark's right jaw. He went down again." Several other people in the place cheered. About that time, some bouncers came over to see what was happening.

"This gentleman on the floor insulted the lady here and she put him down," said Robbie.

"Is that right miss? Is that what happened?" asked one of the bouncers.

"It certainly is," answered Brandy. "Would you please escort this ass hole out the door."

"It would be a pleasure miss," said the bouncer. "You don't need a job do you?" Brandy let out a laugh.

"No, but thanks for the offer," answered Brandy. The bouncers grabbed Clark and escorted him to the door. When he struggled some, one of them put Clark's arm behind his back and told him that if he didn't settle down, he'd break it for him.

"So it looks like you can take care of yourself," said Robbie. "You got a mean left hook. And the right's not bad either."

"I put up with that guy's shit for too long," said Brandy. "He started out as a really nice guy and then somewhere along the way, he got possessive and nasty. He slapped me once. I tried to slap him back but he blocked it. I was lucky today. He was drunk when I hit him. Anyway, he's history."

"Well if we ever run into him when he's sober and he gets nasty, I'll clean his clock for you," said Robbie.

"I think you and I are going to be good friends Robbie Parker," said Brandy.

"I think so too," said Robbie. "The band's back. Let's go dance some more."

"Gladly," said Brandy.

The band played some good songs and they stayed on the dance floor for a long time. They had danced for one slow song not long after they went back to the dance floor and now the band started another one. They had just got going when Tonya showed up. "Mind if I cut in?" she said. "Remember, I said I wanted one slow dance."

"All right, go ahead," said Brandy. "Give him back when you're done." Tonya clung to Robbie very tightly as they danced. When they were done, she took Robbie back to the table and thanked Brandy. Then she was on her way. "Did she have anything to say?" asked Brandy.

"We never said one word while we danced," said Robbie.

"That's surprising," said Brandy. "Well anyway, it's close to midnight. Do you want to dance some more?"

"I've had enough," said Robbie. "But I'll stay if you want."

"I've had enough too," said Brandy. "Dancing with you is fun but it's a lot of work too. How bout we go get some pizza. I know this place that has real good pizza. They sell it by the slice too if you don't want to get a whole pizza."

"That's fine by me," said Robbie. "Let's go."

It took them around fifteen minutes to get to the pizza parlor. Robbie was impressed. The pizza was really good. They could have gotten beer with their pizza, but both of them had a soda instead. They talked a lot about their lives before they first left home.

"I was basically a tom boy," said Brandy. "I never wanted to do girl things. I liked sports, especially baseball. I wanted to play baseball so bad, but they wouldn't let me. I ended up playing softball in school. I played third or short."

"That's interesting," said Robbie. "I was a baseball player. I played little league and up to American Legion ball. We never had any girls playing either. I never heard of any girls who wanted to play."

"So what position did you play?" asked Brandy.

"When I first started, I played second base," started Robbie. "The next year I went to shortstop. My last year of little league, I was a pitcher."

"I bet you had a mean curveball," said Brandy.

"I did," said Robbie. "I threw it three different ways. I had a good sinker too." When I played Teener ball at 13, I played second base. The next year I was at short and at 15, I pitched."

"Were you a good hitter?" asked Brandy.

"I've always batted lead-off, third, or clean-up," answered Robbie.

"So you can hit too," said Brandy. "How was Legion ball?"

"Legion ball was a good experience," answered Robbie. "I soon found out that I just couldn't blow the ball by the hitters. I learned how to really pitch. I had a good coach."

"Well maybe we can get out the gloves when the weather warns up," said Brandy. "You can show me what you got."

"I look forward to it," said Robbie. "I'll probably go home some weekend sometime and I'll bring back my glove and some balls. I'll get my bat too. I haven't thrown a ball for a year or so. When's the last time you threw a ball?"

"It's been longer than that for me," answered Brandy. "But it won't take us long to get loosened up."

"Let's finish up and get home if you don't mind," said Robbie. "I'm about to fall asleep."

"I'm getting tired too," said Brandy.

~~~~

When they got back to the apartment, Robbie thanked Brandy for a pleasant evening and went straight to his bed. He was asleep immediately. The next thing he knew, he was waking up to the sound of coffee percolating. He looked at his watch. It was 9 AM. He threw on a robe and went to the kitchen. Brandy was sitting on the couch sipping coffee. All she had on was a short robe. "Morning, how did you sleep?" asked Brandy.

"Like a baby," answered Robbie. "I went right to sleep and the next thing I hear is the coffee being made."

"Well you sure did a lot of cussing in your sleep," said Brandy. "I thought I could cuss, but I can't hold a candle to what you were saying last night."

"What was I saying?" asked Robbie.

"Well I didn't get all of it at any one time," said Brandy. "Seemed like I got woke up and caught a few words and then I went back to sleep. Then the same thing happened again. That happened a couple of times last night. Fuck was the word you used the most. Mother fuckers came in second. The rest was a lot of shits and damns. You know, the more common stuff."

"I'm sorry," said Robbie. "I had no idea I was doing that. My folks never said anything about anything like that when I was at home. The times that I spent the night with girls, they never said I did that. That seems strange. I really slept well last night. If I dreamed at all, I never knew it. If I do that again, come into my room and wake me up. Just give me a nudge and then stand back."

"Why do I need to stand back?" asked Brandy.

"Well if I was dreaming about the war, I might think you were the enemy or something," said Robbie. "I could wake up and take a swing at you or something worse. I'm sorry. I hope I'm not scaring you."

"I've heard about guys sleeping with a gun under their pillow when they get home," said Brandy.

"Well I don't have a gun with me," said Robbie. "Don't worry. If I get wacko, I'll get myself to a shrink." Robbie poured himself a cup of coffee. He took a sip. "Hey, you make good coffee," said Robbie. "How bout I make us some bacon and scrambled eggs for breakfast?"

"Sounds good," said Brandy. "I don't like my eggs runny."

"Neither do I," said Robbie. Robbie fixed breakfast and they ate.

"You did good with the bacon," said Brandy. "Just the way I like it. Nice and crispy but not burnt. The eggs are good too." After they ate, Robbie did the dishes and Brandy sat at the table sipping coffee.

"I'm going to take a shower now," said Robbie. "I feel a little sweaty. Should have taken one last night before bed."

"Would you like some company?" asked Brandy. Robbie was a little surprised by Brandy's question. He gave her a hard look and then smiled.

"Brandy, you are a very attractive woman and any guy who's not dead would jump at the chance to take a shower with you," said Robbie. "But I don't think we should be doing that just yet."

"So you mean there's a chance we could do it later?" asked Brandy.

"I'm not dead Brandy," said Robbie. "You will be very hard to resist." Brandy didn't say a word. She got up off her chair and walked to her room. Right before she entered her room, she slipped off her robe so Robbie could see her backside naked as she entered her room.

"I better make this a cold shower," Robbie said to himself as he closed the bathroom door.

~~~~

Classes would start tomorrow so Robbie got out his alarm clock and checked it to make sure he wouldn't oversleep in the morning. He really wanted to get out and walk around the neighborhood, but it was very cold outside and there was a chance of snow. Brandy went to visit some friends for the day and told Robbie she wouldn't be back till late. Robbie decided to write some letters. He wrote one to Carl Sims telling him that he was in Cincinnati now and that they should get together sometime. Another letter he wrote to Larry Johnson. Larry was still in Vietnam, but he should be getting short. Robbie hadn't been following the news about the war closely, but he knew that Nixon's troop withdrawals had started. The 3rd Marine Division had left in late 1969, but the 1st Marine Division was still there. Some Army units had been withdrawn too. All of this worried Robbie. He had not had much experience working with the ARVN's. All he ever heard was that they were useless. If they were taking over areas where the Americans had been, the remaining American troops could be in some real trouble. "Get all this out of your head Robbie," he said to himself. "You're home now." Robbie started having some flashbacks. He tried to get them out of his head but couldn't. He went to his bed and curled up into a ball. The next thing he knew, Brandy was standing next to his bed smiling at him.

"So you went to bed without me again," said Brandy. "How was your day?"

"Whoa, I must have fallen asleep," said Robbie. "I wrote some letters and that's all I remember."

"So are you hungry?" asked Brandy. "I haven't eaten dinner yet. There's still some chili. I'll heat it up. Do you want some?"

"What time is it?" asked Robbie.

"It's seven," answered Brandy.

"Wow, I slept a good while," said Robbie. "I haven't eaten since breakfast. I guess I am hungry. How bout I make us a grilled cheese sandwich too?"

"Sounds good," said Brandy. "Maybe there's a movie on we can watch." Brandy put the chili on the stove and turned on the TV looking for a movie. Robbie got busy with the sandwiches. They had their choice of three movies. One was a war movie, "In Love and War." Then there were two John Wayne movies, "The Quiet Man," and "Stagecoach." They decided to watch both of the John Wayne movies. They would watch one for fifteen minutes and then switch to the other one for fifteen minutes. "Why do you think people like John Wayne?" asked Brandy. "I never really liked him."

"Well I'm no critic," started Robbie. "But you've got to admit, He's not an ugly man. He's a big man. He walks with that swagger and there's the way he says his lines. Some folks like that. Just listen to his lines. Next time he says something, try to imagine what it would be like if he said it differently. They were watching "The Quiet Man" now. John Wayne was having some words with Maureen O'Hara. Brandy said John Wayne's line several different ways.

"I guess the way he said it was the best," said Brandy. "Mary Kate, DANAHER!" Before either of the movies were done, they switched channels. The NFL playoffs were going on. Brandy wasn't a real football fan either, but they watched the rest of the game that was on.

~~~~

The first day of classes went well for Robbie. His instructors were nice and seemed very knowledgeable. The classes were small so none of the students should feel neglected. The first week breezed by. Robbie felt good about the school. He and some of the other people in his class were going out Saturday afternoon to get a few beers. He and Brandy were having some coffee Saturday morning when the phone rang. Brandy answered it. "It's for you Robbie," said Brandy. "It's your mother."

"Hi Mom, what's up?" asked Robbie.

"I just called to make sure you're doing o.k. down there," said Mary.

"Everything's good Mom," said Robbie. "Are you and Dad o.k.?"

"We're fine," said Mary. "I also wanted to let you know that Debbie Ryan called. She's the girl you were dating before you left, isn't she?"

"Yes Mom, that was Debbie," said Robbie.

"Well she asked if I would give her your address and phone number," said Mary. "I gave them to her. Is that all right with you?"

"Yes mom, that's fine," said Robbie. "I thought about calling or writing her, but I haven't done it yet."

"Well you should expect a call or a letter from her very soon," said Mary. "I think that girl loves you son. I don't know what happened between you two, but I think she is very sorry about it. So, how's you roommate? Is school o.k.?"

"You'll have to meet my roommate Mom," said Robbie. "She is one very nice girl. She's got a mean left hook too. I'll tell you about that another time. School is o.k. so far. Classes are small and the instructors are nice."

"I'm glad all is well for you son," said Mary. "I'll let you go now. We love you."

"I love you too Mom. Talk to you later, goodbye," said Robbie.

"Goodbye son," said Mary.

"So I am one very nice girl?" asked Brandy.

"Yes you are girl," said Robbie. "You try to come on like a hard ass, but you're not. You're gentle and sweet." Robbie was going to say more but before he could get any words out, Brandy had come over to him and slipped her tongue down his throat. Robbie thought about pulling away, but didn't. An hour later, they were holding each other on the couch.

"So that Debbie girl, is she the girl who had her house broken into?" asked Brandy.

"That's her," answered Robbie.

"Does she love you?" asked Brandy.

"I don't know," answered Robbie. "My mom thinks that she does. She called the house to get my address and phone number."

"Do you think you love her?" asked Brandy.

"When we first met, we said that we didn't want a serious relationship," said Robbie. "I have strong feelings for her but I do not think that I really love her. I was in love twice before and there was no doubt in my mind that I was in love. I might fall in love with her some day, but for now I'm convinced it was lust."

"Will you lust after her when you go back home on a weekend or semester break?" asked Brandy.

"Probably," answered Robbie. "Speaking of lust and such, I hope you're on the pill. I usually don't have unprotected sex."

"I'm on the pill and this is the first time in years that I've had unprotected sex," said Brandy. "Pretty sure I don't have the clap or something worse." Brandy had her back against Robbie's chest and Robbie had his arms around her. He gently caressed her breasts. She turned to face him. She straddled his lap and shoved her breasts into his face. His mouth found hers and they started all over again. It seemed it would never end. They finally lay on the couch exhausted. They smiled at each other but did not kiss. "I noticed all of your scars Robbie," said Brandy. "I hope they don't hurt you anymore."

"The only one that hurts is my left thigh," said Robbie. "The bone was shattered. Sometimes it aches a lot. I think this colder weather makes it worse sometimes. Maybe someday it won't bother me anymore."

"I hope so," said Brandy. "So you weren't thinking about Debbie while we were doing it, were you?"

Robbie got up off the couch and took Brandy by the hand and pulled her up off the couch. He led her over to a full sized mirror that was in the hallway. "Now look in that mirror," said Robbie.

"O.k., I'll look in the mirror," said Brandy. She looked at herself in the mirror and then looked at Robbie. "O.k., I've looked," said Brandy.

"Tell me what you see," said Robbie.

"I see me of course," said Brandy.

"Of course you see yourself, but how do you look?" asked Robbie.

"I look pretty damn good," said Brandy.

"That's right. You look pretty damn good," said Robbie. "Now how could I be with you and be thinking about someone else? I don't think that would be possible."

"You know the right things to say Robbie Parker," said Brandy. She wrapped herself around him and they were at it again. After a good while they were in the shower. They spent some time in the shower and then dried each other off.

"I'm supposed to meet some people from my class at some bar this afternoon," said Robbie. "Would you want to go?"

"Sure, I'll go," said Brandy. "I didn't have anything planned today. Should we get a sandwich here or get something at the bar?"

"I'm hungry but I can wait till we get to the bar if you can," said Robbie.

"What time are you meeting them?" asked Brandy.

"They said two o'clock," said Robbie. "If you're really hungry, we can eat something here or just go early to the bar and eat something before the rest of them get there. It's 12:30 now. What do you want to do?"

"I already did that three times," answered Brandy. "Let's just go early and grab something there. What is this place we're going to anyway?"

"It's just some small neighborhood bar," said Robbie. "The other people have been there and they say it's a nice place and they have good hamburgers."

"Well let's get ready and go," said Brandy. "I always appreciate a good hamburger. Anyone who doesn't is un-American or a communist."

"Don't talk like that girl. You're getting me excited again," said Robbie. Brandy smiled at him and went into her room and got dressed. Robbie did the same.

Robbie found the bar with no problems. It was small, but it was a nice place. Several people were sitting at the bar watching a basketball game. There were a few booths and some tables, all of which were empty. They picked a table and sat down. An older woman came over from the bar and asked what they wanted to drink. Brandy ordered a Michelob. Robbie ordered a Strohs. "You young folks want hi or lo?" asked the bartender.

"We'll just take lo," replied Robbie. "We're not 21 yet."

"I'm s'posed to card you but I can see that you're not high school kids," said the bartender.

"We're definitely not high school kids," said Robbie. "We're studying to become morticians."

"Jesus God, are you serious?" asked the bartender.

"Yes I am," answered Robbie. "They'll be six more of us in here shortly. Would it be all right if we pulled two tables together?"

"Sure, go ahead," said the bartender. She walked back over to the bar to get the beer. She yelled across the bar to someone named Barney. "Hey Barney, we got us some folks here that are gonna be morticians," yelled the bartender. "You'll be needin'em soon."

"I'm not that far gone you old bitch," said Barney. The other folks in the bar let out a laugh. There were some menus on the table. Robbie and Brandy studied them while the bartender was getting the beer. She returned with the beer shortly.

"You two want somethin' to eat?" the bartender asked.

"I'll have a cheeseburger with everything on it and some onion rings," said Brandy.

"I'll have the same," said Robbie. "Ma'am, may I ask your name?"

"I'm Polly," she answered.

"Well Polly, This young woman is Brandy and I'm Robbie," said Robbie. "We're pleased to meet you. So tell me Polly. Are your cheeseburgers good?"

"Best damn cheeseburgers around this town," answered Polly. "Way better'n that shit you get at McDonalds or them other fast food dumps."

"Thank you Polly, I just know they'll be good," said Robbie. "I bet them onion rings'll be good too."

"None better," said Polly as she walked away and went into the kitchen.

"So what do you think of this place?" asked Robbie.

"I like it," answered Brandy. "It's cozy in here. It's not all loud and everything like big places. It's not far from our apartment either. If we would happen to drink too much while we were here, a cab wouldn't cost too much. If we weren't too drunk, we could probably walk if we had to."

"I like it too. It kind of reminds me of the Legion post back home," said Robbie. "It's mostly older folks and it's nice and quiet." They hadn't talked another ten minutes when the other people from Robbie's class arrived. They saw Brandy and Robbie and went to the tables Robbie had grabbed. They all introduced themselves and sat down. They heard Polly yell across the room again.

"Hey Barney, they're ready for you now," said Polly.

"I done told you old woman. I'm not goin' anywhere just yet," said Barney. Everyone let out another laugh.

Polly came over and took their order. After she had everyone's order, she asked them a question. "So all a you are really gonna be working on dead folks?" asked Polly.

"Yes we are," answered one of the others. "Someone's gotta do it."

"I don't think I could do that," said Polly. "It would give me the creeps."

"Well dead folks are usually very quiet and don't cause much trouble," said Brandy.

"Ha Ha," said Polly as she walked back to the bar.

Of the six people from Robbie's class, three were male and three were female. Robbie didn't expect that there would be many women in this line of work. The six seemed to be couples. They did not know Brandy as she was a semester ahead of them, but they had seen her at the school. They had a good time at the bar. They all finally left around six. Brandy was concerned about Robbie driving, but he assured her that he was all right to drive. "We've been here all this time and I only had three beers," said Robbie. "I guess I talked more than I drank." They got back home with no trouble. They both sprawled out on the ends of the couch. Brandy dozed off after a bit. She woke up a short while later. "I'm hungry again," she said. "I'm making a sandwich. You want one?"

"Stay put," said Robbie. "I'll make them for us. What would you like?"

"Don't matter. Whatever we got is fine," said Brandy. Robbie made some sandwiches and took one to Brandy. He also brought her a glass of milk.

"If you don't want the milk, I'll drink it," said Robbie.

"I'll drink it. I should drink more of it," said Brandy. "I like the whole stuff, not that skim stuff."

Both of them spent Sunday studying. Later in the day, Robbie wrote a letter home and asked his parents if they would send him his baseball glove and some balls. The next week at school breezed by quickly. Robbie enjoyed his classes and really liked his classmates. When he got home from class on Friday, there was a letter from Debbie waiting on him. He put his books in his room and then sat down on the couch and read the letter.

Dear Robbie,

I am ashamed of myself for the way I acted when we were at that party. I am not sure why I acted that way. Maybe it was because it happened not long after the attempted break-in at the house. Words cannot explain how badly I feel about my actions. I know that you are a kind and gentle man. I have missed you more than I can say. I loved the times we spent together. I hope we can see each other again.

You mother is a very nice person and I enjoyed talking with her. I can tell by talking to her that you have a close and loving family. I hope you are doing well at your school. I am confident that you would do well no matter what you would become.

Anna is having a great time being a stripper. She finally got Tina talked into doing it too. Tina is happy with the money and of course she likes the men. Sharon has got herself a new boyfriend. He's in Law School.

I met him the other day. He's a nice guy. He looks like a lawyer too. She doesn't get to see him all of the time because he studies so much, but I think that she works him over when they get together.

Robbie, I sincerely hope to hear from you. Please write me. I miss you terribly.

Love,
Debbie

Robbie was sitting on the couch with the letter still in his hand when Brandy got home. She threw her books and things on her bed and then went to refrigerator and got a beer. She sat down on the other end of the couch and looked at Robbie. "I bet that letter's from Debbie," said Brandy.

"Yep, it is," said Robbie.

"She misses you and loves you, right," said Brandy.

"Well she misses me and is sorry for how she acted, but she doesn't come out and say she loves me," said Robbie.

"Let me read it," said Brandy.

"'No," said Robbie. "You are a nosey girl, aren't you?"

"Hey, you already told me what she said," said Brandy. "I might as well read it. Come on, give it here. I'll tell you if she loves you or not."

"What the hell, go ahead," said Robbie. Robbie handed the letter to Brandy. She sat there and gave the letter a good once over.

"Oh hell yes, that girl loves you," said Brandy. "There's no doubt about it." Brandy slipped over next to Robbie. "Now if she were here, she be doing this," said Brandy as she started kissing Robbie on the ear and neck. Then she eased her way to his mouth. "Then she'd be doing this," said Brandy as she pulled Robbie's shirt off of him. She took off her blouse and bra and straddled him. Then she'd do this," said Brandy as she rubbed her breasts against his chest as she locked her mouth on his.

"Then I'd be doing this," said Robbie as he picked her up and carried her to his room. A good while later, they were soaking in the tub. They slowly washed each other. When they were finished, they went to their separate rooms and got dressed. Robbie just put on some jeans and a sweatshirt. Brandy was wearing some nicer clothes. Robbie kind of stared at her.

"I won't be here this evening," said Brandy. "I have a date."

"That's interesting," said Robbie. "We just had some great sex and now you're going on a date. Don't take it the wrong way. It doesn't bother me. I have just never met anyone like you."

"Any you will never meet anyone like me," said Brandy. "I don't have a ring on my finger and I do what I want and when I want. But I'll tell you this Robbie, if I ever do find the right man, I will commit myself totally to him."

"You're a good woman Brandy. I consider you a true friend. I am glad I know you," said Robbie. "I hope your date is a good person." Brandy came over to Robbie and gave him a big hug.

"You're a true friend Robbie," said Brandy. "Now since I'll be out of your hair this evening, you'll have plenty of time to answer Debbie's letter." Just then, the door bell rang. "That's my date," said Brandy as she went out the door. "Don't wait up."

Robbie decided he was hungry and looked in the refrigerator. He decided he would make himself some pork chops, fried potatoes, and green beans. The meal didn't take long to prepare. He sat at the kitchen table and ate. He did the dishes when he was finished eating, and then he put a load of laundry in the washing machine. He got his pen and paper and sat down at the table. He thought and thought. Writing this letter would be harder than he thought. "I really like Debbie, but here I am having sex with my roommate," Robbie said to himself. "Maybe I should think like Brandy does. There's no ring on my finger. Well here goes."

Dear Debbie,

I was glad to get your letter. I have missed you too. I kept telling myself to call or write you but I didn't. I am ashamed of myself for not doing so. The two incidents that happened were very close together and I can understand why you would be upset. I do not enjoy hitting people, but sometimes force is the only thing certain people understand. I greatly enjoyed our times together and I'm sure we will have many more of them. I will probably come home Easter weekend and we can see each other then. Our spring break time is somewhere around the end of April and early May. I know I will be home then for sure and we will see each other.

So far, I like my classes and I have made many new friends. Not all people who want to be morticians are "dead" heads. Pardon the pun. I hope you're are doing well with your classes too. Let's hope that since Anna and

Tina are making good money as strippers, they don't decide to drop out of
school. Tell Sharon I hope her lawyer friend works out.
   I miss you and will be so glad when we see each other again,

Love,

Robbie

Robbie sealed up the letter and took it to the mailbox. His wash load was done so he put it in the dryer. He sat around and watched TV for a while. There was a Jimmy Stewart movie on and it was a western. After the movie, he took a shower and went to bed. It seemed like it took him hours to get to sleep. He'd been asleep for a good while when he saw S/Sgt. Rojas. Rojas handed him a K-bar. The next thing Robbie knew, he was sticking the knife into the gut of an NVA soldier. He heard someone shouting. Then he heard a sound that was like the crack of a whip. Then there was a scream. He sat up in bed. There was another crack and a scream. Robbie finally realized that the noises were real and he was now awake. They were coming from Brandy's room. He heard Brandy yell. "I'll cut your balls off if I get the chance you piece of shit." He threw on his jeans and grabbed his cane. As he was running to her room, he heard a man's voice. "Shut up bitch. You know you like it."

When Robbie entered Brandy's room, he saw that Brandy was tied to her bed. She was face down and some very big man was standing at the end of the bed with a leather belt in his right hand. He was about to hit Brandy with the belt again. Robbie came up behind him and hooked his cane around the man's neck and pulled him backwards off of Brandy and onto the floor. Before the man could react, Robbie was on him beating him senseless. Brandy was able to turn her head enough and see what was happening. When Robbie was sure that the man was unconscious, he got off of him and untied Brandy. She wrapped her arms around him and began crying. She quit after a few minutes. "Is he dead?" asked Brandy.

"No, just unconscious," answered Robbie.

"I want to kill him," said Brandy.

"We can't do that," said Robbie. "We need to call the police. Can you call them while I make sure this guy stays unconscious?"

"Can I cut his nuts off first?" asked Brandy.

"No, but that's what he deserves," answered Robbie. Brandy put on a robe and called the police. They must have been in the area because they were there in ten minutes. Brandy answered the door when they arrived.

"I'm officer Dalton and this is officer Sharp," said Dalton. "Now what do we have here?"

"I'm Brandy Wisecup and this is my apartment," started Brandy. "I went on a date with that guy who's on the floor in my room. We came back here to have sex. He slapped me so hard that it knocked me out for a little while." Brandy showed them her face. It was red and starting to bruise. "The next thing I know is I'm tied to my bed face down and this guy is whipping me with his belt." The officers were taking notes. They went to Brandy's room. The guy was still unconscious on the floor.

"Who are you?" officer Dalton asked Robbie.

"I'm Robbie Parker," started Robbie. "I share this apartment with Brandy. I was asleep in my room when I heard screaming and the sound of a whip or something. I heard that fella say, "shut up, you know you like it bitch." I came into her room and saw her tied to the bed and him getting ready to hit her again. I knocked him off of her and knocked him unconscious."

"What's this guy's name?" asked Dalton.

"It's Paul Jordan," answered Brandy. Officer Sharp found Paul's pants on the floor and checked his wallet.

"Yep, that's Paul Jordan all right," said Sharp. "You're lucky lady. This guy has been picked up several times for assaulting women. Seems the other women always drop the charges. That's why he's still around."

"Well I won't be dropping any charges," said Brandy. "If this son of a bitch comes near me again, I'm gonna cut his nuts and his dick off. I have a camera. Robbie you take some pictures of me in case they need them for evidence."

"We have a camera ma'am," said Dalton. "We'll take some pictures." Jordan was coming to now. Dalton stood him up and put the cuffs on him. Jordan never said a word. Dalton read him his rights and they took him to the cruiser still naked. They put Jordan's clothes in a bag and they put a blanket over Jordan. Sharp stayed at the cruiser and Dalton came back with the camera. He took several pictures of Brandy's face and then her backside. He also took pictures of her wrists and legs where she had been tied. "I'm sorry this happened to you Brandy," said Dalton. "Maybe now he can go to jail and be someone's girlfriend. If you want medical attention, I'll get a squad over here."

"I have plenty of first aid stuff," said Brandy. "I'll be all right."

"Hope you get healed up," said Dalton. "Bye now."

After Dalton left, Brandy got her camera and had Robbie take some pictures. "Why do you want pictures now?" asked Robbie. "The cops have pictures."

"I want them to remind me of what I got myself into tonight," said Brandy. Robbie took the pictures and then they did what they could for Brandy's injuries. She was lucky that Robbie woke up when he did. She could have been very seriously injured. They stood and looked at each other for a while after Brandy put away the first aid kit. "I want to go to sleep now," said Brandy. "Can I sleep with you Robbie? I need to hold on to someone tonight."

"Sure you can," said Robbie as he led her to his room.

"I'll have to sleep on my side," said Brandy. "It's hurts a good bit on my backside. We can sleep facing each other?"

"That's fine," said Robbie. They undressed, climbed into bed, and held each other. They were asleep in no time.

Chapter Sixteen

Robbie woke up the next morning to the sound of coffee percolating. He got up, put on a robe, and went to the bathroom. When he came out of the bathroom, Brandy was sitting on the couch having some coffee.

"Morning Robbie, how did you sleep?" asked Brandy. "I slept really good. I can't believe I slept that good." Robbie got himself some coffee.

"I slept good too," said Robbie. "I didn't do any cussing or anything last night, did I?"

"If you did, I didn't hear it," answered Brandy. "When I woke up, we were still holding and facing each other. I thought you might wake up when I got out of bed, but you didn't. How does my face look? I haven't looked in the mirror yet. I've kind of been afraid to." Robbie sat down close to Brandy on the couch and took a good look at her face.

"It's still a little red and it's slightly bruised just below your cheek," said Robbie. "I think that a little extra make-up would cover it up no problem."

"Well take a look at my ass," said Brandy. "It feels sore back there." Brandy stood up and pulled up her robe so Robbie could see her backside.

"The swelling has really gone down," said Robbie. "The skin was not broken too badly so I don't think there will be any noticeable marks when it heals."

"It was a good thing you woke up when you did," said Brandy. "Robbie, thank you for saving me. I would still like to cut off his nuts and dick."

"That's totally understandable," said Robbie. "I hit that son of a bitch more than enough times to knock him out. Let's hope he gets put away for a long time.

Want some pancakes for breakfast? I make good pancakes. We can have some sausage, pancakes, and eggs."

"Sure, why not?" said Brandy. "Living with you could make me fat. If I start getting fat, promise me you'll help me work it off."

"Of course I will help you," said Robbie. "You know, I was thinking about joining a gym or something. I really need to build up my upper body strength, especially on my left side. I saw an ad for this one place that only costs ten bucks a month. They're supposed to have all kinds of weights and machines. Would you be interested in something like that?"

"I had a membership at a gym once," said Brandy. "I went religiously for the first three months. Then I got away from it. I didn't like the people there. They were so concerned about their looks. This place had mirrors on almost every wall. It was kind of sickening."

"Well if you go with me, you won't have to worry about other people," said Robbie. "We could work out together. What do you say?"

"We can give it a try," said Brandy. "Do you have any workout clothes?"

"I have T-shirts, sweat pants, and sneakers," answered Robbie. "That's good enough to start isn't it?"

"Yes it is," answered Brandy. "Maybe later on you'll want some gloves and a weight belt."

"So do you have workout stuff?" asked Robbie.

"I still have my stuff," answered Brandy. "So what are you going to do today?"

"I was just going to lounge around and do some studying," answered Robbie. "Are you doing anything?"

"No, I'll just do some studying too," said Brandy. "Maybe I'll make a us a nice dinner today too. Do you have any requests?"

"I'm sure whatever you do will be good," said Robbie. "I can eat about anything anyway. I've never had heartburn in my life either. Spicey stuff won't hurt me."

"Well I'll think on it," said Brandy.

Robbie got busy making breakfast. Brandy was impressed with his pancakes. "You made the pancakes from scratch didn't you?" asked Brandy. "I don't remember seeing any boxes of mix around here."

"Yep, they're from scratch," said Robbie. "My mother taught me."

"Well they were really good," said Brandy. "I don't usually eat my eggs over easy, but these were good too. Are you sure you weren't a cook in the Marines?"

"I did cook some in the Corps," said Robbie. "I heated up my C-rats."

"What are C-rats like?" asked Brandy. "In the movies, the men are always bitching about their rations."

"They're not that bad," answered Robbie. "The best one is the "beans and franks," or "beans and weanies," or whatever it's called. It's just like the pork and beans that you get at the store with pieces of hot dog in it. It's not bad. Then there's spaghetti, ham and limas, and—. Damn, I can't remember right now. But there is one that I will never forget. It was called "beef slices with potatoes and gravy." We called it "beef and rocks," or "beef and shrapnel." It was nasty. I never knew a potato could be that hard and nasty. In each box of C-rats, you also got a little packet. Inside the packet was a little pack of smokes, 4 cigarettes. Then there was some instant coffee and some hot cocoa. We also got a little thing of toilet paper, some matches, and a heat tab or two. Sometimes, there was fruit."

"What's a heat tab?" asked Brandy.

"It's just some little tablet thing that you burned to heat up your food," answered Robbie. "You used an empty C-rat can and made yourself a little stove. Oh, we also got a small can that had crackers and peanut butter or cheese in it."

"So when you weren't out in the bush, did you have a mess hall or whatever you call it?" asked Brandy.

"Depends on where you were," answered Robbie. "If you were at some small fire base out in the middle of nowhere, you got C-rats. If you were at a bigger combat base, there would be a mess hall."

"How was the food at the mess halls," asked Brandy.

"Not as good as momma's," answered Robbie. "I just never thought about it. I just ate it. They always had good coffee though. They had better coffee over there than we had at stateside mess halls."

"Why would that be?" asked Brandy. "Shouldn't they be able to make it better stateside?"

"I just think it's the way they make it," said Robbie. "My dad told me that the coffee was always better in the field."

"So your dad was a Marine too?" asked Brandy.

"Yes he was," answered Robbie.

"My dad was in the Army Air Corps," said Brandy. "He was a bombardier on a B-17. They got shot down towards the end of the war and he was a POW for a short while. That's enough military talk. Would you put some of this cream on my backside?" Brandy had a tube of some first aid cream in her pocket.

"Sure, come over here and stand in front of me," said Robbie. Robbie sat on the couch and Brandy stood in front of him. Robbie rubbed the cream on her backside.

"You're enjoying this aren't you?" said Brandy.

"Hey, I'm not dead," said Robbie. "But I wish that I didn't need to do this."

"Well when it gets better, I'll probably have you check it out and make sure it's all right," said Brandy.

"I'll do my best," said Robbie. "Now I'll get these dishes cleaned up." Robbie started on the dishes. Brandy went into her room and came back with a book. She laid down on her belly on the couch. She pulled up her robe so her backside was exposed.

"You don't care if I study like this do you?" asked Brandy. "I think if I leave my ass uncovered, it'll heal quicker. You don't mind, do you?"

"Not one bit," said Robbie. "You can study like that all day if you want." Brandy looked over at Robbie and smiled. Then she put her nose in the book. Robbie finished the dishes and went to his room. He put on some jeans, a flannel shirt, and some socks. He didn't bother with any shoes. He grabbed a book and went to a chair in the living room and studied. At first he thought he would be distracted, but he wasn't. About three hours later, the phone rang. Robbie answered it. It was Brandy's father. Robbie introduced himself to him on the phone and then handed it to Brandy.

"Hi Daddy, what's up?" asked Brandy.

"Nothing Baby," answered her father. "I called because your mother and I will be in Cincinnati in a couple of weeks and we thought we could all go to dinner. Would that be all right with you?

"Sure Daddy, that would be nice," answered Brandy. "Would it be o.k. if Robbie went with us?"

"If you want him to come it's all right with us Baby," said her father. "Now I won't keep you. We love you."

"I love you too Daddy, goodbye," said Brandy. "Hey Daddy, would you bring my ball glove with you? Robbie and I will be playing catch some when we get a nice day."

"Sure Baby, I'll go round it up now so I don't forget," said her father. "Bye now."

Brandy hung up the phone and looked at Robbie. "My folks will be coming down here in a couple of weeks. We will be going out to dinner with them if it's all right with you."

"That sounds nice," said Robbie. "Will we go to a really nice place?"

"Yes we will," answered Brandy. "My folks don't go cheap when they go to dinner."

"Well I'll make sure my good clothes are cleaned and pressed," said Robbie.

"You won't need a suit," said Brandy. "Some nice slacks and a nice shirt and tie with a sweater would be good."

"Tell you what. I'll get my good stuff out this afternoon and you can take a look at it," said Robbie. "If you think I need something else, you can take me shopping. I need more nice clothes anyway. Now, I noticed you didn't tell your father about what happened. It's really none of my business, but if we're going to dinner with them, I don't want to slip up and say something."

"I'll tell Daddy when I think the time is right," said Brandy. "I'm not quite sure how he would react. He might want to go down to the jail and kill that guy. He's not one to turn the other cheek. Especially where his family is concerned. I sure hope my face is better. One time at a softball game in high school, this man said some bad things to me after a play. His daughter was on the other team. My dad yanked him out of the stands and took him out back in the parking lot. He politely asked the man to refrain from such verbal abuse. He told him that if he didn't, he wouldn't mind going to jail for working him over. The man was quiet after that."

"I think your dad and I will get along great," said Robbie. "So I was thinking about making a sandwich. You want one?"

"I'll just take a half of one," said Brandy. "There's some grapes in the frig. We can munch on them too." Robbie made the sandwiches and poured them a glass of milk. They sat at the kitchen table and ate. "I think I'll do something with chicken for dinner," said Brandy. "Got some breasts and I know how guys like breasts."

"I'm a dark meat kind of guy," said Robbie. "But like I said before, I'll eat anything. Are we talking about chicken?" Brandy laughed a little and went back to studying. Robbie cleaned up the table and went back to studying.

Brandy fixed them a fine dinner. She took the chicken breasts and pounded them a while to tenderize them. Then she did something with mayonnaise and mustard and some garlic. Robbie was very impressed. She made enough for two days too.

After dinner, Robbie did the dishes and then both of them went back to studying. At close to bedtime, Brandy took a shower. Robbie took one as soon as she was finished. After he brushed his teeth, he got into bed. He was just about asleep when Brandy came into his room. "May I sleep with you again tonight?" asked Brandy. "I still need someone to hold onto."

"Sure, I'll hold you," said Robbie. Brandy got into bed. They laid facing and holding each other.

"Thanks for doing this Robbie," said Brandy. "I need to be held."

"I'll hold you whenever you need it," said Robbie. "Let me know if I do anything strange tonight." They were asleep in no time.

The next morning, Brandy spent a good bit of time making sure her makeup was all right. She had an earlier class than Robbie and was leaving while he was still eating breakfast. They both were done with their classes at three o'clock. They got home about the same time. Robbie asked Brandy if she would go take a look at a gym with him and she agreed. "We'll just look around today and see what they have," said Robbie. "I want to talk with someone and see if they can help me get started properly."

"Fine, let's go," said Brandy. The gym was about fifteen minutes away. Robbie was impressed by all of their equipment. They had plenty of free weights and machines. There were plenty of treadmills and elliptical machines too. One of the employees showed them around. "We also have different classes too," said the employee. "My name's Josh. There's aerobics and yoga. We also have a guy who teaches judo. The judo costs extra."

"I'll need someone to help me get started with the weights," said Robbie. "I don't want to look like Arnold. I just need to build up some more upper body strength."

"No problem, anyone of the employees here would be glad to get you started," said Josh. "How about you Miss? What are you after?"

"Just wanting to stay in shape," said Brandy. "Nothing hardcore."

"We'll take care of you," said Josh. "So are you joining?"

"I believe we will," said Robbie. They went into an office and filled out some paperwork.

"You're all set," said Josh. "Just use that slip of paper till your membership card comes in the mail." They thanked Josh and then left.

On the way home Brandy talked a little about athletic women. "You know Robbie, a lot of very athletic women don't have big boobs," said Brandy. "Is it because they didn't have them when they started or they worked them off? I'd hate to make mine smaller."

"Gee, I never thought about that," said Robbie. "I guess I've never seen a tennis player or a figure skater with big boobs. I wouldn't worry about that if I were you. We're not going to work that much or that hard. If I notice that you're getting smaller, I'll tell you. You know, I've heard that if you have good pecs, you're boobs will stand up better. You didn't worry about this when you played ball did you?"

"No, they were smaller then," said Brandy. "They grew some after high school."

"Well take my word for it. They are really nice now," said Robbie. Brandy looked over at him and smiled. Nothing else was said till they got home. Dinner was quick and easy. All they had to do was heat up everything from last night. Robbie did the dishes after dinner and they both studied.

They went to the gym three times the first week and four times the second. Josh got Robbie started properly. After the second visit, Josh turned him loose. Brandy had been spending most of her time on the treadmill and some other machines, but she decided to start lifting weights too. She and Robbie worked out together and spotted for each other. Also, in the first two weeks, they were able to figure out when the gym was crowded and when it wasn't. They always went when it wasn't crowded.

Brandy slept with Robbie every night for two weeks. There was no sex. She wanted to be held and Robbie obliged her.

When Brandy's parents came, they went to dinner at a very extravagant restaurant. Robbie had never been to a place this fancy. There was so much silverware on the table that Robbie didn't know where to start. "I get confused too," said Brandy's mother. "Start from the outside and work your way in." They had wine with dinner too. No one bothered to check any ID's. Robbie had never drunk wine before. The wine they had was a chardonnay. Robbie decided he liked it. Brandy's father was a very nice man. He and Robbie got along really well. They didn't swap any war stories, but WW mentioned that he was bombardier during the war and had been a POW for a short while. He said that he was upset by the way the Vietnam Vets had been treated although he didn't understand the war. That was it for the military talk. Robbie mentioned that he was working for Abner Fulbright and WW was sure that he knew Abner. Brandy's mother Ellen, asked Robbie how he and Brandy got along sharing the apartment. Robbie assured them that the two of them got along great. Ellen also spent a lot of time telling Brandy about everything that was going on back home. They had a pleasant evening. When the check came, Robbie requested that he pay for his part. WW would have no part of it.

"You're our guest," said WW. When they took Brandy and Robbie back home, WW remembered that Brandy's ball glove was in the trunk of the car. He got it out and they were on their way.

"You have some nice folks," said Robbie after they were inside. "Looks like you got a nice glove too. First nice day we get, we'll throw some. Hey, I just thought of something. Would you want to go to the Reds Opening Day game?"

"Yeh, that would be fun," said Brandy. "I've never been to a Reds game. I've been to see the Indians and there's a minor League team in Toledo I've seen. Sure, I'll go see the Reds."

"Well I'll try to remember to get tickets as soon as they're available," said Robbie. "Hope they have a good team this year. I haven't followed them much the last couple of years. I do like Crosley Field, but I guess this will be the last season for it. They're building that new place. Riverfront Stadium I think it's called, or something like that. Anyway, we'll have a good time."

~~~~

The next two months breezed by quickly. Robbie was doing very well at school. He and Brandy went to the gym regularly. Brandy quit worrying about her breasts getting smaller. They had one real nice day in the middle of March so they went to a park that was close by and played catch. Robbie was impressed with Brandy. She had a good curveball too. There were some younger boys in the park too. They were shagging some fly balls. They didn't shag a whole lot after Brandy and Robbie arrived. They spent a lot of time watching Brandy. They must not have known that a girl who looked like that could throw a baseball like that. "I bet them young boys would really like your batting stance," said Robbie.

"We'll have to find out," said Brandy. "Let's get us a bat or two and bring it next time it's nice."

"Sounds good," said Robbie. "Maybe we can round up enough kids to have some batting practice or something. We'll see if you can hit as good as you throw."

"I can," said Brandy. "You'll see." They stayed in the park for a couple of hours and then went back home. The next weekend was nice so he and Brandy went out and bought a couple of bats. They went to the park and played catch for a while. Some of the same young boys showed up so Robbie got them all together and they took some batting practice. Robbie pitched first. Brandy batted first. She could hit. Robbie didn't bare down hard on her, but she did well. Robbie let all the young boys take a turn batting and then he took a turn. Brandy pitched to him. The young boys were so busy looking at Brandy that they weren't watching where the balls went when Robbie hit them. They only had three balls between them so they had to stop once in a while and look for the balls. When they finished, the young boys were eager to know when they were coming back.

Easter was getting closer. It was at the end of March this year. Robbie had written to Debbie telling her when he'd be home. His parents were also looking forward to seeing him. He knew he wanted to see Debbie, but he still wasn't sure about his feelings. He and Brandy hadn't slept together since her parents took them to dinner. Brandy hadn't dated anyone else either. He kind of missed her being with him even though they weren't having sex. Did he have strong feelings for Brandy? He knew that he did. Was it more than friendship?

School was closed for Good Friday so they had a three day weekend. Brandy and Robbie both left to go home after their last class on Thursday. Brandy was already gone when Robbie got back from his last class. He wished that he had seen her to tell her goodbye and that he'd miss her. He packed a few things and then headed home.

When Robbie got home, his folks were still sitting at the dinner table eating. Robbie gave his mom a kiss, and shook his dad's hand. He threw his stuff into his room and joined them at the table.

"Glad you're home son," said Mary. "We're having spaghetti, one of your favorites."

"Great mom," said Robbie. "I haven't had any since I left for school."

"So what have you been eating?" asked Mary. "Are you learning to cook for yourself?"

"I cook some, but Brandy's such a good cook that I don't have to very often," said Robbie. "We have a deal. She cooks and I do dishes. Works out good. When she cooks, she makes enough for two days, so no one has to cook every day."

"I'd say she's a good cook," said Robert. "Doesn't look like you've lost any weight."

"I haven't weighed myself since I left, but I doubt if I've lost any," said Robbie. "So how have you two been? Have you been dancing? How's the Legion and the VFW?"

"We're still the same and everyone at the Legion and the VFW is the same," said Robert. "Ole Jessie's been asking about you and how you're doing. Every once in a while he gets on this "I'm gonna die soon" kick and talks about making arrangements. He wants you to take care of things for him."

"Gee, my first request," said Robbie. "Well I'll probably stop at the VFW sometime this weekend. Maybe I'll see him. If I don't and you see him after I'm gone, tell him I'll be back for spring break around the end of April and early May. If he's in a hurry, tell him to call Abner."

"Are you going to see Debbie while you're home?" asked Mary.

"Yes, we'll be going out Saturday night," answered Robbie.

"So did something happen between you two?" asked Mary. "I know she was upset when she called here."

"Well I told you all about them guys breaking into her house," said Robbie. "Well we went to a New Year's Eve party at some philosophy professor's house. There was a lot of pot and other drugs there. I was not comfortable there and wanted to leave but Debbie talked me into staying for a while. Anyway, the professor was a horse's ass. He kept giving me shit about the war and stuff. I asked him to leave me alone. I really ticked him off when I gave him my opinion about philosophy professors. He kept sticking his finger on my chest. I asked him to stop two times. He didn't so I grabbed his finger and bent it backwards. After I let it go, he said he was a brown belt and was gonna kick my ass. I told him to come on. He threw a punch and missed. He hit a door frame and broke some bones in his hand. Then he tried to kick me. I got ahold of his leg and had him dancing on one foot. He cussed me so I smacked the side of his knee with my elbow. He went down hard. He said he was calling the law on me. I said no, that I was gonna call the law. I told him his university would really like it when they found out their professor had a bunch of drugs at his house and probably some underage drinkers. Anyway, Debbie was upset by all of this."

"I don't see why," said Robert. "I would have kicked the guys ass. You didn't do anything wrong. She had no reason to be upset."

"I agree," said Mary. "I'm sure you two will work it out if you want to."

"She said she was sorry about everything," said Robbie. "We'll see how it goes."

~~~~

Friday night, Robbie and Robert went to the VFW for a couple of beers. Ole Jessie had already been there earlier in the day. They told Jake to tell Jessie that Robbie would be back for spring break at the end of April and early May. Randy

White came in and had a couple of shots at the bar and left without giving anybody a hard time. Robbie knew that Randy had seen him, but Randy acted like he had never seen Robbie before. "I wonder what's up with Randy tonight?" asked Robbie. "He didn't get into it with anyone."

"Hard to tell," said Robert. "Maybe he's been smoking some of that wacky tobaccy and has mellowed out." Robbie let out a laugh. "Do any of them people in your school smoke that stuff?"

"If they do, they don't do it around me," answered Robbie. "Every once in a while, a bunch of us go to this small neighborhood bar. No one ever talks about smoking pot or any drugs."

"I was watching the news the other night and they're saying that the Army has a real bad problem with drugs over there," said Robert. "It's not just that pot. They say a lot of our boys are getting hooked on heroin. You think the Marines got a problem too?"

"I don't know dad," answered Robbie. "I never saw much drug use of any kind when I was there. We had them new guys get killed that one time. We were pretty sure they were sitting around smoking pot when a mortar round landed in the middle of them. Three of them got killed and the fourth one had part of his left arm blown off. We figured that was what they were doing cause I caught them smoking pot in our tent and threw them out earlier that day. Hell they just got in country and got to our base that day. So anyway, if others were doing drugs, they didn't do them around me."

"Well on the news the other day, they had this whole squad of soldiers and they were all smoking that shit," said Robert. "This was on national TV. Why would their officers and NCO's let them do that if the stuff is illegal?"

"I don't know dad," answered Robbie. "Maybe even though them boys smoke that stuff, they can still do their job. I really don't know anything about the stuff. Maybe the officers are afraid they'll get fragged if they do anything."

"I've heard about fraggings too," said Robert. "I never seen it, but I heard of guys taking out bad officers in combat during the war. That's different than killing some officer back at the rear because he won't let you smoke pot or whatever. I was lucky, the officers I had never had me do anything that they didn't do too. How were your officers?"

"Most of them were all right," said Robbie. "Sometimes we went through them so fast that you never got a chance to see if they were any good or not. We had some good NCO's. Most of them were on their second tour. If we had a green officer, they looked after him."

"That's how it's supposed to be," said Robert. "The NCO's are the one's that get things done. Let's go home now. I feel the need to see your mother."

When they got home, Mary greeted them right at the door. She gave Robert a kiss and then went to Robbie. "There was a call for you while you were gone," started Mary. "It was from Debbie. Her father died earlier today from a massive heart attack. She won't be able to see you this weekend. I gave her our condolences."

"That's bad news," said Robbie. "I know she had a very tight family. That would be hard to handle." Robbie didn't say anything else. He went straight to his room.

Robbie thought he slept well during the night. He had some dreams about Brandy. He knew that he missed her. When he got up the next morning, Mary told him he had done a lot of yelling during the night. "What was I yelling?" asked Robbie.

"Well you shouted "incoming" several times," answered Mary. "You did a lot of talking about the m---f----rain. You were cursing the leeches too."

"It's weird that I would do that and not know it," said Robbie. "I know I had some good dreams about something else. I hope I didn't scare you."

"You didn't scare us," said Robert. "We'll let you know when and if you ever do anything scary." Robbie didn't do much of anything all day. Sunday morning, they all got up and went to early Mass. Mary fixed a nice dinner. Jake Canton and his wife were invited for dinner. As soon as Robbie finished dinner, he packed up and left for school.

~~~~

When he got the apartment, Brandy was already there. She was sitting on the couch sipping a beer. Robbie threw his things into his room and joined her. "So how was your Easter?" asked Brandy.

"It was all right I guess," said Robbie.

"You said that with such enthusiasm," said Brandy. "How was Debbie?"

"I didn't get to see her," answered Robbie. "Her father died sometime Friday."

"That's terrible," said Brandy. "On Good Friday too."

"She had a real close family too," said Robbie. "It'll be tough on them."

"Well it was tough on me not being with you Robbie," said Brandy. "I missed you. I never thought I would say this to you, but I believe I am love with you. I couldn't wait to get back."

Robbie never said a word. He slid over next to her and put his arms around her. They started kissing. It seemed the kisses would never end. They found their way to Brandy's room and made love for most of the night. When they woke up late the next morning, they discovered that they were already late for class. Brandy put some coffee on the stove while they hurriedly got dressed. They both filled a travel mug and went to their cars. Robbie held her and kissed her passionately in the parking lot beside her car. They almost went back to the apartment.

That week was almost like being on a honeymoon. They never left the apartment except to go to class. Robbie had gotten his tickets for opening day to see the Reds. Their seats were right behind home plate and not far up in the stands. They would be able to tell what every pitch was. Opening day was on a Monday. Robbie had two classes that day. He told his instructors that he wouldn't be there but he wouldn't get behind on anything. The instructors were not dummies. They knew it was opening day for the Reds. "We should probably just shut down that day," said one of his instructors. "I wouldn't mind going myself. They have a brand new manager this year and some rookies. I think they'll do it this year."

"We can hope," said Robbie.

Robbie and Brandy took a taxi to the ball field that day. They didn't want to fight with the traffic. Robbie took his cane with him. His leg ached some. They had a great time at the game. The Reds beat the Expos 5 – 1 and Jim Merritt was the winning pitcher. They sat in the stands for a while and let the crowd filter out. They were almost out of the stadium. Robbie was looking for a pay phone so they could call a cab. He spotted a phone and was headed for it when he saw someone that he thought he recognized. He was a very big black man. He was using a cane and he was holding hands with a small girl. He wore a Reds hat. Robbie thought and thought. He knew who the man was. He took Brandy's hand and they went over to the black man. He positioned himself right in front of the man and stopped.

"S/Sgt. Benjamin," said Robbie.

"Parker," shouted the man. "Jesus H. Christ, I woulda never thought I'd see you again. Betty Jean, this man here saved your daddy's life."

"Really Daddy?" said Betty Jean.

"Really," said Benjamin as he reached out and shook Robbie's hand. Betty Jean went over to Robbie and gave him a hug.

"Thank you for saving my daddy," said Betty Jean.

"Damn Parker, what brings you here besides opening day?" asked Benjamin.

"I go to school down here," answered Robbie.

"Is this your woman?" asked Benjamin.

"Yes, she is my woman," said Robbie. "Brandy, I'd like to introduce you to one of my Platoon Sergeants from Vietnam." They shook hands.

"I'm very pleased to meet you," said Brandy. "So Robbie here saved your life?"

"Yes he did Brandy," said Benjamin. "He probably saved the whole platoon that day. So you two are coming over to my house for dinner. I won't take no for an answer. You can follow me in your car."

"We came in a taxi," said Robbie.

"Well my car's way over to the back of the lot," said Benjamin. "You'll ride with us and I'll take you home after." They all went to his car and twenty minutes later, they were at his house. They went inside and Benjamin introduced them to his mother. "Momma, this is the man that saved my life over there," said Benjamin. The woman practically ran over to Robbie and hugged him and kissed his cheek several times.

"Thank you for saving my boy," said Mrs. Benjamin. "You are sure welcome at this house any time."

"Thank you Mrs. Benjamin," said Robbie. "And this is Brandy." Mrs. Benjamin went to Brandy and hugged and kissed her too. " You all sit down and talk while I work on dinner," said Mrs. Benjamin. "Son, git your guests a beer. We got plenty in the frig."

"We got Hudepohl," said Benjamin. "It's a cheap beer but it's not bad."

"That's all right with us," said Robbie. "So tell me, what is your first name?" I know it's not S/Sgt."

"It's Bobby. Not Robert, just Bobby," said Bobby. "Now I think your first name is Robert but they call you Robbie. Is that right?"

"Yes that's right," said Robbie. "So how have things been for you since you've been home?"

"They're a lot better now," said Bobby. "It was bad when I first got back. It's a long story."

"We got time," said Robbie. "Sometimes it helps to talk."

"Well I was a big football star around here when I was in high school," started Bobby. "I had a scholarship to play for Cincinnati. I wanted to be a Marine. I didn't want to go to college and play football. Jean, she was my high school sweetheart. We got married after I had all my training done. Then I got orders for Vietnam. She was pregnant when I left. I never realized it till too late that she was a real climber. She wanted more and more all the time. She was convinced that I was going to be a college star and go to the NFL. Why she stayed with me for as long as she did, I'll never know. Betty Jean was born when I was over there. That was in 1966. When I got back, I found out that Jean had been running around on me. I stayed with her anyway. I felt guilty about joining the Corps in the first place. I got orders to go back and that's when she just took off. I got no idea where she is or what's she doing. She don't care about Betty Jean here at all. Momma been raising her. I decided to make the Corps my career. I was on my third tour when I was your Platoon Sergeant. Most folks thought it was my second tour but it was my third. After I got my Medical Discharge, I came home. I tried to find Jean but couldn't. I was mad at the world for a long time. I did some serious drinking for a while. Then I finally decided that I had a daughter to raise. I straightened myself out. We're not rich folks but we're happy."

"Are you working somewhere?" asked Robbie.

"I got a job at the VA," answered Bobby. "The pay's not great, but we got good benefits. What with my disability and getting health care at the VA, we're doing o.k. How bout you? What are you up to?"

"Well this might shock you," said Robbie. "Brandy and I are both studying to be morticians."

"Say what? Really? Whoa! I couldn't do that," said Bobby.

"Somebody's got to do it," said Robbie. "May as well be us."

"I guess so," said Bobby. "I see you got that cane. Looks like they got you too."

"They did," said Robbie. "More than once too."

Brandy had been quiet and was just listening to everything. Now she decided to speak. "So Bobby, would you tell me how Robbie saved your life?" asked Brandy. "I know he doesn't talk much about the war. Would you tell me please?"

"I will if you don't mind Robbie," said Bobby.

"Oh go ahead, we'll see what your version is like," said Robbie.

"All right, here goes," started Bobby. "Parker, Robbie that is, had just gotten in country. It was his first patrol. Our platoon was in a staggered column when we got ambushed from two sides. Robbie was about halfway back in the column right behind the machine gunner. I was working my way back through the column and directing the men's fire. Robbie's rifle had been shot up. He had checked on the machine gunner and he was dead. The A-gunner was dead too. I was right beside Robbie when I was hit in the thigh. It clipped the femoral artery. I would have bled to death if Robbie hadn't taken my belt and put a tourniquet on my leg. I was hit in the right arm too. He wrapped it up too. Then this crazy man, got the machine gun and some ammo off of the dead gunner and worked his way toward the enemy. When he fired at them, some of them got up and ran. Crazy man here stood up and charged after them firing the machine gun as he went. A bullet grazed his left shoulder but he kept going. He threw some grenades during all of this too. They started calling him "Pitcher" after this because of how well he threw them grenades. Anyway, he killed a bunch of them that day. They were working their way around us and if he hadn't done what he done, the platoon could have been wiped out. So what do you think Robbie? Does that sound about right?"

"That's close," said Robbie.

"Robbie got himself a medal for that," said Bobby. "He got the Bronze Star."

"How bout no more talk about over there," said Robbie. "Hope I don't sound rude."

"That's all right," said Bobby. "It took me a long time before I would talk about over there. So, you're in for a real treat for dinner."

"Why's that?" asked Robbie.

"Cause momma's making her world famous recipe today," said Bobby.

"What would that be?" asked Brandy.

"Why fried chicken a course," said Bobby. "Don't you folks know that us folks always eat fried chicken." They all laughed.

Mrs. Benjamin called them to the table. Robbie was really impressed with the food. Brandy thought the chicken was the best she ever had or ever would have. "I've got to know what you did to this chicken to make it so good," said Brandy.

"Nothin' to it child," said Mrs. Benjamin. "Soak it in buttermilk for a day. Then roll it in flour and fry like always with salt and pepper or whatever seasonings you like."

"I'm going to try it," said Brandy. "Next time we go to the grocery, we're getting some chickens."

"So Bobby, do you remember Sims?" asked Robbie.

"Yeh, I remember him," said Bobby. "He was your squad leader."

"That's him. He just lives over near Covington," said Robbie. "We been writing back and forth. He got himself married and works at his uncle's lumber yard. Maybe we could all get together sometime."

"That would be all right," said Bobby. "It would be nice to see some of the guys you served with. It'd be nice to know who made it and who didn't."

They finished their food and talked a while longer and then Bobby took them home. They exchanged phone numbers and said they would stay in touch. It was getting a little late, so Robbie and Brandy got into the shower together. It was a long shower. They finally got out and dried each other off. They put on some robes, sat on the couch and turned on the TV. Nothing was on that they wanted to watch. Brandy turned off the TV and then went over and sat on Robbie's lap. She looked into his eyes and smiled. "You're a good a man Robbie Parker, and you're my man," said Brandy. "I'll be with you as long as you'll have me." She opened her robe and put one of his hands on her breasts. Robbie picked her up and took her to his room.

~~~~

Spring break was only two weeks away. They would have two weeks off before the next semester started. Brandy had it in her head that they ought to go somewhere special or something. "I'd like to go to the beach or somewhere special," said Brandy when they got home Monday afternoon. "I don't mean like where all the other kids go for spring break and party and carry on. I don't want to be around a bunch of drunk or high kids. I want to be with you and just you. There's this little island close to Savannah that my folks go to once in a while. They have a friend down there who owns a house and lets them use it from time to time. I think it's called Tybee Island. My folks like it because it's quiet and laid back. How bout I ask my folks about it?"

"Are you sure your parents wouldn't mind that we would be sleeping together?" asked Robbie.

"My parents already know that we have sex," said Brandy. "I told them when I was home for Easter. I also told them that you were the man I was going to marry."

"When is this marriage going to happen?" asked Robbie.

"There's no rush," answered Brandy. "Whenever you're ready. I know you have strong feelings for me and you probably do love me but you might not be sure yet. I can wait Robbie. I'll wait as long as it takes."

Robbie was speechless. He knew that he loved Brandy. He just didn't want to admit it. "I do love you Brandy," said Robbie. "I have been afraid to admit it. I have been afraid because of what happened to the other women I loved. I sort of felt like I was cursed."

"You are not cursed Robbie," said Brandy. "Nothing will happen to me. I won't allow it." They hugged each other tightly.

The next day, Brandy got on the phone with her parents and asked them if they would ask their friend about the house on Tybee Island. They assured Brandy that they would do this for her. Her father called back on Friday and told them the news. They could have the house from April 26 to May 3. They were totally elated. They went out to celebrate. They went out to dinner and then went dancing. Robbie didn't tell Brandy that it was also his birthday until they were about to leave the club. "I'll give you your present when we get home," said Brandy. She did.

The next Monday, Robbie received a letter from Debbie. He went into his room, closed the door, sat on the bed and read it.

Dear Robbie,

Things have been very hectic here. We had to delay the funeral for several days because we have so many relatives all over the country. My father was very well liked by everyone. My mother is crushed by his death. She has decided that she doesn't want to live here anymore. Her sister in Florida invited her to live with her. She accepted. We had someone who always wanted to buy our house. We called them and my mother accepted their offer. I cannot afford to stay here and go to school. I will go to Florida too and transfer my credits to a Florida school. We have had yard sales so we won't have a lot to take to Florida with us. We will be leaving as soon as this semester is over.

I doubt if we will see each other again. I want you to know that I truly loved the times we were together. You are a good person Robbie Parker. I hope you have a good life.

Love,
Debbie

Brandy came home right after Robbie had finished the letter. She saw that his door was closed and gave it a gentle knock. "Come on in," said Robbie. Brandy saw the letter.

"So what's Debbie got to say?" asked Brandy.

"Well she told me about the funeral," started Robbie. "Her mom sold the house and they're moving to Florida and living with her aunt. She can't afford to stay here. She wished me well. That's all."

"That was nice of her," said Brandy. "Hey, we need to go shopping sometime real soon. I need a bathing suit. I bet you need one too."

"I do," said Robbie. "Why don't we go after dinner? Or why don't we go eat somewhere and then shop? What would you want to do?"

"We can eat out," said Brandy. "I don't mind getting out of cooking once in a while."

They went to a mall. There was a Chinese restaurant there so they ate Chinese. There were a lot of stores and they all had their line of spring clothing out. "You'll have to model the suits for me," said Robbie as they got started.

"I don't mind," said Brandy. "You can model for me too."

Brandy couldn't make up her mind on which suit to buy. Robbie thought she was gorgeous in all of them. She got it narrowed down to two suits. Both of them were very revealing and the colors really suited her. "Get them both," said Robbie. "I like them both."

"All right, it's your turn now," said Brandy. They moved to the men's clothing area and Robbie picked out some trunks to model. He ended up getting two pair also.

Brandy's whole family were members in AAA. Brandy had a trip ticket made up so they would know the best way to get to Tybee. They studied it every day. They didn't go to the gym this week but they did go to the park and play catch and have some batting practice. The young boys were glad to see Brandy again.

The trip to Tybee would take twelve hours or more. Brandy wanted to take her Volkswagen because it got good mileage. Robbie convinced her that his Olds would be much more comfortable. They took the Olds. They left for Tybee Island early Saturday morning. They drove several hours and stopped somewhere for lunch. Then they drove a few more and spent the night at a motel. They were both in awe as they drove through Savannah the next morning. It was a beautiful city. They were really surprised when they arrived on Tybee. The beach looked really nice based on what they could see of it from the road. There were no big high rise hotels and downtown Tybee was only about a square block. They remembered that they had passed a visitor's center and they went back to it. The lady on duty got them some maps and showed them exactly where their house was located. She also gave them several magazines and literature that told them about all the restaurants and activities. The owners of the house would be meeting them at ten o'clock which was in about a half hour. They made sure they knew where the house was located and then drove around exploring the island for a bit. "This is really nice," said Brandy. "It looks nice and laid back. This will be nice."

"I agree," said Robbie. "We'll have a good time here."

They headed to their house which was located on Chatham Avenue. There was no one there, but as soon as they got out of the car, another car pulled in. A nice looking middle aged woman got out and went to them. "Hi, I'm Sondra and I assume you're Brandy and Robbie," said Sondra as she shook their hands.

"Yes we are," said Brandy. "This looks like a very nice place and location."

"It is," said Sondra. "We just love it down here. Here's a couple of keys for you. The keys work the front and back door. Let's go in and I'll show you around." They went inside.

"Oh my but this is nice," said Brandy.

"It surely is," said Sondra. "Now there's two bedrooms both with queen sized beds." She quickly showed them the rooms. "The main bedroom is a master bedroom and it has its' own bathroom," said Sondra. "It has a jetted tub and shower in it. There is another bathroom between in the hallway leading to the other bedroom. The kitchen has everything you need. There's a TV in each bedroom and the living room. We have cable. Let's go out back." They went out back to see that this house had its' own dock and pier. "This is what we call the backwater," said Sondra. "That's the Atlantic over there to the left. This is called Tybee Creek here. There's a hot tub by the house. Those bicycles go with the place too. Feel free to use them. Do you have any questions?"

"I think we're good," said Brandy.

"O.k., I'll be back around ten o'clock next Sunday when you check out," said Sondra. "I hope you enjoy our island. I know you will." Sondra waved goodbye and left.

"This place is beautiful," said Brandy. "No wonder my folks come down here. Let's get unpacked and check out the place."

"I know what I want to check out," said Robbie. Brandy smiled at him and led him to the master bedroom. An hour later they were unloading the car. It didn't take long as they hadn't taken much. "Let's go out for just a bit," said Robbie. "I want to check out the water." They went out on the pier. There were a few people kayaking and some fisherman were on the other side of the creek. Robbie spotted something about halfway out in the water. Then he saw several things. "Those are dolphins," said Robbie. "We got dolphins out there. Great!" They watched the dolphins a good while and then decided to take off on the bikes. Robbie put a map of the streets in a pocket. Everywhere they went they were amazed. This was a nice place. They were able to ride the bikes on the beach without getting stuck in the sand. They rode north and when they got to the northern end of the island, they saw some ships full of freight heading into Savannah on the river. They stopped and watched for a while. They didn't realize it but the tide was coming in. As they headed back the way they had come, the beach was shrinking. "Maybe there's a tide chart in one of those magazines that the lady gave us," said Robbie. "We'll know when we can ride on the beach. I don't understand tides."

"I don't either," said Brandy. "It's got to do with the moon or something."

They got off the beach and started riding all over the island on the streets. They were amazed at all the types of houses. They all looked so cozy. After a while they decided they were hungry and went looking for a restaurant. On the way to a place to eat, they passed a small grocery store. "We can buy breakfast food and just eat out for lunch and dinner if you want," said Robbie. "Whatever you want is all right with me. I never mind fixing breakfast. We can get some beer too so we can have some at the house."

"I wonder what the drinking age is down here," said Brandy.

"I don't know," said Robbie. "We can just try to buy some and if they let us have it, we'll know they think we're old enough."

They passed a small liquor store on the way to a restaurant. They picked a place that was right in downtown Tybee. At the restaurant, they asked the waitress what the drinking age on Tybee was. It was 21. The waitress told them which places carded on a regular basis and which ones didn't. She told them that the older guy who worked at the liquor store almost never carded. After the meal, they went back to the house. "So what do you want to do about food Brandy?" asked Robbie.

"What you said was good," said Brandy. "We can take the car and get some groceries. I think it would be nice to set out on our pier and drink coffee in the morning. Maybe we'll see some more dolphins. Then we'll go to that liquor store and see if we can get some beer. I thought I saw an older guy in there when we went past it on our bikes. I have an idea if you won't be offended. It's about getting some beer."

"I doubt I'd be offended," said Robbie. "What is it?"

"Well let's take your cane with us," said Brandy. "Act like your leg really hurts and is giving you a hard time. Maybe you can let it slip out that you're a veteran. Maybe the guy will be sympathetic to veterans and let us have the beer."

"I already thought of that," said Robbie. "I got a set of dog tags I keep in the car. I can wear them too."

"You're as devious as me Robbie Parker," said Brandy. They kissed a little and got in the car. They bought enough breakfast food for several days and plenty of coffee and orange juice. They went ahead and got some lunch things too. Then they went to the liquor store. The older man was still there. Brandy went ahead of Robbie and held the door for him to make things look even better. Robbie kind of limped along and groaned every once in a while. The older man spoke.

"Are you gonna be all right young man," he said. "If you want, I'll get you a chair and you can just sit down and tell me what you want. I'll get if for you."

"I would really appreciate that sir," said Robbie. "My leg is acting up again." The man went somewhere in the back and came back with a folding chair. He unfolded it and set it down close to Robbie. Then he saw Robbie's dog tags.

"Are you one of them Vietnam Vets?" the man asked.

"Yes sir, I am," answered Robbie. "Just got discharged not long ago, Medical Discharge."

"What was you in son, and please don't call me sir? I used to work for a living," said the man.

"I was in the Marines and I can tell by the way you talk that were a Marine too," said Robbie.

"Yes son, I was. I was in WW2 and Korea," said the man. "I woulda made it a career but I got shot up at Chosin Reservoir. Damn near kilt me. Said after that I'd never live where it was cold again. Is this your first time here?"

"Yes it is," answered Robbie. "Brandy, my girlfriend here, well her parents are friends with people who have a house down here and they're letting us use it. This is just our first day but we really like it here."

"It's nice here. I actually live over on Wilmington Island," said the man. "It does get crowded here in the summer and on the weekends when the weather is good. Seems like the whole city of Savannah comes out sometimes. You're lucky. It's early in the season. My names Sam Shelby. What's yours?"

"I'm Robbie Parker and this is Brandy Wisecup," said Robbie. They all shook hands .

"Now Robbie Parker. What can I get for you?" asked Sam.

"You don't carry the same beer we have back home," said Robbie. "I do see some Pabst in your cooler."

"We sell a lot of that down here," said Sam. "Will a case be enough?"

"That'll do for now," said Robbie. Robbie paid Sam and Sam carried the beer out to his car.

"Robbie, I figure you're not 21 but you're close," said Sam. "I figure if a man can fight for his country, he ought to be allowed to have a drink if he wants one. Semper Fi."

"Semper Fi Sam," said Robbie and they went back to the house.

"What's Semper Fi?" asked Brandy.

"That's the Marine Corps motto," answered Robbie. "It's actually Semper Fidelis. It means always faithful.

"All right," said Brandy. They put the groceries away and grabbed a beer. They went out on their pier and hoped to see some more dolphins. They got to kissing and soon they were back in the house. A couple of hours later they were back on the pier. The tide was high now. The dolphins must have come in with the tide because they were everywhere. Some even swam up close to their pier. The water was fairly clear and they could see the dolphin's eyes. Several dolphins had young ones with them. "I could watch them for hours," said Brandy. "They are so beautiful and graceful in the water. It's hard to believe they are mammals. They can really hold their breath a long time."

They watched the dolphins until they were gone and then decided to just walk around the neighborhood. They discovered that there was a restaurant just down the road from them. They walked till almost dark and then headed to the restaurant. It was called AJ's. They could sit inside or outside. It was a little windy but they sat outside anyway. They saw a few more dolphins when they were eating. They had a good meal and headed back to their house. When they got back, they decided they would try out the hot tub. Neither one of them had ever been in a hot tub. There was a small privacy fence on one side of it but not the other. The back of it was close to the house and it was open toward the water. The house to the side where there was no fence appeared to be empty. They got in with their bathing suits on, but they were soon removed. The hot tub got a work out that evening.

Every day was like this. They did whatever they wanted and had a great time. One day they were worn out from too much hot tub time and laying in bed watching TV when President Nixon came on. He announced that the Army was going into Cambodia. He was tired of the NVA always attacking and then going back across the border where it was safe. The U.S. was going in there and do some damage and be out in a few weeks. "Oh my God," said Brandy after she listened to Nixon. "He's expanding the war. There will be a lot of protesting over this. Oh my God. What do you think about this Robbie?"

"I don't know what to think," said Robbie. "It was always that way. They were always sneaking back across the border of Laos or Cambodia. If they were going to do this, why didn't they do it years ago? I just don't know. I just don't know. Let's hope they don't get into a real big mess over there and we don't have a big mess here. I know there will be some heavy protesting going on. It's scary to think about. Let's try not to let it ruin our break."

"I'll try not to think about it but it will be hard," said Brandy. "If you start having funny or odd feelings and think you're losing your mind, just let me hold you. I'll hold you till it passes."

"You're a good woman Brandy," said Robbie. "I will have to marry you one of these days."

"What did you say Robbie Parker?" asked Brandy.

"You know perfectly well what I said Brandy Wisecup," said Robbie.

"I was just making sure," said Brandy.

The rest of their week flew by but they had a wonderful time. They decided that Tybee Island would always be their special place. They took their time going home. They spent Sunday night somewhere in Virginia. They slept in and didn't get to Cincinnati till late on Monday. They unloaded the car and took everything to the apartment. They just threw their things in their rooms, got a beer, and sat down on the couch. Robbie turned on the TV and went through the channels. A special news bulletin was on. Four students had been killed at a war protest at Kent State University.

Chapter Seventeen

Before another word came out of the mouth of the newsperson, Brandy started crying uncontrollably. Robbie held her, but the crying didn't stop. The newsperson continued. "Four students were killed and nine were wounded during an anti-war protest at Kent State University. The National Guard had been called in by Governor James Rhodes after rioting and looting had happened a couple days before in downtown Kent. When the Guard finally arrived in Kent, the ROTC building had been set on fire. Firemen and Police were having a hard time fighting the fire because they were being pelted with rocks and other things. Fire hoses were also cut. As of now, no one knows if there was an order for the Guard to fire into the unarmed crowd. There is also a rumor that a shot was fired at the Guard before they opened fire. That has not been confirmed."

"I don't understand," cried Brandy. "Why was the National Guard there in the first place? We have the right to peaceful protest and gatherings in this country."

"Yes we do," said Robbie. "But the downtown looting and the burning of the ROTC building was not something I would consider peaceful. I am not taking sides in this. We should wait until we here all that happened before we condemn the Guard or the students."

"Why would the Guard even have live ammunition?" asked Brandy. "Shouldn't they have just used tear gas and billy clubs or something?"

"I don't know anything about riot control," answered Robbie. "I do know this though. If you give a young man a rifle and some live ammunition and get him scared, bad things will happen. I'd say the Guard was scared too. There were 2000 or so kids and the kids were throwing rocks and bottles at them and cursing them. That would be scary to me. This is going to cause riots all over the country."

"I have friends who go to Kent State," said Brandy. "I need to find out if they are o.k. or not."

"I would call everybody I know," said Robbie. "I wouldn't go near any college campus for a good while." Brandy cried for a good while longer and then called her parents. She was on the phone on and off for over a couple of hours. She finally got good news. None of her friends were anywhere near the trouble at Kent State. Some of them had left town after the rioting in downtown Kent and others had stayed in their dorms during the shootings. "I was thinking that I would go home for a couple of days before classes start again," said Robbie. "Maybe you should go home too. I bet your parents would be glad to see you."

"I was just home Easter," said Brandy. "I don't know if I want to go home or not."

"Well you could go with me and meet my parents," said Robbie. "I know they'd like to meet you."

"What would the sleeping arrangements be at your house?" asked Brandy. "What would they think if we slept together?"

"They know that I'm no priest," said Robbie. "I have never taken a girl to the house and slept with her. I can call them and see what they say."

"I could go and we wouldn't have to sleep together," said Brandy. "Why don't we just go and see how it goes. I guess I'd like to meet your parents. A girl should meet her future in-laws sometime before the wedding." Robbie let out a little laugh. Brandy tried to laugh but she started crying again.

Robbie called home and told his parents that he would be there tomorrow and he was bringing Brandy with him. Mary said they would be glad to meet her. Brandy and Robbie slept together that night. They didn't have sex. Several times during the night, Robbie woke up to hear Brandy crying. Each time he just tried to hold her tighter. They got up early the next morning and had a big breakfast.

Then they were on their way. Every once in a while they tried to find some music on the radio. It seemed that every time they did, there was a new report of rioting and protests breaking out all across the country. They decided to leave the radio off.

Robert was working 1st trick and was gone when Robbie and Brandy got to Columbus. Mary saw them pull in the driveway and went out to meet them. She went straight to Robbie and gave him a hug and kiss on the cheek. Then she did the same to Brandy. "You must be Brandy," said Mary. "I'm Robbie's mother Mary and I'm so glad to meet you. Robbie's dad Robert is working 1st trick today and will be home this afternoon. Let's go in and get acquainted. Robbie can bring in anything you may have packed." Robbie took their bags and put them in his room. Then they all sat down at the kitchen table. "Would you two like some coffee?" asked Mary. "I can make a fresh pot."

"That sounds good Mrs. Parker," said Brandy. "I could use a cup."

"Me too," said Robbie.

"Call me Mary," said Mary to Brandy. "You're Robbie's friend and now you're my friend." Brandy nodded her head. Mary got the pot ready and put it on the stove. "So do you two like sharing the apartment? I see you haven't killed each other yet."

"We get along really well Mary," said Brandy. "It's good that we do because Robbie is the man I'm going to marry. Excuse me for being blunt."

"Oh, all right, is that so Robbie?" asked Mary. "Is she going to marry you?"

"Yes mom, she is," answered Robbie. "She hasn't told me when though. Just kidding Mom. We will get it figured out. We do know that we love each other."

"Well I'm happy for the both of you," said Mary as she got up and gave Brandy a hug and a kiss on the cheek. "You two are a beautiful couple. Your children will be good looking too."

"We might wait a little on that Mom," said Robbie.

"Don't wait too long," said Mary. "They grow up and leave home before you know it. So Brandy, how do you like your school?"

"It's all right Mary," said Brandy. "My family has been in the business for years and they expect me to carry it on."

"Do you have any brothers or sisters?" asked Mary.

"Two younger sisters," answered Brandy. "And they don't want anything to do with the business. They're hoping to get married to men who do not work on corpses. That's fine with me. I have big plans. I'll be running the business one day. Robbie's going to become partners with Fulbright and take over one day. We'll open up other places across the state. We'll have a crematorium too. Crematoriums will be popular one day soon."

"You're an ambitious person," said Mary. "Maybe that will happen for you."

"You sure are ambitious Brandy," said Robbie. "You never said anything like that to me before."

"It just came out," said Brandy. "I'm talking years down the road. Wouldn't it be nice if we could just own several places.? We'd have good people working for us and you and I could relax and do whatever we wanted. Like maybe spend time down at Tybee, or go to the Caribbean, or anywhere we wanted."

"Yes, that would be nice," said Robbie. "That will take a lot of hard work and effort for that to happen."

"We're both hard workers," said Brandy. "It could happen for us." The coffee was ready now. Mary poured each of them a cup.

"You two have heard about Kent State, haven't you?" asked Mary.

"Yes we have Mom," answered Robbie. Brandy got teary eyed. "Brandy has some friends up there and she was worried about them. She made some calls and all of them are all right."

"It's a sad thing," said Mary. "I suppose it will be a long time before we find out all the facts."

"It probably will," said Robbie. "But in the meantime, there's bound to be more trouble. I just hope no one gets hurt. Can we change the subject?"

"Please do," said Brandy. "I don't want to cry anymore."

"All right, now Mom, how would you feel if Brandy and I sleep together while we're here?" asked Robbie. Brandy seemed a little startled that Robbie asked this question so soon.

"I would say that you two have already been intimate," said Mary. "It won't bother me or your father. What would your parents say if you two wanted to sleep together at their house?"

"I've already told them that we're having sex," answered Brandy. "I've also told them that Robbie is the man I'm going to marry."

"What did they say to that?" asked Mary.

"They know that I am serious," answered Brandy.

They drank their coffee and chatted some more. After a while, Robbie took Brandy on a walk around the neighborhood. Before he got to Mrs. Wilson's house, he told her the story about the dog and how it tore his pants and that she had called the law on him. Then he told her about Mrs. Wilson giving him the finger at times when he walked past her house. "Just wait," said Robbie. "Soon you'll hear that dog of hers barking," said Robbie. "She'll come over to the window to see what it's barking at." When they were about to Mrs. Wilson's house, they could hear the dog barking. When they got closer, they could see the dog in the window. Sure enough, a few seconds later and Mrs. Wilson came to see what the dog was barking at. Robbie waved to her. Her hand started to come up, but apparently when she saw Brandy with him, the middle finger didn't come up. She walked away from the window.

"That woman doesn't like you," said Brandy.

"No, she doesn't," said Robbie. "I'll get over it though." They walked all around the neighborhood. Robbie took her to the park and showed her where he used to play ball. They went past his old school. As they started back towards home, a police cruiser pulled up beside them. It was Jerry Tomlinson. He got out and shook Robbie's hand. Robbie introduced him to Brandy.

"I saw you on the sidewalk and I thought I'd stop and tell you something," said Jerry. "There won't be any trial for them two that broke into that girls' house. They copped a plea. Not sure how much time they got, but they won't be around for a while."

"Thanks Jerry. I appreciate that," said Robbie. "I didn't want to come back for a trial. I would have if necessary."

"Well I gotta be going," said Jerry. "Hey, if I was you, I wouldn't go anywhere near the Ohio State Campus. They haven't had any trouble yet, but after what happened at Kent State, they're expecting trouble at campuses all across the country."

"Thanks Jerry. We'll be staying away," said Robbie. "Try to keep yourself safe." Jerry waved and took off. "That was the cop who came for the dog incident and when Debbie's house was broke into," said Robbie. "I went to school with Jerry."

"He seems like a nice guy," said Debbie. "I bet it's tough on them now. People see that blue uniform and all they think of is PIG. I don't like that."

"I don't either," said Robbie. "Somebody's got to prove to me that they're a pig or whatever before I call them that. Let's get back now. It's lunch time. They went back and had lunch. Robbie asked Brandy if she would mind seeing the place where he worked. She didn't mind, so they went to Fulbright's. Abner was in his office when they arrived. He rushed out and shook Robbie's hand when he saw him. "This is Brandy Wisecup," said Robbie. "She's from Toledo."

"I think I know your father," said Abner. "They call him WW, don't they?"

"Yes they do," said Brandy. "He thought he knew you too."

"So have you been busy Abner?" asked Robbie.

"Average," answered Abner. "I did get a call not long ago from a man who said he knew you. Said his name was Jessie something or other. Anyway, he wanted to go ahead and get his plans taken care of. We got it done. You must have made an impression on him somewhere."

"I met him at the VFW," said Robbie. "Everybody said he was a cranky old fart. I started talking to him and we've been friends ever since. He was Marine too. So was his son. His son was killed on Guadalcanal."

"I told you that you'd do well in this business," said Abner. "So what are you two up to? Are you on a break or something?"

"Yes, we're on our break between semesters," said Robbie. "Classes start again next week."

"Well I hope there's no trouble down there," said Abner. "They're thinking there'll be trouble all over the country at campuses."

"Well it's pretty small at our place," said Robbie. "We'll stay away from UC and all the other universities. Mind if I show Brandy around?"

"No, help yourself," said Abner. Robbie took Brandy all around and showed everything.

"I like this place," said Robbie. "It seems more homey. It doesn't look like a big assembly line place. It's more personable."

"Our place is kind of like this too," said Brandy. "We'll have to keep this in mind when we become rich and famous and have a bunch of places. We won't want that assembly line look."

"No, we'll want it to look like a place that your grandmother would have been happy to go to," said Robbie. "Well we've seen everything. Let's go tell Abner goodbye and thank him."

Abner had gone to another room. They found Abner and told him goodbye and thanked him for allowing the tour. Robbie drove around town for a while and showed Brandy the sights. When they got home, Robert was already there. He and Mary were sitting out back having a beer. Robbie and Bandy went out back. Robbie introduced Brandy to Robert. Then he got two more chairs and then got Brandy and him a beer.

"Just how did you do it son?" asked Robert. "How did get this beautiful girl?"

"I got good genes dad," answered Robbie. "Women appreciate men with good genes. I think she latched onto me first."

"That's true," said Brandy. "I went after Robbie and I got him. He's mine to stay now."

"That sounds serious," said Robert.

"It is," said Brandy.

"Sounds like you got it all figured out," said Robert.

"I'm working on it," said Brandy.

"Well it's nice that you're a positive thinker," said Robert. "So many folks never have a plan or a goal in life. Sounds like you'll do well."

"We will do well because we will be together," said Brandy.

"Am I missing something here?" asked Robert. "You two didn't get married did you?"

"Not yet Dad, but we will," said Robbie. "It might be a while, but it will happen."

"It's a good thing your mother had me bring home some more beer," said Robert. "We might need it tonight. I think we should celebrate."

"I'm making something special for dinner tonight," said Mary. "I can't pronounce it, but it looks good in the picture."

"Brandy's a real good cook too," said Robbie. "I haven't lost any weight at school." Mary excused herself and headed to the kitchen.

"I'll help you in the kitchen if you don't mind Mary," said Brandy.

"You're our guest," said Mary. "Sit down and relax."

"I don't mind," said Mary. "I like it in the kitchen. We can talk and Robbie and his dad can talk. I'm sure they'd like a little man talk."

"O.k., come on," said Mary. "We'll study this recipe together."

The men got to talking and ran out of beer. Robbie went inside and got them another one. Robbie didn't want to talk about Kent State or anything like that so he told Robert about opening day.

"We had a good time down there dad," said Robbie. "I guess they'll be moving to that new place about mid-season."

"I guess the Bengals'll be playing there too," said Robert. "I don't watch much pro football but since they have a team now, maybe I should."

"I ran into a man I knew in Vietnam," said Robbie. "He was my Platoon Sergeant when I first got there. We ended up going to his house for dinner. His mother makes the best fried chicken I've ever had. Don't tell Mom I said that."

"What's he been up to since he's been home?" asked Robert.

"He works at the VA," started Robbie. "He was going to make the Corps a career. He was on his third tour when he was wounded. He got a Medical Discharge. When he was in high school, he was a big football star and had a scholarship to UC. He wanted to join the Marines instead. He married his childhood sweetheart after training. Then he got orders to Vietnam. She was pregnant. The baby was born in '66 on his first tour. His wife started running around on him. He stayed with her anyway. He said she was still convinced that he was going to be a big football star and go to the NFL. After he got orders to go back over there again, she took off and left the kid. His mother raised the kid while he was gone. When he came back, he tried to find his wife but couldn't. He was on his third tour and was my Platoon Sergeant when he was badly wounded. He said he had a bad time for a good while. Too much drinking and such. He finally decided that he had a daughter to raise and he's doing o.k. now."

"That's good," said Robert. "That would be tough though. You want to make the Corps a career and then get a Medical Discharge. Well I hope the best for him and his kid."

"Brandy's a ball player too dad," said Robbie. "She can hit and she can field and throw. She wanted to play baseball when she was a kid but they wouldn't let her. She was on the softball team in school. We went to a park a few times. I didn't bare down on her, but she can hit my stuff."

"Well maybe one of these days they'll let girls play baseball," said Robert. "They had women's teams during the war. I heard some of them women were really good, but I never saw them. After the war, they pretty much faded away. All the big stars that were gone for the war came back home. You know, I don't know if I could hit a softball or not. They throw that ball underhanded and it comes at you uphill, not downhill like a baseball. Some of them pitchers are pretty darn fast too. There're only 45 feet from the plate too. They throw curves and other pitches too. So, what did you think of the Reds?

They got that new fella Sparky Anderson. That shortstop is a rookie and there's a rookie pitcher that's a reliever I think."

"Dave Concepcion is the rookie shortstop," said Robbie. "He did good. That pitcher is Don Gullet. They didn't use him. They say he's real fast and a lefty."

"I got me a feeling that this might be the year for them," said Robert. "Remember when we went to the series back in '61?"

"Yes I do dad," answered Robbie. "That was a good time." Mary called the men to dinner.

"What did you ladies talk about while we were outside?" asked Robert.

"Why we talked about you men," answered Mary.

"Was it good?" asked Robbie.

"Yes it was," answered Brandy. They all sat down. Robbie pulled out a chair for Brandy and Robert pulled one out for Mary. They all kind of stared at the main dish for a while.

"That sure looks pretty," said Robert. "What's it called?"

"It's prosciutto wrapped chicken," answered Mary. "I'm not sure on that pronunciation." Everything was passed and they dug in.

"Oh my, you've outdone yourself again," said Robert. "This stuff is excellent. We should be drinking some kind of wine or something."

"It is good isn't it," said Mary after she took a bite. Brandy and Robbie agreed that it was very good. "I have a cheesecake for dessert too."

"I must be royalty eating like this," said Robert. "This is really by God good. I bet the Prince of Wales don't get food this good." That was the last of the talking. Everyone tore into their food. When they were finished, Brandy and Mary cleared the table. Mary put on some coffee and Brandy got some dessert plates. When the coffee was done, they drank a little and talked before they had their dessert. Mary had made some kind of strawberry topping for the cheesecake. The cheesecake and the topping was excellent. They drank a little more coffee after their dessert was gone. After a while, to everyone's surprise, Robbie got up and started doing the dishes. They all gave him a strange look.

"Hey, I'm used to doing the dishes after Brandy cooks," said Robbie. "I don't mind." Brandy got up and helped him.

"You two are going to have to visit more often," said Robert. "We get to eat good and then you clean up."

There was still some daylight left after dinner. Robbie and Brandy took another walk. Robbie saw a couple of people driving by that he thought he remembered. They waved back but kept going. They got back to the house a little after dark. Mary and Robert were nowhere to be seen. "Where are your parents?" asked Brandy.

"They're probably having some more dessert," answered Robbie. "That's nice," said Brandy. "I hope we're like that after twenty years. My folks never show any affection that I can see. He never kisses Mom when he goes to work or comes home or any other time."

"Maybe they're hot lovers when they're alone," said Robbie. "They go to that house in Tybee. That's a romantic place."

"It surely is," said Brandy. "Maybe they are hot lovers." Robbie and Brandy went to the living room and turned on the TV and kept the volume low. The news was long gone so there was nothing on about Kent State or any other problems. Robbie went through the channels and found a movie. It was a Western. The TV was on but they really didn't watch it much. They did a lot of kissing and fondling. They heard someone making their way to the living room so they slowed down a bit.

"Don't mind me," said Robert. "I'll be out of your way in a minute." Robert went to the kitchen. They heard the refrigerator door open and close. Robert made his way back to his room. They didn't see Robbie's parents the rest of the evening.

"Why don't we take a shower and go to bed," said Robbie. "You can go first. I'll show you where everything is." Brandy thought that was a good idea. Robbie turned off the TV and showed Brandy where everything was in the bathroom. After she was finished, Robbie took a quick shower and joined Brandy in his room.

"Does it feel strange with your parents in the house?" asked Brandy.

"Maybe a little but I'll get past it," said Robbie. He did get past it and soon they were all over each other. Apparently, it didn't bother Brandy either. When they woke in the morning, they were still holding each other. They loved each other again before they left the room. Mary was in the kitchen drinking coffee. Robert had already gone to work. Mary poured them some coffee.

"What would you like for breakfast?" asked Mary. "Your father had French toast and some bacon and eggs."

"Sounds good to me," said Robbie.

"Me too," said Brandy. "But please don't make me as much as you make Robbie. He eats a bigger breakfast than I do."

"All right," said Mary. "So how long will you be here?"

"I figure we'll stay tonight and go back in the morning," said Robbie.

"All right, I'll see if I can come up with another good recipe for dinner tonight," said Mary. "Or maybe we'll just grill some steaks. I might need to send you to the store."

"Robbie really likes spaghetti," said Brandy. "I can make you a good sauce. I don't mind."

"Take my word for it Mom," said Robbie. "Brandy is a good cook."

"Well if you don't mind, it's all right with me," said Mary. "Let's check and make sure we have everything you need." Everything was there except one thing or maybe two. Brandy said that she needed some red wine for the sauce and that they should have a nice red wine to drink with the meal.

"The wine we need is not an expensive wine," said Brandy. "I always use a chianti."

"Well Robbie can take us to the store so we can get the wine," said Mary. "I'll have to buy it since you two are not 21 yet. I'll get some different kinds of lettuce too so we can have a nice salad."

After breakfast, they all got in Robbie's car and headed to the store. They found the wine all right. It was even the brand that Brandy usually used. "I better get a corkscrew too," said Mary. "If we even have one in the house, I have no idea where it would be. Let's get some Italian bread too. We can make some garlic bread."

When they got home, Brandy got busy making the sauce. Mary wrote down everything Brandy did and all of the ingredients too. The sauce would have to simmer for two or three hours and then it would be done. "After the sauce has simmered, we'll just let it cool and then put it in the frig," said Brandy. "Then all we'll have to do is cook our pasta and heat the sauce back up. We can make the garlic bread and salads while we're cooking the pasta."

"I didn't think about a dessert," said Mary. "Should I make something. I do have some mint chocolate chip ice cream in the frig."

"That should be just fine," said Brandy. "Believe me, this stuff is so good and you'll eat so much of it that you won't even think about a dessert."

"Confident, aren't you," said Robbie.

"About certain things, yes," said Brandy. "My cooking is one of them. Another one is you."

Robbie looked at her and smiled.

It was lunch time now so Mary fixed them all something to eat. After the meal, Brandy and Robbie went for a nice long walk. They ended up at the park. They were almost to the park, when two police cruisers came flying. They didn't have their sirens on. They pulled into the park and headed toward a small group of people who were sitting on the ground in a circle. Robbie and Brandy figured they were smoking pot. As soon as they saw the cruisers, they scattered. Brandy and Robbie stayed back and watched. Not one of the group was apprehended. Brandy and Robbie tried not to laugh. The cruisers left after the officers caught their breath. Robbie thought he recognized someone on one of the ball diamonds and went to it. It was his old Legion coach. There were a couple of others on the field too. He saw Robbie too and come over to him. They shook hands. "How have you been Coach?" asked Robbie. "Got you some new prospects?"

"Yes I do Robbie," said coach. "Now you need to tell me who this gorgeous girl is."

"Coach, this drop dead gorgeous woman is my very dear friend Brandy Wisecup." said Robbie.

"I'm pleased to meet you Brandy," said coach. "I'm Robbie's old Legion ball coach. My real name is Art, but everyone just calls me Coach."

"Well I'm pleased to meet you too Coach," said Brandy. They shook hands.

"That fella on the left is fast but he has no control," said coach. "The other one has a great curveball but he doesn't know when to throw it. I'm working with them a little. So how've you been? How was Vietnam? I heard you were back. They said you got shot up some."

"I did get shot up some Coach," said Robbie. "Got a Medical Discharge. Doing all right though. Brandy and I are both studying to be morticians."

"You don't say," said Coach. "Who'd a thunk that? Well I guess somebody's gotta do it. If you got the stomach for it, why not?"

"Have you ever had any girls wanting to play baseball around here coach?" asked Brandy. Coach kind of looked at her strangely.

"I don't believe so," said Coach.

"I'll bet you a beer that Brandy can throw more strikes than those two on the field right now," said Robbie. "What do you say?" Have we got a bet?"

"Got a glove with you Brandy?" asked Coach.

"I'll just borrow one from one of them two," said Brandy. "So let me see. Each of us will throw six pitches. Robbie can borrow your glove, Coach. He'll catch and you can be the ump."

"Do you want to warm up any Brandy?" asked Coach.

"Those two should be warmed up already," said Brandy. "They can go first. When I'm up, I'll take four warm up pitches."

"Confident, isn't she," said coach.

"Yes she is," said Robbie. Robbie got coach's glove and the one with the speed and no control went first. Out of six pitches, he got one over the plate, but just barely. It was just in on the outside corner and almost high. The other one threw two strikes. They were belt high fastballs and a good hitter would have hit them over the fence. Brandy took the mound. She was right handed. She threw her warm up pitches nice and easy. Then she got down to business. The first pitch came in fast. It was a strike at the knees on the inside corner. The next pitch was a strike on the inside corner just below the letters. The third pitch was a strike at the knees on the outside corner. The fourth pitch was a strike at the knees on the inside corner. This pitch was a slider. The fifth pitch was a sinker and a strike at the knees on the outside corner. Her sixth pitch was a curveball that came in right at a right handed batter's shoulder. At the last second it broke down and away just catching the outside corner at the knees.

"Holy mackerel," said coach. "Girl, you need to talk to Sparky Anderson. They might need you over in Cincinnati. What kind of beer do you like Robbie?"

"Cold," answered Robbie. The two pitchers weren't the least bit concerned that Brandy had outdone them. Their eyes were glued to her.

"You boys put your tongues back in your mouths now," said Coach. "Let's get back to work. Robbie, I'll get you that beer."

"Nice seeing you again Coach," said Robbie. "Good luck this season." Robbie and Brandy headed back home.

Everyone stuffed themselves at dinner that evening. No one even mentioned dessert. "That was some really good sauce," said Mary. "I got your recipe now and I'll be making it from now on."

"I'm glad you liked it," said Brandy. "I got the recipe from my grandmother. She loved to cook."

"You are a very good cook Brandy," said Robert. "I'd eat some more but I don't think I can. This wine is good too. We don't drink wine around here. Maybe we should once in a while. That stuff really went good with the spaghetti."

"Certain wines go with certain foods," said Brandy. "I still like my beer, but I appreciate a good wine once in a while." Robbie jumped up and started on the dishes. Mary just about fell out of her chair when Robert got up and helped him. Mary and Brandy just looked at each other and smiled. Nothing was said.

That night, Brandy and Robbie made love for a very long time. They finally fell asleep in each other's arms. The next morning after breakfast, they kissed Mary goodbye and headed back to Cincinnati. After they got to the apartment, they just spent the day lounging around. In the afternoon, Brandy got a call from a friend from back home. She was going to Washington D.C. for a big demonstration and wanted to know if Brandy would like to go. Brandy told her she'd call her back. She hung up the phone and sat down beside Robbie on the couch. "Robbie, a friend of mine called," started Brandy. "There's going to be a huge demonstration in Washington D.C. and she wants to know if I want to go too. I'm not sure if I do or not."

"Brandy, I can't and wouldn't tell you what to do," said Robbie. "But you know what happened at Kent State. If there's a big demonstration at Washington D.C., it won't be any National Guard out there. That's the nation's capital. They'll be real troops and hundreds of riot police. If it would get out of hand, it could get real ugly. I would hate it if something happened to you."

"I would hate that too," said Brandy. "Somehow, I just don't think that it would stay peaceful, especially after Kent Stare. I'll call her back." Brandy called her friend and told her she wouldn't be going and wished her the best.

There were demonstrations and riots happening all over the country. On May 8, eleven students were bayoneted by the New Mexico National Guard at the University of New Mexico. There were no fatalities. On May 9, 100,000 people demonstrated at Washington, D.C. On May 14, 2 students were killed and 12 were wounded at Jackson State University. There was a nationwide student strike. Campuses and schools all over the country were closed. Back in Ohio, the National Guard was sent to Ohio University in Athens, Ohio. The country was in a terrible mess.

A Gallup Poll had been taken immediately after the shootings at Kent State. Of the respondents answering, 58 percent blamed the students for the shootings, 11 percent blamed the National Guard, and 31 percent had no opinion. President Nixon established the President's Commission on Campus Unrest. This was known as the Scranton Commission. A report was issued in September 1970. The report concluded that the Ohio National Guard shootings on May 4, 1970 were unjustified. It stated that even if the guardsmen faced danger, it was not a danger that called for lethal force. Kent State was the last time that guardsmen had loaded rifles.

Also in September 1970, 24 students and 1 faculty member were indicted for the burning of the ROTC building. They became known as the "Kent 25." One student was found guilty and two others pleaded guilty. One was acquitted and the rest were dismissed.

Eight members of the Ohio National Guard were indicted, but the charges were dismissed in 1974. The Guardsmen said they fired because they feared for their lives. The prosecutor decided the case was too weak. Civil actions were then taken against the guardsmen, the State of Ohio, and the President of Kent State. After an 11 week trial, there were unanimous verdicts for the plaintiffs. This was overturned by a Court of Appeals. On remand, the civil case was settled in return for a total of $675,000 to all plaintiffs by the State of Ohio. The defendants had to publicly state that they regretted what had happened.

Chapter Eighteen

Classes started on Monday as scheduled without any problems. Nothing was mentioned in any of Robbie's classes about all of the problems in the country. Some of the people in Brandy's classes talked about Kent State, but it was mostly business as usual. When Robbie got home that afternoon, there was a letter waiting on him. It was from Carl Sims. Carl had invited him over for the next weekend or whatever weekend Robbie was available. He also gave Robbie his new phone number. When Brandy got home a little later, Robbie gave her the news. "My friend Carl Sims invited me down next weekend," said Robbie. "He lives just outside of Covington. Would you want to go with me?"

"Who's Carl Sims?" asked Brandy. "If you've mentioned him before, I don't remember him right now."

"He was my squad leader in Vietnam," said Robbie. "We became good friends over there. He was a ball player too."

"Sure, I'll go with you if Carl doesn't mind," said Brandy. "I feel like getting away from the big city for a while."

"I'll call him later this evening and tell him we're coming," said Robbie. "It'll be good to see him. On my first patrol, I had to put a dressing on Carl's ass."

"Wasn't your first patrol the one that you saved Bobby Benjamin?" asked Brandy.

"Yes it was," answered Robbie. "I was busy that day."

"Sounds like we'll have an interesting visit," said Brandy. "I think I'll get started on dinner."

Brandy went to the kitchen and got started on dinner. Robbie sat on the couch and did some studying. He didn't want to turn on the TV because it was time for the news and he didn't want to hear any news of any kind. As he studied, he would sneak a few looks at Brandy as she worked in the kitchen. One time he looked and she was bent over getting some pans out of a cupboard. He watched her form for a few seconds and then made his way into the kitchen. He got behind her and began feeling her all over. He gently kissed her neck and ears. He slowly pulled down her jeans and then her panties. He got down on his knees and slowly kissed her backside. As he stood back up, he dropped his own jeans and underwear. He turned her to face him and their mouths locked together. He picked her up and sat her on the counter. As they made love, pans were flying all over.

After they were done, Robbie picked her up and carried her to the couch. They lay there holding each other. "Thank you Robbie Parker," said Brandy. "I think I needed that. I love you Robbie."

"I love you too, Brandy Wisecup," said Robbie. "I needed that too, and when you bent over in the kitchen, I just couldn't help myself."

"I'll remember that," said Brandy. "I'll try not to bend over too much in public. We might get arrested." They started kissing and soon they were at it again. "I guess we'll be eating late tonight," said Brandy after they were finished. "Why don't you go ahead and call Carl while I'm cooking?"

"I will," said Robbie. Robbie got to the phone and called. A woman answered the phone. "This is Robbie Parker," said Robbie. "I'm calling for Carl Sims."

"I'm Carl's wife Sally," said Sally. "He's just outside. I'll get him for you." Carl picked up the phone a moment later.

"Is that you pitcher?" asked Carl.

"Yep, it's me," said Robbie. "I'm calling to let you know I'll be down this weekend."

"That's great," said Carl. "Bring a glove with you."

"I will," said Robbie. "Would it be all right if I brought my girl with me?"

"Sure, Sally'd probably like some female company," said Carl. "You're not afraid of staying in a trailer are you?"

"No, but I've never been in one," said Robbie.

"Well we're living in this trailer and I'm building us a house a little at a time," said Carl. "I hope to have the house done before the baby comes."

"So you're gonna be a daddy," said Robbie. "That's great. I bet you'll be a great dad."

"I hope so," said Carl. "Me and Sally want to have a bunch of kids."

"Well I've never been much of a carpenter but maybe I can help a little with the house this weekend," said Robbie. "You can just tell me what to do or what to hold and I'll do it. Brandy can help too."

"So your girl don't mind manual labor?" asked Carl.

"I don't know but we'll find out," said Robbie. "I'll tell you this though, She's a hell of a ball player. You'll see. I'm gonna hang up now. We'll have all weekend to yak. So give me directions and I'll see you Saturday morning." Carl gave Robbie the directions to his place and then they hung up.

"Well you'll meet Carl Saturday morning," said Robbie. "His wife's name is Sally and she's pregnant. They're living in a trailer and Carl's building them a house. We'll take our gloves too."

It was nine o'clock before they had finished eating and Robbie got the dishes done. They took a shower together and then went to bed. They made love one more time before falling asleep. Brandy was awakened about 3 AM. Robbie was dreaming and was shouting, "mother fuckin' rain, God damned fuckin' rain." Brandy held him tightly for a while and he quit yelling. A little while later, he yelled, "incoming." Brandy shook him a little and he woke. "What is it?" he asked Brandy. "Was I dreaming or something?"

"Yes you were dreaming," said Brandy. "At first you were cursing the rain. Then you yelled, 'Incoming!' "

"Sorry, I was thinking about Carl and that got me thinking about over there," said Robbie. "I'll be all right. Let's get back to sleep."

The rest of the night was uneventful. When Robbie got up for his first class, Brandy had already gone. He found a note from her beside the coffee pot. It said "I love you Robbie Parker." Robbie smiled and poured himself some coffee. The rest of the week flew by. After breakfast Saturday morning, they headed to Carl's place. Carl had given good directions and they found the place easily. Robbie stopped at a store right before they got there and purchased a case of beer. He figured they might need it. When they pulled into Carl's driveway, Carl was outside working on the house. His wife Sally was with him and handing him nails. Carl was on the roof but when he saw Robbie, he went to the edge of the roof and jumped off. He rolled when he hit the ground and got up and ran over to Robbie's car. Robbie got out and they shook hands and hugged for a while.

"You're lookin' good Pitcher," said Carl. "Sally, this is my friend Robbie Parker and his girl."

"I'm Brandy Wisecup," said Brandy. "I'm so pleased to meet the two of you." Brandy went to Sally and gave her a hug and then hugged Carl."

"Pitcher, you got yourself a fine lookin' woman," said Carl. "Brandy, Robbie tells me you're a hell of ball player. We'll see after while."

"I brought something with me," said Robbie as he went to the car and took out the case of beer. "I figured we might need this later."

"We just might," said Carl. "I'll get this in the frig right now to keep it cold. Come on inside. I'll show you the place." They went inside and Carl put the beer in the frig. Then he gave them a quick tour of the trailer. "It's not much, but it's all we need right now," said Carl. "This'll be your room over there. It's got a full sized bed too. Bathroom's right over there in the hallway." After the tour, they all went outside and sat on the deck. Sally got them all a cup of coffee. "So tell me Pitcher, how's mortician school?" asked Carl.

"It's just dead," answered Robbie. They all laughed. "So why don't you show me what to do and maybe we can do a little on the house."

"You're my guest. I shouldn't be working my guest right off," said Carl.

"Don't bother me any," said Robbie. "Are you game Brandy?"

"Sure, why not?" said Brandy. "I can drive a nail and cut a board. Get me some knee pads and I'll help you on the roof."

Carl produced some knee pads so Brandy got on the roof. The plywood was already nailed down. They put on some felt paper and then started nailing on shingles. Robbie was impressed. Brandy swung that hammer like she was a regular construction worker. The house was going to be a four bedroom ranch with a simple roof. With three of them working, they had one side of the roof done in no time. Sally kept them supplied with nails and drinking water. Carl and Robbie took turns bringing the shingles up the ladder. When the one side was done, Carl decided that was enough for the day. "That would have taken me two weekends to do by myself," said Carl. "You guys were a great help. Let's have something to eat. Then we can throw a few balls and then drink some of that beer." Sally made them some lunch. Brandy helped her in the kitchen.

"So how does it feel being pregnant?" Brandy asked Sally.

"It was o.k. till I started getting the morning sickness," said Sally. "I been lucky. I've only had it mostly in the morning. I guess some women get it all the time."

"So with four bedrooms you must be planning on several kids," said Brandy.

"We are," said Sally. "We both came from big families. We won't be rich, but we'll be happy. We're building the house a little at a time so we don't have to go into debt. We got the land cheap too. Carl's dad knew the man that owned it. We got ten acres and it's all woods but up here where the house is. It's beautiful here and quiet."

"It does look nice," said Brandy. "I bet you have deer in your yard at times."

"We do," said Sally. "They're fun to watch but when we have our garden, we'll have to keep them out of it. Carl won't shoot them. He says he'll never shoot anything again unless it's trying to shoot him. So how did you meet Robbie?"

"I needed a person to share expenses on an apartment," said Brandy. "I put up a note on the bulletin board at school and Robbie called. We're roommates. We're lovers too."

"That's great," said Sally. "So are you studying to be a mortician too?"

"Yes I am," answered Brandy. "My family has been in the business since 1870. I'm carrying on the tradition."

"I don't think I could do that," said Sally.

"It's not for everyone, but someone's gotta do it," said Brandy.

"So when are you and Robbie tying the knot?" asked Sally.

"We haven't set a date yet," answered Brandy. "It'll probably be after we both get done with school. I'm finished at the end of the year and Robbie will have one more semester after that. So it won't be long."

"Are you having a big wedding?" asked Sally.

"We haven't discussed that, but I'd be happy if we just eloped," said Brandy. "I don't need all that fancy stuff. Robbie's all I need."

"That's what we kind of did," said Sally. "We just went to the Justice of the Peace. We went to Myrtle Beach for a honeymoon. It was fun."

"That sounds nice," said Brandy. "I'm sure we'll do something for a honeymoon. We spent some time at a house on Tybee Island a while back. That was wonderful."

"I've never been there but I know people who have and they just love it," said Sally. "Well everything's ready guys. Let's eat."

After lunch, Robbie and Carl got out the gloves while the girls did the dishes. The men didn't talk much when they first started throwing. After a while they talked some. "You'll never guess who I saw at opening day," said Robbie.

"I give up, who?" asked Carl.

"S/Sgt. Benjamin," said Robbie. "He was there with his little girl."

"I never knew he was from around here," said Carl. "He never hung around much with us. I guess it was easier that way."

"I never knew he was from Cincinnati either," said Robbie. "He was a big high school football star and had a scholarship to UC. He joined the Corps instead."

"He must have really wanted to be a Marine if he gave up a scholarship," said Carl.

"He married his high school sweetheart too," started Robbie. "She was convinced that one day he would be an NFL star. Anyway, their girl was born in '66 when he was on his first tour. His wife started running around on him but he stayed with her. When he went back the second time, she took off. His momma raised the girl while he was gone. He was on his third tour when he was with us."

"So what's he doing now?" asked Carl.

"He's got a job at the VA," answered Robbie. "His momma lives with him. He said with his disability pay and job, he gets by all right. He had some problems drinking too much and such but got straightened out. His momma makes the best fried chicken I ever had."

"Sally makes damn good fried chicken too," said Carl. "She soaks it in buttermilk or something. Anyway, it's good." Brandy came out with her glove and joined them. Sally sat on the deck and watched. Carl let her get loosened up a bit. "Show me what you got girl," said Carl. Brandy threw him a big curve. "Damn girl, that's good," said Carl. "What else you got?" Brandy threw him a sinker and then a slider. Carl was impressed. "If they allowed women baseball players, you'd be one of the first ones drafted," said Carl. "You're not bad to look at either. The batters would be looking at you and not paying attention to the ball." Brandy smiled and threw him another curve.

They played catch for around an hour and then they decided it was time to drink beer. The boys got a little drunk and told war stories. Brandy drank a little and laughed at some of the stories. Sally didn't drink because she was pregnant. After a few hours, they decided they were hungry. Sally was figuring on making dinner. Robbie asked if there was a pizza place around. He would get them some pizza if no one objected. No one did. There was a pizza place not too far away. Sally called in the order and she and Brandy went to pick it up. The boys were in no shape to drive. They wolfed down the pizza and the boys continued their drinking. The girls did some talking while the boys drank.

"Does Robbie ever have any nightmares?" Sally asked Brandy.

"He does once in a while," answered Brandy. "Just the other night he woke me up. He was cursing the rain. Then he was yelling "incoming." He has others. He's never done anything weird though. Has Carl?"

"He has nightmares sometimes," said Sally. "He's walked in his sleep a few times, but he hasn't done that for a while now." Just then, Carl walked over to the girls.

"Robbie says I gotta show you my ass," said Carl half slurring the words. "Ole Pitcher here had to put a dressing on my ass that one day." He never said another word. He turned facing away from the girls and dropped his drawers. "Whaddaya think? Is that a nice ass or not," said Carl.

"Yes it's nice," said Brandy. "Looks like it healed very nicely." The girls laughed a little. Carl pulled his pants back up, turned and bowed to the girls, and then went back to his chair. "So why do you call Robbie Pitcher?" asked Brandy.

"Cause of the way he can throw a grenade," answered Carl. "I never seen nobody who could throw a grenade like him. He's good. Blew the shit outta them that day."

The boys went back to their talking and the girls got back to theirs. Finally about 1 AM, they decided it was time for bed. Sally and Carl went straight to bed. Brandy and Robbie took a quick shower and then went to bed. Robbie had a buzz on but he wasn't drunk. He and Brandy made love before they fell asleep.

They woke up the next morning to the sound of hammering. Carl had gotten up and was working on the house. Brandy and Robbie threw on their clothes and went out to help. Carl saw them and came over to them. "Let's have some coffee and breakfast," said Carl. "I was just getting in a few licks while the coffee was brewing. Didn't wake you did I?"

"Don't matter," said Robbie. "It was past time to get up anyway." They had their coffee and breakfast and were back on the roof. Robbie and Carl took turns carrying the shingles up the ladder. Brandy nailed them down and Sally kept them supplied with nails and water. The roof was completely done in a few hours. They had some lunch and then did a little work on the inside of the house. Late in the afternoon, Robbie and Brandy were thinking about leaving. Sally announced that she was fixing dinner and they had to stay. They had fried chicken with mashed potatoes and gravy.

"You're a good cook Sally," said Robbie. "Carl's gonna weigh 300 pounds some day."

"Glad you like it," said Sally. "My momma taught me. My daddy was a big man and he liked his food."

"You soaked the chicken in buttermilk didn't you?" asked Brandy. "We had some chicken not long ago that was just like this."

"Yes I did," answered Sally. "Plus the chicken wasn't store bought. We got them from a farmer down the road. Carl does him favors from time to time and he give us a chicken once in a while."

"Sounds like you have good neighbors," said Brandy. "I do like your place."

"Well you two are welcome here anytime," said Sally. "I do hope to see you again."

"Maybe we can come again sometime and help with the house," said Robbie.

"I'll be doing some serious work in three weeks to a month," said Carl. "The main thing was the roof and we got that done this weekend. I can't thank you two enough. If you're serious about coming, I'll call when I get everything I need."

"We'll be here," said Brandy. "We really enjoyed helping you. Maybe one day we'll build ourselves a house."

They finished their meal and said their goodbyes. Brandy sat very close to Robbie on the trip home. "Sally and Carl are nice people aren't they?" said Brandy. "I liked helping them. I hope he can get the house done before the baby comes."

"He will if I have anything to say about it," said Robbie. "It's not far down there. I wouldn't mind going once or twice a month to help out."

"Pull over," said Brandy. "I want to kiss you for a while."

"I can't. This is a freeway," said Robbie. "You're not supposed to pull over unless it's an emergency."

"Well this is an emergency, now pull over," said Brandy. Robbie did as instructed. As soon as he got stopped, she was all over him. They had been making out for about ten minutes when a patrol car pulled up behind them. Robbie just happened to see him pulling over and convinced Brandy to slow down a bit. The patrolman walked up to Robbie's car.

"Are you having a problem?" asked the patrolman.

"Yes officer, the engine was overheating so I pulled over to let it cool off a bit," said Robbie. The patrolman looked hard at Brandy.

"I can see why it overheated," said the patrolman. "Get moving as soon as you can. Have a nice day." The officer tipped his hat and went back to his car.

"Nice fella," said Robbie. "We better get moving." Brandy gave him a kiss on the cheek and then they took off. The patrol car pulled out right after they left.

Robbie's leg ached a good bit for the next couple of days. He took his cane with him to class every day that week. That weekend, a bunch from the school decided to go back to the neighborhood bar. It was the same group of people who went the last time. Polly was there and had to quiz all of them about their chosen vocation. She and Barney exchanged a few harsh but friendly words again. Some of the people wanted to talk about Kent State and the other demonstrations that had been happening. Brandy and Robbie changed the subject several times but the conversation always went back to Kent State. One of the students mentioned something about Calley and the My Lai Massacre. They wanted to know what Robbie thought about it.

"I don't know that much about it," said Robbie. "I know it happened in '68 but the Army didn't make it public knowledge until last year sometime. I know a lot of people were killed and I think Calley's being charged with murder."

"How could someone do that?" asked one of the girls. Her name was Anna.

"It could happen," answered Robbie. "You give a young man a loaded weapon and get him tired, scared, and pissed off, bad things can happen. Now can we please not talk about any of this stuff?"

"This stuff is what's going on in our country right now," Anna said. "Things like this need to be talked about so they don't happen again."

"Us talking about them will not change anything," said Robbie. "Now if you want to have a peaceful demonstration somewhere, go ahead. Just make sure there are no hotheads there. The National Guard wouldn't have even been sent to Kent State if there hadn't been rioting and looting in downtown Kent. That wasn't very peaceful. And burning down the ROTC building was just plain arson. And we don't know for sure what orders were given to Calley."

"See Robbie, we're talking about it," said Anna. "This is good." Brandy could see that Robbie was getting a little ticked off.

"I think we've talked enough about the country's problems," said Brandy. "Now let's move on to something else. You are upsetting Robbie."

"We're sorry," said Anna. "Sometimes we forget that he is a veteran and maybe had to do bad things."

"That's it," said Robbie. "We're leaving. You all can talk all you want now." Robbie and Brandy left.

"I'm sorry about this," said Robbie as they were driving home. "I would have stayed if you wanted. I could have ignored them."

"I didn't want to talk about any of that stuff either," said Brandy. "We're going to be hearing it on the news forever. There will probably be demonstrations all over until all the boys get home and maybe even after that. Some of those POW's have been there for a lot of years. I hope they make it home."

"So do I," said Robbie. "Now let's snuggle on the couch and see if we can find a movie to watch."

~~~~

During the next week, Anna and several of the other students were constantly apologizing to Robbie. The first time around was all right, but after that, Robbie was tired of it and told them that it wasn't necessary for them to apologize in the first place. They were entitled to their own thoughts and opinions. If they conflicted with his, then so be it.

The next weekend, the same group that went to the neighborhood bar, decided to go bowling. Brandy and Robbie went too. Only one person in the group had ever bowled before and knew how to keep score. He did his best to show the others what he knew. They bowled two games. There were eight of them altogether and they had two lanes side by side. Brandy's first game was a 75 and Robbie's was a 99. They did better on the second game with an 85 and a 105. They didn't throw any gutter balls and not one of the group threw a strike. All of them went to a diner for dinner. Afterwards, they went their separate ways. Brandy and Robbie went home. When they got home, there was a letter for Robbie waiting. It was from someone named Johnson in Detroit. Robbie remembered that he had written Larry Johnson sometime back but hadn't heard back from him. When he saw that Larry's name wasn't on the return address, he started thinking the worst. He sat on the couch and slowly opened the letter. Brandy figured it was bad news but sat close to him. The letter went as follows.

Dear Robbie,

I am Larry's older sister. I am writing to inform you that Larry was killed almost three weeks ago. I got your address when Larry's personal affects arrived. I know that you and Larry were good friends. He often talked about you in his letters. He said you were his white boy. He was just kidding. Larry didn't get along too well with white folks but I know he liked you. This is why I am writing you. You might have never found out if I hadn't written. We all miss Larry terribly. He had big plans for when he got home. He was going to college and major in business. I have to stop now because I can't quit crying. Thank you for being my brother's friend.

Sincerely,

Loni Johnson

Robbie put his arms around Brandy and started crying. He cried for a good fifteen minutes. Robbie hardly spoke the rest of the day. That night, they held each other tightly as they drifted off to sleep. About two in the morning, Brandy was awakened. Robbie was very restless. He rolled from side to side and then flipped onto his back and then back onto his stomach several times. He started shouting, "get down, get down, get down, stay the fuck down. Ammo, ammo, get me some fuckin' ammo. Tell that FO to get some arty workin'. That 82's killin' us." Then he was still and quiet. It took Brandy a while, but she got back to sleep.

When Robbie woke up the next morning, Brandy was sitting on the edge of the bed next to him. She was naked and had a coffee cup in her hand. "Good morning man of mine," said Brandy. "You had a rough night last night."

"Put down that coffee and come here," said Robbie. Brandy sat down her cup and Robbie pulled her to him. An hour later, they were eating breakfast. "I know I had some dreams last night," said Robbie. "I didn't scare you, did I?"

"No, I wasn't scared," said Brandy. "You were very restless for a little while and then you shouted some things. Then it was over."

"I was thinking about Larry," said Robbie. "And that got me going about over there."

"That place will be with you probably for the rest of your life," said Brandy. "But you're a strong man Robbie Parker. And you're a good man. Plus you're my man." Robbie sat down his coffee cup and got up from the table. He went to Brandy, picked her up out of her chair, and took her to the living room floor. They made love till they were exhausted.

That afternoon, they took their gloves, balls, and bats to the park and had some batting practice and shagged some fly balls and grounders. Some teenage boys were there and they joined Brandy and Robbie. Of course the boys spent most of their time looking at Brandy. A couple of the young boys had girlfriends with them. The young girls got a little jealous.

~~~~

Two weeks later, they were at Carl's place. He'd gotten some of his material and was ready for the help. Robbie took another case of beer. The work they were doing didn't go as fast as the roof. There was a lot of board cutting and measuring. They worked all morning till lunch and then a couple of hours after lunch. They drank a couple of beers before they got out the gloves. They threw for less than an hour and then drank beer. This time they didn't drink as hard and fast as they did the first weekend they were there, but the boys still got a buzz. Robbie told Carl about Larry Johnson. Carl had known Larry but not as well as Robbie. Carl knew that Larry was a good man in the bush.

Sally and Brandy fixed them a fine meal for dinner. After dinner, they all sat out back of the house and watched the wildlife. There were several deer with new fawns. The deer knew they were being watched but didn't mind. A red tailed hawk swooped down after a chipmunk, but missed. "There's a little stream just a little back in the woods there," said Carl. "It don't usually run dry. I'm thinking I might make myself a pond. I'd stock it with bluegills and bass. Them bluegills are good eatin'. Did you ever eat bluegills?"

"I never been fishing in my life," said Robbie. "My dad took me shooting and that was about it for my outside activities except baseball."

"Well you need to take up fishing," said Carl. "It's relaxing. Don't matter if you catch fish or not. Have you ever fished Brandy?"

"My family has a house on Kelley's Island," said Brandy. "That's on Lake Erie. We fish for walleyes up there. I've caught some. What I like to catch up there is sheephead. They fight a lot harder than walleye."

"What's a sheephead?" asked Carl.

"It's actually a fresh water drum," answered Brandy. "Not sure why they call them sheephead. A real sheephead is a salt water fish. They catch them down South."

"Well if you'd hook into a big catfish, you'd have your hands full," said Carl. "They just tug and tug and tug. My dad caught a 40 pound shovelhead once. Big booger."

They stayed out back and watched the wildlife till it got dark. They thought about staying out longer, but the mosquitos were getting bad. "Remember how bad them things were over there?" asked Carl.

"I do," answered Robbie. "Took a long time to get used to them. If I could keep them off my ears, I was all right. They could still eat me up but if I couldn't hear them I didn't care."

"Same for me," said Carl. "They're not usually this bad. We've had some rain and there must be water laying in a few places. When it dries up, they won't be bad."

They went to bed early that night. The next morning they were up early and hammering away. By the time dinner rolled around, they had most of the plywood on the outside walls. They had another good dinner and said their goodbyes. Carl had a cousin who would be helping him run the electric in the house. Then Carl would run the plumbing. Brandy and Robbie would be down when Carl was ready to hang the windows.

The next month seemed to fly by. Robbie and Brandy were doing well at school. They went to a couple of Reds' games and hung out with their usual crowd some. At each game, they looked around to see if maybe Bobby Benjamin was there. He was not. Carl had called and they were going down to help hang windows the next Saturday. It was Thursday and for some reason, Robbie decided to pick up a newspaper. He scanned the headlines on the front page and turned the page. He was shocked to see a picture of Bobby Benjamin in the middle of the second page. Then he read the headline above the picture. "Local Vietnam Vet Commits Suicide," it read. Then it went on to tell how he was a big football hero in high school and then joined the Corps. His wife was mentioned but not much was said about her. It said how he had served three tours of duty in Vietnam and now worked at the VA. No one suspected him of having any mental or personal problems. He was leaving a daughter behind.

Robbie couldn't believe what he had just read. Bobby seemed all right to him when they had met. Why would he kill himself? He loved his little girl. Robbie didn't understand. When he got home, Brandy was already there. He went to her and hugged her. "Bobby Benjamin killed himself," said Robbie. "I saw it in the paper." Brandy started crying.

"Why would he do that?" said Brandy. "He's got that little girl. He loved that girl. I don't understand."

"I don't understand either," said Robbie. "He seemed o.k. to me when we visited. He said he had a drinking problem sometime back but straightened out. His momma and daughter must be in hell about this." They didn't talk a lot that evening. They turned on the TV once but they were talking about some demonstration somewhere so they turned it off.

~~~~

Their minds seemed to get clearer when they headed back to Carl's Saturday morning. "I like it when we go to Carl's," said Robbie. "He and I were in the same shit, but my mind seems to set itself free when we're down there."

"I kind of feel that way too," said Brandy. "It's kind of like a family thing. It makes me feel good."

They stopped and got some beer like they usually did, but this time they got some steaks and some food to go with the steaks. Carl was already working when they pulled into the driveway. Sally greeted them with a cup of coffee. "Better get this stuff in the frig," said Robbie as he headed inside. "I saw a grill here somewhere."

"Robbie brought some steaks," said Sally to Carl.

"You didn't need to be doing that," said Carl. "You're my guests."

"You've been feeding us some good meals," said Brandy. "We wanted to help out."

"You've been helping with the house," said Carl. "You've saved me a bunch of time and money."

"Don't argue with us Carl," said Robbie. "You're eating steak today. I'm sure you like steak. Plus they go real good with beer."

"They go good with a shot of bourbon too," said Carl. "We'll have a shot of bourbon with dinner too. Now are you guys gonna drink coffee all day or get to work?"

"Show me what needs done," said Robbie. "I figure I can hang a window, but if you want it straight and proper, you best show me."

"Two of us will work on the windows," said Carl. "I have some things the other person can do. Now who's doing windows?"

"You and Robbie go ahead and do the windows," said Brandy. "Show me what else you need done."

It took all of the morning and part of the afternoon to get the windows installed. Carl made sure everything was perfect. When they were done working for the day, they played a little catch and then drank beer. Brandy volunteered to cook the steaks. "I like mine medium rare," announced Brandy. "If anybody wants theirs different speak up now." No one spoke up. The steaks were done in no time. After the meal, Carl pulled out a bottle of bourbon.

"We'll have us a shot of this now," said Carl. "Just sip it and enjoy it. Don't be slamming it down. That's for fools who don't really enjoy it. They just want to get drunk. Carl poured everyone but Sally a shot.

"This is pretty good stuff," said Brandy after she took a sip. "I think it could really grow on you."

"I like it too," said Robbie. "What kind of bourbon is it?"

"This is Jim Beam," answered Carl. "It's smoother and lighter than some bourbons. Did you know that all bourbon is made in Kentucky?"

"I never knew that," said Robbie. "I guess that's why it's called Kentucky Bourbon."

"They been making bourbon down here for years," said Carl. "I guess at one time when people didn't have any money, they used whiskey for money."

"Is there any moonshining going on around here?" asked Brandy.

"I have relatives that make it," said Carl. "They do it for themselves. There are some people that make it to sell, but I stay away from them. I hear some folks up in the hills are growing pot. They say it's a good cash crop and less work than whiskey."

"Yeh, as long as they don't get caught," said Sally.

Brandy and Robbie seemed to enjoy the bourbon, so after the dishes were done, they had another shot while they sat out back and watched the deer. "We can't do much work tomorrow," said Carl. "Gotta save up a few more bucks and then I can get the siding. That might be another month."

"Well give me a call and we'll be down to help," said Robbie.

"Why don't you come down in a couple of weeks and we can go fishing," said Carl.

"I don't know anything about fishing, but I'm willing to learn," said Robbie. "Don't I need a fishing license."

"You won't need one where we'll be going," said Carl. "It's private land."

"How about poles and such?" asked Robbie.

"I got enough stuff for everybody," said Carl. "I got casting reels, spinning reels, and push button for rookies."

"What'll we be fishing for?" asked Brandy.

"Catfish," answered Carl. "We'll see if we can get us a big shovelhead."

The next morning after breakfast, They helped Carl pick up scrap wood and such around the house and then they were on their way.

Chapter Nineteen

The next two weeks of school seemed to go fast. Brandy and Robbie spent a lot of time in the gym and at the park. Robbie was considering taking Judo lessons. He thought it might help him be more flexible on his left side. He had never said anything to Brandy, but there were times when his upper left back seemed to tighten up a lot. He knew it was from his wound. Sometimes his workout at the gym helped it but sometimes it didn't. When he told Brandy that he was thinking of taking Judo lessons, she thought that it was a good idea if it would help him.

The next weekend, they decided they would go dancing. They hadn't been dancing for a good while and missed it. Saturday night, they went to a club where they had gone before. The place looked totally different to them. It had been completely remodeled. They found themselves a table right before the band started. They ordered a beer and it arrived right as the band started. The lead singer walked up to his microphone and just stood there for a few minutes. After a few minutes of quiet, some of the patrons started yelling. "C'mon, play something." The lead singer smiled for a moment and then the band started. The first song they played was an anti-war song.

The crowd sang along and cheered through every verse. That is maybe everybody but Robbie and Brandy. "I came here to dance," said Robbie. "Not to listen to anti-war music. Maybe we should go somewhere else."

"Let's let them do another song or two," said Brandy. "Maybe they'll get away from that stuff."

"O.k., we'll see what they do," said Robbie. It took a long time for the cheering to die down after the song was over. Finally the band played another song. Robbie's eyes rolled back when they got started. It was another anti-war song.

"Let's go," said Robbie. "I've heard enough." Brandy agreed and they left. "Where would you like to go now?" asked Robbie.

"There's this club not far from here," said Brandy. "I've never been to it but whenever I've gone by on the weekends, the place looks packed."

"Well let's give it a try," said Robbie. It didn't take long to get there. The place looked packed. It took them a good while to find a parking spot in the lot. When they got inside, the first thing they noticed was that a lot of the guys were wearing cowboy boots and hats. A lot of the women had on their boots too. "I'd say this a country music place," said Robbie. "Are we staying?"

"Sure, maybe they'll play some of that new country rock type stuff," said Brandy. "We should be able to dance to some of that stuff. Let's find us a table." They looked all over and every table was occupied. They were about to give up when they heard someone say, "You can sit here jarhead." They looked around and spotted the man who spoke.

"What did you say?" said Robbie.

"I said you can sit here jarhead," the man said.

"How did you know I was a jarhead?" asked Robbie.

"You carry yourself like a jarhead," said the man. "Now you and your lovely woman sit yourself down. I'm Dave Simpson and this is my wife Marie."

"I'm Robbie Parker and this is Brandy Wisecup," said Robbie. They all shook hands and then Brandy and Robbie sat down.

"So how does a jarhead carry himself?" asked Robbie.

"Like he knows what's going on around him at all times," said Dave. "I was a Marine too. When did you get back from over there?"

"I left there late summer last year, but I was in the hospital at Pearl Harbor for a good while healing up," said Robbie. "I was with the 5th Marines at An Hoa."

"I got back not long after the '68 TET," said Dave. "I was with the 3rd division. I was a forward observer. I bounced around from unit to unit."

"I was just a grunt," said Robbie. Robbie couldn't take his eyes off of Marie. He could tell that she was part oriental but he didn't want to say anything that could be offensive. Marie was beautiful. She saw that Robbie was mesmerized by her.

"I am Vietnamese and French," said Marie. "I was born in Hanoi. My family moved to Okinawa when I was very small. That's where I met Dave."

"She's a looker isn't she," said Dave.

"She surely is," said Robbie. "So what have you been doing since you got home?"

"I'm a cop but I'm trying to make it as a personal trainer," said Dave.

"I imagine it's tough being a cop right now with everything the way it is," said Brandy.

"Yes it's tough," said Dave. "If I could punch out people every time I was called a "Pig," my knuckles would probably be broken on a regular basis." A waitress came and took their orders. Just as the drinks arrived, the band came out on the stage and got tuned up. The first song they played was "All my exes live in Texas."

Brandy grabbed Robbie and took him to the dance floor. "Let's do a little two steppin'," said Brandy. "Maybe we can fancy it up a bit too." They were the first ones on the dance floor but soon they were joined by a few other couples. The next song was a good dancing song too. The next one was a slow song. It was Conway Twitty's "Make Believe." When it was over, they went back to their table.

"You two are very good out there," said Dave. "Don't you think so honey?" "Yes they are good," said Marie. "Maybe you can teach us."

"Sure, why not?" said Brandy. They drank some of their drinks and then all of them went out on the dance floor. Several couple were out there, but it wasn't crowded yet. Dave and Marie did what Brandy and Robbie told them. A few songs later, they were dancing like they had been doing it for years. They were on the floor for a half hour or so before they went back to their table. They had just sat down when some big fella wearing a cowboy hat and boots came over to the table.

"How bout a dance lovely lady?" he said to Brandy.

"No thank you," said Brandy politely.

"Oh come on girl," said the man. "I seen how good you were out there. I got me some good moves too. Let's go."

"I already told you no," said Brandy. "Now would you please move on?"

"All right girl, but you don't know what you're missin'," said the man as he left.

"I hope I don't get more of that tonight," said Brandy.

"Well you are a beautiful woman Brandy," said Robbie. "It stands to reason that men should want to dance with you." Brandy smiled and leaned over to Robbie and gave him a kiss. Marie gave Dave a kiss too.

"So what are you doing with yourself since you've been back?" asked Dave.

"Both of us are attending the Cincinnati College of Mortuary Science," answered Robbie.

"Wow, that's interesting," said Dave. "I hope it works out for you."

"My family's been in the business since 1870," said Brandy. "I'm carrying on the tradition."

"How about you Robbie?" said Dave. "Are you carrying on a tradition?"

"No, my dad works at a factory and my mother is a housewife," said Robbie. "I wanted a profession that is always needed by everyone sooner or later."

"That's right," said Marie. "We will all die sooner or later and someone must take care of us."

"So how about you Marie?" asked Brandy. "Are you into anything special?"

"I am a teacher," answered Marie. "I teach math at a junior high school."

"That's great," said Brandy. "Do the kids behave for you?"

"They do," said Marie. "It's hard to believe the way things are now, but I haven't had any trouble."

"Maybe they know your husband is a cop," said Brandy.

"Maybe, but a lot of people dislike cops nowadays," said Marie. "I think it's just luck that I have well behaved students."

They talked a little more and then went to the dance floor. They danced a few songs and then the band took a break. They said it would be fifteen minutes but they didn't get back for a half hour. When the band started back up, they were on the dance floor. They danced for around a half hour and then sat down. They had just sat down when the fella that had wanted to dance with Brandy came back to the table. He was a little drunk. He had another guy with him. "How bout you and me now babe?" the man said.

"I'm not your babe," said Brandy. "I told you no before and no still means no. Now piss off."

"Hey bitch, you got no call to talk like that," said the man. Robbie was about to get involved. Brandy gave him a look and he knew that she was handling this.

"Tell you what," started Brandy. "Take your dick out and put it in my hand. I'll show you something that you've never seen before."

"What's that darlin'?" asked the man.

"The other end of it," said Brandy. "Now get the fuck away from me before you get yourself hurt."

"Damn, you're a sassy bitch," said the man. As soon as the word bitch came out of his mouth, Brandy stood and faced him. She hit him square in the nuts with a right uppercut. When he went down to his knees, she hit him with a left hook to the jaw. Down he went."

"Do you always let your women do your fightin' for you?" asked the other man.

"Move on before I break you in half," said Robbie. The man ignored Robbie.

"So who's the good lookin' slope?" said the other man. "Don't s'pose she'll dance either."

Dave stood now. "You will immediately apologize to my wife," said Dave. "And I mean right fuckin' now."

"Hey, fuck you man," said the man. "I don't apologize to anyone for anything." He reared back with his right and took a swing at Dave. Robbie wasn't quite sure what had happened because it was so quick. The man was flat on his back with Dave's foot on his throat.

"Now apologize to my wife," said Dave.

"All right man, I'm sorry. I'm sorry," said the man.

"I said apologize to my wife, not me," said Dave. "Her name is Marie."

"All right Marie, I'm sorry," he said.

"A little louder," said Dave. "I don't think she heard you."

"I'M SORRY," yelled the man. Dave took his foot away from the man's throat and let him get up. As he was getting up, a couple of bouncers showed up.

"What's goin' on?" one of the bouncers asked.

"This pig on the floor wouldn't leave me alone so I took care of him," said Brandy. "That other fool insulted Marie and took a swing at Dave. Dave took care of him. Now would you please escort these two out the door?"

"Of course Miss," said the bouncer. The bouncers helped the man on the floor stand up and escorted the two of them to the door.

"You're pretty feisty Brandy," said Dave. "I guess Robbie doesn't get to throw any punches with you around." Brandy let out a laugh.

"What did you do to get that man down so quick?" asked Robbie. "It happened so fast I couldn't tell."

"I'm also a judo instructor," said Dave. "Marie can handle herself too."

"Are you the instructor at the gym not far from here?" asked Robbie.

"Yes I am," answered Dave. "That's the only place I teach right now."

"Well we're members of that club," said Robbie. "I was thinking about taking judo lessons. I was thinking it would help my back."

"I think it would," said Dave. "Get signed up and I'll teach you what I know. So what's going on with your back?"

"It's my left upper back," answered Robbie. "I got shot and the bullet went through my shoulder blade, the lung, and then tore up two ribs on the way out."

"I could see how that would give you problems," said Dave. "Do you have any more wounds that give you problems?"

"I got shot through the stomach, but that one doesn't bother me," answered Robbie. I got shot through both legs but no bones were hit so that doesn't bother me. The one that does bother me the most is my left thigh. When I got shot there, the bone was really shattered. I have to use a cane sometimes."

"You'd never know that by the way you dance," said Marie.

"My leg will probably ache some tomorrow after all this dancing," said Robbie. "I've gotten used to it."

"Well we'll be careful and see what your body can handle," said Dave.

"I'm not looking to be an expert," said Robbie. "I'd like to learn some basic throws and some exercises that might help my back."

"I'll see what I can do," said Dave. "Now I think it's time to dance again." They danced until the band took another break. After the break, they were back on the floor. The band was playing some of the newer songs that were considered country rock. Brandy and Robbie decided that they liked the music. An hour later, both couples decided that they had enough dancing for the evening and were going home. Marie said that she would like to invite Brandy and Robbie over for dinner sometime.

"We'd love to," said Brandy. "Robbie and I are available every evening, not just the weekends."

"I work days but sometimes those days end up being long," said Dave. "I work some weekends too. Give us a number and we'll call you when I know what my schedule is." Brandy gave them their phone number and they all went home.

On Monday, they got a call from Marie. They were invited to dinner on Thursday evening. They accepted. Brandy thought they should take something so she took a nice arrangement of flowers. Marie fixed a very good oriental meal. She told them what everything was called, but they forgot. Robbie and Dave swapped a few war stories and Brandy and Marie hit it off well. Hot tea was the main drink with dinner but there was sake if anyone wanted it. "I've never had sake," said Brandy. "I'll try some."

"Me to," said Robbie. Both of them decided that they didn't like it. Marie was not offended. The meal was delicious and Brandy was after Marie for recipes. After dinner they sat around and talked. Everyone was asked about their families. Marie was born in Hanoi. She was an only child. Her father was French and was a business man. They left Vietnam a year before the French were defeated at Dien Bien Phu. They did well in Okinawa.

"That's where I met her," said Dave. "I was on Okinawa for a while before I went to Vietnam. We hit it off good and she was still there when I left Vietnam. We were married a few months later. So how did you two meet?"

"I was looking for a place to live while going to school and Brandy had a note on the school bulletin board and was looking for someone to share expenses. I called her and here we are."

"So when are you two getting married?" asked Marie. "Anyone who sees you two together knows you're getting married sometime."

"Probably when we're both out of school," said Robbie. "Brandy is done at the end of this year and I have one more semester."

"How will you handle it when she goes home and you're still here?" asked Dave.

"I'm sure we'll see each other on weekends and holidays," said Brandy. "We'll get it worked out."

"So Robbie, was your dad a Marine?" asked Dave.

"Yes he was," answered Robbie. "He signed up in 1942 right after high school graduation. He was only 17. He and my mom were sweethearts in school. They got married when he got home."

"That's about the same for me," said Dave. "My dad signed up the day after Pearl Harbor. He and mom got married right after he got back home."

"Brandy's dad was a bombardier on a B-17," said Robbie. "He was a POW near the end of the war."

They all talked about their families for a while longer and then Robbie and Brandy decided not to overstay their welcome. "We'll have you over to our apartment soon," said Robbie. "Brandy is an excellent cook too. We'll give a call or we can talk when I start my judo lessons next week."

"Sounds good," said Dave. "Thanks for coming and once again, thanks for the dance lessons."

"You're most welcome," said Brandy. "Thank you so much for having us over. We enjoyed your company."

~~~~

When Saturday morning rolled around, they were on their way to Carl's. Carl told them that they didn't need to get there until late afternoon. He always did his cat-fishing right before dark and a few hours into the night. When they arrived, Carl had several rods and reels on display. "We'll do some practicing and see what you two can handle," said Carl. "Let's have some coffee first." Sally got them all a cup. "I don't usually drink coffee this late in the day but the caffeine will help keep me awake tonight," said Carl. "I don't do any drinking when I'm going fishing. I take my fishing seriously." They had their coffee and then Carl started with Brandy. He fixed her up with a nice long rod and a spinning reel. He tied on a sinker and demonstrated several different casts. "You can't always cast the same way," said Carl. "Could be trees or brush in the way." After several more casts, he handed the rod and reel to Brandy. It took her a few casts, but she did all right. "Now you move over some and practice some more," said Carl. "Pick a spot and try to put your sinker right on it." Then Carl worked with Robbie. He had him using a long rod with a spinning reel too. Robbie did well and then Carl had him practice hitting a spot. They practiced for ten or fifteen minutes. Carl thought they were doing o.k. Then he showed them how to tie a proper knot on a fishing line. It took both of them a few tries, but they got it down pat. "Now take that sinker off your line and tie on this snap on swivel," said Carl. "I have leaders with hooks made up. When we are ready to fish, we just snap on a sinker and one of the leaders. Put on the bait and then give it a cast."

"What are we using for bait?" asked Brandy.

"Mostly night crawlers," answered Carl. "I got some minnows too. I'll show you how to put them on the hook when we're at the creek."

They had a late dinner and after the dishes were done, they loaded up and headed to the creek. Sally wasn't going to fish, but she went along. They went in Carl's car. Carl had blankets for them to sit on and a couple of lanterns. He also had plenty of bug spray. "It'll only take ten or fifteen minutes to get where we're going," said Carl. "We're going on my Uncle's land. He has a couple hundred acres right beside the creek. A hundred of it is woods, and he rents out a hundred acres to some farmer. The farmer usually plants corn or soy beans. He's got corn in this year. It's pretty tall already." It wasn't long until they turned onto some dirt road. There were a few houses on both sides of the road. After about a mile, they turned onto a smaller dirt road. "This is his place," said Carl. "There creek's back there a little ways. This dirt road is right in the middle of his land." The cornfield was on the left and the woods were on the right. Right at the end of the cornfield, the road forked to the left and right. Carl was about to turn right when he stopped and looked to his left. "What the f---," said Carl. "Do you see what I see over in those last few rows of corn?" Everyone looked over at the corn.

"That's pot," said Brandy. "Let's see how much there is." They all got out and went to the cornfield.

"Son of a bitch, there's a whole lotta that stuff," said Carl. "It looks like it goes on the whole length of the field."

"Yeh, and back here by the creek bank, no one would notice it," said Robbie. "Do you suppose that farmer's making some extra money?"

"I don't know the man personally," said Carl. "My uncle's known him for years. What do you reckon I should do?"

"I'd get ahold of your Uncle tomorrow and tell him what we found back here," said Robbie. "This stuff wouldn't be his, would it?"

"My Uncle's a redneck through and through," said Carl. "There's no way this stuff could be his."

"Well you better tell him in the morning," said Robbie. "It's his land. He can decide how he wants to handle it."

"Sounds good, let's go fishing," said Carl.

They got back in the car and went a couple of hundred yards on the right fork of the dirt road. There was a spot where Carl usually parked just off the dirt road. He parked the car and they all grabbed some gear and walked the twenty five yards to the creek bank. "This is a beautiful place," said Brandy. "And the water looks so clear." Carl took them to some good spots. He got them baited up and showed them likely spots to cast their bait. He explained to Robbie how to properly set the hook. He also explained that catfish have sharp fins and to be careful handling them.

It was about an hour before dark. None of them had any strikes for the first hour. Carl was about to light the lanterns when they heard a car or truck coming down the dirt road toward the creek. They could tell by the sound that the vehicle turned onto the left fork. It sounded like it had gone just a little way and then stopped. They heard two car doors open and close. "Everyone be quiet," said Carl. "There shouldn't be anyone else here. I told my uncle we'd be here and he said no one else would be fishing that he knew of. I'm gonna slip over that way and see if I can tell who it is."

"I'll go with you," said Robbie.

"Better stay here with the girls," said Carl. "Never know what could happen. Besides, I know every foot of this place." Carl went back over to the car and gently opened the trunk. He pulled out a machete."

"What are gonna do with that?" whispered Brandy.

"Hopefully nothing," answered Carl. Then he slipped off toward the other vehicle. It was dark now. There was a half moon so Carl could see fairly well. He slipped to within fifty yards of the vehicle. It was a pickup truck. He could hear two men talking. They were in the corn rows. He could see their flashlights flickering. He slipped up closer and got the license number of the truck. He could tell that the truck was a '68 Chevy ½ ton. It was red and had a dented passenger side door. He thought for a moment. "I know whose truck this is," Carl said to himself. "Think Carl, think." Then it came to him. This truck belonged to some guy who was his cousin's friend. He had seen the truck at his Uncle's house. Carl quietly slipped away. He wasn't all the way back to the others when he heard the pickup start up and leave. The others heard the truck leaving too. Carl slowly approached the others. "Let's stay quiet for a little while longer and make sure they're long gone," said Carl.

After another five minutes, they decided that they truck was long gone. Carl lit the lanterns. "Well did you find out anything?" asked Robbie.

"There was two of them and they were checking on their pot," said Carl. "They had a '68 red Chevy pickup. I got the license number and I've seen that truck around. It belongs to a friend of my cousin. My Uncle's really gonna like all this."

"So what do we do now?" asked Brandy.

"We fish," said Carl. "Tomorrow I give the news to my Uncle."

It wasn't long till they started getting some strikes. Brandy caught the first fish. It was a fourteen inch channel cat. Not long after that, Robbie hooked one too. It was the same size as Bandy's. Brandy caught another one a few minutes later. As she was reeling it in, Carl hooked onto something that was a little bigger. He got it in all right. It was a ten pound shovelhead. That was the biggest fish they caught that night. Brandy caught another channel cat and Robbie pulled in a five pound shovelhead. Carl caught a six pound channel cat. It was around midnight. They decided they had enough fish and headed home. After they got the gear put away, Carl got busy cleaning the fish. He was pretty slick with a filet knife. Robbie and Brandy volunteered to help, but Carl was so quick that it wasn't necessary. They put the filets in the refrigerator and then Carl took the fish guts and bones out toward the woods and buried them. Then they all washed up and got the fish smell off of them. They all drank a few beers and then went to bed.

The next morning after breakfast, Carl decided to drive over to his uncle's house and give him the news. Robbie went with him. Brandy stayed with Sally. It only took fifteen minutes to get to Carl's Uncle's house. He was not a church going man so Carl knew he would be home. His Uncle was sitting on the front porch having some coffee. Carl and Robbie went to the porch. "Uncle Bill, this is my friend Robbie," said Carl. "We were in Vietnam together." Robbie and Bill shook hands.

"Pleased to meet you son," said Bill. "Did you do any good last night?"

"We did good Uncle Bill," said Carl. "Caught some channel cats and some shovelheads. I got some other stuff to tell you. I don't think you'll like it."

"Well spill it out," said Bill.

"Someone's growing marijuana in the cornfield on your place," started Carl. "We saw it when we got back to where the road forks. It's mixed in with the corn on the last few rows next to the creek bank."

"Son of a bitch, who in the hell would be doing that?" said Bill.

"Well when we were fishing at my usual spot, right at dark, a red pickup came in," said Carl. "Two guys got out and checked out the pot. I slipped up and got the license number and make. I seen that truck before Uncle Bill. It belongs to a friend of Steve."

"Steve better not be mixed up with that shit," said Bill. "I'll skin his ass alive and then have the law take him to jail."

"What's that farmer's name that rents the land from you?" asked Carl. "You don't suppose he's mixed up in this too do you?"

"I'm gonna find that our right now," said Bill. "I'll go call him and tell him he better get over here PDQ. Steve's not here right now, but he'll be home this afternoon." Bill went inside and called the farmer. His wife said he was out in the barn but she would get him over there as soon as she could. Twenty minutes later, the farmer arrived. He was a very old man. Robbie guessed that he was at least eighty years old. He walked all bent over and very slow. His name was Charlie Hanson. He slowly made his way to Bill.

"What's so important that you need me over here?" asked Charlie.

"I'll get right to the point," started Bill. "Are you growing pot on my land?"

"Pot, what's that?" asked Charlie.

"Marijuana," said Bill. "Marifuckingjuana."

"Marijuana, that's that stuff them hippies smoke isn't it?" asked Charlie.

"Yes, that's the stuff," said Carl.

"Well why in the hell would I be growing that stuff?" asked Charlie.

"Because it's worth a lot of money," answered Bill. "Now are you growing it on my land?"

"Jesus H. Christ no," answered Charlie. "I wouldn't know nothing about growing that stuff. I don't even know what it looks like."

"Well someone's planted some in your last few rows of corn next to the creek bank," said Bill.

"Are we gonna call the law?" asked Charlie. "That shit's agin the law isn' it?"

"It surely is," said Bill. "I gotta talk to one of my sons first. Then I'm calling the law. Now Charlie, don't be telling anyone about this. We don't want word getting out that we know about the pot."

"I won't even tell the wife," said Charlie. "Probly scare her to death. She'd be thinking that some big drug outfit was moving into the area."

"All right Charlie, you can head home now," said Bill. "I'll keep you posted on what's going on." Charlie nodded his head and walked back to his car. "You boys may as well take off," said Bill. "I'll let you know what's going on. Steve better pray he's not mixed up in this." Carl and Robbie headed back to Carl's place.

"I know my Uncle," said Carl s they were heading home. "He might just skin Steve alive if he's tied in with this."

"Hopefully that fella with the red truck is doing this without Steve's knowl-edge," said Robbie. "I'd say Uncle Bill will find out even if he has to beat it out of Steve."

"Are you up for a fish fry today?" asked Carl.

"Sure, we caught them fish. May as well eat them," said Robbie.

"Good, I got a fryer and we can have coleslaw and baked beans," said Carl. "I like my fish on rye bread. Will that suit you?"

"Sounds good," said Robbie. "Have we still got some beer?"

"There's plenty," said Carl. "Every time you came down, you brought a case of beer with you. There's still plenty left. Why don't we skip lunch today and eat an early dinner?"

"That sounds good too," said Robbie. "We can throw a few balls when we get back and then start on the beer." That's just what they did. After about an hour of catch, they started on the beer. Just as they started on the beer, the phone rang. It was Uncle Bill. Carl went to the phone. "Uncle Bill, what's up?" said Carl.

"Steve got home a little while ago and we had a nice long talk," started Bill. "He swears he don't know nothin' about that pot. He said he took that other fella back to the creek a few times fishin'. Anyway, I called the law. They sent out an unmarked car and I took them over to the cornfield. They're gonna keep an eye on that fella with the red pickup and stake out the cornfield for a while. If they don't have no luck staking the place out, then they'll go in and cut down all the pot and destroy it. I hope they catch someone. I can't believe someone had the balls to do that on my land."

"Well maybe they will catch someone," said Carl. "Will you keep me posted? I won't go fishing down there for a while."

"That deputy I talked to says he knows you so if you want to go fishing down there, go right ahead," said Bill. "They won't bother you."

"All right, thanks for calling," said Carl. "Good luck." Carl hung up the phone and told everyone what Bill had said. "Now it's time for beer," said Carl.

After a few beers, Carl got his fryer ready. Sally had made the coleslaw and the baked beans were in the oven. "I use corn flour instead of corn meal," said Carl. "I like it better. I think you will too." Carl thought the oil was ready and he put in a small piece of fish to try it out. It was ready. It didn't take long to fry the fish. They were eating in no time. Robbie had never had catfish before. He was surprised that it was so good. Brandy had eaten catfish before, but she thought this was better than what she had before. "Sometimes, them big ole cats can be strong," said Carl. "These here are just fine." They finished their meal and cleaned up. Sally packed some fish in some ice for them to take home. "It'll still be awhile before I can do more to the house, but we can go fishing again whenever you want," said Carl. "Just give us a call."

~~~~

Robbie took a couple of Judo lessons the next week. After the first lesson he wasn't sure he should be doing this. After the second lesson, he was sure that he shouldn't. His leg hurt him a lot when he was learning the throws. He figured it would be better for his leg not to be doing this. Dave fully understood. He showed Robbie some exercises that he thought would help his back. A couple of weeks later, Brandy and Robbie had Dave and Marie over for dinner. Brandy fixed a fine meal. The two couples were becoming very good friends. They made plans to go out dancing together at least once a month.

A week later, Brandy had the urge to go fishing again so they called Carl. Robbie stopped at a store and got some more beer and some rye bread. They had a late dinner and went to the creek. They could see that the pot was still there and getting taller. "Don't look like they've caught anyone yet," said Carl. "Wonder how long they'll wait before they cut it down?"

"Hard to tell," said Brandy. "They probably can't afford to have a stakeout for a long time."

"Oh well, let's fish," said Robbie.

About a half hour before dark, they started catching some fish. Carl had hooked into something that he said was really big when they heard a vehicle coming down the dirt road. They all got quiet. Carl kept on fighting his fish. They heard doors opening and closing. Five minutes later, Carl was still fighting his fish. A shot rang out, and then another one. "Everybody get down and take cover behind something," said Robbie. Another shot rang out. Then several more were fired.

"That last one was a 9mm," said Carl. "The rest were .357's." Carl was hunkered down next to the water, still fighting his fish. Another shot rang out and Carl's car was hit. "Son of a bitch, everybody stay down," said Carl. It was quiet for the next few moments. Then all of them could hear someone running through the brush toward them. Carl still had his fish on. He opened the tackle box and took out a metal stringer. He hooked it to his rod and then hooked it to some tree roots on the creek bank. He slipped over to Robbie. "I think there's two of them coming this way," said Carl. "Let's get behind the car. They'll either run past the car or see if they can start it and take off. Let's jump them when they get here."

"Carl, they have guns," said Robbie. "We don't."

"They won't expect it," said Carl. "Someone is behind them. They don't know we're here. You girls hug the ground and don't move." The runners got closer and closer. When they finally saw Carl's car, they stopped. One of them said. "What the fuck. That must belong to whoever's chasing us. Let's shoot out the tires." They approached the car from the front. Robbie and Carl were directly behind it. One man shot out the left front tire. The other man went to shoot out the right front. They could hear the hammer of his pistol strike an empty chamber.

"Son of a bitch," he said. "I need to reload."

"You dumbass, you never carry a full load do you?" Said the other one. "I'll take care of it." They could hear the hammer cock. Click, the hammer struck an empty chamber. "Well shit, let's get moving," said the other one. "I know these woods. They'll never catch us." The two men started moving again. As soon as they got past the rear of the car, Robbie and Carl sprang on them. When Robbie's man went down, he dropped his pistol. Robbie picked up the pistol and cracked him over the head with it. He was knocked unconscious. Carl's man dropped his pistol too. Carl quickly took the pistol and threw it to the side. The man had gone down face first. Carl turned him over and started beating on him. He was knocked unconscious but Carl kept beating on him. Robbie grabbed Carl's arms.

"I think he's unconscious," said Robbie. "You don't need to beat him to death."

"Nobody, and I mean nobody shoots my car," said Carl. "Mother fucker's gonna pay." Carl went through the man's pockets. There was a big roll of bills. Carl checked out the car where the bullet had struck it. The bullet had gone through the grill and hit the radiator. Carl unrolled the bills and counted. There was $2000 in the roll. "I'm taking $500," said Carl. "That should get me a new tire, grill, and radiator." Carl took the rest of the money, rolled it back up and put it back in the man's pocket. A few minutes later, an unmarked cruiser pulled up. Two deputies were in it. "Are you looking for these two?" asked Carl.

"Yes we are," answered one of the deputies. "I'm Deputy Stark and this is Deputy Smith. We had the place staked out. Them two were harvesting some of the marijuana. We told them to freeze and they started shooting. How did you catch them?"

"We heard them running this way," said Carl. "We hunkered down. Robbie and I hid behind the car. Them two stopped and shot out the left front tire. They were gonna shoot out the right front, but they both needed to reload. They decided to take off. I heard one of them say that he knew these woods and you'd never catch them. Anyway when they took off again, we jumped them."

"This one looks like he got jumped several times," said Deputy Smith.

"He tripped," said Carl. "Several times."

"Did either of you touch their weapons?" asked Deputy Stark.

"I used the one over here to knock this one out," answered Robbie.

"I grabbed that one over there and threw it," said Carl.

"Are you ladies all right?" asked Deputy Stark.

"We were scared for a while," answered Sally. "But we're o.k. now."

"Holy shit, I still got a fish on," said Carl. Carl ran over and checked his pole. The fish was still on. Carl played the fish while the deputies took statements from the others. The two men had regained consciousness and were cuffed and given their rights. The Deputies put them in the cruiser. The deputies needed a formal statement from Carl but he was still playing his fish. He finally landed it. He got his scale out of the tackle box. It was a 30 pound shovelhead. He put it on the metal stringer and gave the deputy his statement. The two men in the back seat of the cruiser gave Carl and Robbie some very nasty looks. One of them yelled out. "We know your faces. We'll get you sons a bitches."

Carl yelled back. "We used to kill people for a living you stupid fuck. If I even see your face anywhere near me or anyone in my family, I'll send you straight to hell."

"I never heard that, did you Deputy Stark?" asked Deputy Smith.

"I didn't hear anything," said Deputy Stark. "We'll be going now. I'll have a car come and pick you up. I'll have a wrecker take your car where you want."

"They can just take it to my house," said Carl. "I'll be fixing it myself." The deputy made some calls on his radio and then they were on their way.

"We may as well fish some more while we're waiting," said Carl.

"I don't feel much like fishing now," said Brandy. "I'll just watch."

Carl went back to fishing. Sally sat down next to him and put her arm around him. Robbie put his line out and Brandy sat close to him. "I was afraid," said Brandy. "Someone could have gotten killed or really hurt."

"I know," said Robbie. "There's some bad people out there." They didn't talk any more till the wrecker and their car arrived. When they got back to Carl's place, they put the gear away and Carl cleaned his fish. Then they had some beer. "How will you be able to get to work now?" asked Robbie.

"I'll call my Uncle in the morning," answered Carl. "He'll lend me his pick up. He'll be happy to know what happened tonight too. That reminds me Pitcher. Since when is a pistol a gun. You said that they had guns and we didn't."

"Just lost my head in the heat of battle," said Robbie. "It won't happen again." Carl laughed and took another sip of beer. They drank a few more beers and then went to bed. None of them woke up the next morning till around ten. They had some breakfast and then Robbie and Brandy left for home.

"I suppose there'll be a trial or something for them two," said Carl before they left. "I reckon we'll all have to testify."

"What would we say?" asked Brandy.

"The truth," started Robbie. "We were fishing at the creek. We heard shooting and then took cover. Carl's car was hit. Two men came running toward us. They stopped and shot out the front tire. When they took off again, Carl and I jumped them. Then the deputies showed up."

"Sounds good to me," said Carl. "Them two'll go to jail for a good while. Shooting at the law carries a long penalty in this state."

"Well give me a call when you need help on the house again," said Robbie. "We'll be here."

Robbie and Brandy didn't talk much on the way home. When they got to the apartment, they laid down together on the couch and just relaxed. "I hope something like that never happens again," said Brandy. "I was afraid. And you two guys tackling them two when they had guns."

"We were closer than you and we knew that their pistols were empty," said Robbie. "We're not fools, but we would have probably gone after them anyway."

"I was thinking that too Robbie Parker," said Brandy. "I don't want a dead hero. I want to get married and have babies with you."

"I want that too," said Robbie. "I've been thinking about that a lot. I suppose your dad will be wanting you to go right to work with him after you graduate."

"Yes he will," said Brandy. "And you'll have another semester and then you'll work for Abner. I guess we should do some serious thinking on what we'll be doing."

"I agree," said Robbie. "In the meantime, I think I'll do some serious kissing with the woman I love. It wasn't long until their clothes went flying. They fell asleep on the couch in each other's arms. When Robbie woke up in the morning, he heard coffee percolating. Brandy was naked in the kitchen getting ready to make breakfast. Robbie didn't need any motivation. "We're already late for class," said Brandy. "We forgot to set the alarm last night."

"We might as well be later for a worthy cause," said Robbie.

"What cause is that?" asked Brandy.

"Cause I want you right now," said Robbie.

An hour later, they were finishing their breakfast. They both made it to their classes before their classes were completely over. The next few weeks went by quickly. They hooked up with Dave and Marie a couple of times. Carl had called and said that he got his car fixed and even had a hundred bucks of the $500 left over. He still needed to save up some more money before buying anything else for the house. Break between the second and third semester was fast approaching.

Brandy wanted Robbie to see where she lived in Toledo. They would also spend some time at the house on Kelley's Island. Robbie was all right with this. They had almost two weeks off and he would have time to visit his folks again. They would go north first and then go down to Columbus.

Chapter Twenty

B randy's house was in a very nice section of town. It was a huge two story stone house with a huge yard. There was a swimming pool out back. "That's some house," said Robbie when he first saw it.

"It is," said Brandy. "It doesn't look it, but it's a very old house. My dad's dad had it built. The inside has been remodeled over the years and newer windows have been put it. I don't think that my dad could have afforded this house if he hadn't inherited it. We did have the swimming pool put in. My mother inherited the house on Kelley's island from her parents. Maybe one day our kids will inherit nice places."

"I hope so," said Robbie. Brandy took Robbie inside. Her dad was still at work, but her mother and two younger sisters were there. Brandy's sisters were very attractive young women and Robbie remembered that Brandy had said that neither of them wanted anything to do with the funeral parlor. Robbie thought that they would have no trouble finding husbands. Brandy gave Robbie a tour of the house and the yard and then they went to the funeral parlor. Robbie was kind of surprised. It was a nice place. It was like Fulbright's, only bigger. Brandy's dad was busy with some customers so they didn't get a chance to chat. They left the parlor and Brandy gave Robbie a quick tour of Toledo. Then they went back home.

When WW got home, they had a nice dinner and chatted. There were no questions about sleeping arrangements. There were five bedrooms in the house and each one had its' own bathroom with tub and shower. Brandy's bed even had some kind of canopy thing on it. Robbie hoped they wouldn't get too rambunctious and tear it down. They didn't. After staying at the house for three days, they went to Kelley's Island. Brandy's parents were going to go too, but one of WW's employees got really sick and WW had to work. They drove over to Marblehead and took the ferry to the island. It was late in the tourist season, so not many people were on the ferry. The house was just a two bedroom cottage but Robbie liked it. They had bicycles and could ride all over the place. What Robbie really liked was that he was there alone with Brandy. The houses that were close to them were all vacant. They had a great time for two full days and then went back to Toledo. They spent the night at Brandy's house and then took off for Columbus.

While they were on their way to Columbus, they heard on the radio that there had been a bombing at the University of Wisconsin-Madison. Someone packed a Ford van with explosives and was trying to blow up the Army Math Research Center. They missed their target and blew up the physics lab. A young researcher was killed and another person was seriously injured. "When is this going to end?" cried Brandy. "I don't understand. I just don't understand."

"I don't understand either," said Robbie. "They want to stop the war, so what do they do? They make war themselves. Blowing up innocent people won't help anything." Robbie turned off the radio.

Mary and Robert were both home when Brandy and Robbie arrived. They did the usual hugging and kissing and then went inside. Robbie put their things in his room and then they sat out back and had a beer. "So how have things been for you two at school?" asked Robert. "It's probably not like the big campuses or anything is it?"

"No dad, we don't have all the trouble like the other places," said Robbie. "Mortician trainees are a quiet bunch." They all laughed.

"We had some excitement down in Kentucky when we were visiting a friend of Robbie's," said Brandy. "There was some shooting."

"Was anyone hurt?" asked Mary.

"Carl's car got shot," said Robbie.

"Carl, he's your friend from Vietnam isn't he?" asked Robert.

"Yes he is Dad," answered Robbie. "He lives not far from Covington. We've been going down and helping him build his house. Brandy's good with a hammer."

"So why was there shooting?" asked Mary.

"Carl took us out fishing," started Robbie. "His uncle has a couple of hundred acres beside this creek. It's half woods and half farmland. He rents the farmland to some old farmer. The first day we went fishing, we saw that there was marijuana growing along with some rows of corn. Carl told his uncle and he told the law. Carl recognized a pickup that we saw down there and the law kept watch on the owner of the pickup and staked out the field. A while later we went fishing again. We go in the evening and night for catfishing. Anyway, right before dark, we heard some shooting. Carl's car took a hit in the radiator. We heard two guys running our way. We had the girls take cover and Carl and I hid behind the car. When those two got to the car, they shot the front left tire and was gonna shoot the right front, but they needed to reload. They took off again. Carl and I knew that they hadn't reloaded. When they got past us, we jumped them and knocked them out. Then the law arrived. They had the place staked out. When they saw the guys harvesting the pot, they told them to freeze. The guys started shooting and took off. Oh yeah, Carl had a 30 pound shovelhead on his line the whole time this was going on."

"So you've never been fishing before that I know of," said Robert. "Did you do any good?"

"We both did," said Brandy. "We had a nice fish fry."

"Well there's a dance at the Legion on Saturday night," said Robert. "Do you reckon you two will be here?"

"We can be," said Robbie. "What do you say Brandy? Will we be here or do you want to get back to Cincinnati?"

"We might as well stick around," said Brandy. "Come next Monday and we'll be back to the same old grind."

"Brandy's only got one more semester and then she graduates," said Robbie.

"Will you be going right to work with your father?" asked Mary.

"I will," answered Brandy. "Robbie and I have a lot of things to figure out. He has another semester after me and then he'll be working for Abner. We want to get married sometime before too long."

"You two are smart people," said Mary. "You'll get it worked out. So are there any requests for dinner tonight?"

"Why don't we go out tonight?" said Robbie. "I'll buy. We don't need to go fancy. We could go to a pizza parlor if you want."

"Let's make sure it serves beer," said Robert. "I feel thirsty this evening."

They went to the parlor where Robbie and Maria used to go. Robbie felt a little guilty when they first got there. He told everyone that this was where he and Maria used to go. He told them he brought them here for the good pizza, not because he and Maria frequented the place.

The pizza was good. They ate their fill and had three pitchers of beer. The boys weren't drunk, but they wouldn't have passed a balloon test. Mary drove home. She had only had two glasses of beer. They watched a little TV and then showered and went to bed. Brandy was worried that they were making too much noise as they were making love, but she could hear Robert and Mary being noisy so she quit worrying about it.

They just lounged around in the morning. After lunch they walked over to the park. A little league game was about to start. "Let's watch for a while," said Robbie. It was o.k. with Brandy. They kept waiting for the game to start. They heard someone say that the umpire hadn't shown up and no one knew why. After a while, Robbie's old Legion ball coach showed up and went on the field to talk to the coaches. The umpire had a death in the family and wouldn't be there. He had a previous engagement too and couldn't do it. Then he saw Robbie sitting in the bleachers. He left the coaches and went to Robbie.

"They need your help Robbie," said the coach. "The umpire had a death in the family and can't be here. I have something I have to do. Could you ump this game for them?"

"What do you say Brandy?" asked Robbie. "Would you mind?"

"Go ahead," said Brandy. "I can watch your ass when you squat down." Robbie laughed and then went out to meet the coaches. They agreed that Robbie could ump and the game started. The first three innings were uneventful. The home team had a pitcher who was big for a twelve year old. His dad was the coach. The twelve year old had a good curve ball and the other batters couldn't hit it. They were fooled into swinging at some bad pitches. In the fourth inning, the visiting team coach must have told his boys to start taking more pitches. They did and the pitcher walked the first two hitters. The third batter took the first three pitches. They were balls. The young pitcher gave Robbie some nasty looks and asked Robbie if he needed glasses. Robbie ignored him. The next pitch was a strike. The boy threw a fastball and it caught the outside corner at the knees. He threw a curve on the next pitch and it was a ball.

"What the hell's wrong with you ump?" said the pitcher. "Are you fucking blind?" Robbie walked out to the mound.

"You're out of the game," said Robbie. The pitcher cursed Robbie some more. "Coach, get this person off the field or I'll call the game a forfeit." The boy's coach ran out on the field.

"What the hell are you doing?" said the coach. "You can't do that. Are you fucking crazy?"'

"You'll not talk to the umpire this way," said Robbie. "You have forfeited the game." The coach was furious now. He got in Robbie's face cursing him. "You're not setting a good example for the boys coach," said Robbie. The coach took a swing at Robbie. Robbie still had on his mask and he let the coach connect. Robbie was sure that he heard some bones in the coach's hand snap. "Better get to the hospital," said Robbie. "I heard some bones break." Robbie took off his mask now. The coach sucked up his pain and took another swing at Robbie with his left. Before the coach knew it, he was flat on his back. "Now lay there for a while and try to get some sense back in your head," said Robbie. Several people in the stands were cursing Robbie but others were cheering him. The coach of the other team came over and thanked Robbie for calling the game.

"You did a good job son," said the coach. "These kids don't need a bad influence like that. I feel sorry for that pitcher. He could do good if it weren't for his old man. Thanks again."

Robbie gave his equipment to someone and then went over to Brandy. "Well what did you think?" asked Robbie. "Did I do good?"

"You were wonderful," said Brandy. "You'd be a real good umpire. Maybe you should do this in the evenings for the kids. And what was that move you put on that coach? He went down quick."

"I learned a little bit from my judo lessons," said Robbie. "It was just a basic throw. Let's get out of here before someone else gets nasty." They walked back to the house. Robert was home from work and dinner was about ready.

"So what did you two do today?" asked Mary.

"We had some real fun," said Brandy. "Robbie umpired a little league game."

"Did the parents yell at you?" asked Robert.

Before Robbie could speak, Brandy spoke. "One of the pitchers cursed Robbie and Robbie threw him out of the game and said if he didn't get off the field, the game would be a forfeit," said Brandy. "The boy's father was the coach and he had words with Robbie. He took a swing at Robbie and Robbie still had his mask on. I think he's got some broken fingers. Then he took another swing and Robbie used some judo on him and put him down quick. Anyway, the game was a forfeit."

"Sounds like you had an interesting day son," said Mary. "Since when do you know judo?"

"I took a couple of lessons and learned some basic throws," said Robbie. "I didn't take any more lessons because it hurts my leg."

Saturday rolled around and all of them went to the Legion dance. They had an older band that played a lot of swing music. Robert and Mary were having a blast. Brandy and Robbie had a blast too. They got to where they were trying to outdo each other on the dance floor. Robert and Mary would do a big move and Robbie and Brandy would try to outdo it. Sometimes they did. Sometimes they didn't. A good bit of the time, they were the only couples on the dance floor. The other people would rather watch them than dance themselves. They stayed until the band quit. Robert was ready to leave. He was very tired. Robbie's leg was hurting him.

They got up the next morning and after breakfast, they headed back to Cincinnati. When they got to the apartment, they threw their stuff in their rooms and laid down on the couch. Robbie turned on the TV and went through the channels. There was a news flash. There had been an anti-war demonstration in Los Angeles. 20,000 – 30,000 Mexican Americans participated in it. The police were attacked with clubs and guns and three people were killed. Robbie turned off the TV.

~~~~

Classes seemed to be easier now for Robbie. He felt like he already knew what the instructors were teaching, but he also knew that he had to go by the numbers to get his degree. Brandy felt the same way. When they went out to dinner with Dave and Marie, Marie announced that she was pregnant. Brandy and Robbie were very happy for them. At the end of the first month of the semester, they got a call from Carl. He told them that there was going to be a trial for the two men they had knocked out. They would all be called to testify.

The trial was on a Monday. Brandy and Robbie told their instructors what they were doing and hopefully the trial wouldn't last long. They went to Carl's place and spent Sunday night. The trial started at 9 AM on Monday. Carl, Robbie, Sally, and Brandy were all witnesses for the prosecution. Carl was the first witness called. The prosecutor asked Carl to tell, in his own words, what happened that night.

"We were fishing on my uncle's property and it was close to dark," started Carl. "We heard some shooting. I told everyone to get low and find some cover. We heard more shots. My car was struck by a bullet. We heard some people running toward us through the brush. Robbie and I hid behind the car and the girls stayed hidden as best they could. When the two men got close to our car, they went to it and stopped. One of them shot out the left front tire and the other was going to shoot out the right front but his pistol was empty. The other fella went to shoot it but then his pistol was empty. They decided to take off again. When they got past the car, Robbie and I tackled them. Robbie knocked the one on his side out with the man's pistol. He had dropped it when he went down. The one on my side dropped his pistol too. I threw the pistol to the side and knocked him out with my fists. Then the two deputies arrived."

"Did you hear any of any conversations the two men had?" asked the Prosecutor.

"When the two of them got close to the car, I head one of the say, "What the fuck. This car must belong to whoever's chasing us. Let's shoot out the tires," Carl began. "That's when the left front tire was shot out and they tried to shoot out the right front, but they both needed to reload. One of them called the other one a dumbass for not having a full load. And when they took off again, one of them said, "I know these woods. They'll never catch us.""

"Are these the guns that the two suspects were carrying?" asked the Prosecutor as he showed Carl the guns.

"Yes they are," answered Carl.

"Did you know that there was marijuana growing in the cornfield on your uncle's property?" asked the Prosecutor.

"Yes I did," answered Carl. "We had gone fishing on my uncle's property about a month before all this. We saw the marijuana that Saturday evening."

"What did you do after you saw the marijuana?" asked the Prosecutor.

"We went fishing," answered Carl.

"Then what happened?" asked the Prosecutor.

"About dark, we heard a vehicle coming down the dirt road and go over by the cornfield," said Carl. "I slipped over to see what was going on."

"What was going on?" asked the Prosecutor.

"There was a red Chevy pickup truck. Two men had gotten out and were in the cornfield," answered Carl. "I could see their flashlight flickering. I got the license number of the truck and slipped away."

"What happened after that?" asked the Prosecutor.

"After a while, the pickup left and we went back to fishing," answered Carl.

"What did you do the next morning?" asked the Prosecutor.

"Robbie and I went to my uncle's house and told him that there was marijuana growing in the cornfield on his property," answered Carl.

"What did your uncle do then?" asked the Prosecutor.

"He called the farmer who rents the field from him," answered Carl.

"Then what did your uncle do?" asked the Prosecutor.

"After he talked with the farmer, he told me to go ahead and go back home," said Carl. "He'd call us and keep us informed of everything."

"Did he call you later?" asked the Prosecutor.

"Yes he did," answered Carl.

"What did he say when he called?" asked the Prosecutor.

"He said that he had called the law," answered Carl. "The law would keep an eye on the owner of the red pickup and stake out the cornfield. He said we could keep going fishing because a deputy knew who I was and they wouldn't bother me."

"No further questions your honor," said the Prosecutor. The Defense Attorney took over now.

"You must be some kind of hero to tackle someone who was allegedly carrying a pistol," said the defense attorney. "Why did you tackle them?"

"We had heard shooting and we heard them running toward us," started Carl. "They shot out one tire of my car and were going to shoot out another. And there was no alleged to it. Them two had pistols."

"One of my client's face was beaten up pretty good," said the defense attorney. "How did that happen?"

"He went down face first when I tackled him," answered Carl.

"You punched on him to knock him out didn't you?" asked the defense attorney.

"Yes I did," answered Carl.

"How many punches did you throw?" asked the attorney.

"I didn't count them," answered Carl.

"What did you think the shooting was about when you first heard it?" asked the defense attorney.

"Objection," said the Prosecutor. "Calls for speculation from the witness."

"Objection sustained," said the Judge.

"So you and your friend tackled two men you heard running through the brush without knowing what was going on?" asked the defense attorney.

"Them two men shot my car," answered Carl. "I didn't ask them to shoot my car."

"I understand that you are a Vietnam veteran," said the defense attorney.

"This has nothing to do with the case," said the Prosecutor.

"It doesn't," said the Judge. "Whether the witness is a veteran or not has nothing to do with this case. Move on."

"I'm saying that maybe since this man is a veteran, maybe he thought he was still out in the jungle and my clients were VC or NVA," said the defense attorney.

"You're on shallow ground," said the Judge. "One more piece of crap like this, and I do mean crap, I'll see you in my chambers."

"Sorry your honor, no further questions," said the defense attorney.

Robbie was the next witness called. The questions from the Prosecutor were almost identical to the ones he asked Carl. Robbie's answers were identical to Carl's. Then the defense attorney had his turn.

"I have no questions for this witness your honor," started the defense attorney. "This witness and the previous witness have obviously rehearsed their testimony."

"One more comment like that and I'll find you in contempt," said the Judge. "Witness, you may step down."

Brandy was the next witness. The questions from the Prosecutor were the same ones asked Carl and Robbie. Brandy was truthful and testified that she hadn't seen that much. She had heard the shooting and the men running toward them, but she was hugging the ground and behind some trees and didn't see everything. Sally's testimony was the same. The defense attorney did not question the girls.

The next two witnesses were the deputies. They testified that they had the cornfield staked out and that when the suspects were seen harvesting the marijuana, they told them to freeze, they were the law. The suspects opened fire on the deputies and fled on foot. Both deputies had identical stories. They stated that they got in their cruiser and then found that the suspects had been apprehended by the two male witnesses.

The defense attorney tried to make it look like the deputies had no idea what the suspects were doing and only shot at the deputies in self defense. The two suspects were found guilty of growing the marijuana and attempted murder of the deputies. Sentencing would be in one week.

They were all glad that the trial was over. They stopped at a diner and had a meal before going back to Carl's. When they got to Carl's, they had a couple of beers. Then Brandy and Robbie headed back to Cincinnati. "I'll call you and tell you what them two got for a sentence," said Carl before they left. "They'll be gone for a long time. Attempted murder of a lawman is some serious shit. They'll get 20 years at least, maybe more."

"Well give us a call when you're ready for help with the house," said Robbie. "We'll be down."

"I will," said Carl. "Should be in less than a month."

When Robbie and Brandy got home, the kind of vegged out for a while. They had dozed off on the couch when the phone rang. Robbie answered it. "Oh hello WW, I'll get Brandy for you," said Robbie.

"Hi Daddy," said Brandy. "Is everything all right?"

"Yes it is with us Baby, but I need to talk with you about something," said WW.

"O.k. Daddy, go ahead," said Brandy.

"Well you know that I go to Cincinnati at times to visit a good friend of mine," said WW. "I've never mentioned this to you, but this person is a very good friend from the war. We were on the same B-17. We were POW's together. When our plane was hit, Richard was wounded and his chute was torn off. We bailed out together and held onto each other. The Germans picked us up quickly. Anyway, Richard is also a mortician. He has his own funeral parlor in Cincinnati. His son was killed in Vietnam. His wife had left him years earlier and remarried. She married a very wealthy man. Richard has no close relatives. He needs help at his place."

"What can I do to help daddy?" asked Brandy.

"I found out that Richard is dying from cancer," said WW. "He might not make it six more months. I would like it if you would work with him when you graduate."

"Of course I will daddy," said Brandy. "He's your friend and I will help him all I can. Give me his address and I will go soon and introduce myself."

"You're a good daughter Baby," said WW. "A man couldn't ask for better." WW gave Brandy all the information and then said his goodbyes."

"So is everything all right?" Robbie asked Brandy.

"Everything is o.k. at home but my daddy's friend needs help," said Brandy.

"Is there anything I can do?" asked Robbie.

"Not just yet," answered Brandy. "Daddy's friend Richard is a good friend from the war. They were on the same B-17 and were POW's together. I guess Richard's chute was torn off. Richard was wounded when their plane was hit. Daddy and he bailed out holding onto each other and using daddy's chute. Richard has a funeral parlor too. His son was killed in Vietnam and his wife left him years ago and married a very wealthy man. Richard is dying of cancer and might not last six months. Daddy asked me if I would work with Richard after I graduate. That's what I'll do. I'll go introduce myself sometime this week."

"I'll go with you," said Robbie. "Maybe I can help too."

"You're a good man Robbie Parker," said Brandy. "I will love you forever."

"I will love you forever too, Brandy Wisecup," said Robbie.

~~~~

When they went to class the next day, they found out that they hadn't really missed too much. They both got home in the early afternoon and Brandy decided they should go meet WW's friend Richard. They found his place with no problems. It was a nice looking place and was about the size of WW's parlor in Toledo. The front door was unlocked so they went in looking for Richard. They found him in an office in the back. They could see that at one time, Richard was a bull of a man. They could also see that something was eating away at him. Maybe it was the cancer or maybe chemotherapy. He was now just a shell of a man. He got up from his desk and walked over to Brandy. "I'm WW's daughter Brandy, and this gentleman is my fiancé Robbie Parker," said Brandy. They all shook hands.

"I'm so glad to finally meet WW's daughter," said Richard. "He said you were a good looking woman. He is wrong. You're a drop dead gorgeous woman. You two will make some beautiful babies. Did you know that your father saved my life?"

"He told me that your chute was torn off and you bailed out together when your plane was hit," said Brandy.

"That's not all he did," said Richard. "After we landed, he kept me from bleeding to death. When the Germans came, one of the soldiers, a very young boy, I'd say he was maybe sixteen. Anyway, this young boy was going to shoot me. I speak a little German. My last name is Zoeller. He said I was already wounded and would die anyway. He aimed his rifle at my head. Your father knocked him down and threw his rifle away. The boy got up and got his rifle and was going to shoot the both of us. Another German soldier, an older man, maybe 40 or so, stopped him. He told the boy that they weren't going to shoot prisoners. The boy argued with him and the older soldier knocked him down and took his rifle from him. I don't know what happened to the boy after that. They put us on a truck and took us to a POW camp. The war ended a few months later."

"I'm glad you and my daddy made it out of the war," said Brandy. "Did you know that my daddy asked me to help you out?"

"I didn't know that," said Richard. "We talked awhile back. I told him the cancer is killing me. Your father is a good man. He knew I could use some help."

"Well Richard, I actually have my Associates Degree," said Brandy. "I'll have my Bachelor's at the end of this semester. I can do anything here that needs to be done. I can help out in the evenings or on the weekends if needed."

"I don't have a degree yet," said Robbie. "But I've worked in a funeral parlor and I will help any way I can."

"You two are good people," said Richard. "The people I have working for me are not bad people. It's just that they need constant direction. I'm tired of having to tell people what to do over and over. They've been here a good while but they are not leaders if you know what I mean."

"I know just what you mean," said Robbie. "Here's our phone number. You can call us anytime you need us. We are available every evening and weekend. Some days we get out of class early afternoon. We will try to be here when you need us."

"I will look forward to working with the two of you," said Richard. "Now I must go. I have chemotherapy this afternoon."

"Do you need a ride to the hospital?" asked Brandy.

"I have a friend who takes me back and forth," said Richard. "It was nice meeting the both of you. I must go now. I see that my ride is here."

"Don't hesitate to call when you need us," said Brandy. Richard's friend helped him to his car and they left. Robbie and Brandy headed back to their apartment.

"You've never introduced me as your fiancé before," said Robbie.

"I know," said Brandy. "It sounded good didn't it?"

"It did," said Robbie. "I haven't gotten you a ring."

"I don't need one," said Brandy. "A little gold band will do when the time comes."

The very next day, they got a call from Richard. He needed them as soon as they could get there. Brandy had gotten home before Robbie. As soon as Robbie got home, they took a shower together and then went to Richard's place. Richard was in his office and was almost crying. Brandy went to him. "What is it Richard?" asked Brandy. "Is something wrong"

"All of my help gave me a two week notice today," cried Richard. "They all know I have the cancer are afraid for their jobs. What can I do?"

"Don't worry about a thing," said Brandy. "Robbie and I can get you all the help you'll need. There are several people at the school who need a job. Some of them already have their Associates Degrees and are working on their Bachelors. I bet we'll have no problem getting people. I can set up a schedule. If you need morning help, I can schedule people who don't have classes in the morning. Same for the afternoon. People who don't have afternoon classes can work afternoons. Any of us can work evenings."

"You'd do that for me?" asked Richard.

"Of course, you're my daddy's good friend," said Brandy. "Good friends always help friends." Richard got up from his desk and gave Brandy a huge hug. Then he hugged Robbie and shook his hand."

"You two are wonderful people," said Richard. "I wish my son was alive and could meet you. You'd have liked him."

"I'm sure we would," said Brandy. "Now is there anything else we can do for you today?"

"No, I have everything covered for this week," said Richard. "I just wanted you to come here today so I could talk with you face to face."

"We appreciate that too," said Robbie. "We'll be going now and if anything changes, don't hesitate to call us. We'll get right to work finding some more help."

"I can't thank you enough," said Richard. "Good luck."

The next day at school, both of them went right to work finding help for Richard. They had a work force rounded up in no time. Several of the other students lived in Cincinnati and would love to work at Richard's place. Several of them also had their Associates Degree. At the end of the week, Brandy and Robbie had all of the students meet at Richard's place so they could all get acquainted. Richard was tickled. One of his regular employees was there when they all arrived. He had seen Brandy and Robbie and knew that they were going to help at the place. He asked Brandy what was going on with all of the others. When she told him what they were doing, he quit right then. "Tell that old man I'm outta here," he said as he was leaving. "He can mail my check." Richard was glad that the man had quit.

"He wasn't much help," said Richard. "He was worse than a two year old. Had to be told everything all the time. Don't know why I kept him around."

"Well you have plenty of help now," said Brandy. She introduced Richard to all of his new help. "I'll be setting up schedules," said Brandy. "You'll have help whenever you need it. All of us can work when we don't have classes and most of us have Associates Degrees. All of us can work evenings and weekends if necessary."

"Well Brandy, I'd like it if you could start next week," said Richard. "You can come to the office when you don't have class. You can help me with customers and help with the books. Bring Robbie with you when you can."

"I'll be here Monday as soon as classes are over," said Brandy. "We all want to thank you for this opportunity. This will give some of us some good experience. That will look very good on a resume."

"I can't thank you enough," said Richard. "I know we will all work very well together." They all shook Richard's hand again and left.

"This is a good thing you're doing," said Robbie as they were driving back home. "Call Daddy when we get home and give him the news."

"I will after I have my way with you," said Brandy as she nibbled on his ear. Robbie almost ran a red light trying to get home in a hurry. After they had made love, Brandy called Daddy. WW was very pleased.

"You've always been a good girl Baby," said WW. "Now you're a wonderful woman. I hope Robbie knows he's getting the best."

"He does Daddy," said Brandy. "I'll call you in a couple of weeks and let you know how things are working out. Bye now."

"Bye Baby, We love you," said WW.

"Love you too Daddy," said Brandy.

~~~~

They got a call from Carl Saturday morning. The two men had been sentenced to 20 years. Carl mentioned that he was a little concerned that those two might be working for someone else. He had never mentioned this before, but he now thought that those two weren't smart enough to be drug dealers. Nothing was mentioned about this at the trial. Maybe they were afraid to rat out who they worked for. Maybe the law had questioned them about this and got nowhere. Anyway, Carl said he would try and get this out of his head. It would be a while before he had enough money to work more on the house, but Robbie and Brandy would be welcome anytime.

~~~~

Brandy and Robbie were both at Richard's place early Monday afternoon. Some customers were coming in at 3 PM. Richard introduced his new help and let them take charge. Richard was very impressed with the both of them. Everything was settled in no time. There would be a viewing Tuesday evening and the funeral would be Wednesday morning. Just when they had everything settled and those customers were gone, a phone call came in and an appointment was set up for Tuesday morning. Brandy had no classes Tuesday morning and would be there. They ended up having four funerals this week. Richard was very happy with his new help. Brandy had scheduled everyone perfectly. At the end of the new help's first week, the employees who had given two week's notice went ahead and quit. Richard would not miss them. Before they had left on Friday, Robbie saw that a lawn service was doing the grounds for Richard. Robbie went looking in a building out back and found a lawn mower and a weedeater. There were also different kinds of trimmers. He went to Richard. "How much are you paying that lawn service?" asked Robbie. "I bet it's too much."

"It is too much," said Richard. "But they've been reliable and our mower gave out sometime back. I don't think that weedeater runs either."

"I can get that mower and trimmer running," said Robbie. "I could take care of the grounds for you. Do you have a contract with the lawn service?"

"I didn't sign one this year," said Richard. "I told them about my condition and they agreed to work on a week to week basis."

"Well if you'd like, you can give them a two week notice," said Robbie. "I'll have everything up and running by then."

"All right young man," said Richard. "I'll call their supervisor Monday morning."

Monday afternoon, Robbie worked on the mower and trimmer while Bandy took care of things in the office. Robbie needed a couple of parts for the mower. The trimmer just needed a spark plug. He made some phone calls and went to get the parts. Before they left for the day, the mower and trimmer were running properly. The rest of the week went well. They had three funerals and everything went like clockwork. Richard felt so good about everything. He said at the end of the week that he almost forgot he had cancer.

Chapter Twenty-One

About a week after the two men had been sentenced, Carl started noticing a beat up black van. It would go down the road past his place. He would see it two or three times every evening. Whenever it went past, it seemed that two men inside the van were eyeballing his place pretty hard. It worried him some. He didn't want to scare Sally so he never mentioned it to her. He had an M-1 Carbine that he had inherited from his father. It had two magazines and plenty of ammo with it. Carl had said that he would never shoot at anything ever again unless it was shooting at him, but the van was worrying him. One day when Sally was out back hanging up some laundry, Carl loaded the two magazines and put them and the rifle under his side of the bed. He put it in far enough that Sally couldn't see it unless she got down on her hands and knees and looked. Carl made up his mind that the next time the van went down the road, he would run out and ask them what the hell they wanted.

The van didn't go by the next week at all. On Saturday morning, Carl was out doing a few things to the house. Sally was inside doing some cleaning. Carl had been inside the new house and had just come out the front door when the black van went by the place. Carl ran after the van yelling. "What the hell do you want?" The van was almost past his place. It stopped and backed up. Carl was about twenty feet from the van and started walking toward it. When he got closer, the passenger side window opened. The driver of the van kept his hands on the steering wheel. Before Carl could speak, the passenger of the van stuck a pistol out the window and fired three quick shots. Carl was struck in the chest and stomach area. The van sped off. Sally ran outside when she heard the shooting.

She spotted Carl laying beside the road in pools of his blood. The van was out of sight. Sally checked to see that he was alive and ran inside to call 911. An ambulance and a Sheriff's Deputy were there within ten minutes. Sally had worked on Carl as best she could to stop or slow the bleeding. Carl was bleeding from his mouth too.

A team of nurses and doctors were ready for the ambulance and they went right to work on Carl as soon as they got him on the operating table. Sally was hysterical. She kept asking everyone that she saw if Carl was going to live. Everyone told her that the best doctors around were working on Carl and they would do everything in the world that was possible for him. Hours rolled by. Finally Sally got herself glued back together and made some calls. She called her folks and told them what had happened. Carl's folks had been gone for some time so she called his Uncle. Then she called Robbie. She knew that he would want to know.

Brandy and Robbie had slept in some and were just having their morning coffee when the phone rang. Brandy answered the phone. "This is Sally. I need Robbie," Sally said. "This is an emergency." Brandy handed the phone to Robbie.

"Yes, what is it Sally?" asked Robbie.

"Carl's been shot," cried Sally. Robbie almost broke out in tears.

"Is he all right now?" asked Robbie.

"He's still in surgery," cried Sally. "He's been in there a long time. He was shot three times. They won't tell me anything except that they have their best doctors working on him."

"I'll be down there as quick as I can," said Robbie. "Pray for Carl."

"What is it?" asked Brandy. "What happened?"

"Someone shot Carl," answered Robbie. "He's still in surgery."

"Oh my God, why would anyone shoot Carl?" cried Brandy. She sat down and started crying uncontrollably.

"Get ready," said Robbie. "We're going down there."

Robbie was lucky that he didn't get a speeding ticket on the way to the hospital. He had gone over 90mph on a few stretches of the highway. When they arrived at the hospital, Carl was still in surgery. Sally and Carl's uncle were sitting in a waiting area. They were both crying. Robbie and Brandy went to Sally and hugged her. "They shot him three times," cried Sally. "Why, why would anyone want to shoot my Carl?"

"I don't know," said Robbie. "But if I find out who did this before the law does, he won't be around for long." Brandy gave Robbie a strange look when he said this, but she never said anything. They all sat down and had a good cry.

Another hour later, a surgeon came out to the waiting area. "I'm Doctor Shultz," he began. "There was damage to his right lung, stomach, and liver. I have done everything possible. I have faith that he will pull through. If he makes it through the night, I am sure he will be all right. You have my prayers."

"Thank you Doctor," said Sally. "When can I see him?"

"He will be moved to I.C.U. shortly," said the Doctor. "You will be able to see him then, but he will be unconscious for a long time. He might not wake till tomorrow morning."

"Thank you Doctor," said Sally. The Doctor then left.

They all waited a few minutes and then went to the I.C.U. Carl had tubes and IV's sticking out all over the place. A Deputy came and wanted to talk with Sally. She went out into the hall and talked with him. She explained to him that she had been inside cleaning when she heard the shots. She then ran outside and found Carl bleeding beside the road. A vehicle had sped down the road but it was out of sight by the time she got outside. The Deputy also asked her if anything strange or different had happened around their place or anywhere. Sally told him that there was nothing that she knew of. The Deputy informed her that an armed guard would be placed just outside Carl's door until Carl left the hospital. Somehow the local news found out about everything and were all over the place. They tried to keep questioning Sally. Robbie could see that she was extremely upset and very politely informed the reporters that it would be in their best interest if they would back off. There was a TV in the waiting room. When the evening news came on, the attempted murder of Carl Sims was the main topic. "That's just great," Robbie said to himself. "Now that shooter knows for sure that Carl isn't dead. He might try again."

They all went to the cafeteria and tried to eat. Most of them were so nervous that they couldn't. Sally just had some coffee. "I'll be staying here till after he wakes up," said Sally. "And I know he will wake up. The rest of you should go home."

"No way," said Robbie. "I'll be right here till Carl wakes up and tells me himself that he'll be all right. Brandy, you can go back home."

"Carl's my friend too," said Brandy. "I'm not leaving." Carl's Uncle was the only one to leave. The guard came and posted himself on a chair beside the door of the I.C.U. He informed them that he would be there till 11 PM and then he would be replaced. Then at 7 AM, another man would take over. The nurse was nice and allowed them to bring in more chairs so all three of them could sit in the I.C.U.

They had small talk on and off, but no one could carry a conversation very well. When the new guard arrived at 11PM, they all decided they would go get some coffee to help them stay awake. There was another big waiting room way down the hall that had several different vending machines. They got some coffee and sat down and talked a little. Then they headed back to the I.C.U. As soon as they turned a corner to go into the hall where Carl was located, Robbie saw that something was wrong. The guard looked like he was slumped over in his chair. "You girls stay back and keep quiet," whispered Robbie. "Something's not right. I'll check it out." Brandy started to speak. "Please, keep quiet," whispered Robbie. "Don't ask questions. Just keep quiet."

Robbie took off his shoes so he wouldn't be heard walking. When he got closer to the guard, he could see blood on the guard's head. Robbie saw that he had a 9mm Beretta. Robbie slowly took it from the holster and carefully chambered a round. He moved slowly and quietly and entered the room. Two men were inside pulling Carl's tubes and IV's out of him. There wasn't much light in the room but Robbie could make out the two men and what they were doing. He couldn't see if they had any weapons or not. "Stop right there or I'll blow your fucking heads off," said Robbie. The two men were startled at first. They quit what they were doing and stood up straight. Then they started turning around. Robbie could tell that they were reaching for something as they were turning around. Both of the men apparently had pistols stuck in their belts. Robbie could now make out the pistols in their hands as they were turning. He fired at the one on the right. The bullet struck the man in the side of his head and he went down. Before Robbie could fire at the other man, the man fired at Robbie. Robbie was knocked back a little but got off a shot as he was being knocked backwards. His bullet struck the man in the forehead. He went down hard.

It was quiet for a short while and then gobs of people came running down the hall to see what had happened. The police had been called and had a car in the area. They were there in no time. Robbie had put the 9mm down on the floor so no one would think that he was a shooter. Several nurses saw the dead bodies and took off screaming. One older nurse remained calm. She hooked Carl's IV's and tubes back up and checked his vitals to make sure he was o.k. Then she looked at Robbie. "Young man, you've been shot," said the nurse. "We better get you to emergency." The policeman, Sally, and Brandy all came into the I.C.U. at the same time. Brandy saw that Robbie had been shot and tried to hug him as best she could. His right shoulder was all bloody. She began crying. Sally ignored the two bodies on the floor and made sure Carl was all right.

"Can anyone here tell me what happened?" asked the policeman.

"I can," answered Robbie.

"Make it quick," said the nurse. "You're going to surgery."

"I'm all right nurse," said Robbie. "I been shot before. This one is nothing. That shoulder will be good as new in no time." Robbie got with the policeman and told him all that had happened. The cop thanked Robbie and left. As they were getting Robbie on a stretcher to take him to surgery, Robbie swore he heard Carl say something. "Just wait a minute," said Robbie. "I think Carl said something. Carl looked like he was asleep but Robbie saw his hand make a motion for Robbie to come over to him. Robbie went to him and bent down so Carl could talk into his ear if he wanted.

"Old black van," whispered Carl. "Old black van."

"All right, we can go now," Robbie said to the nurse.

"What did he say?" asked Sally.

"It wasn't anything I could make out," said Robbie. "But this is a good sign. He's gonna make it all right. I know he is."

Brandy followed Robbie to his surgery. The nurse showed her where the waiting room was. The guard who had been knocked out was taken to the emergency room. He needed several stitches in his head. Carl was taken to a different room so the dead bodies could be removed and the mess cleaned up. A new guard had been posted.

Robbie was not in surgery very long. The 9mm bullet had not done much damage. Robbie was awake and in a room in no time. He was still groggy, but he was awake. Brandy sat beside his bed holding his hand while he babbled a little. After a short while, the affects of the anesthesia were gone. Robbie looked at Brandy and smiled. "Give me a good kiss woman," said Robbie. Brandy gave Robbie a good long kiss. Then he wanted another one. His hands were finding their way all over her.

"We can't be doing that," said Brandy. "You've been shot."

"I've been shot," said Robbie. "I'm not dead. Now come here."

Brandy went over and made sure the door to Robbie's room was closed. Then she undressed and slipped under the sheets with him. "You stay still," said Brandy. "I'll do all the work." They had been at it for a good while when they heard the door open. It was a nurse.

"Oh excuse me," she said. "I was just checking to see how my patient is doing. I see he's doing fine." The nurse smiled and left the room.

"That'll give her a story to tell," said Robbie.

"I bet something like this happens all the time," said Brandy. "Now keep still. You've been shot." They fell asleep in each other's arms. They were awakened the next morning by a young nurse.

"Excuse me, I hate to wake you," said the nurse. "You two looked so peaceful laying there. There's a cop outside that needs to speak with you. I'll leave the room so you can get dressed ma'am." Brandy got dressed quickly and opened the door for the cop. It was Deputy Stark.

"What can we do for you Deputy Stark?" asked Robbie.

"We're trying to find out if the two men you were forced to shoot had any ties to the gentlemen you testified against," said the Deputy.

"I would have no idea," said Robbie. "But if they were mixed up with them two, that would be a reason to try to kill Carl."

"I understand Carl whispered something in your ear before you were taken to surgery," said the Deputy.

"He did," said Robbie. "But it wasn't anything that I could understand. It wasn't even a good mumble. I can't even pronounce what he said. I figure he was still under the affects of the anesthesia and was babbling some."

"Well would you try and repeat it?" asked the deputy.

"All right, here goes. Whafrumpupingrubbleton," said Robbie. "That's about the best I can do."

"All right, good enough," said the Deputy. "Carl is awake now. I've already talked to him."

"Does he know who shot him?" asked Robbie.

"He said that he was out front and some car was going down the road," started the Deputy. "The two men in the car stopped and yelled out the window that they needed some directions to a friend's house. When he got close to the car, the passenger of the car produced a pistol and shot him. He said it happened so fast that he didn't get the make of the car, only that it was red. We showed him pictures of the two men from last night. Carl confirmed that those were the same men from the red car. We will still keep a guard posted."

"It's good that he identified those two," said Robbie. "Can you keep us informed if you find out that all of them were working together?"

"I will," said the Deputy. "I'll be on my way now. If you think of anything, anything at all, no matter how unimportant it might seem, please get ahold of me. Here's my card."

"Thank you Deputy. We will," said Robbie. The Deputy left.

"I gotta go see Carl," said Robbie. "I'm going now."

"You better make sure you're allowed to get out of bed," said Brandy.

"Hey, I'm shot, not dead," said Robbie.

"You proved that very well last night," said Brandy. "Let's go." They made their way to Carl's room. Robbie's young nurse gave him a stern look when they walked past her, but she didn't say anything. Sally was with Carl holding his hand when Brandy and Robbie walked in.

"I hear you saved my ass last night Pitcher," said Carl. "We both thank you."

"Such a nice ass too," said Robbie. "So when you breaking out of here?"

"They tell me it'll be a little while," said Carl. "I hope I don't get too far behind on the house."

"We'll help you all we can," said Brandy. "We are so glad you are all right. I guess you two Marines are hard to kill."

"I guess we are," said Carl. "Them little fuckers over there couldn't get it done and neither can these crazies over here. I could sure use some coffee. Ask that nurse if I can have some coffee." Sally tracked down a nurse and asked about some coffee for Carl. Sally was informed that Carl couldn't have caffeine of any kind until the doctor said it's all right. Sally came back and told Carl the news.

"Damn, I miss my morning coffee," said Carl. "Why don't you girls go have some. Me and Pitcher can jaw while you're gone. The girls went for coffee.

As soon as the girls were out of sight, Carl asked Robbie if he remembered what he had told him last night. "I do," answered Robbie. "You said old black van."

"That's what I said," said Carl. "Them two was driving a beat up old back van when they shot me. I had seen it going up and down the road some. It looked like they were eyeballing my place pretty good. I made up my mind I was gonna ask them what the hell they were doing. It didn't go by for a week. Then Saturday morning, it came back. I went over to it and that's when they shot me."

"Why didn't you tell the law?" asked Robbie.

"Cause I was hoping to track them two down myself after I got better," said Carl. "Now I want to find that van and see if them two own it or it belongs to someone else. Would you please not tell this to anyone?"

"I won't Carl," said Robbie. "You got my word."

"So when will you get out of here?" asked Carl.

"I see no reason why I can't leave today," said Robbie. "It doesn't hurt unless I move it too much. I don't know what else they can do for me except tell me to take it easy. Now is this hospital bill gonna hurt you bad?"

"I have good insurance," said Carl. "It should pay for most of this. I'll pay for what's left when I can. If they have to take payments, then they'll take payments. How about you?"

"I'll be making payments as best I can," said Robbie. "I don't have insurance. I go to the VA for my health care. Haven't been since I first got signed up." A nurse came into the room and informed them that Carl had enough talking for a while and needed to rest.

"All I been doing is laying here resting," said Carl. "I don't think I can get any more rested."

"I'll not argue with you young man," said the nurse. She gave Carl a stern look. Robbie waved goodbye and headed back to his room. Sally and Brandy were in the hall and headed toward Carl's room.

"That nurse in there says Carl's gotta be quiet and rest some more," said Robbie. "I'm going back to my room." Sally slipped into Carl's room and Robbie and Brandy went to Robbie's room. The young nurse came in right after them.

"They'll be bringing you some breakfast shortly," she said. "Do you feel like eating?"

"I can eat," said Robbie. "How soon can I get out of here?"

"You've been shot," said the nurse. "Maybe you should stick around for awhile."

"I been shot before," said Robbie. "Here I'll show you." Robbie got up off the bed and pulled up his hospital robe so the nurse could see the scars on his legs. "Been shot once in the right leg and twice in the left," said Robbie. Then he pulled the robe up around his neck. "I got shot in the stomach and this one up here went through my shoulder blade and through the lung and tore up two ribs on the way out," said Robbie. "This little thing I got last night is nothing." Brandy was laughing now. "What are you laughing about darlin'?" asked Robbie.

"Well, my dear, you're naked under that thing," said Brandy. "You've been giving this young lady a private tour of your anatomy." Robbie pulled his robe back down.

"I didn't mind at all," said the young nurse. "After you have some breakfast, I'll find your doctor and see what he says."

"That'll be another story for that young girl to tell," said Brandy. They both laughed a little.

After Robbie had finished his breakfast, a young doctor came to his room. "I'm Doctor Moore," he said. "They tell me you're ready to get out of here."

"I am Doc," said Robbie. "I feel all right. I don't need to be here taking up space that might be needed for someone else."

"That's good logic," said the doctor. The doctor gave Robbie a once over. "You can go now," said the doctor. "Everything looks good. I'll give a prescription for some antibiotics. I want to see you back here in a week. My office is easy to find. Stop in and the prescription will be ready. Schedule yourself an appointment while you're there."

"I will Doc and thank you," said Robbie. Robbie's clothes were tracked down and he dressed and found the doctor's office. He made the appointment and got the prescription. Then he went to the billing office. Robbie told them who he was and he'd like to see what his bill was and make a payment. They informed him that his bill hadn't even been made yet. He could check back another time. They went to Sally and told her they were headed home. Carl was asleep. Sally told them that she would be staying with her folks for a while. They headed to Robbie's car. On the way to the car in the parking lot, Robbie spotted an old beat up black van. When they got close to it, Robbie could see that the doors were unlocked. "Hold on a minute," said Robbie. "I gotta check on something in this van."

"Robbie, what the hell are you doing?" asked Brandy. "This has got something to do with them two from last night doesn't it?"

"I promised Carl I wouldn't say," said Robbie. "But you've already figured it out. He said the ones that shot him were driving an old beat up black van. I'm checking to see if there's a registration in it."

"Why didn't he tell that to the law?" asked Brandy.

"Because he wanted to track them down himself when he got better," said Robbie. "Now he won't have to. Robbie found the registration in the glove box. He read it carefully. "Holy shit, this van belongs to that old farmer who rents the land from Carl's uncle."

"Holy shit is right," said Brandy. "Do you suppose he's the ring leader?"

"I don't know, but I'm sure Carl will want to find out when he gets better," said Robbie.

"So you're not telling this to the law?" asked Brandy.

"I can't," answered Robbie. "I promised Carl and I will not break a promise."

"You already broke one when you told me about the van," said Brandy.

"No I didn't," said Robbie. "You figured that out on your own."

"What do you think Carl will do when he finds this out?" asked Brandy.

"Carl is no fool," said Robbie. "He won't do anything that'll get him sent to prison. He loves Sally and he can't wait for that baby to come. Things will be all right."

When they got home, they were all over each other. "Be gentle now," said Robbie. "I've been shot." Brandy let out a laugh and had her way with him. Afterwards, they lay in bed holding each other as best they could so as not to aggravate Robbie's wound. "Are you going to tell your parents you've been shot?" asked Brandy.

"I better," said Robbie. "You probably will if I don't."

"That's right," said Brandy. "Parents should be told when things happen to their children."

Robbie got up and went to the phone. Robert answered. "Hi Dad. How've you been?" asked Robbie.

"Your mother and I are fine," answered Robert. "Is everything all right down there?"

"Oh, I got shot," said Robbie.

"Say what, shot, is it serious? Are you in the hospital?" asked Robert.

"I'm home dad," started Robbie. "It was just in the right shoulder. It happened last night. Do you remember me telling you about those two fellas that Carl and I knocked out? The ones who were growing the pot?"

"I remember," said Robert. "Go on."

"Well there was a trial and we all had to testify," said Robbie. "They found them two guilty of growing the pot and also guilty of attempted murder because they shot at the two deputies. Anyway, a couple weeks after them two were sentenced, Carl was shot. He was in his front yard by the road and some people drove by and shot him. He was hit three times. He's o.k. now but they weren't sure if he would make it or not. That night after his surgery he was in I.C.U. I was at the hospital with Brandy and Carl's wife Sally. They had a guard posted outside Carl's door because they were afraid that when they found out that Carl wasn't dead, the shooters would try again. It was all over the local news. It was late when the girls and I went down the hall to get some coffee. When we got back, I could see that something was wrong. I told the girls to be quiet and stay put. The guard had been knocked out. I took his pistol and went into Carl's room. Two men were in there pulling Carl's IV's and tubes out of him. They were armed. I killed them and I got hit in the shoulder."

"Damn Son, you saved Carl's life," said Robert. "You're a brave man Son. I'm so proud of you. So they must think that those two were linked to the ones you testified against."

"I think so Dad," said Robbie. "Now you'll go easy when you tell Mom all of this won't you?"

"I will Son," said Robert. "How's Brandy handling this?"

"She's doing good Dad," answered Robbie. "She's a good woman."

"Do you need anything?" asked Robert. "Can we do anything for you? I know your mother will want to see you after I tell her. You should figure on us coming down my next day off."

"It'll be good to see you," said Robbie. "I have an appointment next weekend to see the doctor who worked on my shoulder but that shouldn't take long. Just call me when you're coming. We'll be here. Now make sure you tell mom real easy like."

"I will son," said Robert. "You just make sure you don't sit around feeling bad because you shot those two men. They got what they deserved."

"I won't Dad," said Robbie. "Goodbye now."

"Bye Son. We love you," said Robert.

"Love you too Dad, goodbye," said Robbie.

"Well how did it go?" asked Brandy.

"I talked to my dad," said Robbie. "He'll tell Mom and he promised he would do it gently."

"Well speaking of gently, you come on back in here," said Brandy. "I'll give you some more gentleness."

Mary had been sitting under a hair dryer and hadn't known that Robbie called. She came out to the living room. Robert was sitting on the couch watching TV. Mary sat down on his lap. They kissed a little. "Our son called," said Robert.

"Is everything all right?" asked Mary. "Something's wrong. You have a strange look on your face. Tell me." Robert turned off the TV.

"Our son has been a hero again," said Robert. "Two men tried to kill his friend Carl and he saved him."

"There's more to this story than that," said Mary. "Come on, get it out."

"This will be a long story now," said Robert. "So be patient and listen. Do you remember when Brandy and Robbie told us about the two pot growers?"

"Yes, I remember. Go on," said Mary.

"Well those two were convicted of pot growing and attempted murder of the deputies," said Robert. "Robbie and all of them had to testify at the trial. Two weeks after they were sentenced, someone drove by Carl's house and shot him. They weren't sure if he would live or not. It was all over the local news. They put a guard outside Carl's door because they feared that the shooters would try again. Robbie was at the hospital with Carl's wife, Sally, and Brandy. Late that night, they went down the hall to get some coffee. When they got back, Robbie saw that the guard had been knocked out. He told the girls to stay quiet and out of the way. He took the guard's pistol and went into Carl's room. Two men were in there pulling Carl's IV's and tubes out. They were armed. There was a shootout. Robbie killed the two men but he got hit in the right shoulder. He had surgery right away and is already home. He and Brandy are fine. Carl is fine too."

"I'm going down to see our son," said Mary. "We'll be going on your next day off."

"I already told him that," said Robert.

"Our poor boy, he got shot all those times in Vietnam and comes home only to get shot again," said Mary. "How much of that can a body take?"

"He's a strong man," said Robert. "And he's a good man. We raised him right."

~~~~

The next week went by quickly. There were three funerals and everyone did a good job. Robbie did the best that he could with only one arm. Robbie's parents would be down Saturday afternoon. Robbie's appointment was at nine in the morning. Brandy went with him. After his appointment, they went to see Carl. Carl was doing really well. He couldn't talk them into letting him go home though. He was just glad that he could drink coffee now. Brandy and Sally went to the ladies room so Robbie saw his chance to tell Carl about the back van. "I know who owns that black van," said Robbie.

"Who's the son of a bitch?" asked Carl.

"It's that old farmer who rents the land from your Uncle," answered Robbie.

"You're shitting me," said Carl.

"No, I'm not," said Robbie. "That van was in the lot when I left the other day. It was unlocked and I found the registration. His name is on it."

"Jesus H. Christ, that old man sure played dumb when my Uncle asked him about the pot," said Carl. "I'll be doing some serious thinking on how to handle this."

"Well don't get yourself put in prison," said Robbie. "You got Sally and a baby on the way. They need you."

"I need them too," said Carl. "Whatever I do will get it done proper. I won't be going to no prison."

"Remember that when you have a weak moment," said Robbie. "Maybe the old man had no idea what was going on. Maybe he knew them guys and just lent them the van."

"I'll get to the bottom of it," said Carl. "So how's Brandy doing? Is she upset about you getting shot?"

"We're doing good," said Robbie. "She's a good woman."

"When you gonna marry that girl?" asked Carl.

"Probably as soon as I finish school," answered Robbie. "She's done at the end of this semester and I have one more. It won't be long."

"I expect to be at the wedding," said Carl. "That is unless you two elope."

"I guess we'll do what Brandy wants to do," said Robbie. "Her folks live up in Toledo. That's a long way for you if we do it up there."

"No distance is too far for you my friend," said Carl. "Maybe the baby'll be here by then."

"Are you wanting a boy or a girl?" asked Robbie.

"Healthy is all I want," said Carl. "Sally feels the same." The girls came back now.

"What did you two talk about while we were gone?" asked Sally.

"We talked about Brandy and Robbie getting married and where it will happen," said Carl.

"Where's it going to happen?" asked Brandy.

"I said that was up to you Brandy," said Robbie. "You might want to do it at Toledo since that's where you're from."

"And what if I want to elope?" asked Brandy.

"We can do that too," answered Robbie. "As long as I get you, it doesn't matter when or where." Brandy grabbed Robbie gently and gave him a nice big kiss.

"Calm down you two," said Carl. "This is not your hotel room." Brandy gave Robbie another kiss and then let go of him.

"Be gentle on him," said Carl. "He's been shot."

"I've been getting plenty of gentleness," said Robbie.

"I figured so," said Carl. "It'll be a while before I can get some gentleness." They all laughed. Robbie and Brandy visited for a little while longer. Then they let

Carl know that they had to leave because Robbie's parents were coming down for a visit. They told Carl that they would be back for a visit a soon as they could.

~~~~

When Robbie's parents arrived at the apartment. Mary had herself a good cry. It took a good half hour for her to get control of herself. Once she was all right, nothing more was said about the shootings. Brandy told them all about Richard Zoeller and how he was a good friend of her father. She told how her father had saved Richard during the war and that her and Robbie and other students were helping out at his funeral parlor. Brandy made them a really nice dinner. When it came time for them to leave, Mary did a little more crying. She gave Robbie and Brandy a good hug. Robert gave Brandy and Robbie a good hug too and then they were on their way.

"We're lucky Robbie," said Brandy. "We have pretty good parents. Some people have terrible parents or only one parent or no parents at all."

"Yes, we are lucky," said Robbie. "Speaking of lucky, how about we go get lucky right now?" Brandy ran to the bedroom tearing off her clothes as she went. Robbie wasn't as fast. Brandy helped him when he got beside the bed.

~~~~

School went well the next week and they had three more funerals. Everything was going well. They went to see Carl on Saturday. The nurses said that Carl was doing better than expected and could possibly get out in a week. If he did, he would have to take it very easy and check in regularly with his surgeons. There were two of them. One of them had worked on Carl's lung and the other one had done his stomach and liver. Carl was excited about leaving.

Carl did get released the next week. Robbie was worried that Carl would do something stupid and go after the old man, but Carl didn't. He followed his doctors instructions to the letter. Three more weeks went by and Carl was allowed to do a lot more. He could go back to work in another week if he didn't do any heavy lifting. The day before he went back to work, he decided to pay a certain old farmer a visit. He got the M-1 Carbine into the car without Sally knowing it.

"I got something to do," Carl said to Sally. "I'll be back shortly." Before Sally could say anything, Carl was out the door and leaving. There was an old pickup in the driveway when Carl pulled into Charlie Hanson's driveway. Carl took a good look around and then got out of his car. He carried the carbine so it could be plainly seen by anyone who was looking at him. Carl took his time and slowly moved to the front porch of the house. He eyeballed every window and corner to see if he was being watched. He could see no one in the front part of the house. He slipped around to the back door. Through a window, he could see Charlie setting at the kitchen table. There was an old revolver on the table in front of him. Carl opened the back door and rushed in. Charlie didn't seem surprised at all to see Carl.

"I knew you was back home," said Charlie. "I knew you'd get it figured out and come for me. Go ahead, shoot me and get it over with. I'm ready to die."

"Why are you so ready to die old man?" asked Carl. "Nobody's ready to die."

"I am," said Charlie. "I got prostate cancer and it'll kill me if you don't. Your way is quicker."

"Looks like maybe you were gonna do it yourself," said Carl.

"I've tried but I just can't do it," said Charlie.

"So how did you get tied up with them pot growers?" asked Carl.

"They came by one day. They seemed like real nice boys," said Charlie. "They convinced me that they'd never get caught growing that stuff and they would give me a good piece of the profits. I'm in debt somethin' awful. I got this damn cancer and I didn't want to leave the wife with a huge debt so I agreed. I never knowed they was crazy. I never dreamed they would shoot at them deputies and then try to kill you. Go ahead and kill me. You got the right."

"Where's your wife right now?" asked Carl.

"She's playing bingo somewhere," answered Charlie. "She plays bingo once a week."

"Well Charlie, I'm not gonna to kill you," said Carl. "You can do it yourself or let the cancer take you. I'll tell you something though Charlie. If you got life insurance, you better check your policy. Some of them don't pay off for suicide." Carl left and went back home. He thought he heard a shot as he was pulling away but he didn't go back to check. The next day at work, they had him in an office doing some paperwork. He'd been at work for a couple of hours when his Uncle came in to the office.

"I just heard on the radio that old Charlie Hanson killed himself," said his Uncle. "His wife came home from bingo and found him dead at the kitchen table."

"That's a shame," said Carl. "What'll happen to his corn on your place?"

"I suppose the wife will pay someone to harvest it for her," said his Uncle. "I'll wait a little while before I talk with her about it." Carl didn't say anything else. His uncle left the office and Carl went back to work.

Chapter Twenty-Two

It didn't take Robbie's shoulder long to heal. He was doing about anything he wanted in no time. Carl was coming along fine too. The only person who wasn't doing well was Richard Zoeller. He had decided to quit his chemotherapy. He believed that it was killing him quicker than the cancer. He rarely came to the office anymore, but he was excited about the Reds. They had won the pennant and were going to the World Series. He hoped to take in a game when they played in Cincinnati. He had tickets for one of the games, but when the day of the game came, he felt too bad to go. He gave the tickets to some friends. The Reds lost the Series to the Orioles.

They were very busy at the funeral parlor clear up to Thanksgiving. Brandy and Robbie both wanted to see their parents for the holiday, but they were just too busy. Brandy was running the place and she didn't feel right about leaving, even for a day. They had Thanksgiving dinner at their apartment. Both sets of parents came. Brandy fixed a nice feast. Robbie helped her all he could but he didn't know anything about turkeys and dressing and such. Mary and Robert came a little early and helped out some. They had a good time on Thanksgiving day. There was a funeral on Friday so Brandy and Robbie both had to work.

The first two weeks of December were steady. They had four funerals the first week but only two the second week. At the end of the second week, Brandy and Robbie were at home relaxing and just enjoying each other's company. The phone rang. Brandy answered it. "This is Tony Giraldi," he started. "I have seen you but we have not been formally introduced. I am Richard's friend. You have seen me when I picked him up for this appointments."

"Yes, I remember seeing you," said Brandy. "How can I help?"

"Richard passed away today," said Tony.

"Oh, I'm deeply sorry," said Brandy.

"Before he died, he gave me a letter," said Tony. "It says what he wants done for his funeral and everything. He wants you to personally handle everything."

"It will be an honor," said Brandy.

"After the funeral, there will be a reading of the will and it is requested that you attend," said Tony. "He also has requested that your father be present."

"I will get ahold of my father and let him know," said Brandy. "Has the body been transported yet?"

"Yes it has," said Tony. "I am with him right now at the funeral home."

"I will be there as soon as I can," said Brandy. "I'll read Richard's letter and make sure I do everything he has requested. I should be there within half an hour." Brandy hung up the phone and told Robbie the news. They cleaned up and went straight to the funeral parlor. Tony was there with the letter. The letter went as follows.

> *Brandy,*
>
> *I do not want anything fancy. I want a viewing with a short service at the parlor and then to the graveyard. The VFW will provide a color guard and fire a salute. I have some pictures I would like displayed. They are my son and old war buddies. There are none of my ex-wife. I wouldn't display them anyway. I would like it if WW would say a few short words. There will be no preachers. I was never a religious man. I have my casket picked out. Tell people to donate to cancer research instead of flowers. It has been a great pleasure knowing you.*
>
> *Richard*

"We'll do what he has requested," said Brandy. "Today is Saturday. Everything will happen on Tuesday morning. That will give us time for the obituary to be read in the papers. Has an obituary been written?"

"I have written one," said Tony. "I wrote is not long ago. We knew he would die soon. All I had left to do was put in the date of death. The local papers already have it. We just need to let them know the time and date of everything."

"We'll take care of that," said Brandy. "Let's figure on 11AM Tuesday morning."

"I'll get with Richard's lawyer so he can set a time for the reading of the will," said Tony. "I will tell you the time for the reading when I see you Tuesday."

"Thank you for everything Tony," said Brandy. "We'll get right to work now." Tony left and Robbie got everything ready for Brandy. Brandy went straight to a telephone and called her father. WW answered the phone.

"Hi Daddy," said Brandy. "I have some sad news. Richard has died."

"Well he's not in pain anymore," said WW. "When is everything?"

"There will be a viewing at the parlor at 11AM on Tuesday," started Brandy. "He asked that you say a few words at the viewing. He requested that there be no preacher as he was never a religious man. Then to the graveyard. The VFW will provide a color guard. There will be a reading of the will after the graveyard. Richard's friend Tony is in contact with Richard's lawyer for this."

"O.k. Baby, we'll see you then," said WW.

"Hey Daddy, if you'd like to come on Monday, you can spend the night at our apartment," said Brandy. "That way you won't have to rush around Tuesday morning."

"That's probably what we'll do baby," said WW. "We'll see you then."

~~~~

Robbie had never seen so many people for a funeral. There were hundreds of people at the viewing. Only about half of them went in the procession to the graveyard, but it was still a huge procession. Richard was one well known and well liked person.

They met with the lawyer back at the funeral parlor. Brandy was a little nervous. She had never been to one of these, and wasn't sure why she was even there. She wasn't a relative or anything. The lawyer was an older man, but he was very nice and polite. He asked if everyone was ready to start. "This is the 'Last Will and Testament of Richard Alvin Zoeller,' " he began. "I wrote it for him and it was duly witnessed. It is a simple will. It is short, concise and to the point. I will read now."

I Richard Alvin Zoeller, being of sound mind, my body is not too sound, but my mind is. I do hereby bequeath the following.

To my dearest friend Tony Giraldi, I leave my house, my personal car, and $50,000.

> *To my newest friend Brandy Wisecup, I leave my business and all of*
> *the assets that go with it.*
>   *All legal fees for everything have been taken care of.*

Signed – Richard Alvin Zoeller

Brandy was totally dumbfounded. She just sat there and cried. WW went to her and hugged her. The lawyer asked if there were any questions. No one had any. He handed everyone his card and said they could reach him anytime and he would get busy on any necessary paperwork. Before he left, he reminded everyone that the legal fees had already been paid. Tony shook everyone's hand and then left. Brandy just sat there. She couldn't believe what had just happened. Robbie was still at the parlor and waiting in another room. When he saw the lawyer and Tony leave, he went to Brandy. "What is it Brandy?" asked Robbie. "You look like you saw a ghost or something."

"Richard left this place to me," said Brandy.

"Are you serious?" asked Robbie. "Did he? Really?"

"Yes he did," said Brandy. "I don't understand. Why would he do that?"

"Because he liked you Baby," said WW. "You impressed him. He knew that you are a good person. You'll take care of your customer's needs."

"Maybe he left it to me because of you Daddy," said Brandy.

"That's possible," said WW. "But if he'd have left it to me, I would have given it to you anyway. Face it baby, you are a full fledged business person now. People will work for you now."

"I suppose I should get with that lawyer and get everything taken care of," said Brandy. "I'll set up an appointment with him on Wednesday."

"Your mother and I will be going home now," said WW. "Congratulations Baby. You're still my little girl even if you do have your own business now."

"I love you Daddy," said Brandy.

"We love you too Baby," said WW. "Bye now."

Brandy and Robbie spent the rest of the day trying to figure out how they were going to handle things. Brandy would have her Bachelor's Degree in a couple of weeks and Robbie would have his Associate's Degree. An Associate's Degree is all that is required by the State of Ohio. Robbie was expecting to work for Fulbright's in Columbus after he got his degree. How would they work this out now that Brandy was the owner of the funeral home in Cincinnati?

Robbie really wanted to get his Bachelor's Degree so they decided that for the time being, Robbie would attend school for another semester and get his Bachelor's. Brandy would run the funeral parlor and Robbie would be there as much as he could. Over Christmas break, Robbie would go home and have a talk with Abner Fulbright and see where he stood with Abner. Brandy would also make sure that her employees would know how to handle things in her absence.

The day after Richard's funeral, Brandy had a meeting with all of her employees and informed them that she was now the new owner of the business. Things would basically be the same because Brandy had been running the place already. On Wednesday, she met with Richard's lawyer. Everything was taken care of with no problems. Richard had been a very good business man and kept very good books. There was a good inventory on hand of all supplies and there was a generous amount of money on hand. Brandy asked the lawyer about changing the name of the place and the lawyer advised that she go ahead and change the name. She decided it would be called the Wisecup Parker Funeral Home. Richard had expected the name to be changed and set aside money for a new sign.

~~~~

The two weeks before Christmas were very busy for them. They had five funerals the first week and then four the second. They had a funeral on December 23rd and another December 26th. Brandy was glad for the business but she felt bad because Christmas didn't seem special this year. They were so busy with work that they didn't really have time for each other. They set up a small Christmas tree and exchanged some gifts, but neither of them really felt that they had the Christmas spirit.

Right after Christmas, Robbie went home for a couple of days. Brandy stayed and would go visit her family for a couple of days after Robbie returned. When Robbie got home, he apologized for not being home on Christmas day and gave his parents the news about Brandy being given the funeral home. "You don't need to apologize for not being here on Christmas," said Mary. "You're with Brandy now and there's a business to run. Young men are supposed to leave home sometime."

"I love you guys," said Robbie.

"We love you too Son," said Mary and Robert.

"I've got to see Abner Fulbright while I'm home," said Robbie. "If Brandy and I are going to get married, we'll need to figure out how we're going to do things. I was expecting to work for Abner for a while."

"Maybe Abner won't need you for a while," said Robert. "You'll get it figured out. You have another semester of school to get your Bachelor's if you do want your Bachelor's."

"I'm getting my Bachelor's," said Robbie. "I know that the State only requires an Associate's but I want the better degree. Some day the State might change things."

"Well let's sit down and eat," said Robert. "Your mother made a great meal yesterday and we have tons of leftovers. We'll be eating on this turkey and ham for several days."

The next day, Robbie paid Abner a visit. He got a big surprise when he went into Abner's office. Abner looked like he had aged twenty years. Robbie went to him and shook his hand, but didn't say anything about Abner's appearance. Abner spoke first. "I look like shit, don't I," said Abner. "There's something going on inside me and they can't figure out what it is. I've had test after test. I'm about tired of getting stuck. So how's school?"

"I have my Associate's Degree and I'll have my Bachelors at the end of the next semester," said Robbie.

"Are you still with that good looking girl you brought over here?" asked Abner.

"Yes I am," answered Robbie. "We'll be getting married one of these days."

"Well what are you waiting for?" asked Abner.

"We've got a lot to figure out," said Robbie. "She owns her own funeral parlor now and I was expecting to work for you for a while. Her funeral home is in Cincinnati."

"Just how did she end up with her own place?" asked Abner. "I thought her father had his own place in Toledo. She'd run that place sooner or later."

"It's a long story," said Robbie.

"I got time," said Abner. "Tell me."

"Well Brandy's dad had a war buddy in Cincinnati who had a funeral parlor too," started Robbie. "WW saved his life during the war and they were great friends ever since. Anyway, this fella was dying of cancer and he needed some help. Brandy and I worked with him all we could. He liked Brandy so well that when he died, he left her the place."

"He probably did like her, but she got the place because her dad saved his life during the war," said Abner. "Anyway, you two will be well off one day. She has that place in Cincinnati and her dad will probably leave her his place too. Yes sir, you two will do well. If they don't find out what's wrong with me soon, I'm liable to die. I have no family who wants this place. I'll end up selling it. Hell, maybe you'll buy it. That would be something wouldn't it. A young couple like you and Brandy owning three funeral parlors."

"You won't be going anywhere Abner," said Robbie. "They'll find out what's wrong with you and get you fixed up."

"I might just sell the place anyway before too long," said Abner. "I've been at this for a good while and I'm getting tired of it. I'd like to set back and take it easy for a while. Spend some time with the wife for a change. If you bought this place, you and Brandy could get yourself some good people to run the places for you and you could do about anything you wanted. That's what I would do if I was you."

"That would be nice," said Robbie. "But I still say you're not going anywhere."

"It's nice that you think that," said Abner. "Now I hate to cut your visit short, but I'm feeling poorly and I best get home and lay down."

"Well I hope you feel better soon," said Robbie. "I'll see you at the end of the next semester."

Robbie and his dad went to the VFW later that day. Ole Jessie was there and they had a good visit. Jesse had been telling all of his old friends that if they wanted a good deal on a funeral, they should go to Fulbright's because that's where Robbie would work. After a few shots, Jessie's wife called and said it was time for Jesse to get home. Robbie and Robert had one more beer and then went home. They had another great meal of leftovers.

Robbie had a hard night that night. He couldn't get the war out of his head. He didn't understand why. He hadn't even thought about the war for a long time. He did a lot of screaming and yelling during the night. "Shoot that fucker," he yelled several times. "They're coming. They're coming. Send'em to hell. Ammo, ammo, get me some fuckin' ammo. Grenade! RPG's! Shit, there's more of them. I can't kill them fast enough. Mother fuckers!"

Mary wanted to run to Robbie's room every time he yelled, but Robert told her stay put. "He'll be all right when he wakes up," said Robert. "We'll just stay here and listen. If we hear anything that sounds bad, like he's breaking things or anything, I'll take care of it."

The next morning at breakfast, Robbie seemed perfectly normal. "You had a hard night son," said Robert. "You were having some bad dreams."

"I was?" said Robbie. "I don't remember them at all. I know I was thinking about the war some before I fell asleep and I couldn't quit thinking about it, but if I was dreaming at all, I don't remember. I do remember thinking about Brandy. I was thinking that we should go ahead and set a date."

"That's wonderful," said Mary. "You two are so good together. That Brandy loves you so much. I can tell."

"Well I'll let you know what we're going to do as soon as I know for sure," said Robbie. "As soon as I get back, she'll go visit her folks for a couple of days. Having your own business kind of ties you down some."

"It does," said Robert. "But you two will get everything figured out. So how was Abner Fulbright? You never said how your visit with him was."

"Abner's not in good health at all," said Robbie. "When I saw him, he looked twenty years older than when I saw him last. He said they can't find out what's wrong with him."

"Sounds like something serious," said Robert. "Let's hope they get it figured out."

Robbie ate his breakfast and then headed back to Cincinnati. When he got home, Brandy was there waiting for him. She ran to him and they kissed till they were out of breath. "I missed you Robbie," said Brandy. "I missed you a lot."

"I missed you too Brandy," said Robbie as he picked her up and carried her to bed. They made love like they had never made love before. They fell asleep in each other arms for a couple of hours after they were finished. Robbie woke up first. When Brandy woke up, he had his head propped up with his right arm and was looking into her eyes. "I think we should go ahead and set the date," said Robbie. "I think we should be married."

"I want that too," said Brandy. "What kind of wedding do you want?"

"I will do whatever you want," said Robbie. "If you want a big wedding it's o.k. If you want a Justice of the Peace it's o.k."

"I don't want all that fuss," said Brandy. "I just want you. I'll go see my folks for a couple of days and then we'll get a Justice when I get back if that's o.k. with you."

"It's o.k. with me," said Robbie. "How will your parents feel about this? Maybe WW wants to give you away."

"Daddy will not mind what I do," said Brandy. "He might be glad that he won't have a big wedding to pay for. Momma will cry a little, but she'll get over it. I'll tell them as soon as I get up there."

"So how were things at work?" asked Robbie.

"We've got some good people working for us," said Brandy. "I trust them already. So how was Abner?"

"Abner's in bad shape," answered Robbie. "They can't seem to find out what's wrong with him. He looks terrible. He even talked about selling his place."

"I hope he gets better," said Brandy. "But who knows? Maybe we will buy his place someday. We'll have his place, our place here, and I'm sure daddy will give me his place. We can let people run them for us and we can do whatever we want."

"Abner said the same thing," said Robbie. "Who knows? All of this could happen. So when you get back and we get married, are we going on a honeymoon?"

"You still have school," said Brandy. "We can go on a belated honeymoon as soon as the semester is over."

"Where should we go?" asked Robbie.

"I was thinking we would go to Tybee," answered Brandy. "I loved that place and I know you did too."

"I did," said Robbie. "Do you think we could get that same house?"

"I'll go to work on that while I'm in Toledo," said Brandy.

They spent most of the rest of the day in bed. They did get up around 7 PM and had something to eat. Brandy left early the next morning for Toledo and Robbie went to the funeral home. Everything went smoothly at the parlor. There would be four funerals for the week.

Robbie had a hard time getting to sleep the first night Brandy was gone. He kept reaching for her but she wasn't there. He finally fell asleep. He had some good dreams about Brandy and Tybee. They had made love several times and were sitting out on the dock drinking coffee and watching dolphins. When he woke up the next morning, he was hugging a pillow. Robbie didn't feel like making his own breakfast so he went to a diner. The day went smoothly again and Robbie had more good dreams about Brandy that night.

~~~~

When Brandy got home, her father was already there. She sat her parents down and told them the news about her and Robbie. Her mother cried a little and WW let her know that whatever she did was all right with him. WW said that he would pay for their honeymoon. Brandy asked him if he could see about getting them the house in Tybee. WW immediately made some phone calls. The owner of the house in Tybee wasn't home, but she would call WW tomorrow.

WW took the family out for dinner that night to celebrate the good news. Brandy's sisters brought their boyfriends too. One of them was dating a graduate student who was working on his PhD in Chemical Engineering and the other one was dating a lawyer who had just passed his Bar exam. He had several job offers and was making up his mind. They had a nice evening but Brandy thought her sister's men were a little "stuffed shirt."

The next day, the owner of the Tybee house called and said that the house would be available for the second and third week of May. WW told her to book it for Brandy and Robbie. Brandy spent the night in Toledo and then headed back to Cincinnati early the next morning. Robbie was at the parlor when Brandy got home. She called him and he came right home. They went to a jewelry store and picked out some wedding bands. Then they made arrangements for a blood test so they could get their marriage license. Then they went out and had a nice dinner. When they got back home there was a message on the answering machine from Dave and Marie. Brandy called them back. They were invited over to Dave and Marie's for a small New Year's Eve dinner and party. They accepted.

They had a good time at Dave and Marie's. There were two other couples there too. Their names were Martha and Tom Scranton and Julie and Bob Tarlton. Martha had been a Navy nurse in Vietnam and Tom had been on a river patrol boat. Bob Tarlton had been with the Air Cavalry in Vietnam. They all got along very well. Robbie told everyone about Brandy's good fortune and Brandy told everyone that she and Robbie would be married as soon as they got their blood test results. Marie fixed an excellent meal. No one got really drunk although Robbie was sure that the men shouldn't be driving home. They made it to midnight and sang Auld Lang Syne. All of the women helped Marie clean up before everyone went home. The men swapped a few war stories while the women cleaned up.

~~~~

The blood test results came back in a couple of days so Brandy and Robbie went to get their marriage license. Robbie asked Brandy if he could ask Carl to witness the wedding. "I know we are just going to a Justice of the Piece," said Robbie. "But Carl is my friend and I'd like for him to be there."

"That's fine by me," said Brandy. "Give him a call and see if he can get up here. He can be the best man and Sally can be Maid of Honor."

"I'll call him as soon as we get home," said Robbie.

As soon as they got home, Robbie made the call. Sally answered the phone. "Sally, this is Robbie," started Robbie. "Brandy and I are getting married. We'd like it if you and Carl could attend."

"We would love to," said Sally. "When and where will it be?"

"Well it won't be anything fancy," said Robbie. "We're just going to the Justice of the Peace here in town. You two can be witnesses. We'd like to have the wedding as soon as you two can get here."

"I'll have Carl call you as soon as he gets home," said Sally. "He should be home by 5:00 PM."

The phone rang at 5:05. "So Pitcher, you're getting it done," said Carl. "I can get off work day after tomorrow. Just give me a time, a place, and directions and we'll be there."

"Don't worry about getting dressed up," said Robbie. "Just come as you are."

"We'll be there," said Carl. Robbie gave him the necessary information.

Robbie called his parents that evening to let them know about the wedding. Mary cried a little bit and Robert told Robbie that he knew that Robbie would be a good husband and father when the time came. They also had some sad news for Robbie. Abner Fulbright's wife called and asked them to let Robbie know that Abner had Lou Gehrig's disease. He wasn't expected to live much longer. The Funeral Home would go up for sale in a couple of weeks. Robbie was to have a chance to purchase the place before it went on the market. Abner's wife also gave them the name and number of the lawyer who was handling Abner's affairs. Robbie almost cried but he kept the tears back. Robbie changed the subject and told his parents about the belated honeymoon. They chatted a little more and then said goodbye. Robbie didn't look very happy when he hung up the phone.

"What is it Robbie?" asked Brandy. "Aren't your parents happy for us?"

"That's not it," answered Robbie. "They're happy for us. They just let me know that Abner Fulbright doesn't have long to live. He has Lou Gehrig's disease."

"That's so sad," said Brandy. "I know you two got to be good friends."

"His place is going up for sale in a couple of weeks," started Robbie. "They're letting me have first chance to buy it before it goes on the market. Could we even afford it?"

"We would have to talk to a bank, but I'm sure we can afford it," said Brandy. "We have plenty of money in our operations account so we would have a good down payment. I can't see why a bank wouldn't give us a loan. Why don't you make a call tomorrow morning and let whoever is handling Abner's affairs know that we are interested."

"I kind of feel guilty about this," said Robbie. "I kind of feel like a buzzard sitting in a tree just waiting for something to die."

"You don't need to feel guilty," said Brandy. "It's not your fault that Abner is not well. If you don't buy the place, someone else will. Abner thought enough of you to give you first chance. His family will need the money too."

"I guess you're right," said Robbie. "Abner's family will need the money. I'll call that lawyer in the morning."

At nine o'clock the next morning Robbie called Abner's attorney. He made an appointment to meet with him the next Saturday. Then they both went to the funeral home and made sure everything was running smoothly. Then they went back home and acted like a young couple that was about to get married. After a couple of hours of acting nervous, they put on some nice clothes and went to the courthouse. Carl and Sally were to meet them at 1PM and they were there waiting for them. They exchanged hugs and kisses and handshakes and then went inside and got it done. Robbie took all of them for a nice meal at a fancy restaurant. They even had a bottle of champagne. Sally even took a small sip. After the meal, Carl and Sally went back home and Brandy and Robbie went to their apartment. They made love for hours.

Robbie skipped a couple of classes this week and Brandy had confidence in her crew and was home whenever Robbie was home. When Saturday came, they made the trip to Columbus. Abner's lawyer was a very thorough man. Everything was laid out perfectly. Brandy and Robbie were pleased with the numbers they saw and let the lawyer know that they would be talking to a bank on Monday. They exchanged business cards with the lawyer and then went to visit Abner.

Brandy was not with Robbie when he saw Abner the last time and she was plainly upset when she saw how bad Abner looked. Abner saw that she was upset. "I know I look bad girl," said Abner. "It's just the way things are sometimes. I don't like it but there's nothing I can do about it. I had a good life. If I had it to do over again, I wouldn't change a thing. Of course if I did, I wouldn't want this damn disease. Now I know you two will do this place right. Young Robbie there's already got himself a good reputation around here."

"So how's your wife holding up?" asked Robbie.

"She has a good cry every once in a while, but she's holding up," said Abner. "She has a spell once in a while where she wishes that we would have done this or would have gone there. I imagine a lot of folks get like that." They had some more small talk and then Abner said he was tired and needed to lie down.

It was lunch time when they got to Robbie's parents house. Mary and Robert were just getting ready to eat. They had not expected a visit from Robbie so soon. Robbie had called and told them about the wedding but he hadn't told them that he was coming to Columbus for a meeting with Abner's lawyer. They were glad to see the both of them.

"So how does it feel being married?" Robert asked them.

"It feels real good," said Robbie. "Every time I see Brandy I just want her more and more."

"I feel that way too," said Brandy. "I bet you two felt that way at first too."

"We still do," said Mary.

"So why the visit?" asked Robert. "Is something going on that we should know about?"

"We met with Abner's lawyer this morning," said Robbie. "We're going to buy his place. We'll be talking to a bank on Monday."

"That's great," said Mary. "But how will you handle two places that are not in the same town?"

"We haven't discussed that yet," said Brandy, "But we have a good crew in Cincinnati and I can trust them to run the place. We can let them take care of Cincinnati while we get this place here running good."

"If I remember right, I had some people from Columbus in a class of mine last semester," said Robbie. "I saw some of their work and they did good work. Maybe they are in the area and looking for work. Of course we will have to see if any of Abner's employees will want to stay. One thing for sure though. We'll need a place to live in Columbus for a while."

"Your mother and I would love it if you stayed with us while you were looking for a place," said Robert. "Isn't that right Woman?"

"I'd love the company," said Mary. "You two are welcome here anytime and for however long is needed."

"Well we'll talk to the bank on Monday and let you know what's going on," said Robbie. "We'll spend the night and then head back to Cincinnati in the morning. Would you guys want to go out for dinner this evening?"

"I already had a new recipe planned for this evening," said Mary. "We can go out another time. I do need to get a few things from the grocery. Brandy and I can go after lunch and you men can sit around and drink beer if you want."

"Sounds good to me," said Robert. "I got some of that Hudepohl that they make over in Cincinnati. It's not the best beer in the world but it's cheap and drinkable."

"I've had some dad," said Robbie. "I can drink it."

The girls went to the store and the men sat down in front of the TV and found a football game. It was an NFL playoff game. The boys didn't really want to watch it but there wasn't a decent movie on. When the first quarter ended, Robbie thought he heard some strange noises. They got louder and louder. Then the sounds were unmistakable. Robbie could hear the "whop whop whop" of helicopter blades. He had a strange look on his face, but a few minutes after the helicopters passed, the strange look left.

"What is it Son?" asked Robert. "Did them helicopters get your thoughts going?"

"I haven't heard any choppers for a while Dad," said Robbie. "They did get my thoughts going."

"You probably did spend a lot of time on them choppers didn't you?" asked Robert.

"That's mostly how we got around Dad," said Robbie. "Choppers do a lot of things, but there's two things that I will never forget. They either take you some-place bad or get you out of someplace bad." Robbie went outside to see if the choppers were out of sight yet. In the distance to the west, Robbie could see two Hueys and and a Chinook. "What the hell are them things doing around here?" Robbie asked himself. "Probably some reserve unit somewhere flying around." Robbie went back inside.

"Did you spot them Son?" asked Robert.

"I did," answered Robbie. "It was a Chinook and two Hueys. Must be some Army Reserve unit or something."

"Well we've had some News helicopters fly over from time to time," said Robert. "They really like it when there's a high speed chase or something going on. Well anyway, I hope you're not upset cause I have something that we need to talk about."

"Well I'm not upset," said Robbie. "Now what is it that we need to talk about?"

"One of these days your mother and I won't be around anymore," started Robert. "You need to know where all the important papers and such are."

"That's fine dad, but you're not going anywhere for a good while," said Robbie. "Hell you're only 45 and you look in good shape to me."

"I know I look like I'm in good shape but at my last doctor visit, my blood pressure was pretty high," said Robert. "I've never had high blood pressure before. I check it at home at least once a week. Sometimes it's high, sometimes it isn't. That doctor wants me to take medication for it. I been arguing with him about it. Some of that stuff messes up your love life. If I couldn't make love to your mother, it would make me feel worthless. I know when a man gets old, he can't carry on like a teenager. I'm just not ready to give that up yet."

"Well maybe there's different medications," said Robbie. "Maybe you'll find one that doesn't slow you down. You really should try and do what the doctor says dad. High blood pressure can cause a stroke or a heart attack or something bad. I'm sure mom would rather have you alive than dead. They say exercise and such can help high blood pressure too. Plus certain foods are good for it. You'll get it figured out. You gotta stick around and help us with the grandkids."

"So when are these grandkids coming?" asked Robert.

"Probably not for a couple of years, but they're coming so stick around," said Robbie.

"All right, I will," said Robert. "But you still need to know where the important stuff is. Now follow me." They went into Robert and Mary's bedroom. Robert went to the closet. It was a huge closet. It covered one wall of the bedroom. There were two doors on the right side and two doors on the left. "The right side is your mothers and the left is mine," said Robert. "Now stick your head in there and look at the back wall right in the middle." Robbie did as instructed. There was a small safe in there. "That thing's bolted to the floor and the back wall," said Robert. "Plus it's fireproof." Robert took a pen and some paper and wrote down the combination and handed it to Robbie. "Everything's in there," said Robert. "Your mother and I both have wills and they are in there. The deed to the house and the title to the car are in there. All of our banking information is in there. Our insurance policies are in there. You name it, and it's in there. There's even some very expensive jewelry in there that your mother inherited from her mother and other relatives. We've never had a credit card and we owe absolutely nothing right now. I'm sure there's other things in there but I can't remember all of them right now. Anyway, now you know where everything is."

"Well let's hope I don't need to get in there for a good while," said Robbie. The men heard a door open and close. "The women must be back. Let's go find out what we're eating this evening." The men went to the kitchen.

"So what are we having this fine evening?" asked Robert.

"Lamb chops with garlic mashed potatoes and roasted asparagus," answered Mary. "We have a nice cabernet too."

"That's wine isn't it?" asked Robert.

"You know it is," said Mary.

"So are you making a fancy dessert too?" asked Robert.

"Not today dear," said Mary. "You'll have to suffer with some mint chocolate chip ice cream."

"I can live with that," said Robert.

"You boys go back to your game while Brandy and I make some nice appetizers," said Mary. The boys did as instructed.

Robbie had never had lamb chops before. When he saw how rare they were, he was a little hesitant to take a bite. After the first bite, he knew that he was eating something very good. "These are really good Mom," said Robbie. "You outdid yourself again. I like my steaks medium. Maybe I'll try eating them rare from now on."

"I never made lamb chops until today," said Mary. "I did a lot of reading and research before I decided to make them. Most of the books say that you don't want to overcook the lamb. If you do, it will get strong and muttony. I've never had mutton either, but I always heard that it was kind of strong."

"Well you did good woman," said Robert. "You did real good."

After the meal and cleanup, they all sat around the table for hours and talked. Finally around 10 PM, Robert decided he better get cleaned up and get to bed. He was working first trick in the morning. Mary and he went to their room. Brandy and Robbie watched TV for a half hour or so and then went to their room.

Robert was already gone when Brandy and Robbie got up the next morning. Mary fixed them a big breakfast and they were on their way. They didn't talk much until they got away from Columbus. Brandy spoke first. "What did you and your dad talk about while we were at the grocery?" asked Brandy.

"My dad told me that he's having trouble with high blood pressure," said Robbie. "He's upset because he's always been healthy. The doctor wants him to take medication for it but Dad is putting it off because the medication can slow down his love life."

"You mother and I talked about that too," said Brandy. "You mother would rather have him take the medication and be alive instead of not taking it and having a stroke or heart attack."

"I told him that too," said Robbie. "I think I got him convinced that he should at least try the medication. I also told him that there were different medications. Maybe one of them will work for him and not slow him down."

"Did he tell you about the safe and all the important papers?" asked Brandy.

"Yes he did," said Robbie. "I have the combination in my wallet right now."

"Well let's hope we don't need it for a long time to come," said Brandy.

They spent most of the day lounging around taking it easy. They made love a couple of times in the afternoon and then ordered a pizza for dinner. After the pizza, they laid in bed for hours talking about how their life together was going to be and how many kids they were going to have. They fell asleep in each other's arms.

When Robbie woke up the next morning, he heard Brandy in the shower so he joined her. An hour later, Robbie made them pancakes, sausage, and eggs for breakfast. They needed groceries because they had been so busy with other things so they went shopping right after the dishes were done. After they got back and the groceries were put away, Brandy called her dad and told him about Abner Fulbright. He was sorry about Abner, but he knew that Brandy and Robbie would be able to handle two places.

Robbie had a class at 8 AM on Monday so they went to the bank right after Robbie's class. They took every piece of paperwork that they thought the bank would want to see. Everything went smoothly. The loan officer told them that he was sure that the loan would be approved. They should know something before the end of the week.

The week seemed to fly by. Thursday at noon they got a call from the bank. The loan had been approved and they needed to sign the necessary paperwork. They went right to the bank. As soon as they got back to the apartment, Robbie called Fulbright's and said that he would like to have a meeting with all of Abner's employees on Saturday morning. Robbie also found the phone number of the student who had been in a class of his and was from Columbus. He called him and told him the situation. Robbie told him that there was possible employment for him and would he attend the meeting with the others on Saturday. His name was John Merrill. He informed Robbie that he would be looking forward to their meeting.

Friday night, they went out dancing to celebrate. They invited Marie and Dave too. Marie and Dave invited Martha and Tom and they in turn, invited Julie and Bob. They went to the club where Marie and Dave had learned how to dance. They had a great time. There was no trouble from anyone wanting to dance with the women. About eleven, Brandy and Robbie told everyone they had to leave because they had a meeting in Columbus in the morning. Marie was tired and ready to leave anyway. The rest of them had had enough dancing too. As they were leaving, Julie and Bob asked Brandy and Robbie if it would be possible to meet with them early next week. Julie's father was in bad shape and they had been discussing funeral plans. An appointment was set up for Monday at 10 AM.

~~~~

The meeting on Saturday morning did not go very well. Abner's employees had no intention of working for Robbie or Brandy and everyone of them gave their two week's notice. Robbie thanked them for coming to the meeting and the two week notice. He then informed them that John Merrill would be in charge any-time that he or Brandy was not present during their last two weeks. John was very pleased that Robbie had faith in him. He also knew some other people who had the proper credentials and were seeking gainful employment. Robbie told John that if he could get ahold of these people today, he would interview them if they could come to the parlor on such short notice. John went right to work on the phone. He knew four people and was able to track down two of them. Interviews were set up for 1PM and 2 PM. It was 11AM now. Robbie gave John some money and told him to go get them all some Chinese food for lunch. Robbie called home and told his mother to expect another visit from them this evening.

The two interviews went well. Brandy and Robbie both liked the two people. They told them that they would start as soon as the other employee's two week notices were up. It would be sooner if things weren't working out. Brandy and Robbie were about to leave when John told them that he had gotten ahold of the other two potential employees. They would be available to be interviewed that afternoon. Robbie told John to have them come in as soon as possible and not worry too much about their appearances on such short notice.

The first one showed up in a half hour. Her name was Marsha Hayes. She was an attractive woman, probably in her early 30's. She had graduated from

Cincinnati College of Mortuary Science five years ago. She was employed at another funeral home in town and wanted to leave because she was tired of the other employees, all of whom were male, always questioning her ability. Brandy and Robbie could tell that she seemed more at ease when she found out that a woman was one of the owners. They liked her and told her she would start at the end of the two week's notice from the other employees.

A half hour later, the other person arrived. He was an older man, probably in his late 40's or early 50's. His name was Sam Toler. He had retired from the Army after 20 years. He spent his last years in grave's registration. He had his Associate's Degree in mortuary science from another school and had just graduated a month ago. He had taken a month off before looking for work. He interviewed well and was told that he would start in a couple of weeks.

Before leaving for Robbie's parent's house, Brandy and Robbie had a nice long talk with John. They wanted to make sure that he knew that he was in charge during their absence. If the employees who had given two week's notice were not performing up to par, they should be encouraged to perform or move on. John said he was ready for the task. If anything needed their attention, he was to call them without hesitation. Cincinnati was not that far away.

They talked almost the whole way to Robbie's parent's house. "I find it hard to believe that all of those people didn't want to work for us," said Brandy. "You worked with those people. Does it seem weird to you that they quit?"

"It does," said Robbie. "I always thought we got along together. I never had any problems with any of them. Maybe they thought that one of them would buy the place. I don't know. Anyway, it looks like we already have a decent crew."

"If they're as good as our other crew, we'll be in great shape," said Brandy. "You know, we're going to have to figure out where we'll be living. We can't stay in the apartment forever. Oh, I guess we could stay there as long as we want, but we should have our own place as soon as we figure things out. I'd like a nice house. Wouldn't you? It doesn't have to be big or fancy. A two bedroom with a nice kitchen and living room. A nice yard so the kids will have room to play. What would you like Robbie?"

"All of that sounds good to me," said Robbie. "I like Cincinnati. I could live there. I like Columbus too."

"I really like Cincinnati," said Brandy. "We can get us a house there and stay at your parents' place when we come to Columbus. Then as time goes on, we can get a bigger place when more kids come."

"How soon are these kids coming?" asked Robbie.

"Sometime after we get our first house," answered Brandy. "Now pull over."

"We're almost there," said Robbie.

"I know," said Brandy. "But I want to kiss you a bunch right now, so pull over." Robbie found a place to pull over. As soon as the Olds was in park, Brandy was all over him. Fifteen minutes later, they pulled into the driveway.

They had a good meal and visit. They were on their way back to Cincinnati the next morning.

Chapter Twenty-Three

Robbie had class on Monday morning so Brandy handled the meeting with Julie and Bob. Everything went well and the plans were made for Julie's father. Julie and Bob were impressed with Brandy. Julie's father died the next week. It wasn't long after his funeral that the Wisecup Parker Funeral Home started getting a lot of calls and were setting up appointments. Julie and Bob had put out the word about Brandy and Robbie. They must have had a lot of friends because fifty calls were received the next week. Half of the calls resulted in confirmed plans.

The next two months went very well for them. John was doing well in Columbus and had no problems and Cincinnati was good too. Brandy and Robbie had two good crews and felt totally confident in them. They spent a lot of time house hunting.

One evening they were sitting on the couch kissing when the phone rang. Brandy answered it. "Well hello Daddy," said Brandy. "It's nice to hear from you."

"It's good to talk with you too Baby," said WW. "I've got some news for you."

"Well what is it Daddy?" asked Brandy.

"I'm going to get a crematory," said WW. "I believe that this business is going to increase greatly over the next 20 years."

"You're probably right Daddy," said Brandy. "It's cheaper than traditional funerals and one day there might not be any more space in graveyards. Can you afford it Daddy?"

"I believe so Baby," said WW. "I think that it would pay for itself before too long. I just have to find out about zoning and laws and everything. You know if I do this, you can use it too. Maybe I won't put it up here in Toledo. Maybe I'll put it in Columbus. That would be a more central location."

"This sounds good Daddy," said Brandy. "Robbie and I have been house hunting. No luck yet."

"Well keep looking Baby," said WW. "You'll find one and you'll know it's the right one when you see it. I'll let you go now. I'll call you when everything is all set on the crematory. We love you."

"Love you too Daddy, goodbye," said Brandy. Brandy hung up the phone. "Daddy's going to get a crematory," said Brandy.

"That's probably a wise move," said Brandy. "I'd say the need will increase a lot over the next several years."

"He says he might even put it in Columbus," said Brandy. "And we can all use it."

"That would be good too," said Robbie. "And he could let others use it too. Of course there would be a fee. Man, I just can't believe how smooth things are going. It almost seems too good to be true."

"It does, doesn't it?" said Brandy. "All we need now is our house."

~~~~

Robbie rarely watched the news or read the paper because he was always afraid there would be some anti-war stuff going on. He wasn't wrong. Protests were still happening all over the country. One particular day, he bought a newspaper for the sole purpose of looking at the real estate section. He opened the paper and was scanning the pages when something on the third page caught his eye. There had been an operation by the South Vietnamese forces called Lam Son 719. The South Vietnamese forces had invaded Laos to stop infiltration from the north. The south had gotten their asses totally kicked. American forces were only involved as support. A lot of American helicopters and their crews had been lost. The South lost a lot of their best troops. Robbie just shook his head and threw the newspaper in the nearest trash can.

~~~~

Some good news came the next Monday. Carl Sims had called to say Sally had given birth to a healthy nine pound boy. They named him Carl Robert Sims. Two days later, Brandy and Robbie went to see the new addition to Carl's family. Brandy looked like a natural mother as she held the baby. Robbie was a little clumsy at first. He was probably like most young men holding a baby for the first time. He was afraid he might break it. "So is there a certain reason that Carl's middle name is Robert?" asked Robbie.

"There certainly is," answered Carl. "You saved my ass Pitcher. Carl Jr. wouldn't have a daddy if it weren't for you."

"Well I'm deeply honored," said Robbie.

"So when are you two gonna get busy and crank out some kids?" asked Carl.

"As soon as we get our house," said Brandy. "We've been looking. It won't be long."

"So how are you two handling everything?" asked Sally. "Robbie's still in school and you have the business. It must be very hectic."

"It seems like it should be," said Brandy. "But we have very good employees. They know what to do and when to do it. It's almost too good to be true. My father is getting a crematory so the business should get even better. Robbie's school will be over shortly too. We'll be going on our belated honeymoon toward the end of the month. I have a good feeling that we'll find our house as soon as we get back."

"Where are you going for your honeymoon?" asked Sally.

"Tybee Island," answered Brandy. "We loved it down there. I'm getting excited just thinking about it." Carl Jr. started whining a bit. Sally knew it was feeding time. She sat down on the couch and pulled out a breast. Carl Jr. got down to business. Robbie was mesmerized watching the baby. He imagined what it would be like watching Brandy feed their own baby. Carl tapped him on the shoulder.

"Let's go outside and have a beer and talk for awhile," said Carl. Carl went to the frig and got a couple of beers for them. They went out on the front porch. "So have you been watching the news at all?" asked Carl.

"No, not really. I did see in a paper where the South Vietnamese got their asses kicked on an operation into Laos," said Robbie. "I don't keep up with stuff. I'm tired of hearing about protests all the time."

"Well I saw somewhere that the 1st Marine Division is pulling out this spring," said Carl. "Troop strength over there will be down to 150 some thousand."

"Let's hope that a bunch more don't get killed waiting to be withdrawn," said Robbie. "I know I wouldn't want to be the last one killed if I was over there. I'm guessing that the North will just bide their time and wait till we're gone and then take over. The South won't be able to stop them. Hell, let's talk about something else. Looks like the house is coming along."

"I'm doing o.k.," said Carl. "Getting shot slowed things down some but it'll be done before too long."

"Brandy and I'll give you a hand whenever we can," said Robbie. "I know she likes using a hammer. I bet when we get our house she'll have all kinds of plans."

"Hey, before I forget to tell you, that old farmer shot himself," said Carl.

"You're shitting me," said Robbie. "Why do you supposed he did that?"

"I paid him a visit right before I went back to work," said Carl. "He told me all about the pot growers and how he was in bad debt and such. He said he never knew they was crazy. Anyway, he was dying of prostate cancer. He expected me to kill him. He did it himself right after I left. His wife was out playing bingo and found him dead at the kitchen table."

"I'm glad that you didn't do anything stupid," said Robbie.

"I probably could have when I first found out about that van, but I had plenty of time to think when I was healing up," said Carl. "Anyway, that's all past now."

"So how's the lumber business doing now?" asked Robbie.

"Good, there's a lot of new construction going on all over the place," said Carl. "We've had a time keeping up with orders. I hope this keeps up for a while. They say when there's a lot of house building and other construction, the economy is doing good. So how's your business, dead?"

"Yep, and it gets deader all the time," said Robbie. They both had a laugh.

They had brought some groceries with them and Brandy fixed a nice dinner for them that evening. "I figured you could use a little break," said Brandy. "There'll be enough leftovers for a couple more meals for you." After dinner, the men cleaned up. Brandy and Robbie were going to head home. Carl insisted that they stay the night.

"I think you should stay," said Carl. "You can get a small taste of what it'll be like having a baby in the house. I'm lucky. I don't have tits and can't feed the baby. I still get woke up though."

That night, Brandy and Robbie were awakened two times by the baby crying. They couldn't get right back to sleep after the second time, so they took advantage of being awake and made love. After coffee and breakfast the next morning, they headed back to Cincinnati. "We'll come down and help with the house after we get back from Tybee," said Robbie. "We'll have you in the house in no time."

~~~~

The semester ended and Robbie received his Bachelor's Degree. They made sure everything was in order and then left for Tybee. They had a wonderful time in Tybee. The weather was almost perfect the whole time. They saw plenty of dolphins and even fished a little off their pier. They caught some black sea bass, some whiting, and some sheephead. Neither of them wanted to clean fish so they let them all go. Robbie bought a crab net just to see if he could even catch a blue crab. They caught several crabs of legal size and turned them loose too. They had heard that blue crab was very tasty but it looked like it would be a good chore to get the meat off one.

They almost cried when it was time to leave. The house was taken for the rest of the month by others so they couldn't stay there. They actually went to some rental agencies and asked about other places. There was nothing available on the back water until the fall. They sucked it up and went home. Everything had gone smoothly in their absence so they went down to Carl's the first weekend back. Carl had gotten a lot done. All that was left to do was painting and some linoleum. Sally had decided that they should wait on carpeting. Big throw rugs would be just fine in the living room. Robbie discovered that he wasn't a very good painter, but the job got done. Brandy was slow but she was very good. Carl painted like he had been a painter his whole life. One more day of painting and they could move into the house.

Carl finished up the painting and they moved everything out of the trailer and into the house the next weekend. It took Sally a little while to decide how she wanted furniture arranged. After a few moves, she gave up. "I'll get it figured out over time," Sally said. "I expect we'll have more things over time too. Just think, we get to sleep in our new house tonight."

"What will you do with the trailer?" asked Brandy.

"We'll sell it," said Carl. "Should get $2000 out of it. It's in decent shape."

"We should go home so you can spend the first night in your new house alone," said Robbie.

"Nonsense, if it weren't for you two we wouldn't be getting into the house till fall or later," said Sally. "Plus Carl might not even be here. You're staying the night and that's that."

"Well we'll order some pizza for dinner tonight," said Robbie. "I don't imagine anyone feels like cooking after moving all that stuff today."

If the baby made any noise that night, it didn't wake Brandy or Robbie. When they woke up the next morning, Sally was sitting on the couch feeding the baby and Carl was in the kitchen making coffee and getting breakfast ready. Carl made everyone ham and cheese omelets with hash browns. Robbie was surprised. They said their goodbyes after breakfast and then headed back to Cincinnati. Brandy talked Robbie into driving around and doing some house hunting. They were in a suburb on the west side of town. Both of them saw the house at the same instance. It was a ranch house with a lot that must have been a quarter of an acre. There was a chain link fence around the yard. It had a two car garage and looked like it might have at least three bedrooms. The realtor sign was out front but there was an additional sign. There was an open house today from 12 to 4. It was 11:30 AM now. They would bide their time and take a look at the house at 12. They saw a woman in the house and the woman saw them too. She came out and introduced herself. She was the realtor and she would answer any questions they had if they were there for the house. The house was a three bedroom, two bath, and had a full basement. There was the two car garage, a large kitchen and dining area. The living room was also large.

Right at 12, the realtor let them come into the house. Both of them knew right away that this was to be their house. The furnace was only two years old and the house had central air conditioning. The master bathroom had a shower and bathtub plus a double vanity. As far as the realtor knew, this was a nice neighborhood and all the people got along well. Brandy cornered the realtor and asked her every question imaginable. Other people were coming in now but Brandy wouldn't let the woman get away. After Brandy had acquired the information she wanted, she let the realtor go and talk with other potential customers. "I've got all the information we need," said Brandy to Robbie. "I've got the asking price, the taxes, the school district, and everything imaginable. Let's go home and figure out how much we will offer and how much we can afford. I have the realtor's number at this house so if we come up with a number before she leaves, we can call her." Robbie agreed and they went to their apartment.

Brandy was good with numbers and budgets. She had it figured out in no time. She also knew the bank interest rates and figured out their monthly payment if their offer was accepted and they put so much money down. Robbie was agreeable on her numbers. It was only 3 PM so Brandy called the realtor at the house and made their offer. According to the realtor, there had been no other offers yet. She would relay their offer to the owner after the open house and get back with them as soon as she had heard something. They were so excited that they couldn't sit still. They tried to watch TV but couldn't. They tried to drink a beer but it didn't hit the spot. At 5:30 PM, the phone rang. It was the realtor. "I have given your offer to the owner," said the realtor. "Your offer was $3000 less than the asking price. The owner wants at least $1500 more than your offer. Is that agreeable to you?"

"Yes it is," answered Brandy.

"Good, come to the office tomorrow afternoon at 2 PM and we'll do the paperwork," said the realtor.

"We'll be there," said Brandy. She hung up the phone. "We've got us a house. I bet a beer will go down a lot better now." Robbie got them another beer. "You know we'll have to buy a lot of stuff," said Brandy. "We've been living in this furnished apartment all this time."

"It'll be fun shopping for stuff with you," said Robbie. "We don't have to get everything all at once. The most important things come first, like a bed." Brandy took that as a hint and led Robbie to bed. He went willingly.

All of the paperwork and such at the realtor and the bank took almost a week. They would get the keys to the house the next Monday. Brandy called her parents and told them the news. WW knew they would need a lot furniture and things. He had a good friend who had a furniture store. He made a call to him and told him that anything Brandy wanted would be charged to him. Robbie called his parents and they said they would buy them a stove and refrigerator. It was now the third week in May. They were supposed to give a two week's notice on their apartment. Since they had been good renters, the landlord didn't worry about it. The apartment would be rented as soon as they were out of it. They were confident that their loan would be approved. They went to the furniture store and picked out some things. A bed, kitchen table and chairs, couch, easy chair, coffee table, and some lamps would be delivered Tuesday morning. A refrigerator and stove would come on Wednesday.

The loan was approved with no problems. They got a surprise on the day they started moving in. There was a washer and dryer downstairs. The owner had decided he didn't want them and just left them. They were in good working order. They didn't have many personal belongings so it didn't take long for them to move in. The things from the furniture store arrived on schedule too. They had a great time in their new bed the first night.

Whenever they weren't working, they were out shopping for things for the house. The needed another bed so they could have company over so that was one of the first things they bought. The first two weeks at the new house, Robbie did a lot of driving back and forth to Columbus. He would leave early Monday morning, spend a good bit of the day at the funeral home, and then stop in at his parent's house for a bit. Then he went back to Cincinnati. He did this on Thursday too. He did this for a month before he decided it wasn't necessary. The Columbus crew was good. John was a good leader and Marsha was an exceptional worker. Sam was very good too. WW was working out the plans for the Crematory in Columbus and hopefully it would be in operation shortly.

~~~~

Brandy was serious about wanting kids with Robbie. They had the house now and she was ready. Whenever she was in her fertile period, neither of them spent much time at work. Three months after they had moved into the house, Brandy announced that she was pregnant. She was so happy. They would have a dinner party and invite all of their friends. She would ask Carl and Sally, Dave and Marie, Martha and Tom, and Julie and Bob. Everyone could make it. Carl and Sally could spend the night if necessary. They could rig up something for Carl Jr. to sleep in if necessary.

Brandy made a prime rib with all the trimmings. Everyone had a great time. The women couldn't resist Carl Jr. except when it was time for him to eat. Marie didn't handle the baby as much as the others. Her baby was already wearing her out and she still had a good ways to go until it arrived. Carl and Sally had brought a bassinet with them in case they ended up spending the night. It was a good thing they did. All of the men drank a little too much and the women had to drive them home. Sally didn't want to drive so they spent the night. For some reason, Carl Jr. slept the whole night through. Sally had to wake him up to eat in the morning. Maybe all that handling wore him out.

It wasn't long until Brandy started having some morning sickness. It wasn't all in the morning either. She handled it very well and didn't take it out on Robbie. As soon as her morning sickness was over, she got her sex drive back. Robbie didn't mind.

Business was really taking off. The crematory was in operation and business was booming. If this kept up, they would have to add another one. Maybe they would put one in Cincinnati. The rest of the year seemed to fly by. They went to Robbie's parents' house for Thanksgiving and Brandy made Christmas dinner at their house. Both sets of parents came. They stayed home for New Years. Brandy started worrying that she was gaining too much weight, but Robbie kept telling her that she was beautiful. The winter wasn't bad but it seemed to go on forever. Spring finally arrived. Brandy was glad to get out of the house more but she was still worried about her looks. The baby would arrive in April and she was ready.

On April 10, an 8 ½ pound healthy baby girl was born. She was named Mary Lou Parker. It didn't dawn on them until after the birth that this was also Robbie's birthday. He was now 22. The delivery went well and Brandy was home in three days. Of course the in-laws spent a lot of time visiting. Robbie had been a nervous wreck during the delivery. He had called Carl and Sally and they were there in the waiting room helping him keep calm. Carl had remembered what a wreck he had been when Carl Jr. was born.

Robbie stayed home for several days and waited on Brandy hand and foot. She kept telling him that he didn't need to do this or that, but he wouldn't quit so she just let him. When he did go to work, he called her regularly making sure everything was all right. He finally got settled down after a couple of weeks. He felt so good one day that he decided he would stop off at a local bar and have a beer before he went home. He went into the place and took a seat at the bar. There was a TV above the bar and just his luck, it was time for the news. He ordered a beer and took a sip. The news started. The big story was that the North Vietnamese had invaded the south and had taken the whole northern province of Quang Tri and some other key places. They were calling this the "Easter Offensive." There were thousands of refugees fleeing south. The south was hoping that with U.S. air power and naval gunfire, they could retake everything. The bartender was watching the news too. "Could you change the channel?" asked Robbie.

"What's a matter fella? You don't wanna know what's goin' on in the world?" said the bartender.

"I don't mind most of the world," said Robbie. "Right now I don't want to know about that place."

"Are you one a them war protesters?" asked the bartender. "You sure as hell don't look like one a them."

"I'm not a protester," said Robbie. "I was over there a while back."

"So are you one a them Vietnam Veterans Against the War?" asked the bartender.

"No, I'm not one of them either," said Robbie. "I'm just some guy who doesn't want to hear about that place right now."

"So what were you fella?" asked the bartender. "I bet you was a Marine."

"Yes I was a Marine. Now would you change the channel?" asked Robbie. The bartender mumbled something and changed the channel. The same thing was on the next channel. He changed it again and it was there too.

"That's all the channels I got fella, sorry," said the bartender. "I won't pay for cable. I'll just turn it off for awhile."

"Thank you," said Robbie. The bartender tried to have a conversation with Robbie but Robbie mostly ignored him. He finished his beer and headed home. By the time he had gotten home, he had forgotten about the news and his mind was on Brandy and Mary Lou. Mary Lou was asleep and Brandy was feeling amorous. "Should we be doing this so soon?" asked Robbie.

"I need it," said Brandy. "I'm all right down there. It will be all right. Both of them needed it and they were all over each other. Robbie had never had a woman's breast leak milk on him before. He didn't mind. As soon as they were finished, Mary Lou woke up and let them know what time it was. Robbie started on something for dinner while Brandy fed Mary Lou.

~~~~

Everything was still running smoothly at work, but Robbie decided that he should go to Columbus at least once a week to check on things. They had been extremely busy ever since the crematory had been in operation. On the first trip to Columbus, John told Robbie that they should consider hiring another person, maybe even two. They were putting in a lot of time and he didn't want to lose anyone because they were putting in too much time. Robbie agreed and told John to take care of it. Robbie talked to all of the employees while he was there. Marsha was in very good spirits. She had gotten herself engaged and would be married in a couple of months. When she told this to Robbie, he told her she could have some time off for a honeymoon. She gave him a hug and kissed his cheek.

Now that Robbie had more available time, he and Brandy took turns going to work in Cincinnati. Robbie would go in on Monday and Brandy would go in on

Tuesday. She pumped off breast milk so Robbie could feed Mary Lou while she was gone. On Wednesday, they all made the trip to Columbus. Of course they always stopped and visited Robbie's parents. On Thursday Robbie went to work and Brandy would go in on Friday. If Saturdays were necessary, they took turns. Things were working out really well.

Both of Brandy's sisters got engaged. They both wanted big expensive weddings. WW told them that he would only spring for one big one so if they were serious, it would have to be a double wedding. They agreed and the wedding was set for June 15. The girls couldn't decide on where to have the wedding so Brandy's mother suggested they have it at their house. They did.

It was a huge wedding. It was totally catered and WW hired a very good band. Brandy and Robbie hadn't danced for a while and they had a great time. Mary Lou didn't get neglected. Most of the women couldn't wait their turn to hold her.

Brandy and Robbie stayed for a couple of days after the wedding to visit. When they got back home, there was a message on the answering machine from Carl Sims. He wanted Robbie to return his call. Robbie got the car unloaded and things put away then called Carl. "What's up Carl," said Robbie. "Sorry we haven't talked for a while."

"I was wondering if you'd like to come down and do some fishing," said Carl. "The creek's looking good and we should have some luck."

"That sounds good," said Robbie. "I think Brandy and I could use some time away from the city. I'll call you in the middle of the week and we'll be down if there's nothing going on that needs our attention."

"Look forward to seeing you," said Carl. "Oh, and Sally's pregnant again."

"That's good news," said Robbie. "You guys said you wanted a big family and you're off to a good start. I'll call you Wednesday."

"Talk to you then, bye now," said Carl.

Nothing serious was happening so Brandy and Robbie made the trip to Carl's. Brandy was glad to get away for a while. The first thing they noticed when they got to Carl's was that the trailer was gone. After handshakes and hugs and kissed, they all had a seat in the shade. Little Carl was a real pistol. He was fifteen months old now and was into everything. Keeping up with him was a full time job.

"So I see the trailer's gone," said Robbie. "You got rid of it pretty quick."

"Yeh, I put up a note at the lumber yard and it sold in less than a week," said Carl. "Got $2000 for it too. I had three people wanting it, but only one of them come up with the $2000. Paid me cash and got it the very next day. Got my hospital bill paid off."

"That's great," said Robbie. "I paid mine off sometime back. We have some insurance now. I expect we'll be having another kid before too long. We want a big family too."

"Speaking of families, I'm going inside and feed Mary Lou," said Brandy. "There's a few flies out and I don't want to swat flies while I'm feeding." The women went inside and took little Carl with them. The boys stayed outside and talked.

"You heard about Jane Fonda?" asked Carl.

"You mean the actress?" asked Robbie. "What about her?"

"Well she went over to North Vietnam," answered Carl.

"You're shitting me," said Robbie. "Why the hell would she do that?"

"She's a really big anti-war person," said Carl. "She's over there slandering our politicians and the military."

"Fuck her," said Robbie. "Maybe they'll fucking keep her. There's nothing wrong with being a peaceful protester, but that's going way too far."

"They're calling her "Hanoi Jane," said Carl. "Sounds like a good name to me."

"Well I'll tell you one thing," said Robbie. "I don't watch a lot of TV and we don't go to the movies much, but I'll never watch another Jane Fonda movie again."

"Same for me," said Carl. "Damn bitch. She's got balls bigger than us put together."

"I guess I should keep up with the news once in a while," said Robbie. "Ignoring it all the time won't make things go away."

"Speaking of things going away, let's see if we can make a couple of beers go away," said Carl. The boys drank a couple of beers then played some catch. They had a good dinner and then the boys went fishing. The girls stayed home. Brandy and Sally had a good visit. Little Carl kept them busy and they were glad when it was his bed time.

"So what does Robbie think about Jane Fonda?" Sally asked Brandy.

"Why should Robbie be thinking about Jane Fonda?" asked Brandy.

"You don't know, do you?" asked Sally.

"Know what?" asked Brandy.

"Well Jane Fonda went over to North Vietnam," said Sally.

"Why would she do that?" asked Brandy.

"She's a big anti-war person," said Sally. "I guess you two haven't kept up with the news."

"We rarely watch the news," said Brandy. "Robbie's so tired of hearing about protests and stuff so we don't bother with it. I guess maybe we should keep up once in a while."

"Well Carl got pretty upset when he heard about her over there slandering us over here," said Sally. "He's tired of this whole mess too. He figures the north will take over as soon as we get completely out of there. And then all those boys got killed or crippled for nothing."

"Robbie figures the same thing," said Brandy. "I know he thinks the north will take over but he hasn't said anything about all the killed and wounded. Robbie's got a strong mind. I think he'll be all right when it happens."

The boys did well at the creek. Carl had some lures and showed Robbie where and how to catch bass. The caught several nice sized smallmouths before they fished for catfish. They caught several nice sized channel cats and went back home around eleven. The girls were awake and waiting on them when they got home. Carl let Robbie take a shot at filleting. Robbie did well and the fish were cleaned in no time. They all sat around and talked for an hour and then cleaned up and went to bed. After breakfast the next morning, Brandy and Robbie went back to Cincinnati.

Chapter Twenty-Four

Summer and fall flew by. Robbie was doing better at keeping up with the news. The South Vietnamese finally retook Quang Tri and the other cities the North had taken. Nixon had gotten himself reelected by a huge margin but there was something going on called "Watergate." Robbie wasn't quite sure what that was, but it was always on the news. Thanksgiving came and Brandy fixed a fine meal with all the trimmings. Both sets of in-laws came.

As Christmas got closer, Brandy and Robbie were really getting into the Christmas spirit. This would be Mary Lou's first Christmas and they wanted it to be special. This was tough for Robbie because Vietnam was constantly in the news. For some reason, the peace talks between the U.S., the North Vietnamese, and the South Vietnamese weren't going well. Nixon started a huge bombing campaign against the North. For around two weeks, the U.S. just bombed the living hell out of the North. Robbie ignored this as much as he could and they had a very nice Christmas. They would almost need another room in the house for all the toys and things that Mary Lou received. They were invited to a New Year's party but decided to stay home instead.

~~~~

All of that bombing must have done something because some type of agreement was reached and in early 1973, the POW's started coming home. The whole country was glad that their ordeal was finally over. There were still a lot of men who were unaccounted for. After the POW's had been home for a while, the country found out how they had been tortured and mistreated. "Hanoi Jane" came out and said that these men were a bunch of liars. This was a statement she later regretted having made.

Sally gave birth to another fine boy in February. They named him Samuel Thomas Sims. Samuel was Carl's father's name and Thomas was Sally's father's name. Brandy and Robert paid them a visit a few days after the birth.

Business was doing exceptionally well. It was doing so well that they decided to get another crematory. This one would be in Cincinnati. When they finally had it in operation two months later, it got a lot of use. One Saturday morning in June, they were enjoying each other's company when the phone rang. It was Brandy's mother. WW had had a severe stroke and was not expected to live. Robbie got ahold of the employees in Cincinnati and told them that they might be gone for several days. Brandy and Robbie loaded up enough clothes and for several days and then left for Toledo.

WW died before they got there. When they did arrive in Toledo, Brandy's mother was a total wreck. Brandy's sisters were upset too but did a good job of concealing it. WW had let it be known that he wanted cremated. After the cremation, he just wanted a small memorial service at the funeral home. The body was transported to the crematory in Columbus. Two days later, they had the memorial service. Brandy's mother was still a wreck and she showed no signs of getting better.

As WW had told everyone a few years before, he left the funeral business to Brandy. To the sisters, he left money. Brandy thought that the sisters might be jealous and raise hell but they didn't. They had always said that they wanted nothing to do with the funeral business and they meant it. Their husbands were on the fast track to becoming wealthy men.

Brandy did a good job hiding her feelings too. She only cried one time at the memorial service. They stayed with Brandy's mother for another two days, but she made it clear that she did not want them there. The sisters had volunteered to stay with her also, but she had told them the same thing.

Brandy had a meeting with the employees at the funeral home. They were all intending to stay. WW had a good crew and pretty much let them run the show anyway. The only thing different now would be that Brandy was the owner.

Brandy had been pretty sure that she was pregnant again so when they got back home, she made an appointment and had it confirmed. They were both very happy. They went right to work thinking of names. Then they decided they had plenty of time for that.

Brandy made a trip to Toledo once a week to see how her mother was doing. The first two weeks, Brandy was worried that her mother would need professional help. She was very withdrawn and becoming incoherent. The third week she seemed to snap out of it and was acting totally normal. Brandy was confident that her mother would be all right. Brandy was about to make the trip to Toledo on the fourth week when the phone rang as she was almost to the door. It was her younger sister. Their mother had just died. A severe heart attack was suspected but they wouldn't know for sure until the body was examined. Brandy was the oldest and the sisters were looking to her for guidance on what to do. Brandy told them that she did not feel it was necessary for an autopsy. Their mother was dead. What she died from was not important. Anyone who knew her would say that she died from grief.

Brandy and Robbie made the trip to Toledo. Brandy's mother was to be cremated and a small memorial service was to be held. Brandy took care of everything. Brandy's mother had a will and the three sister's read it after the memorial service. It was their mother's wish that everything would be sold and the money divided equally among the three girls. Brandy was sure that her sisters would be upset by this since WW had given her his business. There were some very harsh words exchanged, but the sisters finally agreed to go along with their mother's wishes. The three of them decided that they each could take whatever they wanted from the house and property before it went on the market. There was nothing that Brandy wanted so she let her sisters have anything they wanted.

The house on Kelley's Island sold within a week of being listed. The next week there were several offers on the house. It took another two weeks, but everything got settled. Brandy had hired a good lawyer and made sure everything was done properly. When the girls got their share of the money, Brandy was sure that she might not see her sisters ever again.

~~~~

Mary Lou was fifteen months old now and got into everything. She was beginning to talk some too. Robbie truly enjoyed playing with her. It didn't matter what they did. He loved it. Brandy loved watching them play. He and Brandy were still trading off days at work and making a trip to Columbus once a week. They thought about a weekly trip to Toledo, but decided against it. Their manager would call if something needed their attention.

All that was on the news most of the time was "Watergate." Robbie was so sick of hearing about it. In November, Nixon gave a speech and stated, "I am not a crook." By this time, the whole world figured he was guilty of something. Thanksgiving and Christmas came and went and the new year started. In February, Brandy and Robbie were blessed with a beautiful, healthy baby girl. They named her Louise Ellen Parker. Mary Lou seemed a little jealous of all the attention given to the new addition, but she got over it quickly. Sally announced that she was pregnant again when she and Carl came up for a visit.

Brandy and Robbie couldn't have asked for a better life. Their businesses were doing very well and they had great employees. They could probably stay home and collect their money, but neither of them were like that. They wanted their employees to see them. Showing themselves and giving good encouragement really paid off for them. When Louise was a few months older, they started making a trip to Toledo once a week. Brandy had buried the hatchet with her sisters and they stayed with one of them on their Toledo trips.

It seemed like the "Watergate" hearings would never end. Finally, Nixon resigned in August of 74. The country wasn't surprised, but was still shocked. No President had ever resigned before. Vice President Spiro Agnew had resigned in 73 but most people never knew who he was anyway. Gerald Ford had become President and one of the first things he did was pardon Nixon. Robbie had never heard of Gerald Ford. He figured that since he had never heard of him, maybe he would be a good President. Maybe someone who hasn't been in the spotlight or been in trouble would do a good job. The country would find out.

Fall seemed to go by quickly. Sally had delivered another baby boy in September. They named him James Alex Sims. Brandy and Robbie visited with them for a couple days to help around the house. Carl was a proud father. He never expected to start out with three boys, but he wouldn't trade them for anything.

The holiday season was once again upon them. Brandy had a good cry one day when she was missing her parents. Robbie held her tightly and let her have at it. Mary Lou didn't understand why mommy was crying. She was too young when Gramma and Grampa Wisecup died. She only knew Gramma and Grampa Parker.

They got some sad news right before Thanksgiving. Marie had called and told them that Dave had been ill for a good while. They had discovered that he had some rare form of leukemia. His outlook wasn't good. Robbie was extremely upset by this. "Dave's a big strong man," said Robbie. "Look at his lifestyle. The man was in perfect shape. Just why would he have leukemia?"

"I couldn't tell you," said Brandy. "I've been hearing about Vietnam veterans getting sick a lot and having strange cancers and things. Why would that be?"

"Maybe it was that stuff they sprayed all over the place to defoliate the jungle," said Robbie. "I think they call it Agent Orange. If that stuff could kill a jungle in no time, it sure as hell couldn't be good for a human body."

"Did you get sprayed with that stuff?" asked Brandy.

"No, but I've been where it was used," answered Robbie. "That stuff got used a lot. Let's get over and see Dave and Marie soon. I don't know what we can say that would help anything, but they're our friends."

"I'll call Marie tomorrow and see if she'd like some company," said Brandy. Brandy called Marie the next evening. "Would you mind some company?" Brandy asked Marie.

"I would like that very much," answered Marie. "I could use some help with Dave."

"What can we do to help?" asked Brandy.

"He's talking about killing himself," said Marie. "The doctors keep telling him that there's nothing they can do and he should get his affairs in order. He does not want me to see him die like that. He wants to go out on his own terms. I believe that if we can talk him out of this and he hangs on longer, maybe they will come up with a possible cure or something."

"We will try our best," said Brandy. "Scientists and researchers are always finding out new things. How soon should we come over?"

"Tomorrow evening will be fine," said Marie.

"We'll be there," said Brandy. As soon as Brandy got off the phone, she told Robbie what was going on with Dave. Robbie was extremely upset. He didn't say much the rest of the evening.

Marie greeted them at the door when they arrived the next evening. Marie was holding their two and a half year old daughter Annette. She was beautiful. She had dark hair like her mother and her father's blue eyes. Dave was half asleep on the sofa. He sat up slowly when they came into the living room. He tried to get up and shake Robbie's hand. Robbie told him to stay put and went to him. "So, they tell me you're not doing too well," said Robbie. "And you're thinking about doing yourself in."

Dave, Marie, and Brandy were shocked when those words came out of Robbie's mouth. Brandy was about to scold Robbie for being so blunt when

Marie spoke. "That's just what he needs," said Marie. "Someone who won't beat around the bush and gets right to the point. Go ahead Robbie. You're getting off to a good start."

"Yeh, go ahead old man," said Dave. "Go ahead and give me hell."

"I'm not gonna give you hell Dave," said Robbie. "Now you just look over here." Robbie pointed to Marie and Annette. "See these two beautiful people here. You love them and they love you. They want you around. Now quit listening to this crap about there's no chance for you and such. You've got to hang on no matter how long it takes. Could be that some new cure might be found."

"All this is easy for you to say," said Dave. "You're not the one dying."

"No, it's not easy for me to say," said Robbie. "Now quit that dying shit. Hell, you were a Marine and you made it through hell. If you can do that, you can do anything." Dave began to cry. Marie started crying too. Brandy took Annette from Marie and Marie sat with Dave and on the sofa and they cried together. Brandy cried too. Robbie tried to hold his tears back but had no luck. Annette cried too.

"I love you baby," Dave said to Marie. "I'll hang on for you as long as it takes."

"I love you too," said Marie. "We'll make it through this."

After they all had a good cry, they sat around and talked about earlier days. They did a good job of not talking about the present situation. Dave got very tired and went to bed after a couple of hours. Brandy and Robbie talked with Marie for another half hour before they went home. They assured Marie that they would be there when they were needed.

~~~~

Mary and Robert had invited them to their house for Thanksgiving so they went. They had new beds for the children so they could spend the night too. Mary fixed a tremendous feast and they ate till they couldn't eat anymore. Brandy and Robbie cleaned up and let Mary and Robert play with the kids. Mary Lou couldn't get enough of Grampa. The kids got worn out and went to bed early. Robert and Mary went to bed early too. Brandy and Robbie went to bed too, but they didn't do any sleeping for a good while. Both of them had decided it was time to get started on another baby. This was a good time to start.

Robert had taken Friday off and was up at daylight. He let Mary sleep in and made coffee. Robbie heard the coffee percolating and got up. He let Brandy and the kids sleep. Robert handed him a cup of coffee as he entered the kitchen. "Here you go Son," said Robert. "It's the nectar of the Gods."

"I don't know about that but you make good coffee Dad," said Robbie as he took a sip.

"Yep, your mother taught me," said Robert. "So how are you all doing? Is everything going good for you?"

"Dad, you wouldn't believe how well things are going," said Robbie. "We've got such good people working for us that we could set home all the time if we wanted. They know what to do and they do it. It's amazing."

"I'm happy for you Son," said Robert. "Most folks struggle to get by or hate their jobs. So business must be dead, right?"

"Yeh dad, and it gets deader all the time," said Robbie. "So how's work for you and how's your blood pressure doing?"

"Work is just work," said Robert. "I do it cause we gotta eat. I don't hate it, but I don't like it either. My blood pressure is better. We try to eat better and your mother and I do a lot of walking. I never knew we had so many new neighbors."

"Well that's good Dad," said Robbie. "You and Mom should take a nice trip sometime. You know. Someplace romantic or something. I recommend Tybee Island, Georgia. We've been there twice and we just love it. You will too. It's small and it's not full of high rise hotels. Go in the late spring or early fall. That's an off season."

"We've been talking about going somewhere," said Robert. "Your mother has mentioned the Caribbean."

"That sounds good," said Robbie. "I'd just make sure I didn't go during hurricane season." Mary came into the kitchen now.

"I see you men have your coffee," said Mary. "Do you want me to start some breakfast?"

"No mom. Sit down. Have some coffee and tell us about your trip to the Caribbean." said Robbie.

"Oh, so you've been blabbing," said Mary to Robert. "I was thinking about the U.S. Virgin Islands. You don't need a passport to go there. They have several all inclusive places and it looks beautiful there. I think we'd have a good time."

"I'd have a good time anywhere with you woman," said Robert. Brandy came into the kitchen now with the kids. Mary Lou jumped up on Robert's lap. Mary took Louise.

"So you all continue your conversation while I rustle up some breakfast," said Brandy. "Everybody's getting scrambled eggs and bacon. So when is this Caribbean trip?"

"It'll be some time soon," said Mary. "I'll be talking to a travel agent next week."

"I'm sure you'll love it down there," said Brandy. "If you ever do decide to try Tybee, just let me know and I'll get a hold of the owners of the house where we stayed."

They ate their breakfast and Mary packed them a bunch of leftovers to take with them. "We'll never be able to eat all of this stuff," said Mary. "I'll still be freezing some of this even after what I send with you. I guess a 22 pound turkey was plenty." There was a lot of hugs and kisses and Brandy and Robbie and the kids left for Cincinnati.

Brandy and Robbie got busy with their Christmas shopping the next week. They decided not to make any trips to Toledo or Columbus until after Christmas unless something came up. Robbie and Brandy were very generous. They gave all of their employees a nice Christmas bonus. They had been calling Marie once a week to see how Dave was doing. She said he was doing all right and had not talked anymore about suicide. A week before Christmas, they put up their Christmas tree. Of course the kids helped decorate it. Everything was going well and they were all in the Christmas spirit. It was Christmas Eve and Robbie was reading "The Night Before Christmas" when the phone rang. It was Marie. Brandy answered the phone. Marie was crying and struggling to get out her words. She finally got them out. Dave had just died. He was feeling really terrible and Marie had taken him to the hospital. He died a few minutes after they arrived at the hospital. Would Brandy and Robbie take care of the arrangements for him? Dave said before he died that he wanted a viewing and a short service at the funeral home. The American Legion would supply a color guard. The Police might have one too. Dave was very well liked on the force and he had lot of veteran friends.

Christmas at the Parker house wasn't as enthusiastic as was expected , but Robbie did his best. He played with the kids and their new toys almost all day. Brandy made a fine meal and they even had a nice wine with the meal.

Dave's funeral was huge. Besides all of his family and friends, a huge portion of the Police and Fire Department was there. Several people had fine words about Dave at the service. Marie did well and was able to control her tears. Brandy and Robbie and a lot of the other people could not. When the funeral was over,

Brandy asked Marie if she would like it if she stayed with her or would she want to stay with her and Robbie. She thanked Brandy and told her that Dave's parents would be staying with her for awhile. Brandy told her that she would call her soon and see how she was doing.

Robbie took Dave's death really hard. He wanted reasons why a young, strong, and active man should die from some rare cancer. In the days after Christmas and after New Years, Robbie visited the VA in Cincinnati and talked to several men who were in waiting rooms for doctor appointments. Some of them had some type of skin disorder. Everyone one of them had handled Agent Orange or had been exposed to it. One of the men had Parkinson's disease. He was only 26 years old. Another man said he kept having chest pain and they couldn't figure out why.

When they resumed trips to Columbus after New Years, Robbie visited the VA hospital in Columbus. Several of the men had the same ailments as the men at Cincinnati. When Robbie got back home, he found out who his U.S. Congressman was and wrote him a letter. He introduced himself and asked the Congressman if he could find out if there had been any research on Agent Orange and how it could affect people. Robbie was surprised. He got a letter back in less than two weeks. The Congressman did not know of any research but he would do his best to find out. Then he thanked Robbie for his letter.

A month went by and there was nothing from the Congressman. After the fifth week, a letter arrived. The Congressman had not found anything but was still investigating. "At least he used the word "investigating," Robbie said to himself.

~~~~

Before January was over, Brandy announced that she was pregnant again. They got a baby sitter and went out for a nice dinner to celebrate. They did some more celebrating that night at home. Winter wasn't bad that year but it had some very cold days. Robbie was getting pretty good at guessing the temperature. His leg hurt a lot more when it was very cold. Spring finally came. Robbie got tickets for opening day for the Reds. Marie watched the kids for them. Marie had been doing well and volunteered. Having three kids around would keep her mind off other things.

After the POW's came home, Robbie had gotten away from keeping up with the news again. Brandy and the kids were out in the back yard one nice spring evening so Robbie decided to catch the news. He was in shock when he watched the news. The North Vietnamese had captured Saigon. The U.S. Embassy had been evacuated. Robbie sat there crying as he watched news clips of the helicopters taking people out. Mary Lou walked into the living room and saw him. She yelled out, "mommy, mommy, daddy's crying, daddy's crying." Brandy heard her and came running into the living room.

"What is it Robbie?" she asked. "What's wrong?"

"That damn war's finally over," said Robbie. "The North captured Saigon and they've evacuated the U.S. Embassy." Brandy held Louise and sat down with Robbie and watched the news clips. She cried a few tears too.

"So do you think the U.S. will do anything now?" asked Brandy.

"No, the country's had enough of that place," said Robbie. "It's over. Now everybody can sit down and point fingers at each other and say, "that was all your fault," or "we should have done it this way," or "why didn't we do that?" A lot of us poor dumb slobs who went over there will wonder for the rest of our lives why the hell we went over there in the first place. Then we'll cry about all of our friends who got killed or crippled." Robbie looked at Brandy and smiled. "Don't worry beautiful. I'll be all right," he said.

The next weekend, they went down to visit Carl. Little Carl was four years old now and was already interested in baseball. The men played some catch with him and let him hit a few balls. He had a plastic ball and bat. Then the men got out the real stuff and played catch. They had been throwing for awhile before either of them spoke. Carl spoke first. "So what do you think of this designated hitter stuff?" asked Carl.

"What are you talking about?" asked Robbie. "What's a designated hitter?"

"Man, you're not keeping up with stuff are you," said Carl. "A designated hitter bats for the pitcher."

"Well why would someone hit for the pitcher?" asked Robbie.

"Cause the pitcher doesn't hit for himself," answered Carl. "Man, where have you been? They started doing that in the American League last year or the year before. They got all these high paid free agent pitchers now and they don't want them to get hurt batting or running the bases. Most of them can't hit anyway."

"That's a bunch of shit," said Robbie. "The pitcher hitting is part of the game. What do they do in the World Series?"

"Well when they play at the National League park, they don't use a designated hitter," answered Carl. "When they play at the American League park, they use the designated hitter."

"I watch a Reds game once in a while," said Robbie. "I guess I don't watch any American League games. I won't now anyway. That's just plain wrong. They're ruining the game. Most big league pitchers were probably stars at hitting and pitching before they came up to the show. Man, that pisses me off."

"Well talking about keeping up with stuff, you know Saigon fell don't you?" asked Carl.

"Yeh, I know that," answered Robbie. "I imagine that'll keep my head spinning for a good while. Hey, I never told you that Dave Simpson died. He had some rare form of leukemia."

"That's tough," said Carl. "They had that little girl too."

"Marie is doing all right," said Robbie. "I was trying to see if there was any research on that shit they sprayed to kill the jungle. I figure if it can kill a jungle, it can't be good for people."

"They'll probably get that figured out after. we'll all dead and gone," said Carl. "They used asbestos for years before they found out it was bad for you."

"Well I wrote my congressman," said Robbie. "He says he's investigating."

"Don't hold your breath waiting for an answer," said Carl.

"I won't," said Robbie. "So how is it having three little boys around all the time? I bet they're a handful."

"They are, but they're good boys," said Carl. "They mind us and they behave when we go somewhere. How's the girls?"

"They're good too," said Robbie. "I bet this next baby will be a girl too. Don't matter, as long as it's healthy."

The men spent the rest of the day drinking beer and telling war stories. There was plenty of beds and room in Carl's house so they spent the night. After breakfast, Robbie, Brandy, and the girls went back to Cincinnati.

Robbie got a surprise when they got home. There was a letter from his congressman waiting for him. Robbie sat down on the sofa and opened it. There were a lot of big words and such, but the letter did have a point. In 1970, some research was done on one of the defoliants used in Vietnam. It was discovered that it caused cancer in laboratory animals so it's use was discontinued. Other defoliants were used after this but they were discontinued in 1971. Robbie was glad that he received the letter. "Vietnam was the laboratory and we were the rats," Robbie said to himself.

Chapter Twenty-Five

Robbie made up his mind that he was going to find out if Agent Orange could be connected to certain cancers or diseases in the troops who served in Vietnam. He wasn't sure where to start. He had already talked with several men at the VA's in Cincinnati and Columbus. Some of them were experiencing some problems. Robbie decided that he would start making a list of the veterans. It would have their name and where they now lived. Then it would have their branch of service, the dates they were in country, where they were in country, their MOS(Military Occupational Skill) and what they actually did in country, if they were a smoker or nonsmoker, and if they had any health issues, did anyone one in their family have the same health issues? He would also get their phone numbers if they would give them.

Robbie went back to the VAs and talked to men whenever he had the chance. Some of the men were hesitant to talk with him when he told them he was keeping a list. When they finally understood what he was trying to do, most of them were glad to talk with him. The list kept getting larger and larger. Robbie was surprised to find out that several of them had cancers. Some of them had names that Robbie couldn't spell or pronounce, but lung and throat cancer was very prevalent among the men. Some of them were nonsmokers too. These men were in their mid twenties. Why should they have these cancers?

Robbie also visited the VFW's and the American Legion Posts in Cincinnati. He was surprised that their membership did not include very many Vietnam veterans. Robbie spent a lot of time talking with WW2 and Korean veterans. There were also a few WW1 veterans. Robbie always had a hard time staying sober when he visited the posts. The old timers were always wanting to buy him drinks. They were always saying that they needed the Vietnam vets because the old farts were dying out. Robbie had always told them his name but had never told them what he did for a living. He was sitting at a table with a couple of old timers one evening. The old timers were discussing George Patton. One of them thought he was the greatest general ever. The other one didn't care for Patton at all. They had just exchanged some arguments when one of them looked at Robbie and asked. "Are you related to them people who run that Wisecup Parker Funeral Home?"

"I am," answered Robbie. "I'm Parker and Wisecup is my wife."

"Son of a bitch, I've been needing to talk with you people but I never got up the nerve," said the man. "Wife's been bugging me for some time to buy some plan or something so it's already paid for when the time comes. My name's Fred Jackson."

"Well you know my name is Parker," said Robbie. "My full name is Robert W. Parker. The W doesn't stand for anything and everyone calls me Robbie. Robbie shook Fred's hand. "And you are?" Robbie said to the other man.

"I'm Tom Blankenship," the man said as he shook Robbie's hand. "So how in the hell did you get into the funeral business?"

"I decided I wanted to do something that there would always be a demand for, no matter what," said Robbie. "People are always gonna die, no if's, ands. or buts. Someone's gotta take care of the bodies."

"That true," said Fred. "Don't handling dead folks bother you?"

"I filled enough body bags overseas," said Robbie. "Of course death bothers me, but I accept it."

"Did you go to school for this?" asked Tom.

"Yes I did," answered Robbie. "I went to the Cincinnati College of Mortuary Science."

"So when should I talk to you folks about a plan?" asked Fred.

"You just call the number in the phone book anytime and we'll set up an appointment," said Robbie. We'll go over everything with you. I'm sure you'll be glad you got it done."

"Will I be talking to you or your wife?" asked Fred.

"Either one of us or both of us," said Robbie. "My wife went to the same school I did."

"All right, I'll be calling maybe tomorrow," said Fred. "Now don't get upset with my wife. She can be a tight assed bitch when it comes to money. She'll want to go cheap if she can."

"That's not a problem," said Robbie. "You're the customer. We'll do what you want. Now you might want to think about this too. We have a crematory. Cremation is a lot cheaper than a regular funeral."

"I never thought about that," said Fred. "I guess I'll be dead. Getting burned shouldn't hurt."

"No, it won't hurt," said Robbie.

"You better check into this too Tom," said Fred. "That bitch of yours just might kill you one day."

"Hey now, watch that," said Tom. "No one calls her a bitch but me. She wouldn't kill me herself anyway. She'd hire it done." Robbie had another beer with the two men and then went home.

The next day, Fred called the funeral home and made an appointment. Fred and Tom must have put out the word about Robbie and there were several calls to the funeral home. Appointments were made and plans were sold.

Robbie continued his visits to the VA in Cincinnati and Columbus. He also visited the VA in Toledo. His list kept growing. He was at the VA in Cincinnati talking with some veterans when one of them said that he should talk with this guy named Bob Alverez. Bob was a Vietnam veteran and been the head of the local "Vietnam Veterans Against the War." The man told Robbie that Bob knew a lot of veterans and would probably be glad to give Robbie their names. He didn't know Bob's phone number, but he was sure it would be in the phone book.

It took Robbie a couple of days to track down Bob Alverez. Robbie explained what he was trying to do and Bob agreed to meet with him. They would meet at a small diner that both of them knew. When Robbie walked into the diner, there were a couple of people sitting at the counter and a lone man sitting in a booth at the far of end of the place. He had very long brown hair and wore a fatigue shirt that had peace signs all over it. His hair looked like it hadn't been washed for a good while. He also had a short scraggly beard and mustache. Robbie walked over to him and stretched out his hand. "I'm Robbie Parker and you're Bob Alverez I assume," said Robbie.

Bob reluctantly shook Robbie's hand. "Yep, I'm Bob," he said. "Have a seat. I bet you were a jarhead weren't you. You still look like one."

"Yes, I was a Marine," said Robbie. "Just what were you?"

"I was in the Air Force," said Bob. "I was a mechanic. I worked on planes."

"Where were you stationed over there?" asked Robbie.

"I was at Da Nang," answered Bob. "I suppose you were a grunt and was out humping in all that shit."

"I was," said Robbie. "You got something against grunts?"

"No I don't," said Bob. "Sometimes I think they got something against me cause I was in the rear with the gear."

"I got nothing against any man who went over there," said Robbie. "Neither one of us got drafted and we did what we were ordered to do. The guys in the field couldn't get by without the guys in the rear doing their jobs."

"Does it bother you that I protested against the war?" asked Bob.

"No, that was your right," said Robbie. "As long as you didn't hurt anyone or damage property I have no problem with you."

"We'll get along fine," said Bob. "So explain to me what it is you're trying to do."

"I'm trying to find out if Agent Orange could be the cause of some of the health issues Vietnam veterans are having," said Robbie. "I'm keeping a list of veterans and where they were in country and if they have issues or not. I have a long list now and there are a lot of men with problems. I intend to keep in touch with them over time and see if anything has changed."

"So what will you do with your list?" asked Bob.

"When I think the time is right, I'll send it to my Congressman or whoever I think might take a good look at it and see that these men have two things in common," said Robbie. "They were all in Vietnam and they were all exposed to Agent Orange. So maybe, just maybe, Agent Orange could be the cause of their problems."

"Go for it man," said Bob. "Tell you what I can do. I'll sit down and get you a list of all the veterans I know. I'll try to have their phone numbers for you too. Have you been to the VA at all?"

"I go out there all the time," answered Robbie.

"Well I heard they're starting this group thing for Vietnam vets who are having problems," said Bob. "I don't mean health issues. I mean they are having trouble adjusting back to civilian life and can't get past their war experiences. You should go to that thing."

"Well I have a nightmare once in a while, but I have no big problems that I know of," said Robbie. "Maybe I will go. I can get some more vets for my list while I'm there."

"I'll have you that list in a couple of days," said Bob. "Give me your address and I'll send it to you. I want you to get ahold of me in a few months and let me know how you're doing."

"I will," said Robbie. Robbie wrote down his address. They shook hands again and they both left the diner. Robbie went home and called the VA and asked about the Vietnam veteran group meeting that was coming up. It would be meeting next Tuesday evening at 7 PM and he would be welcome to attend. A counselor would be there and would be in charge of the group. Robbie told Brandy about the group and that he was planning to attend.

"Are you sure you want to go to that meeting?" asked Brandy. "If a bunch of guys sit around and talk about all their bad experiences over there it might get to thinking about yours more often. Do you want that?"

"I'll be all right," said Robbie. "I'll be all right."

Tuesday came and Robbie went to the meeting. The counselor's name was Bart Kline and he had his PhD in Psychology. He told everyone not to be afraid of his title. There were twenty men and one woman in the group. The counselor asked them all to tell everyone their names and what branch of the service they had been in. Robbie was the only Marine. The woman had been a Navy nurse and another man had been in the Navy and had been on a river patrol boat. The rest of the men had all been in the Army. One of them had been with the artillery and the rest were grunts. Bart told them that they could talk about anything they wanted, no matter how trivial it might seem. They were there to talk about their problems and if it was a problem for them, it was not trivial. He asked if anyone would like to start. No one volunteered so Bart picked a man and asked him to start. The man slumped down in his chair and almost cried. After a few minutes, he started. His name was Ed Jackson.

"My company was out on this operation," he started. "We had been out for a couple of weeks and taken several casualties. We had also killed several VC. We had no contact for a day or so after this when we came up on this vill. As we got closer, we took some fire for a minute or two then it got quiet. We did a sweep of the vill. We found no weapons or VC, but we knew this was a VC controlled vill because there were no young men. It was mostly real old men and women and kids. There were a few women with babies. We discovered a huge supply of rice hidden under some of the hootches. We destroyed the rice. We set up a perimeter while our interpreter was talking with some of the people. Our CO and the Platoon Commanders were in the center of the vill with the interpreter. Out of nowhere, I saw this little girl with something in her hand running towards them. She couldn't have been more than ten or twelve. I was armed with a shotgun. She was about fifteen feet from me and I could tell that she was about to throw a hand grenade. I fired just as her arm went back to throw. The blast caught her in the face and threw her down. Somehow she landed on the grenade. When it went off, it tore her completely in two. I had hit the deck. The top half of her body came down and landed on me. I had blood and guts all over me. I didn't move for a little while. Someone came over and pulled the body off of me. I got up on my knees and took a look. There was this faceless partial body with guts hanging out beside me and it was some little girl. I flipped out. My Platoon Sergeant finally punched me out to shut me up. I was out of the bush on the next chopper. They kept me at the rear for a couple of weeks before I went back to the bush. I never had any problems after that. I finished my tour and came home. I didn't have any problems for a good while, but now all I see is that little girl's face being blown off and her body and guts all over me. I can't sleep at night. I can't hardly concentrate at work. I tried drinking, but that didn't help. She's there whether I'm drunk or sober."

"That was a bad experience Ed," said Bart. "We're all glad that you survived the war. Did you ever think who might have gotten killed if you hadn't shot that girl?"

"I do all the time," answered Ed. "Probably would have gotten the CO and all the Platoon Commanders and the interpreter. I know I saved them, but I still can't get that girl out of my mind."

"Would you feel the same way if it had been a man about to toss a grenade?" asked Bart.

"I doubt it," said Ed. "I would have probably laughed it off."

"Well try not to think of that little girl as a little girl," said Bart. "Try to think of her as someone who wanted you dead." Ed was crying now.

"I can try," cried Ed. "I will try. I can't live like this."

"We'll help you all we can, won't we group?" said Bart.

"Sure we will," some of the group replied.

The next person to speak was the Navy nurse. She kind of stared at Robbie a couple of times but Robbie wouldn't make eye contact with her. She had been a surgical nurse and spent her tour working on ripped up men. After the war, she resigned her commission and took a job at a local hospital. Things were going well until one day there was a severe car accident involving several cars. A lot of badly hurt people were brought to the hospital. As she helped with the surgeries, old memories started coming back. They wouldn't go away. After a year, she quit nursing and got an accounting degree. She now works for a big firm in town. She still has trouble with nightmares and memories. She won't get married because she's afraid that one day her husband might have to go off to war.

The next person to speak was the man who was with artillery in the Army. His name was Brian. He told how his firebase was being overrun and they loaded beehive rounds and fired them into the VC. Bodies were everywhere and ripped to pieces. Two of his best friends were killed when a mortar round landed in their parapet during a fire mission. The explosion started a fire and the ammo bunker that kept the rounds and powder went off. He was thrown through the air and a bunch of men were just disintegrated. No distinguishable body parts could be found.

No one else wanted to speak. Bart practically begged them but no one would speak. Finally Robbie spoke. "I spent a lot of time in the bush and have seen a lot of death," started Robbie. "I've killed a lot and I've been shot up some. Got the holes in me to prove it. All that death helped me choose my vocation."

"What is it that you do?" asked Bart.

"I'm a mortician," answered Robbie.

"You're shitting me." said Ed.

"No, that's what I do," said Robbie. "Someone's gotta do it and I can handle it."

"So you're immune to death?" asked Bart.

"No, I just accept it," answered Robbie. "I don't like it but I accept it. I lost a lot of friends over there and have lost some since they've come back. One of my friends killed himself and another died of a rare cancer. The cancer is one of the reasons I came here tonight."

"So tell us why you came." said Bart.

"I believe that there's a link between Agent Orange and some of the health issues that a lot of Vietnam veterans are experiencing," said Robbie. "I believe that if that stuff can kill a jungle, it can't be good for human beings."

"So what have you been doing?" asked Bart.

"I've just been keeping a list of veterans and where and what they did over there and if they have any health issues," said Robbie. "Did they smoke or not and does anyone else in their family have the same health issues. I have maybe two hundred names now and I'd say ten percent of them are having a health issue that seems unexplained. There's a lot of skin disorders and cancers. I want more research done to see if Agent Orange might cause these problems."

"Well good luck with that," said Bart. "You might be on to something. Anytime you spray something to kills weeds around the house, it tells you not to get it on your skin and what to do if it does. Agent Orange was a hell of a lot stronger than household weed killer. I think all of you should give your names to our Marine here. He might do you some good someday."

No one else spoke so Bart told them that would be it till next month. They could call the VA and find the date and time when it was set up. Everyone gave Robbie all the information he wanted. The Navy nurse went last. She introduced herself to Robbie. "I'm Sheila Roberts," she began. "I helped operate on you in DaNang. Your Captain said he would tear off the doctor's arms and beat him to death with them if he didn't work on you. I see you recovered well."

"So that was you," said Robbie. "Thank you. I know they didn't expect me to live."

"I also knew Helen Carter," Sheila said. "She was there till her tour ended and she went to Pearl Harbor. She wrote me a letter and told me about this Marine she had met. His name was Robbie."

"That was me," said Robbie. "We met when I was in the hospital for other wounds. We got to be good friends. We fell in love. After I healed up at Pearl Harbor, I got a Medical Discharge. I spent some time with her before I went home. I intended to see her again. She didn't write for a while. One day I got a letter from her father. She found out she had bone cancer. It was too far advanced. She went out surfing one day and didn't come back. They found her body later."

"That's terrible," said Sheila. "I always liked her. So how are you doing?"

"I'm fine," answered Robbie. "I have a beautiful wife and two gorgeous daughters. My wife is pregnant again."

"I'm happy for you," said Sheila. "Maybe someday I'll have all that."

"You will," said Robbie. "Someday the right fella will come along and your fears will go away."

"Will we see you next meeting?" asked Sheila.

"I'll be here," said Robbie. "I'll see you then." Robbie gave her a hug and they left.

When Robbie got home, the girls were already in bed. Brandy was sitting on the sofa waiting for him. Robbie went to her and sat down beside her. He began kissing her passionately. The next thing Brandy knew, they were in the shower making love. After the shower, the dried each other off. "So how was your meeting?" asked Brandy. "Did something happen to make you horny?"

"Your sheer beauty does that my darling," said Robbie.

"Thank you for the compliment my dear," said Brandy. "I needed it. I'm feeling ugly and fat again."

"You've never been ugly and fat in your life woman," said Robbie. "You've always been beautiful. You even have a glow about you in your ninth month."

"Talk like that needs rewarded," said Brandy. They made it to the bed and made love again. When they were finished, Brandy asked Robbie one more time about his meeting.

"It was all right," started Robbie. "Some of those people have some real problems. You'll never guess who I met at the meeting."

"How would I know?" asked Brandy. "Tell me."

"Well one of the people at the meeting had been a Navy nurse," said Robbie. "She recognized me. She helped operate on me the last time I got shot up."

"That's amazing," said Brandy. "How is she doing now?"

"She quit being a nurse," said Robbie. "It was bringing back too many memories. She works for an accounting firm now. She won't get married because she thinks her husband will go off to war."

"That's sad," said Brandy. "Maybe if she keeps going to the meetings and talks about her trouble, things will get better."

"I think so too," said Robbie. "So how were you and the girls this evening?"

"Mary Lou wanted to play with you something awful," said Brandy. "She tried to stay awake for you but didn't. Louise was a good girl. Your new daughter has been kicking a lot."

"Are you sure it's a girl?" asked Robbie.

"Yes I am," said Brandy. "There's no doubt. And before I forget, Carl called. Sally's pregnant again. They'd like us to come down next weekend."

"Are you up to it?" asked Robbie. "I know it's not far but I don't want you to be uncomfortable."

"I'll be all right," said Brandy. "I know where all the places to pee are if I gotta go. Besides, the girls just love playing with those boys."

~~~~

They made the trip to Carl's the next weekend. They had a good visit. Robbie told Carl what he was trying to do about Agent Orange. Carl thought it was a great idea. Carl knew a lot of Vietnam vets in the area and would help Robbie by getting their information from them if they would give it. Carl and Robbie slipped away and did a little fishing. The creek was up a little and they weren't doing any good so they didn't stay very long. When they got back, the kids were playing and Sally and Brandy were sitting on the porch drinking iced tea and talking about all of their aches and pains during pregnancy. Carl surprised everyone. He fixed dinner that evening. It was just meatloaf with mashed potatoes, gravy, and green beans, but it was good. Even the kids wolfed it down. Robbie did the dishes after dinner. There was a Walt Disney movie on that evening. It was "Old Yeller." They had some popcorn and watched the movie. There wasn't a dry eye in the house when Old Yeller got killed. The kids cheered up when there was a new puppy at the end. They spent the night and left the next morning after breakfast.

"I'll get you that list," said Carl as they were leaving. "I'll have it all written down and mail it to you."

~~~~

The next meeting at the VA got scheduled and Robbie attended. There were some new faces, but a couple of the other ones didn't show. The Navy man who had been on river patrol boats and another one of the army grunts didn't show. Sheila and Ed were both there. The artilleryman wasn't there when they started, but he came shortly after they started. He apparently was drunk. When he spoke, his words were slurred. Bart asked him right off if he'd been drinking. "What the hell is it to you?" he answered. "You're not my mother."

"No, I'm not your mother," said Bart. "But if I was your mother, I'd tell you to get your head out of your ass and straighten up." Everyone was surprised when Bart said that. Bart looked at all the surprised faces. "Come on people, you know the answers to your problems are not at the bottom of a bottle," said Bart. "They're still there when the booze wears off." Brian looked like he was about to puke. Robbie got up and helped him to the nearest restroom. Brian puked his guts out. They were lucky to get to the toilet in time. After all the puke came out, Brian had some dry heaves. Robbie didn't stand too close to Brian, but he could see that there was some blood in Brian's puke. Brian was finally able to stand. He looked at Robbie.

"Get away from me man," said Brian. "I don't need nobody who handles stiffs helping me."

"Fine, I'll leave you alone in all your glory," said Robbie. "By the way, you were puking up some blood. You might want to have that checked out."

"I been drinking whiskey all day man," said Brain. "Sometimes that happens when I drink all day."

"Well keep it up and maybe you'll be a customer before too long," said Robbie.

"Get the fuck away from me man," said Brain. "Just get the fuck away."

"All right," said Robbie. "I hope the rest of your evening is pleasant." Robbie left and went back to the group.

"How's our boy?" asked Bart.

"Oh, he puked his guts out," said Robbie. "He puked up some blood too. He says that happens when he drinks whiskey all day long."

"I guess he has the right to kill himself if he wants to," said Bart. "Is he coming back?"

"I couldn't tell you," answered Robbie. "He told me to get away from him and not politely either. He said he didn't want anyone who handles stiffs being around him."

Brian must have slipped out another door because he wasn't seen again by anyone at the meeting. The meeting went well this time. All of the new people had gory stories to tell about their experiences. A guy named Sid was there from the last meeting and talked about doing a lot of drugs over there and how he thought the drugs helped him cope with his situation. He said that his whole platoon was high when they charged up some hill. Not one of their platoon was hit, but the other platoons in the company took a lot of casualties. "That was just plain dumb luck," Robbie told him. "That pot or whatever you were on didn't protect you. Maybe it made you feel like you didn't care, but it didn't protect you."

"Maybe not caring is protection," said Sid. "Didn't you smoke that shit over there?"

"No I didn't," answered Robbie. "I wanted to know what was going on around me at all times."

"Did others in you unit smoke that shit?" asked Sid.

"I figure some did back at the firebase but if they did, they didn't do it around me," answered Robbie. "I know no one did that shit out in the bush. Not in my platoon they didn't. We did have some new guys get killed back at the base. Four of them were smoking pot when an 82 round landed in the middle of them. The one that didn't get killed got part of his left arm blown off. They had just got in country. Someone had to send a nice letter to their mammas and lie some about how they died."

"You musta been one a them gung ho fuckers," said Sid. "You mighta got fragged if you was in our unit."

Bart could tell that Robbie was really getting pissed. "Sid I suggest you change the tone of your voice and speak to Robbie properly before he gets up and hurts you," said Bart. "I did some research on some of you. For instance, Sid, I found out that you were a slacker and just barely got an honorable discharge. Whenever you weren't in the bush, you were always on company punishment. They would have gotten rid of you but they needed bodies and you had a pulse. Just why are you here? We don't smoke pot at these meetings."

"Hey man, I seen some bad shit. It bothers me," said Sid. "So did you look up Mr. gung ho?"

"Yes I did," said Bart. "Robbie, would you mind if I told everyone your record?"

"If it'll shut up this worm, go ahead," said Robbie. Sid shook his head.

"Well people, Robbie is a thrice decorated man," said Bart. "He has two Bronze Stars and a Silver Star. He also has three Purple Hearts. He was given a Medical Discharge because of his wounds."

"I knew he was some gung ho fuck," said Sid. Just as Sid had finished his words, he was laying on the floor. Robbie had charged over and hit him on his right jaw. He hit the floor hard. Robbie went back and sat down. When Sid could get up, he did and walked out.

"I'm sorry folks," said Robbie. "That was not a proper thing for me to do."

"Hey, the son of a bitch deserved it," said Ed. "If you hadn't cold cocked him, I would have. I knew guys like him over there. You never knew if they'd be there when you needed them. We had a few guys who smoked that stuff but most of us were too scared. I smoked it some when I got back. I'm glad I didn't do it over there. I'd be dead for sure."

The rest of the meeting went well. After it was over, Ed asked Robbie, Sheila, and another man if they wanted to go have a beer or two. The other man's name was Charlie. They all went to a small neighborhood bar that was close to the VA. There was only one person at the bar when they entered the place. They found a table. Robbie went to the bar and got them all a beer. All of them were very curious about Robbie's profession and just bombarded him with questions. He was glad to answer them. Then he had them all tell about what they were doing with their lives. They all knew Sheila's story so Charlie spoke. He had jumped from one factory job to another. He couldn't seem to get along with any of his supervisors. He was always questioning them and they didn't like it. "Well Charlie, maybe you should try to make it sound like you're not questioning your supervisor," said Robbie. "Convince him that you're interested in helping the company in any way you can and you have ideas that could be helpful. Be nice about it. He'll listen if you're nice."

"I guess I could give that a try," said Charlie. "Maybe one day I'll be the supervisor."

"Keep that attitude," said Robbie. "Now tell us about you Ed. What are you doing with yourself?"

"I work for the B&O Railroad," started Ed. "I run a switching engine."

"That sounds interesting," said Sheila. "Trains always interested me. My folks always brought us to town when the old steam engines made runs."

"Well they still have a steam engine that makes a run once in a while for show," said Ed. "They're something to see. I was on the road for a while and run the big trains with all them engines. Some of them trains were over a mile and half long and had six engines."

"How can you control all the engines from one engine?" asked Sheila.

"There's a cable that connects one engine to another," answered Ed. "You can control up to six engines like this."

"I bet it takes a long time to get stopped if you're going 50 mph and you have a train that's well over a mile long," said Sheila.

"It sure does," said Ed. "You have to know exactly what you're doing. You've got to know every bit of the track you're on. Everything comes into play, like if you're going uphill or downhill or on curves. Part of your train can be in dips so your train can be stretching out and coming together at the same time. You've got to control it or you could bust a knuckle or pull out a drawbar. Pull out a drawbar and you'll have a derailment."

"What's a knuckle and drawbar?" asked Sheila.

"I'm sure you've seen trains being coupled together on TV," said Ed. "The knuckles are the moveable parts of the coupler. They are open when the cars are being coupled together. When they come together, a pin drops in the couplers and the knuckle stays shut. The drawbar fastens the coupler to the railcar."

"This is fascinating," said Sheila. "Why is it that you run a switching engine now?"

"I was on the road for a while," started Ed. "I made great money but I was never home to spend it. I lost some girlfriends because I was never home. I had a chance to bid on a yard job and I took it. I like it fine. It's not glamorous like the road but I sleep in my own bed every night and I still make good money."

"I guess I wouldn't like the road that well either," said Sheila. "It probably is glamorous at first, but I'd miss my own bed. So Ed, do you live by yourself now?"

"Yes, I do," answered Ed. "I rent a little house not far from here. It's small, but it's nice and I have a small yard and everything. Got good neighbors too."

"It sounds nice," said Sheila. "Maybe you could show it to me sometime."

"That would be nice," said Ed. Sheila excused herself and went to the ladies room.

"That girl likes you," said Charlie after Sheila was gone.

"She does," added Robbie. "You best ask her out. Nothing fancy, maybe for a cup of coffee or lunch to start."

"Hell, take her down to the switching yard and give her a tour," said Charlie. "That woman likes trains." Sheila came back to the table now. They had finished their beer. Sheila was up so she went to the bar and got them another one.

"What did you boys talk about while I was gone?" asked Sheila.

"Why we talked about you," said Robbie. "We can see that you like Ed and we're convinced he should ask you out." Ed was totally embarrassed.

"So Ed, are you going to ask me out?" asked Sheila.

Ed regained his composure. "Yes I am," said Ed. "I'd like to take you to lunch or dinner in the near future whenever it's convenient for you."

"I'm available every evening after 5 PM and all day every weekend," said Sheila.

"I have an idea," said Ed. "I'll pick you up and give you a tour of the rail yard. Then we can get some dinner. How about I pick you up at 4 PM Saturday?"

Sheila reached into her purse and produced a pen and some paper. She wrote down her address and handed it to Ed. "That will be just fine," said Sheila as she handed her address to Ed. They finished their beer and then they all went their separate ways. Brandy was up waiting on Robbie.

"How was it this evening?" asked Brandy after Robbie had smothered her with kisses.

"Oh, it was all right," started Robbie. "I punched out some slime ball and another guy was sick drunk and puked his guts out. Then me and three of the others went for a couple of beers. And here I am."

"So did the nurse have a beer with you?" asked Brandy.

"Yes she did," answered Robbie. "There was me, Sheila, Ed, and Charlie. Sheila and Ed have a date next Saturday."

"That's nice for them," said Brandy. "Now why did you punch someone out?"

"Well there was this guy who kept talking about doing drugs and such over there," started Robbie. "He kept bugging me about guys in my outfit doing drugs and such. Anyway, he said I was a gung ho fuck so I punched him out. He left after that."

"Were you a gung ho fuck?" asked Brandy. Brandy was nibbling Robbie's ear when she asked him this."

"I am a gung ho fuck when it comes to you woman," said Robbie as he picked her up and carried her to bed.

~~~~

The next week, Robbie received a list of Vietnam veterans from Carl. It had all the information he needed. A few days later, he received a list from Bob Alverez. It was a huge list. It only had their names and phone numbers, so Robbie started making calls. It took him two weeks to get a hold of everyone. When he had all the information needed, he sat down and started figuring percentages. His list had over 600 names on it. Over twelve percent of the men on the list were experiencing some type of unexplained health issue. Robbie did some research and tried to find out how many men served in Vietnam over the years. The numbers were staggering. The highest troop strength during the war was over 500,000. Over the years, men were doing their tours and being rotated out. Men were killed or wounded and were replaced. The total number of men who served in Vietnam was well over 2 million and maybe closer to 3 million. How many of these men had been exposed to Agent Orange? Was it just the grunts and the men on the ground or was anyone who was over there exposed to it?

Robbie made his list as orderly as he could and made several copies of it. Then he sent a copy of it to his Congressman. He included a letter with the list. It was short and simple. It just stated that twelve percent of the people on his list were experiencing health issues. If twelve percent of his 600 person list had issues, surely a lot of other people who served in Vietnam were having issues or might have them later on.

~~~~

At the next meeting of the Vietnam veterans at the VA, Ed and Sheila showed up together. Apparently, they had hit it off and enjoyed each other's company. Sid was there too. His personality was totally different. When he arrived, he went over to Robbie and shook his hand. He apologized for being an asshole at the last meeting. Someone said that Brian was found dead in an alley somewhere. He hadn't been beaten or robbed. They had heard that he died from alcohol poisoning. There was a couple of new faces there too. The meeting went well and Robbie, Charlie, Sheila, and Ed went for a beer at the same bar they had visited last time. Charlie and Robbie could tell that Ed and Sheila were good for each other. They all had a good time and left after a couple of beers. Sheila and Ed left together.

Chapter Twenty-Six

Robbie attended the monthly meetings at the VA and continued keeping his list. Robbie began noticing that he was starting to have more nightmares and wondered if he should continue attending the meetings. He decided that he would keep attending the meetings if the nightmares didn't get any worse. In September, Sara Jean Parker was born. Mary Lou and Louise helped with the new addition as best they could.

Brandy and Robbie had a nice long serious talk about a month after Sara was born. Both of them decided that three children would be enough. Brandy was a little surprised that Robbie was not concerned that he didn't have a son. All Robbie wanted was for all of them to be healthy. Three beautiful girls would do just fine.

Business was still doing extremely well. Robbie went to the office almost every day. When Sara was a little older, he and Brandy started trading off days again. They made a trip to either Columbus or Toledo once a week. Of course they visited Robbie's parents every time they went to Columbus.

Robbie had been driving his 60 Olds all these years and Brandy convinced him that they should get a family type car. She had sold her VW a year or so ago and bought a mid sized Ford. Robbie would not part with the olds. He would keep it forever he said, but he did go out and buy a full sized station wagon.

When Christmas came, they thought that they might have to put a room addition on the house because of all the things the girls received, but Brandy was very efficient. She sorted out old toys and such that the girls didn't play with anymore and gave them to local charities.

Carl's fourth son, Zachary Beaumont Sims, was born in January of 1976. The Parkers went for a visit a week after Sally was released from the hospital. Carl wondered who in the hell was pulling into his driveway when he saw the station wagon and not the olds. They had a good visit. The boys and girls got along great. Little Carl kept telling everyone that he would be starting school in the fall. He was sure he wouldn't like school. It would take away from playing baseball. The next morning after breakfast, the Parkers headed home.

They were on a stretch of four lane highway not far from home. Mary Lou and Louise were asleep in the back seat and Brandy was holding Sara in the front seat. A semi-trailer was in front of Robbie and wasn't doing the speed limit so Robbie got over in the passing lane to pass him. As he was passing the semi, he noticed that the semi was starting to weave a little. Robbie gave the car some more acceleration so he could get past the semi. As he got up even with the cab of the truck, the truck made a severe swerve to the left. The driver of the truck had dozed off. When he heard his truck make contact with Robbie's car, he woke up and jerked his steering wheel hard to the right. It was too late though. The station wagon was forced into the median. There was a big dip between opposing lanes. Robbie's car turned sideways and then flipped over and over several times before stopping at the bottom of the dip. The semi had run off the road on the other side and down an embankment. When it finally stopped, it caught fire.

Three days later, Robbie finally awakened. He had no idea where he was or what had happened. A nurse had been in the room and when she saw that he was waking up, she yelled for a doctor. The doctor was there in a few minutes. He walked over beside Robbie's bed. "Mr. Parker, I'm Dr. Tull," he said. "Do you know where you are and what has happened?"

Robbie tried to think. Then he started remembering. "There was this truck and he hit us," said Robbie. "Where's Brandy? Where're my kids?"

"Mr. Parker, I have some terrible news for," started the doctor. "Your family was killed in the accident. The truck driver was killed too."

"Oh God no, no, no, that can't be," cried Robbie. "That can't be." Robbie tried to get out of bed but the doctor held him down.

"You cannot get out of bed Mr. Parker," said the doctor. "You have been severely injured. You have a severe concussion, several broken ribs, and one of your lungs was punctured. We had to remove some of your small intestine because it was damaged beyond repair. Plus your left leg was broken. The leg alone will take a long time to heal because it was broken where you had been previously injured." Robbie struggle with the doctor and tried to get up again.

"I've got to find my family," cried Robbie. "I know they're alive and here somewhere."

"Mr. Parker, I'm going to have to sedate you if you insist on getting out of bed," said the doctor.

"You better knock me out cause I'm getting out of this bed," said Robbie. The nurse was standing by with a needle of something. She stuck it in one of Robbie's IV's. He was asleep in a few seconds. The doctor went out to a waiting room. Robbie's parents, Carl, and Marie were there. Robert got up from his chair.

"How's my son doing doctor?" asked Robert.

"As we told you before, he has some severe injuries," said the doctor. "Those will heal well in time. But right now, he refuses to believe that his family is gone. He kept trying to get out of bed and I was forced to sedate him. He will only be out for a couple of hours. You may all go into his room and be there when he wakes up if you wish. I'll have someone get some more chairs."

"Thank you doctor," said Robert. Mary was crying. She had been crying almost continuously since they had gotten the news of the accident. Even Carl had been crying. Marie had done her crying earlier and was now able to control it. The chairs arrived and they went into the ICU room where Robbie was. He woke up a couple of hours later. The first person he saw was his mother next to the bed and crying her eyes out. She wanted to hug Robbie so much but knew that she couldn't.

"What am I going to do momma? What am I going to do?" said Robbie. "Everybody I love dies. What am I going to do?"

"I don't know son," said Mary. "I just don't know. We'll do our best to help you through this. We all love you so very much."

Robbie was crying hard now. "I love all of you too," cried Robbie. Mary leaned over and gave Robbie as lightly of a hug as she could. Robert did the same. Then Marie did the same and was followed by Carl. They all did some more crying. In a few minutes, Robbie fell back asleep. Robert was worried about Robbie going back to sleep so soon so he went for the nurse. She explained to him that Robbie was still extremely weak and even though their conversations had been short, it had probably worn Robbie out. All of them decided they would go to the cafeteria and get some coffee and something to eat. None of them had much of an appetite so they just had some coffee.

While Robbie had been asleep, there had been a shift change. The nurse keeping watch over him was a middle aged hard looking woman. She wasn't pretty but she wasn't ugly either. She looked like she was a person who wouldn't take any crap from anyone else. She had checked on Robbie and had made her other rounds and had come back to check on him again. When she got into his room, Robbie had awakened and was yanking out his tubes and IV's. She ran over to his bed and stopped him.

"Just what the hell are you doing young man?" she said. "Nobody's gonna kill themselves on my watch and I mean nobody." She began replacing everything. Robbie yanked on one of the tubes again. The nurse grabbed his arm and bit it. Robbie let go of the tube.

"I told you nobody's gonna kill themselves on my watch and I meant it," screamed the nurse. "Now you settle down or I'll fill you full of something that'll knock you out and I mean PDQ."

"Just leave me alone. I got nothing to live for," said Robbie.

"How bout all them folks that were here just a while ago?" said the nurse. "I'm sure them folks love you and want you around."

"You don't understand. Just leave me alone," yelled Robbie.

"Young man, I'm gonna tell you the story of my life," started the nurse. "And you're gonna listen. Act like you're ignoring me and I'll bite that arm again. Now lay there and listen." She hesitated for a second and then started. "I was sixteen years old and my boyfriend was 17 in the middle of 1944. We were sure we would get married after we got out of school. My boyfriend decided that he had to do his part and he joined the Marine Corps. He was afraid he might miss out. Well he didn't miss out. He was on Okinawa. He got shot up some but it wasn't too bad. We got married after he got out when he was healed up. He decided he would stay in the Reserves. Our son was born in 1948. Ralph, that was my husband's name, got called up during Korea. He got killed at the Chosin Reservoir. A few years later, I remarried. We had a daughter. One day as she was walking home from school, she was hit and killed by a drunk driver while she was in a crosswalk. She was only 8 years old. My husband went nuts and killed himself. Then to top all of this off, my son had to prove he was a man and ran off and joined the Marine Corps. He was killed at Khe Sanh." The nurse didn't say anything else for a while. Then she spoke. "Now don't be telling me that you're the only person who lost loved ones and such," said the nurse. "If I catch you even looking cross-eyed at any of the tubes or IV's, I'll give you a whoppin' worse that any your daddy ever give you." The nurse turned around to leave and saw Mary, Robert, Marie, and Carl there. She smiled at them and walked out. Mary went over to Robbie's bed first. Robert left the room for a minute and talked with the nurse.

"Was that story true?" Robert asked her.

"It doesn't matter if it is or isn't, but it's a good tear jerker isn't it?" said the nurse.

"It sure is," said Robert. "The way you told it, I believed it. So was it true?"

"It all was but one part," said the nurse. "My son wasn't killed at Khe Sanh. I just said that because Khe Sanh is so well known. He was killed in some jungle in 1968."

"I'm sorry for your losses ma'am," said Robert.

"Don't feel sorry for me," said the nurse. "I had my times of misery and I healed. You and them others gotta help your boy now. He'll need all the help he can get." Robert went back to Robbie's room. He went over to Robbie. Robbie looked him in the eyes.

"Dad, do you think that story the nurse told me was true?" asked Robbie.

"I know it was," answered Robert. "There was only one untruth in it."

"What was that?" asked Robbie.

"Her son wasn't killed at Khe Sanh," answered Robert. "He was killed out in some jungle. She just said Khe Sanh because everyone's heard of it."

Robbie had Brandy and the kids cremated and had no memorial service. This upset Brandy's sisters, but at the time, Robbie didn't care.

Robbie healed well and was released from the hospital in three weeks. He still had to take it very easy. He had a cast on his leg. Mary tried to convince Robbie to stay with them in Columbus but Robbie insisted on going home. Robert and Mary took him home. They stayed with him for a few days. Mary cooked several things for Robbie so he wouldn't have to cook for a while. He was sad when they left but he wanted to be by himself. It was tough. He kept looking for Brandy and kids but they weren't there. He cried every time he went into the girls rooms. Every night he reached for Brandy but she wasn't there. He had several good cries every day.

While all of this was going on, he was constantly bombarded with shyster lawyers trying to get him to sue the trucking company. Some of them even showed up at the house. It was all Robbie could do to keep from hurting them. The trucking company's insurance had paid for everything without question. Suing them wouldn't bring back his family.

Marie called Robbie one day and volunteered to help him with things around the house. She came over and they rounded up all of the clothing and toys and donated them to different charities. Robbie was reluctant to depart with Brandy's clothing, but he finally did. They wouldn't fit Marie, but maybe she could find them a home. The visits from Marie were nice at first, but when Marie brought Annette with her, Robbie would start thinking about the girls and cry.

Finally the cast came off after over two months. Robbie started going back to the office. He wouldn't buy another car so he drove his olds. He made a trip to Columbus one week, and the next week, he went to Toledo. When he made his first trips to Toledo, he would visit Brandy's sisters. After a while, he quit. He stayed involved in work as much as he could to help keep his mind busy. He also kept up with his Vietnam veterans list. He did not attend any more of the monthly meetings at the VA.

Marie would call him at least once a month and ask how he was doing. After about six months, they would go out to lunch or something. Both of them knew that there would never be anything romantically between them. They were just becoming very good friends.

Two months later, Robbie got a call from Sheila and Ed. They were getting married and hoped he would attend if he was up to it. Robbie went to the wedding and took Marie with him. It was actually a fair sized wedding. Sheila had been an only child and her folks wanted to do this for her. They had a band and everything. Robbie danced a little but had to quit because his leg was hurting him badly. He still danced very well and everyone was amazed at his ability. That is, everyone but Marie. She already knew he was a master. Ed's older brother was the best man at the wedding and he had taken an interest in Marie. He asked for Robbie's permission to dance with her. "Don't ask me, ask her," said Robbie.

Very politely, he spoke. "Miss, I am Ed's brother John and I would be deeply honored if you would dance with me," said John.

"John, I am Marie and I will gladly dance with you," said Marie. John took her arm and escorted her to the dance floor. John wasn't a good dancer but he was trying.

"John, try to follow me," said Marie. "I will have you dancing well in no time. Do not be embarrassed. I was taught by a master."

"I bet the master was Robbie, wasn't it?" said John.

"Yes it was," said Marie. "He taught my husband and I how to dance a few years back. My husband died sometime back."

"I am sorry for your loss," said John.

"My daughter and I both miss him," said Marie. "Now follow me." Marie took the lead and it wasn't long until John was doing very well. They danced several dances before he escorted her back to the table.

During the last dance, John spoke forwardly. "Marie, you are a very attractive and nice woman. I would like to get to know you much better," said John. "Is there a chance that we could go out in the near future?"

"John, you've been a perfect gentleman and you may call on me anytime," said Marie. When the dance was over, John escorted her back to the table. Marie reached into her purse and took out paper and pen and gave John her address and phone number.

"I will call you tomorrow evening after I know my work schedule," said John. John shook Robbie's hand and then went over and sat next to Ed and Sheila.

"So you'll be going on a date soon," said Robbie. "That's great."

"He's a perfect gentleman," said Marie. "He didn't even flinch when I said I had a daughter. I think it will be nice. I believe I'm finally ready to go out again."

"I'm happy for you. So can we go now?" said Robbie. "My leg is killing me."

"Sure, we can leave now," said Marie. They both went over, wished Ed and Sheila well, and were on their way.

~~~~

Robbie felt good one summer day after work and he decided to stop off at a bar after work and have a beer. He sat there at the bar nursing his beer when he decided he would have a shot of bourbon with it. He remembered how he liked the bourbon that day down at Carl's. He slowly sipped the bourbon. It was as good as he had remembered. He still had half a beer left when a man and woman came in and sat at the bar too. They were probably in their 30's. They were about four stools away from Robbie. They ordered their drinks and then commenced arguing. They were getting loud and obnoxious. Robbie thought he might tell them to knock it off, but after a while it seemed pretty funny to him. He was almost done with his beer when he heard a loud cracking noise. The woman had slapped the man across his face and almost knocked him off his stool. He regained his composure and yelled several cuss words at her and then slapped her cross the face. It didn't phase her one bit. She got in his face and went to cussing him. He slapped her again. Again it didn't phase her. Then he stood up and gave her a right to the jaw. Down off the bar stool she went but she wasn't out. Robbie got up and went over to him.

"Don't be hitting women when I'm around," said Robbie.

"Who the fuck are you?" said the man. "Get away from me before you get some of the same."

"Come on, give me some of the same you asshole," said Robbie. The man took a swing at Robbie with his right. Robbie blocked it and gave him a left to the jaw. Down he went off the bar stool. He was out cold. The woman was up now and got in Robbie's face.

"Who the hell are you?" she screamed. "Mind you own damn business." Then she bent down and held the man in her arms. Robbie went back to his stool. The bartender came over to him.

"Them two are married," he said. "They do that all the time in here. I just leave them alone." Robbie shrugged his shoulders. He finished his drinks and paid the bill. He left the bartender a tip.

"Thanks for the entertainment," Robbie said to everyone as he went out the door.

~~~~

Robbie's parents decided not to worry about hurricane season and went to the Virgin Islands in July. They stayed for a full week and had a wonderful time. They had been home for a few days and decided to pay Robbie a visit. Robert had taken three week's vacation all at once and still had days off. They called Robbie and told him they would be down on a Wednesday around noon. Noon came and they weren't there. Then two came and then three. Robbie started to worry. His parents had never been late for anything ever in their lives. He called their house and there was no answer. Then he really started thinking the worst. He was about to call the State Patrol when the phone rang. Robbie's worst fears were confirmed. There had been a traffic accident. Robbie's parents had been killed. No other vehicles were involved. It was believed that his father had had a severe heart attack. Robert and Mary died in the crash. They had ran off the highway, through a guardrail, and crashed into a huge oak tree. It was believed he might have been doing 70mph at impact. Robbie dropped the phone and fell to the floor. He cried openly for a few minutes. The officer on the phone heard the crying and stayed on the line. Finally, Robbie was able to get back on the phone and get the necessary information from the officer. He then called the funeral parlor and informed them the bodies would be transported to Columbus after he identified them.

Robert and Mary both had wills and instructions on how everything was to be handled. Robbie did exactly as they instructed. There would be a viewing, a service at the funeral home, and then on to the grave yard. There would be a color guard from the Legion and the VFW. Both Robert and Mary were very well liked and it was a huge funeral. Robbie did his best to keep from crying but he couldn't stop. It took a long time after the graveyard to get away from all of the people who wanted to pay their respects. The funeral had started at 1 PM that day and Robbie finally got to his parents house at 8 PM. He cried himself to sleep on the sofa.

The next day, he went over all of his parents important papers and such. Robbie knew he would own the house but he had no idea that his dad had carried that much life insurance on Mary and himself. Robert had insured himself for $100,000 and Mary for $50,000. It took a lot crying and some time, but Robbie got everything settled. Now he had two houses. What was he going to do with them? Which one should he live in? He didn't want either of them empty for fear of vandalism. It would take a while longer to go through all of his parents things, so he figured he should try to get someone in his house in Cincinnati at least while he sorted things out. He asked the neighbors if they would keep an eye on the place for a few days until he could get back.

When he got back to Cincinnati, he thought and thought about who he should call first. He didn't want to hire some professional house sitter. He decided to call Marie and ask her if she knew of someone. Marie knew of someone. It was her. She would be glad to house sit for him. She'd been living in an apartment for a long time now and it would be great to be in a house for a while. Her lease had been up for some time and she was paying month to month because she was thinking about moving out. This would help her make up her mind. Robbie was all for it. He helped her get settled in and then went back to Columbus.

Robbie and his dad were close to the same size. Robbie went through all of his clothes and kept what he wanted for himself. The rest would go to a charity or the Salvation Army. All of Mary's clothes would go there too. He kept all of her jewelry. He got out the M-1 and gave it a once over. His dad had kept it cleaned and oiled. Robbie decided he would like to go shoot some, but where would he go. He made some calls and found out there was a range at Deer Creek State Park. The next day he went shooting. He had a hard time keeping from crying as he was shooting. There were other shooters at the range and they were all very interested in what Robbie was shooting. He held back his tears as he talked to several of them. He even let some young boy fire a couple of rounds. Robbie fired seventy five rounds that day and he could feel it in his shoulder. There were times when he was firing that he could see the NVA and VC that he had shot at before.

He broke the rifle down and cleaned it before he left the range. The young shooter who he had let fire the rifle watched him as he tore it down and cleaned it. Robbie gave the boy a little lecture on how important it was to make sure his weapon was clean and in working order. Robbie cried almost the whole trip back to Columbus.

That evening, Robbie decided to get out of the house and visit the Legion. He figured that it was possible he might drink too much so he called a cab. There were several men at the Legion who knew Robert and Robbie and were at the funeral. They came over and gave their condolences again. Robbie had a couple of beers with some of them and took a cab to the VFW.

Jake Canton was tending bar when Robbie walked in. He gave Robbie his condolences and told him his beer was on the house. "What if I want some bourbon to go with it?" asked Robbie.

"It's on the house too," said Jake. Just as Jake went to get Robbie's drinks, Ole Jessie came in. Jessie couldn't move well but he went to Robbie and sat next to him.

"I've heard you had some hard times," said Jessie. "It'll take time and you won't think it, but you'll heal." Jake showed up with Robbie's drinks. "So are you drinking a man's drink now?" asked Jessie.

"I've decided I like bourbon," said Robbie. "Wanna join me?"

"Sure, I'll have some," said Jesse. "Haven't had any bourbon for years. Still drinking Jack." Jake brought Jessie's drink and sat down with them. Jake had poured himself some bourbon too."

They talked and had a good time. Robbie was feeling a lot better and it just wasn't the alcohol. Three drinks later, Jessie's wife called and said for them to send him home. Jesse surprised everyone. This time he wasn't going back home just yet.

"I'll be taking a cab when I leave," said Robbie. "I'll make sure you get home." Three more drinks later and Robbie was ready to go. He wasn't really too drunk, but he sure shouldn't be driving a car. Someone else called them a cab. Jake was drunk and couldn't." Jesse's wife was a little upset when he got home, but she kept her mouth shut. Someone at the VFW had called and told her that Jessie needed to be with a friend who had recently suffered great losses.

Jessie died the next week. He had purchased a plan from Fulbright a good while back and everything was set up. Even though Jessie had been an old grouch, he was well liked and it was a fair sized funeral. When everything was over, Jessie's wife went to Robbie and thanked him for being Jessie's friend.

Robbie had everything possible taken care of at the house. All he had to do now was decide where he wanted to live. He thought on it for another week and decided on Columbus. He asked the neighbors to watch the house again and he went back to Cincinnati. Marie had really enjoyed staying in the house. Annette like it too. She had made several new friends in the neighborhood. Robbie took all of them out to dinner that evening. They went to a pizza parlor. They had a little small talk before Robbie asked them about the house. "So would you two like to live in the house all the time?" he asked.

"Oh boy, could we?" asked Annette.

"I love your house," said Marie. "I just love it."

"Well here's what I propose," started Robbie. "Give your landlord notice and when your time is up at the end of the month, you move in here."

"We don't have much to move," said Marie. "The apartment is furnished. We had to sell most everything when David died."

"Well this house is already furnished," said Robbie. "You'll be all set."

"How much will the rent be?" asked Marie.

"Here's what we are going to do," started Robbie. "You will not pay any rent. You will put the utilities in your name and pay them. I'll pay all the taxes and upkeep."

"I couldn't do that," said Marie. "That's way too generous."

"Look, I have more money than I need," said Robbie. "I don't need your money. I just need you in this house. Dave was a Marine and Marines look out for each other and their families. Do we have a deal?"

"Yes, we have a deal," said Marie as she went to Robbie and hugged him. Annette hugged him too.

"Now there's only one more condition," said Robbie. "I'll be living in Columbus and come to Cincinnati possibly once a week or every other week. I'll be staying here when I do if it's all right."

"Of course it's all right," said Marie. "We'll always be happy to see you."

"So, not to change the subject, but how's John doing?" asked Robbie.

"John is a good man and he is doing fine," said Marie. "We are taking things a step at a time. I like him. He likes Annette too."

"That's wonderful," said Robbie. "How's Ed and Sheila doing?"

"They are just like school kids in love," said Marie. "They are so good for each other. I heard stories about what Ed had been through over there and I hear now that he rarely even thinks about it."

"That is so good," said Robbie. "That is so good. So will you need a truck or anything to help you get moved?"

"No, I told you we didn't have much," said Marie. "I'll be able to get everything in maybe three trips in the car. I have a station wagon now." When she said station wagon, Robbie cried for a little bit. Marie realized why Robbie was crying and gave him a hug. Annette gave him one too.

Marie was in the house at the end of the month and Robbie was settled in Columbus. He went to the funeral parlor every day at first, but then decided he wasn't needed. His crew was very good. He spent a lot of time walking around the neighborhood and at the park. The lady with the Jack Russell had moved out and a young couple now lived in the house. The next week, the house on Robbie's right went up for sale. In two weeks it was sold. The original owners were moving to Florida. A young couple around Robbie's age had bought it. They had no children. Robbie introduced himself when they first moved in. They seemed like very nice people. He was a loan officer at a bank and she worked part time as a secretary. Robbie began to notice after the first week they moved in that on some days, there was a different car in the driveway. When the woman wasn't working and when no different cars were in the driveway, she was always sunbathing in the back yard. She always wore a very skimpy two piece bathing suit. This woman was drop dead gorgeous and she didn't mind showing it. One day when there was a different car in their driveway, Robbie was sitting in the back yard drinking a beer. The car pulled out of the driveway and a few minutes later, the neighbor lady came out to lay in the sun. She saw Robbie outside and went over to him. "That beer looks good," she said. "Could I join you?"

"Sure," said Robbie not wanting to be impolite. He went inside and returned with the beer. He opened it and handed it to her. She sat down in a lawn chair beside Robbie.

"Would you like to put some suntan lotion on my back?" she asked Robbie.

"No I wouldn't," said Robbie.

"Don't you like my back?" she asked Robbie.

"Your back is just fine," said Robbie.

"Well what do you think of these?" she asked as she stood up and untied her bikini top fully exposing her rather large but very well shaped breasts.

Robbie stared at them for a moment. "They are very beautiful," said Robbie. "You are a very beautiful woman."

"You can have me," said the woman. "My husband and I have an open marriage."

"What does that mean?" asked Robbie.

"It means that we can see other people whenever we want," she answered. "My husband does this all the time too."

"I'm happy for you," said Robbie. "It's good to see that you have taken your marriage vows seriously."

"You're not fooling me," she said. "I know you want me. I'll go back home, but remember, you can have me anytime you want."

"Thank you, I appreciate that," said Robbie. The woman went back to her yard tying her bathing suit top as she went. She laid in the sun and hoped that Robbie was watching. He wasn't. He went inside. Robbie had a very hard time getting to sleep that night. He wasn't thinking about his neighbor. She had reminded him of Brandy. Their shapes were very similar. He cried himself to sleep.

For the next two weeks, the lady next door laid in the sun every day except on the weekend. Her husband was home then. Robbie sometimes heard them in the house. They always left the windows open. They sure liked their sex and they liked it loud. Robbie was amazed that two people who screwed everyone else would still have the hots for each other like that. He wondered if the other neighbors minded.

About a month later in the middle of the afternoon, a police car pulled into the neighbor's driveway. The woman was in the backyard sunbathing. Some words were spoken that Robbie couldn't hear. They escorted her into the house and the next thing Robbie knew, she was being escorted from the house to the back seat of the cruiser. She was in handcuffs and she had put on some clothes.

Robbie found out later that she and her husband had been arrested for prostitution. Apparently, he set up her clients at the bank. In other words, he was her pimp.

Chapter Twenty-Seven

For the next year, Robbie made a weekly trip to Cincinnati. It wasn't because of the business. His employees were great and took care of everything. They rarely needed to consult him. He always stopped in and told everyone what a great job they were doing. Robbie wanted to make sure his friends were doing well. He would take Marie and Annette out to dinner when he was in town. Sometimes, John would go with them when he was available. Sheila and Ed were still doing well. Robbie talked to Bart at the VA and asked how the group meetings were going. Bart told him that he thought they had made some progress.

The holidays were a lonely time for Robbie. He always got invited somewhere but it wasn't the same as being with Brandy and the kids. He loved it when he visited Carl and Sally and the four boys, but inside, it made him sad. In Columbus, he began getting himself more involved in the community. He helped with charities and got involved with the Chamber of Commerce. He was becoming very well known and very well liked. Some people tried to get him to run for city council but he would have no part of that. He thought that he might coach a little league team but decided against that after he remembered the incident when he umpired a game.

The next year, Marie called Robbie and announced that she and John were getting married. Robbie was so happy for them. "Do you have a plan on where you will live?" asked Robbie after he congratulated her.

"We haven't discussed that yet," said Marie. "John lives in a apartment and he has talked about buying a house."

"Why don't you all live in my house while you're making up your mind and saving your money," said Robbie. "It would be my wedding gift to you."

"You are good man," said Marie. "I know why Brandy loved you so much. I will talk with John and tell him what you said."

"I can tell him if you'd like," said Robbie. "I can tell him on my visit next week. When is the wedding?"

"We haven't set a date yet, but it will be next month for sure," said Marie.

"That's plenty of time for John to chew on this," said Robbie. "I hope he's not one of those guys who figures he's the man and everything is his responsibility."

"I guess we'll find out when you get here," said Marie.

"And another thing, if you two need someone to take care of Annette while you go on a honeymoon, I can be available," said Robbie.

"You are such a good man Robbie," said Marie. "You really are."

"Why thank you and I'll see you next Tuesday," said Robbie.

Tuesday rolled around and Robbie took all of them to dinner. John had to ask for time off to be with them. Robbie started the conversation at the restaurant. "So John, Marie tells me you two are getting married," started Robbie. "Congratulations, Marie is a fine woman and from what I see, you are a fine man. I'm sure you two will be, oh, sorry, I mean you three, will be happy together." Robbie reached out and shook John's hand.

"Thank you Robbie," said John. "Marie is a wonderful woman and Annette is a beautiful daughter. I'm sure we will be happy together."

"All right, now I'm going to get to the point," said Robbie. "You three can live in my house for as long as is necessary. It will be under the same conditions as it is now between Marie and myself. This will give you plenty of time to save money and buy your own place."

"What are your conditions with Marie?" asked John. "We've never talked about her staying in your house. How much is the rent?"

"I do not charge Marie any rent," started Robbie. "The utilities are in her name and she pays them. I pay the taxes and upkeep. Marie is my friend. Her husband was a Marine and Marines take care of each other and their families. I also stay at the house when I come to town once a week or every other week."

"That's way too generous Robbie," said John. "I would feel guilty about that."

"Swallow your pride and consider it a wedding gift," said Robbie. "I'm a wealthy man. I do not need the money. I take care of my friends."

"In that case it would be an honor to live in your house," said John. "And you will stay with us when you are in town."

~~~~

Marie and John had a beautiful wedding. Ed was the best man and Sheila was the Maid of Honor. Robbie was the first one after John to kiss the bride. They went on a two week honeymoon and Robbie took care of Annette. They had a great time. They went to ball games and the zoo and just had a really good time. Robbie was actually a little sad when Marie and John got home and he had to leave.

Robbie didn't make any trips to Cincinnati for the next two months. He thought they should have the house to themselves. Living together can be a real adjustment for some folks. When Robbie did come to town, he wanted to take them all to dinner, but Marie would have no part of it. She fixed a fine meal. Robbie could see that John and Marie were deeply in love. He was happy for them.

Robbie was continuously involved in something with the community for the next several years. He was also considered a very available widower with plenty of money. Every time he went to a meeting or some type of gathering, women were all over him. His new friends were always trying to fix him up with someone. Robbie mostly ignored them. He did go on a date every once in a while, but there was not usually a second date. There was no one that Robbie wanted. Brandy was gone.

Robbie was walking downtown one afternoon when he thought he saw someone he recognized. She saw him at the same time. They stood and stared at each other for a moment. There was a man with her. Robbie walked over to her. "Are you Debbie Ryan?" he asked.

"I used to be," answered Debbie. "It's Debbie Carnes now. And you are Robbie Parker. You still look the same."

"You look good too," said Robbie. "Is this your husband?"

"Yes, this is my husband," said Debbie. "Robbie Parker, this is my husband Paul Carnes." They shook.

"I'm pleased to meet you Paul and I'm glad to see you again Debbie," said Robbie. "Have you two got time for a cup of coffee or a drink. We can talk a little if you have time."

"That would be nice," said Debbie. They found a café and sat at a table. No one wanted a drink so they had some coffee.

"So you're the guy who was there when two guys broke into Debbie's house," said Paul. "She told me all about that. That was something. And she also told me about that professor."

"I can see that you two don't keep secrets," said Robbie. "So where did you two meet and why are you here now?"

"We met at school in Florida," started Debbie. "We dated a good while and fell in love and got married. We have two boys now. They're with Paul's folks while we came here for a visit. Paul is an electrical engineer and I teach 4th grade. How have you been all this time?"

Robbie almost cried but he held the tears back. "I met my wife at school in Cincinnati," started Robbie. "We had three beautiful girls. My wife and the girls were killed in a traffic accident." Robbie couldn't hold back the tears.

"I'm so sorry," said Debbie. "I didn't know. I'm so sorry."

"It's been a little while but I'm not over it yet," said Robbie. "My parents died in a car accident too. I'm living in their old house. I have a house in Cincinnati too. I guess you could say I'm a rich man. I own three funeral homes and two crematories. I'd trade it all to get my Brandy and girls back."

"I'm so sorry," said Debbie. "I don't know what I'd do if something happened to Paul and the boys."

"You never will know until it happens and always hope that it never will," said Robbie. "It's hard to get over. I may never get over it. So I'm done sobbing now. Why are you two here?"

"We're supposed to be meeting Tina and Anna this afternoon," said Debbie. "It would be great if you would join us. I know they'd get a kick out of seeing you."

"I've got nothing planned," said Robbie. "I'll join you if Paul doesn't mind."

"You're most welcome," said Paul. "We better get moving. Where is it we're meeting them?"

"It's one of these downtown bistros," said Debbie. "I can't remember the name but I know right where it is and what it looks like." They left the café and headed to the bistro. As soon as they entered the place they spotted Tina and Anna. Tina and Anna spotted them and ran over to them. They exchanged hugs and kisses and then the boys were introduced. Debbie introduced Paul first. Tina and Anna stared at Robbie for a moment.

"I know who this is," said Anna. "You're Robbie Parker." Robbie wanted to say that maybe she didn't recognize him with his clothes on but he didn't.

"Yes, it's me Robbie," Robbie said. Anna grabbed him and tried to ram her tongue down his throat but he politely kept her at bay. Tina was a little more subtle. She just hugged Robbie and gave him a kiss on the lips with no tongue. They all sat down. Tina and Anna turned their attention to Debbie now and yakked about a hundred miles an hour. After they got the information out of Debbie they wanted, they turned to Robbie. Robbie went through the stories again about the deaths of his wife and kids and parents. They wanted to know all about his business and how he was doing. After a while, Robbie and Debbie questioned Tina and Anna. Apparently, they were now partners in a "Gentleman's Club." They had the best looking girls in town and were very successful. They didn't dance very much anymore, unless someone requested them. When they did dance, it was for a premium price.

"So did you ever try that other business we discussed one day?" asked Robbie.

"I did for a little while," said Anna. "I almost got busted one time but this real nice cop let me go. I had to be real nice to him if you know what I mean."

"We know what you mean," said Debbie. "So are you ladies working tonight or can we do something?"

"We have to be back at the club by ten or eleven tonight," said Tina. "How about we go dancing. Robbie used to be a great dancer."

"I still am," said Robbie. "But my leg was broken where I got shot and it hurts quite a bit sometimes. I have to take it a little easier than before."

"So Paul, are you a dancer?" asked Tina.

"I get by, but I'd wager that I'm nothing like Robbie here from what I've heard," said Paul.

"Well it's settled," said Anna. "We'll meet at that club over on third street at eight. We can have a couple of drinks before the band starts." Tina and Anna left.

"Would you like to have dinner with us," asked Debbie.

"No, I wouldn't want intrude," said Robbie. "You two enjoy yourselves and I'll see you at the club." Robbie excused himself and headed home. He dug out some clothes to wear and laid them out. He fixed himself some dinner and then took a shower after he cleaned up. When it was time to go, he called a cab.

Debbie and Paul were already at the club and had a table when Robbie arrived. Anna and Tina were not there yet. They went ahead and ordered some drinks. A half hour later, Anna and Tina arrived. Both of them were dressed in very tight and very revealing dresses. There was not a whole lot left for the imagination. Robbie couldn't help himself. "Those are some really nice dresses that you ladies almost have on," said Robbie.

"You like them don't you Robbie?" said Anna. "You're not fooling me."

"Hey, I'm not dead," said Robbie. "A man would have to be dead for more than ten years not to notice you. Then he'd probably still have a heart attack even though he's already dead."

"I got the first dance with you Robbie Parker," said Tina. "I was the first one to dance with you when we first met. And you remember what happened that night."

"I'm not senile," said Robbie. "You don't forget times like that." Anna and Tina ordered some drinks. The band started playing fifteen minutes later. True to her word, Tina grabbed Robbie and took him to the dance floor. They were the only ones on the dance floor and they had room to move and move they did. Tina had picked up some newer moves and Robbie was worried that they might be asked to leave because they might be considered obscene. No one did and when the song was over, the whole place cheered them. Tina kept him on the dance floor for another song and another after that. Then the band played a slow song. Tina couldn't have gotten pulled any tighter unless she was actually under Robbie's skin. Robbie felt himself getting aroused. Tina could feel him too. She kept rubbing against him making things worse. Her tongue in his ear didn't help either. When the song ended, Robbie had to pry her off of him. Tina smiled and grabbed his ass as they went back to the table.

"That was very entertaining," said Debbie. "Can you top that Anna?"

"We'll find out shortly," said Anna.

"Give me a few songs to rest my leg," said Robbie. "I need to get some blood in my leg. A good bit of my blood went someplace else." They all let out a laugh. Debbie and Paul got up and danced. They looked good together. Paul wasn't a master, but he did well and anyone could see that Debbie was in love with this man. A few songs later, Anna took Robbie to the dance floor. Some of her moves were even more obscene that Tina's, but no one cared. In fact, they enjoyed them. They danced a couple of songs before the band played another slow song. It was the same as it was with Tina. Robbie got aroused and Anna did everything but actually put her hands in his pants. The rest of the evening went like this. Tina and Anna had said that they were supposed to be at their club by ten or eleven. When ten thirty came, both of them tried to talk Robbie into leaving with him. Robbie had not been with a woman since Brandy's death a very long time ago. He kept saying to himself that he would feel guilty if he went with them. Finally he gave in to his libido and went with them. They said their good-byes to Debbie and Paul and left.

They went to Anna's place. Robbie didn't even get to look around before they were all over him. He had never been with two women at once and wasn't sure he really liked it, but he blanked out those thoughts and let his libido go to work. The next morning, all three of them were lying every which way across the bed. Robbie woke up first. He was getting up to relieve himself. Anna grabbed him and tried to pull him back to bed. "Look, I gotta go and go now or there'll be stuff in the bed that you don't want," said Robbie. Anna let go of him. When he got back to the bed, Tina was awake now and they started all over again. A good while later, Robbie found his clothes and got himself dressed. The girls were still in bed. He called himself a cab and headed to the door.

"We need to do this again," said Anna before he got out the door.

"Thank you but I don't believe we will," said Robbie as he closed the door.

Robbie felt guilty for a very long time after that. Finally a couple of months later, he convinced himself that Brandy wouldn't have wanted him to become a priest.

~~~~

During the next year, Robbie loosened up quite a bit. He started dating some. He tried and tried, but the women he dated were not Brandy. He wanted Brandy. Nobody was like Brandy. He still kept dating, but there was not usually a second date. He even had sex once in a while, but it was totally meaningless. Robbie kept himself busy with the community and charities. The next spring, there would be a huge fund raiser in town. Very wealthy people in town would be attending. Besides the generous donations that would be given, there would also be an auction. Some of the men would put themselves up for bid and women would bid on them for a night out. Robbie was practically coerced into this, but he gave in and let himself be auctioned. There were hundreds of very wealthy people at the auction. Robbie was the fourth man to be auctioned. The man before him had gone for $2000, so the auctioneer started the bidding at $2000. It wasn't long and it was up to $10,000. A lot of older ladies were bidding for Robbie. He hoped some younger woman would rescue him. A voice came from the crowd, "$15,000." Everyone looked around to see who had bid. A young dark skinned woman with jet black hair moved to the front of the crowd. "$15,000," she said again. This woman was beautiful. Robbie looked around to see if any other hands were up to outbid her. There were none. "Sold for $15,000," said the auctioneer.

Robbie got off the stage and went to her. "I'm Robbie Parker and you are very beautiful," said Robbie. "I am at your service."

"I am Naomi Thomas and yes, you are at my service," she said. She took Robbie by the hand and led him to the front door. A limo was waiting for them. The driver opened a back door and let them in. No words were spoken. The limo stopped in front of the Hyatt Regency. They got out and she led him to the elevator. When the elevator door closed, she put her arms around his neck and kissed him several times. Then she backed away as if nothing had happened. The elevator stopped on the top floor. She was staying in the penthouse. She opened the door and they went inside. She put down her purse and wrapped her arms around Robbie's neck again and began kissing him. Then she backed away. "I want you to undress me," she said. "I want it slow and easy."

"I can do that," said Robbie as he went to work. Robbie did this very delicately. After every move there was a soft kiss somewhere. The slower he worked, the more aroused she got. She started undressing Robbie too.

A couple of hours later, they lay in bed caressing each other. "I will tell you right now that I will not get involved with any one person," said Naomi. "You are a very good lover Robbie Parker."

"Thank you Naomi Thomas," said Robbie. "May I ask you some questions about yourself?"

"You may ask but I might not answer," said Naomi. "I will tell you a few things about myself. I am from India. My father was British and Indian and my mother was Indian and Polynesian. We live in Calcutta. My family is very wealthy. I will not tell you what we do. I work for the company and I go all over the United States doing things for the company. That is all I will tell you now, but you can ask questions if you'd like."

"All right, how often do you get to Columbus?" asked Robbie.

"About every two months," answered Naomi.

"Maybe we could get together again," said Robbie.

"That might be possible," answered Naomi. "What is it that you do?"

"I own some funeral parlors and crematories," said Robbie.

"That is very honorable. Do you have a business card with you?" asked Naomi.

"I do," answered Robbie and he got up and got a card for Naomi. "Maybe we could have dinner too if I see you again."

"That's possible," said Naomi. "We will have dinner here shortly. I will call room service. Now I want you to make love to me again." Robbie did not need any coaxing.

After they were finished, Naomi ordered some room service. She didn't get dressed, but she did put on a robe. She had another robe for Robbie. As Robbie put on the robe, he had some questions he wanted to ask Naomi. "Why did you bid on me?" asked Robbie. "There were other men there."

"You are a good looking man and you didn't act all macho when you were on the stage," answered Naomi. "I liked that."

"I know you said your family was wealthy, but $15,000 is a lot of money," said Robbie.

"It was for charity," said Naomi.

"Don't you have a lot of poor people in your country?" asked Robbie. "Couldn't they use that money over there?"

"You are asking too many questions Robbie Parker," said Naomi. "But I will tell you this. My family spends a huge amount of money in my country helping the needy."

"Will I be spending the night with you?" asked Robbie.

"Not his time," answered Naomi. "Maybe if we see each other again we may spend the night together."

"Do you do things like this on a regular basis?" asked Robbie.

"That is none of your business," answered Naomi. "I have not asked you about your personal life other than what you do."

"Fair enough. Do you like to dance?" asked Robbie.

"I do," answered Naomi. "Are you a good dancer?"

"Yes I am," answered Robbie. "Maybe if I see you again we can go dancing."

"That would be nice," answered Naomi. Room service arrived and they ate their meal. There was a little small talk while they were eating, but Naomi was very elusive and wouldn't say much of anything. After the meal, they made love one more time. When they were finished, she told Robbie it was time for him to leave. Her driver would take him anywhere he wanted to go. She gave him a kiss on the cheek as he left the room.

Robbie's car was over where the charity auction had been so he had the driver take him to his car. When he got home, he opened up a beer and sat down on the sofa. "What just happened?" he asked himself. "If I told someone what I had just been through, they wouldn't believe me. It's not every day that some drop dead gorgeous woman bids $15,000 for you and then takes you to her hotel for some meaningless sex.

~~~~

The next month, Robbie decided it was time to get a crematory in Toledo. As busy as they were with the ones in Columbus and Cincinnati, it would pay for itself in no time. Robbie got ahold of his manager in Toledo and told him to get started on it. The rest of the month went by quickly. At the end of the month, he made a trip to Cincinnati and visited Marie, John, and Annette when he was in town. He told them the story about the auction and Naomi. He was right. They didn't believe him at first. But then they figured that a story like that was too strange to be untrue. They had a good visit. John told him that Sheila and Ed were still acting like school kid lovers.

Robbie was still collecting names for his list. He had not heard back from his Congressman after he sent him the last list. It didn't matter. Robbie still had plenty of copies. He was having a lot of nightmares again. They began to worry him. As far as he knew, he really didn't think about the war much, but apparently it was still in his head and let him know it from time to time. For several nights in a row, he had the same dream. He could see himself throwing a grenade at an NVA soldier. The grenade went off just as it almost hit the soldier. He was blown to bits. In another dream, he couldn't get the leeches off of himself. Whenever he did get rid of one, another one would get on him someplace else. He was getting weak from loss of blood. Then it started raining. It rained and rained and rained. He was so shriveled up that he looked like an accordion. He got so shriveled that the leeches couldn't hold on to him anymore. He had to take a leak, but he was so shriveled up that he couldn't find his dick. When he woke up from this dream, he found that he was in the shower. He turned off the water and immediately checked for his dick. It was there, and it was fine. Just how in the hell had he gotten himself in the shower? He was asleep, just how in the hell did he get in the shower?

For the next week, he had some dreams, but they were not nightmares. They were dreams of Brandy and the kids. He kept reaching for Brandy, but she wasn't there.

At the end of the next month, he got a call from Naomi. She would be in town the next Friday and they could get together if he wished. Robbie would meet her at the same room at the Hyatt Regency at 6 PM. "My car will pick you up," said Naomi.

"No, I'll drive to the hotel myself," said Robbie. "I don't know where you actually live so you don't need to know where I live."

"That's fine. I'll see you at six on Friday," said Naomi.

Robbie cleaned up the olds a little and dug out some nice clothes. He intended to take Naomi to dinner and then dancing if she would agree.

Friday came and Robbie was at her door promptly at 6 PM. When she came to the door, she was wearing some very sexy lingerie. She pulled Robbie inside and wrapped her arms around him and began kissing him. Robbie politely pulled her away from him. "We have plenty of time for that later. In fact we can do that all night long if you want," said Robbie.

"Don't you want me?" asked Naomi. "I thought you would like the lingerie."

"I do like the lingerie and what's in it," said Robbie. "But we're going to dinner and then we're going dancing."

"Maybe we could have a quick one first?" said Naomi.

"All right, you win," said Robbie. It wasn't very quick, but they got it done. They cleaned up a bit and got dressed. Robbie informed her that they would be taking his olds and not her limo. She had never been in an olds and seemed excited about it. Robbie opened the door for her and when he got behind the wheel, she slid over next to him.

"I believe this is how young girls ride with their boyfriends in this country," she said.

"That's right," said Robbie. "So am I your boyfriend?"

"You are tonight," said Naomi. She let out a giggle. They went to G. Michael's in German Village for their dinner. Robbie let the valet park the olds. Robbie hadn't asked Naomi if she was Hindu or Muslim. He found out that she wasn't Hindu when she ordered her food. She ordered some beef tenderloin with crab meat on top of it. Robbie had always heard that Hindu's didn't eat beef. He didn't know for sure, but he wasn't going to ask her about her religion. They had a good meal with some good wine and then went to a club for some dancing. It was the same club where he had met Debbie and the other girls. The band was about to start and they found a table and got some drinks ordered.

Robbie didn't like the first song the band played so he didn't dance. The second song was all right so he escorted Naomi to the dance floor. Robbie was impressed. Naomi followed him really well. Robbie could see that she was enjoying herself. They danced for two more songs and then Robbie explained to her that he had to give his leg a rest. When they got back to the table, Naomi wanted him to tell her all about his leg injury. "You're getting personal, aren't you?" asked Robbie.

"Well, you're my boyfriend tonight," said Naomi. "It will be all right."

"All right, but you might have to answer some personal questions too," said Robbie. Robbie told her he had been in the Marine Corps and had been wounded in Vietnam. He also told her how his leg had been broken again in a traffic accident. He didn't say one word about Brandy and the kids. She wanted to know more about Vietnam but he told her that he would not talk about the war. Telling her that he got wounded was enough. They sat out a few songs and then got back on the dance floor. After a couple of songs, the band played a slow song. They were practically glued together. She could feel Robbie getting aroused. They looked into each other's eyes. "We'll take care of that later," said Robbie.

After another dance, they went back to their table. Just as they sat down, Anna and Tina showed up. "We saw you on the dance floor," said Anna. "Thought we'd come over and say hi." The girls were wearing some very revealing dresses again.

"That was nice of you," said Robbie. "Anna, Tina, this is Naomi Thomas." The girls kind of shook hands.

"So how you did you get tied up with Robbie here?" asked Tina.

"I bought him at an auction," answered Naomi. "He was very expensive."

"Well you'll find out that he's worth it if you haven't found out already," said Anna.

"He was worth it," said Naomi. "You two may join us if you'd like."

"Thanks, but we're meeting some people," said Anna. "They should be already here. We'll go find them now. Tootles." Anna and Tina left.

"What does tootles mean?" asked Naomi.

"Goodbye, I guess," said Robbie. "I don't hear it very often."

"I notice you didn't say those girls last names," said Naomi.

"That's because I don't know their last names," said Robbie. "Those were some interesting dresses that those girls almost had on weren't they?"

"Yes they were," said Naomi. "Did you like them?"

"Hey, I'm not dead," answered Robbie.

"Have you been with those girls?" asked Naomi.

"You know that I have," answered Robbie. "Now let's go dance some more." After two more songs, the band announced it was time for a break. They went back to their table. The fifteen minute break turned into a half hour like they usually do. Robbie and Naomi were back on the floor as soon as they started up. They would dance several dances and then rest Robbie's leg. When the band took its' next break, Naomi said that she had enough and wanted to get back to the hotel. Robbie obliged her.

They didn't make love all night, but close to it. They must have fallen asleep around 4 AM. When they woke up around ten, she had her way with him one more time and then they ordered room service for breakfast. After breakfast, she told Robbie it was time for him to leave. She gave him a kiss and told him that she might call him again in a couple of months or so.

Three and a half months went by and Robbie hadn't heard from Naomi. He knew there would never be anything serious between them, but he liked her and her company. Her elusiveness was something else. At the end of the fourth month, Naomi called him. She apologized for not calling for such a long time, but she explained that her parents had both been ill and she had been in India. Robbie met her at the same hotel room on a Friday evening. They had some very intense sex before they went out to dinner. They went dancing again, but this time it was at a different club. Robbie spent the night with her again, but got a big surprise when they got up Saturday morning. She was not leaving till Sunday and they could spend the whole day together. They had room service for breakfast.

"Do you like baseball?" Robbie asked her after breakfast.

"I do," answered Naomi.

"Would you like to see a game today?" asked Robbie.

"That would be nice," answered Naomi. "We can eat hotdogs and drink beer."

"We can," said Robbie. "Columbus has a minor league team called the Columbus Clippers. I believe they have a home game this afternoon. I'll give you a tour of the area. I'll even show you my house."

"That's not necessary," said Naomi.

"I don't mind," said Robbie. "It's just an average house in the suburbs, nothing fancy."

The only places that Naomi knew in Columbus were the places her driver took her for business. She never paid attention to anything as she rode around in the limo. Robbie took her all over the place. They spent some time at the park where Robbie used to go with Maria. Then they went to Robbie's house. Naomi said that she liked Robbie's house but she wondered why he didn't have a big fancy house like wealthy people. "I may be wealthy according to some folks, but I don't need things like some people do," said Robbie. "I like my olds. I don't need a new fancy car. I like this house. It works for me just fine.

"How long have your parents been gone?" asked Naomi. The question surprised Robbie because he hadn't said one word about his parents. "This was their house wasn't it?"

"Yes, it was their house. I was raised here," said Robbie. "They have been gone for a few years now."

"You haven't said anything about your wife," said Naomi. Robbie was startled by this question. Then he saw that he was still wearing his wedding band. He had never taken it off. A few tears slipped out. Naomi was looking at some pictures on the living room wall. They were pictures of Robbie, Brandy, and the girls. "Your family was very beautiful." Robbie busted loose with the tears now. He went into his bedroom and got himself a handkerchief. He stayed in the bedroom till he regained his composure. The he came out.

"That was my wife Brandy, and my three girls," sobbed Robbie. "Mary Lou was the oldest, then Louise Ellen, and then Sara Jean. I lost them in a traffic accident. A semi-trailer driver fell asleep and ran us off the road. That's when my leg was broken. It's been a long time, but I don't think I'll ever get over it."

"I'm sorry for your losses," said Naomi. "Maybe I shouldn't be here in this house."

"You are most welcome in my house," said Robbie. "How about I make us a sandwich and then we can head to the ballpark."

"Do you have any bologna?" asked Naomi. "I have never had it and I'd like to try it. I hear it's bad for you."

"A woman who wants bologna. That's something," said Robbie. "I do have some and I hear it's supposed to be bad for you. So are hotdogs and we're gonna eat some of them today." Robbie made some sandwiches and they had them, some chips, and a glass of milk for lunch. Then they left for the ballpark.

The Clippers weren't a contender this year and the stands were not crowded. Robbie got them seats behind home plate and not too far up. "I like these seats," said Robbie. "We can see what the pitcher's throwing."

"What do you mean what the pitcher is throwing?" asked Naomi'

"You don't know much about baseball do you?" said Robbie.

"No, I don't, but I like it," said Naomi. "Now tell me."

"Well the pitcher can throw the ball different ways and make it do different things," started Robbie. "There's curves, knuckleballs, sinkers, sliders, just all kinds of stuff. I'll show you when the game gets going. You'll be able to see the ball doing different things."

After a couple of innings, Naomi started telling Robbie what pitches the pitcher had thrown. They ate some hotdogs and drank some beer. It was an exciting game. Some home runs were hit and some bases were stolen. There was almost a fight once when the Columbus pitcher brushed back an opposing batter. He didn't miss his head by much. The batter shouted a few choice words at the pitcher and started to the mound but his coach stopped him. The batter ended up hitting a double. Columbus lost 2 to 1 but they had a good time.

After the game, Robbie took her to a hamburger joint for dinner. Naomi enjoyed it. Robbie spent the night with her again. The next morning after breakfast, they parted ways. She also told Robbie that it was likely that they wouldn't see each other again. Her parents were not well and she would probably have to stay in India and run the business. She was the oldest daughter and there were no sons. "I have greatly enjoyed our time together," she said to Robbie. "I know you will have a good life." Robbie kissed her one more time and left.

Every two months, Robbie hoped that Naomi would call, but she didn't. After six months, he quit hoping and just considered himself lucky to have met her.

~~~~

Robbie paid Carl a visit. The movie "Apocalypse Now" had been out for a good while. Robbie and Carl kept hearing that is was such a good movie about Vietnam. It was playing and Robbie and Carl went. When it was over and they walked out of the theater, they looked at each. Almost in unison, they said, "What the fuck was that?"

"That was a waste of money," said Carl.

"Maybe it was supposed to be a comedy," said Robbie. "I don't understand. Why would anyone say that this was a great picture? I don't get it."

"Well look at it this way," said Carl. "Maybe it's the worst movie you'll ever see. That way all of the movies you see from now on will be better."

"Let's get some beer and head home," said Robbie. They stopped at a carry out and got some beer. They sat around on the porch drinking their beer and watched the boys play. Robbie told Carl about the dream he had where it rained so much and he was shriveled up so much he couldn't find his dick. Carl had an idea for him.

"Next time you have that dream, dream that you have a stick in your hand," said Carl. "Poke that stick in your asshole and shove it in some so you can grab your dick." The stick made Robbie cringe a little, but it got him laughing. Then Robbie told Carl all about Naomi.

"You are always getting the good looking woman," said Carl. "What's up with that?"

"I'm pretty," said Robbie. They both had a good laugh. They drank a couple of beers then played some catch. After they tossed for a while, they got out the plastic stuff for the boys. Little Carl was getting a lot better.

"Did you know that everybody but the pros are using aluminum bats now?" said Carl.

"I never knew that," said Carl. "What's that all about?"

"I have no idea," said Carl. "Maybe they think they're saving trees. Them things sound awful when they hit a ball. You expect a good crack and then there's this plunk sound. Hard to get used to."

"Maybe we're getting old," said Robbie. "Do you remember your folks always saying how things used to be. Well that's us now."

"I guess it is," said Carl.

Chapter Twenty-Eight

Annette had a baby sister now. Marie and John were deeply in love. When Robbie visited them after the baby was born, Marie and John asked Robbie if they could buy his house. They loved the house and the neighborhood. The school system was good too. Robbie agreed to sell them the house. A price was agreed upon. "I do have one little condition," said Robbie. "And it's not about me staying here when I come to Cincinnati. How long of a loan would you get from a bank, 15, 20 years?"

"I would figure on 15 years," said John.

"All right, 15 years it is," said Robbie. "There will be no interest. We'll figure out the monthly payments and you will pay directly to me. How does that sound?"

"Too good to be true," said Marie. "That's way too generous."

"Look, I don't owe a thing on this house," said Robbie. "I paid it off a good while back. You two will be responsible for taxes and upkeep now."

"I don't know what to say," said John.

"Don't say anything," said Robbie. "Just think of all the money you'll save over fifteen years."

"I've never met a man like you Robbie," said John. "You are the kindest, and most generous person I have ever met, or even heard about. How can I ever re-pay you?"

"Just make your monthly payments and maybe name a son after me after you run out of the names you use. Just kidding," said Robbie.

A year later, John David Jackson was born. A year and half later, Robert James Jackson was born.

Robbie continued to keep himself busy in the community. He hadn't been with a woman since Naomi had gone. People kept trying to fix him up and women were always flirting with him, but he kept his distance. He was home one day watching a Reds game when he decided to get out his ball glove and oil it up. I had been a good glove and had lasted a lot of years, but it was time to retire it. Robbie put the glove and oil away and headed to a sporting goods store. He had just parked his car and was almost to the door. An attractive woman was coming out the door with a young boy. The boy had a new glove on his hand and baseball in it. As she cleared the door, some young looking man ran by them at a dead run and grabbed the woman's purse off of her shoulder. She let out a yell. Robbie was only a few feet away. He ran to the boy. "Excuse me son, I'm going to borrow your baseball for a second," said Robbie. The boy and his mother didn't know what to say. The purse snatcher was still running flat out. Robbie took a quick windup and let the ball fly. The ball struck the purse snatcher on the back side of his right knee. His leg buckled and down he went. Robbie ran over to him and grabbed his arms and pulled them behind his back. The man struggled but Robbie was too strong for him. Robbie sat on him as he undid his belt and used it to tie the man's arms behind him. Robbie was sitting on him when the boy ran over. The boy wanted to kick the man. "No, you can't do that son," said Robbie. The baseball was laying beside the man and Robbie handed it to the boy. "Here's your ball back son," said Robbie. "It might be scuffed some. I'll get you another one. Now go tell your mother to call the law. And here's her purse back." The boy took his ball and the purse and went back to his mother. Someone else had already called the law. There must have been a cruiser in the area because they were there in no time. The officers cuffed the snatcher and gave Robbie his belt back. They took statements from everyone and then left with the snatcher.

Robbie had heard the woman tell the officer that her name was Cindy. He didn't think about it at first, but then he got to looking at her. Robbie stood in front of her. "Cindy Tyler," he said. "Is that you?"

"Yes Robbie Parker, it's me," she said. "Only I don't go by Tyler now. It's Alexander. And thank you for helping us. You always were a good ball player. How long's it been now, fifteen years of so?"

"I guess so," said Robbie. 'How have you been? What have you been up to? How's your family? I have an idea. Why don't we have lunch one day next week?"

"I have a better idea," started Cindy. "You can come over to our place for dinner this evening. We live in my parent's old house. Is 6 PM all right?"

"I'll be there and thank you," said Robbie. "It sure is nice to see you after all this time."

Robbie was a little nervous as he was killing time before going to dinner at Cindy's. Cindy was the first girl he ever dated and the first girl he ever had sex with. Was there a Mr. Alexander? Robbie didn't have any wine to take with him so he took some beer instead. Maybe Cindy drank beer. Maybe her husband drank beer.

Robbie pulled into her driveway at exactly 6 PM. The boy saw him and ran out to welcome him. "What kind of car is that?" asked the boy. "It looks old."

"It is old Son, and what is your name?" asked Robbie.

"It's Billy," he answered.

"Well Billy, I'm Robbie and I'm glad to meet you," said Robbie. "This car is a 1960 Oldsmobile. They don't make them like this anymore."

"It sure looks big," said Billy.

"There's plenty of room in there," said Robbie.

"Come on in, Mom's in the kitchen," said Billy. Robbie followed Billy into the house and into the kitchen. Cindy had on an apron and was stirring something on the stove.

"I hope you like spaghetti," said Cindy. "That's what we're having this evening."

"I love spaghetti," said Robbie. "My mother and -----." Robbie couldn't finish.

"You were saying, Robbie?" said Cindy.

"I'm sorry Cindy. Give me a minute," said Robbie. Robbie forced himself to hold back his tears. "My wife used to make the best sauce. It was to die for. She's no longer with us."

"I'm sorry Robbie," said Cindy. "I didn't mean to get you upset. Maybe I should have made something else?"

"No, it's o.k. It's just taking me a really long time to get over things." said Robbie. "I go for a long time and I'm all right and then I get in a slump for a while."

"Well maybe after dinner, you and I can set down and unload everything on each other," said Cindy. "I see you brought some beer. Would you like one now? I have some red wine too. It's a chianti and it goes well with Italian food."

"The wine is fine," said Robbie. "I brought the beer because I didn't have anything else to bring. I was always taught that when you get an invite for dinner, you should bring some wine or something."

"Billy, put the beer in the frig and get Robbie the wine and a corkscrew," said Cindy. "We can sip a little wine while the pasta is cooking." Robbie opened the wine and poured them a small glass. The wine was good. It reminded him of Brandy.

They had some small talk as they ate. Robbie wanted to ask if there was a Mr. Alexander, but he kept his mouth shut. Cindy would tell him sooner or later. Billy finished his food and asked to be excused. Cindy let him go. He went into the living room and turned on the TV. In a couple of minutes, he was yelling, "Mom, Mom, it's on TV."

"What's on TV?" asked Cindy.

"What happened today at the store," said Billy. "They're talking about some man who threw a baseball and knocked down a purse snatcher. They said some-one in the store recognized Robbie. They thought it would be a good news story and called them up. Robbie got up from the table and went to the living room. They were still talking about it. Then the news lady summed it up like this. "Robert W. Parker, local businessman, was at the right place at the right time. Parker had witnessed a woman's purse being snatched. The woman's young son had just purchased a baseball and glove from a local sporting goods store. Parker grabbed the baseball from the young boy and threw it at the snatcher as he was running away. The ball struck the snatcher, knocking him down. Parker ran over, tied him up with his belt, and sat on him till police arrived. Robert Parker, the city thanks you. And the Reds can always use another pitcher."

"That's real nice," said Robbie. "They have my name plastered all over the place. It'll probably be in the paper too."

"You did make one hell of a pitch," said Cindy. "Maybe the Reds will be af-ter you."

"Yes and maybe that fella will be out looking for some revenge," said Robbie. "He won't be locked up all that long for purse snatching. He'll probably be out on bail before it gets dark. I'm sorry. Didn't mean to be gloom and doom. Cindy, you make a great sauce. If it's all right with you, I could eat some more."

"I'm glad you like it," said Cindy. "Eat as much as you want. I always make a big pot and eat for a couple of days or so and then freeze the rest."

"We always did that too," said Robbie. Robbie ate till he couldn't eat any-more. Cindy cleared the table and put the dishes in the sink.

"I can do clean up," said Robbie. "That's how we always did it. She cooked and I cleaned up."

"No, I'll do them later," said Cindy. "Let's just sit back, enjoy the wine, and talk. So Robbie, are you dying to ask me about Mr. Alexander?"

"I figured you would tell me when you were ready," said Robbie.

"I guess I am ready," started Cindy. "You know how I was in high school. Well I was the same way after that for a while. I slept with anyone who paid me a little attention and some who didn't. Then I met Bill. I had started college at Ohio University. All I did was party. I went to this party one night with some of my friends. Bill was there. People were ignoring him. He had short hair and we all knew he was in the military. I started talking to him. He was the nicest, kindest person, I had ever met. He swept me off of my feet. I had never felt like that before. He was an Army Officer and was about to go to training to be a helicopter pilot. He was on a two week leave. We got married right before his leave was up. He left for training and I joined him as soon as we could get housing. That man loved me and I loved him, but I found out that he loved flying more than anything. Not long after his training, he got orders for Vietnam. He flew those gunships, whatever they are. We met in Hawaii for an R&R. He got shot down 2 times during his tour but never got a scratch. I followed him around from base to base after his tour like a good Army wife, but I knew he was restless. About this time, I was pregnant with Billy. He got orders to go back over there. He was killed during that operation when the South Vietnamese invaded Laos, Lam Son 719 I think they called it. I went back home and lived with my parents for a while. I think I cried for two years. I finally moved out and got myself a job after Billy was a couple of years old. Have I talked too much yet?"

"No, go ahead," said Robbie, "I have a lot to tell you too."

"Well, a few years ago, I met another man," started Cindy. "We dated a while and he was very nice. I finally decided to marry him. He had asked me several times. The first year was fine, but then he changed. He got very possessive and mean. He hit me more than once. I had him jailed. I didn't have to dump him. He dumped me. He just took off one day and never came back. We finally got divorced later on. When my folks died, I moved into the house and here I am. I work as a secretary and Billy is my life. There, now you know my life story. I see you still have that Olds. That sure is a nice back seat." They both laughed. "So tell me about your life after school."

"Well you know I joined the Marines," started Robbie. "I was still dating Maria. We saw each other on my first leave. We intended to get married after I got out of the Marines. Maria was killed in an armed robbery at a convenience store while I was in Vietnam."

"I wasn't here when that happened," said Cindy. "I never knew that. I'm so sorry."

"Well I was in the hospital recovering from wounds and I met a nurse," Robbie began again. "When her tour ended, she was sent to Pearl Harbor. I was badly wounded later on and after I was well enough to travel, they sent me to Pearl Harbor. I got a Medical Discharge when I was well enough to travel home. I spent some time with Helen before I went home. We wrote back and forth but then her letters stopped. I got a letter from her father telling me that she had died. She had an advanced bone cancer. She went out surfing one day and didn't come back. They found her body later."

"Robbie, that's terrible," said Cindy. "How many times did you get shot anyway?"

"Well the first time, a bullet just grazed my left shoulder," started Robbie. "The second time, a bullet went through both of my legs. The last time, I was hit three times. The first one hit me in the stomach and passed through just missing my spine. As I tried to get up, another one hit me in the back, passed through my left lung, and tore up some ribs on the way out. As I was laying there, another bullet hit me in the left thigh shattering the bone."

"Robbie, that's a lot of wounds," said Cindy. "Don't they have some rules on how many times you can get wounded before they send you home?"

"They do," said Robbie. "In the Marines, they'll send you out after three times. That's was what they did to me. It was my third time, even though I was hit three times when it happened. Sometimes after a guys been hit a couple of times, they'll give him an easy job in the rear. I didn't ask for that. There was no safe place over there. You can get shot or blown up just about anywhere over there."

"So what did you do after Helen died?" asked Cindy.

"Well, I was accepted at the Cincinnati School of Mortuary Science," said Robbie. "I started there winter semester of 1970. I worked for a local funeral parlor while I was home."

"How did you ever decide to become a mortician?" asked Cindy.

"I wanted to do something that there would always be a demand for, no matter what," answered Robbie. "That was it. Everybody dies and there are no exceptions. I met Brandy, my wife at school. We shared an apartment at first to help with expenses. Then we fell in love. We finally got married. We worked for a friend of her father's at a funeral home in Cincinnati to help out. The man was dying of cancer. When he died, he left the business to Brandy. Brandy's dad saved the man's life during WW2. I was figuring to work for Fulbright's here in town. Abner became ill and sold his place. I bought it. Brandy's dad had his funeral home in Toledo. He put a crematory in Columbus. Later on, he died and left the business to Brandy. We added a crematory in Cincinnati, and later on, I added one in Toledo. We had such good employees, we never had to go to work at all if we didn't want to. Brandy and I had three beautiful girls. We lived in a nice house in Cincinnati. One day we were on a four lane, and a semi ran us off the road. Brandy and the girls were killed. I got torn up pretty good but I'm still here. The truck driver got killed. Not long after that, my folks were killed when my dad had a heart attack and ran off the road and slammed into a huge tree. I still have good cries about all of this. I live in the old house and some friends of mine are buying the house in Cincinnati. Now you know it all."

"We're a pair, aren't we?" said Cindy. "Maybe we should call "The Guinness Book of World Records" and see if we have the records for the most tragedy in our lives."

"So how is your life with just you and Billy?" asked Robbie. "I'm sure you get lonely at times. I do. I don't think that will ever stop."

"Well, Billy's on a ball team and I go to the games," said Cindy. "I just try to keep a positive attitude. Sometimes, I get asked out. Sometimes I go. Sometimes I don't. There's not usually a second date."

"I've been there and done that," said Robbie. "So when does Billy have another ball game? I'd like to go."

"They're playing Tuesday evening at the park," said Cindy. "The game starts at 6 PM."

"I believe I'll be there," said Robbie. "Now I think I've over stayed my welcome. I will see you Tuesday."

"You're welcome here anytime Robbie Parker," said Cindy. "It was really nice to see you again and talk. I enjoyed it."

It was three days till Tuesday. Robbie went home and rounded up all of his baseball equipment. He had two wooden bats, ten baseballs, and his old glove. He never did get that new glove purchased. The purse snatcher interrupted that. Billy didn't live that far away. Maybe he and Billy could play some catch and shag some fly balls some time. Robbie put everything in the trunk of the olds. That night, he had several dreams about Brandy. Again he reached for her and she wasn't there.

Robbie's manager had called him on Saturday and told them that there was something he needed to sign. He would leave it on his desk and Robbie could go sign it whenever he wanted. It was Sunday evening and Robbie had just remembered that he needed to sign something. He got in the olds and drove to the funeral parlor. It had just gotten dark. He was inside and he had just signed the paper. He looked out a window and he thought he saw someone in the shadows. He watched. Someone was outside slashing the tires on a hearse. Robbie thought about calling the law. "No, I'll handle this myself," he said to himself. He looked around the place and found something he could use to tie up the man. He had grabbed the cords off of some drapes. They would do.

Robbie slipped out a back door. He took off his shoes so he would be quieter as he snuck up on the man. Robbie was able to get on one side of the hearse while the man was on the other. The man had slashed the tires on the driver side and was working on the rear tire on the passenger side. As he finished that tire and was working his way to the front tire, Robbie crouched down and got to the front of the car. When the man bent down to slash the tire, Robbie was able to slip behind him and stand up. He lightly tapped the man on the shoulder. As the man stood up and turned, Robbie gave him a right to the jaw. The young man hit the pavement and was out cold. The man had a knife in his right hand, but Robbie was so quick that he never had a chance to slash or stab at Robbie. Robbie tied his legs together and tied his arms so they were strapped to his sides and couldn't move. Then he threw him over his shoulder and carried him inside.

It was several minutes later when the young man came to. He looked around to see where he was. There were caskets all around him. He couldn't do much more than wiggle a little. He turned his head from side to side. Then he realized that he was in a casket. He started screaming at the top of his lungs. Robbie walked over to the casket. "You fucked with the wrong person boy," said Robbie. The young man screamed a collection of cusswords at Robbie. "Have it your way," said Robbie as he closed the lid of the casket. He could hear the muffled screams coming from inside the casket. Robbie opened the lid. "Don't be shitting your pants in there boy," said Robbie. Then he closed the lid again. Robbie let a half hour go by. He opened the lid again. "How we doing in there boy?"

"Fuck you, you son of a bitch," yelled the man. "You're fucking nuts."

"Nuts huh, I'll show you fucking nuts," said Robbie. There was a long hall in the parlor that was at least seventy feet long and had a twelve foot ceiling. There were no chandeliers hanging from the ceiling in it. The lights in it were recessed.

There was a casket leaning against the wall at one end of the hallway. Robbie pulled the young man out of the casket and carried him down the hall to the casket. He stood him up and tied him to the casket. Robbie had all of his baseballs in a bucket. He paced off sixty feet six inches from the young man and turned around. "Now I'll show you fucking nuts," said Robbie. Robbie took one of the baseballs out of the bucket. He looked at the young man as if getting a sign from a catcher. He took a windup and let the ball fly. It was heading right for the man's face. The young man was screaming. At the last second, the ball broke down to the man's right just missing his right arm. "That was my curve ball," said Robbie. "I'm a little rusty." Robbie grabbed another ball and took a windup. At the last second the ball tailed up to the right and just missed the man's head. The man was screaming and crying.

"That was a fastball," said Robbie.

"What do you want from me you crazy fuck?" he screamed.

"Crazy fuck huh, I'll show you crazy," said Robbie. Robbie grabbed another ball and let go with another fastball. The ball struck the man right in the gut. "How's that for crazy?" asked Robbie.

"Come on, let me go. I won't fuck with you no more," said the young man.

"That didn't sound very convincing," said Robbie. Robbie grabbed another ball from the bucket. "This one will be a knuckle ball. I never know where that sucker is gonna go. Robbie let it fly. It fluttered around some and hit the man on his left thigh."

"That's enough. I mean it. I won't fuck with you ever again," sobbed the young man.

"All right, now repeat after me. I, state your name, agree never to fuck with Robbie Parker ever again. If I do, I will be hunted down and possibly killed. Go on now, say it."

"I, Roger Salyer, agree never to fuck with Robbie Parker again. If I do, I will be hunted down and possibly killed," he said.

"Now Roger, do you believe that I am capable of killing you?" asked Robbie.

"Yes I do, I believe you're capable of about anything," cried Roger.

"It's good that you believe that," said Robbie. "Have you ever killed anyone?"

"Hell no," answered Roger.

"Well I have," said Robbie. "I killed five men in my first firefight in Vietnam. Don't know how many I killed after that. Maybe thirty or forty. The reason I'm telling you this Roger is because I want you to know that killing comes easy to me.

If you're in some gang or something and you think that since you said you wouldn't fuck with me anymore, maybe your friends can do it. Well Roger, I'd kill them without batting an eye, and then I'd kill you. I also have lots of friends who are good at killing. Are you getting my meaning Roger?"

"I am. I will not fuck with you ever again and no one I know will ever fuck with you," cried Roger.

"I know about punks like you Roger," said Robbie. "If something happened to you, you would not be missed by anyone. I could put you in my crematory and no one would ever know or find out. I'd just sweep your ashes into the street. Now are we done for the evening?"

"Yes, yes, I will never fuck with you again," cried Roger.

"How about my tires?" asked Robbie.

"I'll get you some brand new tires," said Roger. Robbie took Roger's knife and cut the cords that were keeping him tied. Robbie kept the knife.

"I believe you can find your way out of here and get home," said Robbie. "Now di di mao." The young man kept his eyes on Robbie.

"What the hell is di di mao?" asked Roger.

"Loosely translated, it means "get the fuck outta here," answered Robbie. Roger ran out.

Robbie didn't call the law about the slashed tires. He spent the night thinking about what he had done. What was he? Maybe he was nuts. Then he began to think about all the men he had killed. How many did he actually kill? Then he had a dream about Brandy. The next day when Robbie's crew came to work, there were four new tires on the pavement beside the hearse.

That afternoon when Robbie's mail arrived, he got a letter from his Congressman. A class action suit had been filed in 1979 on behalf of Vietnam veterans. It was against the herbicide manufacturers who had made Agent Orange. It was settled out of court now and there was a fund called "The Agent Orange Settlement Fund." It was for $200 million and it was to be paid to Vietnam veterans over several years. "That's something at least," said Robbie to himself. "How many of them will die waiting on that money?"

~~~~

Tuesday came and Robbie was at the game. He sat with Cindy in the stands. Billy was pitching so Robbie and Cindy sat right behind home plate so they could see all the pitches. Billy was a little wild, but he had some good stuff and he was fast.

The wildness helped him some. Some of the batters were a little afraid of him. Billy only gave up three hits, and he had eight strikeouts. His team still lost 2 to 1. The other pitcher wasn't that good. Billy's team just wasn't hitting the ball that day. Robbie gave Billy a few pointers after the game. Robbie told him that he would play catch with him any time he wanted and show him how to throw some different pitches. Billy was all for that. He knew Robbie could pitch after seeing what he did to that purse snatcher.

Billy's team played two games a week. Billy always pitched one of them. When he wasn't pitching, he played third base. They played catch and shagged some balls at least once a week and Robbie attended at least one game every week. Robbie really enjoyed the games, but he had a hard time putting up with some of the parents. They way they screamed and yelled was pathetic. You would have thought this was Yankee Stadium and the Yankees were losing. It took all the strength that Robbie could muster at times to keep from getting into it with some of the parents.

They were at a game one day when Robbie saw someone he recognized. It was the coach who had hit Robbie the day he umpired a game. Robbie still had his mask on and had let the man hit him. Some bones got broken. The man didn't recognize Robbie or at least acted like he didn't. When they left the park that day, Robbie told Cindy and Billy the whole story about him. Fall came and baseball season ended for Billy. After a couple of weeks, Robbie was missing Billy. He started thinking of some reasons to see Billy and Cindy.

Robbie hadn't realized it, but school had started. Billy was a fair sized boy and he was playing football. He was a defensive back. He was quick and made a lot of tackles and had a few interceptions. Robbie wasn't a big football fan, but he enjoyed watching Billy. Billy was getting popular with the girls too. He was getting to an age where young people don't want to hang around with their parents. Cindy gave him several lectures on birth control and even gave the boy a bunch of rubbers. Billy always told her not to worry because he would always think with the right head.

The games were always on Friday night. Billy had football practice every day after school. Sometimes, the coach made them practice Saturday if they performed badly Friday night. Robbie took them to dinner on Saturday once in a while. Sometimes Billy's girlfriend would go with them.

Football season ended and basketball season started. Billy didn't play basketball, but his new girlfriend was a cheerleader so he had to go to all the home games. He was driving now and didn't need to be hauled around. Thanksgiving was getting close. Robbie started feeling lonely. Monday before Thanksgiving, Cindy called him and invited him over. He accepted.

Thanksgiving day, he arrived at Cindy's house with a couple bottles of good white wine. He put the wine in the frig and helped Cindy any way he could. Then he noticed something. Billy wasn't there. "Where's Billy?" asked Robbie.

"He's at his girlfriends house," said Cindy. "It's just you and me."

"I guess I didn't start dating till later," said Robbie. "I would have never wanted to be away from home on Thanksgiving."

"I didn't want him to go either, but I let him make his own decision," said Cindy. "Don't worry. It'll be all right. Why don't you open up a bottle of wine? We can have a glass and watch the Macy's Parade for a while before we eat." Robbie opened a bottle and poured them a glass. They sat down on the couch. They weren't real close together, but they weren't far apart either. After a few sips, Cindy slipped a little closer to Robbie. Robbie sat his wine glass on the coffee table. Cindy did the same. She looked into Robbie's eyes for a moment and then pressed her mouth gently to his. He responded well so she continued. After a few minutes, she pulled away and picked up her wine glass. "I think we should do that more often," said Cindy.

Robbie wasn't sure what to say. He picked up his glass of wine, took a sip, and then said, "O.K." They sipped their wine and watched the parade for a while. Cindy decided that the turkey had set long enough and asked Robbie to do the carving. He had just finished carving when Billy showed up.

"I kind of felt guilty about not being here, so I came home," said Billy. "Besides, Sandy got into a big argument with her folks and I didn't want to listen to it."

"Well, let's eat," said Cindy. Cindy was a very good cook. Robbie ate his fill and then had some more. After the meal, he helped Cindy clean up. After clean up, they watched TV. "Miracle on 34th Street" was on so they all watched it. When it was over, Robbie decided he should leave. He thanked Cindy for the fine meal. He shook Billy's hand and walked to the door. Cindy walked to the door with him. As he stood in the doorway, he spoke. "How would you like to help me with some Christmas shopping next week?"

"I would like that," answered Cindy. "I am available every day after five."

"I'll be here Tuesday just after five," said Robbie. "We'll get some dinner too."

"That will be nice," said Cindy. "I'll see you then." Robbie pulled her to him and kissed her gently. Then he nodded his head and said goodbye and was on his way.

Robbie slipped down to see Carl on Saturday. There was a movie about Vietnam that had been out for a while and it was supposed to be the "Best Picture of the Year" for 1986. Robbie and Carl went to see it. "It was "Platoon." "Not a bad movie," Robbie said as they came out of the theater. "What did you think?"

"Tom Berenger played a good asshole," answered Carl . "Them guys sure smoked a lot of dope when they were in the rear and sometimes when they were in the field. I don't remember our guys getting high too much."

"That's cause they didn't," said Robbie. "Or if they did, they didn't do it around us. Anyway it brought back some old memories. Probably have me some nightmares tonight."

"Yeh, me too," said Carl. "Hey, have you ever thought about going to D.C. and seeing "The Wall?"

"I have a little," replied Robbie. "But I'm not sure I want to go. I still remember the names of most of the guys we knew who got killed. I don't need to see it on a wall to remind me. It's nice they finally did something for us though."

"That's how I feel too," said Carl. "So, do you have any concrete plans for Christmas? You know you're always welcome here."

"I know," said Robbie. "I figure I'll get down here. I need to see Marie and John and Ed and Sheila. I've kind of been seeing someone too."

"How do you kind of see someone?" asked Carl.

"I guess I am seeing someone," said Robbie. "She's the first girl I ever dated in high school. We met one day when she had her purse snatched."

"I saw that on the news down here," said Carl. "I should have said something then."

"Well the woman who had her purse snatched was the first girl I ever dated," said Robbie. "She has a son around Carl's age. Her first husband was a helicopter pilot in the Army. He was killed. She remarried several years later and this guy was a jerk. He left her. Anyway, her son is a ball player. He pitches and plays third. I went to a lot of the games. When school started he played football. I went to those games. I was at her house for Thanksgiving dinner."

"I bet she's a looker," said Carl. "You always get good looking women."

"She is," said Robbie. "She's really kept her looks all these years. She even looks better than before."

"Is she a good cook?" asked Carl.

"Yes she is," answered Robbie.

"Well there you go," said Carl. "I never did tell you what my dad used to say about my mom, did I?"

"No you didn't. What was it he used to say?" asked Robbie.

"He always said, she's not much to look at but she can fuck and make biscuits," said Carl.

"What did your mom think of that?" asked Robbie.

"She didn't mind. She knew she wasn't a looker, but her and dad loved each other and that's what counted," said Carl. Carl and Robbie drank a little beer and had a little bourbon that night. Robbie went back to Columbus in the morning after breakfast.

~~~~

Robbie picked up Cindy at five on Tuesday. The first people on his shopping list was Carl and his family. Robbie knew that the four boys were all baseball players, so they would be easy to buy for. Or at least that's what he thought. They went to a sporting goods store. In fact, it was the store where Cindy's purse had been snatched. Robbie wanted to get them things he knew they liked and would use, like gloves and bats. But what type of gloves would they like?

"May I make a suggestion?" asked Cindy.

"Sure, I could use some help," said Robbie.

"This store is a big chain, right?" asked Cindy.

"I'm sure it is," answered Robbie.

"Well, I'd get all of them a gift certificate," said Cindy. "That way they can pick out what they want."

"That's a wise move," said Robbie and that's what he did. Then they went to a home goods store. Robbie picked out a nice set of cookware for Sally and asked Cindy's opinion.

"I like it," said Cindy. "It looks like it will last. I would use a set like that if it was mine." Robbie purchased the cookware and then they went for dinner.

"Where would you like to eat?" asked Robbie.

"Anywhere is fine," answered Cindy. "We don't have to go expensive. A diner would be fine with me."

"A diner it is," said Robbie. There was a diner a few blocks away. The daily special was chicken and noodles. Both of them had the special. They had some small talk while they ate. Robbie knew that he wanted to get Carl a new rod and reel for Christmas. There was a store just off South High Street that sold hunting and fishing equipment. Robbie told the salesman that he wanted the best medium weight spinning reel he had and the best graphite rod in the store. He also got two spools of fishing line. Carl could put on whichever one he wanted. They went out to the car. Robbie opened her door as he always did for women. "One family down and a bunch to go," said Robbie. "We'll shop some more in a few days if you don't mind."

"No, I don't mind," said Cindy. "I enjoy your company. I think we should spend more time together."

"I think that too," said Robbie. "I'll see what I can do." He leaned over and kissed Cindy gently. Then he moved back over behind the wheel. Cindy slid over next to him. Before he got the car started, she had her arms around his neck and was kissing him. She kissed him hard for about five minutes. Then she slid over to her own side and fastened her seatbelt. The olds didn't have seatbelts when Robbie first bought it. He installed them after he was in the wreck with the station wagon. He didn't always use them, but they were there. Sooner or later, a state law would probably be passed requiring the wearing of seatbelts.

They stopped off for a drink at a bistro before they went home. Cindy had a glass of white wine and Robbie had a beer. There was a dance coming up at the VFW and Robbie asked Cindy if she'd like to go. She was thrilled about it. She hadn't been dancing for years. They finished their drinks and headed home. Robbie kissed her goodbye and said he'd pick her up Saturday at noon to go shopping if that was all right. It was.

On Saturday, Robbie wanted to shop for Marie and John and their children. Robbie told Cindy all about each of the family members and then turned her loose at a big department store. It took some time, but Cindy found suitable gifts for all of them. Then they went for a late lunch. Robbie wanted to shop for Ed and Sheila that day too. "I want something really special for these two," said Robbie. "Sheila was a nurse and helped operate on me when I was wounded that last time over there. Ed is a veteran and was having some hard times till he got hooked up with Sheila."

"How about we go to a jewelry store," started Cindy. "We might find a clock or something that you can have something engraved on it. Something like how they are the best of friends and how much you love them or something like that."

"Sounds good to me," said Robbie. They went to a jewelry store. They found a very nice clock that could have things engraved on it. Cindy wasn't sure about her idea when she saw the price of the clock. "It's only money," said Robbie. "I have plenty of it and my friends are worth it."

"All right, I guess I've been used to living on a tight budget all these years," said Cindy. Robbie told the clerk what to engrave on the clock and they said it would be done by Monday afternoon. Robbie said he would pick it up Tuesday. "If we're done shopping for the day, why don't we go back to my place," said Cindy. "I'll make us some dinner."

"Or we could just order a pizza later if you want," said Robbie.

"Well let's go home and we'll see what we want to do later," said Cindy.

When they got home, Billy and his girlfriend were sitting on the sofa in the living room. By the looks of things, they had been doing some heavy making out. Robbie gave Billy a look. "So boys are wearing lipstick now," said Robbie. Cindy let out a laugh. Billy pulled out a handkerchief and wiped off his face and lips. Cindy looked at Billy's girlfriend and then whispered in her ear.

"Maybe you should go to the bathroom and fasten your bra strap," said Cindy. The young girl turned red, got up, and went to the bathroom.

"That was good timing Mom," said Billy.

"Looks like it to me," said Cindy. "You should have been in your room and not on the sofa. There's more privacy in there. I hope you remember that you told me you would always think with the right head."

"I remember Mom," said Billy. "So how are you two getting along? Are you having sex yet?"

Without any hesitation at all, Cindy replied. "We had sex two times in the back seat of Robbie's olds before we left the last store. It was wonderful."

"Way to go Mom," said Billy. Billy's girlfriend came back to the living room.

"I think you better take me home now," she said to Billy.

"All right, there's too many people here now anyway," said Billy. They headed to the door. "I'll be back in a few minutes Mom. Don't get too involved while I'm gone. It would be awkward for me to catch my mother doing the nasty." Robbie couldn't help himself. He started laughing. Cindy joined him. Billy and his girlfriend shook their heads as they went out the door.

"He's a good boy," said Robbie. "He'll be a good man."

"I think so too," said Cindy. Then she went to Robbie and began kissing him. They kissed for several minutes and then pulled apart. "Do you know what I'd like for Christmas Robbie Parker?" asked Cindy.

"No, what would you like Cindy Alexander?" said Robbie.

"I'd like to wake up with you in my bed Christmas morning," said Cindy.

"I'd like that too," said Robbie and he pulled her back to him and kissed her some more. They had just pulled apart when Billy got back home. He never said a word. He just went straight to his room. Cindy and Robbie sat on the sofa and watched TV for a while. When they decided they were hungry, they ordered a pizza. Billy helped them eat it when it arrived. Billy wanted to have a few private words with Robbie. He asked his mother if she would give them a few minutes alone. She went to her room. Robbie had no idea what Billy wanted. He thought Billy was going to give him a lecture about his mother. He was very surprised when Billy began.

"Robbie, I know you think I might be too young to be even thinking about this, but I believe that I want to join the Army or the Marines after I graduate," started Billy. "I know I do not want to go to college or a trade school. We couldn't afford that anyway. I want to serve my country. I know my father was killed in Vietnam and you were badly wounded, but I know that you believed you were serving your country."

"I did believe I was serving my country when I joined the Marines," said Robbie. "After the shots get fired, you're not concerned about serving your country. You're concerned about keeping yourself and your friends alive. That's what it's all about, staying alive. Vietnam was a big mess. I may never know what to believe about that place. I have nightmares sometimes about things that happened over there. The public back home didn't help things either. There were riots and protests for years during the war. Veterans coming home were spit on by anti-war people. It took a long time for the country to heal and it's still not healed. Vietnam veterans were exposed to Agent Orange and they finally decided that it could be linked to some cancers and other health issues. Billy, I'm sorry. I didn't mean to get started yakking about Vietnam. I do believe serving your country is an honorable thing. During WW2, we didn't have any choice except to go to war. If we hadn't, we might be speaking Japanese or German today. You're are a smart young man. When the time comes, you will make the right decision. I'll tell you this right now though. You need to talk this out with your mother. You don't want to come home the day after you turn eighteen and tell her you just joined the Army or Marines. Have I said enough?"

"You have," answered Billy. "I will have a talk with Mom when the time is right and I don't mean the day before or the day after I enlist."

"You're a good person Billy," said Robbie. "You'll make a fine soldier or Marine."

"So should I join the Army or the Marines?" asked Billy. "They always say Marines are the best and the first to go."

"Well, I believed we were the best," said Robbie. "But if you talk to some Army Rangers, I'm sure they'll tell you that they're the best. One thing you should always remember. Everybody's blood is red."

"Thanks for talking with me Robbie. Mom, you can come back out now," shouted Billy. "I've got a little home work I can work on. See you in the morning."

"So what was so important that I couldn't hear?" asked Cindy when she came back."

"Billy will talk with you when the time is right," said Robbie. "And now I think you and I should have a serious talk. You said that you wanted to wake up with me in your bed Christmas morning. That can happen, but if it does, I want us to be husband and wife."

"Oh Robbie, are you serious?" cried Cindy.

"Yes I am," aid Robbie. "I want us to be married. I hope you want that too."

"I do. I do," cried Cindy. "I want it more than anything in the world." Cindy went to Robbie and kissed him till they were out of breath. "When can we be married?"

"I was thinking that we could do it a few days before Christmas," said Robbie. "We could spend a couple of days in a nice hotel. Then we could spend Christmas Eve at your house. The day after Christmas, we could go on a honeymoon. We can go wherever you'd like."

"We don't have to get married in a church if you don't want," said Cindy. "A Justice of the Peace will do for me."

"That's fine for me too," said Robbie. "I would like some of my friends to be there if it's all right with you."

"That's all right by me," said Cindy.

"Tomorrow, we'll go pick out some rings and I'll let my friends know what we're doing," said Robbie. Then he kissed Cindy goodbye. "I'll pick you up at ten Monday morning," said Robbie as he was leaving. "Call in sick or something for your job."

Cindy told Billy their plans the next morning. He was very happy for his mother. She had not even been out with a good man for a long time before Robbie showed up.

Robbie spent Sunday calling his friends. He got a real surprise when he talked to Ed and Sheila. Ed had gotten himself ordained. He didn't do any hard core preaching or anything. He got himself ordained so he could perform marriages in the state of Ohio. He would be honored to perform the ceremony. That was great. They would have the service at Robbie's house. After Robbie talked with everyone, they would set the date. Sally said that Carl had to run into town for something, but they would definitely be at the wedding. Marie and John and the kids would be there too.

Monday morning, Cindy and Robbie went to the jewelry store where they had purchased the clock. They got their rings picked out and the clock was finished so they took it with them. They went out to a nice restaurant for lunch to celebrate getting officially engaged. "So where would you like to go for a honeymoon?" asked Robbie.

"It doesn't matter as long as I'm with you," said Cindy.

"Well then we're going to one of those Sandals places," said Robbie. "We can go talk to a travel agent right after lunch if you'd like."

"Sure, that sounds good," said Cindy. "They make those places sound so inviting on the commercials." They went to a travel agent right after lunch and got everything booked. All they had to do now was set the date for wedding.

In a couple of days, they had the date set. The wedding would be at Robbie's house on December 22nd. They would spend two nights at the Hyatt Regency and then go to Cindy's house Christmas Eve. The day after Christmas, they would leave for the Bahamas. Robbie would use his wedding to pass out the Christmas gifts he had purchased for his friends. There would be some champagne and a little drinking at the house, but not a lot as Robbie and Cindy would want to get to the hotel.

Robbie told Cindy that she could quit her job anytime she wanted if that's what she wanted to do. She gave her boss a two week's notice, but they told her it wasn't necessary so she left her job after a week. She helped Robbie finish up his shopping. "I still need to get something for you and Billy," said Robbie when they were finished shopping for Robbie's friends.

"Just having us for your family now is gift enough," said Cindy. "So we won't be able to go to the dance at the VFW now."

"We can go dancing anytime you want now," said Robbie.

"We'll probably do some dancing in the Bahamas," said Cindy. "Now I was wondering about our houses. Which one should we live in?"

"It's entirely up to you," said Robbie. "My house is bigger. All of us would have more space there. We can live in mine and rent yours or sell it if you want. I don't need the money. We can do whatever you want."

"Living in your house would be fine," said Cindy. "But I'd like to keep my house, even if we don't rent it. Maybe someday I can give it to Billy or he can live there when he first gets married or something. Course, he might not want to live so close to his mother after he's married."

"That might be true," said Robbie. "But it shouldn't matter if you don't visit too often and such. Young folks like their parents, but they don't want them around too much."

"Did you parents hang around much or interfere when you first got married?" asked Cindy.

"No, they were good parents," said Robbie. "They were in Columbus and we were in Cincinnati. Brandy's folks were in Toledo. It was nice."

"I love you Robbie Parker," said Cindy.

"I love you too Cindy Alexander," said Robbie. They held each other and kissed for a while.

Chapter Twenty-Nine

The days before the wedding were a blur. They had gone by so fast. Robbie made a trip to Toledo and then to Cincinnati to see all of his employees and personally give them their Christmas Bonus. All of them were overjoyed that Robbie had found love again too. The night before the wedding, Robbie was a nervous wreck. Ed and Sheila were there and were spending the night at his house. Ed got a few beers into Robbie and calmed him down. Robbie was wondering if Cindy was nervous too. She was. She didn't hardly sleep at all that night.

It was a warm day for December, 65 degrees. They set up in the back yard, but nothing fancy. There were some chairs and some coolers that had champagne and other spirits in them. The time finally came. Robbie stood out back and waited. Carl was his best man and Sheila was Maid of Honor. A car pulled into the driveway. Billy went around and opened the door for his mother. She was beautiful. Robbie thought of Brandy and how beautiful she was when they got married, even though they had just gone to the Justice of the Peace. He knew that if Brandy was looking down on him, she would be happy for him. Cindy and Robbie were so happy during the ceremony that they cried some. This started everyone crying. Ed had to take a second and wipe the tears from his eyes so he could read the vows to them. When Robbie and Cindy kissed at the end of the service, it was a very long kiss. Champagne was opened and toasts were made. Robbie passed out all of his Christmas gifts to everyone before he and Cindy left for the hotel. The gifts that they received would be opened when they got back from the hotel or after they returned from the Bahamas.

When they got to their hotel room, Robbie picked up Cindy and carried her inside. The next day around noon, they finally had to come up for air and get some food. They ordered room service. They stayed locked together the rest of the day and night. They didn't check out of their room until exactly 11 AM which was check out time. Then they found a café downtown and had some breakfast. Billy was over at his girlfriend's house when they got home so they took advantage of his absence. They had purchased a nice piece of beef ribeye roast and Cindy prepared some prime rib and the trimmings for Christmas Eve dinner. They drank wine and flirted with each other as she worked in the kitchen. There would be enough prime rib left for Christmas dinner too. When they woke up Christmas morning, Robbie looked into Cindy's eyes. "You got your Christmas gift," he said. "It's Christmas morning and I am definitely in your bed." Cindy smiled and had her way with him.

They all had a great time Christmas day. Robbie had gotten gifts for Cindy and Billy even though Cindy had said that it wasn't necessary. They had to get up early and catch their flight the next day. They spent some time talking to Billy and making sure they had all the bases covered. They would be gone for two weeks. There was plenty of food in the house and they left Billy plenty of money so he could eat out if he wanted. If there was some sort of emergency, he could get a hold of the travel agency or call Carl. Not one word was mentioned about Billy's girlfriend.

The flight to the Bahamas was uneventful. When they arrived at Sandals, they were truly impressed with the way everything looked. The beach was beautiful. Their room was beautiful. They had a Jacuzzi in their room and their own small private pool just outside their room. They were in heaven. After several days in their room, they decided to look around some. They were sitting at an outside bar having some tropical drinks and just looking around. "I think we're the oldest people here," said Cindy.

"We might be, but you're the best looking woman here," said Robbie. He leaned over and kissed her. As he pulled back from her, an older couple, maybe in their 60s walked passed them holding hands.

"Do you suppose we'll be doing that when we're that old?" said Cindy.

"We might," said Robbie. "But I'm more likely to have my hands on your ass." Cindy took Robbie's hand and led him back to their room.

They had a wonderful time at Sandals. They ate good food and danced a lot. They spent some time at the beach, but not a lot. Whenever Robbie would look at Cindy for too long in her bathing suit, he had to take her back to their room.

~~~~

When they arrived back home, it was mid morning. Billy was in school. They were surprised. The house was not a mess. There was not one dirty dish in the sink. There was no big pile of dirty clothes in Billy's room. His bed was even made. They sat down on the sofa and relaxed. They had a little jet lag. They fell asleep on the sofa for a couple of hours. When Robbie woke up, Cindy was on his lap gently kissing him and nibbling on his ear. He picked her up and carried her to bed. They were holding each other in bed when Billy got home from school.

"Welcome back," he said. "Hope you had a nice time. Don't mind me. Continue with what you were doing." Cindy and Robbie let out a laugh.

The next day, they went to Robbie's house and opened their Christmas and wedding gifts. Then they started figuring where everything would go when they moved into Robbie's house.

The next day, they started the move to Robbie's house. Robbie wasn't worried about money so he hired a mover. He told the mover to tell his crew that Cindy was the boss. It took two days to get everything arranged the way Cindy wanted it, but Robbie admitted that what she had done was a big improvement. They cleaned and painted Cindy's house and put up a "For Rent" sign.

Cindy loved it that Robbie was around most of the time. Robbie had such good employees that he could stay home all he wanted and right now, he wanted to be with Cindy. Spring rolled around and so did baseball season. Billy was better than last season. He had learned what Robbie had taught him. He played Legion ball in the summer too. When school started, he played football again. He had gotten a little taller and they had him playing quarterback. He did well during the season. He was only sacked twice and only threw two interceptions the whole season. All the girls were after him. Billy never let it get to his head. He was only a junior, but some of the smaller colleges were keeping an eye on him.

When baseball season started again, Billy had a fastball that was at least 90mph. There were very few boys in high school who could throw 90. He had a great season. The coach at Ohio University talked to him and asked him to come down next year. Billy thanked him and said he'd see how things were going.

When football season started the next year, Billy was always in the headlines. He wasn't that big, 6'2" and 180 lbs., but he could throw a football like nobody around had seen before. When the season ended, some big colleges were after him. Billy knew he was joining the Marines but he never said a word to the scouts and coaches. A day after football season ended, Billy sat down with his mother and had a talk. He informed her that he would be joining the Marines right after graduation. Cindy cried a little but she was not surprised. She knew he would make a good Marine.

Billy turned 18 in early May and enlisted. He would be leaving two weeks after graduation. Robbie got a call from Carl about this time. Young Carl had enlisted in the Marines and would be going to Boot Camp two weeks after graduation. Maybe Carl and Billy would end up in the same platoon. When they took Billy to the airport, there were plenty of tears. Billy's girlfriend went with them and she couldn't quit crying.

It was a couple of weeks before they got a letter from Billy. They hadn't killed him yet, but it was tough. Carl Sims was in his platoon too. They were becoming good friends. He would write whenever he could find time. After Boot Camp was infantry training. Carl's MOS was machine gunner and Billy was a rifleman. They had a short leave after training and then were to report to Camp Lejeune, 2nd Marine Division.

When they picked up Billy at the airport, Cindy had a good cry. He and Robbie shook hands and had a hug. They went home and fed Billy a good home cooked meal. Then they knew that he would want to be with his girlfriend. After dinner, he took a quick shower and headed to his girl's place. He wanted to surprise her. He had not told her exactly when he'd be home. Cindy had another good cry. It wasn't more than a couple of hours and Billy came back home. They were surprised he was back.

"What's up?" asked Robbie. "Isn't your girl home."

"No, she's not home," said Billy. "She's out on a date. Her parents said she's been seeing several different guys since I been gone."

"Sounds to me like she wasn't the faithful type," said Robbie. "Stuff like that happens a lot. Absence doesn't always make the heart grow fonder. Better to find out now. At least you weren't in some hole getting shot at and finding out."

"I'll find me another girl," said Billy. "There's plenty of them out there."

"So maybe tomorrow if you're not out girl hunting, you and I can sit down and compare Boot Camps," said Robbie.

"I'd like that," said Billy. "So you think we could all have a beer?"

"Yes we can," said Cindy. "If my son can wear a uniform, he can have a beer if he wants one." They drank a couple of beers and then Billy said he wanted to go to bed. Cindy and Robbie went to bed too, but they didn't sleep.

The next day, Billy and Robbie compared their Boot Camps. Not a whole lot had changed, except that it was longer now and the Drill Instructors were not allowed to hit the recruits. Billy had fired "expert" on the rifle range. That was very good for someone who had never fired any type of weapon in his life. They had lunch and Billy left. When he got home around midnight, he had a big smile on his face.

The next morning at breakfast, Cindy asked him about his evening. Billy proceeded to tell her about all the girls he had met and only one of them had a last name. "You don't need to explain further," said Cindy.

It came time for Billy to report to Camp Lejeune. They took him to the airport and Cindy had another good cry.

Billy was a good son and wrote home often. He had a couple of girlfriends down there and he and Carl Sims were in the same unit. Things were good so far.

The house next to Robbie's had been empty ever since the loan officer and his wife were busted for prostitution. There was a rumor going around the neighborhood that it had been sold. A sold sign had not been put up with the realtor sign. Robbie and Cindy were having some coffee one morning when they heard a knock on the front door. They both went to see who it was. There were three older women and three older men on the front porch. Robbie opened the door. "What can I do for you folks?" asked Robbie. All of them gave Robbie their names and where they lived. Robbie remember seeing some of them when he used to walk around the neighborhood.

"We know you make a good living and we were hoping that you could help us out," said one of the men.

"I like to help folks," said Robbie. "What is it that I can do for you?"

"Well, I'm sure you've heard the rumor that the house next to you has been sold," said the man.

"Yes, I've heard that," said Robbie. "What of it?"

"Well, some colored people have bought it," said the man.

"Colored people, what do you mean? We're colored too. What color are they?" said Robbie.

"I mean darkies," said the man. "We don't want their kind around here. Next thing you know, property values will go down and this place will be a slum."

"And you know this for a fact?" asked Robbie.

"It's always that way when them people move in," said the man.

"First they were colored, then they were darkies, and now they're them people," said Robbie. "What's a matter with you? Are you afraid to use the "N" word.

"All right, we don't want any niggers in the neighborhood," said the man.

"Well how about the "F" word. Do you ever use it?" asked Robbie. "Now get the "Fuck" off my property and I mean right fucking now." The old folks were totally flabbergasted. They had no idea what to say. They turned around and left.

"I guess you told them," said Cindy.

"I guess I did," said Robbie.

~~~~

A week later, a black couple started moving in. Cindy and Robbie went over and introduced themselves and welcomed them to the neighborhood. They also offered to help any way they could. The new couple was Jerome and Natalie Johnson. They didn't have time to talk much because a moving van would soon arrive. Robbie and Cindy got out of their way. Later on, Cindy could see that they were dead tired from moving all day and invited them to dinner. They accepted.

They talked a lot as they ate. Jerome was from Detroit and had gotten a job in Columbus in Employee Services. Natalie would be working as a part time grocery clerk. They had a son who was in the Army and was a driver on an "Abrams" tank. Cindy and Robbie told them all about themselves. Then Robbie remembered that his friend Larry Johnson was from Detroit. He asked Jerome if he and Larry were by some chance related. They were. Larry was Jerome's first cousin. Then Robbie told how he and Larry had been good friends and Larry's sister had written him that Larry had been killed. Jerome was also a Vietnam veteran. He had been with the Air Cavalry at the Ia Drang Valley on LZ X-Ray.

They all became very good friends. They went out to dinner together from time to time and had cookouts. Not too many of the other neighbors made up to them, but they didn't care. Jerome had also been a baseball player. He was a centerfielder. He and Robbie played catch a lot. Jerome understood why Larry had always referred to his white boy as "Pitcher" in his letters. Robbie could throw a baseball wherever he wanted. It was most likely the same for a hand grenade.

~~~~

One evening, as the country watched the news, a gloomy report was given. The ruler of Iraq, Saddam Hussein, had invaded Kuwait. President Bush and allies of the U.S. would not tolerate that and action would be taken. Robbie and Cindy, Carl and Sally, and Jerome and Natalie all waited to get word from their sons.

Other Books by Michael E. Cook

<u>The Sean O'Rourke Series</u>

A Killer for the Common Good

A Killer For The Common Good – Lawman

O'Rourke's Revenge

O'Rourke's Law or No Law at All

<u>Coming Soon</u>

Quiet Times?

About the Author

Michael E. Cook (Mike), was born in Chillicothe, Ohio and grew up loving and playing baseball. After high school graduation in 1969, Mike served 4 years in the U.S. Marine Corps. In Vietnam, Mike was a Field Radio Operator in a Forward Observation Team, and was attached to the companies of the 3rd Battalion 5th Marines. During the "Easter Offensive" of 1972, Mike was with 2nd ANGLICO (Air and Naval Gunfire Liaison Company) and was attached to South Vietnamese Marines as a Naval Gunfire Spotter. After military service, Mike attended and graduated from Ohio University, Athens, Ohio and received a BA with a major in Psychology. "I did not pursue my major," Mike says. "The more classes I took, the more I disliked Psychology." At Ohio University, Mike met Eleanor, his wife of 40 years.

After college, Mike worked as a maintenance man, and then a brakeman and locomotive engineer on the B&O Railroad. When the division was shut down, Mike took a job at a snack food manufacturer, and retired after 31 years of service and was Plant Manager for almost 30 years. "Pitcher," is Mike's first attempt at writing outside the Western genre. He currently has 4 books of "The Sean O'Rourke Series" published, and is working on a 5th.

Mike's hobbies are fishing, turkey hunting, and shooting. He has two grown children and two grandchildren. He resides with his wife on their 31 acre mini-farm in southwest central Ohio.

www.ingramcontent.com/pod-product-compliance
Lightning Source LLC
Chambersburg PA
CBHW020817180626
46814CB00001B/2